TALES OF MYSTERY & THE SUPERNATURAL

General Editor: David Stuart Davies

BULLDOG DRUMMOND
THE CARL PETERSON QUARTET

BULLDOG DRUMMOND

THE CARL PETERSON QUARTET

by 'Sapper'

with an Introduction by
David Stuart Davies

WORDSWORTH EDITIONS

In loving memory of
MICHAEL TRAYLER
the founder of Wordsworth Editions

1

Readers who are interested in other titles from
Wordsworth Editions are invited to visit our website at
www.wordsworth-editions.com

For our latest list and a full mail-order service contact
Bibliophile Books, 5 Thomas Road, London E14 7BN
Tel: +44 0207 515 9222 Fax: +44 0207 538 4115
e-mail: orders@bibliophilebooks.com

This edition published 2007 by
Wordsworth Editions Limited
8B East Street, Ware, Hertfordshire SG12 9HJ

ISBN 978 1 84022 620 1

Typeset in Great Britain by Antony Gray
Printed by Clays Ltd, St Ives plc

CONTENTS

INTRODUCTION

Captain Hugh 'Bulldog' Drummond was the prototype of all the sleuthing adventurers who ambushed the bookshelves in the first half of the twentieth century. He inspired numerous crime solvers from Sidney Horler's Tiger Standish to Leslie Charteris' The Saint to Dick Barton and beyond, and indeed he could well have been the father of James Bond.

Born as a literary character just after the First World War when readers needed pace, excitement and escapism in their crime fiction, Drummond was neither as cerebral as Sherlock Holmes nor as self-contained, cunning and aristocratic as Lord Peter Wimsey (although like Wimsey he did have a trusty and useful manservant), but he had a bluff, good-hearted nature, great energy and above all staunch patriotism and tremendous courage.

His creator, Herman Cyril McNeille (1888–1937), known as Sapper, was already a successful writer before he set forth on the Drummond saga. McNeille served in the Royal Engineers during the war and was awarded the Military Cross. His short stories concerning the conflict were raw and vivid and were described by one contemporary reviewer as 'far more terrible than anything Kipling or Stephen Crane or Tolstoy or Zola ever imagined'. These stories first appeared in the *Daily Mail*, and it was the newspaper's proprietor, Lord Northcliffe, who suggested that the author used the pseudonym, Sapper (the official term for a private in the Royal Enginers), presumably to lend the stories greater authenticity. The stories were collected as *The Lieutenant and Others* (1915) and *Sergeant Michael Cassidy* (1915). Both collections sold over 200,000 copies within a year.

Despite the theatrical, almost comic-book nature of Drummond's characterisation, he was actually based on a real person: McNeille's good friend Gerald Fairlie, an officer in the Scots Guards and a noted amateur boxer.

We first meet Captain Hugh Drummond, DSO, MC, ex-British

army, at breakfast looking over an advertisement that he has placed in the paper: 'Demobilised officer, finding peace incredibly tedious, would welcome diversion. Legitimate if possible; but crime, if of a comparatively humorous description, no objection. Excitement essential.' In this ad, the author captures the mood of thousands of men who had returned from the dangerous, frightening but often exhilarating field of war to the routine dullness of civilian life. The first two books were written by an officer just home from the front line and written primarily – as he himself might have put it – for others of his ilk.

Drummond is a man's man in an era when that was what a man was supposed to be. He has all the virtues and vices of his class and time. He is scrupulously honest, trustworthy, fearless and loves a good fight; but he is also a casual and good-natured bigot. His attitude to foreigners and Jews would today have the political correctness brigade blowing a collective gasket. The critic T. J. Binyon, writing of the novels in *The Oxford Companion to Crime & Mystery Writing* (1999) observes: '[Sapper's] work with its reactionary political views, anti-Semitism, and curious blend of chivalry and brutality, belongs to the inter-war years and is scarcely acceptable to the modern reader.'

I feel that the modern reader, while not accepting Drummond's stance, should be able to place it in an historical context. The officer class was wary and concerned. Britain had just fought a bloody war with the Germans and the brutal and merciless Bolshevik revolution in Russia, which took place in 1918, seemed to pose another dark if distant threat to those of Sapper's breed. Britain needed to be defended and protected against such perceived dangers, and Drummond and his cronies were the chaps who were up for the job. To them all foreigners were the enemy. That is why, for example, one can find such outrageous statements in the Drummond books as his observation in the first novel that Russia was a place ruled by a clique of 'homicidal, alien Jews'.

Perhaps the images of the horror of the war so vivid still in Sapper's mind prompted him to match these in his Drummond stories, which can be very graphic in their violence. In the first novel, *Bulldog Drummond*, we find Drummond forcing one of the villains into a bath of acid from which he emerges with his clothes burned off and 'mad with agony'. In *The Black Gang*, perhaps the most violent of the quartet in this volume, two Jews who have been working as white slavers are told by a masked Drummond, 'My friends and I do not like your trade, you swine,' before being flogged with a cat o' nine tails 'within an inch of their lives'.

Much later and with greater subtlety, and yet with the same implied horrific violence, Ian Fleming included such scenes in his James Bond novels.

The Bulldog Drummond stories serve not only as entertaining, racy, thud and blunder thrillers but also as an interesting, if not palatable, historical reflection of upper-class attitudes to foreigners and Jews at the time. It is interesting to note that this seam of xenophobia and anti-Semitism fades significantly after the first two books in the series as memories of the war begin to fade.

Sapper's great skill as a writer did not lie in the characterisation department. His characters tended to veer towards caricature. Drummond himself appears rather oafish in a likeable sort of way and uses dialogue which could almost have been spouted by Lord Peter Wimsey or, indeed, Bertie Wooster:

> 'You priceless old bean,' boomed Hugh affably. 'I gathered from the female bird punching the what-not outside that the great brain was heaving – but my dear old lad, I have come to report a crime . . . '
> (*The Black Gang*)

Physically, Drummond is typical hero material. He is a little under six feet tall, very broad (his bulk is referred to often) and muscular; he is an excellent boxer (like his model Gerald Fairlie) and 'a lightning and deadly shot'. However, Sapper informs us that 'His best friend would not have called him good-looking, but he was the fortunate possessor of that cheerful type of ugliness which inspires immediate confidence in its owner.'

The other various regulars in the series are Toby Sinclair, army pal Peter Darrell, 'who usually came home with the milk each morning but often turned out to play cricket for Middlesex', Ted Jerningham 'who fell in love with a different girl daily' and in particular his best friend, the monocled Algy Longworth whose behaviour, that of an upper class twit, is included mainly, one must assume, for comic effect:

> 'Well – er – ' mimicked Algy, 'there's a big element of risk – er – don't you know, and I mean – er - we're sort of pledged to bung you through the window, old man, if you talk such consolidated drivel.'
> (*Bulldog Drummond*)

There is also his dedicated and servile manservant, James Denny who drops his aitches as an indication of his lower status in the first novel, but seems to recover perfect English for the rest.

Then there is Phyllis, a beautiful girl (of course) – the damsel in distress in the first novel – who becomes Mrs Drummond. After the marriage Phyllis, whom Drummond refers to as 'old thing', plays less of an active role in his exploits and yet seems to be placed in danger in every outing.

There is also a tame policeman, Inspector MacIver [or, in *The Black Gang*, McIver] of Scotland Yard who, in traditional fashion, is always two or three steps behind Drummond.

The first four books in the series feature the super-villain Carl Peterson. He is a mixture of all the notable scheming literary master-minds who have plagued society through the years. In him you can note elements of Professor Moriarty, Dr Fu Manchu, Goldfinger, Dr No and even Mocata, the villain in Dennis Wheatley's *The Devil Rides Out*. Like these malevolent luminaries, Peterson is a criminal genius whose desire for greed and world domination grows through the four novels. He has the great facility of disguise, which allows him to present himself convincingly as being of any nationality. His chameleon appearances are one of the joys of the story. Sapper never tells you directly that a certain character is indeed Peterson. However we are sometimes alerted to the fact by his seemingly unbreakable habit of tapping his left knee with his left middle finger.

> Even his most fearless accomplices had been known to confess that Peterson's inhuman calmness sent cold shivers down their backs.
>
> (*Bulldog Drummond*)

Peterson's constant companion is the sinister but beautiful Irma, who is originally presented as his daughter, a claim that is both dubious and risible. It's possibly an idea Sapper took from Sax Rohmer's Fu Manchu books. However, it clear that Peterson and Irma are lovers.

All the stories feature the classic confrontations between hero and villain whichhave now become part of literary culture. Both men indulge in civilised and smooth conversations, as though they were discussing items on the menu before they indulge in a pleasant meal together rather than wanting to destroy the other:

> 'It is a little difficult to know what to do with you, young man,' said Peterson, gently, after a long silence. 'I knew you had no tact.'

Drummond leaned back in his chair and regarded his host with a faint smile.

'I must come to you for lessons, Mr Peterson. Though I frankly admit,' he added genially, 'that I have never been brought up to regard the forcible abduction of a harmless individual and a friend who is sleeping off the effects of what low people call a jag as being typical of that admirable quality.'

(Bulldog Drummond)

If characterisation is not Sapper's strong point, plotting and dramatic action are. Each story unfolds in an exciting, page-turning fashion, with surprising twists, while the author cleverly dovetails the various elements of the plot to construct a thrilling scenario. It is no wonder that Bulldog Drummond very quickly became a film star – but more of that later.

It is in *Bulldog Drummond* (1920) that our hero first encounters Carl Peterson when the villain is involved in a plot to deliver England into the hands of the evil Communists – purely for financial gain, of course, for Peterson is above politics. The story features the archetypal damsel-in-distress scenario and introduces Drummond to his future wife.

In *The Black Gang* (1922) the Communist revolutionaries return again and receive even harsher treatment from Drummond & Co. In his second outing, Drummond is a much smoother operator, more skilful in his duplicity, fooling both the police and the bad guys. He and his cronies have become vigilantes, acting as a law unto themselves, punishing those whose aim is to bring about the downfall of democracy in the country. As Drummond says to the fellow who is about to be whipped for his perceived misdeeds, 'We merely anticipate the law.'

In *The Third Round* (1926) Sapper introduces an element of science fiction to spice up the plot with the discovery of a process for cheaply synthesising diamonds. Professor Goodman has developed a method of creating perfect diamonds for 'a fiver'. Of course the diamond industry wishes this process to be kept under wraps permanently. A Mr Blackton, who has a habit of tapping his left knee with his left middle finger, is employed by the Metropolitan Diamond Syndicate to silence Professor Goodman, who just so happens to be Algy Longworth's prospective father-in-law. It isn't long before Bulldog Drummond is involved in the matter. As Peterson, now disguised as another character observes: 'Drummond again – always Drummond.'

At the climax when Peterson and Drummond face each other yet again, this time with Drummond having the upper hand, our hero suggests that the two men settle their differences by fighting each other atop a glacier in Switzerland, a scenario that brings to mind the titanic struggle between those other two great adversaries of crime fiction Sherlock Holmes and Professor Moriarty, who fought to the death on a ledge overlooking the Reichenbach Falls, also in Switzerland. We shall probably never know whether this was a deliberate allusion on Sapper's part or not. However, it is satisfying to think so.

Sapper continued with the boxing/sparring imagery for the title of the next episode in the Drummond saga, *The Final Count* – the one in which Carl Peterson meets his just deserts. The element of pseudo-science introduced in the previous novel is enhanced further in this story in which the volatile invention in question almost takes us into the realms of penny dreadful serials, the world of stolen formulas and deadly scientific discoveries. Here we are dealing with a poison which brings about instantaneous death. One has only to touch the powerful liquid to die: 'It is a destructive force so terrible no other nation would make war against it.' There are other fantastic elements in the story also, such as the grotesque spider sent to Phyllis. It is as large as a puppy and hisses loudly as Drummond tries to attack it.

In *The Final Count*, which was published in 1925 but apparently records 'the amazing happenings of the summer of 1927', Sapper adapts a different narrative style. The story is told in the first person by a character called John Stockton who joins Drummond and his pals in their exploits. Therefore, this time around, the reader is not privy to the machinations of Peterson and Irma. In this adventure, Peterson adopts another impenetrable persona that is only revealed in the closing pages. The highly dramatic and spectacular finale aboard an airship headed out to sea is very cinematic in concept and perhaps this is not surprising because *The Third Round* had already been filmed in 1924 and so it is likely that Sapper wrote this new novel with the hope that it too would reach the screen. However it did not happen until 1938, the year following Sapper's death.

With *The Final Count*, Sapper and Drummond collectively rid the world of one of the most effective and engaging arch-fiends, Carl Peterson. However his lover Irma is still alive at the end and ready to pick up the cudgels on his behalf: 'You have killed the man I loved, Hugh Drummond,' she said. 'But do not think it is the end.' And so the fight continues.

Jack Buchanan, the debonair song-and-dance man, played Bulldog Drummond in *The Third Round* (1925), but he was not the first screen Drummond. This distinction goes to English matinée idol Carlyle Blackwell who played the character in the 1922 movie, *Bulldog Drummond*. However it wasn't until the advent of the talking cinema that the screen incarnation of Hugh Bulldog Drummond took off, and for about a decade from 1929 there was a spate of Drummond movies.

In 1929 Ronald Colman, perhaps the best screen Drummond, took the role in *Bulldog Drummond*, based on the first novel. Colman returned in 1934 in *Bulldog Drummond Strikes Back*.

During the Thirties old Bulldog was played on screen by Kenneth MacKenna, Ray Milland and John Howard, John Lodge and Ralph Richardson. In general the movies were lighter in tone than the novels and tended to use original plots, although *Bulldog Drummond Escapes* (1937), with Milland, was a reworking of the original novel, and *Bulldog Drummond's Peril* (1938), with Howard, was based on *The Third Round*. *Arrest Bulldog Drummond* (1938), again with Howard, was based on *The Final Count*.

Taken in the right spirit, making allowances for the elements of narrow-minded jingoism in the novels, the Bulldog Drummond stories remain good fun. They are not deep or intellectual, but they are well-constructed adventure stories for grown-up boys and girls. As Algy himself might have said, 'They were designed purely to while away a wearisome hour, don't you know.' And they do that very well.

DAVID STUART DAVIES

BULLDOG DRUMMOND

Prologue

In the month of December, 1918, and on the very day that a British Cavalry Division marched into Cologne, with flags flying and bands playing as the conquerors of a beaten nation, the manager of the Hôtel Nationale in Berne received a letter. Its contents appeared to puzzle him somewhat, for having read it twice he rang the bell on his desk to summon his secretary. Almost immediately the door opened, and a young French girl came into the room.

'Monsieur rang?' She stood in front of the manager's desk, awaiting instructions.

'Have we ever had staying in the hotel a man called le Comte de Guy?' He leaned back in his chair and looked at her through his pince-nez.

The secretary thought for a moment and then shook her head.

'Not as far as I can remember,' she said.

'Do we know anything about him? Has he ever fed here, or taken a private room?'

Again the secretary shook her head.

'Not that I know of.'

The manager handed her the letter, and waited in silence until she had read it.

'It seems on the face of it a peculiar request from an unknown man,' he remarked as she laid it down. 'A dinner of four covers; no expense to be spared. Wines specified, and if not in hotel to be obtained. A private room at half-past seven sharp. Guests to ask for room X.'

The secretary nodded in agreement.

'It can hardly be a hoax,' she remarked after a short silence.

'No.' The manager tapped his teeth with his pen thoughtfully. 'But if by any chance it was, it would prove an expensive one for us. I wish I could think who this Comte de Guy is.'

'He sounds like a Frenchman,' she answered. Then after a pause: 'I suppose you'll have to take it seriously?'

'I must.' He took off his pince-nez and laid them on the desk in front of him. 'Would you send the *maître d'hôtel* to me at once?'

Whatever may have been the manager's misgivings, they were certainly not shared by the head waiter as he left the office after receiving his instructions. War and short rations had not been conducive to any particularly lucrative business in his sphere; and the whole sound of the proposed entertainment seemed to him to contain considerable promise. Moreover, he was a man who loved his work, and a free hand over preparing a dinner was a joy in itself. Undoubtedly he personally would meet the three guests and the mysterious Comte de Guy; he personally would see that they had nothing to complain of in the matter of the service at dinner . . .

And so at about twenty minutes past seven the *maître d'hôtel* was hovering round the hall-porter, the manager was hovering round the *maître d'hôtel*, and the secretary was hovering round both. At five-and-twenty minutes past the first guest arrived . . .

He was a peculiar-looking man, in a big fur coat, reminding one irresistibly of a codfish.

'I wish to be taken to Room X.' The French secretary stiffened involuntarily as the *maître d'hôtel* stepped obsequiously forward. Cosmopolitan as the hotel was, even now she could never hear German spoken without an inward shudder of disgust.

'A Boche,' she murmured in disgust to the manager as the first arrival disappeared through the swing doors at the end of the lounge. It is to be regretted that that worthy man was more occupied in shaking himself by the hand, at the proof that the letter was *bona fide*, than in any meditation on the guest's nationality.

Almost immediately afterwards the second and third members of the party arrived. They did not come together, and what seemed peculiar to the manager was that they were evidently strangers to one another.

The leading one – a tall gaunt man with a ragged beard and a pair of piercing eyes – asked in a nasal and by no means inaudible tone for Room X. As he spoke a little fat man who was standing just behind him started perceptibly, and shot a bird-like glance at the speaker.

Then in execrable French he too asked for Room X.

'He's not French,' said the secretary excitedly to the manager as the ill-assorted pair were led out of the lounge by the head waiter. 'That last one was another Boche.'

The manager thoughtfully twirled his pince-nez between his fingers.

'Two Germans and an American.' He looked a little apprehensive. 'Let us hope the dinner will appease everybody Otherwise – '

But whatever fears he might have entertained with regard to the furniture in Room X, they were not destined to be uttered. Even as he spoke the door again swung open, and a man with a thick white scarf around his neck, so pulled up as almost completely to cover his face, came in. A soft hat was pulled down well over his ears, and all that the manager could swear to as regards the newcomer's appearance was a pair of deep-set, steel-grey eyes which seemed to bore through him.

'You got my letter this morning?'

'M'sieur le Comte de Guy?' The manager bowed deferentially and rubbed his hands together. 'Everything is ready, and your three guests have arrived.'

'Good. I will go to the room at once.'

The *maître d'hôtel* stepped forward to relieve him of his coat, but the Count waved him away.

'I will remove it later,' he remarked shortly. 'Take me to the room.'

As he followed his guide his eyes swept round the lounge. Save for two or three elderly women of doubtful nationality, and a man in the American Red Cross, the place was deserted; and as he passed through the swing doors he turned to the head waiter.

'Business good?' he asked.

No – business decidedly was not good. The waiter was voluble. Business had never been so poor in the memory of man . . . But it was to be hoped that the dinner would be to Monsieur le Comte's liking . . . He personally had superintended it . . . Also the wines.

'If everything is to my satisfaction you will not regret it,' said the Count tersely. 'But remember one thing. After the coffee has been brought in, I do not wish to be disturbed under any circumstances whatever.' The head waiter paused as he came to a door, and the Count repeated the last few words. 'Under no circumstances whatever.'

'*Mais certainement*, Monsieur le Comte . . . I, personally, will see t o it . . . '

As he spoke he flung open the door and the Count entered. It cannot be said that the atmosphere of the room was congenial. The three occupants were regarding one another in hostile silence, and as the Count entered, they, with one accord, transferred their suspicious glances to him.

For a moment he stood motionless, while he looked at each one in turn. Then he stepped forward . . .

'Good evening, gentlemen' – he still spoke in French – 'I am honoured at your presence.' He turned to the head waiter. 'Let dinner be served in five minutes exactly.'

With a bow the man left the room, and the door closed.

'During that five minutes, gentlemen, I propose to introduce myself to you, and you to one another.' As he spoke he divested himself of his coat and hat. 'The business which I wish to discuss we will postpone, with your permission, till after the coffee, when we shall be undisturbed.'

In silence the three guests waited while he unwound the thick white muffler; then, with undisguised curiosity, they studied their host. In appearance he was striking. He had a short dark beard, and in profile his face was aquiline and stern. The eyes, which had so impressed the manager, seemed now to be a cold grey-blue; the thick brown hair, flecked slightly with grey, was brushed back from a broad forehead. His hands were large and white; not effeminate, but capable and determined: the hands of a man who knew what he wanted, knew how to get it and got it. To even the most superficial observer the giver of the feast was a man of power: a man capable of forming instant decisions and of carrying them through . . .

And if so much was obvious to the superficial observer, it was more than obvious to the three men who stood by the fire watching him. They were what they were simply owing to the fact that they were not superficial servers of humanity; and each one of them, as he watched his host, realised that he was in the presence of a great man. It was enough: great men do not send fool invitations to dinner to men of international repute. It mattered not what form his greatness took – there was money in greatness, big money. And money was their life . . .

The Count advanced first to the American.

'Mr Hocking, I believe,' he remarked in English, holding out his hand. 'I am glad you managed to come.'

The American shook the proffered hand, while the two Germans looked at him with sudden interest. As the man at the head of the great American cotton trust, worth more in millions than he could count, he was entitled to their respect . . .

'That's me, Count,' returned the millionaire in his nasal twang. 'I am interested to know to what I am indebted for this invitation.'

'All in good time, Mr Hocking,' smiled the host. 'I have hopes that the dinner will fill in that time satisfactorily.'

He turned to the taller of the two Germans, who without his coat seemed more like a codfish than ever.

'Herr Steinemann, is it not?' This time he spoke in German.

The man whose interest in German coal was hardly less well known than Hocking's in cotton, bowed stiffly.

'And Herr von Gratz?' The Count turned to the last member of the party and shook hands. Though less well known than either of the other two in the realms of international finance, von Gratz's name in the steel trade of Central Europe was one to conjure with.

'Well, gentlemen,' said the Count, 'before we sit down to dinner, I may perhaps be permitted to say a few words of introduction. The nations of the world have recently been engaged in a performance of unrivalled stupidity. As far as one can tell that performance is now over. The last thing I wish to do is to discuss the war – except in so far as it concerns our meeting here tonight. Mr Hocking is an American, you two gentlemen are Germans. I' – the Count smiled slightly – 'have no nationality. Or rather, shall I say, I have every nationality. Completely cosmopolitan . . . Gentlemen, the war was waged by idiots, and when idiots get busy on a large scale, it is time for clever men to step in . . . That is the *raison d'être* for this little dinner . . . I claim that we four men are sufficiently international to be able to disregard any stupid and petty feelings about this country and that country, and to regard the world outlook at the present moment from one point of view and one point of view only – our own.'

The gaunt American gave a hoarse chuckle.

'It will be my object after dinner,' continued the Count, 'to try and prove to you that we have a common point of view Until then – shall we merely concentrate on a pious hope that the Hôtel Nationale will not poison us with their food?'

'I guess,' remarked the American, 'that you've got a pretty healthy command of languages, Count.'

'I speak four fluently – French, German, English, and Spanish,' returned the other. 'In addition, I can make myself understood in Russia, Japan, China, the Balkan States, and – America.'

His smile, as he spoke, robbed the words of any suspicion of offence. The next moment the head waiter opened the door, and the four men sat down to dine.

It must be admitted that the average hostess, desirous of making a dinner a success, would have been filled with secret dismay at the general atmosphere in the room. The American, in accumulating his millions, had also accumulated a digestion of such an exotic and tender character that dry rusks and Vichy water were the limit of his capacity.

Herr Steinemann was of the common order of German, to whom food is sacred. He ate and drank enormously, and evidently considered that nothing further was required of him.

Von Gratz did his best to keep his end up, but as he was apparently in a chronic condition of fear that the gaunt American would assault him with violence, be cannot be said to have contributed much to the gaiety of the meal.

And so to the host must be given the credit that the dinner was a success. Without appearing to monopolise the conversation he talked ceaselessly and well. More – he talked brilliantly. There seemed to be no corner of the globe with which he had not a nodding acquaintance at least, while with most places he was as familiar as a Londoner with Piccadilly Circus. But to even the most brilliant of conversationalists the strain of talking to a hypochondriacal American and two Germans – one greedy and the other frightened – is considerable; and the Count heaved an inward sigh of relief when the coffee had been handed round and the door closed behind the waiter. From now on the topic was an easy one – one where no effort on his part would be necessary to hold his audience. It was the topic of money – the common bond of his three guests. And yet, as he carefully cut the end of his cigar, and realised that the eyes of the other three were fixed on him expectantly, he knew that the hardest part of the evening was in front of him. Big financiers, in common with all other people, are fonder of having money put into their pockets than of taking it out. And that was the very thing the Count proposed they should do – in large quantities . . .

'Gentlemen,' he remarked, when his cigar was going to his satisfaction, 'we are all men of business. I do not propose therefore to beat about the bush over the matter which I have to put before you, but to come to the point at once. I said before dinner that I considered we were sufficiently big to exclude any small arbitrary national distinctions from our minds. As men whose interests are international, such things are beneath us. I wish now to slightly qualify that remark.' He turned to the American on his right, who with his eyes half closed was thoughtfully picking his teeth. 'At this stage, sir, I address myself particularly to you.'

'Go right ahead,' drawled Mr Hocking.

'I do not wish to touch on the war – or its result; but though the Central Powers have been beaten by America and France and England, I think I can speak for you two gentlemen' – he bowed to the two Germans – 'when I say that it is neither France nor America with whom they desire another round. England is German's main enemy; she always has been, she always will be.'

Both Germans grunted assent, and the American's eyes closed a little more.

'I have reason to believe, Mr Hocking, that you personally do not love the English?'

'I guess I don't see what my private feelings have got to do with it. But if it's of any interest to the company you are correct in your belief.'

'Good.' The Count nodded his head as if satisfied. 'I take it, then, that you would not be averse to seeing England down and out.'

'Wal,' remarked the American, 'you can assume anything you feel like. Let's get to the showdown.'

Once again the Count nodded his head; then he turned to the two Germans.

'Now you two gentlemen must admit that your plans have miscarried somewhat. It was no part of your original programme that a British Army should occupy Cologne . . . '

'The war was the act of a fool,' snarled Herr Steinemann. 'In a few years more of peace we should have beaten those swine . . . '

'And now – they have beaten you.' The Count smiled slightly. 'Let us admit that the war was the act of a fool if you like, but as men of business we can only deal with the result . . . the result, gentlemen, as it concerns *us*. Both you gentlemen are sufficiently patriotic to resent the presence of that army at Cologne, I have no doubt. And you, Mr Hocking, have no love on personal grounds for the English . . . But I am not proposing to appeal to financiers of your reputation on such grounds as those to support my scheme . . . It is enough that your personal predilections run with and not against what I am about to put before you – the defeat of England . . . a defeat more utter and complete than if she had lost the war . . . '

His voice sank a little, and instinctively his three listeners drew closer.

'Don't think that I am proposing this through motives of revenge merely. We are businessmen, and revenge is only worth our while if it pays. This will pay. I can give you no figures, but we are not of the type who deal in thousands, or even hundreds of thousands. There is a force in England which, if it be harnessed and led properly, will result in millions coming to you . . . It is present now in every nation – fettered, inarticulate, uncoordinated . . . It is partly the result of the war – the war that the idiots have waged . . . Harness that force, gentlemen, co-ordinate it, and use it for your own ends . . . That is my proposal. Not only will you humble that cursed country to the dirt, but you will taste of power such as few men have tasted before . . . ' The Count stood up, his eyes blazing. 'And I – I will do it for you.'

He resumed his seat, and his left hand, slipping off the table, beat a tattoo on his knee.

'This is our opportunity – the opportunity of clever men. I have not got the money necessary: you have . . . ' He leaned forward in his chair, and glanced at the intent faces of his audience. Then he began to speak . . .

Ten minutes later he pushed back his chair.

'There is my proposal, gentlemen, in a nutshell. Unforeseen developments will doubtless occur; I have spent my life overcoming the unexpected. What is your answer?'

He rose and stood with his back to them by the fire, and for several minutes no-one spoke. Each man was busy with his own thoughts, and showed it in his own particular way. The American, his eyes shut, rolled his toothpick backwards and forwards in his mouth slowly and methodically; Steinemann stared at the fire, breathing heavily after the exertions of dinner: von Gratz walked up and down – his hands behind his back – whistling under his breath. Only the Comte de Guy stared unconcernedly at the fire, as if indifferent to the result of their thoughts. In his attitude at that moment he gave a true expression to his attitude on life. Accustomed to play with great stakes, he had just dealt the cards for the most gigantic gamble of his life . . . What matter to the three men, who were looking at the hands he had given them, that only a master criminal could have conceived such a game? The only question which occupied their minds was whether he could carry it through. And on that point they had only their judgment of his personality to rely on.

Suddenly the American removed the toothpick from his mouth, and stretched out his legs.

'There is a question which occurs to me, Count, before I make up my mind on the matter. I guess you've got us sized up to the last button; you know who we are, what we're worth, and all about us. Are you disposed to be a little more communicative about yourself? If we agree to come in on this hand, it's going to cost big money. The handling of that money is with you. Wal – who are you?'

Von Gratz paused in his restless pacing and nodded his head in agreement; even Steinemann, with a great effort, raised his eyes to the Count's face as he turned and faced them . . .

'A very fair question, gentlemen, and yet one which I regret I am unable to answer. I would not insult your intelligence by giving you the fictitious address of – a fictitious Count. Enough that I am a man whose livelihood lies in other people's pockets. As you say, Mr Hocking, it is going to cost big money; but compared to the results the costs will be a flea-bite . . . Do I look – and you are all of you used to judging men – do I look the type who would steal the baby's money-box which lay on the mantelpiece, when the pearls could be had for opening the safe? . . . You will have to trust me, even as I shall have to trust you . . . You will have to trust me not to divert the money which you give me as working expenses into my own pocket . . . I shall have to trust you to pay me when the job is finished . . . '

'And that payment will be – how much?' Steinemann's guttural voice broke the silence.

'One million pounds sterling – to be split up between you in any proportion you may decide, and to be paid within one month of the completion of my work. After that the matter will pass into your hands . . . and may you leave that cursed country grovelling in the dirty . . . ' His eyes glowed with a fierce, vindictive fury; and then, as if replacing a mask which had slipped for a moment, the Count was once again the suave, courteous host. He had stated his terms frankly and without haggling: stated them as one big man states them to another of the same kidney, to whom time is money and indecision or beating about the bush anathema.

'Take them or leave them.' So much had he said in effect, if not in actual words, and not one of his audience but was far too used to men and matters to have dreamed of suggesting any compromise. All or nothing: and no doctrine could have appealed more to the three men in whose hands lay the decision . . .

'Perhaps, Count, you would be good enough to leave us for a few minutes.' Von Gratz was speaking. 'The decision is a big one, and . . . '

'Why, certainly, gentlemen.' The Count moved towards the door. 'I will return in ten minutes. By that time you will have decided – one way or the other.'

Once in the lounge he sat down and lit a cigarette. The hotel was deserted save for one fat woman asleep in a chair opposite, and the Count gave himself up to thought. Genius that he was in the reading of men's minds, he felt that he knew the result of that ten minutes' deliberation . . . And then . . . What then? . . . In his imagination he saw his plans growing and spreading, his tentacles reaching into every corner of a great people – until, at last, everything was ready. He saw himself supreme in power, glutted with it – a king, an autocrat, who had only to lift his finger to plunge his kingdom into destruction and annihilation . . . And when he had done it, and the country he hated was in ruins, then he would claim his million and enjoy it as a great man should enjoy a great reward . . . Thus for the space of ten minutes did the Count see visions and dream dreams. That the force he proposed to tamper with was a dangerous force disturbed him not at all: he was a dangerous man. That his scheme would bring ruin, perhaps death, to thousands of innocent men and women, caused him no qualm: he was a supreme egoist. All that appealed to him was that he had seen the opportunity that existed, and that he had the nerve and the brain to turn that opportunity to his own advantage. Only the necessary money was lacking . . . and . . . With a quick movement he pulled out his watch. They had had their ten minutes . . . the matter was settled, the die was cast . . .

He rose and walked across the lounge. At the swing doors was the head waiter, bowing obsequiously . . .

It was to be hoped that the dinner had been to the liking of Monsieur le Comte . . . the wines all that he could wish . . . that he had been comfortable and would return again . . .

'That is improbable.' The Count took out his pocket-book. 'But one never knows; perhaps I shall.' He gave the waiter a note. 'Let my bill be prepared at once, and given to me as I pass through the hall.'

Apparently without a care in the world the Count passed down the passage to his private room, while the head waiter regarded complacently the unusual appearance of an English five-pound note.

For an appreciable moment the Count paused by the door, and a faint smile came to his lips. Then he opened it, and passed into the room . . .

The American was still chewing his toothpick; Steinemann was still breathing hard. Only von Gratz had changed his occupation, and he was sitting at the table smoking a long thin cigar. The Count closed the door, and walked over to the fire-place . . .

'Well, gentlemen,' he said quietly, 'what have you decided?'

It was the American who answered.

'It goes. With one amendment. The money is too big for three of us: there must be a fourth. That will be a quarter of a million each.'

The Count bowed.

'Yep,' said the American shortly. 'These two gentlemen agree with me that it should be another of my countrymen – so that we get equal numbers. The man we have decided on is coming to England in a few weeks – Hiram C. Potts. If you get him in, you can count us in too. If not, the deal's off.'

The Count nodded, and if he felt any annoyance at this unexpected development he showed no sign of it on his face.

'I know of Mr Potts,' he answered quietly. 'Your big shipping man, isn't he? I agree to your reservation.'

'Good,' said the American. 'Let's discuss some details.'

Without a trace of emotion on his face the Count drew up a chair to the table. It was only when he sat down that he started to play a tattoo on his knee with his left hand.

* * *

Half an hour later he entered his luxurious suite of rooms at the Hôtel Magnificent.

A girl, who had been lying by the fire reading a French novel, looked up at the sound of the door. She did not speak, for the look on his face told her all she wanted to know.

He crossed to the sofa and smiled down at her.

'Successful . . . on our own terms. Tomorrow, Irma, the Comte de Guy dies, and Carl Peterson and his daughter leave for England. A country gentleman, I think, is Carl Peterson. He might keep hens and possibly pigs.'

The girl on the sofa rose, yawning.

'Mon Dieu! What a prospect! Pigs and hens – and in England! How long is it going to take?'

The Count looked thoughtfully into the fire.

'Perhaps a year – perhaps six months . . . It is in the lap of the gods . . . '

Chapter 1

In which he takes tea at the Carlton and is surprised

I

Captain Hugh Drummond, D.S.O., M.C., late of His Majesty's Royal Loamshires, was whistling in his morning bath. Being by nature of a cheerful disposition, the symptom did not surprise his servant, late private of the same famous regiment, who was laying breakfast in an adjoining room.

After a while the whistling ceased, and the musical gurgle of escaping water announced that the concert was over. It was the signal for James Denny – the square-jawed ex-batman – to disappear into the back regions and get from his wife the kidneys and bacon which that most excellent woman had grilled to a turn. But on this particular morning the invariable routine was broken. James Denny seemed preoccupied, distrait.

Once or twice he scratched his head, and stared out of the window with a puzzled frown. And each time, after a brief survey of the other side of Half Moon Street, he turned back again to the breakfast table with a grin.

'What's you looking for, James Denny?' The irate voice of his wife at the door made him turn round guiltily. 'Them kidneys is ready and waiting these five minutes.'

Her eyes fell on the table, and she advanced into the room wiping her hands on her apron.

'Did you ever see such a bunch of letters?' she said.

'Forty-five,' returned her husband grimly, 'and more to come.' He picked up the newspaper lying beside the chair and opened it out.

'Them's the result of that,' he continued cryptically, indicating a paragraph with a square finger, and thrusting the paper under his wife's nose.

'Demobilised officer,' she read slowly, 'finding peace incredibly tedious, would welcome diversion. Legitimate, if possible; but crime, if of a comparatively humorous description, no objection. Excitement essential. Would be prepared to consider permanent job if suitably impressed by applicant for his services. Reply at once Box X10.'

She put down the paper on a chair and stared first at her husband and then at the rows of letters neatly arranged on the table.

'I calls it wicked,' she announced at length. 'Fair flying in the face of Providence. Crime, Denny – crime. Don't you get 'aving nothing to do with such mad pranks, my man, or you and me will be having words.' She shook an admonitory finger at him, and retired slowly to the kitchen. In the days of his youth, James Denny had been a bit wild, and there was a look in his eyes this morning – the suspicion of a glint – which recalled old memories.

A moment or two later Hugh Drummond came in. Slightly under six feet in height, he was broad in proportion. His best friend would not have called him good-looking, but he was the fortunate possessor of that cheerful type of ugliness which inspires immediate confidence in its owner. His nose had never quite recovered from the final one year in the Public Schools Heavyweights; his mouth was not small. In fact, to be strictly accurate, only his eyes redeemed his face from being what is known in the vernacular as the Frozen Limit.

Deep-set and steady, with eyelashes that many a woman had envied, they showed the man for what he was – a sportsman and a gentleman. And the combination of the two is an unbeatable production.

He paused as he got to the table, and glanced at the rows of letters. His servant, pretending to busy himself at the other end of the room, was watching him surreptitiously, and noted the grin which slowly spread over Drummond's face as he picked up two or three and examined the envelopes.

'Who would have thought it, James?' he remarked at length. 'Great Scot! I shall have to get a partner.'

With disapproval showing in every line of her face, Mrs Denny entered the room, carrying the kidneys, and Drummond glanced at her with a smile.

'Good morning, Mrs Denny,' he said. 'Wherefore this worried look on your face? Has that reprobate James been misbehaving himself?'

The worthy woman snorted. 'He has not, sir – not yet, leastwise. And if so be that he does' – her eyes travelled up and down the back of the hapless Denny, who was quite unnecessarily pulling books off shelves and putting them back again – 'if so be that he does,' she continued grimly, 'him and me will have words – as I've told him already this morning.' She stalked from the room, after staring pointedly at the letters in Drummond's hand, and the two men looked at one another.

'It's that there reference to crime, sir, that's torn it,' said Denny in a hoarse whisper.

'Thinks I'm going to lead you astray, does she, James?'

Hugh helped himself to bacon. 'My dear fellow, she can think what she likes so long as she continues to grill bacon like this. Your wife is a treasure, James – a pearl amongst women; and you can tell her so with my love.' He was opening the first envelope, and suddenly he looked up with a twinkle in his eyes. 'Just to set her mind at rest,' he remarked gravely, 'you might tell her that, as far as I can see at present, I shall only undertake murder in exceptional cases.'

He propped the letter up against the toast-rack and commenced his breakfast. 'Don't go, James.' With a slight frown he was studying the typewritten sheet. 'I'm certain to want your advice before long. Though not over this one . . . It does not appeal to me – not at all. To assist Messrs. Jones & Jones, whose business is to advance money on note of hand alone, to obtain fresh clients, is a form of amusement which leaves me cold. The waste-paper basket, please, James. Tear the effusion up and we will pass on to the next.'

He looked at the mauve envelope doubtfully, and examined the postmark. 'Where is Pudlington, James? And one might almost ask – why is Pudlington? No town has any right to such an offensive name.' He glanced through the letter and shook his head. 'Tush! Tush! And the wife of the bank manager too – the bank manager of Pudlington, James! Can you conceive of anything so dreadful? But I'm afraid Mrs Bank Manager is a puss – a distinct puss. It's when they get on the soul-mate stunt that the furniture begins to fly.'

Drummond tore up the letter and dropped the pieces into the basket beside him. Then he turned to his servant and handed him the remainder of the envelopes.

'Go through them, James, while I assault the kidneys, and pick two or three out for me. I see that you will have to become my secretary. No man could tackle that little bunch alone.'

'Do you want me to open them, sir?' asked Denny doubtfully.

'You've hit it, James – hit it in one. Classify them for me in groups. Criminal; sporting; amatory – that means of or pertaining to love; stupid and merely boring; and as a last resort, miscellaneous.' He stirred his coffee thoughtfully. 'I feel that as a first venture in our new career – ours, I said, James – love appeals to me irresistibly. Find me a damsel in distress; a beautiful girl, helpless in the clutches of knaves. Let me feel that I can fly to her succour, clad in my new grey suiting.'

He finished the last piece of bacon and pushed away his plate. 'Amongst all that mass of paper there must surely be one from a lovely maiden, James, at whose disposal I can place my rusty sword. Incidentally, what has become of the damned thing?'

'It's in the lumber-room, sir – tied up with the old humbrella and the niblick you don't like.'

'Great heavens! Is it?' Drummond helped himself to marmalade. 'And to think that I once pictured myself skewering Huns with it. Do you think anybody would be mug enough to buy it, James?'

But that worthy was engrossed in a letter he had just opened, and apparently failed to hear the question. A perplexed look was spreading over his face, and suddenly he sucked his teeth loudly. It was a sure sign that James was excited, and though Drummond had almost cured him of this distressing habit, he occasionally forgot himself in moments of stress.

His master glanced up quickly, and removed the letter from his hands. 'I'm surprised at you, James,' he remarked severely. 'A secretary should control itself. Don't forget that the perfect secretary is an it: an automatic machine – a thing incapable of feeling . . . '

He read the letter through rapidly, and then, turning back to the beginning, he read it slowly through again.

MY DEAR BOX X10 – *I don't know whether your advertisement was a joke: I suppose it must have been. But I read it this morning, and it's just possible, X10, just possible, that you mean it. And if you do, you're the man I want. I can offer you excitement and probably crime.*

I'm up against it, X10. For a girl I've bitten off rather more than I can chew. I want help – badly. Will you come to the Carlton for tea tomorrow afternoon? I want to have a look at you and see if I think you are genuine. Wear a white flower in your buttonhole.'

Drummond laid the letter down, and pulled out his cigarette-case. 'Tomorrow, James,' he murmured. 'That is today – this very afternoon. Verily I believe that we have impinged upon the goods.' He rose and stood looking out of the window thoughtfully. 'Go out, my trusty fellow, and buy me a daisy or a cauliflower or something white.'

'You think it's genuine, sir?' said James thoughtfully.

His master blew out a cloud of smoke. 'I *know* it is,' he answered dreamily. 'Look at that writing; the decision in it – the character.

She'll be medium height, and dark, with the sweetest little nose and mouth. Her colouring, James, will be – '

But James had discreetly left the room.

2

At four o'clock exactly Hugh Drummond stepped out of his two-seater at the Haymarket entrance to the Carlton. A white gardenia was in his buttonhole; his grey suit looked the last word in exclusive tailoring. For a few moments after entering the hotel he stood at the top of the stairs outside the dining-room, while his eyes travelled round the tables in the lounge below.

A brother-officer, evidently taking two country cousins round London, nodded resignedly; a woman at whose house he had danced several times smiled at him. But save for a courteous bow he took no notice; slowly and thoroughly he continued his search. It was early, of course, yet, and she might not have arrived, but he was taking no chances.

Suddenly his eyes ceased wandering, and remained fixed on a table at the far end of the lounge. Half hidden behind a plant a girl was seated alone, and for a moment she looked straight at him. Then, with the faintest suspicion of a smile, she turned away, and commenced drumming on the table with her fingers.

The table next to her was unoccupied, and Drummond made his way towards it and sat down. It was characteristic of the man that he did not hesitate; having once made up his mind to go through with a thing, he was in the habit of going and looking neither to the right hand nor to the left. Which, incidentally, was how he got his D.S.O.; but that, as Kipling would say, is another story.

He felt not the slightest doubt in his mind that this was the girl who had written him, and, having given an order to the waiter, he started to study her face as unobtrusively as possible. He could only see the profile, but that was quite sufficient to make him bless the moment when more as a jest than anything else he had sent his advertisement to the paper.

Her eyes, he could see, were very blue; and great masses of golden brown hair coiled over her ears, from under a small black hat. He glanced at her feet – being an old stager; she was perfectly shod. He glanced at her hands, and noted, with approval, the absence of any ring. Then he looked once more at her face, and found her eyes were fixed on him.

This time she did not look away. She seemed to think that it was her turn to conduct the examination, and Drummond turned to his tea while the scrutiny continued. He poured himself out a cup, and then fumbled in his waistcoat pocket. After a moment he found what he wanted, and taking out a card he propped it against the teapot so that the girl could see what was on it. In large block capitals he had written 'BOX X10'. Then he added milk and sugar and waited.

She spoke almost at once. 'You'll do, X10,' she said, and he turned to her with a smile.

'It's very nice of you to say so,' he murmured. 'If I may, I will return the compliment. So will you.'

She frowned slightly. 'This isn't foolishness, you know. What I said in my letter is literally true.'

'Which makes the compliment even more returnable,' he answered. 'If I am to embark on a life of crime, I would sooner collaborate with you than – shall we say? – that earnest eater over there with the tomato in her hat.'

He waved vaguely at the lady in question and then held out his cigarette-case to the girl. 'Turkish on this side – Virginian on that,' he remarked. 'And as I appear satisfactory, will you tell me who I'm to murder?'

With the unlighted cigarette held in her fingers she stared at him gravely. 'I want you to tell me,' she said at length, and there was no trace of jesting in her voice, 'tell me, on your word of honour, whether that advertisement was *bona fide* or a joke.'

He answered her in the same vein. 'It started more or less as a joke. It may now be regarded as absolutely genuine.'

She nodded as if satisfied. 'Are you prepared to risk your life?'

Drummond's eyebrows went up and then he smiled. 'Granted that the inducement is sufficient,' he returned slowly, 'I think that I may say that I am.'

She nodded again. 'You won't be asked to do it in order to obtain a halfpenny bun,' she remarked. 'If you've a match, I would rather like a light.'

Drummond apologised. 'Our talk on trivialities engrossed me for the moment,' he murmured. He held the lighted match for her, and as he did so he saw that she was staring over his shoulder at someone behind his back.

'Don't look round,' she ordered, 'and tell me your name quickly.'

'Drummond – Captain Drummond, late of the Loamshires.' He leaned back in his chair, and lit a cigarette himself.

'And are you going to Henley this year?' Her voice was a shade louder than before.

'I don't know,' he answered casually. 'I may run down for a day possibly, but – '

'My dear Phyllis,' said a voice behind his back, 'this is a pleasant surprise. I had no idea that you were in London.'

A tall, clean-shaven man stopped beside the table, throwing a keen glance at Drummond.

'The world is full of such surprises, isn't it?' answered the girl lightly. 'I don't suppose you know Captain Drummond, do you? Mr Lakington – art connoisseur and – er – collector.'

The two men bowed slightly, and Mr Lakington smiled. 'I do not remember ever having heard my harmless pastimes more concisely described,' he remarked suavely. 'Are you interested in such matters?'

'Not very, I'm afraid,' answered Drummond. 'Just recently I have been rather too busy to pay much attention to art.'

The other man smiled again, and it struck Hugh that rarely, if ever, had he seen such a cold, merciless face.

'Of course, you've been in France,' Lakington murmured. 'Unfortunately a bad heart kept me on this side of the water. One regrets it in many ways – regrets it immensely. Sometimes I cannot help thinking how wonderful it must have been to be able to kill without fear of consequences. There is art in killing, Captain Drummond – profound art. And as you know, Phyllis,' he turned to the girl, 'I have always been greatly attracted by anything requiring the artistic touch.' He looked at his watch and sighed. 'Alas! I must tear myself away. Are you returning home this evening?'

The girl, who had been glancing round the restaurant, shrugged her shoulders. 'Probably,' she answered. 'I haven't quite decided. I might stop with Aunt Kate.'

'Fortunate Aunt Kate.' With a bow Lakington turned away, and through the glass Drummond watched him get his hat and stick from the cloak-room. Then he looked at the girl, and noticed that she had gone a little white.

'What's the matter, old thing?' he asked quickly. 'Are you feeling faint?'

She shook her head, and gradually the colour came back to her face. 'I'm quite all right,' she answered. 'It gave me rather a shock, that man finding us here.'

'On the face of it, it seems a harmless occupation,' said Hugh.

'On the face of it, perhaps,' she said. 'But that man doesn't deal with face values.' With a short laugh she turned to Hugh. 'You've stumbled right into the middle of it, my friend, rather sooner than I anticipated. That is one of the men you will probably have to kill . . .'

Her companion lit another cigarette. 'There is nothing like straight-forward candour,' he grinned. 'Except that I disliked his face and his manner, I must admit that I saw nothing about him to necessitate my going to so much trouble. What is his particular worry?'

'First and foremost the brute wants to marry me,' replied the girl.

'I loathe being obvious,' said Hugh, 'but I am not surprised.'

'But it isn't that that matters,' she went on. 'I wouldn't marry him even to save my life.' She looked at Drummond quietly. 'Henry Lakington is the second most dangerous man in England.'

'Only the second,' murmured Hugh. 'Then hadn't I better start my new career with the first?'

She looked at him in silence. 'I suppose you think that I'm hyster-ical,' she remarked after a while. 'You're probably even wondering whether I'm all there.'

Drummond flicked the ash from his cigarette, then he turned to her dispassionately. 'You must admit,' he remarked, 'that up to now our conversation has hardly proceeded along conventional lines. I am a complete stranger to you; another man who is a complete stranger to me speaks to you while we're at tea. You inform me that I shall probably have to kill him in the near future. The statement is, I think you will agree, a trifle disconcerting.'

The girl threw back her head and laughed merrily. 'You poor young man,' she cried; 'put that way it does sound alarming.' Then she grew serious again. 'There's plenty of time for you to back out now if you like. Just call the waiter, and ask for my bill. We'll say goodbye, and the incident will finish.'

She was looking at him gravely as she spoke, and it seemed to her companion that there was an appeal in the big blue eyes. And they were very big: and the face they were set in was very charming – especially at the angle it was tilted at, in the half-light of the room. Altogether, Drummond reflected, a most adorable girl. And ador-able girls had always been a hobby of his. Probably Lakington possessed a letter of hers or something, and she wanted him to get it back. Of course he would, even if he had to thrash the swine to within an inch of his life.

'Well!' The girl's voice cut into his train of thought and he hurriedly pulled himself together.

'The last thing I want is for the incident to finish,' he said fervently. 'Why – it's only just begun.'

'Then you'll help me?'

'That's what I'm here for.' With a smile Drummond lit another cigarette. 'Tell me all about it.'

'The trouble,' she began after a moment, 'is that there is not very much to tell. At present it is largely guesswork, and guesswork without much of a clue. However, to start with, I had better tell you what sort of men you are up against. Firstly, Henry Lakington – the man who spoke to me. He was, I believe, one of the most brilliant scientists who have ever been up at Oxford. There was nothing, in his own line, which would not have been open to him, had he run straight. But he didn't. He deliberately chose to turn his brain to crime. Not vulgar, common sorts of crime – but the big things, calling for a master criminal. He has always had enough money to allow him to take his time over any coup – to perfect his details. And that's what he loves. He regards a crime as an ordinary man regards a complicated business deal – a thing to be looked at and studied from all angles, a thing to be treated as a mathematical problem. He is quite unscrupulous; he is only concerned in pitting himself against the world and winning.'

'An engaging fellah,' said Hugh. 'What particular form of crime does he favour?'

'Anything that calls for brain, iron nerve, and refinement of detail,' she answered. 'Principally, up to date, burglary on a big scale, and murder.'

'My dear soul!' said Hugh incredulously. 'How can you be sure? And why don't you tell the police?'

She smiled wearily. 'Because I've got no proof, and even if I had . . . ' She gave a little shudder, and left her sentence unfinished. 'But one day, my father and I were in his house, and, by accident, I got into a room I'd never been in before. It was a strange room, with two large safes let into the wall and steel bars over the skylight in the ceiling. There wasn't a window, and the floor seemed to be made of concrete. And the door was covered with curtains, and was heavy to move – almost as if it was steel or iron. On the desk in the middle of the room lay some miniatures, and, without thinking, I picked them up and looked at them. I happen to know something about miniatures, and, to my horror, I recognised them.' She paused for a moment as a waiter went by their table.

'Do you remember the theft of the celebrated Vatican miniatures belonging to the Duke of Melbourne?'

Drummond nodded; he was beginning to feel interested.

'They were the ones I was holding in my hand,' she said quietly. 'I knew them at once from the description in the papers. And just as I was wondering what on earth to do, the man himself walked into the room.'

'Awkward – deuced awkward.' Drummond pressed out his cigarette and leaned forward expectantly. 'What did he do?'

'Absolutely nothing,' said the girl. 'That's what made it so awful.

' "Admiring my treasures?" he remarked. "Pretty things, aren't they?" I couldn't speak a word: I just put them back on the table.

' "Wonderful copies," he went on, "of the Duke of Melbourne's lost miniatures. I think they would deceive most people."

' "They deceived me," I managed to get out.

' "Did they?" he said. "The man who painted them will be flattered."

'All the time he was staring at me, a cold, merciless stare that seemed to freeze my brain. Then he went over to one of the safes and unlocked it. "Come here, Miss Benton," he said. "There are a lot more – copies."

'I only looked inside for a moment, but I have never seen or thought of such a sight. Beautifully arranged on black velvet shelves were ropes of pearls, a gorgeous diamond tiara, and a whole heap of loose, uncut stones. And in one corner I caught a glimpse of the most wonderful gold chaliced cup – just like the one for which Samuel Levy, the Jew moneylender, was still offering a reward. Then he shut the door and locked it, and again stared at me in silence.

' "All copies," he said quietly, "wonderful copies. And should you ever be tempted to think otherwise – ask your father, Miss Benton. Be warned by me; don't do anything foolish. Ask your father first." '

'And did you?' asked Drummond.

She shuddered. 'That very evening,' she answered. 'And Daddy flew into a frightful passion, and told me never to dare to meddle in things that didn't concern me again. Then gradually, as time went on, I realised that Lakington had some hold over Daddy – that he'd got my father in his power. Daddy – of all people – who wouldn't hurt a fly: the best and dearest man who ever breathed.' Her hands were clenched, and her breast rose and fell stormily.

Drummond waited for her to compose herself before he spoke again. 'You mentioned murder, too,' he remarked.

She nodded. 'I've got no proof,' she said, 'less even than over the burglaries. But there was a man called George Dringer, and one evening, when Lakington was dining with us, I heard him discussing this man with Daddy.

' "He's got to go," said Lakington "He's dangerous!"

'And then my father got up and closed the door; but I heard them arguing for half an hour. Three weeks later a coroner's jury found that George Dringer had committed suicide while temporarily insane. The same evening Daddy, for the first time in his life, went to bed the worse for drink.'

The girl fell silent, and Drummond stared at the orchestra with troubled eyes. Things seemed to be rather deeper than he had anticipated.

'Then there was another case.' She was speaking again. 'Do you remember that man who was found dead in a railway-carriage at Oxhey station? He was an Italian – Giuseppe by name; and the jury brought in a verdict of death from natural causes. A month before, he had an interview with Lakington which took place at our house: because the Italian, being a stranger, came to the wrong place, and Lakington happened to be with us at the time. The interview finished with a fearful quarrel.' She turned to Drummond with a smile. 'Not much evidence, is there? Only I *know* Lakington murdered him. I *know* it. You may think I'm fanciful – imagining things; you may think I'm exaggerating. I don't mind if you do – because you won't for long.'

Drummond did not answer immediately. Against his saner judgment he was beginning to be profoundly impressed, and, at the moment, he did not quite know what to say. That the girl herself firmly believed in what she was telling him, he was certain; the point was how much of it was – as she herself expressed it – fanciful imagination.

'What about this other man?' he asked at length.

'I can tell you very little about him,' she answered. 'He came to The Elms – that is the name of Lakington's house – three months ago. He is about medium height and rather thick-set; clean-shaven, with thick brown hair flecked slightly with white. His forehead is broad, and his eyes are a sort of cold grey-blue. But it's his hands that terrify me. They're large and white and utterly ruthless.' She turned to him appealingly. 'Oh! don't think I'm talking wildly,' she implored. 'He frightens me to death – that man: far, far worse than Lakington. He would stop at nothing to gain his ends, and even Lakington himself knows that Mr Peterson is master.'

'Peterson!' murmured Drummond. 'It seems quite a sound old English name.'

The girl laughed scornfully. 'Oh! the name is sound enough, if it was his real one. As it is, it's about as real as his daughter.'

'There is a lady in the case, then?'

'By the name of Irma,' said the girl briefly. 'She lies on a sofa in the garden and yawns. She's no more English than that waiter.'

A faint smile flickered over her companion's face; he had formed a fairly vivid mental picture of Irma. Then he grew serious again.

'And what is it that makes you think there's mischief ahead?' he asked abruptly.

The girl shrugged her shoulders. 'What the novelists call feminine intuition, I suppose,' she answered. 'That – and my father.' She said the last words very low. 'He hardly ever sleeps at night now; I hear him pacing up and down his room – hour after hour, hour after hour. Oh! it makes me mad . . . Don't you understand? I've just got to find out what the trouble is. I've got to get him away from those devils, before he breaks down completely.'

Drummond nodded, and looked away. The tears were bright in her eyes, and, like every Englishman, he detested a scene. While she had been speaking he had made up his mind what course to take, and now, having outsat everybody else, he decided that it was time for the interview to cease. Already an early diner was having a cocktail, while Lakington might return at any moment. And if there was anything in what she had told him, it struck him that it would be as well for that gentleman not to find them still together.

'I think,' he said, 'we'd better go. My address is 60a, Half Moon Street; my telephone 1234 Mayfair. If anything happens, if ever you want me – at any hour of the day or night – ring me up or write. If I'm not in, leave a message with my servant Denny. He is absolutely reliable. The only other thing is your own address.'

'The Larches, near Godalming,' answered the girl, as they moved towards the door. 'Oh! if you only knew the glorious relief of feeling one's got someone to turn to . . . ' She looked at him with shining eyes, and Drummond felt his pulse quicken suddenly. Imagination or not, so far as her fears were concerned, the girl was one of the loveliest things he had ever seen.

'May I drop you anywhere?' he asked, as they stood on the pavement, but she shook her head.

'No, thank you. I'll go in that taxi.' She gave the man an address, and stepped in, while Hugh stood bareheaded by the door.

'Don't forget,' he said earnestly. 'Any time of the day or night. And while I think of it – we're old friends. Can that be done? In case I come and stay, you see.'

She thought for a moment and then nodded her head. 'All right,' she answered. 'We've met a lot in London during the war.'

With a grinding of gear wheels the taxi drove off, leaving Hugh with a vivid picture imprinted on his mind of blue eyes, and white teeth, and a skin like the bloom of a sun-kissed peach.

For a moment or two he stood staring after it, and then he walked across to his own car. With his mind still full of the interview he drove slowly along Piccadilly, while every now and then he smiled grimly to himself. Was the whole thing an elaborate hoax? Was the girl even now chuckling to herself at his gullibility? If so, the game had only just begun, and he had no objection to a few more rounds with such an opponent. A mere tea at the Carlton could hardly be the full extent of the jest . . . And somehow deep down in his mind, he wondered whether it was a joke – whether, by some freak of fate, he had stumbled on one of those strange mysteries which up to date he had regarded as existing only in the realms of shilling shockers.

He turned into his rooms, and stood in front of the mantelpiece taking off his gloves. It was as he was about to lay them down on the table that an envelope caught his eye, addressed to him in an unknown handwriting. Mechanically he picked it up and opened it. Inside was a single half-sheet of notepaper, on which a few lines had been written in a small, neat hand.

There are more things in Heaven and Earth, young man, than a capability for eating steak and onions, and a desire for adventure. I imagine that you possess both: and they are useful assets in the second locality mentioned by the poet. In Heaven, however, one never knows – especially with regard to the onions. Be careful.

Drummond stood motionless for a moment, with narrowed eyes. Then he leaned forward and pressed the bell.

'Who brought this note, James?' he said quietly, as his servant came into the room.

'A small boy, sir. Said I was to be sure and see you got it most particular.' He unlocked a cupboard near the window and produced a tantalus. 'Whisky, sir, or cocktail?'

'Whisky I think, James.' Hugh carefully folded the sheet of paper and placed it in his pocket. And his face as he took the drink from his man would have left no doubt in an onlooker's mind as to why, in the past, he had earned the name of 'Bulldog' Drummond.

Chapter 2

In which he journeys to Godalming and the game begins

I

'I almost think, James, that I could toy with another kidney.' Drummond looked across the table at his servant, who was carefully arranging two or three dozen letters in groups. 'Do you think it will cause a complete breakdown in the culinary arrangements? I've got a journey in front of me today, and I require a large breakfast.'

James Denny supplied the deficiency from a dish that was standing on an electric heater.

'Are you going for long, sir?' he ventured.

'I don't know, James. It all depends on circumstances. Which, when you come to think of it, is undoubtedly one of the most fatuous phrases in the English language. Is there anything in the world that doesn't depend on circumstances?'

'Will you be motoring, sir, or going by train?' asked James prosaically. Dialectical arguments did not appeal to him.

'By car,' answered Drummond. 'Pyjamas and a tooth-brush.'

'You won't take evening clothes, sir?'

'No. I want my visit to appear unpremeditated, James, and if one goes about completely encased in boiled shirts, while pretending to be merely out for the afternoon, people have doubts as to one's intellect.'

James digested this great thought in silence.

'Will you be going far, sir?' he asked at length, pouring out a second cup of coffee.

'To Godalming. A charming spot, I believe, though I've never been there. Charming inhabitants, too, James. The lady I met yesterday at the Carlton lives at Godalming.'

'Indeed, sir,' murmured James noncommittally.

'You damned old humbug,' laughed Drummond, 'you know you're itching to know all about it. I had a very long and interesting talk with her, and one of two things emerges quite clearly from our conversation. Either, James, I am a congenital idiot, and don't know enough to come in out of the rain; or we've hit the goods. That is what I propose to find out by my little excursion. Either our legs, my friend, are being pulled till they will never resume their normal shape; or that advertisement has succeeded beyond our wildest dreams.'

'There are a lot more answers in this morning, sir.' Denny made a movement towards the letters he had been sorting. 'One from a lovely widow with two children.'

'Lovely,' cried Drummond. 'How forward of her!' He glanced at the letter and smiled. 'Care, James, and accuracy are essential in a secretary. The misguided woman calls herself lonely, not lovely. She will remain so, as far as I am concerned, until the other matter is settled.'

'Will it take long, sir, do you think?'

'To get it settled?' Drummond lit a cigarette and leaned back in his chair. 'Listen, James, and I will outline the case. The maiden lives at a house called The Larches, near Godalming, with her papa. Not far away is another house called The Elms, owned by a gentleman of the name of Henry Lakington – a nasty man, James, with a nasty face – who was also at the Carlton yesterday afternoon for a short time. And now we come to the point. Miss Benton – that is the lady's name – accuses Mr Lakington of being the complete IT in the criminal line. She went even so far as to say that he was the second most dangerous man in England.'

'Indeed, sir. More coffee, sir?'

'Will nothing move you, James?' remarked his master plaintively. 'This man murders people and does things like that, you know.'

'Personally, sir, I prefer a picture-palace. But I suppose there ain't no accounting for 'obbies. May I clear away, sir?'

'No, James, not at present. Keep quite still while I go on, or I shall get it wrong. Three months ago there arrived at The Elms *the* most dangerous man in England – the IT of ITs. This gentleman goes by the name of Peterson, and he owns a daughter. From what Miss Benton said, I have doubts about that daughter, James.' He rose and strolled over to the window. 'Grave doubts. However, to return to the point, it appears that some unpleasing conspiracy is being hatched by IT, the IT of ITs, and the doubtful daughter, into which Papa Benton has been unwillingly drawn. As far as I can make out, the suggestion is that I should unravel the tangled skein of crime and extricate papa.'

In a spasm of uncontrollable excitement James sucked his teeth. 'Lumme, it wouldn't 'alf go on the movies, would it?' he remarked. 'Better than them Red Indians and things.'

'I fear, James, that you are not in the habit of spending your spare time at the British Museum, as I hoped,' said Drummond. 'And your brain doesn't work very quickly. The point is not whether this hideous affair is better than Red Indians and things – but whether it's genuine. Am I to battle with murderers, or shall I find a house-party roaring with laughter on the lawn?'

'As long as you laughs like 'ell yourself, sir, I don't see as 'ow it makes much odds,' answered James philosophically.

'The first sensible remark you've made this morning,' said his master hopefully. 'I will go prepared to laugh.'

He picked up a pipe from the mantelpiece, and proceeded to fill it, while James Denny still waited in silence.

'A lady may ring up today,' Drummond continued. 'Miss Benton, to be exact. Don't say where I've gone if she does; but take down any message, and wire it to me at Godalming Post Office. If by any chance you don't hear from me for three days, get in touch with Scotland Yard, and tell 'em where I've gone. That covers everything if it's genuine. If, on the other hand, it's a hoax, and the house-party is a good one, I shall probably want you to come down with my evening clothes and some more kit.'

'Very good, sir. I will clean your small Colt revolver at once.'

Hugh Drummond paused in the act of lighting his pipe, and a grin spread slowly over his face. 'Excellent,' he said. 'And see if you can find that water-squirt pistol I used to have – a Son of a Gun they called it. That ought to raise a laugh, when I arrest the murderer with it.'

2

The 30 h.p. two-seater made short work of the run to Godalming. Under the dickey seat behind lay a small bag, containing the bare necessaries for the night; and as Drummond thought of the two guns rolled up carefully in his pyjamas – the harmless toy and the wicked little automatic – he grinned gently to himself. The girl had not rung him up during the morning, and, after a comfortable lunch at his club, he had started about three o'clock. The hedges, fresh with the glory of spring, flashed past; the smell of the country came sweet and fragrant on the air. There was a gentle warmth, a balminess in the day that made it good to be alive, and once or twice he sang under his breath through sheer lightheartedness of spirit. Surrounded by the peaceful beauty of the fields, with an occasional village half hidden by great trees from under which the tiny houses peeped out, it seemed impossible that crime could exist – laughable. Of course the thing was a hoax, an elaborate leg-pull, but, being not guilty of any mental subterfuge, Hugh Drummond admitted to himself quite truly that he didn't care a damn if it was. Phyllis Benton was at liberty to continue the jest, wherever and whenever she liked. Phyllis Benton was a very nice girl, and very nice girls are permitted a lot of latitude.

A persistent honking behind aroused him from his reverie, and he pulled into the side of the road. Under normal circumstances he would have let his own car out, and as she could touch ninety with ease, he very rarely found himself passed. But this afternoon he felt disinclined to race; he wanted to go quietly and think. Blue eyes and that glorious colouring were a dangerous combination – distinctly dangerous. Most engrossing to a healthy bachelor's thoughts.

An open cream-coloured Rolls-Royce drew level, with five people on board, and he looked up as it passed. There were three people in the back – two men and a woman, and for a moment his eyes met those of the man nearest him. Then they drew ahead, and Drummond pulled up to avoid the thick cloud of dust.

With a slight frown he stared at the retreating car; he saw the man lean over and speak to the other man; he saw the other man look round. Then a bend in the road hid them from sight, and, still frowning, Drummond pulled out his case and lit a cigarette. For the man whose eye he had caught as the Rolls went by was Henry Lakington. There was no mistaking that hard-lipped, cruel face. Presumably, thought Hugh, the other two occupants were Mr Peterson and the doubtful daughter, Irma; presumably they were returning to The Elms. And incidentally there seemed no pronounced reason why they shouldn't. But, somehow, the sudden appearance of Lakington had upset him! He felt irritable and annoyed. What little he had seen of the man he had not liked; he did not want to be reminded of him, especially just as he was thinking of Phyllis.

He watched the white dust-cloud rise over the hill in front as the car topped it; he watched it settle and drift away in the faint breeze. Then he let in his clutch and followed quite slowly in the big car's wake.

There had been two men in front – the driver and another, and he wondered idly if the latter was Mr Benton. Probably not, he reflected, since Phyllis had said nothing about her father being in London. He accelerated up the hill and swung over the top; the next moment he braked hard and pulled up just in time. The Rolls, with the chauffeur peering into the bonnet, had stopped in such a position that it was impossible for him to get by.

The girl was still seated in the back of the car, also the passenger in front, but the two other men were standing in the road apparently watching the chauffeur, and after a while the one whom Drummond had recognised as Lakington came towards him.

'I'm so sorry,' he began – and then paused in surprise. 'Why, surely it's Captain Drummond?'

Drummond nodded pleasantly. 'The occupant of a car is hardly likely to change in a mile, is he?' he remarked. 'I'm afraid I forgot to wave as you went past, but I got your smile all right.' He leant on his steering-wheel and lit a second cigarette. 'Are you likely to be long?' he asked; 'because if so, I'll stop my engine.'

The other man was now approaching casually, and Drummond regarded him curiously. 'A friend of our little Phyllis, Peterson,' said Lakington, as he came up. 'I found them having tea together yesterday at the Carlton.'

'Any friend of Miss Benton's is, I hope, ours,' said Peterson with a smile. 'You've known her a long time, I expect?'

'Quite a long time,' returned Hugh. 'We have jazzed together on many occasions.'

'Which makes it all the more unfortunate that we should have delayed you,' said Peterson. 'I can't help thinking, Lakington, that that new chauffeur is a bit of a fool.'

'I hope he avoided the crash all right,' murmured Drummond politely.

Both men looked at him. 'The crash!' said Lakington. 'There was no question of a crash. We just stopped.'

'Really,' remarked Drummond, 'I think, sir, that you must be right in your diagnosis of your chauffeur's mentality.' He turned courteously to Peterson. 'When something goes wrong, for a fellah to stop his car by braking so hard that he locks both back wheels is no *bon*, as we used to say in France. I thought, judging by the tracks in the dust, that you must have been in imminent danger of ramming a traction engine. Or perhaps,' he added judicially, 'a sudden order to stop would have produced the same effect.' If he saw the lightning glance that passed between the two men he gave no sign. 'May I offer you a cigarette? Turkish that side – Virginian the other. I wonder if I could help your man,' he continued, when they had helped themselves. 'I'm a bit of an expert with a Rolls.'

'How very kind of you,' said Peterson. 'I'll go and see.' He went over to the man and spoke a few words.

'Isn't it extraordinary,' remarked Hugh, 'how the eye of the boss galvanises the average man into activity! As long, probably, as Mr Peterson had remained here talking, that chauffeur would have gone on tinkering with the engine. And now – look, in a second – all serene. And yet I dare say Mr Peterson knows nothing about it really. Just the watching eye, Mr Lakington. Wonderful thing – the human optic.'

He rambled on with a genial smile, watching with apparent interest the car in front. 'Who's the quaint bird sitting beside the chauffeur? He appeals to me immensely. Wish to Heaven I'd had a few more like him in France to turn into snipers.'

'May I ask why you think he would have been a success at the job?' Lakington's voice expressed merely perfunctory interest, but his cold, steely eyes were fixed on Drummond.

'He's so motionless,' answered Hugh. 'The bally fellow hasn't moved a muscle since I've been here. I believe he'd sit on a hornets' nest, and leave the inmates guessing. Great gift, Mr Lakington. Shows a strength of will but rarely met with – a mind which rises above mere vulgar curiosity.'

'It is undoubtedly a great gift to have such a mind, Captain Drummond,' said Lakington 'And if it isn't born in a man, he should most certainly try to cultivate it.' He pitched his cigarette away, and buttoned up his coat. 'Shall we be seeing you this evening?'

Drummond shrugged his shoulders. 'I'm the vaguest man that ever lived,' he said lightly. 'I might be listening to nightingales in the country; or I might be consuming steak and onions preparatory to going to a night club. So long . . . You must let me take you to Hector's one night. Hope you don't break down again so suddenly.'

He watched the Rolls-Royce start, but seemed in no hurry to follow suit. And his many friends, who were wont to regard Hugh Drummond as a mass of brawn not too plentifully supplied with brains, would have been puzzled had they seen the look of keen concentration on his face as he stared along the white, dusty road. He could not say why, but suddenly and very certainly the conviction had come to him that this was no hoax and no leg-pull – but grim and sober reality. In his imagination he heard the sudden sharp order to stop the instant they were over the hill, so that Peterson might have a chance of inspecting him; in a flash of intuition he knew that these two men were no ordinary people, and that he was suspect. And as he slipped smoothly after the big car, now well out of sight, two thoughts were dominant in his mind. The first was that there was some mystery about the motionless, unnatural man who had sat beside the driver; the second was a distinct feeling of relief that his automatic was fully loaded.

3

At half-past five he stopped in front of Godalming Post Office. To his surprise the girl handed him a wire, and Hugh tore the yellow envelope open quickly. It was from Denny, and it was brief and to the point:

PHONE MESSAGE RECEIVED. AAA. MUST SEE YOU CARLTON TEA DAY AFTER TOMORROW. GOING GODALMING NOW. AAA. MESSAGE ENDS.

With a slight smile he noticed the military phraseology – Denny at one time in his career had been a signaller – and then he frowned. 'Must see you.' She should – at once.

He turned to the girl and inquired the way to The Larches. It was about two miles, he gathered, on the Guildford road, and impossible to miss – a biggish house standing well back in its own grounds.

'Is it anywhere near a house called The Elms?' he asked.

'Next door, sir,' said the girl. 'The gardens adjoin.'

He thanked her, and having torn up the telegram into small pieces, he got into his car. There was nothing for it, he had decided, but to drive boldly up to the house, and say that he had come to call on Miss Benton. He had never been a man who beat about the bush, and simple methods appealed to him – a trait in his character which many a boxer, addicted to tortuous cunning in the ring, had good cause to remember. What more natural, he reflected, than to drive over and see such an old friend?

He had no difficulty in finding the house, and a few minutes later he was ringing the front-door bell. It was answered by a maidservant, who looked at him in mild surprise. Young men in motor-cars were not common visitors at The Larches.

'Is Miss Benton in?' Hugh asked with a smile which at once won the girl's heart.

'She has only just come back from London, sir,' she answered doubtfully. 'I don't know whether . . .'

'Would you tell her that Captain Drummond has called?' said Hugh as the maid hesitated. 'That I happened to find myself near here, and came on chance of seeing her?'

Once again the smile was called into play, and the girl hesitated no longer. 'Will you come inside, sir?' she said. 'I will go and tell Miss Phyllis.'

She ushered him into the drawing-room and closed the door. It was a charming room, just such as he would have expected with Phyllis. Big windows, opening down to the ground, led out on to a lawn, which was already a blaze of colour. A few great oak trees threw a pleasant shade at the end of the garden, and, partially showing through them, he could see another house which he rightly assumed was The Elms. In fact, even as he heard the door open and shut behind him, he saw Peterson come out of a small summer-house and commence strolling up and down, smoking a cigar. Then he turned round and faced the girl.

Charming as she had looked in London, she was doubly so now, in a simple linen frock which showed off her figure to perfection. But if he thought he was going to have any leisure to enjoy the picture undisturbed, he was soon disillusioned.

'Why have you come here, Captain Drummond?' she said, a little breathlessly. 'I said the Carlton – the day after tomorrow.'

'Unfortunately,' said Hugh, 'I'd left London before that message came. My servant wired it on to the post office here. Not that it would have made any difference. I should have come, anyway.'

An involuntary smile hovered round her lips for a moment; then she grew serious again. 'It's very dangerous for you to come here,' she remarked quietly. 'If once those men suspect anything, God knows what will happen.'

It was on the tip of his tongue to tell her that it was too late to worry about that; then he changed his mind. 'And what is there suspicious,' he asked, 'in an old friend who happens to be in the neighbourhood dropping in to call? Do you mind if I smoke?'

The girl beat her hands together. 'My dear man,' she cried, 'you don't understand. You're judging those devils by your own standard. They suspect everything – and everybody.'

'What a distressing habit,' he murmured. 'Is it chronic, or merely due to liver? I must send 'em a bottle of good salts. Wonderful thing – good salts. Never without some in France.'

The girl looked at him resignedly. 'You're hopeless,' she remarked – 'absolutely hopeless.'

'Absolutely,' agreed Hugh, blowing out a cloud of smoke. 'Wherefore your telephone message? What's the worry?'

She bit her lip and drummed with her fingers on the arm of her chair. 'If I tell you,' she said at length, 'will you promise me, on your word of honour, that you won't go blundering into The Elms, or do anything foolish like that?'

'At the present moment I'm very comfortable where I am, thanks,' remarked Hugh.

'I know,' she said; 'but I'm so dreadfully afraid that you're the type of person who . . . who . . . ' She paused, at a loss for a word.

'Who bellows like a bull, and charges head down,' interrupted Hugh with a grin. She laughed with him, and just for a moment their eyes met, and she read in his something quite foreign to the point at issue. In fact, it is to be feared that the question of Lakington and his companions was not engrossing Drummond's mind, as it doubtless should have been, to the exclusion of all else.

'They're so utterly unscrupulous,' she continued hurriedly, 'so fiendishly clever, that even you would be like a child in their hands.'

Hugh endeavoured to dissemble his pleasure at that little word 'even', and only succeeded in frowning horribly.

'I will be discretion itself,' he assured her firmly. 'I promise you.'

'I suppose I shall have to trust you,' she said. 'Have you seen the evening papers today?'

'I looked at the ones that come out in the morning labelled 6 p.m. before I had lunch,' he answered. 'Is there anything of interest?'

She handed him a copy of the *Planet*. 'Read that little paragraph in the second column.' She pointed to it as he took the paper, and Hugh read it aloud.

' "Mr Hiram C. Potts – the celebrated American millionaire – is progressing favourably. He has gone into the country for a few days, but is sufficiently recovered to conduct business as usual." '
He laid down the paper and looked at the girl sitting opposite. 'One is pleased,' he remarked in a puzzled tone, 'for the sake of Mr Potts. To be ill and have a name like that is more than most men could stand . . . But I don't quite see . . . '

'That man was stopping at the Carlton, where he met Lakington,' said the girl. 'He is a multimillionaire, over here in connection with some big steel trust; and when multimillionaires get friendly with Lakington, their health frequently does suffer.'

'But this paper says he's getting better,' objected Drummond. '"Sufficiently recovered to conduct business as usual." What's wrong with that?'

'If he is sufficiently recovered to conduct business as usual, why did he send his confidential secretary away yesterday morning on an urgent mission to Belfast?'

'Search me,' said Hugh. 'Incidentally, how do you know he did?'

'I asked at the Carlton this morning,' she answered. 'I said I'd come after a job as typist for Mr Potts. They told me at the inquiry office that he was ill in bed and unable to see anybody. So I asked for his secretary, and they told me what I've just told you – that he had left for Belfast that morning and would be away several days. It may be that there's nothing in it; on the other hand, it may be that there's a lot. And it's only by following up every possible clue,' she continued fiercely, 'that I can hope to beat those fiends and get Daddy out of their clutches.'

Drummond nodded gravely, and did not speak. For into his mind had flashed suddenly the remembrance of that sinister, motionless figure seated by the chauffeur. The wildest guesswork certainly – no vestige of proof – and yet, having once come, the thought stuck. And as he turned it over in his mind, almost prepared to laugh at himself for his credulity – millionaires are not removed against their will, in broad daylight, from one of the biggest hotels in London, to sit in immovable silence in an open car – the door opened and an elderly man came in.

Hugh rose, and the girl introduced the two men. 'An old friend, Daddy,' she said. 'You must have heard me speak of Captain Drummond.'

'I don't recall the name at the moment, my dear,' he answered courteously – a fact which was hardly surprising – 'but I fear I'm getting a little forgetful. I am pleased to meet you, Captain Drummond. You'll stop and have some dinner, of course.'

Hugh bowed. 'I should like to, Mr Benton. Thank you very much. I'm afraid the hour of my call was a little informal, but being round in these parts, I felt I must come and look Miss Benton up.'

His host smiled absentmindedly, and walking to the window, stared through the gathering dusk at the house opposite, half hidden in the trees. And Hugh, who was watching him from under lowered lids, saw him suddenly clench both hands in a gesture of despair.

It cannot be said that dinner was a meal of sparkling gaiety. Mr Benton was palpably ill at ease, and beyond a few desultory remarks spoke hardly at all: while the girl, who sat opposite Hugh, though she made one or two valiant attempts to break the long silences, spent most of the meal in covertly watching her father. If anything more had been required to convince Drummond of the genuineness of his interview with her at the Carlton the preceding day, the atmosphere at this strained and silent party supplied it.

As if unconscious of anything peculiar, he rambled on in his usual inconsequent method, heedless of whether he was answered or not; but all the time his mind was busily working. He had already decided that a Rolls-Royce was not the only car on the market which could break down mysteriously, and with the town so far away, his host could hardly fail to ask him to stop the night. And then – he had not yet quite settled how – he proposed to have a closer look at The Elms.

At length the meal was over, and the maid, placing the decanter in front of Mr Benton, withdrew from the room.

'You'll have a glass of port, Captain Drummond,' remarked his host, removing the stopper and pushing the bottle towards him. 'An old pre-war wine which I can vouch for.'

Hugh smiled, and even as he lifted the heavy old cut glass, he stiffened suddenly in his chair. A cry – half shout, half scream, and stifled at once – had come echoing through the open windows. With a crash the stopper fell from Mr Benton's nerveless fingers, breaking the finger-bowl in front of him, while every vestige of colour left his face.

'It's something these days to be able to say that,' remarked Hugh, pouring himself out a glass. 'Wine, Miss Benton?' He looked at the girl, who was staring fearfully out of the window, and forced her to meet his eye. 'It will do you good.'

His tone was compelling, and after a moment's hesitation she pushed the glass over to him. 'Will you pour it out?' she said, and he saw that she was trembling all over.

'Did you – did you hear – anything?' With a vain endeavour to speak calmly, his host looked at Hugh.

'That night-bird?' he answered easily. 'Eerie noises they make, don't they? Sometimes in France, when everything was still, and only the ghostly green flares went hissing up, one used to hear 'em. Startled nervous sentries out of their lives.' He talked on, and gradually the colour came back to the other man's face. But Hugh noticed that he drained his port at a gulp, and immediately refilled his glass . . .

Outside everything was still; no repetition of that short, strangled cry again disturbed the silence. With the training bred of many hours in No Man's Land, Drummond was listening, even while he was speaking, for the faintest suspicious sound – but he heard nothing. The soft whispering night-noises came gently through the window; but the man who had screamed once did not even whimper again. He remembered hearing a similar cry near the brickstacks at Guinchy, and two nights later he had found the giver of it, at the edge of a mine-crater, with glazed eyes that still held in them the horror of the final second. And more persistently than ever, his thoughts centred on the fifth occupant of the Rolls-Royce . . .

It was with almost a look of relief that Mr Benton listened to his tale of woe about his car.

'Of course you must stop here for the night,' he cried. 'Phyllis, my dear, will you tell them to get a room ready?'

With an inscrutable look at Hugh, in which thankfulness and apprehension seemed mingled, the girl left the room. There was an unnatural glitter in her father's eyes – a flush on his cheeks hardly to be accounted for by the warmth of the evening; and it struck Drummond that, during the time he had been pretending to look at his car, Mr Benton had been fortifying himself. It was obvious, even to the soldier's unprofessional eye, that the man's nerves had gone to pieces; and that unless something was done soon, his daughter's worst forebodings were likely to be fulfilled. He talked disjointedly and fast; his hands were not steady, and he seemed to be always waiting for something to happen.

Hugh had not been in the room ten minutes before his host produced the whisky, and during the time that he took to drink a mild nightcap, Mr Benton succeeded in lowering three extremely strong glasses of spirit. And what made it the more sad was that the man was obviously not a heavy drinker by preference.

At eleven o'clock Hugh rose and said good night.

'You'll ring if you want anything, won't you?' said his host. 'We don't have very many visitors here, but I hope you'll find everything you require. Breakfast at nine.'

Drummond closed the door behind him, and stood for a moment in silence, looking round the hall. It was deserted, but he wanted to get the geography of the house firmly imprinted on his mind. Then a noise from the room he had just left made him frown sharply – his host was continuing the process of fortification –

and he stepped across towards the drawing-room. Inside, as he hoped, he found the girl.

She rose the instant he came in, and stood by the mantelpiece with her hands locked.

'What was it?' she half whispered – 'that awful noise at dinner?'

He looked at her gravely for a while, and then he shook his head. 'Shall we leave it as a nightbird for the present?' he said quietly. Then he leaned towards her, and took her hands in his own. 'Go to bed, little girl,' he ordered; 'this is my show. And, may I say, I think you're just wonderful. Thank God you saw my advertisement!'

Gently he released her hands, and walking to the door, held it open for her. 'If by any chance you should hear things in the night – turn over and go to sleep again.'

'But what are you going to do?' she cried.

Hugh grinned. 'I haven't the remotest idea,' he answered. 'Doubtless the Lord will provide.'

The instant the girl had left the room Hugh switched off the lights and stepped across to the curtains which covered the long windows. He pulled them aside, letting them come together behind him; then, cautiously, he unbolted one side of the big centre window. The night was dark, and the moon was not due to rise for two or three hours, but he was too old a soldier to neglect any precautions. He wanted to see more of The Elms and its inhabitants; he did not want them to see more of him.

Silently he dodged across the lawn towards the big trees at the end and leaning up against one of them, he proceeded to make a more detailed survey of his objective. It was the same type of house as the one he had just left, and the grounds seemed about the same size. A wire fence separated the two places, and in the darkness Hugh could just make out a small wicket-gate, closing a path which connected both houses. He tried it, and found to his satisfaction that it opened silently.

Passing through, he took cover behind some bushes from which he could command a better view of Mr Lakington's abode. Save for one room on the ground floor the house was in darkness, and Hugh determined to have a look at that room. There was a chink in the curtains, through which the light was streaming out, which struck him as having possibilities.

Keeping under cover, he edged towards it, and at length, he got into a position from which he could see inside. And what he saw made him decide to chance it, and go even closer.

Seated at the table was a man he did not recognise; while on either side of him sat Lakington and Peterson. Lying on a sofa smoking a cigarette and reading a novel was a tall, dark girl, who seemed completely uninterested in the proceedings of the other three. Hugh placed her at once as the doubtful daughter Irma, and resumed his watch on the group at the table.

A paper was in front of the man, and Peterson, who was smoking a large cigar, was apparently suggesting that he should make use of the pen which Lakington was obligingly holding in readiness. In all respects a harmless tableau, save for one small thing – the expression on the man's face. Hugh had seen it before often – only then it had been called shell-shock. The man was dazed, semi-unconscious. Every now and then he stared round the room, as if bewildered; then he would shake his head and pass his hand wearily over his forehead. For a quarter of an hour the scene continued; then Lakington produced an instrument from his pocket. Hugh saw the man shrink back in terror, and reach for the pen. He saw the girl lie back on the sofa as if disappointed and pick up her novel again; and he saw Lakington's face set in a cold sneer. But what impressed him most in that momentary flash of action was Peterson. There was something inhuman in his complete passivity. By not the fraction of a second did he alter the rate at which he was smoking – the slow, leisurely rate of the connoisseur; by not the twitch of an eyelid did his expression change. Even as he watched the man signing his name, no trace of emotion showed on his face – whereas on Lakington's there shone a fiendish satisfaction.

The document was still lying on the table, when Hugh produced his revolver. He knew there was foul play about, and the madness of what he had suddenly made up his mind to do never struck him: being that manner of fool, he was made that way. But he breathed a pious prayer that he would shoot straight – and then he held his breath. The crack of the shot and the bursting of the only electric-light bulb in the room were almost simultaneous; and the next second, with a roar of 'Come on, boys,' he burst through the window. At an immense advantage over the others, who could see nothing for the moment, he blundered round the room. He timed the blow at Lakington to a nicety; he hit him straight on the point of the jaw and he felt the man go down like a log. Then he grabbed at the paper on the table, which tore in his hand, and picking the dazed signer up bodily, he rushed through the window on to the lawn. There was not an instant to be lost; only the impossibility of seeing when suddenly plunged into darkness had enabled him to pull the thing off so far. And before that advantage disappeared he had to be back at The Larches with his burden, no light weight for even a man of his strength to carry.

But there seemed to be no pursuit, no hue and cry. As he reached the little gate he paused and looked back, and he fancied he saw outside the window a gleam of white, such as a shirt-front. He lingered for an instant, peering into the darkness and recovering his breath, when with a vicious phut something buried itself in the tree beside him. Drummond lingered no more; long years of experience left no doubt in his mind as to what that something was.

'Compressed-air rifle – or electric,' he muttered to himself, stumbling on, and half dragging, half carrying his dazed companion.

He was not very clear in his own mind what to do next, but the matter was settled for him unexpectedly. Barely had he got into the drawing room, when the door opened and the girl rushed in.

'Get him away at once,' she cried. 'In your car . . . Don't waste a second. I've started her up.'

'Good girl,' he cried enthusiastically. 'But what about you?'

She stamped her foot impatiently. 'I'm all right – absolutely all right. Get him away – that's all that matters.'

Drummond grinned. 'The humorous thing is that I haven't an idea who the bird is – except that – ' He paused, with his eyes fixed on the man's left thumb. The top joint was crushed into a red, shapeless pulp, and suddenly the meaning of the instrument Lakington had produced from his pocket became clear. Also the reason of that dreadful cry at dinner . . .

'By God!' whispered Drummond, half to himself, while his jaws set like a steel vice. 'A thumbscrew. The devils . . . the bloody swine . . . '

'Oh! quick, quick,' the girl urged in an agony. 'They may be here at any moment.' She dragged him to the door, and together they forced the man into the car.

'Lakington won't,' said Hugh with a grin. 'And if you see him tomorrow – don't ask after his jaw . . . Good night, Phyllis.'

With a quick movement he raised her hand to his lips; then he slipped in the clutch and the car disappeared down the drive . . .

He felt a sense of elation and of triumph at having won the first round, and as the car whirled back to London through the cool night air his heart was singing with the joy of action. And it was perhaps as well for his peace of mind that he did not witness the scene in the room at The Elms.

Lakington still lay motionless on the floor; Peterson's cigar still glowed steadily in the darkness. It was hard to believe that he had ever moved from the table; only the bullet embedded in a tree proved that somebody must have got busy. Of course, it might have been the girl, who was just lighting another cigarette from the stump of the old one.

At length Peterson spoke. 'A young man of dash and temperament,' he said genially. 'It will be a pity to lose him.'

'Why not keep him and lose the girl?' yawned Irma. 'I think he might amuse me – '

'We have always our dear Henry to consider,' answered Peterson. 'Apparently the girl appeals to him. I'm afraid, Irma, he'll have to go . . . and at once . . . '

The speaker was tapping his left knee softly with his hand; save for that slight movement he sat as if nothing had happened. And yet ten minutes before a carefully planned coup had failed at the instant of success. Even his most fearless accomplices had been known to confess that Peterson's inhuman calmness sent cold shivers down their backs.

Chapter 3

In which things happen in Half Moon Street

I

Hugh Drummond folded up the piece of paper he was studying and rose to his feet as the doctor came into the room. He then pushed a silver box of cigarettes across the table and waited.

'Your friend,' said the doctor, 'is in a very peculiar condition, Captain Drummond – very peculiar.' He sat down and, putting the tips of his fingers together, gazed at Drummond in his most professional manner. He paused for a moment, as if expecting an awed agreement with this profound utterance, but the soldier was calmly lighting a cigarette. 'Can you,' resumed the doctor, 'enlighten me at all as to what he has been doing during the last few days?'

Drummond shook his head. 'Haven't an earthly, doctor.'

'There is, for instance, that very unpleasant wound in his thumb,' pursued the other. 'The top joint is crushed to a pulp.'

'I noticed that last night,' answered Hugh noncommittally. 'Looks as if it had been mixed up between a hammer and an anvil, don't it?'

'But you have no idea how it occurred?'

'I'm full of ideas,' said the soldier. 'In fact, if it's any help to you in your diagnosis, that wound was caused by the application of an unpleasant medieval instrument known as a thumbscrew.'

The worthy doctor looked at him in amazement. 'A thumbscrew! You must be joking, Captain Drummond.'

'Very far from it,' answered Hugh briefly. 'If you want to know, it was touch and go whether the other thumb didn't share the same fate.' He blew out a cloud of smoke, and smiled inwardly as he noticed the look of scandalised horror on his companion's face. 'It isn't his thumb that concerns me,' he continued; 'it's his general condition. What's the matter with him?'

The doctor pursed his lips and looked wise, while Drummond

wondered that no-one had ever passed a law allowing men of his type to be murdered on sight.

'His heart seems sound,' he answered after a weighty pause, 'and I found nothing wrong with him constitutionally. In fact, I may say, Captain Drummond, he is in every respect a most healthy man. Except – er – except for this peculiar condition.'

Drummond exploded. 'Damnation take it, and what on earth do you suppose I asked you to come round for? It's of no interest to me to hear that his liver is working properly.' Then he controlled himself. 'I beg your pardon, doctor: I had rather a trying evening last night. Can you give me any idea as to what has caused this peculiar condition?'

His companion accepted the apology with an acid bow. 'Some form of drug,' he answered.

Drummond heaved a sigh of relief. 'Now we're getting on,' he cried. 'Have you any idea what drug?'

'It is, at the moment, hard to say,' returned the other. 'It seems to have produced a dazed condition mentally, without having affected him physically. In a day or two, perhaps, I might be able to – er – arrive at some conclusion . . . '

'Which, at present, you have not. Right; now we know where we are.' A pained expression flitted over the doctor's face: this young man was very direct. 'To continue,' Hugh went on, 'as you don't know what the drug is, presumably you don't know either how long it will take for the effect to wear off.'

'That – er – is, within limits, correct,' conceded the doctor.

'Right; once again we know where we are. What about diet?'

'Oh! light . . . Not too much meat . . . No alcohol . . . ' He rose to his feet as Hugh opened the door; really the war seemed to have produced a distressing effect on people's manners. Diet was the one question on which he always let himself go . . .

'Not much meat – no alcohol. Right. Good morning, doctor. Down the stairs and straight on. Good morning.' The door closed behind him, and he descended to his waiting car with cold disapproval on his face. The whole affair struck him as most suspicious – thumbscrews, strange drugs . . . Possibly it was his duty to communicate with the police . . .

'Excuse me, sir.' The doctor paused and eyed a well-dressed man who had spoken to him uncompromisingly.

'What can I do for you, sir?' he said.

'Am I right in assuming that you are a doctor?'

'You are perfectly correct, sir, in your assumption.'

The man smiled: obviously a gentleman, thought the practitioner, with his hand on the door of his car.

'It's about a great pal of mine, Captain Drummond, who lives in here,' went on the other. 'I hope you won't think it unprofessional, but I thought I'd ask you privately how you find him.'

The doctor looked surprised. 'I wasn't aware that he was ill,' he answered.

'But I heard he'd had a bad accident,' said the man, amazed.

The doctor smiled. 'Reassure yourself, my dear sir,' he murmured in his best professional manner. 'Captain Drummond, so far as I am aware, has never been better. I – er – cannot say the same of his friend.' He stepped into his car. 'Why not go up and see for yourself?'

The car rolled smoothly into Piccadilly, but the man showed no signs of availing himself of the doctor's suggestion. He turned and walked rapidly away, and a few moments later – in an exclusive West End club – a trunk call was put through to Godalming – a call which caused the recipient to nod his head in satisfaction and order the Rolls-Royce.

Meanwhile, unconscious of this sudden solicitude for his health, Hugh Drummond was once more occupied with the piece of paper he had been studying on the doctor's entrance. Every now and then he ran his fingers through his crisp brown hair and shook his head in perplexity. Beyond establishing the fact that the man in the peculiar condition was Hiram C. Potts, the American multimillionaire, he could make nothing out of it.

'If only I'd managed to get the whole of it,' he muttered to himself for the twentieth time. 'That dam' fellah Peterson was too quick.' The scrap he had torn off was typewritten, save for the American's scrawled signature, and Hugh knew the words by heart.

> plete paralysis
> ade of Britain
> months I do
> the holder of
> of five million
> do desire and
>   earl necklace and the
>   are at present
>   chess of Lamp-

k no questions
btained.
AM C. POTTS.

At length he replaced the scrap in his pocket-book and rang the bell.

'James,' he remarked as his servant came in, 'will you whisper "very little meat and no alcohol" in your wife's ear, so far as the bird next door is concerned? Fancy paying a doctor to come round and tell one that?'

'Did he say anything more, sir?'

'Oh! a lot. But that was the only thing of the slightest practical use, and I knew that already.' He stared thoughtfully out of the window. 'You'd better know,' he continued at length, 'that as far as I can see we're up against a remarkably tough proposition.'

'Indeed, sir,' murmured his servant. 'Then perhaps I had better stop any further insertion of that advertisement. It works out at six shillings a time.'

Drummond burst out laughing. 'What would I do without you, O my James,' he cried. 'But you may as well stop it. Our hands will be quite full for some time to come, and I hate disappointing hopeful applicants for my services.'

'The gentleman is asking for you, sir.' Mrs Denny's voice from the door made them look round, and Hugh rose.

'Is he talking sensibly, Mrs Denny?' he asked eagerly, but she shook her head.

'Just the same, sir,' she announced. 'Looking round the room all dazed like. And he keeps on saying "Danger".'

Hugh walked quickly along the passage to the room where the millionaire lay in bed.

'How are you feeling?' said Drummond cheerfully.

The man stared at him uncomprehendingly, and shook his head.

'Do you remember last night?' Hugh continued, speaking very slowly and distinctly. Then a sudden idea struck him and he pulled the scrap of paper out of his case. 'Do you remember signing that?' he asked, holding it out to him.

For a while the man looked at it; then with a sudden cry of fear he shrank away. 'No, no,' he muttered, 'not again.'

Hugh hurriedly replaced the paper. 'Bad break on my part, old bean; you evidently remember rather too well. It's quite all right,' he continued reassuringly; 'no-one will hurt you.' Then after a pause: 'Is your name Hiram C. Potts?'

The man nodded his head doubtfully and muttered 'Hiram Potts' once or twice, as if the words sounded familiar.

'Do you remember driving in a motor-car last night?' persisted Hugh.

But what little flash of remembrance had pierced the drug-clouded brain seemed to have passed; the man only stared dazedly at the speaker. Drummond tried him with a few more questions, but it was no use, and after a while he got up and moved towards the door.

'Don't you worry, old son,' he said with a smile. 'We'll have you jumping about like a two-year-old in a couple of days.'

Then he paused: the man was evidently trying to say something. 'What is it you want?' Hugh leant over the bed.

'Danger, danger.' Faintly the words came, and then, with a sigh, he lay back exhausted.

With a grim smile Drummond watched the motionless figure.

'I'm afraid,' he said half aloud, 'that you're rather like your medical attendant. Your only contribution to the sphere of pure knowledge is something I know already.'

He went out and quietly closed the door. And as he re-entered his sitting-room he found his servant standing motionless behind one of the curtains watching the street below.

'There's a man, sir,' he remarked without turning round, 'watching the house.'

For a moment Hugh stood still, frowning. Then he gave a short laugh. 'The devil there is!' he remarked. 'The game has begun in earnest, my worthy warrior, with the first nine points to us. For possession, even of a semi-dazed lunatic, is nine points of the law, is it not, James?'

His servant retreated cautiously from the curtain and came back into the room. 'Of the law – yes, sir,' he repeated enigmatically. 'It is time, sir, for your morning glass of beer.'

2

At twelve o'clock precisely the bell rang, announcing a visitor, and Drummond looked up from the columns of the *Sportsman* as his servant came into the room.

'Yes, James,' he remarked. 'I think we are at home. I want you to remain within call, and under no circumstances let our sick visitor out of your sight for more than a minute. In fact, I think you'd better sit in his room.'

He resumed his study of the paper, and James, with a curt 'Very good, sir,' left the room. Almost at once he returned, and flinging open the door announced Mr Peterson.

Drummond looked up quickly and rose with a smile.

'Good morning,' he cried. 'This is a very pleasant surprise, Mr Peterson.' He waved his visitor to a chair. 'Hope you've had no more trouble with your car.'

Mr Peterson drew off his gloves, smiling amiably. 'None at all, thank you, Captain Drummond. The chauffeur appears to have mastered the defect.'

'It was your eye on him that did it. Wonderful thing – the human optic, as I said to your friend, Mr – Mr Laking. I hope that he's quite well and taking nourishment.'

'Soft food only,' said the other genially. 'Mr Lakington had a most unpleasant accident last night – most unpleasant.'

Hugh's face expressed his sympathy. 'How very unfortunate!' he murmured. 'I trust nothing serious.'

'I fear his lower jaw was fractured in two places.' Peterson helped himself to a cigarette from the box beside him. 'The man who hit him must have been a boxer.'

'Mixed up in a brawl, was he?' said Drummond, shaking his head. 'I should never have thought, from what little I've seen of Mr Lakington, that he went in for painting the town red. I'd have put him down as a most abstemious man – but one never can tell, can one? I once knew a fellah who used to get fighting drunk on three whiskies, and to look at him you'd have put him down as a Methodist parson. Wonderful the amount of cheap fun that chap got out of life.'

Peterson flicked the ash from his cigarette into the grate. 'Shall we come to the point, Captain Drummond?' he remarked affably.

Hugh looked bewildered. 'The point, Mr Peterson? Er – by all manner of means.'

Peterson smiled even more affably. 'I felt certain that you were a young man of discernment,' he remarked, 'and I wouldn't like to keep you from your paper a minute longer than necessary.'

'Not a bit,' cried Hugh. 'My time is yours – though I'd very much like to know your real opinion of The Juggernaut for the Chester Cup. It seems to me that he cannot afford to give Sumatra seven pounds on their form up to date.'

'Are you interested in gambling?' asked Peterson politely.

'A mild flutter, Mr Peterson, every now and then,' returned Drummond. 'Strictly limited stakes.'

'If you confine yourself to that you will come to no harm,' said Peterson. 'It is when the stakes become unlimited that the danger of a crash becomes unlimited too.'

'That is what my mother always told me,' remarked Hugh. 'She even went farther, dear good woman that she was. "Never bet except on a certainty, my boy," was her constant advice, "and then put your shirt on!" I can hear her saying it now, Mr Peterson, with the golden rays of the setting sun lighting up her sweet face.'

Suddenly Peterson leant forward in his chair. 'Young man,' he remarked, 'we've got to understand one another. Last night you butted in on my plans, and I do not like people who do that. By an act which, I must admit, appealed to me greatly, you removed something I require – something, moreover, which I intend to have. Breaking the electric bulb with a revolver-shot shows resource and initiative. The blow which smashed Henry Lakington's jaw in two places shows strength. All qualities which I admire, Captain Drummond – admire greatly. I should dislike having to deprive the world of those qualities.'

Drummond gazed at the speaker open-mouthed. 'My dear sir,' he protested feebly, 'you overwhelm me. Are you really accusing me of being a sort of wild west show?' He waggled a finger at Peterson. 'You know you've been to the movies too much, like my fellah, James. He's got revolvers and things on the brain.'

Peterson's face was absolutely impassive; save for a slightly tired smile it was expressionless. 'Finally, Captain Drummond, you tore in half a piece of paper which I require – and removed a very dear old friend of my family, who is now in this house. I want them both back, please, and if you like I'll take them now.'

Drummond shrugged his shoulders resignedly. 'There is something about you, Mr Peterson,' he murmured, 'which I like. You strike me as being the type of man to whom a young girl would turn and pour out her maidenly secrets. So masterful, so compelling, so unruffled. I feel sure – when you have finally disabused your mind of this absurd hallucination – that we shall become real friends.'

Peterson still sat motionless save for a ceaseless tapping with his hand on his knee.

'Tell me,' continued Hugh, 'why did you allow this scoundrel to treat you in such an offhand manner? It doesn't seem to me to be the sort of thing that ought to happen at all, and I suggest your going to the police at once.'

'Unfortunately a bullet intended for him just missed,' answered Peterson casually. 'A pity – because there would have been no trace of him by now.'

'Might be awkward for you,' murmured Hugh. 'Such methods, Mr Peterson, are illegal, you know. It's a dangerous thing to take the law into your own hands. May I offer you a drink?'

Peterson declined courteously. 'Thank you – not at this hour.' Then he rose. 'I take it, then, that you will not return me my property here and now.'

'Still the same delusion, I see!' remarked Hugh with a smile.

'Still the same delusion,' repeated Peterson. 'I shall be ready to receive both the paper and the man up till six o'clock tonight at 32A Berners Street; and it is possible, I might even say probable, should they turn up by then, that I shall not find it necessary to kill you.'

Hugh grinned. 'Your kindly forbearance amazes me,' he cried. 'Won't you really change your mind and have a drink?'

'Should they not arrive by then, I shall be put to the inconvenience of taking them, and in that case – much as I regret it – you may have to be killed. You're such an aggressive young man, Captain Drummond – and, I fear, not very tactful.' He spoke regretfully, drawing on his gloves; then as he got to the door he paused. 'I'm afraid that my words will not have much effect,' he remarked, 'but the episode last night *did* appeal to me. I would like to spare you – I would really. It's a sign of weakness, my young friend, which I view with amazement – but nevertheless, it is there. So be warned in time. Return my property to Berners Street, and leave England for a few months.' His eyes seemed to burn into the soldier's brain. 'You are meddling in affairs,' he went on gently, 'of the danger of which you have no conception. A fly in the gearbox of a motorcar would be a sounder proposition for a life insurance than you will be – if you continue on your present course.'

There was something so incredibly menacing in the soft, quiet voice, that Drummond looked at the speaker fascinated. He had a sudden feeling that he must be dreaming – that in a moment or two he would wake up and find that they had really been talking about the weather the whole time. Then the cynical gleam of triumph in Peterson's eyes acted on him like a cold douche; quite clearly that gentleman had misinterpreted his silence.

'Your candour is as refreshing,' he answered genially, 'as your similes are apt. I shudder to think of that poor little fly, Mr Peterson, especially with your chauffeur grinding his gears to pieces.' He held open the door for his visitor, and followed him into the passage. At the other end stood Denny, ostentatiously dusting a book-shelf, and Peterson glanced at him casually. It was characteristic of the man that no trace of annoyance showed on his face. He might have been any ordinary visitor taking his leave.

And then suddenly from the room outside which Denny was dusting there came a low moaning and an incoherent babble. A quick frown passed over Drummond's face, and Peterson regarded him thoughtfully.

'An invalid in the house?' he remarked. 'How inconvenient for you!' He laid his hand for a moment on the soldier's arm. 'I sadly fear you're going to make a fool of yourself. And it will be such a pity.' He turned towards the stairs. 'Don't bother, please; I can find my own way out.'

3

Hugh turned back into his own room, and lighting a particularly noisy pipe, sat down in his own special chair, where James Denny found him five minutes later, with his hands deep in his pockets and his legs crossed, staring out of the window. He asked him about lunch twice without result, and having finally been requested to go to hell, he removed himself aggrievedly to the kitchen. Drummond was under no delusions as to the risks he was running. Underrating his opponent had never been a fault of his, either in the ring or in France, and he had no intention of beginning now. The man who could abduct an American millionaire, and drug him till he was little better than a baby, and then use a thumbscrew to enforce his wishes, was not likely to prove over-scrupulous in the future. In fact, the phut of that bullet still rang unpleasantly in his ears.

After a while he began half-unconsciously to talk aloud to himself. It was an old trick of his when he wanted to make up his mind on a situation, and he found that it helped him to concentrate his thoughts.

'Two alternatives, old buck,' he remarked, stabbing the air with his pipe. 'One – give the Potts bird up at Berners Street; two – do not. Number one – out of court at once. Preposterous – absurd. Therefore – number two holds the field.' He recrossed his legs, and ejected a large wineglassful of nicotine juice from the stem of his pipe on to the carpet. Then he sank back exhausted, and rang the bell.

'James,' he said, as the door opened, 'take a piece of paper and a pencil – if there's one with a point – and sit down at the table. I'm going to think, and I'd hate to miss out anything.'

His servant complied, and for a while silence reigned.

'First,' remarked Drummond, 'put down – "They know where Potts is." '

'Is, sir, or are?' murmured Denny, sucking his pencil.

'Is, you fool. It's a man, not a collection. And don't interrupt, for Heaven's sake. Two – "They will try to get Potts." '

'Yes, sir,' answered Denny, writing busily.

'Three – "They will not get Potts." That is as far as I've got at the moment, James – but every word of it stands. Not bad for a quarter of an hour, my trusty fellah – what?'

'That's the stuff to give the troops, sir,' agreed his audience, sucking his teeth.

Hugh looked at him in displeasure. 'That noise is not, James,' he remarked severely. 'Now you've got to do something else. Rise and with your well-known stealth approach the window, and see if the watcher still watcheth without.'

The servant took a prolonged survey, and finally announced that he failed to see him.

'Then that proves conclusively that he's there,' said Hugh. 'Write it down, James: four – "Owing to the watcher without, Potts cannot leave the house without being seen." '

'That's two withouts, sir,' ventured James tentatively; but Hugh, with a sudden light dawning in his eyes, was staring at the fire-place.

'I've got it, James,' he cried. 'I've got it . . . Five – "Potts must leave the house without being seen." I want him, James, I want him all to myself. I want to make much of him and listen to his childish prattle. He shall go to my cottage on the river, and you shall look after him.'

'Yes, sir,' returned James dutifully.

'And in order to get him there, we must get rid of the watcher without. How can we get rid of the bird – how can we, James, I ask you? Why, by giving him nothing further to watch for. Once let him think that Potts is no longer within, unless he's an imbecile he will no longer remain without.'

'I see, sir,' said James.

'No, you don't – you don't see anything. Now trot along over, James, and give my compliments to Mr Darrell. Ask him to come in and see me for a moment. Say I'm thinking and daren't move.'

James rose obediently, and Drummond heard him cross over the passage to the other suite of rooms that lay on the same floor. Then he heard the murmur of voices, and shortly afterwards his servant returned.

'He is in his bath, sir, but he'll come over as soon as he's finished.' He delivered the message and stood waiting. 'Anything more, sir?'

'Yes, James. I feel certain that there's a lot. But just to carry on with, I'll have another glass of beer.'

As the door closed, Drummond rose and started to pace up and down the room. The plan he had in his mind was simple, but he was a man who believed in simplicity.

'Peterson will not come himself – nor will our one and only Henry. Potts has not been long in the country, which is all to the good. And if it fails – we shan't be any worse off than we are now. Luck – that's all; and the more you tempt her, the kinder she is.' He was still talking gently to himself when Peter Darrell strolled into the room.

'Can this thing be true, old boy,' remarked the newcomer. 'I hear you're in the throes of a brain-storm.'

'I am, Peter – and not even that repulsive dressing-gown of yours can stop it. I want you to help me.'

'All that I have, dear old flick, is yours for the asking. What can I do?'

'Well, first of all, I want you to come along and see the household pet.' He piloted Darrell along the passage to the American's room, and opened the door. The millionaire looked at them dazedly from the pillows, and Darrell stared back in startled surprise.

'My God! What's the matter with him?' he cried.

'I would give a good deal to know,' said Hugh grimly. Then he smiled reassuringly at the motionless man, and led the way back to the sitting-room.

'Sit down, Peter,' he said. 'Get outside that beer and listen to me carefully.'

For ten minutes he spoke, while his companion listened in silence. Gone completely was the rather vacuous-faced youth clad in a gorgeous dressing-gown; in his place there sat a keen-faced man nodding from time to time as a fresh point was made clear. Even so had both listened in the years that were past to their battalion commander's orders before an attack.

At length Hugh finished. 'Will you do it, old man?' he asked.

'Of course,' returned the other. 'But wouldn't it be better, Hugh,' he said pleadingly, 'to whip up two or three of the boys and have a real scrap? I don't seem to have anything to do.'

Drummond shook his head decidedly. 'No, Peter, my boy – not this show. We're up against a big thing; and if you like to come in with me, I think you'll have all you want in the scrapping line before you've finished. But this time, low cunning is the order.'

Darrell rose. 'Right you are, dearie. Your instructions shall be carried out to the letter. Come and feed your face with me. Got a couple of birds from the Gaiety lunching at the Cri.'

'Not today,' said Hugh. 'I've got quite a bit to get through this afternoon.'

As soon as Darrell had gone, Drummond again rang the bell for his servant.

'This afternoon, James, you and Mrs Denny will leave here and go to Paddington. Go out by the front door, and should you find yourselves being followed – as you probably will be – consume a jujube and keep your heads. Having arrived at the booking-office – take a ticket to Cheltenham, say goodbye to Mrs Denny in an impassioned tone, and exhort her not to miss the next train to that delectable inland resort. You might even speak slightingly about her sick aunt at Westbourne Grove, who alone prevents your admirable wife from accompanying you. Then, James, you will board the train for Cheltenham and go there. You will remain there for two days, during which period you must remember that you're a married man – even if you do go to the movies. You will then return here, and await further orders. Do you get me?'

'Yes, sir.' James stood to attention with a smart heel-click.

'Your wife – she has a sister or something, hasn't she, knocking about somewhere?'

'She 'as a palsied cousin in Camberwell, sir,' remarked James with justifiable pride.

'Magnificent,' murmured Hugh. 'She will dally until eventide with her palsied cousin – if she can bear it – and then she must go by Underground to Ealing, where she will take a ticket to Goring. I don't think there will be any chance of her being followed – you'll have drawn them off. When she gets to Goring I want the cottage got ready at once, for two visitors.' He paused and lit a cigarette. 'Above all, James – mum's the word. As I told you a little while ago, the game has begun. Now just repeat what I've told you.'

He listened while his servant ran through his instructions, and nodded approvingly. 'To think there are still people who think military service a waste of time!' he murmured. 'Four years ago you couldn't have got one word of it right.'

He dismissed Denny, and sat down at his desk. First he took the half-torn sheet out of his pocket, and putting it in an envelope, sealed it carefully. Then he placed it in another envelope, with a covering letter to his bank, requesting them to keep the enclosure intact.

Then he took a sheet of notepaper, and with much deliberation proceeded to pen a document which afforded him considerable amusement, judging by the grin which appeared from time to time on his face. This effusion he also enclosed in a sealed envelope, which he again addressed to his bank. Finally, he stamped the first, but not the second – and placed them both in his pocket.

For the next two hours he apparently found nothing better to do than eat a perfectly grilled chop prepared by Mrs Denny, and superintend his visitor unwillingly consuming a sago pudding. Then, with the departure of the Dennys for Paddington, which coincided most aptly with the return of Peter Darrell, a period of activity commenced in Half Moon Street. But being interior activity, interfering in no way with the placid warmth of the street outside, the gentleman without, whom a keen observer might have thought strangely interested in the beauties of that well-known thoroughfare – seeing that he had been there for three hours – remained serenely unconscious of it. His pal had followed the Dennys to Paddington. Drummond had not come out – and the watcher who watched without was beginning to get bored.

About 4.30 he sat up and took notice again as someone left the house; but it was only the superbly dressed young man whom he had discovered already was merely a clothes-peg calling himself Darrell.

The sun was getting low and the shadows were lengthening when a taxi drove up to the door. Immediately the watcher drew closer, only to stop with a faint smile as he saw two men get out of it. One was the immaculate Darrell; the other was a stranger, and both were quite obviously what in the vernacular is known as 'oiled'.

'You prisheless ole bean,' he heard Darrell say affectionately, 'thish blinking cabsh my show.'

The other man hiccoughed assent, and leant wearily against the palings.

'Right,' he remarked, 'ole friend of me youth. It shall be ash you wish.'

With a tolerant eye he watched them tack up the stairs, singing lustily in chorus. Then the door above closed, and the melody continued to float out through the open window.

Ten minutes later he was relieved. It was quite an unostentatious relief: another man merely strolled past him. And since there was nothing to report, he merely strolled away. He could hardly be expected to know that up in Peter Darrell's sitting-room two perfectly sober young men were contemplating with professional eyes an extremely drunk gentleman singing in a chair, and that one of those two sober young men was Peter Darrell.

Then further interior activity took place in Half Moon Street, and as the darkness fell, silence gradually settled on the house.

Ten o'clock struck, then eleven – and the silence remained unbroken. It was not till eleven-thirty that a sudden small sound made Hugh Drummond sit up in his chair, with every nerve alert. It came from the direction of the kitchen – and it was the sound he had been waiting for.

Swiftly he opened his door and passed along the passage to where the motionless man lay still in bed. Then he switched on a small reading-lamp, and with a plate of semolina in his hand he turned to the recumbent figure.

'Hiram C. Potts,' he said in a low, coaxing tone, 'sit up and take your semolina. Force yourself, laddie, force yourself. I know it's nauseating, but the doctor said no alcohol and very little meat.'

In the silence that followed, a board creaked outside, and again he tempted the sick man with food.

'Semolina, Hiram – semolina. Makes bouncing babies. I'd just love to see you bounce, my Potts.'

His voice died away, and he rose slowly to his feet. In the open door four men were standing, each with a peculiar-shaped revolver in his hand.

'What the devil,' cried Drummond furiously, 'is the meaning of this?'

'Cut it out,' cried the leader contemptuously. 'These guns are silent. If you utter – you die. Do you get me?'

The veins stood out on Drummond's forehead, and he controlled himself with an immense effort.

'Are you aware that this man is a guest of mine, and sick?' he said, his voice shaking with rage.

'You don't say,' remarked the leader, and one of the others laughed. 'Rip the bed-clothes off, boys, and gag the young cock-sparrow.'

Before he could resist, a gag was thrust in Drummond's mouth and his hands were tied behind his back. Then, helpless and impotent, he watched three of them lift up the man from the bed, and, putting a gag in his mouth also, carry him out of the room.

'Move,' said the fourth to Hugh. 'You join the picnic.'

With fury gathering in his eyes he preceded his captor along the passage and downstairs. A large car drove up as they reached the street, and in less time than it takes to tell, the two helpless men were pushed in, followed by the leader; the door was shut and the car drove off.

'Don't forget,' he said to Drummond suavely 'This gun *is* silent. You had better be the same.'

At one o'clock the car swung up to The Elms. For the last ten minutes Hugh had been watching the invalid in the corner, who was making frantic efforts to loosen his gag. His eyes were rolling horribly, and he swayed from side to side in his seat, but the bandages round his hands held firm and at last he gave it up.

Even when he was lifted out and carried indoors he did not struggle; he seemed to have sunk into a sort of apathy. Drummond followed with dignified calmness, and was led into a room off the hall.

In a moment or two Peterson entered, followed by his daughter. 'Ah! my young friend,' cried Peterson affably. 'I hardly thought you'd give me such an easy run as this.' He put his hand into Drummond's pockets, and pulled out his revolver and a bundle of letters. 'To your bank,' he murmured. 'Oh! surely, surely not that as well. Not even stamped. Ungag him, Irma – and untie his hands. My very dear young friend – you pain me.'

'I wish to know, Mr Peterson,' said Hugh quietly, 'by what right this dastardly outrage has been committed. A friend of mine, sick in bed – removed; abducted in the middle of the night: to say nothing of me.'

With a gentle laugh Irma offered him a cigarette. '*Mon Dieu!*' she remarked, 'but you are most gloriously ugly, my Hugh!' Drummond looked at her coldly, while Peterson, with a faint smile, opened the envelope in his hand. And, even as he pulled out the contents, he paused suddenly and the smile faded from his face. From the landing upstairs came a heavy crash, followed by a flood of the most appalling language.

'What the — hell do you think you're doing, you flat-faced son of a Maltese goat? And where the — am I, anyway?'

'I must apologise for my friend's language,' murmured Hugh gently, 'but you must admit he has some justification. Besides, he was, I regret to state, quite wonderfully drunk earlier this evening, and just as he was sleeping it off these desperadoes abducted him.'

The next moment the door burst open, and an infuriated object rushed in. His face was wild, and his hand was bandaged, showing a great red stain on the thumb.

'What's this — — jest?' he howled furiously. 'And this damned bandage all covered with red ink?'

'You must ask our friend here, Mullings,' said Hugh. 'He's got a peculiar sense of humour. Anyway, he's got the bill in his hand.'

In silence they watched Peterson open the paper and read the contents, while the girl leant over his shoulder.

To Mr Peterson, The Elms, Godalming.

	£	s.	d.
To hire of one demobilised soldier	5	0	0
To making him drunk (in this item present strength and cost of drink and said soldier's capacity must be allowed for)	5	0	0
To bottle of red ink	0	0	1
To shock to system	10	0	0
TOTAL	£20	0	1

It was Irma who laughed.

'Oh! but, my Hugh,' she gurgled, '*que vous êtes adorable!*'

But he did not look at her. His eyes were on Peterson, who with a perfectly impassive face was staring at him fixedly.

Chapter 4

In which he spends a quiet night at The Elms

I

'It is a little difficult to know what to do with you, young man,' said Peterson gently, after a long silence. 'I knew you had no tact.'

Drummond leaned back in his chair and regarded his host with a faint smile.

'I must come to you for lessons, Mr Peterson. Though I frankly admit,' he added genially, 'that I have never been brought up to regard the forcible abduction of a harmless individual and a friend who is sleeping off the effects of what low people call a jag as being exactly typical of that admirable quality.'

Peterson's glance rested on the dishevelled man still standing by the door, and after a moment's thought he leaned forward and pressed a bell.

'Take that man away,' he said abruptly to the servant who came into the room, 'and put him to bed. I will consider what to do with him in the morning.'

'Consider be damned,' howled Mullings, starting forward angrily. 'You'll consider a thick ear, Mr Blooming Knowall. What I wants to know – '

The words died away in his mouth, and he gazed at Peterson like a bird looks at a snake. There was something so ruthlessly malignant in the stare of the grey-blue eyes, that the ex-soldier who had viewed going over the top with comparative equanimity, as being part of his job, quailed and looked apprehensively at Drummond.

'Do what the kind gentleman tells you, Mullings,' said Hugh, 'and go to bed.' He smiled at the man reassuringly. 'And if you're very, very good, perhaps, as a great treat, he'll come and kiss you good night.'

'Now *that*,' he remarked as the door closed behind them, 'is what I call tact.'

He lit a cigarette, and thoughtfully blew out a cloud of smoke.

'Stop this fooling,' snarled Peterson. 'Where have you hidden Potts?'

'Tush, tush,' murmured Hugh. 'You surprise me. I had formed such a charming mental picture of you, Mr Peterson, as the strong, silent man who never lost his temper, and here you are disappointing me at the beginning of our acquaintance.'

For a moment he thought that Peterson was going to strike him, and his own fist clenched under the table.

'I wouldn't, my friend,' he said quietly, 'indeed I wouldn't. Because if you hit me, I shall most certainly hit you. And it will not improve your beauty.'

Slowly Peterson sank back in his chair, and the veins which had been standing out on his forehead became normal again. He even smiled; only the ceaseless tapping of his hand on his left knee betrayed his momentary loss of composure. Drummond's fist un-clenched, and he stole a look at the girl. She was in her favourite attitude on the sofa, and had not even looked up.

'I suppose that it is quite useless for me to argue with you,' said Peterson after a while.

'I was a member of my school debating society,' remarked Hugh reminiscently. 'But I was never much good. I'm too obvious for argument, I'm afraid.'

'You probably realise from what has happened tonight,' continued Peterson, 'that I am in earnest.'

'I should be sorry to think so,' answered Hugh. 'If that is the best you can do, I'd cut it right out and start a tomato farm.'

The girl gave a little gurgle of laughter and lit another cigarette.

'Will you come and do the dangerous part of the work for us, Monsieur Hugh?' she asked.

'If you promise to restrain the little fellows, I'll water them with pleasure,' returned Hugh lightly.

Peterson rose and walked over to the window, where he stood motionless staring out into the darkness. For all his assumed flipp-ancy, Hugh realised that the situation was what in military phrase-ology might be termed critical. There were in the house probably half a dozen men who, like their master, were absolutely unscrupulous. If it suited Peterson's book to kill him, he would not hesitate to do so for a single second. And Hugh realised, when he put it that way in his own mind, that it was no exaggeration, no *façon de parler*, but a plain, unvarnished statement of fact. Peterson would no more think twice of killing a man if he wished to, than the normal human being would of crushing a wasp.

For a moment the thought crossed his mind that he would take no chances by remaining in the house; that he would rush Peterson from behind and escape into the darkness of the garden. But it was only momentary – gone almost before it had come, for Hugh Drummond was not that manner of man – gone even before he noticed that Peterson was standing in such a position that he could see every detail of the room behind him reflected in the glass through which he stared.

A fixed determination to know what lay in that sinister brain replaced his temporary indecision. Events up to date had moved so quickly that he had hardly had time to get his bearings; even now the last twenty-four hours seemed almost a dream. And as he looked at the broad back and massive head of the man at the window, and from him to the girl idly smoking on the sofa, he smiled a little grimly. He had just remembered the thumbscrew of the preceding evening. Assuredly the demobilised officer who found peace dull was getting his money's worth; and Drummond had a shrewd suspicion that the entertainment was only just beginning.

A sudden sound outside in the garden made him look up quickly. He saw the white gleam of a shirt front, and the next moment a man pushed open the window and came unsteadily into the room. It was Mr Benton, and quite obviously he had been seeking consolation in the bottle.

'Have you got him?' he demanded thickly steadying himself with a hand on Peterson's arm.

'I have not,' said Peterson shortly, eyeing the swaying figure in front of him contemptuously.

'Where is he?'

'Perhaps if you ask your daughter's friend Captain Drummond, he might tell you. For Heaven's sake sit down, man, before you fall down.' He pushed Benton roughly into a chair, and resumed his impassive stare into the darkness.

The girl took not the slightest notice of the new arrival, who gazed stupidly at Drummond across the table.

'We seem to be moving in an atmosphere of cross-purposes, Mr Benton,' said the soldier affably. 'Our host will not get rid of the idea that I am a species of bandit. I hope your daughter is quite well.'

'Er – quite, thank you,' muttered the other.

'Tell her, will you, that I propose to call on her before returning to London tomorrow. That is, if she won't object to my coming early.'

With his hands in his pockets, Peterson was regarding Drummond from the window.

'You propose leaving us tomorrow, do you?' he said quietly.

Drummond stood up.

'I ordered my car for ten o'clock,' he answered. 'I hope that will not upset the household arrangements,' he continued, turning to the girl, who was laughing softly and polishing her nails.

'*Vraiment*! but you grow on one, my Hugh,' she smiled. 'Are we really losing you so soon?'

'I am quite sure that I shall be more useful to Mr Peterson at large, than I am cooped up here,' said Hugh. 'I might even lead him to this hidden treasure which he thinks I've got.'

'You will do that all right,' remarked Peterson. 'But at the moment I was wondering whether a little persuasion now – might not give me all the information I require more quickly and with less trouble.'

A fleeting vision of a mangled, pulplike thumb flashed across Hugh's mind; once again he heard that hideous cry, half animal, half human, which had echoed through the darkness the preceding night, and for an instant his breath came a little faster. Then he smiled, and shook his head.

'I think you are rather too good a judge of human nature to try anything so foolish,' he said thoughtfully. 'You see, unless you kill me, which I don't think would suit your book, you might find explanations a little difficult tomorrow.'

For a while there was silence in the room, broken at length by a short laugh from Peterson.

'For a young man truly your perspicacity is great,' he remarked. 'Irma, is the blue room ready? If so, tell Luigi to show Captain Drummond to it.'

'I will show him myself,' she answered, rising. 'And then I shall go to bed. *Mon Dieu*! my Hugh, but I find your country *très ennuyeux*.' She stood in front of him for a moment, and then led the way to the door, glancing at him over her shoulder.

Hugh saw a quick look of annoyance pass over Peterson's face as he turned to follow the girl, and it struck him that that gentleman was not best pleased at the turn of events. It vanished almost as soon as it came, and Peterson waved a friendly hand at him, as if the doings of the night had been the most ordinary thing in the world. Then the door closed, and he followed his guide up the stairs.

The house was beautifully furnished. Hugh was no judge of art, but even his inexperienced eye could see that the prints on the walls were rare and valuable. The carpets were thick, and his feet sank into them noiselessly; the furniture was solid and in exquisite taste. And it was as he reached the top of the stairs that a single deep-noted clock rang a wonderful chime and then struck the hour. The time was just three o'clock.

The girl opened the door of a room and switched on the light. Then she faced him smiling, and Hugh looked at her steadily. He had no wish whatever for any conversation, but as she was standing in the centre of the doorway it was impossible for him to get past her without being rude.

'Tell me, you ugly man, she murmured, 'why you are such a fool.'

Hugh smiled, and, as has been said before, Hugh's smile transformed his face.

'I must remember that opening,' he said. 'So many people, I feel convinced, would like to say it on first acquaintance, but confine themselves to merely thinking it. It establishes a basis of intimacy at once, doesn't it?'

She swayed a little towards him, and then, before he realised her intention, she put a hand on his shoulder.

'Don't you understand,' she whispered fiercely, 'that they'll kill you?' She peered past him half-fearfully, and then turned to him again. 'Go, you idiot, go – while there's time. Oh! if I could only make you understand; if you'd only believe me! Get out of it – go abroad; do anything – but don't fool round here.'

In her agitation she was shaking him to and fro.

'It seems a cheerful household,' remarked Hugh with a smile. 'May I ask why you're all so concerned about me? Your estimable father gave me the same advice yesterday morning.'

'Don't ask why,' she answered feverishly, 'because I can't tell you. Only you must believe that what I say is the truth – you must. It's just possible that if you go now and tell them where you've hidden the American you'll be all right. But if you don't – ' Her hand dropped to her side suddenly. 'Breakfast will be at nine, my Hugh: until then, *au revoir.*'

He turned as she left the room, a little puzzled by her change of tone. Standing at the top of the stairs was Peterson, watching them both in silence . . .

2

In the days when Drummond had been a platoon commander, he had done many dangerous things. The ordinary joys of the infantry subaltern's life – such as going over the top, and carrying out raids – had not proved sufficient for his appetite. He had specialised in peculiar stunts of his own: stunts over which he was singularly reticent; stunts over which his men formed their own conclusions, and worshipped him accordingly.

But Drummond was no fool, and he had realised the vital importance of fitting himself for these stunts to the best of his ability. Enormous physical strength is a great asset, but it carries with it certain natural disadvantages. In the first place, its possessor is frequently clumsy: Hugh had practised in France till he could move over ground without a single blade of grass rustling. Van Dyck – a Dutch trapper – had first shown him the trick, by which a man goes forward on his elbows like a snake, and is here one moment and gone the next, with no-one the wiser.

Again, its possessor is frequently slow: Hugh had practised in France till he could kill a man with his bare hands in a second. Olaki – a Japanese – had first taught him two or three of the secrets of his trade, and in the intervals of resting behind the lines he had perfected them until it was even money whether the Jap or he would win in a practice bout.

And there were nights in No Man's Land when his men would hear strange sounds, and knowing that Drummond was abroad on his wanderings, would peer eagerly over the parapet into the desolate torn-up waste in front. But they never saw anything, even when the green ghostly flares went hissing up into the darkness and the shadows danced fantastically. All was silent and still; the sudden shrill whimper was not repeated.

Perhaps a patrol coming back would report a German, lying huddled in a shell-hole, with no trace of a wound, but only a broken neck; perhaps the patrol never found anything. But whatever the report, Hugh Drummond only grinned and saw to his men's breakfasts. Which is why there are in England today quite a number of civilians who acknowledge only two rulers – the King and Hugh Drummond. And they would willingly die for either.

The result on Drummond was not surprising: as nearly as a man may be he was without fear. And when the idea came to him as he sat on the edge of his bed thoughtfully pulling off his boots, no question of the possible risk entered into his mind. To explore the house seemed the most natural thing in the world, and with characteristic brevity he summed up the situation as it struck him.

'They suspect me anyhow: in fact, they know I took Potts. Therefore even if they catch me passage-creeping, I'm no worse off than I am now. And I might find something of interest. Therefore, carry on, brave heart.'

The matter was settled; the complete bench of bishops headed by their attendant satellites would not have stopped him, nor the fact that the German front-line trench was a far safer place for a stranger than The Elms at night. But he didn't know that fact, and it would have cut no more ice than the episcopal dignitaries, if he had . . .

It was dark in the passage outside as he opened the door of his room and crept towards the top of the stairs. The collar of his brown lounge coat was turned up, and his stockinged feet made no sound on the heavy pile carpet. Like a huge shadow he vanished into the blackness, feeling his way forward with the uncanny instinct that comes from much practice. Every now and then he paused and listened intently, but the measured ticking of the clock below and the occasional creak of a board alone broke the stillness.

For a moment his outline showed up against the faint grey light which was coming through a window half-way down the stairs; then he was gone again, swallowed up in the gloom of the hall. To the left lay the room in which he had spent the evening, and Drummond turned to the right. As he had gone up to bed he had noticed a door screened by a heavy curtain which he thought might be the room Phyllis Benton had spoken of – the room where Henry Lakington kept his ill-gotten treasures. He felt his way along the wall, and at length his hand touched the curtain – only to drop it again at once. From close beside him had come a sharp, angry hiss . . .

He stepped back a pace and stood rigid, staring at the spot from which the sound had seemed to come – but he could see nothing. Then he leaned forward and once more moved the curtain. Instantly it came again, sharper and angrier than before.

Hugh passed a hand over his forehead and found it damp. Germans he knew, and things on two legs, but what was this that hissed so viciously in the darkness? At length he determined to risk it, and drew from his pocket a tiny electric torch. Holding it well away from his body, he switched on the light. In the centre of the beam, swaying gracefully to and fro, was a snake. For a moment he watched it fascinated as it spat at the light angrily; he saw the flat hood where the vicious head was set on the upright body; then he switched off the torch and retreated rather faster than he had come.

'A convivial household,' he muttered to himself through lips that were a little dry. 'A hooded cobra is an unpleasing pet.'

He stood leaning against the banisters regaining his self-control. There was no further sound from the cobra; seemingly it only got annoyed when its own particular domain was approached. In fact, Hugh had just determined to reconnoitre the curtained doorway again to see if it was possible to circumvent the snake, when a low chuckle came distinctly to his ears from the landing above.

He flushed angrily in the darkness. There was no doubt whatever as to the human origin of that laugh, and Hugh suddenly realised that he was making the most profound fool of himself. And such a realisation, though possibly salutary to all of us at times, is most unpleasant.

For Hugh Drummond, who, with all his lack of conceit, had a very good idea of Hugh Drummond's capabilities, to be at an absolute disadvantage – to be laughed at by some dirty swine whom he could strangle in half a minute – was impossible! His fists clenched, and he swore softly under his breath. Then as silently as he had come down, he commenced to climb the stairs again. He had a hazy idea that he would like to hit something – hard.

There were nine stairs in the first half of the flight, and it was as he stood on the fifth that he again heard the low chuckle. At the same instant something whizzed past his head so low that it almost touched his hair, and there was a clang on the wall beside him. He ducked instinctively, and regardless of noise raced up the remaining stairs on all fours. His jaw was set like a vice, his eyes were blazing in fact, Hugh Drummond was seeing red.

He paused when he reached the top, crouching in the darkness. Close to him he could feel someone else, and holding his breath, he listened. Then he heard the man move – only the very faintest sound – but it was enough. Without a second's thought he sprang, and his hands closed on human flesh. He laughed gently; then he fought in silence.

His opponent was strong above the average, but after a minute he was like a child in Hugh's grasp. He choked once or twice and muttered something; then Hugh slipped his right hand gently on to the man's throat. His fingers moved slowly round, his thumb adjusted itself lovingly, and the man felt his head being forced back irresistibly. He gave one strangled cry, and then the pressure relaxed . . .

'One half-inch more, my gentle humorist,' Hugh whispered in his ear, 'and your neck would have been broken. As it is, it will be very stiff for some days. Another time – don't laugh. It's dangerous.'

Then, like a ghost, he vanished along the passage in the direction of his own room.

'I wonder who the bird was,' he murmured thoughtfully to himself. 'Somehow I don't think he'll laugh quite so much in future – damn him.'

3

At eight o'clock the next morning a burly-looking ruffian brought in some hot water and a cup of tea. Hugh watched him through half-closed eyes, and eliminated him from the competition. His bullet head moved freely on a pair of massive shoulders; his neck showed no traces of nocturnal trouble. As he pulled up the blinds the light fell full on his battered, rugged face, and suddenly Hugh sat up in bed and stared at him.

'Good Lord!' he cried, 'aren't you Jem Smith?'

The man swung round like a flash and glared at the bed.

'Wot the 'ell 'as that got to do wiv you?' he snarled, and then his face changed. 'Why, strike me pink, if it ain't young Drummond.'

Hugh grinned.

'Right in one, Jem. What in the name of fortune are you doing in this outfit?'

But the man was not to be drawn.

'Never you mind, sir,' he said grimly. 'I reckons that's my own business.'

'Given up the game, Jem?' asked Hugh.

'It give me up, when that cross-eyed son of a gun Young Baxter fought that cross down at 'Oxton. Gawd! If I could get the swine – just once again – s'welp me, I'd – ' Words failed the ex-bruiser; he could only mutter. And Hugh, who remembered the real reason why the game had given Jem up, and a period of detention at His Majesty's expense had taken its place, preserved a discreet silence.

The pug paused as he got to the door, and looked at Drummond doubtfully. Then he seemed to make up his mind, and advanced to the side of the bed.

'It ain't none o' my business,' he muttered hoarsely, 'but seeing as 'ow you're one of the boys, if I was you I wouldn't get looking too close at things in this 'ere 'ouse. It ain't 'ealthy: only don't say as I said so.'

Hugh smiled.

'Thank you, Jem. By the way, has anyone got a stiff neck in the house this morning?'

'Stiff neck!' echoed the man. 'Strike me pink if that ain't funny – you're asking, I mean. The bloke's sitting up in 'is bed swearing awful. Can't move 'is 'ead at all.'

'And who, might I ask, is the bloke?' said Drummond, stirring his tea.

'Why, Peterson, o' course. 'Oo else? Breakfast at nine.'

The door closed behind him, and Hugh lit a cigarette thoughtfully. Most assuredly he was starting in style: Lakington's jaw one night, Peterson's neck the second, seemed a sufficiently energetic opening to the game for the veriest glutton. Then that cheerful optimism which was the envy of his friends asserted itself.

'Supposin' I'd killed 'em,' he murmured, aghast. 'Just supposin'. Why, the bally show would have been over, and I'd have had to advertise again.'

Only Peterson was in the dining-room when Hugh came down. He had examined the stairs on his way, but he could see nothing unusual which would account for the thing which had whizzed past his head and clanged sullenly against the wall. Nor was there any sign of the cobra by the curtained door; merely Peterson standing in a sunny room behind a bubbling coffee-machine.

'Good morning,' remarked Hugh affably. 'How are we all today? By Jove! That coffee smells good.'

'Help yourself,' said Peterson. 'My daughter is never down as early as this.'

'Rarely conscious before eleven – what!' murmured Hugh. 'Deuced wise of her. May I press you to a kidney?' He returned politely towards his host, and paused in dismay. 'Good heavens! Mr Peterson, is your neck hurting you?'

'It is,' answered Peterson grimly.

'A nuisance, having a stiff neck. Makes everyone laugh, and one gets no sympathy. Bad thing – laughter . . . At times, anyway.' He sat down and commenced to eat his breakfast.

'Curiosity is a great deal worse, Captain Drummond. It was touch and go whether I killed you last night.'

The two men were staring at one another steadily.

'I think I might say the same,' returned Drummond.

'Yes and no,' said Peterson. 'From the moment you left the bottom of the stairs, I had your life in the palm of my hand. Had I chosen to take it, my young friend, I should not have had this stiff neck.'

Hugh returned to his breakfast unconcernedly.

'Granted, laddie, granted. But had I not been of such a kindly and forbearing nature, you wouldn't have had it, either.' He looked at Peterson critically. 'I'm inclined to think it's a great pity I didn't break your neck, while I was about it.' Hugh sighed, and drank some coffee. 'I see that I shall have to do it some day, and probably Lakington's as well . . . By the way, how is our Henry? I trust his jaw is not unduly inconveniencing him.'

Peterson, with his coffee cup in his hand, was staring down the drive.

'Your car is a little early, Captain Drummond,' he said at length. 'However, perhaps it can wait two or three minutes, while we get matters perfectly clear. I should dislike you not knowing where you stand.' He turned round and faced the soldier. 'You have deliberately, against my advice, elected to fight me and the interests I represent. So be it. From now on, the gloves are off. You embarked on this course from a spirit of adventure, at the instigation of the girl next door. She, poor little fool, is concerned over that drunken waster – her father. She asked you to help her – you agreed; and, amazing though it may seem, up to now you have scored a certain measure of success. I admit it, and I admire you for it. I apologise now for having played the fool with you last night: you're the type of man whom one should kill outright – or leave alone.'

He set down his coffee cup, and carefully snipped the end off a cigar.

'You are also the type of man who will continue on the path he has started. You are completely in the dark; you have no idea whatever what you are up against.' He smiled grimly, and turned abruptly on Hugh. 'You fool – you stupid young fool. Do you *really* imagine that you can beat me?'

The soldier rose and stood in front of him.

'I have a few remarks of my own to make,' he answered, 'and then we might consider the interview closed. I ask nothing better than that the gloves should be off – though with your filthy methods of fighting, anything you touch will get very dirty. As you say, I am completely in the dark as to your plans; but I have a pretty shrewd idea what I'm up against. Men who can employ a thumbscrew on a poor defenceless brute seem to me to be several degrees worse than an aboriginal cannibal, and therefore if I put you down as one of the lowest types of degraded criminal I shall not be very wide of the mark. There's no good you snarling at me, you swine; it does everybody good to hear some home truths – and don't forget it was you who pulled off the gloves.'

Drummond lit a cigarette; then his merciless eyes fixed themselves again on Peterson.

'There is only one thing more,' he continued. 'You have kindly warned me of my danger: let me give you a word of advice in my turn. I'm going to fight you; if I can, I'm going to beat you. Anything that may happen to me is part of the game. But if anything happens to Miss Benton during the course of operations, then, as surely as there is a God above, Peterson, I'll get at you somehow and murder you with my own hands.'

For a few moments there was silence, and then with a short laugh Drummond turned away.

'Quite melodramatic,' he remarked lightly. 'And very bad for the digestion so early in the morning. My regards to your charming daughter, also to him of the broken jaw. Shall we meet again soon?' He paused at the door and looked back.

Peterson was still standing by the table, his face expressionless.

'Very soon indeed, young man,' he said quietly. 'Very soon indeed . . . '

Hugh stepped out into the warm sunshine and spoke to his chauffeur.

'Take her out into the main road, Jenkins,' he said, 'and wait for me outside the entrance to the next house. I shan't be long.'

Then he strolled through the garden towards the little wicket-gate that led to The Larches. Phyllis! The thought of her was singing in his heart to the exclusion of everything else. Just a few minutes with her; just the touch of her hand, the faint smell of the scent she used – and then back to the game.

He had almost reached the gate, when, with a sudden crashing in the undergrowth, Jem Smith blundered out into the path. His naturally ruddy face was white, and he stared round fearfully.

'Gawd! sir,' he cried, 'mind out. 'Ave yer seen it?'

'Seen what, Jem?' asked Drummond.

'That there brute. 'E's escaped; and if 'e meets a stranger – ' He left the sentence unfinished, and stood listening. From somewhere behind the house came a deep-throated, snarling roar; then the clang of a padlock shooting home in metal, followed by a series of heavy thuds as if some big animal was hurling itself against the bars of a cage.

'They've got it,' muttered Jem, mopping his brow.

'You seem to have a nice little crowd of pets about the house,' remarked Drummond, putting a hand on the man's arm as he was about to move off. 'What was that docile creature we've just heard calling to its young?'

The ex-pugilist looked at him sullenly.

'Never you mind, sir; it ain't no business of yours. An' if I was you, I wouldn't make it your business to find out.'

A moment later he had disappeared into the bushes, and Drummond was left alone. Assuredly a cheerful household, he reflected; just the spot for a rest-cure. Then he saw a figure on the lawn of the next house which banished everything else from his mind; and opening the gate, he walked eagerly towards Phyllis Benton.

4

'I heard you were down here,' she said gravely, holding out her hand to him. 'I've been sick with anxiety ever since father told me he'd seen you.'

Hugh imprisoned the little hand in his own huge ones, and smiled at the girl.

'I call that just sweet of you,' he answered. 'Just sweet . . . Having people worry about me is not much in my line, but I think I rather like it.'

'You're the most impossible person,' she remarked, releasing her hand. 'What sort of a night did you have?'

'Somewhat parti-coloured,' returned Hugh lightly. 'Like the hoary old curate's egg – calm in parts.'

'But why did you go at all?' she cried, beating her hands together. 'Don't you realise that if anything happens to you, I shall never forgive myself?'

The soldier smiled reassuringly.

'Don't worry, little girl,' he said. 'Years ago I was told by an old gipsy that I should die in my bed of old age and excessive consumption of invalid port . . . As a matter of fact, the cause of my visit was rather humorous. They abducted me in the middle of the night, with an ex-soldier of my old battalion, who was, I regret to state, sleeping off the effects of much indifferent liquor in my rooms.'

'What are you talking about?' she demanded.

'They thought he was your American millionaire cove, and the wretched Mullings was too drunk to deny it. In fact, I don't think they ever asked his opinion at all.' Hugh grinned reminiscently. 'A pathetic spectacle.'

'Oh! but splendid,' cried the girl a little breathlessly. 'And where was the American?'

'Next door – safe with a very dear old friend of mine, Peter Darrell. You must meet Peter some day – you'll like him.' He looked at her thoughtfully. 'No,' he added, 'on second thoughts, I'm not at all sure that I shall let you meet Peter. You might like him too much; and he's a dirty dog.'

'Don't be ridiculous,' she cried with a faint blush. 'Tell me, where is the American now?'

'Many miles out of London,' answered Hugh. 'I think we'll leave it at that. The less you know, Miss Benton, at the moment – the better.'

'Have you found out anything?' she demanded eagerly.

Hugh shook his head.

'Not a thing. Except that your neighbours are as pretty a bunch of scoundrels as I ever want to meet.'

'But you'll let me know if you do.' She laid a hand beseechingly on his arm. 'You know what's at stake for me, don't you? Father, and – oh! but you know.'

'I know,' he answered gravely. 'I know, old thing. I promise I'll let you know anything I find out. And in the meantime I want you to keep an eye fixed on what goes on next door, and let me know anything of importance by letter to the Junior Sports Club.' He lit a cigarette thoughtfully. 'I have an idea that they feel so absolutely confident in their own power, that they are going to make the fatal mistake of underrating their opponents. We shall see.' He turned to her with a twinkle in his eye. 'Anyway, our Mr Lakington will see that you don't come to any harm.'

'The brute!' she cried, very low. 'How I hate him!' Then – with a sudden change of tone, she looked up at Drummond. 'I don't know whether it's worth mentioning,' she said slowly, 'but yesterday afternoon four men came at different times to The Elms. They were the sort of type one sees tub-thumping in Hyde Park, all except one, who looked like a respectable working man.'

Hugh shook his head.

'Don't seem to help much, does it? Still, one never knows. Let me know anything like that in future at the club.'

'Good morning, Miss Benton.' Peterson's voice behind them made Drummond swing round with a smothered curse. 'Our inestimable friend Captain Drummond brought such a nice young fellow to see me last night, and then left him lying about the house this morning.'

Hugh bit his lip with annoyance; until that moment he had clean forgotten that Mullings was still in The Elms.

'I have sent him along to your car,' continued Peterson suavely, 'which I trust was the correct procedure. Or did you want to give him to me as a pet?'

'From a rapid survey, Mr Peterson, I should think you have quite enough already,' said Hugh. 'I trust you paid him the money you owe him.'

'I will allot it to him in my will,' remarked Peterson. 'If you do the same in yours, doubtless he will get it from one of us sooner or later. In the meantime, Miss Benton, is your father up?'

The girl frowned.

'No – not yet.'

'Then I will go and see him in bed. For the present, *au revoir*.' He walked towards the house, and they watched him go in silence. It was as he opened the drawing-room window that Hugh called after him:

'Do you like the horse Elliman's or the ordinary brand?' he asked. 'I'll send you a bottle for that stiff neck of yours.'

Very deliberately Peterson turned round.

'Don't trouble, thank you, Captain Drummond. I have my own remedies, which are far more efficacious.'

Chapter 5

In which there is trouble at Goring

I

'Did you have a good night, Mullings?' remarked Hugh as he got into his car.

The man grinned sheepishly.

'I dunno what the game was, sir, but I ain't for many more of them. They're about the ugliest crowd of blackguards in that there 'ouse that I ever wants to see again.'

'How many did you see altogether?' asked Drummond.

'I saw six actual like, sir; but I 'eard others talking.'

The car slowed up before the post office and Hugh got out. There were one or two things he proposed to do in London before going to Goring, and it struck him that a wire to Peter Darrell might allay that gentleman's uneasiness if he was late in getting down. So new was he to the tortuous ways of crime, that the foolishness of the proceeding never entered his head: up to date in his life, if he had wished to send a wire he had sent one. And so it may be deemed a sheer fluke on his part, that a man dawdling by the counter aroused his suspicions. He was a perfectly ordinary man, chatting casually with the girl on the other side; but it chanced that, just as Hugh was holding the post office pencil up, and gazing at its so-called point with an air of resigned anguish, the perfectly ordinary man ceased chatting and looked at him. Hugh caught his eye for a fleeting second; then the conversation continued. And as he turned to pull out the pad of forms, it struck him that the man had looked away just a trifle too quickly . . .

A grin spread slowly over his face, and after a moment's hesitation he proceeded to compose a short wire. He wrote it in block letters for additional clearness; he also pressed his hardest as befitted a blunt pencil. Then with the form in his hand he advanced to the counter.

'How long will it take to deliver in London?' he asked the girl . . .

The girl was not helpful. It depended, he gathered, on a variety of circumstances, of which not the least was the perfectly ordinary man who talked so charmingly. She did not say so, in so many words, but Hugh respected her none the less for her maidenly reticence.

'I don't think I'll bother, then,' he said, thrusting the wire into his pocket. 'Good morning . . .'

He walked to the door, and shortly afterwards his car rolled down the street. He would have liked to remain and see the finish of his little jest, but, as is so often the case, imagination is better than reality. Certain it is that he chuckled consumedly the whole way up to London, whereas the actual finish was tame.

With what the girl considered peculiar abruptness, the perfectly ordinary man concluded his conversation with her, and decided that he too would send a wire. And then, after a long and thoughtful pause at the writing-bench, she distinctly heard an unmistakable 'Damn'. Then he walked out, and she saw him no more.

Moreover, it is to be regretted that the perfectly ordinary man told a lie a little later in the day, when giving his report to someone whose neck apparently inconvenienced him greatly. But then a lie is frequently more tactful than the truth, and to have announced that the sole result of his morning's labours had been to decipher a wire addressed to The Elms, which contained the cryptic remark, 'Stung again, stiff neck, stung again', would not have been tactful. So he lied, as has been stated, thereby showing his wisdom . . .

But though Drummond chuckled to himself as the car rushed through the fresh morning air, once or twice a gleam that was not altogether amusement shone in his eyes. For four years he had played one game where no mistakes were allowed; the little incident of the post office had helped to bring to his mind the certainty that he had now embarked on another where the conditions were much the same. That he had scored up to date was luck rather than good management, and he was far too shrewd not to realise it. Now he was marked, and luck with a marked man cannot be tempted too far.

Alone and practically unguarded he had challenged a gang of international criminals: a gang not only utterly unscrupulous but controlled by a mastermind. Of its power as yet he had no clear idea; of its size and immediate object he had even less. Perhaps it was as well. Had he realised even dimly the immensity of the issues he was up against, had he had but an inkling of the magnitude of the plot conceived in the sinister brain of his host of the previous evening, then, cheery optimist though he was, even Hugh Drummond might have wavered. But he had no such inkling, and so the gleam in his eyes was but transitory, the chuckle that succeeded it more whole-hearted than before. Was it not sport in a land flowing with strikes and profiteers; sport such as his soul loved?

'I am afraid, Mullings,' he said as the car stopped in front of his club, 'that the kindly gentleman with whom we spent last night has repudiated his obligations. He refuses to meet the bill I gave him for your services. Just wait here a moment.'

He went inside, returning in a few moments with a folded cheque.

'Round the corner, Mullings, and an obliging fellah in a black coat will shove you out the necessary Bradburys.'

The man glanced at the cheque.

'Fifty quid, sir!' he gasped. 'Why – it's too much, sir . . . I . . . '

'The labourer, Mullings, is worthy of his hire. You have been of the very greatest assistance to me; and, incidentally, it is more than likely that I may want you again. Now, where can I get hold of you?'

'13, Green Street, 'Oxton, sir, 'll always find me. And any time, sir, as you wants me, I'd like to come just for the sport of the thing.'

Hugh grinned.

'Good lad. And it may be sooner than you think.'

With a cheery laugh he turned back into his club, and for a moment or two the ex-soldier stood looking after him. Then with great delib-eration he turned to the chauffeur, and spat reflectively.

'If there was more like 'im, and less like *'im*' – he indicated a stout vulgarian rolling past in a large car and dreadful clothes – 'things wouldn't 'appen such as is 'appening today. Ho! no . . . '

With which weighty dictum Mr Mullings, late private of the Royal Loamshires, turned his steps in the direction of the 'obliging fellah in a black coat'.

2

Inside the Junior Sports Club, Hugh Drummond was burying his nose in a large tankard of the ale for which that cheery pot-house was still famous. And in the intervals of this most delightful pastime he was trying to make up his mind on a peculiarly knotty point. Should he or should he not communicate with the police on the matter? He felt that as a respectable citizen of the country it was undoubtedly his duty to tell somebody something. The point was who to tell and what to tell him. On the subject of Scotland Yard his ideas were nebulous; he had a vague impression that one filled in a form and waited – tedious operations, both.

'Besides, dear old flick,' he murmured abstractedly to the portrait of the founder of the club, who had drunk the cellar dry and then died, 'am I a respectable citizen? Can it be said with any certainty, that if I filled in a form saying all that had happened in the last two days, I shouldn't be put in quod myself?'

He sighed profoundly and gazed out into the sunny square. A waiter was arranging the first editions of the evening papers on a table, and Hugh beckoned to him to bring one. His mind was still occupied with his problem, and almost mechanically he glanced over the columns. Cricket, racing, the latest divorce case and the latest strike – all the usual headings were there. And he was just putting down the paper, to again concentrate on his problem, when a paragraph caught his eye.

STRANGE MURDER IN BELFAST

The man whose body was discovered in such peculiar circumstances near the docks has been identified as Mr James Granger, the confidential secretary to Mr Hiram Potts, the American multimillionaire, at present in this country. The unfortunate victim of this dastardly outrage – his head, as we reported in our last night's issue, was nearly severed from his body – had apparently been sent over on business by Mr Potts, and had arrived the preceding day. What he was doing in the locality in which he was found is a mystery.

We understand that Mr Potts, who has recently been indisposed, has returned to the Carlton, and is greatly upset at the sudden tragedy.

The police are confident that they will shortly obtain a clue, though the rough element in the locality where the murder was committed presents great difficulties. It seems clear that the motive was robbery, as all the murdered man's pockets were rifled. But the most peculiar thing about the case is the extraordinary care taken by the murderer to prevent the identification of the body. Every article of clothing, even down to the murdered man's socks, had had the name torn out, and it was only through the criminal overlooking the tailor's tab inside the inner breast-pocket of Mr Granger's coat that the police were enabled to identify the body.

Drummond laid down the paper on his knees, and stared a little dazedly at the club's immoral founder.

'Holy smoke! laddie,' he murmured, 'that man Peterson ought to be on the committee here. Verily, I believe, he could galvanise the staff into some semblance of activity.'

'Did you order anything, sir?' A waiter paused beside him.

'No,' murmured Drummond, 'but I will rectify the omission. Another large tankard of ale.'

The waiter departed, and Hugh picked up the paper again.

'We understand,' he murmured gently to himself, 'that Mr Potts, who has recently been indisposed, has returned to the Carlton . . . Now that's very interesting . . . ' He lit a cigarette and lay back in his chair. 'I was under the impression that Mr Potts was safely tucked up in bed, consuming semolina pudding, at Goring. It requires elucidation.'

'I beg your pardon, sir,' remarked the waiter, placing the beer on the table beside him.

'You needn't,' returned Hugh. 'Up to date you have justified my fondest expectations. And as a further proof of my good will, I would like you to get me a trunk call – 2 X Goring.'

A few minutes later he was in the telephone box.

'Peter, I have seldom been so glad to hear your voice. Is all well? Good. Don't mention any names. Our guest is there, is he? Gone on strike against more milk puddings, you say. Coax him. Peter. Make a noise like a sturgeon, and he'll think it's caviare. Have you seen the papers? There are interesting doings in Belfast, which concern us rather intimately. I'll be down later, and we'll have a pow-wow.'

He hung up the receiver and stepped out of the box.

'If, Algy,' he remarked to a man who was looking at the tape machine outside, 'the paper says a blighter's somewhere and you know he's somewhere else – what do you do?'

'Up to date in such cases I have always shot the editor,' murmured Algy Longworth. 'Come and feed.'

'You're so helpful, Algy. A perfect rock of strength. Do you want a job?'

'What sort of a job?' demanded the other suspiciously.

'Oh! not work, dear old boy. Damn it, man – you know me better than that, surely!'

'People are so funny nowadays,' returned Longworth gloomily. 'The most unlikely souls seem to be doing things and trying to look as if they were necessary. What is this job?'

Together the two men strolled into the luncheon room, and long after the cheese had been finished, Algy Longworth was still listening in silence to his companion.

'My dear old bean,' he murmured ecstatically as Hugh finished, 'my *very* dear old bean. I think it's the most priceless thing I ever heard. Enrol me as a member of the band. And, incidentally, Toby Sinclair is running round in circles asking for trouble. Let's rope him in.'

'Go and find him this afternoon, Algy,' said Hugh, rising. 'And tell him to keep his mouth shut. I'd come with you, but it occurs to me that the wretched Potts, bathed in tears at the Carlton, is in need of sympathy. I would have him weep on my shoulder awhile. So long, old dear. You'll hear from me in a day or two.'

It was as he reached the pavement that Algy dashed out after him, with genuine alarm written all over his face.

'Hugh,' he spluttered, 'there's only one stipulation. An armistice must be declared during Ascot week.'

With a thoughtful smile on his face Drummond sauntered along Pall Mall. He had told Longworth more or less on the spur of the moment, knowing that gentleman's capabilities to a nicety. Under a cloak of assumed flippancy he concealed an iron nerve which had never yet failed him; and, in spite of the fact that he wore an entirely unnecessary eyeglass, he could see farther into a brick wall than most of the people who called him a fool.

It was his suggestion of telling Toby Sinclair that caused the smile. For it had started a train of thought in Drummond's mind which seemed to him to be good. If Sinclair – why not two or three more equally trusty sportsmen? Why not a gang of the boys?

Toby possessed a V.C., and a good one – for there are grades of the V.C., and those grades are appreciated to a nicety by the recipient's brother officers if not by the general public. The show would fit Toby like a glove . . . Then there was Ted Jerningham, who combined the rôles of an amateur actor of more than average merit with an ability to hit anything at any range with every conceivable type of firearm. And Jerry Seymour in the Flying Corps . . . Not a bad thing to have a flying man up one's sleeve . . . And possibly someone versed in the ways of tanks might come in handy . . .

The smile broadened to a grin; surely life was very good. And then the grin faded, and something suspiciously like a frown took its place. For he had arrived at the Carlton, and reality had come back to him. He seemed to see the almost headless body of a man lying in a Belfast slum . . .

'Mr Potts will see no-one, sir,' remarked the man to whom he addressed his question. 'You are about the twentieth gentleman who has been here already today.'

Hugh had expected this, and smiled genially.

'Precisely, my stout fellow,' he remarked, 'but I'll lay a small amount of money that they were newspapermen. Now, I'm not. And I think that if you will have this note delivered to Mr Potts, he will see me.'

He sat down at a table, and drew a sheet of paper towards him. Two facts were certain: first, that the man upstairs was not the real Potts; second, that he was one of Peterson's gang. The difficulty was to know exactly how to word the note. There might be some mystic password, the omission of which would prove him an impostor at once. At length he took a pen and wrote rapidly; he would have to chance it.

> *Urgent. A message from headquarters.*

He sealed the envelope and handed it with the necessary five shillings for postage to the man. Then he sat down to wait. It was going to be a ticklish interview if he was to learn anything, but the thrill of the game had fairly got him by now, and he watched eagerly for the messenger's return. After what seemed an interminable delay he saw him crossing the lounge.

'Mr Potts will see you, sir. Will you come this way?'

'Is he alone?' said Hugh, as they were whirled up in the lift.

'Yes, sir. I think he was expecting you.'

'Indeed,' murmured Hugh. 'How nice it is to have one's expectations realised.'

He followed his guide along a corridor, and paused outside a door while he went into a room. He heard a murmur of voices, and then the man reappeared.

'This way, sir,' he said, and Hugh stepped inside, to stop with an involuntary gasp of surprise. The man seated in the chair *was* Potts, to all intents and purposes. The likeness was extraordinary, and had he not known that the real article was at Goring he would have been completely deceived himself.

The man waited till the door was closed: then he rose and stepped forward suspiciously.

'I don't know you,' he said. 'Who are you?'

'Since when has everyone employed by headquarters known one another?' Drummond returned guardedly. 'And, incidentally, your likeness to our lamented friend is wonderful. It very nearly deceived even me.'

The man, not ill-pleased, gave a short laugh.

'It'll pass, I think. But it's risky. These cursed reporters have been badgering the whole morning . . . And if his wife or somebody comes over, what then?'

Drummond nodded in agreement.

'Quite so. But what can you do?'

'It wasn't like Rosca to bungle in Belfast. He's never left a clue before, and he had plenty of time to do the job properly.'

'A name inside a breast-pocket might easily be overlooked,' remarked Hugh, seizing the obvious clue.

'Are you making excuses for him?' snarled the other. 'He's failed, and failure is death. Such is our rule. Would you have it altered?'

'Most certainly not. The issues are far too great for any weakness . . . '

'You're right, my friend – you're right. Long live the Brotherhood.' He stared out of the window with smouldering eyes, and Hugh preserved a discreet silence. Then suddenly the other broke out again . . . 'Have they killed that insolent puppy of a soldier yet?'

'Er – not yet,' murmured Hugh mildly.

'They must find the American at once.' The man thumped the table emphatically. 'It was important before – at least his money was. Now with this blunder – it's vital.'

'Precisely,' said Hugh. 'Precisely.'

'I've already interviewed one man from Scotland Yard, but every hour increases the danger. However, you have a message for me. What is it?'

Hugh rose and casually picked up his hat. He had got more out of the interview than he had hoped for, and there was nothing to be gained by prolonging it. But it struck him that Mr Potts's impersonator was a man of unpleasant disposition, and that tactically a flanking movement to the door was indicated. And, being of an open nature himself, it is possible that the real state of affairs showed for a moment on his face. Be that as it may, something suddenly aroused the other's suspicions, and with a snarl of fury he sprang past Hugh to the door.

'Who are you?' He spat the words out venomously, at the same time whipping an ugly-looking knife out of his pocket.

Hugh replaced his hat and stick on the table and grinned gently. 'I am the insolent puppy of a soldier, dear old bird,' he remarked, watching the other warily.' And if I was you I'd put the tooth-pick away . . . You might hurt yourself – '

As he spoke he was edging, little by little, towards the other man, who crouched snarling by the door. His eyes, grim and determined, never left the other's face; his hands, apparently hanging listless by his sides, were tingling with the joy of what he knew was coming.

'And the penalty of failure is death, isn't it, dear one?' He spoke almost dreamily; but not for an instant did his attention relax. The words of Olaki, his Japanese instructor, were ringing through his brain: 'Distract his attention if you can; but, as you value your life, don't let him distract yours.'

And so, almost imperceptibly, he crept towards the other man, talking gently.

'Such is your rule. And I think you have failed, haven't you, you unpleasant specimen of humanity? How will they kill you, I wonder?'

It was at that moment that the man made his mistake. It is a mistake that has nipped the life of many a promising pussy in the bud, at the hands, or rather the teeth, of a dog that knows. He looked away; only for a moment – but he looked away. Just as a cat's nerves give after a while and it looks round for an avenue of escape, so did the crouching man take his eyes from Hugh. And quick as any dog, Hugh sprang.

With his left hand he seized the man's right wrist, with his right he seized his throat. Then he forced him upright against the door and held him there. Little by little the grip of his right hand tightened, till the other's eyes were starting from his head, and he plucked at Hugh's face with an impotent left arm, an arm not long enough by three inches to do any damage. And all the while the soldier smiled gently, and stared into the other's eyes. Even when inch by inch he shifted his grip on the man's knife hand he never took his eyes from his opponent's face; even when with a sudden gasp of agony the man dropped his knife from fingers which, of a sudden, had become numb, the steady, merciless glance still bored into his brain.

'You're not very clever at it, are you?' said Hugh softly. 'It would be so easy to kill you now, and, except for the inconvenience I should undoubtedly suffer, it mightn't be a bad idea. But they know me downstairs, and it would make it so awkward when I wanted to dine here again . . . So, taking everything into account, I think – '

There was a sudden lightning movement, a heave and a quick jerk. The impersonator of Potts was dimly conscious of flying through the air, and of hitting the floor some yards from the door. He then became acutely conscious that the floor was hard, and that being winded is a most painful experience. Doubled up and groaning, he watched Hugh pick up his hat and stick, and make for the door. He made a frantic effort to rise, but the pain was too great, and he rolled over cursing, while the soldier, his hand on the door-knob, laughed gently.

'I'll keep the tooth-pick,' he remarked, 'as a memento.'

The next moment he was striding along the corridor towards the lift. As a fight it had been a poor one, but his brain was busy with the information he had heard. True, it had been scrappy in the extreme, and, in part, had only confirmed what he had suspected all along. The wretched Granger had been foully done to death, for no other reason than that he was the millionaire's secretary. Hugh's jaw tightened; it revolted his sense of sport. It wasn't as if the poor blighter had done anything; merely because he existed and might ask inconvenient questions he had been removed. And as the lift shot downwards, and the remembrance of the grim struggle he had had in the darkness of The Elms the night before came back to his mind, he wondered once again if he had done wisely in not breaking Peterson's neck while he had had the chance.

He was still debating the question in his mind as he crossed the tea-lounge. And almost unconsciously he glanced towards the table where three days before he had had tea with Phyllis Benton, and had been more than half inclined to believe that the whole thing was an elaborate leg-pull . . .

'Why, Captain Drummond, you look pensive.' A well-known voice from a table at his side made him look down, and he bowed a little grimly. Irma Peterson was regarding him with a mocking smile.

He glanced at her companion, a young man whose face seemed vaguely familiar to him, and then his eyes rested once more on the girl. Even his masculine intelligence could appreciate the perfection – in a slightly foreign style – of her clothes; and, as to her beauty, he had never been under any delusions. Nor, apparently, was her escort, whose expression was not one of unalloyed pleasure at the interruption to his *tête-à-tête*.

'The Carlton seems rather a favourite resort of yours,' she continued, watching him through half-closed eyes. 'I think you're very wise to make the most of it while you can.'

'While I can?' said Hugh. 'That sounds rather depressing.'

'I've done my best,' continued the girl, 'but matters have passed out of my hands, I'm afraid.'

Again Hugh glanced at her companion, but he had risen and was talking to some people who had just come in.

'Is he one of the firm?' he remarked. 'His face seems familiar.'

'Oh, no!' said the girl. 'He is – just a friend. What have you been doing this afternoon?'

'That, at any rate, is straight and to the point,' laughed Hugh. 'If you want to know, I've just had a most depressing interview.'

'You're a very busy person, aren't you, my ugly one?' she murmured.

'The poor fellow, when I left him, was quite prostrated with grief, and – er – pain,' he went on mildly.

'Would it be indiscreet to ask who the poor fellow is?' she asked.

'A friend of your father's, I think,' said Hugh, with a profound sigh. 'So sad. I hope Mr Peterson's neck is less stiff by now?'

The girl began to laugh softly.

'Not very much, I'm afraid. And it's made him a little irritable. Won't you wait and see him?'

'Is he here now?' said Hugh quickly.

'Yes,' answered the girl. 'With his friend whom you've just left. You're quick, *mon ami* – quite quick.' She leaned forward suddenly. 'Now, why don't you join us instead of so foolishly trying to fight us? Believe me, Monsieur Hugh, it is the only thing that can possibly save you. You know too much.'

'Is the invitation to amalgamate official, or from your own charming brain?' murmured Hugh.

'Made on the spur of the moment,' she said lightly. 'But it may be regarded as official.'

'I'm afraid it must be declined on the spur of the moment,' he answered in the same tone. 'And equally to be regarded as official. Well, *au revoir*. Please tell Mr Peterson how sorry I am to have missed him.'

'I will most certainly,' answered the girl. 'But then, *mon ami*, you will be seeing him again soon, without doubt . . . '

She waved a charming hand in farewell, and turned to her companion, who was beginning to manifest symptoms of impatience. But Drummond, though he went into the hall outside, did not immediately leave the hotel. Instead, he buttonholed an exquisite being arrayed in gorgeous apparel, and led him to a point of vantage.

'You see that girl,' he remarked, 'having tea with a man at the third table from the big palm? Now, can you tell me who the man is? I seem to know his face, but I can't put a name to it.'

'That, sir,' murmured the exquisite being, with the faintest perceptible scorn of such ignorance, 'is the Marquis of Laidley. His lordship is frequently here.'

'Laidley!' cried Hugh, in sudden excitement. 'Laidley! The Duke of Lampshire's son! You priceless old stuffed tomato – the plot thickens.'

Completely regardless of the scandalised horror on the exquisite being's face, he smote him heavily in the stomach and stepped into Pall Mall. For clear before his memory had come three lines on the scrap of paper he had torn from the table at The Elms that first night, when he had grabbed the dazed millionaire from under Peterson's nose.

> earl necklace and the
> are at present
> chess of Lamp-

The Duchess of Lampshire's pearls were world-famous; the Marquis of Laidley was apparently enjoying his tea. And between the two there seemed to be a connection rather too obvious to be missed.

3

'I'm glad you two fellows came down,' said Hugh thoughtfully, as he entered the sitting-room of his bungalow at Goring. Dinner was over, and stretched in three chairs were Peter Darrell, Algy Longworth, and Toby Sinclair. The air was thick with smoke, and two dogs lay curled up on the mat, asleep. 'Did you know that a man came here this afternoon, Peter?'

Darrell yawned and stretched himself.

'I did not. Who was it?'

'Mrs Denny has just told me.' Hugh reached out a hand for his pipe, and proceeded to stuff it with tobacco. 'He came about the water.'

'Seems a very righteous proceeding, dear old thing,' said Algy lazily.

'And he told her that I had told him to come. Unfortunately, I'd done nothing of the sort.'

His three listeners sat up and stared at him.

'What do you mean, Hugh?' asked Toby Sinclair at length.

'It's pretty obvious, old boy.' said Hugh grimly. 'He no more came about the water than he came about my aunt. I should say that about five hours ago Peterson found out that our one and only Hiram C. Potts was upstairs.'

'Good Lord!' spluttered Darrell, by now very wide awake. 'How the devil has he done it?'

'There are no flies on the gentleman,' remarked Hugh. 'I didn't expect he'd do it quite so quick, I must admit. But it wasn't very difficult for him to find out that I had a bungalow here, and so he drew the covert.'

'And he's found the bally fox,' said Algy. 'What do we do, sergeant-major?'

'We take it in turns – two at a time – to sit up with Potts.' Hugh glanced at the other three. 'Damn it – you blighters – wake up!'

Darrell struggled to his feet and walked up and down the room.

'I don't know what it is,' he said, rubbing his eyes, 'I feel most infernally sleepy.'

'Well, listen to me – confound you . . . Toby!' Hugh hurled a tobacco-pouch at the offender's head.

'Sorry, old man.' With a start Sinclair sat up in his chair and blinked at Hugh.

'They're almost certain to try and get him tonight,' went on Hugh. 'Having given the show away by leaving a clue on the wretched secretary, they must get the real man as soon as possible. It's far too dangerous to leave the – leave the – ' His head dropped forward on his chest: a short, half-strangled snore came from his lips. It had the effect of waking him for the moment, and he staggered to his feet.

The other three, sprawling in their chairs, were openly and unashamedly asleep; even the dogs lay in fantastic attitudes, breathing heavily, inert like logs.

'Wake up!' shouted Hugh wildly. 'For God's sake – wake up! We've been drugged!'

An iron weight seemed to be pressing down on his eyelids: the desire for sleep grew stronger and stronger. For a few moments more he fought against it, hopelessly, despairingly; while his legs seemed not to belong to him, and there was a roaring noise in his ears. And then, just before unconsciousness overcame him, there came to his bemused brain the sound of a whistle thrice repeated from outside the window. With a last stupendous effort he fought his way towards it, and for a moment he stared into the darkness. There were dim figures moving through the shrubs, and suddenly one seemed to detach itself. It came nearer, and the light fell on the man's face. His nose and mouth were covered with a sort of pad, but the cold, sneering eyes were unmistakable.

'Lakington!' gasped Hugh, and then the roaring noise increased in his head; his legs struck work altogether. He collapsed on the floor and lay sprawling, while Lakington, his face pressed against the glass outside, watched in silence.

* * *

'Draw the curtains.' Lakington was speaking. His voice was muffled behind the pad, and one of the men did as he said. There were four in all, each with a similar pad over his mouth and nose. 'Where did you put the generator, Brownlow?'

'In the coal-scuttle.' A man whom Mrs Denny would have had no difficulty in recognising, even with the mask on his face, carefully lifted a small black box out of the scuttle from behind some coal, and shook it gently, holding it to his ear. 'It's finished,' he remarked, and Lakington nodded.

'An ingenious invention is gas,' he said, addressing another of the men. 'We owe your nation quite a debt of gratitude for the idea.'

A guttural grunt left no doubt as to what that nation was, and Lakington dropped the box into his pocket.

'Go and get him,' he ordered briefly, and the others left the room.

Contemptuously Lakington kicked one of the dogs; it rolled over and lay motionless in its new position. Then he went in turn to each of the three men sprawling in the chairs. With no attempt at gentleness he turned their faces up to the light, and studied them deliberately; then he let their heads roll back again with a thud. Finally, he went to the window and stared down at Drummond. In his eyes was a look of cold fury, and he kicked the unconscious man savagely in the ribs.

'You young swine,' he muttered. 'Do you think I'll forget that blow on the jaw?'

He took another box out of his pocket and looked at it lovingly.

'Shall I?' With a short laugh he replaced it. 'It's too good a death for you, Captain Drummond, D.S.O., M.C. Just to snuff out in your sleep. No, my friend, I think I can devise something better than that; something really artistic.'

Two other men came in as he turned away, and Lakington looked at them.

'Well,' he asked, 'have you got the old woman?'

'Bound and gagged in the kitchen,' answered one of them laconically. 'Are you going to do this crowd in?'

The speaker looked at the unconscious men with hatred in his eyes.

'They encumber the earth – this breed of puppy.'

'They will not encumber it for long,' said Lakington softly. 'But the one in the window there is not going to die quite so easily. I have a small unsettled score with him . . . '

'All right; he's in the car.' A voice came from outside the window, and with a last look at Hugh Drummond, Lakington turned away.

'Then we'll go,' he remarked. '*Au revoir*, my blundering young bull. Before I've finished with you, you'll scream for mercy. And you won't get it . . . '

* * *

Through the still night air there came the thrumming of the engine of a powerful car. Gradually it died away and there was silence. Only the murmur of the river over the weir broke the silence, save for an owl which hooted mournfully in a tree near by. And then, with a sudden crack, Peter Darrell's head rolled over and hit the arm of his chair.

Chapter 6

In which a very old game takes place on the Hog's Back

I

A thick grey mist lay over the Thames. It covered the water and the low fields to the west like a thick white carpet; it drifted sluggishly under the old bridge which spans the river between Goring and Streatley. It was the hour before dawn, and sleepy passengers, rubbing the windows of their carriages as the Plymouth boat express rushed on towards London, shivered and drew their rugs closer around them. It looked cold . . . cold and dead.

Slowly, almost imperceptibly, the vapour rose, and spread outwards up the wooded hills by Basildon. It drifted through the shrubs and rose-bushes of a little garden, which stretched from a bungalow down to the water's edge, until at length wisps of it brushed gently round the bungalow itself. It was a daily performance in the summer, and generally the windows of the lower rooms remained shut till long after the mist had gone and the sun was glinting through the trees on to the river below. But on this morning there was a change in the usual programme. Suddenly the window of one of the downstairs rooms was flung open, and a man with a white haggard face leant out drawing great gulps of fresh air into his lungs. Softly the white wraiths eddied past him into the room behind – a room in which a queer, faintly sweet smell still hung – a room in which three other men lay sprawling uncouthly in chairs, and two dogs lay motionless on the hearthrug.

After a moment or two the man withdrew, only to appear again with one of the others in his arms. And then, having dropped his burden through the window on to the lawn outside, he repeated his performance with the remaining two. Finally he pitched the two dogs after them, and then, with his hand to his forehead, he staggered down to the water's edge.

'Holy smoke!' he muttered to himself, as he plunged his head into the cold water; 'talk about the morning after! . . . Never have I thought of such a head.'

After a while, with the water still dripping from his face, he returned to the bungalow and found the other three in varying stages of partial insensibility.

'Wake up, my heroes,' he remarked, 'and go and put your great fat heads in the river.'

Peter Darrell scrambled unsteadily to his feet.

'Great Scott! Hugh,' he muttered thickly, 'what's happened?'

'We've been had for mugs,' said Drummond grimly.

Algy Longworth blinked at him foolishly from his position in the middle of a flower-bed.

'Dear old soul,' he murmured at length, 'you'll have to change your wine merchants. Merciful Heavens! Is the top of my head still on?'

'Don't be a fool, Algy,' grunted Hugh. 'You weren't drunk last night. Pull yourself together, man; we were all of us drugged or doped somehow. And now,' he added bitterly, 'we've all got heads, and we have not got Potts.'

'I don't remember anything,' said Toby Sinclair, 'except falling asleep. Have they taken him?'

'Of course they have,' said Hugh. 'Just before I went off I saw 'em all in the garden, and that swine Lakington was with them. However, while you go and put your nuts in the river, I'll go up and make certain.'

With a grim smile he watched the three men lurch down to the water; then he turned and went upstairs to the room which had been occupied by the American millionaire. It was empty, as he had known it would be, and with a smothered curse he made his way downstairs again. And it was as he stood in the little hall saying things gently under his breath that he heard a muffled moaning noise coming from the kitchen. For a moment he was nonplussed; then, with an oath at his stupidity, he dashed through the door. Bound tightly to the table, with a gag in her mouth, the wretched Mrs Denny was sitting on the floor, blinking at him wrathfully . . .

'What on earth will Denny say to me when he hears about this!' said Hugh, feverishly cutting the cords. He helped her to her feet, and then forced her gently into a chair. 'Mrs Denny, have those swine hurt you?'

Five minutes served to convince him that the damage, if any, was mental rather than bodily, and that her vocal powers were not in the least impaired. Like a dam bursting, the flood of the worthy woman's wrath surged over him; she breathed a hideous vengeance on every one impartially. Then she drove Hugh from the kitchen, and slammed the door in his face.

'Breakfast in half an hour,' she cried from inside – 'not that one of you deserves it.'

'We are forgiven,' remarked Drummond, as he joined the other three on the lawn. 'Do any of you feel like breakfast? Fat sausages and crinkly bacon.'

'Shut up,' groaned Algy, 'or we'll throw you into the river. What I want is a brandy-and-soda – half a dozen of 'em.'

'I wish I knew what they did to us,' said Darrell. 'Because, if I remember straight, I drank bottled beer at dinner, and I'm damned if I see how they could have doped that.'

'I'm only interested in one thing, Peter,' remarked Drummond grimly, 'and that isn't what they did to us. It's what we're going to do to them.'

'Count me out,' said Algy. 'For the next year I shall be fully occupied resting my head against a cold stone. Hugh, I positively detest your friends . . . '

* * *

It was a few hours later that a motor-car drew up outside that celebrated chemist in Piccadilly whose pick-me-ups are known from Singapore to Alaska. From it there descended four young men, who ranged themselves in a row before the counter and spoke no word. Speech was unnecessary. Four foaming drinks were consumed, four acid-drops were eaten, and then, still in silence, the four young men got back into the car and drove away. It was a solemn rite, and on arrival at the Junior Sports Club the four performers sank into four large chairs, and pondered gently on the vileness of the morning after. Especially when there hadn't been a night before. An unprofitable meditation evidently, for suddenly, as if actuated by a single thought, the four young men rose from their four large chairs and again entered the motor-car.

The celebrated chemist whose pick-me-ups are known from Singapore to Alaska gazed at them severely.

'A very considerable bend, gentlemen,' he remarked.

'Quite wrong,' answered the whitest and most haggard of the row. 'We are all confirmed Pussy-foots, and have been consuming non-alcoholic beer.'

Once more to the scrunch of acid-drops the four young men

entered the car outside; once more, after a brief and silent drive, four large chairs in the smoking-room of the Junior Sports Club received an occupant. And it was so, even until luncheon time . . .

'Are we better?' said Hugh, getting to his feet, and regarding the other three with a discerning eye.

'No,' murmured Toby, 'but I am beginning to hope that I may live. Four Martinis and then we will gnaw a cutlet.'

2

'Has it struck you fellows,' remarked Hugh, at the conclusion of lunch, 'that seated around this table are four officers who fought with some distinction and much discomfort in the recent historic struggle?'

'How beautifully you put it, old flick!' said Darrell.

'Has it further struck you fellows,' continued Hugh, 'that last night we were done down, trampled on, had for mugs by a crowd of dirty blackguards composed largely of the dregs of the universe?'

'A veritable Solomon,' said Algy, gazing at him admiringly through his eyeglass. 'I told you this morning I detested your friends.'

'Has it still further struck you,' went on Hugh, a trifle grimly, 'that we aren't standing for it? At any rate, I'm not. It's my palaver this, you fellows, and if you like . . . Well, there's no call on you to remain in the game. I mean – er – '

'Yes, we're waiting to hear what the devil you do mean,' said Toby uncompromisingly.

'Well – er,' stammered Hugh, 'there's a big element of risk – er – don't you know, and there's no earthly reason why you fellows should get roped in and all that. I mean – er – I'm sort of pledged to see the thing through, don't you know, and – ' He relapsed into silence, and stared at the table-cloth, uncomfortably aware of three pairs of eyes fixed on him.

'Well – er – ' mimicked Algy, 'there's a big element of risk – er – don't you know, and I mean – er – we're sort of pledged to bung you through the window, old bean, if you talk such consolidated drivel.'

Hugh grinned sheepishly.

'Well, I had to put it to you fellows. Not that I ever thought for a moment you wouldn't see the thing through – but last evening is enough to show you that we're up against a tough crowd. A damned tough crowd,' he added thoughtfully. 'That being so,' he went on briskly, after a moment or two, 'I propose that we should tackle the blighters tonight.'

'Tonight!' echoed Darrell. 'Where?'

'At The Elms, of course. That's where the wretched Potts is for a certainty.'

'And how do you propose that we should set about it?' demanded Sinclair.

Drummond drained his port and grinned gently.

'By stealth, dear old beans – by stealth. You – and I thought we might rake in Ted Jerningham, and perhaps Jerry Seymour, to join the happy throng – will make a demonstration in force, with the idea of drawing off the enemy, thereby leaving the coast clear for me to explore the house for the unfortunate Potts.'

'Sounds very nice in theory,' said Darrell dubiously, 'but . . . '

'And what do you mean by a demonstration?' said Longworth. 'You don't propose we should sing carols outside the drawing-room window, do you?'

'My dear people,' Hugh murmured protestingly, 'surely you know me well enough by now to realise that I can't possibly have another idea for at least ten minutes. That is just the general scheme; doubtless the mere vulgar details will occur to us in time. Besides, it's someone else's turn now.' He looked round the table hopefully.

'We might dress up or something,' remarked Toby Sinclair, after a lengthy silence.

'What in the name of Heaven is the use of that?' said Darrell witheringly. 'It's not private theatricals, nor a beauty competition.'

'Cease wrangling, you two,' said Hugh suddenly, a few moments later. 'I've got a perfect cerebral hurricane raging. An accident . . . A car . . . What is the connecting-link . . . Why, drink. Write it down, Algy, or we might forget. Now, can you beat that?'

'We might have some chance,' said Darrell kindly, 'if we had the slightest idea what you were talking about.'

'I should have thought it was perfectly obvious,' returned Hugh coldly. 'You know, Peter, your worry is that you're too quick on the uptake. Your brain is too sharp.'

'How do you spell connecting?' demanded Algy, looking up from his labours. 'And, anyway, the damn pencil won't write.'

'Pay attention, all of you,' said Hugh. 'Tonight, some time about ten of the clock, Algy's motor will proceed along the Godalming-Guildford road. It will contain you three – also Ted and Jerry Seymour, if we can get 'em. On approaching the gate of The Elms, you will render the night hideous with your vocal efforts. Stray passers-by will think that you are all tight. Then will come the dramatic moment, when, with a heavy crash, you ram the gate.'

'How awfully jolly!' spluttered Algy. 'I beg to move that your car be used for the event.'

'Can't be done, old son,' laughed Hugh. 'Mine's faster than yours, and I'll be wanting it myself. Now – to proceed. Horrified at this wanton damage to property, you will leave the car and proceed in mass formation up the drive.'

'Still giving tongue?' queried Darrell.

'Still giving tongue. Either Ted or Jerry or both of 'em will approach the house and inform the owner in heartbroken accents that they have damaged his gatepost. You three will remain in the garden – you might be recognised. Then it will be up to you. You'll have several men all round you. Keep 'em occupied – somehow. They won't hurt you; they'll only be concerned with seeing that you don't go where you're not wanted. You see, as far as the world is concerned, it's just an ordinary country residence. The last thing they want to do is to draw any suspicion on themselves – and, on the face of it, you are merely five convivial wanderers who have looked on the wine when it was red. I think,' he added thoughtfully, 'that ten minutes will be enough for me . . . '

'What will you be doing?' said Toby.

'I shall be looking for Potts. Don't worry about me. I may find him; I may not. But when you have given me ten minutes – you clear off. I'll look after myself. Now is that clear?'

'Perfectly,' said Darrell, after a short silence. 'But I don't know that I like it, Hugh. It seems to me, old son, that you're running an unnecessary lot of risk.'

'Got any alternative?' demanded Drummond.

'If we're all going down,' said Darrell, 'why not stick together and rush the house in a gang?'

'No go, old bean,' said Hugh decisively. 'Too many of 'em to hope to pull it off. No, low cunning is the only thing that's got an earthly of succeeding.'

'There is one other possible suggestion,' remarked Toby slowly. 'What about the police? From what you say, Hugh, there's enough in that house to jug the whole bunch.'

'Toby!' gasped Hugh. 'I thought better of you. You seriously suggest that we should call in the police! And then return to a life of toping and ease! Besides,' he continued, removing his eyes from the abashed author of this hideous suggestion, 'there's a very good reason for keeping the police out of it. You'd land the girl's father in the cart, along with the rest of them. And it makes it so devilish awkward if one's father-in-law is in prison!'

'When are we going to see this fairy?' demanded Algy.

'You, personally, never. You're far too immoral. I might let the others look at her from a distance in a year or two.' With a grin he rose, and then strolled towards the door. 'Now go and rope in Ted and Jerry, and for the love of Heaven don't ram the wrong gate.'

'What are you going to do yourself?' demanded Peter suspiciously.

'I'm going to look at her from close to. Go away, all of you, and don't listen outside the telephone box.'

3

Hugh stopped his car at Guildford station and, lighting a cigarette, strolled restlessly up and down He looked at his watch a dozen times in two minutes; he threw away his smoke before it was half finished. In short he manifested every symptom usually displayed by the male of the species when awaiting the arrival of the opposite sex. Over the telephone he had arranged that she should come by train from Godalming to confer with him on a matter of great importance; she had said she would, but what was it? He, having no suitable answer ready, had made a loud buzzing noise indicative of a telephone exchange in pain, and then rung off. And now he was waiting in that peculiar condition of mind which reveals itself outwardly in hands that are rather too warm, and feet that are rather too cold.

'When is this bally train likely to arrive?' He accosted a phlegmatic official, who regarded him coldly, and doubted the likelihood of its being more than a quarter of an hour early.

At length it was signalled, and Hugh got back into his car. Feverishly he scanned the faces of the passengers as they came out into the street, until, with a sudden quick jump of his heart, he saw her, cool and fresh, coming towards him with a faint smile on her lips.

'What is this very important matter you want to talk to me about?' she demanded, as he adjusted the rug round her.

'I'll tell you when we get out on the Hog's Back,' he said, slipping in his clutch. 'It's absolutely vital.'

He stole a glance at her, but she was looking straight in front of her, and her face seemed expressionless.

'You must stand a long way off when you do,' she said demurely. 'At least if it's the same thing as you told me over the 'phone.'

Hugh grinned sheepishly.

'The Exchange went wrong,' he remarked at length. 'Astonishing how rotten the telephones are in Town these days.'

'Quite remarkable,' she returned. 'I thought you weren't feeling very well or something, Of course, if it was the Exchange . . . '

'They sort of buzz and blow, don't you know,' he explained helpfully.

'That must be most fearfully jolly for them,' she agreed. And there was silence for the next two miles . . .

Once or twice he looked at her out of the corner of his eye, taking in every detail of the sweet profile so near to him. Except for their first meeting at the Carlton, it was the only time he had ever had her completely to himself, and Hugh was determined to make the most of it. He felt as if he could go on driving for ever, just he and she alone. He had an overwhelming longing to put out his hand and touch a soft tendril of hair which was blowing loose just behind her ear; he had an overwhelming longing to take her in his arms, and . . . It was then that the girl turned and looked at him. The car swerved dangerously . . .

'Let's stop,' she said, with the suspicion of a smile. 'Then you can tell me.'

Hugh drew into the side of the road, and switched off the engine.

'You're not fair,' he remarked, and if the girl saw his hand trembling a little as he opened the door, she gave no sign. Only her breath came a shade faster, but a mere man could hardly be expected to notice such a trifle as that . . .

He came and stood beside her, and his right arm lay along the seat just behind her shoulders.

'You're not fair,' he repeated gravely. 'I haven't swerved like that since I first started to drive.'

'Tell me about this important thing,' she said a little nervously.

He smiled, and no woman yet born could see Hugh Drummond smile without smiling too.

'You darling!' he whispered, under his breath – 'you adorable darling!' His arm closed around her, and almost before she realised it, she felt his lips on hers. For a moment she sat motionless, while the wonder of it surged over her, and the sky seemed more gloriously blue, and the woods a richer green. Then, with a little gasp, she pushed him away.

'You mustn't . . . oh! you mustn't, Hugh,' she whispered.

'And why not, little girl?' he said exultingly. 'Don't you know I love you?'

'But look, there's a man over there, and he'll see.'

Hugh glanced at the stolid labourer in question, and smiled.

'Go an absolute mucker over the cabbages, what! Plant carrots by mistake.' His face was still very close to hers. 'Well?'

'Well, what?' she murmured.

'It's your turn,' he whispered. 'I love you, Phyllis – just love you.'

'But it's only two or three days since we met,' she said feebly.

'And phwat the divil has that got to do with it, at all?' he demanded. 'Would I be wanting longer to decide such an obvious fact? Tell me,' he went on, and she felt his arm round her again forcing her to look at him – 'tell me, don't you care . . . a little?'

'What's the use?' She still struggled, but, even to her, it wasn't very convincing. 'We've got other things to do . . . We can't think of . . . '

And then this very determined young man settled matters in his usual straightforward fashion. She felt herself lifted bodily out of the car as if she had been a child: she found herself lying in his arms, with Hugh's eyes looking very tenderly into her own and a whimsical grin round his mouth.

'Cars pass here,' he remarked, 'with great regularity. I know you'd hate to be discovered in this position.'

'Would I?' she whispered. 'I wonder . . . '

She felt his heart pound madly against her; and with a sudden quick movement she put both her arms round his neck and kissed him on the mouth.

'Is that good enough?' she asked, very low: and just for a few moments, Time stood still . . . Then, very gently, he put her back in the car.

'I suppose,' he remarked resignedly, 'that we had better descend to trivialities. We've had lots of fun and games since I last saw you a year or two ago.'

'Idiot boy,' she said happily. 'It was yesterday morning.'

'The interruption is considered trivial. Mere facts don't count when it's you and me.' There was a further interlude of uncertain duration, followed rapidly by another because the first was so nice.

'To resume,' continued Hugh. 'I regret to state that they've got Potts.'

The girl sat up quickly and stared at him.

'Got him? Oh, Hugh! how did they manage it?'

'I'm damned if I know,' he answered grimly. 'They found out that he was in my bungalow at Goring during the afternoon by sending round a man to see about the water. Somehow or other he must have doped the drink or the food, because after dinner we all fell asleep. I can just remember seeing Lakington's face outside in the garden, pressed against the window, and then everything went out. I don't remember anything more till I woke this morning with the most appalling head. Of course, Potts had gone.'

'I heard the car drive up in the middle of the night,' said the girl thoughtfully. 'Do you think he's at The Elms now?'

'That is what I propose to find out tonight,' answered Hugh. 'We have staged a little comedy for Peterson's especial benefit, and we are hoping for the best.'

'Oh, boy, do be careful!' She looked at him anxiously. 'I'd never forgive myself if anything happened to you. I'd feel it was all due to me, and I just couldn't bear it.'

'Dear little girl,' he whispered tenderly, 'you're simply adorable when you look like that. But not even for you would I back out of this show now.' His mouth set in a grim line. 'It's gone altogether too far, and they've shown themselves to be so completely beyond the pale that it's got to be fought out. And when it has been,' he caught both her hands in his . . . 'and we've won . . . why, then girl o' mine, we'll get Peter Darrell to be best man.'

Which was the cue for the commencement of the last and longest interlude, terminated only by the sudden and unwelcome appearance of a motor-bus covered within and without by unromantic sightseers, and paper-bags containing bananas.

They drove slowly back to Guildford, and on the way he told her briefly of the murder of the American's secretary in Belfast, and his interview the preceding afternoon with the impostor at the Carlton.

'It's a tough proposition,' he remarked quietly. 'They're absolutely without scruple, and their power seems unlimited. I know they are after the Duchess of Lampshire's pearls: I found the beautiful Irma consuming tea with young Laidley yesterday – you know, the Duke's eldest son. But there's something more in the wind than that, Phyllis – something which, unless I'm a mug of the first water, is an infinitely larger proposition than that.'

The car drew up at the station, and he strolled with her on to the platform. Trivialities were once more banished: vital questions concerning when it had first happened – by both; whether he was quite sure it would last for ever – by her; what she could possibly see in him – by him; and wasn't everything just too wonderful for words – mutual and carried *nem. con.*

Then the train came in, and he put her into a carriage. And two minutes later, with the touch of her lips warm on his, and her anxious little cry, 'Take care, my darling! – Take care!' still ringing in his ears, he got into his car and drove off to an hotel to get an early dinner. Love for the time was over; the next round of the other game was due. And it struck Drummond that it was going to be a round where a mistake would not be advisable.

4

At a quarter to ten he backed his car into the shadow of some trees not far from the gate of The Elms. The sky was overcast, which suited his purpose, and through the gloom of the bushes he dodged rapidly towards the house. Save for a light in the sitting-room and one in a bedroom upstairs, the front of the house was in darkness, and, treading noiselessly on the turf, he explored all round it. From a downstairs room on one side came the hoarse sound of men's voices, and he placed that as the smoking-room of the gang of ex-convicts and blackguards who formed Peterson's staff. There was one bedroom light at the back of the house, and thrown on the blind he could see the shadow of a man. As he watched, the man got up and moved away, only to return in a moment or two and take up his old position.

'It's one of those two bedrooms,' he muttered to himself, 'if he's here at all.'

Then he crouched in the shadow of some shrubs and waited. Through the trees to his right he could see The Larches, and once, with a sudden quickening of his heart, he thought he saw the outline of the girl show up in the light from the drawing-room. But it was only for a second, and then it was gone . . .

He peered at his watch: it was just ten o'clock. The trees were creaking gently in the faint wind; all around him the strange night noises – noises which play pranks with a man's nerves – were whispering and muttering. Bushes seemed suddenly to come to life, and move; eerie shapes crawled over the ground towards him – figures which existed only in his imagination. And once again the thrill of the night stalker gripped him.

He remembered the German who had lain motionless for an hour in a little gully by Hebuterne, while he from behind a stunted bush had tried to locate him. And then that one creak as the Boche had moved his leg. And then . . . the end. On that night, too, the little hummocks had moved and taken themselves strange shapes: fifty times he had imagined he saw him; fifty times he knew he was wrong – in time. He was used to it; the night held no terrors for him, only a fierce excitement. And thus it was that as he crouched in the bushes, waiting for the game to start, his pulse was as normal, and his nerves as steady, as if he had been sitting down to supper. The only difference was that in his hand he held something tight-gripped.

At last faintly in the distance he heard the hum of a car. Rapidly it grew louder, and he smiled grimly to himself as the sound of five unmelodious voices singing lustily struck his ear. They passed along the road in front of the house. There was a sudden crash – then silence; but only for a moment.

Peter's voice came first:

'You priceless old ass, you've rammed the blinking gate.'

It was Jerry Seymour who then took up the ball. His voice was intensely solemn – also extremely loud.

'Preposhterous. Perfectly preposhterous. We must go and apologise to the owner . . . I . . . I . . . absholutely . . . musht apologise . . . Quite unpardonable . . . You can't go about country . . . knocking down gates . . . Out of queshtion . . . '

Half consciously Hugh listened, but, now that the moment for action had come, every faculty was concentrated on his own job. He saw half a dozen men go rushing out into the garden through a side door, and then two more ran out and came straight towards him, They crashed past him and went on into the darkness, and for an instant he wondered what they were doing. A little later he was destined to find out . . .

Then came a peal at the front-door bell, and he determined to wait no longer. He darted through the garden door, to find a flight of back stairs in front of him, and in another moment he was on the first floor. He walked rapidly along the landing, trying to find his bearings, and, turning a corner, he found himself at the top of the main staircase – the spot where he had fought Peterson two nights previously.

From below Jerry Seymour's voice came clearly.

'Are you the pro-propri-tor, ole friend? Because there's been . . . acchident . . . '

He waited to hear no more, but walked quickly on to the room which he calculated was the one where he had seen the shadow on the blind. Without a second's hesitation he flung the door open and walked in. There, lying in the bed, was the American, while crouched beside him, with a revolver in his hand, was a man . . .

For a few seconds they watched one another in silence, and then the man straightened up.

'The soldier!' he snarled. 'You young pup!'

Deliberately, almost casually, he raised his revolver, and then the unexpected happened. A jet of liquid ammonia struck him full in the face, and with a short laugh Hugh dropped his water-pistol in his pocket, and turned his attention to the bed. Wrapping the millionaire in a blanket, he picked him up, and, paying no more attention to the man gasping and choking in a corner, he raced for the back stairs.

Below he could still hear Jerry hiccoughing gently, and explaining to the pro . . . pro . . . pritor that he pershonally would repair . . . inshisted on repairing . . . any and every gateposht he posshessed . . . And then he reached the garden . . .

Everything had fallen out exactly as he had hoped, but had hardly dared to expect. He heard Peterson's voice, calm and suave as usual, answering Jerry. From the garden in front came the dreadful sound of a duet by Algy and Peter. Not a soul was in sight; the back of the house was clear. All that he had to do was to walk quietly through the wicket-gate to The Larches with his semiconscious burden, get to his car, and drive off It all seemed so easy that he laughed . . .

But there were one or two factors that he had forgotten, and the first and most important one was the man upstairs. The window was thrown up suddenly, and the man leaned out waving his arms. He was still gasping with the strength of the ammonia, but Hugh saw him clearly in the light from the room behind. And as he cursed himself for a fool in not having tied him up, from the trees close by there came the sharp clang of metal.

With a quick catch in his breath he began to run. The two men who had rushed past him before he had entered the house, and whom, save for a passing thought, he had disregarded, had become the principal danger. For he had heard that clang before; he remembered Jem Smith's white horror-struck face, and then his sigh of relief as the thing – whatever it was – was shut in its cage. And now it was out, dodging through the trees, let loose by the two men.

Turning his head from side to side, peering into the gloom, he ran on. What an interminable distance it seemed to the gate . . . and even then . . . He heard something crash into a bush on his right, and give a snarl of anger. Like a flash he swerved into the undergrowth on the left.

Then began a dreadful game. He was still some way from the fence, and he was hampered at every step by the man slung over his back. He could hear the thing blundering about searching for him, and suddenly, with a cold feeling of fear, he realised that the animal was in front of him – that his way to the gate was barred. The next moment he saw it . . .

Shadowy, indistinct, in the darkness, he saw something glide between two bushes. Then it came out into the open and he knew it had seen him, though as yet he could not make out what it was. Grotesque and horrible it crouched on the ground, and he could hear its heavy breathing, as it waited for him to move.

Cautiously he lowered the millionaire to the ground, and took a step forward. It was enough; with a snarl of fury the crouching form rose and shambled towards him. Two hairy arms shot towards his throat, he smelt the brute's fetid breath, hot and loathsome, and he realised what he was up against. It was a partially grown gorilla.

For a full minute they fought in silence, save for the hoarse grunts of the animal as it tried to tear away the man's hand from its throat, and then encircle him with its powerful arms. And with his brain cold as ice Hugh saw his danger and kept his head. It couldn't go on: no human being could last the pace, whatever his strength. And there was only one chance of finishing it quickly, the possibility that the grip taught him by Olaki would serve with a monkey as it did with a man.

He shifted his left thumb an inch or two on the brute's throat, and the gorilla, thinking he was weakening, redoubled its efforts. But still those powerful hands clutched its throat; try as it would, it failed to make them budge. And then, little by little, the fingers moved, and the grip which had been tight before grew tighter still.

Back went its head; something was snapping in its neck. With a scream of fear and rage it wrapped its legs round Drummond, squeezing and writhing. And then suddenly there was a tearing snap, and the great limbs relaxed and grew limp.

For a moment the man stood watching the still quivering brute lying at his feet; then, with a gasp of utter exhaustion, he dropped on the ground himself. He was done – utterly cooked; even Peterson's voice close behind scarcely roused him.

'Quite one of the most amusing entertainments I've seen for a long time.' The calm, expressionless voice made him look up wearily, and he saw that he was surrounded by men. The inevitable cigar glowed red in the darkness, and after a moment or two he scrambled unsteadily to his feet.

'I'd forgotten your damned menagerie, I must frankly confess,' he remarked. 'What's the party for?' He glanced at the men who had closed in round him.

'A guard of honour, my young friend,' said Peterson suavely, 'to lead you to the house. I wouldn't hesitate . . . it's very foolish. Your friends have gone, and, strong as you are, I don't think you can manage ten.'

Hugh commenced to stroll towards the house.

'Well, don't leave the wretched Potts lying about. I dropped him over there.' For a moment the idea of making a dash for it occurred to him, but he dismissed it at once. The odds were too great to make the risk worth while, and in the centre of the group he and Peterson walked side by side.

'The last man whom poor Sambo had words with,' said Peterson reminiscently, 'was found next day with his throat torn completely out.'

'A lovable little thing,' murmured Hugh. 'I feel quite sorry at having spoilt his record.'

Peterson paused with his hand on the sitting-room door, and looked at him benevolently.

'Don't be despondent, Captain Drummond. We have ample time at our disposal to ensure a similar find tomorrow morning.'

Chapter 7

In which he spends an hour or two on a roof

I

Drummond paused for a moment at the door of the sitting-room, then with a slight shrug he stepped past Peterson. During the last few days he had grown to look on this particular room as the private den of the principals of the gang. He associated it in his mind with Peterson himself, suave, impassive, ruthless; with the girl Irma, perfectly gowned, lying on the sofa, smoking innumerable cigarettes, and manicuring her already faultless nails; and in a lesser degree, with Henry Lakington's thin, cruel face, and blue, staring eyes.

But tonight a different scene confronted him. The girl was not there: her accustomed place on the sofa was occupied by an unkempt-looking man with a ragged beard. At the end of the table was a vacant chair, on the right of which sat Lakington regarding him with male-volent fury. Along the table on each side there were half a dozen men, and he glanced at their faces. Some were obviously foreigners; some might have been anything from murderers to Sunday-school teachers. There was one with spectacles and the general appearance of an intimidated rabbit, while his neighbour, helped by a large red scar right across his cheek, and two bloodshot eyes, struck Hugh as being the sort of man with whom one would not share a luncheon basket.

'I know he'd snatch both drumsticks and gnaw them simultan-eously,' he reflected, staring at him fascinated; 'and then he'd throw the bones in your face.'

Peterson's voice from just behind his shoulder roused him from his distressing reverie.

'Permit me, gentlemen, to introduce to you Captain Drummond, D.S.O., M.C., the originator of the little entertainment we have just had.'

Hugh bowed gravely.

'My only regret is that it failed to function,' he remarked. 'As I told you outside, I'd quite forgotten your menagerie. In fact' – his glance wandered slowly and somewhat pointedly from face to face at the table – 'I had no idea it was such a large one.'

'So this is the insolent young swine, is it?' The bloodshot eyes of the man with the scarred face turned on him morosely. 'What I cannot understand is why he hasn't been killed by now.'

Hugh waggled an accusing finger at him.

'I knew you were a nasty man as soon as I saw you. Now look at Henry up at the end of the table; he doesn't say that sort of thing. And you do hate me, don't you, Henry? How's the jaw?'

'Captain Drummond,' said Lakington, ignoring Hugh and addressing the first speaker, 'was very nearly killed last night. I thought for some time as to whether I would or not, but I finally decided it would be much too easy a death. So it can be remedied tonight.'

If Hugh felt a momentary twinge of fear at the calm, expressionless tone, and the half-satisfied grunt which greeted the words, no trace of it showed on his face. Already the realisation had come to him that if he got through the night alive he would be more than passing lucky, but he was too much of a fatalist to let that worry him unduly. So he merely stifled a yawn, and again turned to Lakington.

'So it was you, my little one, whose fairy face I saw pressed against the window. Would it be indiscreet to ask how you got the dope into us?'

Lakington looked at him with an expression of grim satisfaction on his face.

'You were gassed, if you want to know. An admirable invention of my friend Kauffner's nation.'

A guttural chuckle came from one of the men, and Hugh looked at him grimly.

'The scum certainly would not be complete,' he remarked to Peterson, 'without a filthy Boche in it.'

The German pushed back his chair with an oath, his face purple with passion.

'A filthy Boche,' he muttered thickly, lurching towards Hugh. 'Hold him the arms of, and I will the throat tear out . . . '

The intimidated rabbit rose protestingly at this prospect of violence; the scarred sportsman shot out of his chair eagerly, the lust of battle in his bloodshot eyes. The only person save Hugh who made no movement was Peterson, and he, very distinctly, chuckled. Whatever his failings, Peterson had a sense of humour . . .

It all happened so quickly. At one moment Hugh was apparently intent upon selecting a cigarette, the next instant the case had fallen to the floor; there was a dull, heavy thud, and the Boche crashed back, overturned a chair, and fell like a log to the floor, his head hitting the wall with a vicious crack. The bloodshot being resumed his seat a little limply; the intimidated bunny gave a stifled gasp and breathed heavily; Hugh resumed his search for a cigarette.

'After which breezy interlude,' remarked Peterson, 'let us to business get.'

Hugh paused in the act of striking a match, and for the first time a genuine smile spread over his face.

'There are moments, Peterson,' he murmured, 'when you really appeal to me.'

Peterson took the empty chair next to Lakington. 'Sit down,' he said shortly. 'I can only hope that I shall appeal to you still more before we kill you.'

Hugh bowed and sat down.

'Consideration,' he murmured, 'was always your strong point. May I ask how long I have to live?'

Peterson smiled genially.

'At the very earnest request of Mr Lakington you are to be spared until tomorrow morning. At least, that is our present intention. Of course, there might be an accident in the night: in a house like this one can never tell. Or' – he carefully cut the end off a cigar – 'you might go mad, in which case we shouldn't bother to kill you. In fact, it would really suit our book better if you did: the disposal of corpses, even in these days of advanced science, presents certain difficulties – not insuperable – but a nuisance. And so, if you go mad, we shall not be displeased.'

Once again he smiled genially.

'As I said before, in a house like this, you never can tell . . . '

The intimidated rabbit, still breathing heavily, was staring at Hugh, fascinated; and after a moment Hugh turned to him with a courteous bow.

'Laddie,' he remarked, 'you've been eating onions. Do you mind deflecting the blast in the opposite direction?'

His calm imperturbability seemed to madden Lakington, who with a sudden movement rose from his chair and leaned across the table, while the veins stood out like whipcord on his usually expressionless face.

'You wait,' he snarled thickly; 'you wait till I've finished with you. You won't be so damned humorous then . . . '

Hugh regarded the speaker languidly.

'Your supposition is more than probable,' he remarked, in a bored voice. 'I shall be too intent on getting into a Turkish bath to remove the contamination to think of laughing.'

Slowly Lakington sank back in his chair, a hard, merciless smile on his lips; and for a moment or two there was silence in the room. It was broken by the unkempt man on the sofa, who, without warning, exploded unexpectedly.

'A truce to all this fooling,' he burst forth in a deep rumble; 'I confess I do not understand it. Are we assembled here tonight, comrades, to listen to private quarrels and stupid talk?'

A murmur of approval came from the others, and the speaker stood up waving his arms.

'I know not what this young man has done: I care less. In Russia such trifles matter not. He has the appearance of a bourgeois, therefore he must die. Did we not kill thousands – aye, tens of thousands of his kidney, before we obtained the great freedom? Are we not going to do the same in this accursed country?' His voice rose to the shrill, strident note of the typical tub-thumper. 'What is this wretched man,' he continued, waving a hand wildly at Hugh, 'that he should interrupt the great work for one brief second? Kill him now – throw him in a corner, and let us proceed.'

He sat down again, amidst a further murmur of approval, in which Hugh joined heartily.

'Splendid,' he murmured. 'A magnificent peroration. Am I right, sir, in assuming that you are what is vulgarly known as a Bolshevist?'

The man turned his sunken eyes, glowing with the burning fires of fanaticism, on Drummond.

'I am one of those who are fighting for the freedom of the world,' he cried harshly, 'for the right to live of the proletariat. The workers were the bottom dogs in Russia till they killed the rulers. Now – they rule, and the money they earn goes into their own pockets, not those of incompetent snobs.' He flung out his arms wildly. 'It is freedom; it is the dawn of the new age.' He seemed to shrivel up suddenly, as if exhausted with the violence of his passion. Only his eyes still gleamed with the smouldering madness of his soul.

Hugh looked at him with genuine curiosity; it was the first time he had actually met one of these wild visionaries in the flesh. And then the curiosity was succeeded by a very definite amazement; what had Peterson to do with such as he?

He glanced casually at his principal enemy, but his face showed nothing. He was quietly turning over some papers; his cigar glowed as evenly as ever. He seemed to be no whit surprised by the unkempt one's outburst: in fact, it appeared to be quite in order. And once again Hugh stared at the man on the sofa with puzzled eyes.

For the moment his own deadly risk was forgotten; a growing excitement filled his mind. Could it be possible that here, at last, was the real object of the gang; could it be possible that Peterson was organising a deliberate plot to try and Bolshevise England? If so, where did the Duchess of Lampshire's pearls come in? What of the American, Hiram Potts? Above all, what did Peterson hope to make out of it himself? And it was as he arrived at that point in his deliberation that he looked up to find Peterson regarding him with a faint smile.

'It is a little difficult to understand, isn't it, Captain Drummond?' he said, carefully flicking the ash off his cigar. 'I told you you'd find yourself in deep water.' Then he resumed the contemplation of the papers in front of him, as the Russian burst out again.

'Have you ever seen a woman skinned alive?' he howled wildly, thrusting his face forward at Hugh. 'Have you ever seen men killed with the knotted rope; burned almost to death and then set free, charred and mutilated wrecks? But what does it matter provided only freedom comes, as it has in Russia. Tomorrow it will be England: in a week the world . . . Even if we have to wade through rivers of blood up to our throats, nevertheless it will come. And in the end we shall have a new earth.'

Hugh lit a cigarette and leaned back in his chair.

'It seems a most alluring programme,' he murmured. 'And I shall have much pleasure in recommending you as manager of a babies' crèche. I feel certain the little ones would take to you instinctively.'

He half closed his eyes, while a general buzz of conversation broke out round the table. Tongues had been loosened, wonderful ideals conjured up by the Russian's inspiring words; and for the moment he was forgotten. Again and again the question hammered at his brain – what in the name of Buddha had Peterson and Lakington to do with this crowd? Two intensely brilliant, practical criminals mixed up with a bunch of ragged-trousered visionaries, who, to all intents and purposes, were insane . . .

Fragments of conversation struck his ears from time to time. The intimidated rabbit, with the light of battle in his watery eye, was declaiming on the glories of Workmen's Councils; a bullet-headed man who looked like a down-at-heels racing tout was shouting an inspiring battle-cry about no starvation wages and work for all.

'Can it be possible,' thought Hugh grimly, 'that such as these have the power to control big destinies?' And then, because he had some experience of what one unbalanced brain, whose owner could talk, was capable of achieving; because he knew something about mob psychology, his half-contemptuous amusement changed to a bitter foreboding.

'You fool,' he cried suddenly to the Russian; and everyone ceased talking. 'You poor damned boob! You – and your new earth! In Petrograd today bread is two pounds four shillings a pound; tea, fifteen pounds a pound. Do you call that freedom? Do you suggest that we should wade to *that*, through rivers of blood?' He gave a contemptuous laugh. 'I don't know which distresses me most, your maggoty brain or your insanitary appearance.'

Too surprised to speak, the Russian sat staring at him; and it was Peterson who broke the silence with his suave voice.

'Your distress, I am glad to say, is not likely to be one of long duration,' he remarked. 'In fact, the time has come for you to retire for the night, my young friend.'

He stood up smiling; then he walked over to the bell behind Hugh and rang it.

'Dead or mad – I wonder which.' He threw the end of his cigar into the grate as Hugh rose. 'While we deliberate down here on various matters of importance we shall be thinking of you upstairs – that is to say, if you get there. I see that Lakington is even now beginning to gloat in pleasant anticipation.'

Not a muscle on the soldier's face twitched; not by the hint of a look did he show the keenly watching audience that he realised his danger. He might have been an ordinary guest preparing to go to bed; and in Peterson's face there shone for a moment a certain un-willing admiration. Only Lakington's was merciless, with its fiendish look of anticipation, and Hugh stared at him with level eyes for a while before he turned towards the door.

'Then I will say good night,' he remarked casually. 'Is it the same room that I had last time?'

'No,' said Peterson. 'A different one – specially prepared for you.

If you get to the top of the stairs a man will show you where it is.' He opened the door and stood there smiling. And at that moment all the lights went out.

2

The darkness could be felt, as real darkness inside a house always can be felt. Not the faintest glimmer even of greyness showed anywhere, and Hugh remained motionless, wondering what the next move was going to be. Now that the night's ordeal had commenced, all his nerve had returned to him. He felt ice-cold; and as his powerful hands clenched and unclenched by his sides, he grinned faintly to himself.

Behind him in the room he could hear an occasional movement in one of the chairs, and once from the hall outside he caught the sound of whispering. He felt that he was surrounded by men, thronging in on him from all sides, and suddenly he gave a short laugh. Instantly silence settled; strain as he would he could not hear a sound. Then very cautiously he commenced to feel his way towards the door.

Outside a car went by honking discordantly, and with a sort of cynical amusement he wondered what its occupants would think if they knew what was happening in the house so near them. And at that moment someone brushed past him. Like a flash Hugh's hand shot out and gripped him by the arm. The man wriggled and twisted, but he was powerless as a child, and with another short laugh Hugh found his throat with his other hand. And again silence settled on the room . . .

Still holding the unknown man in front of him, he reached the foot of the stairs, and there he paused. He had suddenly remembered the mysterious thing which had whizzed past his head that other night, and then clanged sullenly into the wall beside him. He had gone up five stairs when it had happened, and now with his foot on the first he started to do some rapid thinking.

If, as Peterson had kindly assured him, they proposed to try and send him mad, it was unlikely that they would kill him on the stairs. At the same time it was obviously an implement capable of accurate adjustment, and therefore it was more than likely that they would use it to frighten him. And if they did – if they did . . . The unknown man wriggled feebly in his hands, and a sudden unholy look came on to Hugh's face.

'It's the only possible chance,' he said to himself, 'and if it's you or me, laddie, I guess it's got to be you.'

With a quick heave he jerked the man off his feet, and lifted him up till his head was above the level of his own. Then clutching him tight, he commenced to climb. His own head was bent down, somewhere in the regions of the man's back, and he took no notice of the feebly kicking legs.

Then at last he reached the fourth step, and gave a final adjustment to his semiconscious burden. He felt that the hall below was full of men, and suddenly Peterson's voice came to him out of the darkness.

'That is four, Captain Drummond. What about the fifth step?'

'A very good-looking one as far as I remember,' answered Hugh. 'I'm just going to get on to it.'

'That should prove entertaining,' remarked Peterson. 'I'm just going to switch on the current.'

Hugh pressed his head even lower in the man's back, and lifted him up another three inches.

'How awfully jolly!' he murmured. 'I hope the result will please you.'

'I'd stand quite still if I were you,' said Peterson suavely. 'Just listen.'

As Hugh had gambled on, the performance was designed to frighten. Instead of that, something hit the neck of the man he was holding with such force that it wrenched him clean out of his arms. Then came the clang beside him, and with a series of ominous thuds a body rolled down the stairs into the hall below.

'You fool.' He heard Lakington's voice, shrill with anger. 'You've killed him. Switch on the light . . . '

But before the order could be carried out Hugh had disappeared, like a great cat, into the darkness of the passage above. It was neck or nothing; he had at the most a minute to get clear. As luck would have it the first room he darted into was empty, and he flung up the window and peered out.

A faint, watery moon showed him a twenty-foot drop on to the grass, and without hesitation he flung his legs over the sill. Below a furious hubbub was going on; steps were already rushing up the stairs. He heard Peterson's calm voice, and Lakington's hoarse with rage, shouting inarticulate orders. And at that moment something prompted him to look upwards.

It was enough – that one look; he had always been mad, he always would be. It was a dormer window, and to an active man access to the roof was easy. Without an instant's hesitation he abandoned all thoughts of retreat; and when two excited men rushed into the room he was firmly ensconced, with his legs astride of the ridge of the window, not a yard from their heads.

Securely hidden in the shadow he watched the subsequent proceedings with genial toleration. A raucous bellow from the two men announced that they had discovered his line of escape; and in half a minute the garden was full of hurrying figures. One, calm and impassive, his identity betrayed only by the inevitable cigar, stood by the garden door, apparently taking no part in the game; Lakington, blind with fury, was running round in small circles, cursing everyone impartially.

'The car is still there.' A man came up to Peterson, and Hugh heard the words distinctly.

'Then he's probably over at Benton's house. I will go and see.'

Hugh watched the thick-set, massive figure stroll down towards the wicket gate, and he laughed gently to himself. Then he grew serious again, and with a slight frown he pulled out his watch and peered at it. Half-past one . . . two more hours before dawn. And in those two hours he wanted to explore the house from on top; especially he wanted to have a look at the mysterious central room of which Phyllis had spoken to him – the room where Lakington kept his treasures. But until the excited throng below went indoors, it was unsafe to move. Once out of the shadow, anyone would be able to see him crawling over the roof in the moonlight.

At times the thought of the helpless man for whose death he had in one way been responsible recurred to him, and he shook his head angrily. It had been necessary, he realised: you can carry someone upstairs in a normal house without him having his neck broken – but still . . . And then he wondered who he was. It had been one of the men who sat round the table – of that he was tolerably certain. But which . . . ? Was it the frightened bunny, or the Russian, or the gentleman with the bloodshot eye? The only comfort was that whoever it had been, the world would not be appreciably the poorer for his sudden decease. The only regret was that it hadn't been dear Henry . . . He had a distaste for Henry which far exceeded his dislike of Peterson.

'He's not over there.' Peterson's voice came to him from below. 'And we've wasted time enough as it is.'

The men had gathered together in a group, just below where Hugh was sitting, evidently awaiting further orders.

'Do you mean to say we've lost the young swine again?' said Lakington angrily.

'Not lost – merely mislaid,' murmured Peterson. 'The more I see of him, the more do I admire his initiative.'

Lakington snorted.

'It was that damned fool Ivolsky's own fault,' he snarled; 'why didn't he keep still as he was told to do?'

'Why, indeed?' returned Peterson, his cigar glowing red. 'And I'm afraid we shall never know. He is very dead.' He turned towards the house. 'That concludes the entertainment, gentlemen, for tonight. I think you can all go to bed.'

'There are two of you watching the car, aren't there?' demanded Lakington.

'Rossiter and Le Grange,' answered a voice.

Peterson paused by the door.

'My dear Lakington, it's quite unnecessary. You underrate that young man . . . '

He disappeared into the house, and the others followed slowly. For the time being Hugh was safe, and with a sigh of relief he stretched his cramped limbs and lay back against the sloping roof. If only he had dared to light a cigarette . . .

3

It was half an hour before Drummond decided that it was safe to start exploring. The moon still shone fitfully through the trees, but since the two car watchers were near the road on the other side of the house, there was but little danger to be apprehended from them. First he took off his shoes, and tying the laces together, he slung them round his neck. Then, as silently as he could, he commenced to scramble upwards.

It was not an easy operation; one slip and nothing could have stopped him slithering down and finally crashing into the garden below, with a broken leg, at the very least, for his pains. In addition, there was the risk of dislodging a slate, an unwise proceeding in a house where most of the occupants slept with one eye open. But at last he got his hands over the ridge of the roof, and in another moment he was sitting straddlewise across it.

The house, he discovered, was built on a peculiar design. The ridge on which he sat continued at the same height all round the top of the roof, and formed, roughly, the four sides of a square. In the middle the roof sloped down to a flat space from which stuck up a glass structure, the top of which was some five or six feet below his level. Around it was a space quite large enough to walk in comfort; in fact, on two sides there was plenty of room for a deck chair. The whole area was completely screened from view, except to anyone in an aeroplane. And what struck him still further was that there was no window that he could see anywhere on the inside of the roof. In fact, it was absolutely concealed and private. Incidentally, the house had originally been built by a gentleman of doubtful sanity, who spent his life observing the spots in Jupiter through a telescope, and having plunged himself and his family into complete penury, sold the house and observatory complete for what he could get. Lakington, struck with its possibilities for his own hobby, bought it on the spot; and from that time Jupiter spotted undisturbed.

With the utmost caution Hugh lowered himself to the full extent of his arms; then he let himself slip the last two or three feet on to the level space around the glass roof. He had no doubt in his mind that he was actually above the secret room, and, on tip-toe, he stole round looking for some spot from which he could get a glimpse below. At the first inspection he thought his time had been wasted; every pane of glass was frosted, and in addition there seemed to be a thick blind of some sort drawn across from underneath, of the same type as is used by photographers for altering the light.

A sudden rattle close to him made him start violently, only to curse himself for a nervous ass the next moment, and lean forward eagerly. One of the blinds had been released from inside the room, and a pale, diffused light came filtering out into the night from the side of the glass roof. He was still craning backwards and forwards to try and find some chink through which he could see, when, with a kind of uncanny deliberation, one of the panes of glass slowly opened. It was worked on a ratchet from inside, and Hugh bowed his thanks to the unseen operator below. Then he leant forward cautiously, and peered in . . .

The whole room was visible to him, and his jaw tightened as he took in the scene. In an armchair, smoking as unconcernedly as ever, sat Peterson. He was reading a letter, and occasionally underlining some point with a pencil. Beside him on a table was a big ledger, and every now and then he would turn over a few pages and make an entry. But it was not Peterson on whom the watcher above was concentrating his attention; it was Lakington – and the thing beside him on the sofa.

Lakington was bending over a long bath full of some light-brown liquid from which a faint vapour was rising. He was in his shirt sleeves, and on his hands he wore what looked like rubber gloves, stretching right up to his elbows. After a while he dipped a test-tube into the liquid, and going over to a shelf he selected a bottle and added a few drops to the contents of the tube. Apparently satisfied with the result, he returned to the bath and shook in some white powder. Immediately the liquid commenced to froth and bubble, and at the same moment Peterson stood up.

'Are you ready?' he said, taking off his coat and picking up a pair of gloves similar to those the other was wearing.

'Quite,' answered Lakington abruptly. 'We'll get him in.'

They approached the sofa; and Hugh, with a kind of fascinated horror, forced himself to look. For the thing that lay there was the body of the dead Russian, Ivolsky.

The two men picked him up and, having carried the body to the bath, they dropped it into the fuming liquid. Then, as if it was the most normal thing in the world, they peeled off their long gloves and stood watching. For a minute or so nothing happened, and then gradually the body commenced to disappear. A faint, sickly smell came through the open window, and Hugh wiped the sweat off his forehead. It was too horrible, the hideous deliberation of it all. And whatever vile tortures the wretched man had inflicted on others in Russia, yet it was through him that his dead body lay there in the bath, disappearing slowly and relentlessly . . .

Lakington lit a cigarette and strolled over to the fireplace.

'Another five minutes should be enough,' he remarked. 'Damn that cursed soldier!'

Peterson laughed gently, and resumed the study of his ledger.

'To lose one's temper with a man, my dear Henry, is a sign of inferiority. But it certainly is a nuisance that Ivolsky is dead. He could talk more unmitigated drivel to the minute than all the rest of 'em put together . . . I really don't know who to put in the Midland area.'

He leaned back in his chair and blew out a cloud of smoke. The light shone on the calm, impassive face; and with a feeling of wonder that was never far absent from his mind when he was with Peterson, Hugh noted the high, clever forehead, the firmly moulded nose and chin, the sensitive, humorous mouth. The man lying back in the chair watching the blue smoke curling up from his cigar might have been a great lawyer or an eminent divine; some well-known statesman, perhaps, or a Napoleon of finance. There was power in every line of his figure, in every movement of his hands. He might have reached to the top of any profession he had cared to follow . . . Just as he had reached to the top in his present one . . . Some kink in the brain, some little cog wrong in the wonderful mechanism, and a great man had become a great criminal. Hugh looked at the bath: the liquid was almost clear.

'You know my feelings on the subject,' remarked Lakington, taking a red velvet box out of a drawer in the desk. He opened it lovingly, and Hugh saw the flash of diamonds. Lakington let the stones run through his hands, glittering with a thousand flames, while Peterson watched him contemptuously.

'Baubles,' he said scornfully. 'Pretty baubles. What will you get for them?'

'Ten, perhaps fifteen thousand,' returned the other. 'But it's not the money I care about; it's the delight in having them, and the skill required to get them.'

Peterson shrugged his shoulders.

'Skill which would give you hundreds of thousands if you turned it into proper channels.'

Lakington replaced the stones, and threw the end of his cigarette into the grate.

'Possibly, Carl, quite possibly. But it boils down to this, my friend, that you like the big canvas with broad effects, I like the miniature and the well-drawn etching.'

'Which makes us a very happy combination,' said Peterson, rising and walking over to the bath. 'The pearls, don't forget, are your job. The big thing' – he turned to the other, and a trace of excitement came into his voice – 'the big thing is mine.' Then with his hands in his pockets he stood staring at the brown liquid. 'Our friend is nearly cooked, I think.'

'Another two or three minutes,' said Lakington, joining him. 'I must confess I pride myself on the discovery of that mixture. Its only drawback is that it makes murder too easy . . . '

The sound of the door opening made both men swing round instantly; then Peterson stepped forward with a smile.

'Back, my dear. I hardly expected you so soon.'

Irma came a little way into the room, and stopped with a sniff of disgust.

'What a horrible smell!' she remarked. 'What on earth have you been doing?'

'Disposing of a corpse,' said Lakington. 'It's nearly finished.'

The girl threw off her opera cloak, and coming forward, peered over the edge of the bath.

'It's not my ugly soldier?' she cried.

'Unfortunately not,' returned Lakington grimly; and Peterson laughed.

'Henry is most annoyed, Irma. The irrepressible Drummond has scored again.'

In a few words he told the girl what had happened, and she clapped her hands together delightedly.

'Assuredly I shall have to marry that man,' she cried. 'He is quite the least boring individual I have met in this atrocious country.' She sat down and lit a cigarette. 'I saw Walter tonight.'

'Where?' demanded Peterson quickly. 'I thought he was in Paris.'

'He was this morning. He came over especially to see you. They want you there for a meeting at the Ritz.'

Peterson frowned.

'It's most inconvenient,' he remarked with a shade of annoyance in his voice. 'Did he say why?'

'Amongst other things I think they're uneasy about the American,' she answered. 'My dear man, you can easily slip over for a day.'

'Of course I can,' said Peterson irritably; 'but that doesn't alter the fact that it's inconvenient. Things will be shortly coming to a head here, and I want to be on the spot. However – ' He started to walk up and down the room, frowning thoughtfully.

'Your fish is hooked, *mon ami*,' continued the girl to Lakington. 'He has already proposed three times; and he has introduced me to a dreadful-looking woman of extreme virtue, who has adopted me as her niece for the great occasion.'

'What great occasion?' asked Lakington, looking up from the bath.

'Why, his coming of age,' cried the girl. 'I am to go to Laidley Towers as an honoured guest of the Duchess of Lampshire.' She threw back her head and laughed. 'What do you think of that, my friend? The old lady will be wearing pearls and all complete, in honour of the great day, and I shall be one of the admiring house party.'

'How do you know she'll have them in the house?' said Lakington.

'Because dear Freddie has told me so,' answered the girl. 'I don't think you're very bright tonight, Henry. When the young Pooh-ba comes of age, naturally his devoted maternal parent will sport her glad rags. Incidentally the tenants are going to present him with a loving cup, or a baby giraffe or something. You might like to annex that too.' She blew two smoke rings and then laughed.

'Freddie is really rather a dear at times. I don't think I've ever met anyone who is so nearly an idiot without being one. Still,' she repeated thoughtfully, 'he's rather a dear.'

Lakington turned a handle underneath the bath, and the liquid, now clear and still, commenced to sink rapidly. Fascinated, Hugh watched the process; in two minutes the bath was empty – a human body had completely disappeared without leaving a trace. It seemed to him as if he must have been dreaming, as if the events of the whole night had been part of some strange jumbled nightmare. And then, having pinched himself to make sure he was awake, he once more glued his eyes to the open space of the window.

Lakington was swabbing out the bath with some liquid on the end of a mop; Peterson, his chin sunk on his chest, was still pacing slowly up and down; the girl, her neck and shoulders gleaming white in the electric light, was lighting a second cigarette from the stump of the first. After a while Lakington finished his cleaning operations and put on his coat.

'What,' he asked curiously, 'does he think you are?'

'A charming young girl,' answered Irma demurely, 'whose father lost his life in the war, and who at present ekes out a precarious existence in a government office. At least, that's what he told Lady Frumpley – she's the woman of unassailable virtue. She was profoundly sentimental and scents a romance, in addition to being a snob and scenting a future duke, to say nothing of a future duchess. By the mercy of Allah she's on a committee with his mother for distributing brown-paper underclothes to destitute Belgians, and so Freddie wangled an invite for her. *Voilà tout.*'

'Splendid!' said Lakington slowly. 'Splendid! Young Laidley comes of age in about a week, doesn't he?'

'Monday, to be exact, and so I go down with my dear aunt on Saturday.'

Lakington nodded his head as if satisfied, and then glanced at his watch.

'What about bed?' he remarked.

'Not yet,' said Peterson, halting suddenly in his walk. 'I must see the Yank before I go to Paris. We'll have him down here now.'

'My dear Carl, at this hour?' Lakington stifled a yawn.

'Yes. Give him an injection, Henry – and, by God, we'll make the fool sign. Then I can actually take it over to the meeting with me.'

He strode to the door, followed by Lakington; and the girl in the chair stood up and stretched her arms above her head. For a moment or two Hugh watched her; then he too stood upright and eased his cramped limbs.

'Make the fool sign.' The words echoed through his brain, and he stared thoughtfully at the grey light which showed the approach of dawn. What was the best thing to do? 'Make' with Peterson generally implied torture if other means failed, and Hugh had no intention of watching any man tortured. At the same time something of the nature of the diabolical plot conceived by Peterson was beginning to take a definite shape in his mind, though many of the most important links were still missing. And with this knowledge had come the realisation that he was no longer a free agent. The thing had ceased to be a mere sporting gamble with himself and a few other chosen spirits matched against a gang of criminals; it had become – if his surmise was correct – a national affair. England herself – her very existence – was threatened by one of the vilest plots ever dreamed of in the brain of man. And then, with a sudden rage at his own impotence, he realised that even now he had nothing definite to go on. He *must* know more; somehow or other he must get to Paris; he must attend that meeting at the Ritz. How he was going to do it he hadn't the faintest idea; the farthest he could get as he stood on the roof, watching the first faint streaks of orange in the east, was the definite decision that if Peterson went to Paris, he would go too. And then a sound from the room below brought him back to his vantage point. The American was sitting in a chair, and Lakington, with a hypodermic syringe in his hand, was holding his arm.

He made the injection, and Hugh watched the millionaire. He was still undecided as to how to act, but for the moment, at any rate, there was nothing to be done. And he was very curious to hear what Peterson had to say to the wretched man, who, up to date, had figured so largely in every round.

After a while the American ceased staring vacantly in front of him, and passed his hand dazedly over his forehead. Then he half rose from his chair and stared at the two men sitting facing him. His eyes came round to the girl, and with a groan he sank back again, plucking feebly with his hands at his dressing-gown.

'Better, Mr Potts?' said Peterson suavely.

'I – I – ' stammered the other. 'Where am I?'

'At The Elms, Godalming, if you wish to know.'

'I thought – I thought – ' He rose swaying. 'What do you want with me? Damn you!'

'Tush, tush,' murmured Peterson. 'There is a lady present, Mr Potts. And our wants are so simple. Just your signature to a little agreement, by which in return for certain services you promise to join us in our – er – labours, in the near future.'

'I remember,' cried the millionaire. 'Now I remember. You swine – you filthy swine, I refuse . . . absolutely.'

'The trouble is, my friend, that you are altogether too big an employer of labour to be allowed to refuse, as I pointed out to you before. You must be in with us, otherwise you might wreck the scheme. Therefore I require your signature. I lost it once, unfortunately – but it wasn't a very good signature; so perhaps it was all for the best.'

'And when you've got it,' cried the American, 'what good will it be to you? I shall repudiate it.'

'Oh, no! Mr Potts,' said Peterson with a thoughtful smile; 'I can assure you, you won't. The distressing malady from which you have recently been suffering will again have you in its grip. My friend Mr Lakington is an expert on that particular illness. It renders you quite unfit for business.'

For a while there was silence, and the millionaire stared round the room like a trapped animal.

'I refuse!' he cried at last. 'It's an outrage against humanity. You can do what you like.'

'Then we'll start with a little more thumbscrew,' remarked Peterson, strolling over to the desk and opening a drawer. 'An astonishingly effective implement, as you can see if you look at your thumb.' He stood in front of the quivering man, balancing the instrument in his hands. 'It was under its influence you gave us the first signature, which we so regrettably lost. I think we'll try it again . . . '

The American gave a strangled cry of terror, and then the unexpected happened. There was a crash as a pane of glass splintered and fell to the floor close beside Lakington; and with an oath he sprang aside and looked up.

'People-bo,' came a well-known voice from the skylight. 'Clip him one over the jaw, Potts, my boy, but don't you sign.'

Chapter 8

In which he goes to Paris for a night

I

Drummond had acted on the spur of the moment. It would have been manifestly impossible for any man, certainly one of his calibre, to have watched the American being tortured without doing something to try to help him. At the same time the last thing he had wanted to do was to give away his presence on the roof. The information he had obtained that night was of such vital importance that it was absolutely essential for him to get away with it somehow; and, at the moment, his chances of so doing did not appear particularly bright. It looked as if it was only a question of time before they must get him.

But as usual with Drummond, the tighter the corner, the cooler his head. He watched Lakington dart from the room, followed more slowly by Peterson, and then occurred one of those strokes of luck on which the incorrigible soldier always depended. The girl left the room as well.

She kissed her hand towards him, and then she smiled.

'You intrigue me, ugly one,' she remarked, looking up, 'intrigue me vastly. I am now going out to get a really good view of the Kill.'

And the next moment Potts was alone. He was staring up at the skylight, apparently bewildered by the sudden turn of events, and then he heard the voice of the man above speaking clearly and insistently.

'Go out of the room. Turn to the right. Open the front door. You'll see a house through some trees. Go to it. When you get there, stand on the lawn and call "Phyllis". Do you get me?'

The American nodded dazedly; then he made a great effort to pull himself together, as the voice continued:

'Go at once. It's your only chance. Tell her I'm on the roof here.'

With a sigh of relief he saw the millionaire leave the room; then he straightened himself up, and proceeded to reconnoitre his own position. There was a bare chance that the American would get through, and if he did, everything might yet be well. If he didn't – Hugh shrugged his shoulders grimly and laughed.

It had become quite light, and after a moment's indecision Drummond took a running jump, and caught the ridge of the sloping roof on the side nearest the road. To stop by the skylight was to be caught like a rat in a trap, and he would have to take his chance of being shot. After all, there was a considerable risk in using firearms so near a main road, where at any time some labourer or other early riser might pass along. Notoriety was the last thing which Peterson desired, and if it got about that one of the pastimes at The Elms was potting stray human beings on the roof, the inquiries might become somewhat embarrassing.

It was as Hugh threw his leg over the top of the roof, and sat straddle-ways, leaning against a chimney-stack, that he got an idea. From where he was he could not see The Larches, and so he did not know what luck the American had had. But he realised that it was long odds against his getting through, and that his chief hope lay in himself. Wherefore, as has just been said, he got an idea – simple and direct; his ideas always were. It occurred to him that far too few unbiased people knew where he was; it further occurred to him that it was a state of affairs which was likely to continue unless he remedied it himself. And so, just as Peterson came strolling round a corner of the house, followed by several men and a long ladder, Hugh commenced to sing. He shouted, he roared at the top of his very powerful voice, and all the time he watched the men below with a wary eye. He saw Peterson look nervously over his shoulder towards the road, and urge the men on to greater efforts, and the gorgeous simplicity of his manoeuvre made Hugh burst out laughing. Then, once again, his voice rose to its full pitch, as he greeted the sun with a bellow which scared every rook in the neighbourhood.

It was just as two labourers came in to investigate the hideous din that Peterson's party discovered the ladder was too short by several yards.

Then with great rapidity the audience grew. A passing milkman; two commercial travellers who had risen with the lark and entrusted themselves and their samples to a Ford car; a gentleman of slightly inebriated aspect, whose trousers left much to the imagination; and finally more farm labourers. Never had such a titbit of gossip for the local pub been seen before in the neighbourhood; it would furnish a topic of conversation for weeks to come. And still Hugh sang and Peterson cursed; and still the audience grew. Then, at last, there came the police with notebook all complete, and the singer stopped singing to laugh.

The next moment the laugh froze on his lips. Standing by the skylight, with his revolver raised, was Lakington, and Hugh knew by the expression on his face that his finger was trembling on the trigger. Out of view of the crowd below he did not know of its existence, and, in a flash, Hugh realised his danger. Somehow Lakington had got up on the roof while the soldier's attention had been elsewhere; and now, his face gleaming with an unholy fury, Lakington was advancing step by step towards him with the evident intention of shooting him.

'Good morrow, Henry,' said Hugh quietly. 'I wouldn't fire if I were you. We are observed, as they say in melodrama. If you don't believe me,' his voice grew a little tense, 'just wait while I talk to Peterson, who is at present deep in converse with the village constable and several farm labourers.'

He saw doubt dawn in Lakington's eyes, and instantly followed up his advantage.

'I'm sure you wouldn't like the notoriety attendant upon a funeral, Henry dear; I'm sure Peterson would just hate it. So, to set your mind at rest, I'll tell him you're here.'

It is doubtful whether any action in Hugh Drummond's life ever cost him such an effort of will as the turning of his back on the man standing two yards below him, but he did it apparently without thought. He gave one last glance at the face convulsed with rage, and then with a smile he looked down at the crowd below.

'Peterson,' he called out affably, 'there's a pal of yours up here – dear old Henry. And he's very annoyed at my concert. Would you just speak to him, or would you like me to be more explicit? He is so annoyed that there might be an accident at any moment, and I see that the police have arrived. So – er – '

Even at that distance he could see Peterson's eyes of fury, and he chuckled softly to himself. He had the whole gang absolutely at his mercy, and the situation appealed irresistibly to his sense of humour.

But when the leader spoke, his voice was as suave as ever: the eternal cigar glowed evenly at its normal rate.

'Are you up on the roof, Lakington?' The words came clearly through the still summer air.

'Your turn, Henry,' said Drummond. 'Prompter's voice off – "Yes, dear Peterson, I am here, even upon the roof, with a liver of hideous aspect." '

For one moment he thought he had gone too far, and that Lakington, in his blind fury, would shoot him then and there and chance the consequences. But with a mighty effort the man controlled himself, and his voice, when he answered, was calm.

'Yes, I'm here. What's the matter?'

'Nothing,' cried Peterson, 'but we've got quite a large and appreciative audience down here, attracted by our friend's charming concert, and I've just sent for a large ladder by which he can come down and join us. So there is nothing that you can do – nothing.' He repeated the word with a faint emphasis, and Hugh smiled genially.

'Isn't he wonderful, Henry?' he murmured. 'Thinks of everything; staff work marvellous. But you nearly had a bad lapse then, didn't you? It really would have been embarrassing for you if my corpse had deposited itself with a dull thud on the corns of the police.'

'I'm interested in quite a number of things, Captain Drummond,' said Lakington slowly, 'but they all count as nothing beside one – getting even with you. And when I do . . . ' He dropped the revolver into his coat pocket, and stood motionless, staring at the soldier.

'Ah! when!' mocked Drummond. 'There have been so many "whens", Henry dear. Somehow I don't think you can be very clever. Don't go – I'm so enjoying my heart-to-heart talk. Besides, I wanted to tell you the story about the girl, the soap, and the bath. That's to say, if the question of baths isn't too delicate.'

Lakington paused as he got to the skylight.

'I have a variety of liquids for bathing people in,' he remarked. 'The best are those I use when the patient is alive.'

The next instant he opened a door in the skylight which Hugh had failed to discover during the night, and, climbing down a ladder inside the room, disappeared from view.

'Hullo, old bean!' A cheerful shout from the ground made Hugh look down. There, ranged round Peterson, in an effective group, were Peter Darrell, Algy Longworth, and Jerry Seymour. 'Birds-nestin'?'

'Peter, old soul,' cried Hugh joyfully, 'I never thought the day would come when I should be pleased to see your face, but it has! For Heaven's sake get a move on with that blinking ladder; I'm getting cramp.'

'Ted and his pal, Hugh, have toddled off in your car,' said Peter, 'so that only leaves us four and Toby.'

For a moment Hugh stared at him blankly, while he did some rapid mental arithmetic. He even neglected to descend at once by the ladder which had at last been placed in position. 'Ted and us four and Toby' made six – and six was the strength of the party as it had arrived. Adding the pal made seven; so who the deuce was the pal?

The matter was settled just as he reached the ground. Lakington, wild-eyed and almost incoherent, rushed from the house, and, drawing Peterson on one side, spoke rapidly in a whisper.

'It's all right,' muttered Algy rapidly. 'They're half-way to London by now, and going like hell if I know Ted.'

It was then that Hugh started to laugh. He laughed till the tears poured down his face, and Peterson's livid face of fury made him laugh still more.

'Oh, you priceless pair!' he sobbed. 'Right under your bally noses. Stole away. Yoicks!' There was another interlude for further hilarity. 'Give it up, you two old dears, and take to knitting. Miss one and purl three, Henry my boy, and Carl in a nightcap can pick up the stitches you drop.' He took out his cigarette-case. 'Well, *au revoir*. Doubtless we shall meet again quite soon. And, above all, Carl, don't do anything in Paris which you would be ashamed of my knowing.'

With a friendly wave he turned on his heel and strolled off, followed by the other three. The humour of the situation was irresistible; the absolute powerlessness of the whole assembled gang to lift a finger to stop them in front of the audience, which as yet showed no sign of departing, tickled him to death. In fact, the last thing Hugh saw, before a corner of the house hid them from sight, was the majesty of the law moistening his indelible pencil in the time-honoured method, and advancing on Peterson with his notebook at the ready.

'One brief interlude, my dear old warriors,' announced Hugh, 'and then we must get gay. Where's Toby?'

'Having his breakfast with your girl,' chuckled Algy. 'We thought we'd better leave someone on guard, and she seemed to love him best.'

'Repulsive hound!' cried Hugh. 'Incidentally, boys, how did you manage to roll up this morning?'

'We all bedded down at your girl's place last night,' said Peter, 'and then this morning, who should come and sing carols outside but our one and only Potts. Then we heard your deafening din on the roof, and blew along.'

'Splendid!' remarked Hugh, rubbing his hands together, 'simply splendid! Though I wish you'd been there to help with that damned gorilla.'

'Help with what?' spluttered Jerry Seymour.

'Gorilla, old dear,' returned Hugh, unmoved. 'A docile little creature I had to kill.'

'The man,' murmured Algy, 'is indubitably mad. I'm going to crank the car.'

2

'Go away,' said Toby, looking up as the door opened and Hugh strolled in. 'Your presence is unnecessary and uncalled for, and we're not pleased. Are we, Miss Benton?'

'Can you bear him, Phyllis?' remarked Hugh with a grin. 'I mean, lying about the house all day?'

'What's the notion, old son?' Toby Sinclair stood up, looking slightly puzzled.

'I want you to stop here, Toby,' said Hugh, 'and not let Miss Benton out of your sight. Also keep your eye skinned on The Elms, and let me know by phone to Half Moon Street anything that happens. Do you get me?'

'I get you,' answered the other, 'but I say, Hugh, can't I do something a bit more active? I mean, of course, there's nothing I'd like better than to . . . ' He broke off in mild confusion as Phyllis Benton laughed merrily.

'Do something more active!' echoed Hugh. 'You bet your life, old boy. A rapid one-step out of the room. You're far too young for what's coming now.'

With a resigned sigh Toby rose and walked to the door.

'I shall have to listen at the keyhole,' he announced, 'and thereby get earache. You people have no consideration whatever.'

'I've got five minutes, little girl,' whispered Hugh, taking her into his arms as the door closed. 'Five minutes of Heaven . . . By Jove! But you look great – simply great.'

The girl smiled up at him.

'It strikes me, Master Hugh, that you have failed to remove your beard this morning.'

Hugh grinned.

'Quite right, kid. They omitted to bring me my shaving water on the roof.'

After a considerable interval, in which trifles such as beards mattered not, she smoothed her hair and sat down on the arm of a chair.

'Tell me what's happened, boy,' she said eagerly.

'Quite a crowded night.' With a reminiscent smile he lit a cigarette. And then quite briefly he told her of the events of the past twelve hours, being, as is the manner of a man, more interested in watching the sweet colour which stained her cheeks from time to time, and noticing her quickened breathing when he told her of his fight with the gorilla, and his ascent of the murderous staircase. To him it was all over and now finished, but to the girl who sat listening to the short, half-clipped sentences, each one spoken with a laugh and a jest, there came suddenly the full realisation of what this man was doing for her. It was she who had been the cause of his running all these risks; it was her letter that he had answered. Now she felt that if one hair of his head was touched, she would never forgive herself.

And so when he had finished, and pitched the stump of his cigarette into the grate, falteringly she tried to dissuade him. With her hands on his coat, and her big eyes misty with her fears for him, she begged him to give it all up. And even as she spoke, she gloried in the fact that she knew it was quite useless. Which made her plead all the harder, as is the way of a woman with her man.

And then, after a while, her voice died away, and she fell silent. He was smiling, and so, perforce, she had to smile too. Only their eyes spoke those things which no human being may put into words. And so, for a time, they stood . . .

Then, quite suddenly, he bent and kissed her.

'I must go, little girl,' he whispered. 'I've got to be in Paris tonight. Take care of yourself.'

The next moment he was gone.

'For God's sake take care of her, Toby!' he remarked to that worthy, whom he found sitting disconsolately by the front door. 'Those blighters are the limit.'

'That's all right, old man,' said Sinclair gruffly. 'Good huntin'!'

He watched the tall figure stride rapidly to the waiting car, the occupants of which were simulating sleep as a mild protest at the delay; then, with a smile, he rose and joined the girl.

'Some lad,' he remarked. 'And if you don't mind my saying so, Miss Benton, I wouldn't change him if I was you. Unless, of course,' he added, as an afterthought, 'you'd prefer me!'

3

'Have you got him all right, Ted?' Hugh flung the question eagerly at Ted Jerningham, who was lounging in a chair at Half Moon Street, with his feet on the mantelpiece.

'I've got him right enough,' answered that worthy, 'but he don't strike me as being Number One value. He's gone off the boil. Become quite gugga again.' He stood up and stretched himself.' Your worthy servant is with him, making hoarse noises to comfort him.'

'Hell!' said Hugh, 'I thought we might get something out of him. I'll go and have a look at the bird. Beer in the corner, boys, if you want it.'

He left the room, and went along the passage to inspect the American. Unfortunately Jerningham was only too right: the effects of last night's injection had worn off completely, and the wretched man was sitting motionless in a chair, staring dazedly in front of him.

' 'Opeless, sir,' remarked Denny, rising to his feet as Hugh came into the room. 'He thinks this 'ere meat juice is poison, and he won't touch it.'

'All right, Denny,' said Drummond. 'Leave the poor blighter alone. We've got him back, and that's something. Has your wife told you about her little adventure?'

His servant coughed deprecatingly.

'She has, sir. But, Lor' bless you, she don't bear no malice.'

'Then she's one up on me, Denny, for I bear lots of it towards that gang of swine.' Thoughtfully he stood in front of the millionaire, trying in vain to catch some gleam of sense in the vacant eyes. 'Look at that poor devil; isn't that enough by itself to make one want to kill the whole crowd?' He turned on his heel abruptly, and opened the door. 'Try and get him to eat if you can.'

'What luck?' Jerningham looked up as he came back into the other room.

'Dam' all, as they say in the vernacular. Have you blighters finished the beer?'

'Probably,' remarked Peter Darrell. 'What's the programme now?'

Hugh examined the head on his glass with a professional eye before replying.

'Two things,' he murmured at length, 'fairly leap to the eye. The first is to get Potts away to a place of safety; the second is to get over to Paris.'

'Well, let's get gay over the first, as a kick-off,' said Jerningham, rising. 'There's a car outside the door; there is England at our disposal. We'll take him away; you pad the hoof to Victoria and catch the boat train.'

'It sounds too easy,' remarked Hugh. 'Have a look out of the window, Ted, and you'll see a man frightfully busy doing nothing not far from the door. You will also see a racing-car just across the street. Put a wet compress on your head, and connect the two.'

A gloomy silence settled on the assembly, to be broken by Jerry Seymour suddenly waking up with a start.

'I've got the Stomach-ache,' he announced proudly.

His listeners gazed at him unmoved.

'You shouldn't eat so fast,' remarked Algy severely. 'And you certainly oughtn't to drink that beer.'

To avert the disaster he immediately consumed it himself, but Jerry was too engrossed with his brain-storm to notice.

'I've got the Stomach-ache,' he repeated, 'and she ought to be ready by now. In fact I know she is. My last crash wasn't a bad one. What about it?'

'You mean . . .?' said Hugh, staring at him.

'I mean,' answered Jerry, 'that I'll go off to the aerodrome now, and get her ready. Bring Potts along in half an hour, and I'll take him to the Governor's place in Norfolk. Then I'll take you over to Paris.'

'Great ! – Simply great!' With a report like a gun Hugh hit the speaker on the back, inadvertently knocking him down. Then an idea struck him. 'Not your place, Jerry; they'll draw that at once. Take him to Ted's; Lady Jerningham won't mind, will she, old boy?'

'The mater mind?' Ted laughed. 'Good Lord, no; she gave up minding anything years ago.'

'Right!' said Hugh. 'Off you go, Jerry. By the way, how many will she hold?'

'Two beside me,' spluttered the proud proprietor of the Stomach-ache. 'And I wish you'd reserve your endearments for people of your own size, you great, fat, hulking monstrosity.'

He reached the door with a moment to spare, and Hugh came back laughing.

'Verily – an upheaval in the grey matter,' he cried, carefully re-filling his glass. 'Now, boy, what about Paris?'

'Is it necessary to go at all?' asked Peter.

'It wouldn't have been if the Yank had been sane,' answered Drummond. 'As it is, I guess I've got to. There's something going on, young fellahs, which is big; and I can't help thinking one might get some useful information from the meeting at the Ritz tonight. Why is Peterson hand-in-glove with a wild-eyed, ragged-trousered crowd of revolutionaries? Can you tell me that? If so, I won't go.'

'The great point is whether you'll find out, even if you do,' returned Peter. 'The man's not going to stand in the hall and shout it through a megaphone.'

'Which is where Ted comes in,' said Hugh affably. 'Does not the Stomach-ache hold two?'

'My dear man,' cried Jerningham, 'I'm dining with a perfectly priceless she tonight!'

'Oh, no, you're not, my lad. You're going to do some amateur acting in Paris. Disguised as a waiter, or a chambermaid, or a coffee machine or something – you will discover secrets.'

'But good heavens, Hugh!' Jerningham waved both hands in feeble protest.

'Don't worry me,' cried Drummond, 'don't worry me; it's only a vague outline, and you'll look great as a bath-sponge. There's the telephone . . . Hallo!' He picked off the receiver. 'Speaking. Is that you, Toby? Oh! the Rolls has gone, has it? With Peterson inside. Good! So-long, old dear.'

He turned to the others.

'There you are, you see. He's left for Paris. That settles it.'

'Conclusively,' murmured Algy mildly. 'Any man who leaves a house in a motor-car always goes to Paris.'

'Dry up!' roared Hugh. 'Was your late military education so utterly lacking that you have forgotten the elementary precept of putting yourself in the enemy's place? If I was Peterson, and I wanted to go to Paris, do you suppose that fifty people knowing about it would prevent me? You're a fool, Algy – and leave me some more beer.'

Resignedly Algy sat down, and after a pause for breath, Drummond continued:

'Now listen – all of you. Ted – off you go, and raise a complete waiter's outfit, dicky and all complete. Peter – you come with me to the aerodrome, and afterwards look up Mullings, at 13, Green Street, Hoxton, and tell him to get in touch with at least fifty demobilised soldiers who are on for a scrap. Algy – you hold the fort here, and don't get drunk on my ale. Peter will join you, when he's finished with Mullings, and he's not to get drunk either. Are you all on?'

'On,' muttered Darrell weakly. 'My head is playing an anthem.'

'It'll play an oratorio before we're through with this job, old son,' laughed Hugh. 'Let's get gay with Potts.'

Ten minutes later he was at the wheel of his car with Darrell and the millionaire behind. Algy, protesting vigorously at being, as he said, left out of it, was endeavouring to console himself by making out how much money he would have won if he'd followed his infallible system of making money on the turf; Jerningham was wandering along Piccadilly anxiously wondering at what shop he could possibly ask for a dicky, and preserve his hitherto blameless reputation. But Hugh seemed in no great hurry to start. A whimsical smile was on his face, as out of the corner of his eye he watched the man who had been busy doing nothing feverishly trying to crank his car, which, after the manner of the brutes, had seized that moment to jib.

'Get away, man – get away,' cried Peter. 'What are you waiting for?' Hugh laughed.

'Peter,' he remarked, 'the refinements of this game are lost on you.' Still smiling, he got out and walked up to the perspiring driver.

'A warm day,' he murmured. 'Don't hurry; we'll wait for you.' Then, while the man, utterly taken aback, stared at him speechlessly, he strolled back to his own car.

'Hugh – you're mad, quite mad,' said Peter resignedly, as with a spluttering roar the other car started, but Hugh still smiled. On the way to the aerodrome, he stopped twice after a block in the traffic to make quite sure that the pursuer should have no chance of losing him, and, by the time they were clear of the traffic and spinning towards their destination, the gentleman in the car behind fully agreed with Darrell.

At first he had expected some trick, being a person of tortuous brain; but as time went on, and nothing unexpected happened, he became reassured. His orders were to follow the millionaire, and inform head-quarters where he was taken to. And assuredly at the moment it seemed easy money. In fact, he even went so far as to hum gently to himself, after he had put a hand in his pocket to make sure his automatic revolver was still there.

Then, quite suddenly, the humming stopped and he frowned. The car in front had swung off the road, and turned through the entrance of a small aerodrome. It was a complication which had not entered his mind, and with a curse he pulled up his car just short of the gates. What the devil was he to do now? Most assuredly he could not pursue an aeroplane in a motor – even a racer. Blindly, without thinking, he did the first thing that came into his head. He left his car standing where it was, and followed the others into the aerodrome on foot. Perhaps he could find out something from one of the mechanics; someone might be able to tell him where the 'plane was going.

There she was with the car beside her, and already the millionaire was being strapped into his seat. Drummond was talking to the pilot, and the sleuth, full of eagerness, accosted a passing mechanic

'Can you tell me where that aeroplane is going to?' he asked ingratiatingly.

It was perhaps unfortunate that the said mechanic had just had a large spanner dropped on his toe, and his answer was not helpful. It was an education in one way, and at any other time the pursuer would have treated it with the respect it deserved. But, as it was, it was not of great value, which made it the more unfortunate that Peter Darrell should have chosen that moment to look round. And all he saw was the mechanic talking earnestly to the sleuth . . . Whereupon he talked earnestly to Drummond . . .

In thinking it over after, that unhappy man, whose job had seemed so easy, found it difficult to say exactly what happened. All of a sudden he found himself surrounded by people – all very affable and most conversational. It took him quite five minutes to get back to his car, and by that time the 'plane was a speck in the west. Drummond was standing by the gates when he got there, with a look of profound surprise on his face.

'One I have seen often,' remarked the soldier; 'two sometimes; three rarely; four never. Fancy four punctures – all at the same time! Dear, dear! I positively insist on giving you a lift.'

He felt himself irresistibly propelled towards Drummond's car, with only time for a fleeting glimpse at his own four flat tyres, and almost before he realised it they were away. After a few minutes, when he had recovered from his surprise, his hand went instinctively to his pocket, to find the revolver had gone. And it was then that the man he had thought mad laughed gently.

'Didn't know I was once a pickpocket, did you?' he remarked affably. 'A handy little gun, too. Is it all right, Peter?'

'All safe,' came a voice from behind.

'Then dot him one.'

The sleuth had a fleeting vision of stars of all colours which danced before his eyes, coupled with a stunning blow on the back of the head. Vaguely he realised the car was pulling up – then blackness. It was not till four hours later that a passing labourer, having pulled him out from a not over-dry ditch, laid him out to cool. And, incidentally, with his further sphere of usefulness we are not concerned . . .

4

'My dear fellow, I told you we'd get here somehow.' Hugh Drummond stretched his legs luxuriously. 'The fact that it was necessary to crash your blinking bus in a stray field in order to avoid their footling passport regulations is absolutely immaterial. The only damage is a dent in Ted's dicky, but all the best waiters have that. They smear it with soup to show their energy . . . My God! Here's another of them.'

A Frenchman was advancing towards them down the stately vestibule of the Ritz waving protesting hands. He addressed himself in a voluble crescendo to Drummond, who rose and bowed deeply. His knowledge of French was microscopic, but such trifles were made to be overcome.

'Mais oui, Monsieur mon Colonel,' he remarked affably, when the gendarme paused for lack of breath, 'vous comprenez que notre machine avait crashé dans un field des turnipes. Nous avons lost notre direction. Nous sommes hittés dans l'estomacs . . . Comme ci, comme ca . . . Vous comprenez, n'est-ce-pas, mon Colonel?' He turned fiercely on Jerry. 'Shut up, you damn fool; don't laugh!'

'*Mais, messieurs, vous n'avez pas des passeports.*' The little man, torn between gratification at his rapid promotion and horror at such an appalling breach of regulations, shot up and down like an agitated semaphore. '*Vous comprenez; c'est defendu d'arriver en Paris sans des passeports?*'

'Parfaitement, mon Colonel,' continued Hugh, unmoved. 'Mais vous comprenez que nous avons crashé dans un field des turnipes – non; des rognons . . . What the hell are you laughing at, Jerry?'

'*Oignons*, old boy,' spluttered the latter. '*Rognons* are kidneys.'

'What the dickens does that matter?' demanded Hugh. 'Vous comprenez, mon Colonel, n'est-ce-pas? Vive la France ! En-bas les Boches! Nous avons crashé.'

The gendarme shrugged his shoulders with a hopeless gesture, and seemed on the point of bursting into tears. Of course this large Englishman was mad; why otherwise should he spit in the kidneys? And that is what he continued to state was his form of amusement. Truly an insane race, and yet he had fought in the brigade next to them near Montauban in July '16 – and he had liked them – those mad Tommies. Moreover, this large, imperturbable man, with the charming smile, showed a proper appreciation of his merits – an appreciation not shared up to the present, regrettable to state, by his own superiors. *Colonel – parbleu; eh bien! Pourquoi non? . . .*

At last he produced a notebook; he felt unable to cope further with the situation himself.

'*Votre nom, M'sieur, s'il vous plaît?*'

'Undoubtedly, mon Colonel,' remarked Hugh vaguely. 'Nous crashons dans – '

'*Ah! Mais oui, mais oui, M'sieur.*' The little man danced in his agitation. '*Vous m'avez déjà dit que vous avez craché dans les rognons, mais je désire votre nom.*'

'He wants your name, old dear,' murmured Jerry weakly.

'Oh, does he?' Hugh beamed on the gendarme. 'You priceless little bird! My name is Captain Hugh Drummond.'

And as he spoke, a man sitting close by, who had been an amused onlooker of the whole scene, stiffened suddenly in his chair and stared hard at Hugh. It was only for a second, and then he was once more merely the politely interested spectator. But Hugh had seen that quick look, though he gave no sign; and when at last the Frenchman departed, apparently satisfied, he leaned over and spoke to Jerry.

'See that man with the suit of reach-me-downs and the cigar,' he remarked. 'He's in this game; I'm just wondering on which side.'

He was not left long in doubt, for barely had the swing doors closed behind the gendarme, when the man in question rose and came over to him.

'Excuse me, sir,' he said, in a pronounced nasal twang, 'but I heard you say you were Captain Hugh Drummond. I guess you're one of the men I've come across the water to see. My card.'

Hugh glanced at the pasteboard languidly.

'Mr Jerome K. Green,' he murmured. 'What a jolly sort of name.'

'See here, Captain,' went on the other, suddenly displaying a badge hidden under his coat. 'That'll put you wise.'

'Far from it, Mr Green. What's it the prize for – throwing cards into a hat?'

The American laughed.

'I guess I've sort of taken to you,' he remarked. 'You're real fresh. That badge is the badge of the police force of the United States of America; and that same force is humming some at the moment.' He sat down beside Hugh, and bent forward confidentially. 'There's a prominent citizen of New York City been mislaid, Captain; and, from information we've got, we reckon you know quite a lot about his whereabouts.'

Hugh pulled out his cigarette-case.

'Turkish this side – Virginian that. Ah! But I see you're smoking.' With great deliberation he selected one himself, and lit it. 'You were saying, Mr Green?'

The detective stared at him thoughtfully; at the moment he was not quite certain how to tackle this large and self-possessed young man.

'Might I ask why you're over here?' he asked at length, deciding to feel his way.

'The air is free to everyone, Mr Green. As long as you get your share to breathe, you can ask anything you like.'

The American laughed again.

'I guess I'll put my cards down,' he said, with sudden decision. 'What about Hiram C. Potts?'

'What, indeed?' remarked Hugh. 'Sounds like a riddle, don't it?'

'You've heard of him, Captain?'

'Few people have not.'

'Yes – but you've met him recently,' said the detective, leaning forward. 'You know where he is, and' – he tapped Hugh on the knee impressively – 'I want him. I want Hiram C. Potts like a man wants a drink in a dry state. I want to take him back in cotton wool to his wife and daughters. That's why I'm over this side, Captain, just for that one purpose.'

'There seem to me to be a considerable number of people wandering around who share your opinion about Mr Potts,' drawled Hugh. 'He must be a popular sort of cove.'

'Popular ain't the word for it, Captain,' said the other. 'Have you got him now?'

'In a manner of speaking, yes,' answered Hugh, beckoning to a passing waiter. 'Three Martinis.'

'Where is he?' snapped the detective eagerly. Hugh laughed.

'Being wrapped up in cotton wool by somebody else's wife and daughters. You were a little too quick, Mr Green; you may be all you say – on the other hand, you may not. And these days I trust no-one.'

The American nodded his head in approval.

'Quite right,' he remarked. 'My motto – and yet I'm going to trust you. Weeks ago we heard things on the other side, through certain channels, as to a show which was on the rails over here. It was a bit vague, and there were big men in it; but at the time it was no concern of ours. You run your own worries, Captain, over this side.'

Hugh nodded.

'Go on,' he said curtly.

'Then Hiram Potts got mixed up in it; exactly how, we weren't wise to. But it was enough to bring me over here. Two days ago I got this cable.' He produced a bundle of papers, and handed one to Drummond. 'It's in cipher, as you see; I've put the translation underneath.'

Hugh took the cablegram and glanced at it. It was short and to the point:

CAPTAIN HUGH DRUMMOND, OF HALF MOON STREET, LONDON, IS YOUR MAN.

He glanced up at the American, who drained his cocktail with the air of a man who is satisfied with life.

'Captain Hugh Drummond, of Half Moon Street, London, is my man,' he chuckled. 'Well, Captain, what about it now? Will you tell me why you've come to Paris? I guess it's something to do with the business I'm on.'

For a few moments Hugh did not reply, and the American seemed in no hurry for an answer. Some early arrivals for dinner sauntered through the lounge, and Drummond watched them idly as they passed. The American detective certainly seemed all right, but . . . Casually, his glance rested on a man sitting just opposite, reading the paper. He took in the short, dark beard – the immaculate, though slightly foreign evening clothes; evidently a wealthy Frenchman giving a dinner party in the restaurant, by the way the head waiter was hovering around. And then suddenly his eyes narrowed, and he sat motionless.

'Are you interested in the psychology of gambling, Mr Green?' he remarked, turning to the somewhat astonished American. 'Some people cannot control their eyes or their mouth if the stakes are big; others cannot control their hands. For instance, the gentleman opposite. Does anything strike you particularly with regard to him?'

The detective glanced across the lounge.

'He seems to like hitting his knee with his left hand,' he said, after a short inspection.

'Precisely,' murmured Hugh. 'That is why I came to Paris.'

Chapter 9

In which he has a near shave

I

'Captain, you have me guessing.' The American bit the end off another cigar, and leaned back in his chair. 'You say that swell Frenchman with the waiters hovering about like fleas round a dog's tail is the reason you came to Paris. Is he kind of friendly with Hiram C. Potts?'

Drummond laughed.

'The first time I met Mr Potts,' he remarked, 'that swell Frenchman was just preparing to put a thumbscrew on his second thumb.'

'Second?' The detective looked up quickly.

'The first had been treated earlier in the evening,' answered Drummond quietly. 'It was then that I removed your millionaire pal.'

The other lit his cigar deliberately.

'Say, Captain,' he murmured, 'you ain't pulling my leg by any chance, are you?'

'I am not,' said Drummond shortly. 'I was told, before I met him, that the gentleman over there was one of the boys . . . He is, most distinctly. In fact, though up to date such matters have not been much in my line, I should put him down as a sort of super-criminal. I wonder what name he is passing under here?'

The American ceased pulling at his cigar.

'Do they vary?'

'In England he is clean-shaven, possesses a daughter, and answers to Carl Peterson. As he is at present I should never have known him, but for that little trick of his.'

'Possesses a daughter!' For the first time the detective displayed traces of excitement. 'Holy Smoke! It can't be him!'

'Who?' demanded Drummond.

But the other did not answer. Out of the corner of his eye he was watching three men who had just joined the subject of their talk, and on his face was a dawning amazement. He waited till the whole party had gone into the restaurant, then, throwing aside his caution, he turned excitedly on Drummond.

'Are you certain,' he cried, 'that that's the man who has been monkeying with Potts?'

'Absolutely,' said Hugh. 'He recognised me; whether he thinks I recognised him or not, I don't know.'

'Then what,' remarked the detective, 'is he doing here dining with Hocking, our cotton trust man; with Steinemann, the German coal man; and with that other guy whose face is familiar, but whose name I can't place? Two of 'em at any rate, Captain, have got more millions than we're ever likely to have thousands.'

Hugh stared at the American.

'Last night,' he said slowly, 'he was forgathering with a crowd of the most atrocious ragged-trousered revolutionaries it's ever been my luck to run up against.'

'We're in it, Captain, right in the middle of it,' cried the detective, slapping his leg. 'I'll eat my hat if that Frenchman isn't Franklyn – or Libstein – or Baron Darott – or any other of the blamed names he calls himself. He's the biggest proposition we've ever been up against on this little old earth, and he's done us every time. He never commits himself, and if he does, he always covers his tracks. He's a genius; he's the goods. Gee!' he whistled gently under his breath. 'If we could only lay him by the heels.'

For a while he stared in front of him, lost in his dream of pleasant anticipation; then, with a short laugh, he pulled himself together.

'Quite a few people have thought the same, Captain,' he remarked, 'and there he is – still drinking highballs. You say he was with a crowd of revolutionaries last night. What do you mean exactly?'

'Bolshevists, Anarchists, members of the Do-no-work-and-have-all-the-money Brigade,' answered Hugh. 'But excuse me a moment. Waiter.'

A man who had been hovering round came up promptly.

'Four of 'em, Ted,' said Hugh in a rapid undertone. 'Frenchman with a beard, a Yank, and two Boches. Do your best.'

'Right-o, old bean!' returned the waiter, 'but don't hope for too much.'

He disappeared unobtrusively into the restaurant, and Hugh turned with a laugh to the American, who was staring at him in amazement.

'Who the devil is that guy?' asked the detective at length.

'Ted Jerningham – son of Sir Patrick Jerningham, Bart., and Lady Jerningham, of Jerningham Hall, Rutland, England,' answered Hugh, still grinning. 'We may be crude in our methods, Mr Green, but you must admit we do our best. Incidentally, if you want to know, your friend Mr Potts is at present tucked between the sheets at that very house. He went there by aeroplane this morning.' He waved a hand towards Jerry. 'He was the pilot.'

'Travelled like a bird, and sucked up a plate of meat-juice at the end,' announced that worthy, removing his eyes with difficulty from a recently arrived fairy opposite. 'Who says that's nothing, Hugh: the filly across the road there, with that bangle affair round her knee?'

'I must apologise for him, Mr Green,' remarked Hugh. 'He has only recently left school, and knows no better.'

But the American was shaking his head a little dazedly.

'Crude!' he murmured, 'crude! If you and your pals, Captain, are ever out of a job, the New York police is yours for the asking.' He smoked for a few moments in silence, and then, with a quick hunch of his shoulders, he turned to Drummond. 'I guess there'll be time to throw bouquets after,' he remarked. 'We've got to get busy on what your friend Peterson's little worry is; we've then got to stop it – some old how. Now, does nothing sort of strike you?' He looked keenly at the soldier. 'Revolutionaries, Bolshevists, paid agitators last night: international financiers this evening. Why, the broad outline of the plan is as plain as the nose on your face; and it's just the sort of game that man would love . . . ' The detective stared thoughtfully at the end of his cigar, and a look of comprehension began to dawn on Hugh's face.

'Great Scott! Mr Green,' he said, 'I'm beginning to get you. What was defeating me was, why two men like Peterson and Lakington should be mixed up with last night's crowd.'

'Lakington! Who's Lakington?' asked the other quickly.

'Number Two in the combine,' answered Hugh, 'and a nasty man.'

'Well, we'll leave him out for the moment,' said the American. 'Doesn't it strike you that there are quite a number of people in this world who would benefit if England became a sort of second Russia? That such a thing would be worth money – big money? That such a thing would be worth paying through the nose for? It would have to be done properly; your small strike here, and your small strike there, ain't no manner of use. One gigantic syndicalist strike all over your country – that's what Peterson's playing for, I'll stake my bottom dollar. How he's doing it is another matter. But he's in with the big financiers: and he's using the tub-thumping Bolshies as tools. Gad! It's a big scheme' – he puffed twice at his cigar – 'a durned big scheme. Your little old country, Captain, is, saving one, the finest on God's earth; but she's in a funny mood. She's sick, like most of us are; maybe she's a little bit sicker than a good many people think. But I reckon Peterson's cure won't do any manner of good, excepting to himself and those blamed capitalists who are putting up the dollars.'

'Then where the devil does Potts come in?' said Hugh, who had listened intently to every word the American had said. 'And the Duchess of Lampshire's pearls?'

'Pearls!' began the American, when the restaurant door opened suddenly and Ted Jerningham emerged. He seemed to be in a hurry, and Hugh half rose in his chair. Then he sat back again, as with miraculous rapidity a crowd of infuriated head waiters and other great ones appeared from nowhere and surrounded Jerningham.

Undoubtedly this was not the way for a waiter to leave the hotel – even if he had just been discovered as an impostor and sacked on the spot. And undoubtedly if he had been a waiter, this large body of scandalised beings would have removed him expeditiously through some secret buttery-hatch, and dropped him on the pavement out of a back entrance.

But not being a waiter, he continued to advance, while his *entourage*, torn between rage at his effrontery and horror at the thought of a scene, followed in his wake.

Just opposite Hugh he halted, and in a clear voice addressed no-one in particular: 'You're spotted. Look out. Ledger at Godalming.'

Then, engulfed once more in the crowd, he continued his majestic progress, and finally disappeared a little abruptly from view.

'Cryptic,' murmured the American, 'but some lad. Gee! He had that bunch guessing.'

'The ledger at Godalming,' said Hugh thoughtfully. 'I watched Peterson, through the skylight last night, getting gay with that ledger. I'm thinking we'll have to look inside it, Mr Green.'

He glanced up as one of the chucking-out party came back, and asked what had happened.

'*Mon Dieu, m'sieur*,' cried the waiter despairingly. ' 'E vas an impostor, *n'est-ce-pas – un scélerat*; 'e upset ze fish all over ze shirt-front of Monsieur le Comte.'

'Was that the gentleman with the short beard, dining with three others?' asked Drummond gravely.

'*Mais oui, m'sieur.* He dine here always if 'e is in Paris – does le Comte de Guy. *Oh! Mon Dieu! C'est terrible!*'

Wringing his hands, the waiter went back into the restaurant, and Hugh shook silently.

'Dear old Ted,' he murmured, wiping the tears from his eyes. 'I knew he'd keep his end up.' Then he stood up. 'What about a little dinner at Maxim's? I'm thinking we've found out all we're likely to find, until we can get to that ledger. And thanks to your knowing those birds, Mr Green, our trip to Paris has been of considerable value.'

The American nodded.

'I guess I'm on,' he remarked slowly; 'but, if you take my advice, Captain, you'll look nippy tonight. I wouldn't linger around corners admiring the mud. Things kind o' happen at corners.'

2

But on this particular evening the detective proved wrong. They reached Maxim's without mishap, they enjoyed an excellent dinner, during which the American showed himself to be a born conversationalist, as well as a shrewd man of the world. And over the coffee and liqueurs Hugh gave him a brief outline of what had taken place since he first got mixed up in the affair. The American listened in silence, though amazement shone on his face as the story proceeded. The episode of the disappearing body especially seemed to tickle his fancy, but even over that he made no remark. Only when Hugh had finished, and early arrivals for supper were beginning to fill the restaurant, did he sum up the matter as he saw it.

'A tough proposition, Captain – damned tough. Potts is our biggest shipping man, but where he comes on the picture at that moment has me beat. As for the old girl's jewels, they don't seem to fit in at all. All we can do is to put our noses inside that ledger, and see the book of the words. It'll sure help some.'

And as Hugh switched off the electric light in his bedroom, having first seen that his torch was ready to hand in case of emergency, he was thinking of the detective's words. Getting hold of the ledger was not going to be easy – far from it; but the excitement of the chase had fairly obsessed him by now. He lay in bed, turning over in his mind every possible and impossible scheme by which he could get into the secret centre room at The Elms. He knew the safe the ledger was kept in: but safes are awkward propositions for the ordinary mortal to tackle. Anyway, it wasn't a thing which could be done in a minute's visit; he would have to manage at least a quarter or half an hour's undisturbed search, the thought of which, with his knowledge of the habits of the household, almost made him laugh out loud. And, at that moment, a fly pinged past his head . . .

He felt singularly wide-awake, and, after a while, he gave up attempting to go to sleep. The new development which had come to light that evening was uppermost in his thoughts; and, as he lay there, covered only with a sheet, for the night was hot, the whole vile scheme unfolded itself before his imagination. The American was right in his main idea – of that he had no doubt; and in his mind's eye he saw the great crowds of idle, foolish men led by a few hot-headed visionaries and paid blackguards to their so-called Utopia. Starvation, misery, ruin, utter and complete, lurked in his mental picture; spectres disguised as great ideals, but grinning sardonically under their masks. And once again he seemed to hear the toc-toc of machine-guns, as he had heard them night after night during the years gone by. But this time they were mounted on the pavement of the towns of England, and the swish of the bullets, which had swept like swarms of cockchafers over No Man's Land, now whistled down the streets between rows of squalid houses . . . And once again a fly pinged past his head.

With a gesture of annoyance he waved his arm. It was hot – insufferably hot, and he was beginning to regret that he had followed the earnest advice of the American to sleep with his windows shut and bolted. What on earth could Peterson do to him in a room at the Ritz? But he had promised the detective, and there it was – curtains drawn, window bolted, door locked. Moreover, and he smiled grimly to himself as he remembered it, he had even gone so far as to emulate the hysterical maiden lady of fiction and peer under the bed . . .

The next moment the smile ceased abruptly, and he lay rigid, with every nerve alert. Something had moved in the room . . .

It had only been a tiny movement, more like the sudden creak of a piece of furniture than anything else – but it was not quite like it. A gentle, slithering sound had preceded the creak; the sound such as a man would make who, with infinite precaution against making a noise, was moving in a dark room; a stealthy, uncanny noise. Hugh peered into the blackness tensely. After the first moment of surprise his brain was quite cool. He had looked under the bed, he had hung his coat in the cupboard, and save for those two obvious places there was no cover for a cat. And yet, with the sort of sixth sense that four years of war had given him, he knew that noise had been made by some human agency. Human! The thought of the cobra at The Elms flashed into his mind, and his mouth set more grimly. What if Peterson had introduced some of his abominable menagerie into the room? . . . Then, once more, the thing like a fly sounded loud in his ear. And was it his imagination, or had he heard a faint sibilant hiss just before?

Suddenly, it struck him that he was at a terrible disadvantage. The thing, whatever it was, knew, at any rate approximately, his position: he had not the slightest notion where it was. And a blind man boxing a man who could see, would have felt just about as safe. With Hugh, such a conclusion meant instant action. It might be dangerous on the floor: it most certainly was far more so in bed. He felt for his torch, and then, with one convulsive bound, he was standing by the door, with his hand on the electric-light switch.

Then he paused and listened intently. Not a sound could he hear; the thing, whatever it was, had become motionless at his sudden movement. For an appreciable time he stood there, his eyes searching the darkness – but even he could see nothing, and he cursed the American comprehensively under his breath. He would have given anything for even the faintest grey light, so that he could have some idea of what it was and where it was. Now he felt utterly helpless, while every moment he imagined some slimy, crawling brute touching his bare feet – creeping up him . . .

He pulled himself together sharply. Light was essential, and at once. But, if he switched it on, there would be a moment when the thing would see him before he could see the thing – and such moments are not helpful. There only remained his torch; and on the Ancre, on one occasion, he had saved his life by judicious use. The man behind one of those useful implements is in blackness far more impenetrable than the blackest night, for the man in front is dazzled. He can only shoot at the torch: therefore, hold it to one side and in front of you . . .

The light flashed out, darting round the room. Ping! Something hit the sleeve of his pyjamas, but still he could see nothing. The bed, with the clothes thrown back; the washstand; the chair with his trousers and shirt – everything was as it had been when he turned in. And then he heard a second sound – distinct and clear. It came from high up, near the ceiling, and the beam caught the big cupboard and travelled up. It reached the top, and rested there, fixed and steady. Framed in the middle of it, peering over the edge, was a little hairless, brown face, holding what looked like a tube in its mouth. Hugh had one glimpse of a dark, skinny hand putting something in the tube, and then he switched off the torch and ducked, just as another fly pinged over his head and hit the wall behind.

One thing, at any rate, was certain: the other occupant of the room was human, and with that realisation all his nerve returned. There would be time enough later on to find out how he got there, and what those strange pinging noises had been caused by. Just at that moment only one thing was on the programme; and without a sound he crept round the bed towards the cupboard, to put that one thing into effect in his usual direct manner.

Twice did he hear the little whistling hiss from above, but nothing sang past his head. Evidently the man had lost him, and was probably still aiming at the door. And then, with hands that barely touched it, he felt the outlines of the cupboard.

It was standing an inch or two from the wall, and he slipped his fingers behind the back on one side. He listened for a moment, but no movement came from above; then, half facing the wall, he put one leg against it. There was one quick, tremendous heave; a crash which sounded deafening; then silence. And once again he switched on his torch . . .

Lying on the floor by the window was one of the smallest men he had ever seen. He was a native of sorts, and Hugh turned him over with his foot. He was quite unconscious, and the bump on his head, where it had hit the floor, was rapidly swelling to the size of a large orange. In his hand he still clutched the little tube, and Hugh gingerly removed it. Placed in position at one end was a long splinter of wood, with a sharpened point: and by the light of his torch Hugh saw that it was faintly discoloured with some brown stain.

He was still examining it with interest when a thunderous knock came on the door. He strolled over and switched on the electric light; then he opened the door.

An excited night-porter rushed in, followed by two or three other people in varying stages of undress, and stopped in amazement at the scene. The heavy cupboard, with a great crack across the back, lay face downwards on the floor; the native still lay curled up and motionless.

'One of the hotel pets?' queried Hugh pleasantly, lighting a cigarette. 'If it's all the same to you, I wish you'd remove him. He was – ah – finding it uncomfortable on the top of the cupboard.'

It appeared that the night-porter could speak English; it also appeared that the lady occupying the room below had rushed forth demanding to be led to the basement, under the misapprehension that war had again been declared and the Germans were bombing Paris. It still further appeared that there was something most irregular about the whole proceeding – the best people at the Ritz did not do these things. And then, to crown everything, while the uproar was at its height, the native on the floor, opening one beady and somewhat dazed eye, realised that things looked unhealthy. Unnoticed, he lay 'doggo' for a while; then, like a rabbit which has almost been trodden on, he dodged between the legs of the men in the room, and vanished through the open door. Taken by surprise, for a moment no-one moved: then, simultaneously, they dashed into the passage. It was empty, save for one scandalised old gentleman in a nightcap, who was peering out of a room opposite angrily demanding the cause of the hideous din.

Had he seen a native – a black man? He had seen no native, and if other people only drank water, they wouldn't either. In fact, the whole affair was scandalous, and he should write to the papers about it. Still muttering, he withdrew, banging his door, and Hugh, glancing up, saw the American detective advancing towards them along the corridor.

'What's the trouble, Captain?' he asked as he joined the group.

'A friend of the management elected to spend the night on the top of my cupboard, Mr Green,' answered Drummond, 'and got cramp half-way through.'

The American gazed at the wreckage in silence. Then he looked at Hugh, and what he saw on that worthy's face apparently decided him to maintain that policy. In fact, it was not till the night-porter and his attendant minions had at last, and very dubiously, withdrawn, that he again opened his mouth.

'Looks like a hectic night,' he murmured. 'What happened?' Briefly Hugh told him what had occurred, and the detective whistled softly.

'Blowpipe and poisoned darts,' he said shortly, returning the tube to Drummond. 'Narrow escape – damned narrow! Look at your pillow.'

Hugh looked: embedded in the linen were four pointed splinters similar to the one he held in his hand; by the door were three more, lying on the floor.

'An engaging little bird,' he laughed; 'but nasty to look at.'

He extracted the little pieces of wood and carefully placed them in an empty match-box: the tube he put into his cigarette-case.

'Might come in handy: you never know,' he remarked casually.

'They might if you stand quite still,' said the American, with a sudden, sharp command in his voice. 'Don't move.'

Hugh stood motionless, staring at the speaker who, with eyes fixed on his right forearm, had stepped forward. From the loose sleeve of his pyjama coat the detective gently pulled another dart and dropped it into the match-box.

'Not far off getting you that time, Captain,' he cried cheerfully. 'Now you've got the whole blamed outfit.'

3

It was the Comte de Guy who boarded the boat express at the Gare du Nord the next day; it was Carl Peterson who stepped off the boat express at Boulogne. And it was only Drummond's positive assurance which convinced the American that the two characters were the same man.

He was leaning over the side of the boat reading a telegram when he first saw Hugh ten minutes after the boat had left the harbour; and if he had hoped for a different result to the incident of the night before, no sign of it showed on his face. Instead he waved a cheerful greeting to Drummond.

'This is a pleasant surprise,' he remarked affably. 'Have you been to Paris, too?'

For a moment Drummond looked at him narrowly. Was it a stupid bluff, or was the man so sure of his power of disguise that he assumed with certainty he had not been recognised? And it suddenly struck Hugh that, save for that one tell-tale habit – a habit which, in all probability, Peterson himself was unconscious of – he would *not* have recognised him.

'Yes,' he answered lightly. 'I came over to see how you behaved yourself!'

'What a pity I didn't know!' said Peterson, with a good-humoured chuckle. He seemed in excellent spirits, as he carefully tore the telegram into tiny pieces and dropped them overboard.

'We might have had another of our homely little chats over some supper. Where did you stay?'

'At the Ritz. And you?'

'I always stop at the Bristol,' answered Peterson. 'Quieter than the Ritz, I think.'

'Yes, it was quite dreadful last night,' murmured Hugh. 'A pal of mine – quite incorrigible – that bird over there' – he pointed to

Ted Jerningham, who was strolling up and down the deck with the American – 'insisted on dressing up as a waiter.' He laughed shortly at the sudden gleam in the other's eye, as he watched Jerningham go past. 'Not content with that, he went and dropped the fish over some warrior's boiled shirt, and had to leave in disgrace.' He carefully selected a cigarette. 'No accountin' for this dressing-up craze, is there, Carl? You'd never be anything but your own sweet self, would you, little one? Always the girls' own friend – tender and true.'

He laughed softly; from previous experience he knew that this particular form of baiting invariably infuriated Peterson. 'Some day, my Carl, you must tell me of your life, and your early struggles, amidst all the bitter temptations of this wicked world.'

'Some day,' snarled Peterson, 'I'll – '

'Stop.' Drummond held up a protesting hand. 'Not that, my Carl – anything but that.'

'Anything but what?' said the other savagely.

'I felt it in my bones,' answered Drummond, 'that you were once more on the point of mentioning my decease. I couldn't bear it, Carl: on this beautiful morning I should burst into tears. It would be the seventeenth time that that sad event has been alluded to either by you or our Henry; and I'm reluctantly beginning to think that you'll have to hire an assassin, and take lessons from him.' He looked thoughtfully at the other, and an unholy joy began to dawn on his face. 'I see you have thrown away your cigar, Carl. May I offer you a cigarette? No? . . . But why so brusque? Can it be – oh no! surely not – can it be that my little pet is feeling icky-boo? Face going green – slight perspiration – collar tight – only the yawning stage between him and his breakfast! Some people have all the fun of the fair. And I thought of asking you to join me below at lunch. There's some excellent fat pork . . . '

A few minutes later, Jerningham and the American found him leaning by himself against the rail, still laughing weakly.

'I ask no more of life,' he remarked when he could speak. 'Anything else that may come will be an anticlimax.'

'What's happened?' asked Jerningham

'It's happening,' said Drummond joyfully. 'It couldn't possibly be over yet. Peterson, our one and only Carl, has been overcome by the waves. And when he's feeling a little better I'll take him a bit of crackling . . . ' Once again he gave way to unrestrained mirth, which finally subsided sufficiently to allow him to stagger below and feed.

At the top of the stairs leading to the luncheon saloon, he paused, and glanced into the secret place reserved for those who have from early childhood voted for a Channel tunnel.

'There he is,' he whispered ecstatically, 'our little Carl, busy recalling his past. It may be vulgar, Ted: doubtless it is. I don't care. Such trifles matter not in the supreme moments of one's life; and I can imagine of only one more supreme than this.'

'What's that?' asked Ted, firmly piloting him down the stairs.

'The moment when he and Henry sit side by side and recall their pasts together,' murmured Hugh solemnly. 'Think of it, man – think of it! Each cursin' the other between spasms. My hat! What a wonderful, lovely dream to treasure through the weary years!' He gazed abstractedly at the waiter. 'Roast beef – underdone,' he remarked, 'and take a plate of cold fat up to the silence room above. The third gentleman from the door would like to look at it.'

But the third gentleman from the door, even in the midst of his agony, was consoled by one reflection.

'Should it be necessary, letter awaits him.' So had run the telegram, which he had scattered to the winds right under Drummond's nose. And it *was* necessary. The mutton-headed young sweep had managed to escape once again, though Petro had assured him that the wretched native had never yet failed. And he personally had seen the man clamber on to the top of the cupboard . . .

For a moment his furious rage overcame his sufferings . . . Next time . . . next time . . . and then the seventh wave of several seventh waves arrived. He had a fleeting glimpse of the scoundrel Drummond, apparently on the other end of a seesaw, watching him delightedly from outside; then, with a dreadful groan, he snatched his new basin, just supplied by a phlegmatic steward, from the scoundrel next to him, who had endeavoured to appropriate it.

4

'Walk right in, Mr Green,' said Hugh, as, three hours later, they got out of a taxi in Half Moon Street. 'This is my little rabbit-hutch.'

He followed the American up the stairs, and produced his latchkey. But before he could even insert it in the hole the door was flung open, and Peter Darrell stood facing him with evident relief in his face.

'Thank the Lord you've come, old son,' he cried, with a brief look at the detective. 'There's something doing down at Godalming I don't like.'

He followed Hugh into the sitting-room.

'At twelve o'clock today Toby rang up. He was talking quite ordinarily – you know the sort of rot he usually gets off his chest – when suddenly he stopped quite short and said, "My God! What do you want?" I could tell he'd looked up, because his voice was muffled. Then there was the sound of a scuffle, I heard Toby curse, then nothing more. I rang and rang and rang – no answer.'

'What did you do?' Drummond, with a letter in his hand which he had taken off the mantelpiece, was listening grimly.

'Algy was here. He motored straight off to see if he could find out what was wrong. I stopped here to tell you.'

'Anything through from him?'

'Not a word. There's foul play, or I'll eat my hat.'

But Hugh did not answer. With a look on his face which even Peter had never seen before, he was reading the letter. It was short and to the point, but he read it three times before he spoke.

'When did this come?' he asked.

'An hour ago,' answered the other. 'I very nearly opened it.'

'Read it,' said Hugh. He handed it to Peter and went to the door. 'Denny,' he shouted, 'I want my car round at once.' Then he came back into the room. 'If they've hurt one hair of her head,' he said, his voice full of a smouldering fury, 'I'll murder that gang one by one with my bare hands.'

'Say, Captain, may I see this letter?' said the American; and Hugh nodded.

' "For pity's sake, come at once",' read the detective aloud. ' "The bearer of this is trustworthy." ' He thoughtfully picked his teeth. 'Girl's writing. Do you know her?'

'My fiancée,' said Hugh shortly.

'Certain?' snapped the American.

'Certain!' cried Hugh. 'Of course I am. I know every curl of every letter.'

'There is such a thing as forgery,' remarked the detective dispassionately.

'Damn it, man!' exploded Hugh; 'do you imagine I don't know my own girl's writing?'

'A good many bank cashiers have mistaken their customers' writing before now,' said the other, unmoved. 'I don't like it, Captain. A girl in *real* trouble wouldn't put in that bit about the bearer.'

'You go to hell,' remarked Hugh briefly. 'I'm going to Godalming.'

'Well,' drawled the American, 'not knowing Godalming, I don't know who scores. But, if you go there – I come too.'

'And me,' said Peter, brightening up.

Hugh grinned.

'Not you, old son. If Mr Green will come, I'll be delighted; but I want you here at headquarters.'

He turned round as his servant put his head in at the door.

'Car here, sir. Do you want a bag packed?'

'No – only my revolver. Are you ready, Mr Green?'

'Sure thing,' said the American. 'I always am.'

'Then we'll move.' And Peter, watching the car resignedly from the window, saw the American grip his seat with both hands, and then raise them suddenly in silent prayer, while an elderly charlady fled with a scream to the safety of the area below.

They did the trip in well under the hour, and the detective got out of the car with a faint sigh of relief.

'You've missed your vocation, Captain,' he murmured. 'If you pushed a bath-chair it would be safer for all parties. I bolted two bits of gum in that excursion.'

But Drummond was already out of earshot, dodging rapidly through the bushes on his way to The Larches; and when the American finally overtook him, he was standing by a side-door knocking hard on the panels.

'Seems kind of empty,' said the detective thoughtfully, as the minutes went by and no-one came. 'Why not try the front door?'

'Because it's in sight of the other house,' said Hugh briefly. 'I'm going to break in.'

He retreated a yard from the door, then, bracing his shoulder, he charged it once. And the door, as a door, was not . . . Rapidly the two men went from room to room – bedrooms, servants' quarters, even the bathroom. Every one was empty: not a sound could be heard in the house. Finally, only the dining-room remained, and as they stood by the door looking round, the American shifted his third piece of gum to a new point of vantage.

'Somebody has been rough-housing by the look of things,' he remarked judicially. 'Looks like a boozing den after a thick night.'

'It does,' remarked Hugh grimly, taking in the disorder of the room. The tablecloth was pulled off, the telephone lay on the floor. China and glass, smashed to pieces, littered the carpet; but what caught his eye, and caused him suddenly to step forward and pick it up, was a plain circle of glass with a black cord attached to it through a small hole.

'Algy Longworth's eyeglass,' he muttered. 'So he's been caught too.'

And it was at that moment that, clear and distinct through the still evening air, they heard a woman's agonised scream. It came from the house next door, and the American, for a brief space, even forgot to chew his gum.

The next instant he darted forward.

'Stop, you young fool!' he shouted, but he was too late.

He watched Drummond, running like a stag, cross the lawn and disappear in the trees. For a second he hesitated; then, with a shrug of square shoulders, he rapidly left the house by the way they had entered. And a few minutes later, Drummond's car was skimming back towards London, with a grim-faced man at the wheel, who had apparently felt the seriousness of the occasion so acutely as to deposit his third piece of spearmint on the underneath side of the steering-wheel for greater safety.

But, seeing that the owner of the car was lying in blissful uncon-sciousness in the hall of The Elms, surrounded by half a dozen men, this hideous vandalism hurt him not.

Chapter 10

In which the Hun nation decreases by one

I

Drummond had yielded to impulse – the blind, all-powerful impulse of any man who is a man to get to the woman he loves if she wants him. As he had dashed across the lawn to The Elms, with the American's warning cry echoing in his ears, he had been incapable of serious thought. Subconsciously he had known that, from every point of view, it was the act of a madman; that he was deliberately putting his head into what, in all probability, was a carefully prepared noose; that, from every point of view, he could help Phyllis better by remaining a free agent outside. But when a girl shrieks, and the man who loves her hears it, arguments begin to look tired. And what little caution might have remained to Hugh completely vanished as he saw the girl watching him with agonised terror in her face, from an upstairs window, as he dashed up to the house. It was only for a brief second that he saw her; then she disappeared suddenly, as if snatched away by some invisible person.

'I'm coming, darling.' He had given one wild shout, and hurled himself through the door which led into the house from the garden. A dazzling light of intense brilliance had shone in his face, momentarily blinding him; then had come a crushing blow on the back of his head. One groping, wild step forward, and Hugh Drummond, dimly conscious of men all round him, had pitched forward on his face into utter oblivion.

'It's too easy.' Lakington's sneering voice broke the silence, as he looked vindictively at the unconscious man.

'So you have thought before, Henry,' chuckled Peterson, whose complete recovery from his recent unfortunate indisposition was shown by the steady glow of the inevitable cigar. 'And he always bobs up somehow. If you take my advice you'll finish him off here and now, and run no further risks.'

'Kill him while he's unconscious?' Lakington laughed evilly. 'No, Carl, not under any circumstances whatever. He has quite a lengthy score to pay and, by God! he's going to pay it this time.' He stepped forward and kicked Drummond twice in the ribs with a cold, animal fury.

'Well, don't kick him when he's down, guv'nor. You'll 'ave plenty o' time after.' A hoarse voice from the circle of men made Lakington look up.

'You cut it out, Jem Smith,' he snarled, 'or I might find plenty of time after for others beside this young swine.' The ex-pugilist muttered uneasily under his breath, but said no more, and it was Peterson who broke the silence.

'What are you going to do with him?'

'Lash him up like the other two,' returned Lakington, 'and leave him to cool until I get back tomorrow. But I'll bring him round before I go, and just talk to him for a little. I wouldn't like him not to know what was going to happen to him. Anticipation is always delightful.' He turned to two of the men standing near. 'Carry him into my room,' he ordered, 'and another of you get the rope.'

And so it was that Algy Longworth and Toby Sinclair, with black rage and fury in their hearts, watched the limp form of their leader being carried into the central room. Swathed in rope, they sat motionless and impotent, in their respective chairs, while they watched the same process being performed on Drummond. He was no amateur at the game, was the rope-winder, and by the time he had finished, Hugh resembled nothing so much as a lifeless brown mummy. Only his head was free, and that lolled forward helplessly.

Lakington watched the performance for a time; then, wearying of it, he strolled over to Algy's chair.

'Well, you puppy,' he remarked, 'are you going to try shouting again?' He picked up the rhinoceros-hide riding-whip lying on the floor, and bent it between his hands. 'That weal on your face greatly improves your beauty, and next time you'll get two, and a gag as well.'

'How's the jaw, you horrible bit of dreg?' remarked Algy insultingly, and Toby laughed.

'Don't shake his nerve, Algy,' he implored. 'For the first time in his filthy life he feels safe in the same room as Hugh.'

The taunt seemed to madden Lakington, who sprang across the room and lashed Sinclair over the face. But even after the sixth cut no sound came from the helpless man, though the blood was streaming down inside his collar. His eyes, calm and sneering, met those of the raving man in front of him without a quiver, and, at last, Peterson himself intervened.

'Stop it, Lakington.' His voice was stern as he caught the other's upraised arm. 'That's enough for the time.'

For a moment it seemed as if Lakington would have struck Peterson himself; then he controlled himself, and, with an ugly laugh, flung the whip into a corner.

'I forgot,' he said slowly. 'It's the leading dog we want – not the puppies that run after him yapping.' He spun round on his heel. 'Have you finished?'

The rope-artist bestowed a final touch to the last knot, and surveyed his handiwork with justifiable pride.

'Cold mutton,' he remarked tersely, 'would be lively compared to him when he wakes up.'

'Good! Then we'll bring him to.'

Lakington took some crystals from a jar on one of the shelves, and placed them in a tumbler. Then he added a few drops of liquid and held the glass directly under the unconscious man's nose. Almost at once the liquid began to effervesce, and in less than a minute Drummond opened his eyes and stared dazedly round the room. He blinked foolishly as he saw Longworth and Sinclair; then he looked down and found he was similarly bound himself. Finally he glanced up at the man bending over him, and full realisation returned.

'Feeling better, my friend?' With a mocking smile, Lakington laid the tumbler on a table close by.

'Much, thank you, Henry,' murmured Hugh. 'Ah! and there's Carl. How's the tummy, Carl? I hope for your sake that it's feeling stronger than the back of my head.'

He grinned cheerfully, and Lakington struck him on the mouth.

'You can stop that style of conversation, Captain Drummond,' he remarked. 'I dislike it.'

Hugh stared at the striker in silence.

'Accept my congratulations,' he said at length, in a low voice which, despite himself, shook a little. 'You are the first man who has ever done that, and I shall treasure the memory of that blow.'

'I'd hate it to be a lonely memory,' remarked Lakington. 'So here's another, to keep it company.' Again he struck him, then with a laugh he turned on his heel. 'My compliments to Miss Benton,' he said to a man standing near the door, 'and ask her to be good enough to come down for a few minutes.'

The veins stood out on Drummond's forehead at the mention of the girl, but otherwise he gave no sign; and, in silence, they waited for her arrival.

She came almost at once, a villainous-looking blackguard with her, and as she saw Hugh she gave a pitiful little moan and held out her hand to him.

'Why did you come, boy?' she cried. 'Didn't you know it was only a forgery – that note?'

'Ah! was it?' said Hugh softly. 'Was it, indeed?'

'An interesting point,' murmured Lakington. 'Surely if a charming girl is unable – or unwilling – to write herself to her fiancé, her father is a very suitable person to supply the deficiency. Especially if he has been kindly endowed by Nature with a special aptitude for – er – imitating writing.'

Mr Benton, who had been standing outside the door, came lurching into the room.

'Quite ri', Laking – Laking – ton,' he announced solemnly. 'Dreadful thing to sep – separate two young people.' Then he saw Drummond, and paused, blinking foolishly. 'Whash he all tied up for li' that?'

Lakington smiled evilly.

'It would be a pity to lose him, now he's come, wouldn't it?'

The drunken man nodded two or three times; then a thought seemed to strike him, and he advanced slowly towards Hugh, wagging a finger foolishly.

'Thash reminds me, young fellah,' he hiccoughed gravely, 'you never asked my consent. You should have asked father's consent. Mosh incon – inconshiderate. Don't you agree with me, Mishter Peterson?'

'You will find the tantalus in the dining-room,' said Peterson coldly. 'I should say you require one more drink to produce complete insensibility, and the sooner you have it the better.'

'Inshensibility!' With outraged dignity the wretched man appealed to his daughter. 'Phyllis, did you hear? Thish man says I'sh in – inebri . . . says I'sh drunk. Gratui . . . tous inshult . . . '

'Oh, father, father,' cried the girl, covering her face with her hands. 'For pity's sake go away! You've done enough harm as it is.'

Mr Benton tacked towards the door, where he paused, swaying.

'Disgraceful,' he remarked solemnly. 'Rising generation no reshpect for elders and bettersh! Teach 'em lesson, Lakington. Do 'em all good. One – two – three, all ranged in a – in a row. Do 'em good – '

His voice tailed off, and, after a valiant attempt to lean against a door which was not there, he collapsed gracefully in a heap on the floor.

'You vile hound,' said Phyllis, turning like a young tigress on Lakington. 'It's your doing entirely, that he's in that condition.'

But Lakington merely laughed.

'When we're married,' he answered lightly, 'we'll put him into a really good home for inebriates.'

'Married!' she whispered tensely. 'Married! Why, you loathsome reptile, I'd kill myself before I married you.'

'An excellent curtain,' remarked Lakington suavely, 'for the third act of a melodrama. Doubtless we can elaborate it later. In the meantime, however' – he glanced at his watch – 'time presses. And I don't want to go without telling you a little about the programme, Captain Drummond. Unfortunately both Mr Peterson and I have to leave you for tonight; but we shall be returning tomorrow morning – or, at any rate, I shall. You will be left in charge of Heinrich – you remember the filthy Boche? – with whom you had words the other night. As you may expect, he entertains feelings of great friendship and affection for you, so you should not lack for any bodily comforts, such as may be possible in your present somewhat cramped position. Then tomorrow, when I return, I propose to try a few experiments on you, and, though I fear you will find them painful, it's a great thing to suffer in the cause of science . . . You will always have the satisfaction of knowing that dear little Phyllis will be well cared for.' With a sudden, quick movement, he seized the girl and kissed her before she realised his intention. The rope round Drummond creaked as he struggled impotently, and Lakington's sneering face seemed to swim in a red glow.

'That is quite in keeping, is it not,' he snarled, 'to kiss the lady, and to strike the man like this – and this – and this? . . . ' A rain of blows came down on Drummond's face, till, with a gasping sigh, the girl slipped fainting to the floor.

'That'll do, Lakington,' said Peterson, intervening once again. 'Have the girl carried upstairs, and send for Heinrich. It's time we were off.'

With an effort Lakington let his hand fall to his side, and stood back from his victim.

'Perhaps for the present, it will,' he said slowly. 'But tomorrow – tomorrow, Captain Drummond, you shall scream to Heaven for mercy, until I take out your tongue and you can scream no more.' He turned as the German came into the room. 'I leave them to you,

Heinrich,' he remarked shortly. 'Use the dog-whip if they shout, and gag them.'

The German's eyes were fixed on Hugh gloatingly.

'They will not shout twice,' he said in his guttural voice. 'The dirty Boche to it himself will see.'

2

'We appear,' remarked Hugh quietly, a few minutes later, 'to be in for a cheery night.'

For a moment the German had left the room, and the three motionless, bound figures, sitting grotesquely in their chairs, were alone.

'How did they get you, Toby?'

'Half a dozen of 'em suddenly appeared,' answered Sinclair shortly, 'knocked me on the head, and the next thing I knew I was here in this damned chair.'

'Is that when you got your face?' asked Hugh.

'No,' said Toby, and his voice was grim. 'We share in the matter of faces, old man.'

'Lakington again, was it?' said Hugh softly. 'Dear Heavens! If I could get one hand on that . . . ' He broke off and laughed. 'What about you, Algy?'

'I went blundering in over the way, old bean,' returned that worthy, 'and some dam' fellow knocked my eyeglass off. So, as I couldn't see to kill him, I had to join the picnic here.'

Hugh laughed, and then suddenly grew serious.

'By the way, you didn't see a man chewing gum on the horizon, did you, when I made my entrance? Dogrobber suit, and face like a motor-mascot.'

'Thank God, I was spared that!' remarked Algy.

'Good!' returned Hugh. 'He's probably away with it by now, and he's no fool. For I'm thinking it's only Peter and him between us and – ' He left his remark unfinished, and for a while there was silence. 'Jerry is over in France still, putting stamp-paper on his machine; Ted's gone up to see that Potts is taking nourishment.'

'And here we sit like three well-preserved specimens in a bally museum,' broke in Algy, with a rueful laugh. 'What'll they do to us, Hugh?'

But Drummond did not answer, and the speaker, seeing the look on his face, did not press the question.

Slowly the hours dragged on, until the last gleams of daylight had faded from the skylight above, and a solitary electric light, hung centrally, gave the only illumination. Periodically Heinrich had come in to see that they were still secure; but from the sounds of the hoarse laughter which came at frequent intervals through the half-open door, it was evident that the German had found other and more congenial company. At length he appeared carrying a tray with bread and water on it, which he placed on a table near Hugh.

'Food for you, you English swine,' he remarked, looking gloatingly at each in turn. 'Herr Lakington the order gave, so that you will be fit tomorrow morning. Fit for the torture.' He thrust his flushed face close to Drummond's, and then deliberately spat at him.

Algy Longworth gave a strangled grunt, but Drummond took no notice. For the past half-hour he had been sunk in thought, so much so that the others had believed him asleep. Now, with a quiet smile, he looked up at the German.

'How much, my friend,' he remarked, 'are you getting for this?'

The German leered at him.

'Enough to see that you tomorrow are here,' he said.

'And I always believed that yours was a business nation,' laughed Hugh. 'Why, you poor fool, I've got a thousand pounds in notes in my cigarette-case.' For a moment the German stared at him; then a look of greed came into his pig-eyes.

'You hof, hof you?' he grunted. 'Then the filthy Boche will for you of them take care.'

Hugh looked at him angrily.

'If you do,' he cried, 'you must let me go.'

The German leered still more.

'Natürlich. You shall out of the house at once walk.'

He stepped up to Drummond and ran his hands over his coat, while the others stared at one another in amazement. Surely Hugh didn't imagine the swine would really let him go; he would merely take the money and probably spit in his face again. Then they heard him speaking, and a sudden gleam of comprehension dawned on their faces.

'You'll have to undo one of the ropes, my friend, before you can get at it,' said Hugh quietly.

For a moment the German hesitated. He looked at the ropes carefully; the one that bound the arms and the upper part of the body was separate from the rope round the legs. Even if he did undo it the fool Englishman was still helpless, and he knew that he was unarmed.

Had he not himself removed his revolver, as he lay unconscious in the hall? What risk was there, after all? Besides, if he called someone else in he would have to share the money.

And, as he watched the German's indecision, Hugh's forehead grew damp with sweat . . . Would he undo the rope? Would greed conquer caution?

At last the Boche made up his mind, and went behind the chair. Hugh felt him fumbling with the rope, and flashed an urgent look of caution at the other two.

'You'd better be careful, Heinrich,' he remarked, 'that none of the others see, or you might have to share.'

The German ceased undoing the knot, and grunted. The English swine had moments of brightness, and he went over and closed the door. Then he resumed the operation of untying the rope; and, since it was performed behind the chair, he was in no position to see the look on Drummond's face. Only the two spectators could see that, and they had almost ceased breathing in their excitement. That he had a plan they knew; what it was they could not even guess.

At last the rope fell clear, and the German sprang back.

'Put the case on the table,' he cried, having not the slightest intention of coming within range of those formidable arms.

'Certainly not,' said Hugh, 'until you undo my legs. Then you shall have it.'

Quite loosely he was holding the case in one hand; but the others, watching his face, saw that it was strained and tense.

'First I the notes must have.' The German strove to speak conversationally, but all the time he was creeping nearer and nearer to the back of the chair. 'Then I your legs undo, and you may go.'

Algy's warning cry rang out simultaneously with the lightning dart of the Boche's hand as he snatched at the cigarette-case over Drummond's shoulder. And then Drummond laughed a low, triumphant laugh. It was the move he had been hoping for, and the German's wrist was held fast in his vice-like grip. His plan had succeeded.

And Longworth and Sinclair, who had seen many things in their lives, the remembrance of which will be with them till their dying day, had never seen and are never likely to see anything within measurable distance of what they saw in the next few minutes. Slowly, inexorably, the German's arm was being twisted, while he uttered hoarse, gasping cries, and beat impotently at Drummond's head with his free hand. Then at last there was a dull crack as the arm broke, and a scream of pain, as he lurched round the chair and stood helpless in front of the soldier, who still held the cigarette-case in his left hand.

They saw Drummond open the cigarette-case and take from it what looked like a tube of wood. Then he felt in his pocket and took out a match-box, containing a number of long thin splinters. And, having fitted one of the splinters into the tube, he put the other end in his mouth.

With a quick heave they saw him jerk the German round and catch his unbroken arm with his free left hand. And the two bound watchers looked at Hugh's eyes as he stared at the moaning Boche, and saw that they were hard and merciless.

There was a sharp, whistling hiss, and the splinter flew from the tube into the German's face. It hung from his cheek, and even the ceaseless movement of his head failed to dislodge it.

'I have broken your arm, Boche,' said Drummond at length, 'and now I have killed you. I'm sorry about it; I wasn't particularly anxious to end your life. But it had to be done.'

The German, hardly conscious of what he had said owing to the pain in his arm, was frantically kicking the Englishman's legs, still bound to the chair; but the iron grip on his wrists never slackened. And then quite suddenly came the end. With one dreadful, con-vulsive heave the German jerked himself free, and fell doubled up on the floor. Fascinated, they watched him writhing and twisting, until, at last, he lay still . . . The Boche was dead . . .

'My God!' muttered Hugh, wiping his forehead. 'Poor brute.'

'What was that blow-pipe affair?' cried Sinclair hoarsely.

'The thing they tried to finish me with in Paris last night,' answered Hugh grimly, taking a knife out of his waistcoat pocket. 'Let us trust that none of his pals come in to look for him.'

A minute later he stood up, only to sit down again abruptly, as his legs gave way. They were numbed and stiff with the hours he had spent in the same position, and for a while he could do nothing but rub them with his hands, till the blood returned and he could feel once more.

Then, slowly and painfully, he tottered across to the others and set them free as well. They were in an even worse condition than he had been; and it seemed as if Algy would never be able to stand again, so completely dead was his body from the waist downwards. But, at length, after what seemed an eternity to Drummond, who realised only too well that should the gang come in they were almost as helpless in their present condition as if they were still bound in their chairs, the other two recovered. They were still stiff and cramped – all three of them – but at any rate they could move; which was more than could be said of the German, who lay twisted and rigid on the floor, with his eyes staring up at them – a glassy, horrible stare.

'Poor brute!' said Hugh again, looking at him with a certain amount of compunction. 'He was a miserable specimen – but still . . . ' He shrugged his shoulders. 'And the contents of my cigarette-case are half a dozen gaspers, and a ten-bob Bradbury patched together with stamp paper!'

He swung round on his heel as if dismissing the matter, and looked at the other two.

'All fit now? Good! We've got to think what we're going to do, for we're not out of the wood yet by two or three miles.'

'Let's get the door open,' remarked Algy, 'and explore.'

Cautiously they swung it open, and stood motionless. The house was in absolute silence; the hall was deserted.

'Switch out the light,' whispered Hugh. 'We'll wander round.'

They crept forward stealthily in the darkness, stopping every now and then to listen. But no sound came to their ears; it might have been a house of the dead.

Suddenly Drummond, who was in front of the other two, stopped with a warning hiss. A light was streaming out from under a door at the end of a passage, and, as they stood watching it, they heard a man's voice coming from the same room. Someone else answered him, and then there was silence once more.

At length Hugh moved forward again, and the others followed. And it was not until they got quite close to the door that a strange, continuous noise began to be noticeable – a noise which came most distinctly from the lighted room. It rose and fell with monotonous regularity; at times it resembled a brass band – at others it died away to a gentle murmur. And occasionally it was punctuated with a strangled snort . . .

'Great Scott!' muttered Hugh excitedly, 'the whole boiling bunch are asleep, or I'll eat my hat.'

'Then who was it who spoke?' said Algy. 'At least two of 'em are awake right enough.'

And, as if in answer to his question, there came the voice again from inside the room.

'Wal, Mr Darrell, I guess we can pass on, and leave this bunch.'

With one laugh of joyful amazement Hugh flung open the door, and found himself looking from the range of a yard into two revolvers.

'I don't know how you've done it, boys,' he remarked, 'but you can put those guns away. I hate looking at them from that end.'

'What the devil have they done to all your dials?' said Darrell, slowly lowering his arm.

'We'll leave that for the time,' returned Hugh grimly, as he shut the door. 'There are other more pressing matters to be discussed.'

He glanced round the room, and a slow grin spread over his face. There were some twenty of the gang, all of them fast asleep. They sprawled grotesquely over the table, they lolled in chairs; they lay on the floor, they huddled in corners. And, without exception, they snored and snorted.

'A dandy bunch,' remarked the American, gazing at them with satisfaction. 'That fat one in the corner took enough dope to kill a bull, but he seems quite happy.' Then he turned to Drummond. 'Say now, Captain, we've got a lorry load of the boys outside; your friend here thought we'd better bring 'em along. So it's up to you to get busy.'

'Mullings and his crowd,' said Darrell, seeing the look of mystification on Hugh's face. 'When Mr Green got back and told me you'd shoved your great mutton-head in it again, I thought I'd better bring the whole outfit.'

'Oh, you daisy!' cried Hugh, rubbing his hands together, 'you pair of priceless beans! The Philistines are delivered into our hands, even up to the neck.' For a few moments he stood, deep in thought; then once again the grin spread slowly over his face. 'Right up to their necks,' he repeated, 'so that it washes round their back teeth. Get the boys in, Peter; and get these lumps of meat carted out to the lorry. And, while you do that, we'll go upstairs and mop up.'

3

Even in his wildest dreams Hugh had never imagined such a wonderful opportunity. To be in complete possession of the house, with strong forces at his beck and call, was a state of affairs which rendered him almost speechless.

'Up the stairs on your hands and knees,' he ordered, as they stood in the hall. 'There are peculiarities about this staircase which require elucidation at a later date.'

But the murderous implement which acted in conjunction with the fifth step was not in use, and they passed up the stairs in safety.

'Keep your guns handy,' whispered Hugh. 'We'll draw each room in turn till we find the girl.'

But they were not to be put to so much trouble. Suddenly a door opposite opened, and the man who had been guarding Phyllis Benton peered out suspiciously. His jaw fell, and a look of aghast surprise spread over his face as he saw the four men in front of him. Then he made a quick movement as if to shut the door, but before he realised what had happened the American's foot was against it, and the American's revolver was within an inch of his head.

'Keep quite still, son,' he drawled, 'or I guess it might sort of go off.'

But Hugh had stepped past him, and was smiling at the girl who, with a little cry of joyful wonder, had risen from her chair.

'Your face, boy,' she whispered, as he took her in his arms, regardless of the other, 'your poor old face! Oh! that brute, Lakington!'

Hugh grinned.

'It's something to know, old thing,' he remarked cheerily, 'that anything could damage it. Personally I have always thought that any change on it must be for the better.'

He laughed gently, and for a moment she clung to him, unmindful of how he had got to her, glorying only in the fact that he had. It seemed to her that there was nothing which this wonderful man of hers couldn't manage; and now, blindly trusting, she waited to be told what to do. The nightmare was over; Hugh was with her . . .

'Where's your father, dear?' he asked her after a little pause.

'In the dining-room, I think,' she answered with a shiver, and Hugh nodded gravely.

'Are there any cars outside?' He turned to the American.

'Yours,' answered that worthy, still keeping his eyes fixed on his prisoner's face, which had now turned a sickly green.

'And mine is hidden behind Miss Benton's greenhouse unless they've moved it,' remarked Algy.

'Good,' said Hugh. 'Algy, take Miss Benton and her father up to Half Moon Street – at once Then come back here.'

'But Hugh – ' began the girl appealingly.

'At once, dear, please.' He smiled at her tenderly, but his tone was decided. 'This is going to be no place for you in the near future.' He turned to Longworth and drew him aside. 'You'll have a bit of a job with the old man,' he whispered. 'He's probably paralytic by now. But get on with it, will you? Get a couple of the boys to give you a hand.'

With no further word of protest the girl followed Algy, and Hugh drew a breath of relief.

'Now, you ugly-looking blighter,' he remarked to the cowering ruffian, who was by this time shaking with fright, 'we come to you. How many of these rooms up here are occupied – and which?'

It appeared that only one was occupied – everyone else was below . . . The one opposite . . . In his anxiety to please, he moved towards it; and with a quickness that would have done even Hugh credit, the American tripped him up.

'Not so blamed fast, you son of a gun,' he snapped, 'or there sure will be an accident.'

But the noise he made as he fell served a good purpose. The door of the occupied room was flung open, and a thin, weedy object clad in a flannel night-gown stood on the threshold blinking foolishly.

'Holy smoke!' spluttered the detective, after he had gazed at the apparition in stunned silence for a time. 'What, under the sun, is it?'

Hugh laughed.

'Why, it's the onion-eater; the intimidated rabbit,' he said delightedly. 'How are you, little man?'

He extended an arm, and pulled him into the passage, where he stood spluttering indignantly.

'This is an outrage, sir,' he remarked; 'a positive outrage.'

'Your legs undoubtedly are,' remarked Hugh, gazing at them dispassionately. 'Put on some trousers – and get a move on. Now you' – he jerked the other man to his feet – 'when does Lakington return?'

'Termorrow, sir,' stammered the other.

'Where is he now?'

The man hesitated for a moment, but the look in Hugh's eyes galvanised him into speech.

'He's after the old woman's pearls, sir – the Duchess of Lampshire's.'

'Ah!' returned Hugh softly. 'Of course he is. I forgot.'

'Strike me dead, guvnor,' cringed the man, 'I never meant no 'arm – I didn't really. I'll tell you all I know, sir. I will, strite.'

'I'm quite certain you will,' said Hugh. 'And if you don't, you swine, I'll make you. When does Peterson come back?'

'Termorrow, too, sir, as far as I knows,' answered the man, and at that moment the intimidated rabbit shot rapidly out of his room, propelled by an accurate and forcible kick from Toby, who had followed him in to ensure rapidity of toilet.

'And what's he doing?' demanded Drummond.

'On the level, guvnor, I can't tell yer. Strite, I can't; 'e can.' The man pointed to the latest arrival, who, with his nightdress tucked into his trousers, stood gasping painfully after the manner of a recently landed fish.

'I repeat, sir,' he sputtered angrily, 'that this is an outrage. By what right . . . '

'Dry up,' remarked Hugh briefly. Then he turned to the American. 'This is one of the ragged-trousered brigade I spoke to you about.'

For a while the three men studied him in silence; then the American thoughtfully transferred his chewing-gum to a fresh place.

'Wal,' he said, 'he looks like some kind o' disease; but I guess he's got a tongue. Say, flop-ears, what are you, anyway?'

'I am the secretary of a social organisation which aims at the amelioration of the conditions under which the workers of the world slave,' returned the other with dignity.

'You don't say,' remarked the American, unmoved. 'Do the workers of the world know about it?'

'And I again demand to know,' said the other, turning on Drummond, 'the reason for this monstrous indignity.'

'What do you know about Peterson, little man?' said Hugh, paying not the slightest attention to his protests.

'Nothing, save that he is the man whom we have been looking for, for years,' cried the other. 'The man of stupendous organising power, who has brought together and welded into one the hundreds of societies similar to mine, who before this have each, on their own, been feebly struggling towards the light. Now we are combined, and our strength is due to him.'

Hugh exchanged glances with the American.

'Things become clearer,' he murmured. 'Tell me, little man,' he continued, 'now that you're all welded together, what do you propose to do?'

'That you shall see in good time,' cried the other triumphantly. 'Constitutional methods have failed – and, besides, we've got no time to wait for them. Millions are groaning under the intolerable bonds of the capitalist: those millions we shall free, to a life that is worthy of a man. And it will all be due to our leader – Carl Peterson.'

A look of rapt adoration came into his face, and the American laughed in genuine delight.

'Didn't I tell you, Captain, that that guy was the goods?' But there was no answering smile on Hugh's face.

'He's the goods right enough,' he answered grimly. 'But what worries me is how to stop their delivery.'

At that moment Darrell's voice came up from the hall.

'The whole bunch are stowed away, Hugh. What's the next item?'

Hugh walked to the top of the stairs.

'Bring 'em both below,' he cried over his shoulder, as he went down. A grin spread over his face as he saw half a dozen familiar faces in the hall, and he hailed them cheerily.

'Like old times, boys,' he laughed. 'Where's the driver of the lorry?'

'That's me, sir.' One of the men stepped forward. 'My mate's outside.'

'Good,' said Hugh. 'Take your bus ten miles from here: then drop that crowd one by one on the road as you go along. You can take it from me that none of 'em will say anything about it, even when they wake up. Then take her back to your garage; I'll see you later.'

'Now,' went on Hugh, as they heard the sound of the departing lorry, 'we've got to set the scene for tomorrow morning.' He glanced at his watch. 'Just eleven. How long will it take me to get the old buzz-box to Laidley Towers?'

'Laidley Towers,' echoed Darrell. 'What the devil are you going there for?'

'I just can't bear to be parted from Henry for one moment longer than necessary,' said Hugh quietly. 'And Henry is there, in a praise-worthy endeavour to lift the Duchess's pearls . . . Dear Henry!' His two fists clenched, and the American looking at his face, laughed softly.

But it was only for a moment that Drummond indulged in the pleasures of anticipation; all that could come after. And just now there were other things to be done – many others, if events next morning were to go as they should.

'Take those two into the centre room,' he cried. 'Incidentally there's a dead Boche on the floor, but he'll come in very handy in my little scheme.'

'A dead Boche!' The intimidated rabbit gave a frightened squeak. 'Good heavens! You ruffian, this is beyond a joke.'

Hugh looked at him coldly.

'You'll find it beyond a joke, you miserable little rat,' he said quietly. 'if you speak to me like that.' He laughed as the other shrank past him. 'Three of you boys in there,' he ordered briskly, 'and if either of them gives the slightest trouble clip him over the head. Now let's have the rest of the crowd in here, Peter.'

They came filing in, and Hugh waved a cheery hand in greeting.

'How goes it, you fellows,' he cried with his infectious grin. 'Like a company pow-wow before popping the parapet. What! And it's a bigger show this time, boys, than any you've had over the water.' His face set grimly for a moment; then he grinned again, as he sat down on the foot of the stairs. 'Gather round, and listen to me.'

For five minutes he spoke, and his audience nodded delightedly. Apart from their love for Drummond – and three out of every four of them knew him personally – it was a scheme which tickled them to death. And he was careful to tell them just enough of the sinister design of the master-criminal to make them realise the bigness of the issue.

'That's all clear, then,' said Drummond, rising. 'Now I'm off. Toby, I want you to come too We ought to be there by midnight.'

'There's only one point, Captain,' remarked the American, as the group began to disperse. 'That safe – and the ledger.' He fumbled in his pocket, and produced a small india-rubber bottle. 'I've got the soup here – gelignite,' he explained, as he saw the mystified look on the other's face. 'I reckoned it might come in handy. Also a fuse and detonator.'

'Splendid!' said Hugh, 'splendid! You're an acquisition, Mr Green, to any gathering. But I think – I *think* – Lakington first. Oh! yes – most undoubtedly – Henry first!'

And once again the American laughed softly at the look on his face.

Chapter 11

In which Lakington plays his last 'coup'

I

'Toby, I've got a sort of horrid feeling that the hunt is nearly over.'

With a regretful sigh Hugh swung the car out of the sleeping town of Godalming in the direction of Laidley Towers. Mile after mile dropped smoothly behind the powerful two-seater, and still Drummond's eyes wore a look of resigned sadness.

'Very nearly over,' he remarked again. 'And then once more the tedium of respectability positively stares us in the face.'

'You'll be getting married, old bean,' murmured Toby Sinclair hopefully.

For a moment his companion brightened up.

'True, O King,' he answered. 'It will ease the situation somewhat; at least, I suppose so. But think of it, Toby: no Lakington, no Peterson – nothing at all to play about with and keep one amused.'

'You're very certain, Hugh.' With a feeling almost of wonder Sinclair glanced at the square-jawed, ugly profile beside him. 'There's many a slip . . . '

'My dear old man,' interrupted Drummond, 'there's only one cure for the proverb-quoting disease – a dose of salts in the morning.' For a while they raced on through the warm summer's night in silence, and it was not till they were within a mile of their destination that Sinclair spoke again.

'What are you going to do with them, Hugh?'

'Who – our Carl and little Henry?' Drummond grinned gently. 'Why, I think that Carl and I will part amicably – unless, of course, he gives me any trouble. And as for Lakington – we'll have to see about Lakington.' The grin faded from his face as he spoke. 'We'll have to see about our little Henry,' he repeated softly. 'And I can't help feeling, Toby, that between us we shall find a method of ridding the earth of such a thoroughly unpleasing fellow.'

'You mean to kill him?' grunted the other noncommittally.

'Just that, and no more,' responded Hugh. 'Tomorrow morning as ever is. But he's going to get the shock of his young life before it happens.'

He pulled the car up silently in the deep shadows of some trees, and the two men got out.

'Now, old boy, you take her back to The Elms. The ducal abode is close to – I remember in my extreme youth being worse than passing sick by those bushes over there after a juvenile bun-worry . . . '

'But confound it all,' spluttered Toby Sinclair. 'Don't you want me to help you?'

'I do: by taking the buzz-box back. This little show is my shout.'

Grumbling disconsolately, Sinclair stepped back into the car.

'You make me tired,' he remarked peevishly. 'I'll be damned if you get any wedding present out of me. In fact,' and he fired a Parthian shot at his leader, 'you won't have any wedding. I shall marry her myself!'

For a moment or two Hugh stood watching the car as it disappeared down the road along which they had just come, while his thoughts turned to the girl now safely asleep in his flat in London. Another week – perhaps a fortnight – but no more. Not a day more . . . And he had a pleasant conviction that Phyllis would not require much persuasion to come round to his way of thinking – even if she hadn't arrived there already . . . And so delightful was the train of thought thus conjured up, that for a while Peterson and Lakington were forgotten. The roseate dreams of the young about to wed have been known to act similarly before.

Wherefore to the soldier's instinctive second nature, trained in the war and sharpened by his grim duel with the gang, must be given the credit of preventing the ringing of the wedding-bells being postponed for good. The sudden snap of a twig close by, the sharp hiss of a compressed-air rifle, seemed simultaneous with Hugh hurling himself flat on his face behind a sheltering bush. In reality there was that fraction of a second between the actions which allowed the bullet to pass harmlessly over his body instead of finishing his career there and then. He heard it go zipping through the undergrowth as he lay motionless on the ground; then very cautiously he turned his head and peered about. A man with an ordinary revolver is at a disadvantage against someone armed with a silent gun, especially when he is not desirous of alarming the neighbourhood. .

A shrub was shaking a few yards away, and on it Hugh fixed his half-closed eyes. If he lay quite still the man, whoever he was, would probably assume the shot had taken effect, and come and investigate. Then things would be easier, as two or three Boches had discovered to their cost in days gone by.

For two minutes he saw no-one; then very slowly the branches parted and the white face of a man peered through. It was the chauffeur who usually drove the Rolls-Royce, and he seemed unduly anxious to satisfy himself that all was well before coming nearer. The fame of Hugh Drummond had spread abroad amongst the satellites of Peterson.

At last he seemed to make up his mind, and came out into the open. Step by step he advanced towards the motionless figure, his weapon held in readiness to shoot at the faintest movement. But the soldier lay sprawling and inert, and by the time the chauffeur had reached him there was no doubt in that worthy's mind that, at last, this wretched meddler with things that concerned him not had been laid by the heels. Which was as unfortunate for the chauffeur as it had been for unwary Huns in the past.

Contemptuously he rolled Drummond over; then, noting the relaxed muscles and inert limbs, he laid his gun on the ground preparatory to running through his victim's pockets. And the fact that such an action was a little more foolish than offering a man-eating tiger a peppermint lozenge did not trouble the chauffeur. In fact, nothing troubled him again.

He got out one gasping cry of terror as he realised his mistake; then he had a blurred consciousness of the world upside down, and everything was over. It was Olaki's most dangerous throw, carried out by gripping the victim's wrists and hurling his body over by a heave of the legs. And nine times out of ten the result was a broken neck. This was one of the nine.

For a while the soldier stared at the body, frowning thoughtfully. To have killed the chauffeur was inconvenient, but since it had happened it necessitated a little rearrangement of his plans. The moon was setting and the night would become darker, so there was a good chance that Lakington would not recognise that the driver of his car had changed. And if he did – well, it would be necessary to forgo the somewhat theatrical entertainment he had staged for his benefit at The Elms. Bending over the dead man, he removed his long grey driving-coat and cap; then, without a sound, he threaded his way through the bushes in search of the car.

He found it about a hundred yards nearer the house, so well hidden in a small space off the road that he was almost on top of it before he realised the fact. To his relief it was empty, and placing his own cap in a pocket under the seat he put on the driving-coat of his predecessor. Then, with a quick glance round to ensure that everything was in readiness for the immediate and rapid departure such as he imagined Lakington would desire, he turned and crept stealthily towards the house.

2

Laidley Towers was *en fête*. The Duchess, determined that every conceivable stunt should be carried out which would make for the entertainment of her guests, had spared no pains to make the evening a success. The Duke, bored to extinction, had been five times routed out of his study by his indefatigable spouse, and was now, at the moment Hugh first came in sight of the house, engaged in shaking hands with a tall, aristocratic-looking Indian . . .

'How-d'ye-do,' he murmured vacantly. 'What did you say the dam' fellah's name was, my dear?' he whispered in a hoarse undertone to the Duchess, who stood beside him welcoming the distinguished foreigner.

'We're so glad you could come, Mr Ram Dar,' remarked the Duchess affably. 'Everyone is so looking forward to your wonderful entertainment.' Round her neck were the historic pearls, and as the Indian bowed low over her outstretched hand, his eyes gleamed for a second.

'Your Grace is too kind.' His voice was low and deep, and he glanced thoughtfully around the circle of faces near him. 'Maybe the sands that come from the mountains that lie beyond the ever-lasting snows will speak the truth; maybe the gods will be silent. Who knows . . . who knows?'

As if unconsciously his gaze rested on the Duke, who manfully rose to the occasion.

'Precisely, Mr Rum Rum,' he murmured helpfully; 'who indeed? If they let you down, don't you know, perhaps you could show us a card trick?'

He retired in confusion, abashed by the baleful stare of the Duchess, and the rest of the guests drew closer. The jazz band was having supper; the last of the perspiring tenants had departed, and now the bonne-bouche of the evening was about to begin.

It had been the Marquis of Laidley himself who had suggested getting hold of this most celebrated performer, who had apparently never been in England before. And since the Marquis of Laidley's coming-of-age was the cause of the whole evening's entertainment, his suggestion had been hailed with acclamation. How he had heard about the Indian, and from whom, were points about which he was very vague; but since he was a very vague young man, the fact elicited no comment. The main thing was that here, in the flesh, was a dark, mysterious performer of the occult, and what more could a house party require? And in the general excitement Hugh Drummond crept closer to the open window. It was the Duchess he was concerned with and her pearls, and the arrival of the Indian was not going to put him off his guard . . . Then suddenly his jaw tightened: Irma Peterson had entered the room with young Laidley.

'Do you want anything done, Mr Ram Dar?' asked the Duchess – 'the lights down or the window shut?'

'No, I thank you,' returned the Indian. 'The night is still; there is no wind. And the night is dark – dark with strange thoughts, that thronged upon me as I drew nigh to the house – whispering through the trees.' Again he fixed his eyes on the Duke. 'What is your pleasure, Protector of the Poor?'

'Mine?' cried that pillar of the House of Lords, hurriedly stifling a yawn. 'Any old thing, my dear fellow . . . You'd much better ask one of the ladies.'

'As you will,' returned the other gravely; 'but if the gods speak the truth, and the sand does not lie, I can but say what is written.'

From a pocket in his robe he took a bag and two small bronze dishes, and placing them on a table stood waiting.

'I am ready,' he announced. 'Who first will learn of the things that are written on the scroll of Fate?'

'I say, hadn't you better do it in private, Mr Rum?' murmured the Duke apprehensively. 'I mean, don't you know, it might be a little embarrassing if the jolly old gods really do give tongue; and I don't see anybody getting killed in the rush.'

'Is there so much to conceal?' demanded the Indian, glancing round the group, contempt in his brooding eyes. 'In the lands that lie beyond the snows we have nothing to conceal. There is nothing that can be concealed, because all is known.'

And it was at that moment that the intent watcher outside the window began to shake with silent mirth. For the face was the face of the Indian, Ram Dar, but the voice was the voice of Lakington. It struck him that the next ten minutes or so might be well worth while. The problem of removing the pearls from the Duchess's neck before such an assembly seemed to present a certain amount of difficulty even to such an expert as Henry. And Hugh crept a little nearer the window, so as to miss nothing. He crept near enough, in fact, to steal a look at Irma, and in doing so saw something which made him rub his eyes and then grin once more. She was standing on the outskirts of the group, an evening wrap thrown loosely over her arm. She edged a step or two towards a table containing bric-à-brac, the centre of which was occupied, as the place of honour, by a small inlaid Chinese cabinet – a box standing on four grotesquely carved legs. It was a beautiful ornament, and he dimly remembered having heard its history – a story which reflected considerable glory on the predatory nature of a previous Duke. At the moment, however, he was not concerned with its past history, but with its present fate; and it was the consummate quickness of the girl that made him rub his eyes.

She took one lightning glance at the other guests who were craning eagerly forward round the Indian; then she half dropped her wrap on the table and picked it up again. It was done so rapidly, so naturally, that for a while Hugh thought he had made a mistake. And then a slight rearrangement of her wrap to conceal a hard outline beneath, as she joined the others, dispelled any doubts. The small inlaid Chinese cabinet now standing on the table was not the one that had been here previously. The original was under Irma Peterson's cloak . . .

Evidently the scene was now set – the necessary props were in position – and Hugh waited with growing impatience for the principal event. But the principal performer seemed in no hurry. In fact, in his dry way Lakington was thoroughly enjoying himself. An intimate inside knowledge of the skeletons that rattled their bones in the cupboards of most of those present enabled the gods to speak with disconcerting accuracy; and as each victim insisted on somebody new facing the sands that came from beyond the mountains, the performance seemed likely to last indefinitely.

At last a sudden delighted burst of applause came from the group, announcing the discomfiture of yet another guest, and with it Lakington seemed to tire of the amusement. Engrossed though he was in the anticipation of the main item which was still to be staged, Drummond could not but admire the extraordinary accuracy of the character study. Not a detail had been overlooked; not a single flaw in Lakington's acting could he notice. It *was* an Indian who stood there, and when a few days later Hugh returned her pearls to the Duchess, for a long time neither she nor her husband would believe that Ram Dar had been an Englishman disguised. And when they had at last been persuaded of that fact, and had been shown the two cabinets side by side, it was the consummate boldness of the crime, coupled with its extreme simplicity, that staggered them. For it was only in the reconstruction of it that the principal beauty of the scheme became apparent. The element of luck was reduced to a minimum, and at no stage of the proceedings was it impossible, should things go amiss, for Lakington to go as he had come, a mere Indian entertainer. Without the necklace, true, in such an event; but unsuspected, and free to try again. As befitted his last, it was perhaps his greatest effort . . . And this was what happened as seen by the fascinated onlooker crouching near the window outside.

Superbly disdainful, the Indian tipped back his sand into the little bag, and replacing it in his pocket, stalked to the open window. With arms outstretched he stared into the darkness, seeming to gather strength from the gods whom he served.

'Do your ears not hear the whisperings of the night?' he demanded. 'Life rustling in the leaves; death moaning through the grasses.' And suddenly he threw back his head and laughed, a fierce, mocking laugh; then he swung round and faced the room. For a while he stood motionless, and Hugh, from the shelter of the bushes, wondered whether the two quick flashes that had come from his robe as he spoke – flashes such as a small electric torch will give, and which were unseen by anyone else – were a signal to the defunct chauffeur.

Then a peculiar look came over the Indian's face, as his eyes fell on the Chinese cabinet.

'Where did the Protector of the Poor obtain the sacred cabinet of the Chow Kings?' He peered at it reverently, and the Duke coughed.

'One of my ancestors picked it up somewhere,' he answered apologetically.

'Fashioned with the blood of men, guarded with their lives, and one of your ancestors picked it up!' The Duke withered completely under the biting scorn of the words, and seemed about to say something, but the Indian had turned away, and his long, delicate fingers were hovering over the box. 'There is power in this box,' he continued, and his voice was low and thoughtful. 'Years ago a man who came from the land where dwells the Great Brooding Spirit told me of this thing. I wonder . . . I wonder . . . '

With gleaming eyes he stared in front of him, and a woman shuddered audibly.

'What is it supposed to do?' she ventured timidly.

'In that box lies the power unknown to mortal man, though the priests of the Temple City have sometimes discovered it before they pass beyond. Length you know, and height, and breadth – but in that box lies more.'

'You don't mean the fourth dimension, do you?' demanded a man incredulously.

'I know not what you call it, sahib,' said the Indian quietly. 'But it is the power which renders visible or invisible at will.'

For a moment Hugh felt an irresistible temptation to shout the truth through the window, and give Lakington away; then his curiosity to see the next move in the game conquered the wish, and he remained silent. So perfect was the man's acting that, in spite of having seen the substitution of the boxes, in spite of knowing the whole thing was bunkum, he felt he could almost believe it himself. And as for the others – without exception – they were craning forward eagerly, staring first at the Indian and then at the box.

'I say, that's a bit of a tall order, isn't it, Mr Rum Bar?' protested the Duke a little feebly. 'Do you mean to say you can put something into that box, and it disappears?'

'From mortal eye, Protector of the Poor, though it is still there,' answered the Indian. 'And that only too for a time. Then it reappears again. So runs the legend.'

'Well, stuff something in and let's see,' cried young Laidley, starting forward, only to pause before the Indian's outstretched arm.

'Stop, sahib,' he ordered sternly. 'To you that box is nothing; to others – of whom I am one of the least – it is sacred beyond words.' He stalked away from the table, and the guests' disappointment showed on their faces.

'Oh, but Mr Ram Dar,' pleaded the Duchess, 'can't you satisfy our curiosity after all you've said?'

For a moment he seemed on the point of refusing outright; then he bowed, a deep Oriental bow.

'Your Grace,' he said with dignity, 'for centuries that box contained the jewels – precious beyond words – of the reigning Queens of the Chow Dynasty. They were wrapped in silver and gold tissue – of which this is a feeble, modern substitute.'

From a cummerbund under his robe he drew a piece of shining

material, the appearance of which was greeted with cries of feminine delight.

'You would not ask me to commit sacrilege?' Quietly he replaced the material in his belt and turned away, and Hugh's eyes glistened at the cleverness with which the man was acting. Whether they believed it or not, there was not a soul in the room by this time who was not consumed with eagerness to put the Chinese cabinet to the test.

'Supposing you took my pearls, Mr Ram Dar,' said the Duchess diffidently. 'I know that compared to such historic jewels they are poor, but perhaps it would not be sacrilege.'

Not a muscle on Lakington's face twitched, though it was the thing he had been playing for. Instead he seemed to be sunk in thought, while the Duchess continued pleading, and the rest of the party added their entreaties. At length she undid the fastening and held the necklace out, but he only shook his head.

'You ask a great thing of me, your Grace,' he said. 'Only by the exercise of my power can I show you this secret – even if I can show you at all. And you are unbelievers.' He paced slowly to the window, ostensibly to commune with the gods on the subject; more materially to flash once again the signal into the darkness. Then, as if he had decided suddenly, he swung round.

'I will try,' he announced briefly, and the Duchess headed the chorus of delight. 'Will the Presences stand back, and you, your Grace, take that?' He handed her the piece of material. 'No hand but yours must touch the pearls. Wrap them up inside the silver and gold.' Aloofly he watched the process. 'Now advance alone, and open the box. Place the pearls inside. Now shut and lock it.' Obediently the Duchess did as she was bid; then she stood waiting for further instructions.

But apparently by this time the Great Brooding Spirit was beginning to take effect. Singing a monotonous, harsh chant, the Indian knelt on the floor, and poured some powder into a little brazier. He was still close to the open window, and finally he sat down with his elbows on his knees, and his head rocking to and fro in his hands.

'Less light – less light!' The words seemed to come from a great distance – ventriloquism in a mild way was one of Lakington's accomplishments; and as the lights went out a greenish, spluttering flame rose from the brazier. A heavy, odorous smoke filled the room, but framed and motionless in the eerie light sat the Indian, staring fixedly in front of him. After a time the chant began again;

it grew and swelled in volume till the singer grew frenzied and beat his head with his hands. Then abruptly it stopped.

'Place the box upon the floor,' he ordered, 'in the light of the Sacred Fire.' Hugh saw the Duchess kneel down on the opposite side of the brazier, and place the box on the floor, while the faces of the guests – strange and ghostly in the green light – peered like spectres out of the heavy smoke. This was undoubtedly a show worth watching.

'Open the box !' Harshly the words rang through the silent room, and with fingers that trembled a little the Duchess turned the key and threw back the lid.

'Why, it's empty!' she cried in amazement, and the guests craned forward to look.

'Put not your hand inside,' cried the Indian in sudden warning, 'or perchance it will remain empty.'

The Duchess rapidly withdrew her hand, and stared incredulously through the smoke at his impassive face.

'Did I not say that there was power in the box?' he said dreamily. 'The power to render invisible – the power to render visible. Thus came protection to the jewels of the Chow Queens.'

'That's all right, Mr Ram Dar,' said the Duchess a little apprehensively. 'There may be power in the box, but my pearls don't seem to be.'

The Indian laughed.

'None but you has touched the cabinet, your Grace; none but you must touch it till the pearls return. They are there now; but not for mortal eyes to see.'

Which, incidentally, was no more than the truth.

'Look, O sahibs, look; but do not touch. See that to your vision the box is empty . . . ' He waited motionless, while the guests thronged round, with expressions of amazement; and Hugh, safe from view in the thick, sweet-smelling smoke, came even nearer in his excitement.

'It is enough,' cried the Indian suddenly. 'Shut the box, your Grace, and lock it as before. Now place it on the table whence it came. Is it there?'

'Yes.' The Duchess's voice came out of the green fog.

'Go not too near,' he continued warningly. 'The gods must have space – the gods must have space.'

Again the harsh chant began, at times swelling to a shout, at times dying away to a whisper. And it was during one of these latter periods that a low laugh, instantly checked, disturbed the room. It was plainly audible, and someone irritably said, 'Be quiet !' It was not repeated, which afforded Hugh, at any rate, no surprise. For it had been Irma Peterson who had laughed, and it might have been hilarity, or it might have been a signal.

The chanting grew frenzied and more frenzied; more and more powder was thrown on the brazier till dense clouds of the thick vapour were rolling through the room, completely obscuring everything save the small space round the brazier, and the Indian's tense face poised above it.

'Bring the box, your Grace,' he cried harshly, and once more the Duchess knelt in the circle of light, with a row of dimly seen faces above her.

'Open; but as you value your pearls – touch them not.' Excitedly she threw back the lid, and a chorus of cries greeted the appearance of the gold and silver tissue at the bottom of the box.

'They're here, Mr Ram Dar.'

In the green light the Indian's sombre eyes stared round the group of dim faces.

'Did I not say,' he answered, 'that there was power in the box? But in the name of that power – unknown to you – I warn you: Do not touch those pearls till the light has burned low in the brazier. If you do they will disappear – never to return. Watch, but do not touch!'

Slowly he backed towards the window, unperceived in the general excitement; and Hugh dodged rapidly towards the car. It struck him that the séance was over, and he just had time to see Lakington snatch something which appeared to have been let down by a string from above, before turning into the bushes and racing for the car. As it was he was only a second or two in front of the other, and the last vision he had through a break in the trees, before they were spinning smoothly down the deserted road, was an open window in Laidley Towers from which dense volumes of vapour poured steadily out. Of the house party behind, waiting for the light to burn low in the brazier, he could see no sign through the opaque wall of green fog.

It took five minutes, so he gathered afterwards from a member of the house party, before the light had burned sufficiently low for the Duchess to consider it safe to touch the pearls. In various stages of asphyxiation the assembled guests had peered at the box, while the cynical comments of the men were rightly treated by the ladies with the contempt they deserved. Was the necklace not there, wrapped in its gold and silver tissue, where a few minutes before there had been nothing?

'Some trick of that beastly light,' remarked the Duke peevishly. 'For heaven's sake throw the dam' thing out of the window.'

'Don't be a fool, John,' retorted his spouse. 'If you could do this sort of thing, the House of Lords might be some use to somebody.'

And when two minutes later they stared horror-struck at a row of ordinary marbles laboriously unwrapped from a piece of gold and silver tissue, the Duke's pungent agreement with his wife's sentiment passed uncontradicted. In fact, it is to be understood that over the scene which followed it was best to draw a decent veil.

3

Drummond, hunched low over the wheel, in his endeavour to conceal his identity from the man behind, knew nothing of that at the time. Every nerve was centred on eluding the pursuit he thought was a certainty; for the thought of Lakington, when everything was prepared for his reception, being snatched from his clutches even by the majesty of the law was more than he could bear. And for much the same reason he did not want to have to deal with him until The Elms was reached; the staging there was so much more effective.

But Lakington was far too busy to bother with the chauffeur.

One snarling curse as they had entered, for not having done as he had been told, was the total of their conversation during the trip. During the rest of the time the transformation to the normal kept Lakington busy, and Hugh could see him reflected in the wind-screen removing the make-up from his face, and changing his clothes.

Even now he was not quite clear how the trick had been worked. That there had been two cabinets, that was clear – one false, the other the real one. That they had been changed at the crucial moment by the girl Irma was also obvious. But how had the pearls disappeared in the first case, and then apparently reappeared again? For of one thing he was quite certain. Whatever was inside the parcel of gold and silver tissue which, for all he knew, they might be still staring at, it was not the historic necklace.

And he was still puzzling it over in his mind when the car swung into the drive at The Elms.

'Change the wheels as usual,' snapped Lakington as he got out, and Hugh bent forward to conceal his face. 'Then report to me in the central room.'

And out of the corner of his eye Hugh watched him enter the house with one of the Chinese cabinets clasped in his hand . . .

'Toby,' he remarked to that worthy, whom he found mournfully eating a ham sandwich in the garage, 'I feel sort of sorry for our Henry. He's just had the whole complete ducal outfit guessing, dressed up as an Indian; he's come back here with a box containing the Duchess's pearls or I'll eat my hat, and feeling real good with himself; and now instead of enjoying life he's got to have a little chat with me.'

'Did you drive him back?' demanded Sinclair, producing a bottle of Bass.

'Owing to the sudden decease of his chauffeur I had to,' murmured Hugh. 'And he's very angry over something. Let's go on the roof.'

Silently they both climbed the ladder which had been placed in readiness, to find Peter Darrell and the American detective already in position. A brilliant light streamed out through the glass dome, and the inside of the central room was clearly visible.

'He's already talked to what he thinks is you,' whispered Peter ecstatically, 'and he is not in the best of tempers.'

Hugh glanced down, and a grim smile flickered round his lips. In the three chairs sat the motionless, bound figures, so swathed in rope that only the tops of their heads were visible, just as Lakington had left him and Toby and Algy earlier in the evening. The only moving thing in the room was the criminal himself, and at the moment he was seated at the table with the Chinese cabinet in front of him. He seemed to be doing something inside with a penknife, and all the time he kept up a running commentary to the three bound figures.

'Well, you young swine, have you enjoyed your night?' A feeble moan came from one of the chairs. 'Spirit broken at last, is it?' With a quick turn of his wrist he prised open two flaps of wood, and folded them back against the side. Then he lifted out a parcel of gold and silver tissue from underneath.

'My hat!' muttered Hugh, 'what a fool I was not to think of it! Just a false bottom actuated by closing the lid. And a similar parcel in the other cabinet.'

But the American, whistling gently to himself, had his eyes fixed on the rope of wonderful pearls which Lakington was holding lovingly in his hands.

'So easy, you scum,' continued Lakington, 'and you thought to pit yourselves against me. Though if it hadn't been for Irma' – he rose and stood in front of the chair where he had last left Drummond – 'it might have been awkward. She was quick, Captain Drummond, and that fool of a chauffeur failed to carry out my orders, and create a diversion. You will see what happens to people who fail to carry out my orders in a minute. And after that you'll never see anything again.'

'Say, he's a dream – that guy,' muttered the American. 'What pearls are those he's got?'

'The Duchess of Lampshire's,' whispered Hugh. 'Lifted right under the noses of the whole bally house party.'

With a grunt the detective rearranged his chewing gum; then once more the four watchers on the roof glued their eyes to the glass. And the sight they saw a moment or two afterwards stirred even the phlegmatic Mr Green.

A heavy door was swinging slowly open, apparently of its own volition, though Hugh, stealing a quick glance at Lakington, saw that he was pressing some small studs in a niche in one of the walls. Then he looked back at the door, and stared dumbfounded. It was the mysterious cupboard of which Phyllis had spoken to him, but nothing he had imagined from her words had prepared him for the reality. It seemed to be literally crammed to overflowing with the most priceless loot. Gold vessels of fantastic and beautiful shapes littered the floor; while on the shelves were arranged the most wonderful collection of precious stones, which shone and scintillated in the electric light till their glitter almost blinded the watchers.

'Shades of Chu Chin Chow, Ali Baba and the forty pundits!' muttered Toby. 'The dam' man's a genius.'

The pearls were carefully placed in a position of honour, and for a few moments Lakington stood gloating over his collection.

'Do you see them, Captain Drummond?' he asked quietly. 'Each thing obtained by my brain – my hands. All mine – mine!' His voice rose to a shout. 'And you pit your puny wits against me.' With a laugh he crossed the room, and once more pressed the studs. The door swung slowly to and closed without a sound, while Lakington still shook with silent mirth.

'And now,' he resumed, rubbing his hands, 'we will prepare your bath, Captain Drummond.' He walked over to the shelves where the bottles were ranged, and busied himself with some preparations. 'And while it is getting ready, we will just deal with the chauffeur who neglected his orders.'

For a few minutes he bent over the chemicals, and then he poured the mixture into the water which half filled the long bath at the end of the room. A faintly acid smell rose to the four men above, and the liquid turned a pale green.

'I told you I had all sorts of baths, didn't I?' continued Lakington; 'some for those who are dead, and some for those who are alive. This is the latter sort, and has the great advantage of making the bather wish it was one of the former.' He stirred the liquid gently with a long glass rod. 'About five minutes before we're quite ready,' he announced 'Just time for the chauffeur.'

He went to a speaking-tube, down which he blew. Somewhat naturally there was no answer, and Lakington frowned.

'A stupid fellow,' he remarked softly. 'But there is no hurry; I will deal with him later.'

'You certainly will,' muttered Hugh on the roof. 'And perhaps not quite so much later as you think, friend Henry.'

But Lakington had returned to the chair which contained, as he thought, his chief enemy, and was standing beside it with an unholy joy shining on his face.

'And since I have to deal with him later, Captain Drummond, D.S.O., M.C., I may as well deal with you now. Then it will be your friend's turn. I am going to cut the ropes, and carry you, while you're so numbed that you can't move, to the bath. Then I shall drop you in, Captain Drummond, and when afterwards, you pray for death, I shall mercifully spare your life – for a while.'

He slashed at the ropes behind the chair, and the four men craned forward expectantly.

'There,' snarled Lakington. 'I'm ready for you, you young swine.'

And even as he spoke, the words died away on his lips, and with a dreadful cry he sprang back. For with a dull, heavy thud the body of the dead German Heinrich rolled off the chair and sprawled at his feet.

'My God!' screamed Lakington. 'What has happened? I – I – '

He rushed to the bell and pealed it frantically, and with a smile of joy Hugh watched his frenzied terror. No-one came in answer to the ring, and Lakington dashed to the door, only to recoil into the room with a choking noise in his throat. Outside in the hall stood four masked men, each with a revolver pointing at his heart.

'My cue,' muttered Hugh. 'And you understand, fellows, don't you? – he's my meat.'

The next moment he had disappeared down the ladder, and the three remaining watchers stared motionless at the grim scene. For Lakington had shut the door and was crouching by the table, his nerve utterly gone. And all the while the puffed, bloated body of the German sprawled on the floor . . .

Slowly the door into the hall opened, and with a scream of fear Lakington sprang back. Standing in the doorway was Hugh Drummond, and his face was grim and merciless.

'You sent for your chauffeur, Henry Lakington,' he remarked quietly. 'I am here.'

'What do you mean?' muttered Lakington thickly.

'I drove you back from Laidley Towers tonight,' said Hugh with a slight smile. 'The proper man was foolish and had to be killed.' He advanced a few steps into the room, and the other shrank back. 'You look frightened, Henry. Can it be that the young swine's wits are, after all, better than yours?'

'What do you want?' gasped Lakington, through dry lips.

'I want you, Henry – just you. Hitherto you've always used gangs of your ruffians against me. Now my gang occupies this house. But I'm not going to use them. It's going to be just – you and I. Stand up, Henry, stand up – as I have always stood up to you.' He crossed the room and stood in front of the cowering man.

'Take half – take half,' he screamed. 'I've got treasure – I've . . . '

And Drummond hit him a fearful blow on the mouth.

'I shall take all, Henry, to return to their rightful owners. Boys' – he raised his voice – 'carry out these other two, and undo them.'

The four masked men came in, and carried out the two chairs.

'The intimidated rabbit, Henry, and the kindly gentleman you put to guard Miss Benton,' he remarked as the door closed. 'So now we may regard ourselves as being alone. Just you and I. And one of us, Lakington – you devil in human form – is going into that bath.'

'But the bath means death,' shrieked Lakington – 'death in agony.'

'That will be unfortunate for the one who goes in,' said Drummond, taking a step towards him.

'You would murder me?' half sobbed the terrified man.

'No, Lakington; I'm not going to murder you.' A gleam of hope came into the other's eyes. 'But I'm going to fight you in order to decide which of us two ceases to adorn the earth; that is, if your diagnosis of the contents of the bath is correct. What little gleam of pity I might have possessed for you has been completely extinguished by your present exhibition of nauseating cowardice. Fight, you worm, fight; or I'll throw you in!'

And Lakington fought. The sudden complete turning of the tables had for the moment destroyed his nerve; now, at Drummond's words, he recovered himself. There was no mercy on the soldier's face, and in his inmost heart Lakington knew that the end had come. For strong and wiry though he was, he was no match for the other.

Relentlessly he felt himself being forced towards the deadly liquid he had prepared for Drummond, and as the irony of the thing struck him, the sweat broke out on his forehead and he cursed aloud. At last he backed into the edge of the bath and his struggles redoubled. But still there was no mercy on the soldier's face, and he felt himself being forced farther and farther over the liquid until he was only held from falling into it by Drummond's grip on his throat.

Then, just before the grip relaxed and he went under, the soldier spoke once: 'Henry Lakington,' he said, 'the retribution is just.'

Drummond sprang back, and the liquid closed over the wretched man's head. But only for a second. With a dreadful cry, Lakington leapt out, and even Drummond felt a momentary qualm of pity. For the criminal's clothes were already burnt through to the skin, and his face – or what was left of it – was a shining copper colour. Mad with agony, he dashed to the door, and flung it open. The four men outside, aghast at the spectacle, recoiled and let him through. And the kindly mercy which Lakington had never shown to anyone in his life was given to him at the last.

Blindly he groped his way up the stairs, and as Drummond got to the door the end came. Someone must have put in gear the machinery which worked on the fifth step, or perhaps it was automatic. For suddenly a heavy steel weight revolving on an arm whizzed out from the wall and struck Lakington behind the neck. Without a sound he fell forward, and the weight, unchecked, clanged sullenly home. And thus did the invention of which he was proudest break the inventor's own neck. Truly, the retribution was just . . .

'That only leaves Peterson,' remarked the American, coming into the hall at that moment, and lighting a cigar.

'That only leaves Peterson,' agreed Drummond. 'And the girl,' he added as an afterthought.

Chapter 12

In which the last round takes place

I

It was during the next hour or two that the full value of Mr Jerome K. Green as an acquisition to the party became apparent. Certain other preparations in honour of Peterson's arrival were duly carried out, and then arose the question of the safe in which the all-important ledger was kept.

'There it is,' said Drummond, pointing to a heavy steel door flush with the wall, on the opposite side of the room to the big one containing Lakington's ill-gotten treasure. 'And it doesn't seem to me that you're going to open that one by pressing any buttons in the wall.'

'Then, Captain,' drawled the American, 'I guess we'll open it otherwise. It's sure plumb easy. I've been getting gay with some of the household effects, and this bar of soap sort of caught my eye.'

From his pocket he produced some ordinary yellow soap, and the others glanced at him curiously.

'I'll just give you a little demonstration,' he continued, 'of how our swell cracksmen over the water open safes when the owners have been so tactless as to remove the keys.'

Dexterously he proceeded to seal up every crack in the safe door with the soap, leaving a small gap at the top unsealed. Then round that gap he built what was to all intents and purposes a soap dam.

'If any of you boys,' he remarked to the intent group around him, 'think of taking this up as a means of livelihood, be careful of this stuff.' From another pocket he produced an india-rubber bottle. 'Don't drop it on the floor if you want to be measured for your coffin. There'll just be a boot and some bits to bury.'

The group faded away, and the American laughed.

'Might I ask what it is?' murmured Hugh politely from the neighbourhood of the door.

'Sure thing, Captain,' returned the detective, carefully pouring some of the liquid into the soap dam. 'This is what I told you I'd got – gelignite; or, as the boys call it, the oil. It runs right round the cracks of the door inside the soap.' He added a little more, and carefully replaced the stopper in the bottle. 'Now a detonator and a bit of fuse, and I guess we'll leave the room.'

'It reminds one of those dreadful barbarians the Sappers, trying to blow up things,' remarked Toby, stepping with some agility into the garden; and a moment or two later the American joined them.

'It may be necessary to do it again,' he announced, and as he spoke the sound of a dull explosion came from inside the house. 'On the other hand,' he continued, going back into the room and quietly pulling the safe door open, 'it may not. There's your book, Captain.'

He calmly relit his cigar as if safe opening was the most normal undertaking, and Drummond lifted out the heavy ledger and placed it on the table.

'Go out in relays, boys,' he said to the group of men by the door, 'and get your breakfasts. I'm going to be busy for a bit.'

He sat down at the table and began to turn the pages. The American was amusing himself with the faked Chinese cabinet; Toby and Peter sprawled in two chairs, unashamedly snoring. And after a while the detective put down the cabinet, and coming over, sat at Drummond's side.

Every page contained an entry – sometimes half a dozen – of the same type, and as the immensity of the project dawned on the two men their faces grew serious.

'I told you he was a big man, Captain,' remarked the American, leaning back in his chair and looking at the open book through half-closed eyes.

'One can only hope to Heaven that we're in time,' returned Hugh. 'Damn it, man,' he exploded, 'surely the police must know of this!'

The American closed his eyes still more.

'Your English police know most things,' he drawled, 'but you've sort of got some peculiar laws in your country. With us, if we don't like a man – something happens. He kind o' ceases to sit up and take nourishment. But over here, the more scurrilous he is, the more he talks bloodshed and riot, the more constables does he get to guard him from catching cold.'

The soldier frowned.

'Look at this entry here,' he grunted. 'That blighter is a Member of Parliament. What's he getting four payments of a thousand pounds for?'

'Why, surely, to buy some nice warm underclothes with,' grinned the detective. Then he leaned forward and glanced at the name. 'But isn't he some pot in one of your big trade unions?'

'Heaven knows,' grunted Hugh. 'I only saw the blighter once, and then his shirt was dirty.' He turned over a few more pages thoughtfully. 'Why, if these are the sums of money Peterson has blown, the man must have spent a fortune. Two thousand pounds to Ivolsky. Incidentally, that's the bloke who had words with the whatnot on the stairs.'

In silence they continued their study of the book. The whole of England and Scotland had been split up into districts, regulated by population rather than area, and each district appeared to be in charge of one director. A varying number of sub-districts in every main division had each their sub-director and staff, and at some of the names Drummond rubbed his eyes in amazement. Briefly, the duties of every man were outlined: the locality in which his work lay, his exact responsibilities, so that overlapping was reduced to a minimum. In each case the staff was small, the work largely that of organisation. But in each district there appeared ten or a dozen names of men who were euphemistically described as lecturers; while at the end of the book there appeared nearly fifty names – both of men and women – who were proudly denoted as first-class general lecturers. And if Drummond had rubbed his eyes at some of the names on the organising staffs, the first-class general lecturers deprived him of speech.

'Why,' he spluttered after a moment, 'a lot of these people's names are absolute household words in the country. They may be swine – they probably are. Thank God! I've very rarely met any; but they ain't criminals.'

'No more is Peterson,' grinned the American! 'At least not on that book. See here, Captain, it's pretty clear what's happening. In any country today you've got all sorts and conditions of people with more wind than brain. They just can't stop talking, and as yet it's not a criminal offence. Some of 'em believe what they say, like Spindle-shanks upstairs; some of 'em don't. And if they don't, it makes 'em worse: they start writing as well. You've got clever men, intellectual men – look at some of those guys in the first-class general lecturers – and they're the worst of the lot. Then

you've got another class – the men with the business brain, who
think they're getting the sticky end of it, and use the talkers to
pull the chestnuts out of the fire for them. And the chestnuts, who
are the poor blamed decent working-men, are promptly dropped
in the ash-pit to keep 'em quiet. They all want something for
nothing, and I guess it can't be done. They all think they're fooling one another, and what's really going at the moment is that
Peterson is fooling the whole bunch. He wants all the strings in
his hands, and it looks to me as if he'd got 'em there. He's got
the money – and we know where he got it from; he's got the
organisation – all either red-hot revolutionaries, or intellectual
wind-storms, or calculating knaves. He's amalgamated 'em, Captain; and the whole blamed lot, whatever they may think, are really
working for him.'

Drummond, thoughtfully, lit a cigarette.

'Working towards a revolution in this country,' he remarked
quietly.

'Sure thing,' answered the American. 'And when he brings it off, I
guess you won't catch Peterson for dust. He'll pocket the boodle,
and the boobs will stew in their own juice. I guessed it in Paris; that
book makes it a certainty. But it ain't criminal. In a Court of Law he
could swear it was an organisation for selling bird-seed.'

For a while Drummond smoked in silence, while the two sleepers
shifted uneasily in their chairs. It all seemed so simple in spite of the
immensity of the scheme. Like most normal Englishmen, politics
and labour disputes had left him cold in the past; but no-one who
ever glanced at a newspaper could be ignorant of the volcano that
had been simmering just beneath the surface for years past.

'Not one in a hundred' – the American's voice broke into his train
of thought – 'of the so-called revolutionary leaders in this country
are disinterested, Captain. They're out for Number One, and when
they've talked the boys into bloody murder, and your existing social
system is down-and-out, they'll be the leaders in the new one. That's
what they're playing for – power; and when they've got it, God help
the men who gave it to 'em.'

Drummond nodded, and lit another cigarette. Odd things he had
read recurred to him: trade unions refusing to allow discharged
soldiers to join them; the reiterated threats of direct action. And to
what end?

A passage in a part of the ledger evidently devoted to extracts from
the speeches of the first-class general lecturers caught his eye:

'To me, the big fact of modern life is the war between classes . . . People declare that the method of direct action inside a country will produce a revolution. I agree . . . it involves the creation of an army.'

And beside the cutting was a note by Peterson in red ink: 'An excellent man! Send for protracted tour.'

The note of exclamation appealed to Hugh; he could see the writer's tongue in his cheek as he put it in.

'It involves the creation of an army . . . ' [the words of the intimidated rabbit came back to his mind.] 'The man of stupendous organising power, who has brought together and welded into one the hundreds of societies similar to mine, who before this have each, on their own, been feebly struggling towards the light. Now we are combined, and our strength is due to him.'

In other words, the army was on the road to completion, an army where ninety per cent of the fighters – duped by the remaining ten – would struggle blindly towards a dim, half-understood goal, only to find out too late that the whip of Solomon had been exchanged for the scorpion of his son . . .

'Why can't they be made to understand, Mr Green?' he cried bitterly. 'The working-man – the decent fellow – '

The American thoughtfully picked his teeth.

'Has anyone tried to make 'em understand, Captain? I guess I'm no intellectual guy, but there was a French writer fellow – Victor Hugo – who wrote something that sure hit the nail on the head. I copied it out, for it seemed good to me.' From his pocket-book he produced a slip of paper. "The faults of women, children, servants, the weak, the indigent, and the ignorant are the faults of husbands, father, masters, the strong, the rich, and the learned." Wal!' he leaned back in his chair, 'there you are. Their proper leaders have sure failed them, so they're running after that bunch of cross-eyed skaters. And sitting here, watching 'em run, and laughing fit to beat the band, is your pal Peterson!'

It was at that moment that the telephone bell rang, and after a slight hesitation Hugh picked up the receiver.

'Very well,' he grunted, after listening for a while, 'I will tell him.'

He replaced the receiver and turned to the American.

'Mr Ditchling will be here for the meeting at two, and Peterson will be late,' he announced slowly.

'What's Ditchling when he's at home?' asked the other.

'One of the so-called leaders,' answered Hugh briefly, turning over the pages of the ledger. 'Here's his dossier, according to Peterson. "Ditchling, Charles. Good speaker; clever; unscrupulous. Requires big money; worth it. Drinks." '

For a while they stared at the brief summary, and then the American burst into a guffaw of laughter.

'The mistake you've made, Captain, in this country is not giving Peterson a seat in your Cabinet. He'd have the whole caboose eating out of his hand; and if you paid him a few hundred thousand a year, he might run straight and grow pigs as a hobby . . . '

2

It was a couple of hours later that Hugh rang up his rooms in Half Moon Street. From Algy, who spoke to him, he gathered that Phyllis and her father were quite safe, though the latter was suffering in the manner common to the morning after. But he also found out another thing – that Ted Jerningham had just arrived with the hapless Potts in tow, who was apparently sufficiently recovered to talk sense. He was weak still and dazed, but no longer imbecile.

'Tell Ted to bring him down to The Elms at once,' ordered Hugh. 'There's a compatriot of his here, waiting to welcome him with open arms.'

'Potts is coming, Mr Green,' he said, putting down the receiver. 'Our Hiram C. And he's talking sense. It seems to me that we may get a little light thrown on the activities of Mr Hocking and Herr Steinemann, and the other bloke.'

The American nodded slowly.

'Von Gratz,' he said. 'I remember his name now. Steel man. Maybe you're right, Captain, and that he knows something; anyway, I guess Hiram C. Potts and I stick closer than brothers till I restore him to the bosom of his family.'

But Mr Potts, when he did arrive, exhibited no great inclination to stick close to the detective; in fact, he showed the greatest reluctance to enter the house at all. As Algy had said, he was still weak and dazed, and the sight of the place where he had suffered so much produced such an effect on him that for a while Hugh feared he was going to have a relapse. At length, however, he seemed to get back his confidence, and was persuaded to come into the central room.

'It's all right, Mr Potts,' Drummond assured him over and over again. 'Their gang is dispersed, and Lakington is dead. We're all friends here now. You're quite safe. This is Mr Green, who has come over from New York especially to find you and take you back to your family.'

The millionaire stared in silence at the detective, who rolled his cigar round in his mouth.

'That's right, Mr Potts. There's the little old sign.' He threw back his coat, showing the police badge, and the millionaire nodded. 'I guess you've had things humming on the other side, and if it hadn't been for the Captain here and his friends they'd be humming still.'

'I am obliged to you, sir,' said the American, speaking for the first time to Hugh. The words were slow and hesitating, as if he was not quite sure of his speech. 'I seem to remember your face,' he continued, 'as part of the awful nightmare I've suffered the last few days – or is it weeks? I seem to remember having seen you, and you were always kind.'

'That's all over now, Mr Potts,' said Hugh gently. 'You got into the clutches of the most infernal gang of swine, and we've been trying to get you out again.' He looked at him quietly. 'Do you think you can remember enough to tell us what happened at the beginning? Take your time,' he urged. 'There's no hurry.'

The others drew nearer eagerly, and the millionaire passed his hand dazedly over his forehead.

'I was stopping at the Carlton,' he began, 'with Granger, my secretary. I sent him over to Belfast on a shipping deal and – ' He paused and looked round the group. 'Where is Granger?' he asked.

'Mr Granger was murdered in Belfast, Mr Potts,' said Drummond quietly, 'by a member of the gang that kidnapped you.'

'Murdered! Jimmy Granger murdered!' He almost cried in his weakness. 'What did the swine want to murder him for?'

'Because they wanted you alone,' explained Hugh. 'Private secretaries ask awkward questions.'

After a while the millionaire recovered his composure, and with many breaks and pauses the slow, disjointed story continued.

'Lakington! That was the name of the man I met at the Carlton. And then there was another . . . Peter . . . Peterson. That's it. We all dined together, I remember, and it was after dinner, in my private sitting-room, that Peterson put up his proposition to me . . . It was a suggestion that he thought would appeal to me as a businessman.

He said – what was it? – that he could produce a gigantic syndic-alist strike in England – revolution, in fact; and that as one of the biggest shipowners – the biggest, in fact – outside this country, I should be able to capture a lot of the British carrying trade. He wanted two hundred and fifty thousand pounds to do it, paid one month after the result was obtained . . . Said there were others in it . . . '

'On that valuation,' interrupted the detective thoughtfully, 'it makes one million pounds sterling,' and Drummond nodded. 'Yes, Mr Potts; and then?'

'I told him,' said the millionaire, 'that he was an infernal scoundrel, and that I'd have nothing whatever to do with such a villainous scheme. And then – almost the last thing I can remember – I saw Peterson look at Lakington. Then they both sprang on me, and I felt something prick my arm. And after that I can't remember anything clearly. Your face, sir' – he turned to Drummond – 'comes to me out of a kind of dream; and yours, too,' he added to Darrell. 'But it was like a long, dreadful nightmare, in which vague things, over which I had no power, kept happening, until I woke up late last night in this gentleman's house.' He bowed to Ted Jerningham, who grinned cheerfully.

'And mighty glad I was to hear you talking sense again, sir,' he remarked. 'Do you mean to say you have no recollection of how you got there?'

'None, sir; none,' answered the millionaire. 'It was just part of the dream.'

'It shows the strength of the drug those swine used on you,' said Drummond grimly. 'You went there in an aeroplane, Mr Potts.'

'An aeroplane!' cried the other in amazement. 'I don't remember it. I've got no recollection of it whatever. There's only one other thing that I can lay hold of, and that's all dim and muzzy . . . Pearls . . . A great rope of pearls . . . I was to sign a paper; and I wouldn't . . . I did once, and then there was a shot, and the light went out, and the paper disappeared . . . '

'It's at my bank at this moment, Mr Potts,' said Hugh; 'I took that paper, or part of it, that night.'

'Did you?' The millionaire looked at him vaguely. 'It was to pro-mise them a million dollars when they had done what they said . . . I remember that . . . And the pearl necklace . . . The Duchess of . . . ' He paused and shook his head wearily.

'The Duchess of Lampshire's?' prompted Hugh.

'That's it,' said the other. 'The Duchess of Lampshire's. It was saying that I wanted her pearls, I think, and would ask no questions as to how they were got.'

The detective grunted.

'Wanted to incriminate you properly, did they? Though it seems to me that it was a blamed risky game. There should have been enough money from the other three to run the show without worrying you, when they found you weren't for it.'

'Wait,' said the millionaire, 'that reminds me. Before they assaulted me at the Carlton, they told me the others wouldn't come in unless I did.'

For a while there was silence, broken at length by Hugh.

'Well, Mr Potts, you've had a mouldy time, and I'm very glad it's over. But the person you've got to thank for putting us fellows on to your track is a girl. If it hadn't been for her, I'm afraid you'd still be having nightmares.'

'I would like to see her and thank her,' said the millionaire quickly.

'You shall,' grinned Hugh. 'Come to the wedding; it will be in a fortnight or thereabouts.'

'Wedding!' Mr Potts looked a little vague.

'Yes! Mine and hers. Ghastly proposition, isn't it?'

'The last straw,' remarked Ted Jerningham. 'A more impossible man as a bridegroom would be hard to think of. But in the meantime I pinched half a dozen of the old man's Perrier Jouet 1911 and put 'em in the car. What say you?'

'Say!' snorted Hugh. 'Idiot boy! Does one speak on such occasions?'

And it was so . . .

3

'What's troubling me,' remarked Hugh later, 'is what to do with Carl and that sweet girl Irma.'

The hour for the meeting was drawing near, and though no-one had any idea as to what sort of a meeting it was going to be, it was obvious that Peterson would be one of the happy throng.

'I should say the police might now be allowed a look in,' murmured Darrell mildly. 'You can't have the man lying about the place after you're married.'

'I suppose not,' answered Drummond regretfully. 'And yet it's a dreadful thing to finish a little show like this with the police – if you'll forgive my saying so, Mr Green.'

'Sure thing,' drawled the American. 'But we have our uses, Captain, and I'm inclined to agree with your friend's suggestion. Hand him over along with his book, and they'll sweep up the mess.'

'It would be an outrage to let the scoundrel go,' said the millionaire fiercely. 'The man Lakington you say is dead; there's enough evidence to hang this brute as well. What about my secretary in Belfast?'

But Drummond shook his head.

'I have my doubts, Mr Potts, if you'd be able to bring that home to him. Still, I can quite understand your feeling rattled with the bird.' He rose and stretched himself; then he glanced at his watch. 'It's time you all retired, boys; the party ought to be starting soon. Drift in again with the lads, the instant I ring the bell.'

Left alone, Hugh made certain once again that he knew the right combination of studs on the wall to open the big door which concealed the stolen store of treasure – and other things as well; then, lighting a cigarette, he sat down and waited.

The end of the chase was in sight, and he had determined it should be a fitting end, worthy of the chase itself – theatrical, perhaps, but at the same time impressive. Something for the Ditchlings of the party to ponder on in the silent watches of the night . . . Then the police – it would have to be the police, he admitted sorrowfully – and after that, Phyllis.

And he was just on the point of ringing up his flat to tell her that he loved her, when the door opened and a man came in. Hugh recognised him at once as Vallance Nestor, an author of great brilliance – in his own eyes – who had lately devoted himself to the advancement of revolutionary labour.

'Good afternoon,' murmured Drummond affably. 'Mr Peterson will be a little late. I am his private secretary.'

The other nodded and sat down languidly.

'What did you think of my last little effort in the Midlands?' he asked, drawing off his gloves.

'Quite wonderful,' said Hugh. 'A marvellous help to the great Cause.'

Vallance Nestor yawned slightly and closed his eyes, only to open them again as Hugh turned the pages of the ledger on the table.

'What's that?' he demanded.

'This is the book,' replied Drummond carelessly, 'where Mr Peterson records his opinions of the immense value of all his fellow-workers. Most interesting reading.'

'Am I in it?' Vallance Nestor rose with alacrity.

'Why, of course,' answered Drummond. 'Are you not one of the leaders? Here you are.' He pointed with his finger, and then drew back in dismay. 'Dear, dear! There must be some mistake.'

But Vallance Nestor, with a frozen and glassy eye, was staring fascinated at the following choice description of himself: 'Nestor, Vallance. Author – so-called. Hot-air factory, but useful up to a point. Inordinately conceited and a monumental ass. Not fit to be trusted far.'

'What,' he spluttered at length, 'is the meaning of this abominable insult?'

But Hugh, his shoulders shaking slightly, was welcoming the next arrival – a rugged, beetle-browed man, whose face seemed vaguely familiar, but whose name he was unable to place.

'Crofter,' shouted the infuriated author, 'look at this as a description of me.'

And Hugh watched the man, whom he now knew to be one of the extremist members of Parliament, walk over and glance at the book. He saw him conceal a smile, and then Vallance Nestor carried the good work on.

'We'll see what he says about you – impertinent blackguard.'

Rapidly he turned the pages, and Hugh glanced over Crofter's shoulder at the dossier.

He just had time to read: 'Crofter, John. A consummate blackguard. Playing entirely for his own hand. Needs careful watching,' when the subject of the remarks, his face convulsed with fury, spun round and faced him. 'Who wrote that?' he snarled.

'Must have been Mr Peterson,' answered Hugh placidly. 'I see you had five thousand out of him, so perhaps he considers himself privileged. A wonderful judge of character, too,' he murmured, turning away to greet Mr Ditchling, who arrived somewhat opportunely, in company with a thin pale man – little more than a youth – whose identity completely defeated Drummond.

'My God!' Crofter was livid with rage. 'Me and Peterson will have words this afternoon. Look at this, Ditchling.' On second thoughts he turned over some pages. 'We'll see what this insolent devil has to say about you.'

'Drinks!' Ditchling thumped the table with a heavy fist. 'What the hell does he mean? Say you, Mr Secretary – what's the meaning of this?'

'They represent Mr Peterson's considered opinions of you all,' said Hugh genially. 'Perhaps this other gentleman . . .'

He turned to the pale youth, who stepped forward with a surprised look. He seemed to be not quite clear what had upset the others, but already Nestor had turned up his name.

'Terrance, Victor. A wonderful speaker. Appears really to believe that what he says will benefit the working-man. Consequently very valuable; but indubitably mad.'

'Does he mean to insult us deliberately?' demanded Crofter, his voice still shaking with passion.

'But I don't understand,' said Victor Terrance dazedly. 'Does Mr Peterson not believe in our teachings, too?' He turned slowly and looked at Hugh, who shrugged his shoulders.

'He should be here at any moment,' he answered, and as he spoke the door opened and Carl Peterson came in.

'Good afternoon, gentlemen,' he began, and then he saw Hugh. With a look of speechless amazement he stared at the soldier, and for the first time since Hugh had known him his face blanched. Then his eyes fell on the open ledger, and with a dreadful curse he sprang forward. A glance at the faces of the men who stood watching him told him what he wanted to know, and with another oath his hand went to his pocket.

'Take your hand out, Carl Peterson.' Drummond's voice rang through the room, and the arch-criminal, looking sullenly up, found himself staring into the muzzle of a revolver. 'Now, sit down at the table – all of you. The meeting is about to commence.'

'Look here,' blustered Crofter, 'I'll have the law on you . . .'

'By all manner of means, Mr John Crofter, consummate blackguard,' answered Hugh calmly. 'But that comes afterwards. Just now – sit down.'

'I'm damned if I will,' roared the other, springing at the soldier. And Peterson, sitting sullenly at the table trying to readjust his thoughts to the sudden blinding certainty that through some extraordinary accident everything had miscarried, never stirred as a half-stunned Member of Parliament crashed to the floor beside him.

'Sit down, I said,' remarked Drummond affably. 'But if you prefer to lie down, it's all the same to me. Are there any more to come, Peterson?'

'No, damn you. Get it over!'

'Right. Throw your gun on the floor.' Drummond picked the weapon up and put it in his pocket; then he rang the bell. 'I had hoped,' he murmured, 'for a larger gathering, but one cannot have everything, can one, Mr Monumental Ass?'

But Vallance Nestor was far too frightened to resent the insult; he could only stare foolishly at the soldier, while he plucked at his collar with a shaking hand. Save to Peterson, who understood, if only dimly, what had happened, the thing had come as such a complete surprise that even the sudden entrance of twenty masked men, who ranged themselves in single rank behind their chairs, failed to stir the meeting. It seemed merely in keeping with what had gone before.

'I shall not detain you long, gentlemen,' began Hugh suavely. 'Your general appearance and the warmth of the weather have combined to produce in me a desire for sleep. But before I hand you over to the care of the sportsmen who stand so patiently behind you, there are one or two remarks I wish to make. Let me say at once that on the subject of Capital and Labour I am supremely ignorant. You will therefore be spared any dissertation on the subject. But from an exhaustive study of the ledger which now lies upon the table, and a fairly intimate knowledge of its author's movements, I and my friends have been put to the inconvenience of treading on you.

'There are many things, we know, which are wrong in this jolly old country of ours; but given time and the right methods I am sufficiently optimistic to believe that they could be put right. That, however, would not suit your book. You dislike the right method, because it leaves all of you much where you were before. Every single one of you – with the sole possible exception of you, Mr Terrance, and you're mad – is playing with revolution for his own ends: to make money out of it – to gain power . . .

'Let us start with Peterson – your leader. How much did you say he demanded, Mr Potts, as the price of revolution?'

With a strangled cry Peterson sprang up as the American millionaire, removing his mask, stepped forward.

'Two hundred and fifty thousand pounds, you swine, was what you asked me.' The millionaire stood confronting his tormentor, who dropped back in his chair with a groan. 'And when I refused, you tortured me. Look at my thumb.'

With a cry of horror the others sitting at the table looked at the mangled flesh, and then at the man who had done it. This, even to their mind, was going too far.

'Then there was the same sum,' continued Drummond, 'to come from Hocking, the American cotton man – half German by birth; Steinemann, the German coal man; von Gratz, the German steel man. Is that not so, Peterson?' It was an arrow at a venture, but it hit the mark, and Peterson nodded.

'So one million pounds was the stake this benefactor of humanity was playing for,' sneered Drummond. 'One million pounds, as the mere price of a nation's life-blood . . . But at any rate he had the merit of playing big, whereas the rest of you scum, and the other beauties so ably catalogued in that book, messed about at his beck and call for packets of bull's-eyes. Perhaps you laboured under the delusion that you were fooling him, but the whole lot of you are so damned crooked that you probably thought of nothing but your own filthy skins.

'Listen to me.' Hugh Drummond's voice took on a deep, commanding ring, and against their will the four men looked at the broad, powerful soldier, whose sincerity shone clear in his face. 'Not by revolutions and direct action will you make this island of ours right – though I am fully aware that that is the last thing you would wish to see happen. But with your brains, and for your own unscrupulous ends, you gull the working-man into believing it. And he, because you can talk with your tongues in your cheeks, is led away. He believes you will give him Utopia; whereas, in reality, you are leading him to hell. And you know it. Evolution is our only chance – not revolution; but you, and others like you, stand to gain more by the latter . . . '

His hand dropped to his side, and he grinned.

'Quite a break for me,' he remarked. 'I'm getting hoarse. I'm now going to hand you four over to the boys. There's an admirable, but somewhat muddy pond outside, and I'm sure you'd like to look for newts. If any of you want to summon me for assault and battery, my name is Drummond – Captain Drummond, of Half Moon Street. But I warn you that that book will be handed in to Scotland Yard tonight. Out with 'em, boys, and give 'em hell . . .

'And now, Carl Peterson,' he remarked, as the door closed behind the last of the struggling prophets of a new world, 'it's time that you and I settled our little account, isn't it?'

The master-criminal rose and stood facing him. Apparently he had completely recovered himself; the hand with which he lit his cigar was as steady as a rock.

'I congratulate you, Captain Drummond,' he remarked suavely. 'I confess I have no idea how you managed to escape from the somewhat cramped position I left you in last night, or how you have managed to install your own men in this house. But I have even less idea how you discovered about Hocking and the other two.'

Hugh laughed shortly.

'Another time, when you disguise yourself as the Comte de Guy, remember one thing, Carl. For effective concealment it is necessary to change other things beside your face and figure. You must change your mannerisms and unconscious little tricks. No – I won't tell you what it is that gave you away. You can ponder over it in prison.'

'So you mean to hand me over to the police, do you?' said Peterson slowly.

'I see no other course open to me,' replied Drummond. 'It will be quite a *cause célèbre*, and ought to do a lot to edify the public.'

The sudden opening of the door made both men look round. Then Drummond bowed, to conceal a smile.

'Just in time, Miss Irma,' he remarked, 'for settling day.'

The girl swept past him and confronted Peterson.

'What has happened?' she panted. 'The garden is full of people whom I've never seen. And there were two men running down the drive covered with weeds and dripping with water.'

Peterson smiled grimly.

'A slight setback has occurred, my dear. I have made a big mistake – a mistake which has proved fatal. I have underestimated the ability of Captain Drummond; and as long as I live I shall always regret that I did not kill him the night he went exploring in this house.'

Fearfully the girl faced Drummond; then she turned again to Peterson. 'Where's Henry?' she demanded.

'That again is a point on which I am profoundly ignorant,' answered Peterson. 'Perhaps Captain Drummond can enlighten us on that also?'

'Yes,' remarked Drummond, 'I can. Henry has had an accident. After I drove him back from the Duchess's last night' – the girl gave a cry, and Peterson steadied her with his arm – 'we had words – dreadful words. And for a long time, Carl, I thought it would be better if you and I had similar words. In fact, I'm not sure even now that it wouldn't be safer in the long run . . . '

'But where is he?' said the girl, through dry lips.

'Where you ought to be, Carl,' answered Hugh grimly. 'Where, sooner or later, you will be.'

He pressed the studs in the niche of the wall, and the door of the big safe swung open slowly. With a scream of terror the girl sank half-fainting on the floor, and even Peterson's cigar dropped on the floor from his nerveless lips. For, hung from the ceiling by two ropes attached to his arms, was the dead body of Henry Lakington. And even as they watched it, it sagged lower, and one of the feet hit sullenly against a beautiful old gold vase . . .

'My God!' muttered Peterson. 'Did you murder him?'

'Oh, no!' answered Drummond. 'He inadvertently fell in the bath he got ready for me, and then when he ran up the stairs in considerable pain, that interesting mechanical device broke his neck.'

'Shut the door,' screamed the girl; 'I can't stand it.'

She covered her face with her hands, shuddering, while the door slowly swung to again.

'Yes,' remarked Drummond thoughtfully, 'it should be an interesting trial. I shall have such a lot to tell them about the little entertainments here, and all your endearing ways.'

With the big ledger under his arm he crossed the room, and called to some men who were standing outside in the hall; and as the detectives, thoughtfully supplied by Mr Green, entered the central room, he glanced for the last time at Carl Peterson and his daughter. Never had the cigar glowed more evenly between the master-criminal's lips; never had the girl Irma selected a cigarette from her gold and tortoiseshell case with more supreme indifference.

'Goodbye, my ugly one!' she cried, with a charming smile, as two of the men stepped up to her.

'Goodbye,' Hugh bowed, and a tinge of regret showed for a moment in his eyes.

'Not goodbye, Irma.' Carl Peterson removed his cigar, and stared at Drummond steadily. 'Only *au revoir*, my friend; only *au revoir*.'

Epilogue

'I simply can't believe it, Hugh.' In the lengthening shadows Phyllis moved a little nearer to her husband, who, quite regardless of the publicity of their position, slipped an arm round her waist.

'Can't believe what, darling?' he demanded lazily.

'Why, that all that awful nightmare is over. Lakington dead, and the other two in prison, and us married.'

'They're not actually in jug yet, old thing,' said Hugh. 'And some-how . . . ' he broke off and stared thoughtfully at a man sauntering past them. To all appearances he was a casual visitor taking his evening walk along the front of the well-known seaside resort so largely addicted to honeymoon couples. And yet . . . . was he? Hugh laughed softly; he'd got suspicion on the brain.

'Don't you think they'll be sent to prison?' cried the girl.

'They may be sent right enough, but whether they arrive or not is a different matter. I don't somehow see Carl picking oakum. It's not his form.'

For a while they were silent, occupied with matters quite foreign to such trifles as Peterson and his daughter.

'Are you glad I answered your advertisement? ' inquired Phyllis at length.

'The question is too frivolous to deserve an answer,' remarked her husband severely.

'But you aren't sorry it's over?' she demanded.

'It isn't over, kid; it's just begun.' He smiled at her tenderly. 'Your life and mine. . .isn't it just wonderful?'

And once again the man sauntered past them. But this time he dropped a piece of paper on the path, just at Hugh's feet, and the soldier, with a quick movement which he hardly stopped to analyse, covered it with his shoe. The girl hadn't seen the action; but then, as girls will do after such remarks, she was thinking of other things. Idly Hugh watched the saunterer disappear in the more crowded part of the esplanade, and for a moment there came on to his face a look which, happily for his wife's peace of mind, she failed to notice.

With a happy sigh she rose. It *was* just wonderful! And together they strolled back to their hotel. In his pocket was the piece of paper; and who could be sending him messages in such a manner save one man – a man now awaiting his trial?

In the hall he stayed behind to inquire for letters, and a man nodded to him.

'Heard the news ?' he inquired.

'No,' said Hugh. 'What's happened ?'

'That man Peterson and the girl have got away. No trace of 'em.' Then he looked at Drummond curiously. 'By the way, you had something to do with that show, didn't you?'

'A little,' smiled Hugh. 'Just a little.'

'Police bound to catch 'em again,' continued the other. 'Can't hide yourself these days.'

And once again Hugh smiled, as he drew from his pocket the piece of paper:

'Only *au revoir*, my friend; only *au revoir*.'

He glanced at the words written in Peterson's neat writing, and the smile broadened. Assuredly life was still good; assuredly . . .

'Are you ready for dinner, darling?' Quickly he swung round, and looked at the sweet face of his wife.

'Sure thing, kid,' he grinned. 'Dead sure; I've had the best appetiser the old pot-house can produce.'

'Well, you're very greedy. Where's mine?'

'Effects of bachelordom, old thing. For the moment I forgot you. I'll have another. Waiter – two Martinis.'

And into an ash-tray near by, he dropped a piece of paper torn into a hundred tiny fragments.

'Was that a love-letter?' she demanded with assumed jealousy.

'Not exactly, sweetheart,' he laughed back. 'Not exactly.' And over the glasses their eyes met. 'Here's to hoping, kid; here's to hoping.'

THE END

THE BLACK GANG

Chapter 1

In which things happen near Barking Creek

The wind howled dismally round a house standing by itself almost on the shores of Barking Creek. It was the grey dusk of an early autumn day, and the occasional harsh cry of a seagull rising discordantly above the wind alone broke the silence of the flat, desolate waste.

The house seemed deserted. Every window was shuttered; the garden was uncared for and a mass of weeds; the gate leading on to the road, apparently feeling the need of a deficient top hinge, propped itself drunkenly on what once had been a flower-bed. A few gloomy trees swaying dismally in the wind surrounded the house and completed the picture – one that would have caused even the least imaginative of men to draw his coat a little tighter round him, and feel thankful that it was not his fate to live in such a place.

But then few people ever came near enough to the house to realise its sinister appearance. The road – it was little better than a cart-track – which passed the gate, was out of the beaten way; only an occasional fisherman or farm labourer ever used it, and that generally by day when things assumed their proper proportion, and it was merely an empty house gradually falling to pieces through lack of attention. At night they avoided it if possible; folks did say that twelve years ago some prying explorer had found the bones of a skeleton lying on the floor in one of the upstairs rooms with a mildewed rope fixed to one of the beams in the ceiling. And then it had been empty for twenty years.

Even now when the wind lay in the east or north-east and the tide was setting in, there were those who said that you could see a light shining through the cracks in the shutters in that room upstairs, and that, should a man climb up and look in, he'd see no skeleton, but a body with purple face and staring eyes swinging gently to and fro, and tied by the neck to a beam with a rope which showed no trace of mildew. Ridiculous, of course; but then so many of these local superstitions are. Useful, too, in some cases; they afford a privacy from the prying attentions of local gossips far more cheaply and effectively than high walls and bolts and bars.

So, at any rate, one of the two men who were walking briskly along the rough track seemed to think.

'Admirable,' he remarked, as he paused for a moment at the entrance of the weed-grown drive. 'Quite admirable, my friend. A house situated as this one is, is an acquisition, and when it is haunted in addition it becomes a godsend.'

He spoke English perfectly with a slight foreign accent, and his companion nodded abruptly.

'From what I heard about it I thought it would do,' he answered. 'Personally I think it's a damnable spot, but since you were so set against coming to London, I had to find somewhere in this neighbourhood.'

The two men started to walk slowly up the drive. Branches dripping with moisture brushed across their faces, and involuntarily they both turned up the collars of their coats.

'I will explain my reasons in due course,' said the first speaker shortly. 'You may take it from me that they were good. What's that?'

He swung round with a little gasp, clutching his companion's arm.

'Nothing,' cried the other irritably. For a moment or two they stood still, peering into the dark undergrowth. 'What did you think it was?'

'I thought I heard a bush creaking as if – as if someone was moving,' he said, relaxing his grip. 'It must have been the wind, I suppose.'

He still peered fearfully into the gloomy garden, until the other man dragged him roughly towards the house.

'Of course it was the wind,' he muttered angrily. 'For heaven's sake, Zaboleff, don't get the jumps. If you will insist on coming to an infernal place like this to transact a little perfectly normal business you must expect a few strange noises and sounds. Let's get indoors; the others should be here by now. It oughtn't to take more than an hour, and you can be on board again long before dawn.'

The man who had been addressed as Zaboleff ceased looking over his shoulder, and followed the other through a broken-down lattice-gate to the rear of the house. They paused in front of the back door, and on it the leader knocked three times in a peculiar way. It was obviously a prearranged signal, for almost at once stealthy steps could be heard coming along the passage inside. The door was cautiously pulled back a few inches, and a man peered out, only to throw it open wide with a faint sigh of relief.

'It's you, Mr Waldock, is it?' he muttered. 'Glad you've got 'ere at last. This place is fair giving us all the 'ump.'

'Evening, Jim.' He stepped inside, followed by Zaboleff, and the door closed behind them. 'Our friend's boat was a little late. Is everyone here?'

'Yep,' answered the other. 'All the six of us. And I reckons we'd like to get it over as soon as possible. Has he' – his voice sank to a hoarse undertone – 'has he brought the money?'

'You'll all hear in good time,' said Waldock curtly. 'Which is the room?'

''Ere it is, guv'nor.' Jim flung open a door. 'And you'll 'ave to sit on the floor, as the chairs ain't safe.'

Two candles guttered on a square table in the centre of the room, showing up the faces of the five men who sat on the floor, leaning against the walls. Three of them were nondescript specimens of humanity of the type that may be seen by the thousand hurrying into the City by the early business trains. They were representative of the poorer type of clerk – the type which Woodbines its fingers to a brilliant orange; the type that screams insults at a football referee on Saturday afternoon. And yet to the close observer something more might be read on their faces: a greedy, hungry look, a shifty untrustworthy look – the look of those who are jealous of everyone better placed than themselves, but who are incapable of trying to better their own position except by the relative method of dragging back their more fortunate acquaintances; the look of little men dissatisfied not so much with their own littleness as with the bigness of other people. A nasty-faced trio with that smattering of education which is the truly dangerous thing; and – three of Mr Waldock's clerks.

The two others were Jews; a little flashily dressed, distinctly addicted to cheap jewellery. They were sitting apart from the other three, talking in low tones, but as the door opened their conversation ceased abruptly and they looked up at the newcomers with the keen, searching look of their race. Waldock they hardly glanced at; it was the stranger Zaboleff who riveted their attention. They took in every detail of the shrewd, foreign face – the olive skin, the dark, piercing eyes, the fine-pointed beard; they measured him up as a boxer measures up his opponent, or a businessman takes stock of the second party in a deal; then once again they conversed together in low tones which were barely above a whisper.

It was Jim who broke the silence – Flash Jim, to give him the full name to which he answered in the haunts he frequented.

'Wot abaht getting on with it, guv'nor?' he remarked with an attempt at a genial smile. 'This 'ere 'ouse ain't wot I'd choose for a blooming 'oneymoon.'

With an abrupt gesture Waldock silenced him and advanced to the table.

'This is Mr Zaboleff, gentlemen,' he said quietly. 'We are a little late, I am afraid, but it was unavoidable. He will explain to you now the reason why you were asked to come here, and not meet at our usual rendezvous in Soho.'

He stepped back a couple of paces and Zaboleff took his place. For a moment or two he glanced round at the faces turned expectantly towards him; then resting his two hands on the table in front of him, he leaned forward towards them.

'Gentlemen,' he began, and the foreign accent seemed a little more pronounced, 'I have asked you to come here tonight through my good friend, Mr Waldock, because it has come to our ears – no matter how – that London is no longer a safe meeting-place. Two or three things have occurred lately the significance of which it is impossible to disregard.'

'Wot sort of things?' interrupted Flash Jim harshly.

'I was about to tell you,' remarked the speaker suavely, and Flash Jim subsided, abashed. 'Our chief, with whom I spent last evening, is seriously concerned about these things.'

'You spent last night with the chief?' said Waldock, and his voice held a tremor of excitement, while the others leaned forward eagerly. 'Is he, then, in Holland?'

'He was at six o'clock yesterday evening,' answered Zaboleff with a faint smile. 'Today – now – I know no more than you where he is.'

'Who is he – this man we're always hearing about and never seeing?' demanded one of the three clerks aggressively.

'He is – the Chief,' replied the other, while his eyes seemed to bore into the speaker's brain. 'Just that – and no more. And that is quite enough for you.' His glance travelled round the room, and his audience relaxed. 'By the way, is not that a chink in the shutter there?'

'All the safer,' grunted Flash Jim. 'Anyone passing will think the ghost is walking.'

'Nevertheless, kindly cover it up,' ordered Zaboleff, and one of the Jews rose and wedged his pocket-handkerchief into the crack. There was silence in the room while he did so, a silence broken only by the mournful hooting of an owl outside.

'Owls is the only things wot comes to this damned museum,' said Flash Jim morosely. 'Owls and blinkin' fools like us.'

'Stow it, Jim,' snarled Waldock furiously. 'Anyone would think you wanted a nurse.'

'Gentlemen – please.' Zaboleff held up a protesting hand. 'We do not want to prolong matters, but one or two explanations are necessary. To return, then, to these things that have happened recently, and which necessitated a fresh rendezvous for this evening – one which our friend Mr Waldock so obligingly found. Three messengers sent over during the last three weeks bearing instructions and – what is more important – money, have disappeared.'

'Disappeared?' echoed Waldock stupidly.

'Absolutely and completely. Money and all. Two more have been abominably ill-treated and had their money taken from them, but for some reason they were allowed to go free themselves. It is from them that we have obtained our information.'

'Blimey!' muttered Flash Jim; 'is it the police?'

'It is not the police, which is what makes it so much more serious,' answered Zaboleff quietly, and Flash Jim breathed a sigh of relief. 'It is easy to keep within the law, but if our information is correct we are up against a body of men who are not within the law themselves. A body of men who are absolutely unscrupulous and utterly ruthless; a body of men who appear to know our secret plans as well as we do ourselves. And the difficulty of it is, gentlemen, that though, legally speaking, on account of the absurd legislation in this country we may keep within the law ourselves, we are hardly in a position to appeal to the police for protection. Our activities, though allowed officially, are hardly such as would appeal even to the English authorities. And on this occasion particularly that is the case. You may remember that the part I played in stirring up bloodshed at Cowdenbeath a few months ago, under the name of MacTavish, caused me to be deported. So though our cause is legal – my presence in this country is not. Which was why tonight it was particularly essential that we should not be disturbed. Not only are we all up against this unknown gang of men, but I, in addition, am up against the police.'

'Have you any information with regard to this gang?' It was the Jew who had closed the chink in the shutters speaking for the first time.

'None of any use – save that they are masked in black, and cloaked in long black cloaks.' He paused a moment as if to collect his thoughts. 'They are all armed, and Petrovitch – he was one of the men allowed to escape – was very insistent on one point. It concerned the leader of the gang, whom he affirmed was a man of the most gigantic physical strength; a giant powerful as two ordinary strong men. He said . . . Ah! Mein Gott – !'

His voice rose to a scream as he cowered back, while the others, with terror on their faces, rose hurriedly from their seats on the floor and huddled together in the corners of the room.

In the doorway stood a huge man covered from head to foot in black. In each hand he held a revolver, with which he covered the eight occupants during the second or two which it took for half a dozen similarly disguised men to file past him, and take up their positions round the walls. And Waldock, a little more educated than the remainder of his friends, found himself thinking of old tales of the Spanish Inquisition and the Doges of Venice even as he huddled a little nearer to the table.

'Stand by the table, all of you.'

It was the man at the door who spoke in a curiously deep voice, and like sheep they obeyed him – all save Flash Jim. For that worthy, crook though he was, was not without physical courage. The police he knew better than to play the fool with, but these were not the police.

'Wot the – ' he snarled, and got no farther. Something hit him behind the head, a thousand stars danced before his eyes, and with a strangled grunt he crashed forward on his face.

For a moment or two there was silence, and then once again the man at the door spoke.

'Arrange the specimens in a row.'

In a second the seven remaining men were marshalled in a line, while behind them stood six motionless black figures. And then the big man walked slowly down in front of them, peering into each man's face. He spoke no word until he reached the end of the line, and then, his inspection concluded, he stepped back and leaned against the wall facing them.

'A nauseating collection,' he remarked thoughtfully. 'A loathsome brood. What are the three undersized and shivering insects on the right?'

'Those are three of my clerks,' said Waldock with an assumption of angry bravado. 'And I would like to know – '

'In good time you will,' answered the deep voice. 'Three of your clerks, are they; imbued with your rotten ideas, I suppose, and yearning to follow in father's footsteps? Have we anything part-icular against them?'

There was no answer from the masked men, and the leader made a sign. Instantly the three terrified clerks were seized from behind and brought up to him, where they stood trembling and shaking in every limb.

'Listen to me, you three little worms.' With an effort they pulled themselves together: a ray of hope was dawning in their minds – perhaps they were going to be let off easily. 'My friends and I do not like you or your type. You meet in secret places and in your slimy minds you concoct foul schemes which, incredible though it may seem, have so far had more than a fair measure of success in this country. But your main idea is not the schemes, but the money you are paid to carry them out. This is your first and last warning. Another time you will be treated differently. Get out of here. And see you don't stop.'

The door closed behind them and two of the masked men; there was the sound as of a boot being used with skill and strength, and cries of pain; then the door reopened and the masked men re-turned.

'They have gone,' announced one of them. 'We helped them on their way.'

'Good,' said the leader. 'Let us continue the inspection. What are these two Hebrews?'

A man from behind stepped forward and examined them slowly; then he came up to the leader and whispered in his ear.

'Is that so?' A new and terrible note had crept into the deep voice. 'My friends and I do not like your trade, you swine. It is well that we have come provided with the necessary implement for such a case. Fetch the cat.'

In silence one of the men left the room, and as his full meaning came home to the two Jews they flung themselves grovelling on the floor, screaming for mercy.

'Gag them.'

The order came out sharp and clear, and in an instant the two writhing men were seized and gagged. Only their rolling eyes and trembling hands showed the terror they felt as they dragged them-selves on their knees towards the impassive leader.

'The cat for cases of this sort is used legally,' he remarked. 'We merely anticipate the law.'

With a fresh outburst of moans the two Jews watched the door open and the inexorable black figure come in, holding in his hand a short stick from which nine lashes hung down.

'Heavens!' gasped Waldock, starting forward. 'What are you going to do?'

'Flog them to within an inch of their lives,' said the deep voice. 'It is the punishment for their method of livelihood. Five and six – take charge. After you have finished remove them in Number 3 car, and drop them in London.'

Struggling impotently, the Jews were led away, and the leader passed on to the remaining two men.

'So, Zaboleff, you came after all. Unwise, surely, in view of the police?'

'Who are you?' muttered Zaboleff, his lips trembling.

'A specimen hunter,' said the other suavely. 'I am making a collection of people like you. The police of our country are unduly kind to your breed, although they would not have been kind to you tonight, Zaboleff, unless I had intervened. But I couldn't let them have you; you're such a very choice specimen. I don't think somehow that you've worked this little flying visit of yours very well. Of course I knew about it, but I must confess I was surprised when I found that the police did too.'

'What do you mean?' demanded the other hoarsely.

'I mean that when we arrived here we found to our surprise that the police had forestalled us. Popular house, this, tonight.'

'The police!' muttered Waldock dazedly.

'Even so – led by no less a personage than Inspector McIver. They had completely surrounded the house, and necessitated a slight change in my plans.'

'Where are they now?' cried Waldock.

'Ah! Where indeed? Let us trust at any rate in comfort.'

'By heaven!' said Zaboleff, taking a step forward. 'As I asked you before – who are you?'

'And as I told you before, Zaboleff, a collector of specimens. Some I keep; some I let go – as you have already seen.'

'And what are you going to do with me?'

'Keep you. Up to date you are the cream of my collection.'

'Are you working with the police?' said the other dazedly.

'Until tonight we have not clashed. Even tonight, well, I think we are working towards the same end. And do you know what that end is, Zaboleff?' The deep voice grew a little sterner. 'It is the utter, final overthrow of you and all that you stand for. To achieve that

object we shall show no mercy. Even as you are working in the dark –
so are we. Already you are frightened; already we have proved that
you fear the unknown more than you fear the police; already the first
few tricks are ours. But you still hold the ace, Zaboleff – or shall we
say the King of Trumps? And when we catch him you will cease to be
the cream of my collection. This leader of yours – it was what
Petrovitch told him, I suppose, that made him send you over.'

'I refuse to say,' said the other.

'You needn't; it is obvious. And now that you are caught – he will
come himself. Perhaps not at once – but he will come. And then . . .
But we waste time. The money, Zaboleff.'

'I have no money,' he snarled.

'You lie, Zaboleff. You lie clumsily. You have quite a lot of money
brought over for Waldock so that he might carry on the good work
after you had sailed tomorrow. Quick, please; time passes.'

With a curse Zaboleff produced a small canvas bag and held it out.
The other took it and glanced inside.

'I see,' he said gravely. 'Pearls and precious stones. Belonging
once, I suppose, to a murdered gentlewoman whose only crime was
that she, through no action of her own, was born in a different sphere
from you. And, you reptile' – his voice rose a little – 'you would do
that here.'

Zaboleff shrank back, and the other laughed contemptuously.

'Search him – and Waldock too.'

Two men stepped forward quickly.

'Nothing more,' they said after a while. 'Except this piece of
paper.'

There was a sudden movement on Zaboleff's part – instantly
suppressed, but not quite soon enough.

'Injudicious,' said the leader quietly. 'Memory is better. An address,
I see – No. 5, Green Street, Hoxton. A salubrious neighbourhood,
with which I am but indifferently acquainted. Ah! I see my violent
friend has recovered.' He glanced at Flash Jim, who was sitting up
dazedly, rubbing the back of his head. 'Number 4 – the usual'.

There was a slight struggle, and Flash Jim lay back peacefully
unconscious, while a faint smell of chloroform filled the room.

'And now I think we will go. A most successful evening.'

'What are you going to do with me, you scoundrel?' spluttered
Waldock. 'I warn you that I have influential friends, who – who will
ask questions in – in Parliament if you do anything to me; who will
go to Scotland Yard.'

'I can assure you, Mr Waldock, that I will make it my personal business to see that their natural curiosity is gratified,' answered the leader suavely. 'But for the present I fear the three filthy rags you edit will have to be content with the office boy as their guiding light. And I venture to think they will not suffer.'

He made a sudden sign, and before they realised what was happening the two men were caught from behind and gagged. The next instant they were rushed through the door, followed by Flash Jim. For a moment or two the eyes of the leader wandered round the now empty room taking in every detail: then he stepped forward and blew out the two candles. The door closed gently behind him, and a couple of minutes later two cars stole quietly away from the broken-down gate along the cart track. It was just midnight; behind them the gloomy house stood up gaunt and forbidding against the darkness of the night sky. And it was not until the leading car turned carefully into the main road that anyone spoke.

'Deuced awkward, the police being there.'

The big man who was driving grunted thoughtfully.

'Perhaps,' he returned. 'Perhaps not. Anyway, the more the merrier. Flash Jim all right?'

'Sleeping like a child,' answered the other, peering into the body of the car.

For about ten miles they drove on in silence: then at a main cross-roads the car pulled up and the big man got out. The second car was just behind, and for a few moments there was a whispered conversation between him and the other driver. He glanced at Zaboleff and Waldock, who appeared to be peacefully sleeping on the back seat, and smiled grimly.

'Good night, old man. Report as usual.'

'Right,' answered the driver. 'So long.'

The second car swung right-handed and started northwards, while the leader stood watching the vanishing tail-lamp. Then he returned to his own seat, and soon the first beginnings of outer London were reached. And it was as they reached Whitechapel that the leader spoke again with a note of suppressed excitement in his voice.

'We're worrying 'em; we're worrying 'em badly. Otherwise they'd never have sent Zaboleff. He was too big a man to risk, considering the police.'

'It's the police that I *am* considering,' said his companion.

The big man laughed.

'Leave that to me, old man; leave that entirely to me.'

Chapter 2

In which Scotland Yard sits up and takes notice

Sir Bryan Johnstone leaned back in his chair and stared at the ceiling with a frown. His hands were thrust deep into his trouser pockets; his long legs were stretched out to their full extent under the big roll-top desk in front of him. From the next room came the monotonous tapping of a typewriter, and after a while Sir Bryan closed his eyes.

Through the open window there came the murmur of the London traffic – that soothing sound so conducive to sleep in those who have lunched well. But that did not apply to the man lying back in his chair. Sir Bryan's lunch was always a frugal meal, and it was no desire for sleep that made the Director of Criminal Investigation close his eyes. He was puzzled, and the report lying on the desk in front of him was the reason.

For perhaps ten minutes he remained motionless, then he leaned forward and touched an electric bell. Instantly the typewriter ceased, and a girl secretary came quickly into the room.

'Miss Forbes,' said Sir Bryan, 'I wish you would find out if Chief Inspector McIver is in the building. If so, I would like to see him at once; if not, see that he gets the message as soon as he comes in.'

The door closed behind the girl, and after a moment or two the man rose from his desk and began to pace up and down the room with long, even strides. Every now and then he would stop and stare at some print on the wall, but it was the blank stare of a man whose mind is engrossed in other matters.

And once while he stood looking out of the window, he voiced his thoughts, unconscious that he spoke aloud.

'Dash it, McIver's not fanciful. He's the least fanciful man we've got. And yet . . . '

His eyes came round to the desk once more, the desk on which the report was lying. It was Inspector McIver's report – hence his instructions to the secretary. It was the report on a very strange matter which had taken place the previous night, and after a while Sir

Bryan picked up the typed sheets and glanced through them again. And he was still standing by the desk, idly turning over the pages, when the secretary came into the room.

'Chief Inspector McIver is here, Sir Bryan,' she announced.

'Tell him to come in, Miss Forbes.'

Certainly the Inspector justified his Chief's spoken thought – a less fanciful looking man it would have been hard to imagine. A square-jawed, rugged Scotchman, he looked the type to whom Holy Writ was Holy Writ only in so far as it could be proved. He was short and thick-set, and his physical strength was proverbial. But a pair of kindly twinkling eyes belied the gruff voice. In fact, the gruff voice was a pose specially put on which deceived no-one; his children all imitated it to his huge content, though he endeavoured to look ferocious when they did so. In short, McIver, though shrewd and relentless when on duty, was the kindest-hearted of men. But he was most certainly not fanciful.

'What the dickens is all this about, McIver?' said Sir Bryan with a smile, when the door had shut behind the secretary.

'I wish I knew myself, sir,' returned the other seriously. 'I've never been so completely defeated in my life.'

Sir Bryan waved him to a chair and sat down at the desk.

'I've read your report,' he said, still smiling, 'and frankly, McIver, if it had been anyone but you, I should have been annoyed. But I know you far too well for that. Look here' – he pushed a box of cigarettes across the table – 'take a cigarette and your time and let's hear about it.'

McIver lit a cigarette and seemed to be marshalling his thoughts. He was a man who liked to tell his story in his own way, and his chief waited patiently till he was ready. He knew that when his subordinate did start he would get a clear, concise account of what had taken place, with everything irrelevant ruthlessly cut out. And if there was one thing that roused Sir Bryan to thoughts of murder and violence, it was a rambling, incoherent statement from one of his men.

'Well, sir,' began McIver at length, 'this is briefly what took place. At ten o'clock last night as we had arranged, we completely surrounded the suspected house on the outskirts of Barking. I had had a couple of good men on duty there lying concealed the whole day, and when I arrived at about nine-thirty with Sergeant Andrews and half a dozen others, they reported to me that at least eight men were inside, and that Zaboleff was one of them. He had been shadowed the whole way down from Limehouse with another man, and both the watchers were positive that he had not left the house. So I posted my men and crept forward to investigate myself. There was a little chink in the wooden shutters of one of the downstairs rooms through which the light was streaming. I took a glimpse through, and found that everything was just as had been reported to me. There were eight of them there, and an unpleasant-looking bunch they were, too. Zaboleff I saw at the head of the table, and standing next to him was that man Waldock who runs two or three of the worst Red papers. There was also Flash Jim, and I began to wish I'd brought a few more men.'

McIver smiled ruefully. 'It was about the last coherent wish I remember. And,' he went on seriously, 'what I'm going to tell you now, sir, may seem extraordinary and what one would expect in detective fiction, but as sure as I am sitting in this chair, it is what actually took place. Somewhere from close to, there came the sound of an owl hooting. At that same moment I distinctly heard the noise of what seemed like a scuffle, and a stifled curse. And then, and this is what beats me, sir.' McIver pounded a huge fist into an equally huge palm. 'I was picked up from behind as if I were a baby. Yes, sir, a baby.'

Involuntarily Sir Bryan smiled.

'You make a good substantial infant, McIver.'

'Exactly, sir,' grunted the Inspector. 'If a man had suggested such a thing to me yesterday I'd have laughed in his face. But the fact remains that I was picked up just like a child in arms, and doped, sir, doped. Me – at my time of life. They chloroformed me, and that was the last I saw of Zaboleff or the rest of the gang.'

'Yes, but it's the rest of the report that beats me,' said his chief thoughtfully.

'So it does me, sir,' agreed McIver. 'When I came to myself early this morning I didn't realise where I was. Of course my mind at once went back to the preceding night, and what with feeling sick as the result of the chloroform, and sicker at having been fooled, I wasn't too pleased with myself. And then I rubbed my eyes and pinched myself, and for a moment or two I honestly thought I'd gone off my head. There was I sitting on my own front door step, with a cushion all nicely arranged for my head and every single man I'd taken down with me asleep on the pavement outside. I tell you, sir, I looked at those eight fellows all ranged in a row for about five minutes before my brain began to act. I was simply stupefied. And then I began to feel angry. To be knocked on the head by a crew like Flash Jim might happen to anybody. But to be treated like naughty children and sent home to bed was a bit too much. Dammit, I thought, while they were about it, why didn't they tuck me up with my wife.'

Once again Sir Bryan smiled, but the other was too engrossed to notice.

'It was then I saw the note,' continued McIver. He fumbled in his pocket, and his chief stretched out his hand to see the original. He already knew the contents almost by heart, and the actual note itself threw no additional light on the matter. It was typewritten, and the paper was such as can be bought by the ream at any cheap stationer's.

'To think of an old bird like you, Mac' [it ran] 'going and showing yourself up in a chink of light. You must tell Mrs Mac to get some more cushions. There were only enough in the parlour for you and Andrews. I have taken Zaboleff and Waldock, and I dropped Flash Jim in Piccadilly Circus. I flogged two of the others whose method of livelihood failed to appeal to me; the remaining small fry I turned loose. Cheer oh! old son. The fellow in St. James makes wonderful pick-me-ups for the morning after. Hope I didn't hurt you.'

Idly Sir Bryan studied the note, holding it up to the light to see if there was any watermark on the paper which might help. Then he studied the typed words, and finally with a slight shrug of his shoulders he laid it on the desk in front of him.

'An ordinary Remington, I should think. And as there are several thousands in use it doesn't help much. What about Flash Jim?'

McIver shook his head.

'The first thing I did, sir, was to run him to ground. And I put it across him good and strong. He admitted everything: admitted he was down there, but over the rest of the show he swore by everything that he knew no more than I did. All he could say was that suddenly the room seemed full of men. And the men were all masked. Then he got a clip over the back of the head, and he remembers nothing more till the policeman on duty at Piccadilly Circus woke him with his boot just before dawn this morning.'

'Which fact, of course, you have verified,' said Sir Bryan.

'At once, sir,' answered the other. 'For once in his life Flash Jim appears to be speaking the truth. Which puts a funny complexion on matters, sir, if he is speaking the truth.'

The Inspector leaned forward and stared at his chief.

'You've heard the rumours, sir,' he went on after a moment, 'the same as I have.'

'Perhaps,' said Sir Bryan quietly. 'But go on, McIver. I'd like to hear what's on your mind.'

'It's the Black Gang, sir,' said the Inspector, leaning forward impressively. 'There have been rumours going round, rumours which our men have heard here and there for the past two months. I've heard 'em myself; and once or twice I've wondered. Now I'm sure – especially after what Flash Jim said. That gang is no rumour, it's solid fact.'

'Have you any information as to what their activities have been, assuming for a moment it is the truth?' asked Sir Bryan.

'None for certain, sir; until this moment I wasn't certain of its existence. But now – looking back – there have been quite a number of sudden disappearances. We haven't troubled officially, we haven't been asked to. Hardly likely when one realises who the people are who have disappeared.'

'All conjecture, McIver,' said Sir Bryan. 'They may be lying doggo, or they'll turn up elsewhere.'

'They may be, sir,' answered McIver doggedly. 'But take the complete disappearance of Granger a fortnight ago. He's one of the worst of the Red men, and we know he hasn't left the country. Where is he? His wife, I happen to know, is crazy with anxiety, so it doesn't look like a put-up job. Take that extraordinary case of the Pole who was found lashed to the railings in Whitehall with one half of his beard and hair shaved off and the motto "Portrait of a Bolshevist" painted on his forehead. Well, I don't need to tell you, sir, that that particular Pole, Strambowski, was undoubtedly a messenger between – well, we know who between and what the message was. And then take last night.'

'Well, what about last night?'

'For the first time this gang has come into direct contact with us.'

'Always assuming the fact of its existence.'

'Exactly, sir,' answered McIver. 'Well, they've got Zaboleff and they've got Waldock, and they laid eight of us out to cool. I guess they're not to be sneezed at.'

With a thoughtful look on his face Sir Bryan rose and strolled over to the window. Though not prepared to go quite as far as McIver, there were certainly some peculiar elements in the situation – elements which he, as head of a big public department, could not officially allow for an instant, however much it might amuse him as a private individual.

'We must find Zaboleff and Waldock,' he said curtly, without turning round. 'Waldock, at any rate, has friends who will make a noise unless he's forthcoming. And . . . '

But his further remarks were interrupted by the entrance of his secretary with a note.

'For the Inspector, Sir Bryan,' she said, and McIver, after a glance at his chief, opened the envelope. For a while he studied the letter in silence, then with an enigmatic smile he rose and handed it to the man by the window.

'No answer, thank you, Miss Forbes,' he said, and when they were once more alone, he began rubbing his hands together softly – a sure sign of being excited. 'Curtis and Samuel Bauer, both flogged nearly to death and found in a slum off Whitechapel. The note said two of 'em had been flogged.'

'So,' said Sir Bryan quietly. 'These two were at Barking last night?'

'They were, sir,' answered the Inspector.

'And their line?' queried the Chief.

'White Slave Traffic of the worst type,' said McIver. 'They generally drug the girls with cocaine or some dope first. What do you say to my theory now, sir?'

'It's another point in its favour, McIver,' conceded Sir Bryan cautiously: 'but it still wants a lot more proof. And, anyway, whether you're right or not, we can't allow it to continue. We shall be having questions asked in Parliament.'

McIver nodded portentously. 'If I can't lay my hands on a man who can lift me up like a baby and dope me, may I never have another case. Like a baby, sir. Me – '

He opened his hands out helplessly, and this time Sir Bryan laughed outright, only to turn with a quick frown as the door leading to the secretary's office was flung open to admit a man. He caught a vague glimpse of the scandalised Miss Forbes hovering like a canary eating bird-seed in the background: then he turned to the newcomer.

'Confound it, Hugh,' he cried. 'I'm busy.'

Hugh Drummond grinned all over his face, and lifting a hand like a leg of mutton he smote Sir Bryan in the back, to the outraged amazement of Inspector McIver.

'You priceless old bean,' boomed Hugh affably. 'I gathered from the female bird punching the what-not outside that the great brain was heaving – but, my dear old lad, I have come to report a crime. A crime which I positively saw committed with my own eyes: an outrage: a blot upon this fair land of ours.'

He sank heavily into a chair and selected a cigarette. He was a vast individual with one of those phenomenally ugly faces which is rendered utterly pleasant by the extraordinary charm of its owner's expression. No human being had ever been known to be angry with Hugh for long. He was either moved to laughter by the perennial twinkle in the big man's blue eyes, or he was stunned by a playful blow on the chest from a first which rivalled a steam hammer. Of brain he apparently possessed a minimum: of muscle he possessed about five ordinary men's share.

And yet unlike so many powerful men his quickness on his feet was astounding – as many a good heavyweight boxer had found to his cost. In the days of his youth Hugh Drummond – known more familiarly to his intimates at Bulldog – had been able to do the hundred in a shade over ten seconds. And though the mere thought of such a performance now would have caused him to break out into a cold sweat, he was still quite capable of a turn of speed which many a lighter-built man would have envied.

Between him and Sir Bryan Johnstone existed one of those friend-ships which are founded on totally dissimilar tastes. He had been Bryan Johnstone's fag at school, and for some inscrutable reason the quiet scholarship of the elder boy had appealed to the kid of fourteen who was even then a mass of brawn. And when one day Johnstone, going about his lawful occasions as a prefect, discovered young Drummond reducing a boy two years older than himself to a fair semblance of a jelly, the appeal was reciprocated.

'He called you a scut,' said Drummond a little breathlessly when his lord and master mildly inquired the reason of the disturbance. 'So I scutted him.'

It was only too true, and with a faint smile Johnstone watched the 'scutted' one depart with undignified rapidity. Then he looked at his fag.

'Thank you, Drummond,' he remarked awkwardly.

'Rot. That's all right,' returned the other, blushing uncomfortably.

And that was all. But it started then, and it never died, though their ways lay many poles apart. To Johnstone a well-deserved knight-hood and a high position in the land: to Drummond as much money as he wanted and a life of sport.

'Has someone stolen the goldfish?' queried Sir Bryan with mild sarcasm.

'Great Scott! I hope not,' cried Hugh in alarm. 'Phyllis gave me complete instructions about the brutes before she toddled off. I make a noise like an ant's egg, and drop them in the sink every morning. No, old lad of the village, it is something of vast import: a stain upon the escutcheon of your force. Last night – let us whisper it in Gath – I dined and further supped not wisely but too well. In fact I deeply regret to admit that I became a trifle blotto – not to say tanked. Of course it wouldn't have happened if Phyllis had been propping up the jolly old home, don't you know: but she's away in the country with the nightingales and slugs and things. Well, as I say, in the young hours of the morning I though I'd totter along home. I'd been with some birds – male birds, Tumkins' – he stared sternly at Sir Bryan, while McIver stiffened into rigid horror at such an incredible nickname – 'male birds, playing push-halfpenny or some such game of skill or chance. And when I left it was about two a.m. Well, I wandered along through Leicester Square, and stopped just outside Scott's to let one of those watering carts water my head for me. Deuced considerate driver he was too: stopped his horse for a couple of minutes and let one jet play on me uninterruptedly. Well, as I say, while I was lying in the road, steaming at the brow, a motor-car went past, and it stopped in Piccadilly Circus.'

McIver's air of irritation vanished suddenly, and a quick glance passed between him and Sir Bryan.

'Nothing much you observe in that, Tumkins,' he burbled on, quite unconscious of the sudden attention of his hearers. 'But wait, old lad – I haven't got to the motto yet. From this car there stepped large numbers of men: at least, so it seemed to me, and you must remember I'd recently had a shampoo. And just as I got abreast of them they lifted out another warrior, who appeared to me to be unconscious. At first I thought there were two, until I focused the old optics and found I'd been squinting. They put him on the pavement and got back into the car again just as I tottered alongside.

' "What ho, souls," I murmured, "what is this and that, so to speak?"

' "Binged, old bean, badly binged," said the driver of the car. "We're leaving him there to cool."

'And with that the car drove off. There was I, Tumkins, in a partially binged condition alone in Piccadilly Circus with a bird in a completely binged condition.

' "How now," I said to myself. "Shall I go and induce yon water merchant to return" – as a matter of fact I was beginning to feel I could do with another whack myself – "or shall I leave you here – as your pals observed – to cool?"

'I bent over him as I pondered this knotty point, and as I did so, Tumkins, I became aware of a strange smell.'

Hugh paused dramatically and selected another cigarette, while Sir Bryan flashed a quick glance of warning at McIver, who was obviously bursting with suppressed excitement.

'A peculiar and sickly odour, Tumkins,' resumed the speaker with maddening deliberation. 'A strange and elusive perfume. For a long while it eluded me – that smell: I just couldn't place it. And then suddenly I got it: right in the middle, old boy – plumb in the centre of the windpipe. It was chloroform: the bird wasn't drunk – he was doped.'

Completely exhausted, Hugh lay back in his chair, and once again Sir Bryan flashed a warning glance at his exasperated subordinate.

'Would you be able to recognise any of the men in the car if. You saw them again?' he asked quietly.

'I should know the driver,' answered Hugh after profound thought. 'And the bird beside him. But not the others.'

'Did you take the number of the car?' snapped McIver.

'My dear old man,' murmured Hugh in a pained voice, 'who on earth ever does take the number of a car? Except your warriors, who always get it wrong. Besides, as I tell you, I was partially up the pole.'

'What did you do then?' asked Sir Bryan.

'Well, I brought the brain to bear,' answered Hugh, 'and decided there was nothing to do. He was doped, and I was bottled – so by a unanimous casting vote of one – I toddled off home. But Tumkins, while I was feeding the goldfish this morning – or rather after lunch – conscience was gnawing at my vitals. And after profound meditation, and consulting with my fellow Denny, I decided that the call of duty was clear. I came to you, Tumkins, as a child flies to its mother. Who better, I thought, than old Tum-tum to listen to my maidenly secrets? And so . . . '

'One moment, Hugh,' Sir Bryan held up his hand. 'Do you mind if I speak to Inspector McIver for a moment?'

'Anything you like, old lad,' murmured Drummond. 'But be merciful. Remember my innocent wife in the country.'

And silence settled on the room, broken only by the low-voiced conversation between McIver and his chief in the window. By their gestures it seemed as if Sir Bryan was suggesting something to his subordinate to which that worthy officer was a little loath to agree. And after a while a strangled snore from the chair announced that Drummond was ceasing to take an intelligent interest in things mundane.

'He's an extraordinary fellow, McIver,' said Sir Bryan, glancing at the sleeper with a smile. 'I've known him since we were boys at school. And he's not quite such a fool as he makes himself out. You remember that extraordinary case over the man Peterson a year or so ago. Well, it was he who did the whole thing. His complete disability to be cunning utterly defeated that master-crook, who was always looking for subtlety that wasn't there. And of course his strength is absolutely phenomenal.'

'I know, sir,' said McIver doubtfully, 'but would he consent to take on such a job – and do exactly as he was told?'

They were both looking out of the window, while in the room behind them the heavy breathing of the sleeper rose and fell monotonously. And when the whole audience is asleep it ceases to be necessary to talk in undertones. Which was why Sir Bryan and the Inspector during the next ten minutes discussed certain matters of import which they would not have discussed through megaphones at the Savoy. They concerned Hugh and other things, and the other things particularly were of interest. And they continued discussing these other things until, with a dreadful noise like a racing motor back-firing, the sleeper sat up in his chair and stretched himself.

'Tumkins,' he cried. 'I have committed sacrilege. I have slept in the Holy of Holies. Have you decided on my fate? Am I to be shot at dawn?'

Sir Bryan left the window and sat down at his desk. For a moment or two he rubbed his chin thoughtfully with his left hand, as if trying to make up his mind: then he lay back in his chair and stared at his erstwhile fag.

'Would you like to do a job of work, old man?'

Hugh started as if he had been stung by a wasp, and Sir Bryan smiled.

'Not real work,' he said reassuringly. 'But by mere luck last night you saw something which Inspector McIver would have given a good deal to see. Or to be more accurate, you saw some men whom McIver particularly wants to meet.'

'Those blokes in the car you mean,' cried Hugh brightly.

'Those blokes in the car,' agreed the other. 'Incidentally, I may say there was a good deal more in that little episode than you think: and after consultation with McIver I have decided to tell you a certain amount about it, because you can help us, Hugh. You see you're one up on McIver: you have at any rate seen those men and he hasn't. Moreover, you say you could recognise two of them again.'

'Good heavens! Tumkins,' murmured Hugh aghast, 'don't say you want me to tramp the streets of London looking for them.'

Sir Bryan smiled.

'We'll spare you that,' he answered. 'But I'd like you to pay attention to what I'm going to tell you.'

Hugh's face assumed the look of intense pain always indicative of thought in its owner.

'Carry on, old bird,' he remarked. 'I'll try and last the course.'

'Last night,' began Sir Bryan quietly, 'a very peculiar thing happened to McIver. I won't worry you with the full details, and it will be enough if I just give you a bare outline of what occurred. He and some of his men in the normal course of duty surrounded a certain house in which were some people we wanted to lay our hands on. To be more accurate there was one man there whom we wanted. He'd been shadowed ever since he'd landed in England that morning, shadowed the whole way from the docks to the house. And sure enough when McIver and his men surrounded the house, there was our friend and all his pals in one of the downstairs rooms. It was then that this peculiar thing happened. I gather from McIver that he heard the noise of an owl hooting, also a faint scuffle and a curse. And after that he heard nothing more. He was chloroformed from behind, and went straight out of the picture.'

'Great Scott!' murmured Hugh, staring incredulously at McIver. 'What an amazing thing!'

'And this is where you come in, Hugh,' continued Sir Bryan.

'Me!' Hugh sat up abruptly. 'Why me?'

'One of the men inside the room was an interesting fellow known as Flash Jim. He is a burglar of no mean repute, though he is quite ready to tackle any sort of job which carries money with it. And when McIver, having recovered himself this morning, ran Flash Jim to ground in one of his haunts he was quite under the impression that the men who had doped him and the other officers were pals of Flash Jim. But after he'd talked to him he changed his mind. All Flash Jim could tell him was that on the previous night he and some friends had been discussing business at this house. He didn't attempt to deny that. He went on to say that suddenly the room had been filled with a number of masked men, and that he'd had a clip over the back of the head which knocked him out. After that presumably he was given a whiff of chloroform to keep him quiet, and the next thing he remembers is being kicked into activity by the policeman at – ' Sir Bryan paused a moment to emphasise the point – 'at Piccadilly Circus.'

'Good Lord!' said Hugh dazedly. 'Then that bird I saw last night sleeping it off on the pavement was Flash Jim.'

'Precisely,' answered Sir Bryan. 'But what is far more to the point, old man, is that the two birds you think you would be able to recognise and who were in the car, are two of the masked men who first of all laid out McIver and subsequently surrounded Flash Jim and his pals inside.'

'But what did they want to do that for?' asked Hugh in bewilderment.

'That is just what we want to find out,' replied Sir Bryan. 'As far as we can see at the moment they are not criminals in the accepted sense of the word. They flogged two of the men who were there last night, and there are no two men in England who more richly deserved it. They kidnapped two others, one of whom was the man we particularly wanted. Then to wind up, they planted Flash Jim as I've told you, let the others go, and brought McIver and all his men back to McIver's house, where they left them to cool on the pavement.'

For a moment there was silence, and then Hugh began to shake with laughter.

'But how perfectly priceless!' he spluttered when he was able to speak once more. 'Old Algy will burst a blood-vessel when I tell him: you know, Algy, Tumkins, don't you – that bird with the eye-glass, and the funny-looking face?'

Inspector McIver frowned heavily. All along he had doubted the wisdom of telling Drummond anything: now he felt that his misgivings were confirmed. What on earth was the good of expecting such an obvious ass to be of the smallest assistance? And now this raucous hilarity struck him as being positively indecent. But the Chief had insisted: the responsibility was his. One thing was certain, reflected McIver grimly. Algy, whoever he was, would not be the only one to whom the privilege of bursting a blood-vessel would be accorded. And before very long it would be all round London – probably in the papers. And McIver particularly did not want *that* to happen. However, the next instant Sir Bryan soothed some of his worst fears.

'Under no circumstances, Hugh,' he remarked gravely, 'is Algy to be given a chance of bursting any blood-vessel. You understand what I mean. What I have said to you this afternoon is for you alone – and no-one else. We know it: Flash Jim and Co. know it.'

'And the jolly old masked sportsmen know it,' said Hugh.

'Quite,' remarked Sir Bryan. 'And that's a deuced sight too many already. We don't want any more.'

'As far as I am concerned, my brave Tumkins,' cried the other, 'the list is closed. Positively not another participator in the stable secret. But I still don't see where I leap in and join the fray.'

'This way, old boy,' said Sir Bryan. 'McIver is a very strong man, and yet he was picked up last night as he himself says as if he was a baby, by one of these masked men who, judging from a note he wrote, is presumably the leader of the gang. And so we deduce that this leader is something exceptional in the way of strength.'

'By Gad! That's quick, Tumkins,' said Hugh admiringly. 'But then you always did have the devil of a brain.'

'Now you are something very exceptional in that line, Hugh,' continued the other.

'Oh! I can push a fellah's face if it's got spots and things,' said Hugh deprecatingly.

'And what I want to know is this. If we give you warning would you care to go with McIver the next time he has any job on, where he thinks it is likely this gang may turn up? We have a pretty shrewd idea as to the type of thing they specialise in.'

Hugh passed his hand dazedly over his forehead.

'Sort of mother's help you mean,' and McIver frowned horribly. 'While the bird biffs McIver, I biff the bird. Is that the notion?'

'That is the notion,' agreed Sir Bryan. 'Of course you'll have to do exactly what McIver tells you, and the whole thing is most unusual. But in view of the special features of the case . . . What is it, Miss Forbes?' He glanced up at his secretary, who was standing in the doorway, with a slight frown.

'He insists on seeing you at once, Sir Bryan.'

She came forward with a card, which Sir Bryan took.

'Charles Latter.' The frown deepened. 'What the deuce does he want?'

The answer was supplied by the gentleman himself, who appeared at that moment in the doorway. He was evidently in a state of great agitation and Sir Bryan rose.

'I am engaged at the moment, Mr Latter,' he said coldly.

'My business won't take you a minute, Sir Bryan,' he cried. 'But what I want to know is this. Is this country civilised or is it not? Look at what I received by the afternoon post.'

He handed a sheet of paper to the other, who glanced at it casually. Then suddenly the casual look vanished, and Sir Bryan sat down at his desk, his eyes grim and stern.

'By the afternoon post, you say.'

'Yes. And there have been too many disappearances lately!'

'How did you know that?' snapped the chief, staring at him.

For a moment Latter hesitated and changed colour.

'Oh! everyone knows it,' he answered, trying to speak casually.

'Everyone does not know it,' remarked Sir Bryan quietly. 'However, you did quite right to come to me. What are your plans during the next few days?'

'I am going out of London tomorrow to stay with Lady Manton near Sheffield,' answered Latter. 'A semi-political house party. Good heavens! What's that?'

With a snort Hugh sat up blinking.

'So sorry, old lad,' he burbled. 'I snored: know I did. Late hours are the devil, aren't they?'

He heaved himself out of his chair, and grinned pleasantly at Latter, who frowned disapprovingly.

'I don't go in for them myself. Well, Sir Bryan.'

'This matter shall be attended to, Mr Latter. I will see to it. Good afternoon. I will keep this note.'

'And who was that little funny-face?' said Hugh as the door closed behind Mr Latter.

'Member of Parliament for a north country constituency,' answered Sir Bryan, still staring at the piece of paper in his hand. 'Lives above his income. Keenly ambitious. But I thought he was all right.'

The other two stared at him in surprise.

'What do you mean, sir?' asked McIver at length.

'Our unknown friends do not think so, Mac,' answered the chief, handing his subordinate the note left by Latter. 'They are beginning to interest me, these gentlemen.'

'You need a rest, Charles Latter.' [read McIver slowly] 'We have established a home for people like you where several of your friends await you. In a few days you will join them.'

'There are two things which strike one, McIver,' remarked Sir Bryan thoughtfully, lighting a cigarette. 'First and most important: that message and the one you found this morning were written on the same typewriter – the letter "s" is distorted in each case. And, secondly, Mr Charles Latter appears to have inside information concerning the recent activities of our masked friends which it is difficult to see how he came by. Unless' – he paused and stared out of the window with a slight frown – 'unless they are far more conversant with his visiting list than I am.'

McIver's great jaw stuck out as if made of granite.

'It proves my theory, sir,' he grunted, 'but if these jokers try that game on with Mr Latter they won't catch me a second time.'

A terrific blow on the back made him gasp and splutter.

'There speaks my hero-boy,' cried Hugh. 'Together we will out-wit the knaves. I will write and cancel a visit: glad of the chance. Old Julia Manton – face like a horse: house at Sheffield: roped me in, Tumkins – positively stunned me with her verbosity. Ghastly house – but reeks of boodle.'

Sir Bryan looked at him surprised.

'Do you mean to say you are going to Lady Manton's?'

'I was. But not now. I will stick closer than a brother to Mr McIver.'

'I think not, old man. You go. If you'd been awake you'd have heard Latter say that he was going there too. You can be of use sooner than I thought.'

'Latter going to old Julia?' Hugh stared at him amazed. 'My dear old Tum-tum, what a perfectly amazing coincidence.'

Chapter 3

In which Hugh Drummond composes a letter

Hugh Drummond strolled slowly along Whitehall in the direction of Trafalgar Square. His face wore its habitual look of vacuous good humour, and at intervals he hummed a little tune under his breath. It was outside the Carlton that he paused as a car drew up by his side, and a man and a girl got out.

'Algy, my dear old boy,' he murmured, taking off his hat, 'are we in good health today?'

'Passable, old son,' returned Algy Longworth, adjusting his quite unnecessary eyeglass. 'The oysters wilted a bit this morning, but I'm trying again tonight. By the way, do you know Miss Farreydale?'

Hugh bowed.

'You know the risk you run, I suppose, going about with him?'

The girl laughed. 'He seems harmless,' she answered lightly.

'That's his guile. After a second cup of tea he's a perfect devil. By the same token, Algy, I am hibernating awhile in the country. Going to dear old Julia Manton's for a few days. Up Sheffield way.'

Miss Farreydale looked at him with a puzzled frown.

'Do you mean Lady Manton – Sir John's wife?'

'That's the old dear,' returned Hugh. 'Know her?'

'Fairly well. But her name isn't Julia. And she won't love you if you call her old.'

'Good heavens! Isn't it? And won't she? I must be mixing her up with someone else.'

'Dorothy Manton is a well-preserved woman of – shall we say – thirty-five? She was a grocer's daughter: she is now a snob of the worst type. I hope you'll enjoy yourself.'

'Your affection for her stuns me,' murmured Hugh. 'I appear to be in for a cheerful time.'

'When do you go, Hugh?' asked Algy.

'Tomorrow, old man. But I'm keeping you from your tea. Keep the table between you after the second cup, Miss Farreydale.'

He lifted his hat and walked on up the Haymarket, only to turn back suddenly.

' "Daisy," you said, didn't you?'

'No. Dorothy,' laughed the girl. 'Come on, Algy, I want my tea.'

She passed into the Carlton, and for a moment the two men were together on the pavement.

'Lucky she knows the Manton woman,' murmured Hugh.

'Don't you?' gasped Algy.

'Not from Eve, old son. Don't fix up anything in the near future. We shall be busy. I've joined the police and shall require help.'

With a cheery nod he strolled off, and after a moment's hesitation Algy Longworth followed the girl into the Carlton.

'Mad, isn't he – your friend?' she remarked as he came up.

'Absolutely,' he answered. 'Let's masticate an éclair.'

A quarter of an hour later Hugh let himself into his house in Brook Street. On the hall table were three telegrams which he opened and read. Then, having torn them into tiny fragments, he went on into his study and rang the bell.

'Beer, Denny,' he remarked, as his servant came in. 'Beer in a mug. I am prostrate. And then bring me one of those confounded books which people have their names put in followed by the usual lies.'

'*Who's Who*, sir,' said Denny.

'You've got it,' said his master. 'Though who is who in these days, Denny, is a very dark matter. I am rapidly losing my faith in my brother man – rapidly. And then after that we have to write a letter to Julia – no, Dorothy Manton – erstwhile grocer's daughter, with whom I propose to dally for a few days.'

'I don't seem to know the name, sir.'

'Nor did I, Denny, until about an hour ago. But I have it on reliable authority that she exists.'

'But how, sir . . . ' began the bewildered Denny.

'At the moment the way is dark,' admitted Drummond. 'The fog of war enwraps me. Beer, fool, beer.'

Accustomed to the little vagaries of his master, Denny left the room to return shortly with a large jug of beer which he placed on a small table beside Drummond's chair. Then he waited motionless behind his chair with a pencil and writing-block in his hand.

'A snob, Denny; a snob,' said Drummond at length, putting down his empty glass. 'How does one best penetrate into the life and home of a female snob whom one does not even know by sight? Let us reason from first principles. What have we in our repertoire that would fling wide the portals of her house, revealing to our awestruck gaze all the footmen ranged in a row?' He rose suddenly. 'I've got it, Denny; at least some of it. We have old Turnip-top. Is he not a cousin of mine?'

'You mean Lord Staveley, sir,' said Denny diffidently.

'Of course I do, you ass. Who else?' Clasping his replenished glass of beer, Hugh strode up and down the room. 'Somehow or other we must drag him in.'

'He's in Central Africa, sir,' reminded Denny cautiously.

'What the devil does that matter? Julia – I mean Dorothy – won't know. Probably never heard of the poor old thing. Write, fool; take your pen and write quickly.

' "Dear Lady Manton,

' "I hope you have not forgotten the pleasant few days we spent together at Wiltshire Towers this spring." '

'But you didn't go to the Duke's this spring, sir,' gasped Denny.

'I know that, you ass – but no more did she. To be exact, the place was being done up, only she won't know. Go on, I'm going to overflow again.'

' "I certainly have not forgotten the kind invitation you gave to my cousin Staveley and myself to come and stop with you. He, at the moment, is killing beasts in Africa: whereas I am condemned to this unpleasant country. Tomorrow I have to go to Sheffield . . ." '

He paused. 'Why, Denny – why do I have to go to Sheffield? Why in Heaven's name does anyone ever go to Sheffield?'

'They make knives there, sir.'

'Do they? But you needn't go there to buy them. And anyway, I don't want knives.'

'You might just say on business, sir,' remarked his servant.

'Gad! you're a genius, Denny. Put that in. "Sheffield on business, and I wondered if I might take you at your word and come to . . . " Where's the bally woman live? Look it up in *Who's Who*.'

'Drayton House, sir,' announced Denny.

' "To Drayton House for a day or two. Yours very sincerely." '

'That'll do the trick, Denny. Give it to me, and I'll write it out. A piece of the best paper with the crest and telephone number embossed in blue, and the victory is ours.'

'Aren't you giving her rather short notice, sir?' said Denny doubtfully.

Drummond laid down his pen and stared at him sadly.

'Sometimes, Denny, I despair of you,' he answered. 'Even after four years of communion with me there are moments when you relapse into your pristine brain-wallow. If I gave her any longer it is just conceivable – though I admit not likely – that I might get my answer from her stating that she was completely unaware of my existence, and that she'd sent my letter to the police. And where should we be then, my faithful varlet? As it is, I shall arrive at Drayton House just after the letter, discover with horror that I have made a mistake, and be gracefully forgiven by my charming hostess as befits a man with such exalted friends. Now run away and get me a taxi.'

'Will you be in to dinner, sir?'

'Perhaps – perhaps not. In case I'm not, I shall go up to Sheffield in the Rolls tomorrow. See that everything is packed.'

'Will you want me to come with you, sir?'

'No, Denny – not this time. I have a sort of premonition that I'm going to enjoy myself at Drayton House, and you're too young for that sort of thing.'

With a resigned look on his face, Denny left the room, closing the door gently behind him. But Drummond, left to himself, did not at once continue his letter to Lady Manton. With his pen held loosely in his hand he sat at his desk staring thoughtfully at the wall opposite. Gone completely was his customary inane look of good humour: in its place was an expression of quiet, almost grim, determination. He had the air of a man faced with big decisions, and to whom, moreover, such an experience was no novelty. For some five minutes he sat there motionless; then with a short laugh he came out of his reverie.

'We're getting near the motto, my son,' he muttered – 'deuced near. If we don't draw the badger in a few weeks, I'll eat my hat.'

With another laugh he turned once more to his half-finished letter. And a minute or two later, having stamped and addressed the envelope, he slipped it into his pocket and rose. He crossed the room and unlocked a small safe which stood in the corner. From it he took a small automatic revolver which he dropped into his coat pocket, also a tiny bundle of what looked like fine black silk. Then, having relocked the safe, he picked up his hat and stick and went into the hall.

'Denny,' he called, pausing by the front door.

'Sir,' answered that worthy, appearing from the back premises.

'If Mr Darrell or any of them ring up I shall be tearing a devilled bone tonight at the Savoy grill at eleven o'clock.'

Chapter 4

In which Count Zadowa gets a shock

Number 5, Green Street, Hoxton, was not a prepossessing abode. A notice on one of the dingy downstairs windows announced that Mr William Atkinson was prepared to advance money on suitable security: a visit during business hours revealed that this was no more than the truth, even if the appearance of Mr Atkinson's minion caused the prospective borrower to wonder how he had acquired such an aggressively English name.

The second and third floors were apparently occupied by his staff, which seemed unduly large considering the locality and quality of his business. Hoxton is hardly in that part of London where large sums of money might be expected to change hands, and yet there was no doubt that Mr William Atkinson's staff was both large and busy. So busy indeed were his clerks that frequently ten and eleven o'clock at night found them still working hard, though the actual business of the day downstairs concluded at six o'clock – eight Saturdays.

It was just before closing time on the day after the strange affair down at Barking that a large, unkempt-looking individual presented himself at Mr Atkinson's office. His most pressing need would have seemed to the casual observer to be soap and water, but his appearance apparently excited no surprise in the assistant downstairs. Possibly Hoxton is tolerant of such trifles.

The clerk – a pale, anaemic-looking man with an unhealthy skin and a hook nose – rose wearily from his rest.

'What do you want?' he demanded morosely.

'Wot d' yer think!' retorted the other. 'Cat's meat?'

The clerk recoiled, and the blood mounted angrily to his sallow face.

'Don't you use that tone with me, my man,' he said angrily. 'I'd have you to know that this is my office.'

'Yus,' answered the other. 'Same as it's your nose sitting there like a lump o' putty stuck on to a suet pudding. And if I 'ave any o' your lip, I'll pull it off – see. Throw it outside, I will, and you after it – you parboiled lump of bad tripe. Nah, then – business.' With a blow that shook the office he thumped the desk with a huge fist. 'I ain't got no time to waste – even if you 'ave. 'Ow much?'

He threw a pair of thick hobnailed boots on to the counter, and stood glaring at the other.

'Two bob,' said the clerk indifferently, throwing down a coin and picking up the boots.

'Two bob!' cried the other wrathfully. 'Two bob, you miserable Sheenie.' For a moment or two he spluttered inarticulately as if speech was beyond him; then his huge hand shot out and gripped the clerk by the collar. 'Think again, Archibald,' he continued quietly, 'think again and think better.'

But the assistant, as might be expected in one of his calling, was prepared for emergencies of this sort. Very gently his right hand slid along the counter towards a concealed electric bell which communicated with the staff upstairs. It fulfilled several purposes, that bell: it acted as a call for help or as a warning, and according to the number of times it was pressed, the urgency of the matter could be interpreted by those who heard it. Just now the clerk decided that two rings would meet the case: he disliked the appearance of the large and angry man in whose grip he felt absolutely powerless, and he felt he would like help – very urgently. And so it was perhaps a little unfortunate for him that he should have allowed an ugly little smirk to adorn his lips a second or two before his hand found the bell. The man facing him across the counter saw that smirk and lost his temper in earnest. With a grunt of rage he hit the other square between the eyes, and the clerk collapsed in a huddled heap behind the counter with the bell still unrung.

For a few moments the big man stood motionless, listening intently. From upstairs came the faint tapping of a typewriter; from outside the usual street noises of London came softly through the two closed doors. Then, with an agility remarkable in one so big, he vaulted the counter and inspected the recumbent assistant with a professional eye. A faint grin spread over his face as he noted that gentleman's condition, but after that he wasted no time. So quickly and methodically in fact did he set about things, that it seemed as if the whole performance must have been cut and dried beforehand, even to the temporary indisposition of the clerk. In half a minute he was bound and gagged and deposited under the counter. Beside him the big man placed the pair of boots, attached to which was a piece of paper which he took from his pocket. On it was scrawled in an illiterate hand –

Have took a fare price for the boots, yer swine.

Then quite deliberately the big man forced the till and removed some money, after which he once more examined the unconscious man under the counter.

'Without a hitch,' he muttered. 'Absolutely according to Cocker. Now, old lad of the village, we come to the second item on the programme. That must be the door I want.'

He opened it cautiously, and the subdued hum of voices from above came a little louder to his ears. Then like a shadow he vanished into the semi-darkness of the house upstairs.

* * *

It was undoubtedly a house of surprises, was Number 5, Green Street. A stranger passing through the dingy office on the ground floor where Mr Atkinson's assistant was wont to sit at the receipt of custom, and then ascending the stairs to the first story would have found it hard to believe that he was in the same house. But then, strangers were not encouraged to do anything of the sort.

There was a door at the top of the flight of stairs, and it was at this door that the metamorphosis took place. On one side of it the stairs ran carpetless and none too clean to the ground floor, on the other side the picture changed. A wide passage with rooms leading out of it from either side confronted the explorer – a passage which was efficiently illuminated with electric lights hung from the ceiling, and the floor of which was covered with a good plain carpet. Along the walls ran rows of book-shelves stretching, save for the gaps at the doors, as far as a partition which closed the further end of the passage. In this partition was another door, and beyond this second door the passage continued to a window tightly shuttered and bolted. From this continuation only one room led off – a room which would have made the explorer rub his eyes in surprise. It was richly – almost luxuriously furnished. In the centre stood a big roll-top writing-desk, while scattered about were several armchairs upholstered in green leather. A long table almost filled one side of the room, a table covered with every imaginable newspaper. A huge safe flush with the wall occupied the other side, while the window, like the one outside, was almost hermetically sealed. There was a fireplace in the corner, but there was no sign of any fire having been lit, or of any preparations for lighting one. Two electric heaters attached by long lengths of flex to plugs in the wall comprised the heating arrangements, while a big central light and half a dozen movable ones illuminated every corner of the room.

In blissful ignorance of the sad plight of the clerk below, two men were sitting in this room, deep in conversation. In a chair drawn up close to the desk was no less a person than Charles Latter, M.P., and it was he who was doing most of the talking. But it was the other man who riveted attention: the man who presumably was Mr Atkinson himself. He was seated in a swivel chair which he had slewed round so as to face the speaker, and it was his appearance which caught the eye and then held it fascinated.

At first he seemed to be afflicted with an almost phenomenal stoop, and it was only when one got nearer that the reason was clear. The man was a hunchback, and the effect it gave was that of a huge bird of prey. Unlike most hunchbacks, his legs were of normal length, and as he sat motionless in his chair, a hand on each knee, staring with unwinking eyes at his talkative companion, there was something menacing and implacable in his appearance. His hair was grey; his features stern and hard; while his mouth reminded one of a steel trap. But it was his eyes that dominated everything – grey-blue and piercing, they seemed able to probe one's innermost soul. A man to whom it would be unwise to lie – a man utterly unscrupulous in himself, who would yet punish double dealing in those who worked for him with merciless severity. A dangerous man.

'So you went to the police, Mr Latter,' he remarked suavely. 'And what had our friend Sir Bryan Johnstone to say on the matter?'

'At first, Count, he didn't say much. In fact he really said very little all through. But once he looked at the note his whole manner changed. I could see that instantly. There was something about the note which interested him . . . '

'Let me see it,' said the Count, holding out his hand.

'I left it with Sir Bryan,' answered the other. 'He asked me to let him keep it. And he promised that I should be all right.'

The Count's lips curled.

'It would take more than Sir Bryan Johnstone's promise, Mr Latter, to ensure your safety. Do you know whom that note was from?'

'I thought, Count,' said the other a little tremulously – 'I thought it might be from this mysterious Black Gang that one has heard rumours about.'

'It was,' replied the Count tersely.

'Heavens!' stammered Latter. 'Then it's true; they exist.'

'In the last month,' answered the hunchback, staring fixedly at his frightened companion, 'nearly twenty of our most useful men have disappeared. They have simply vanished into thin air. I know, no matter how, that it is not the police: the police are as mystified as we are. But the police, Mr Latter, whatever views they may take officially, are in all probability unofficially very glad of our friends' disappearance. At any rate until last night.'

'What do you mean?' asked the other.

'Last night the police were baulked of their prey, and McIver doesn't like being baulked. You know Zaboleff was sent over?'

'Yes, of course. That is one of the reasons I came round tonight. Have you seen him?'

'I have not,' answered the Count grimly. 'The police found out he was coming.'

Mr Latter's face blanched: the thought of Zaboleff in custody didn't appeal to him. It may be mentioned that his feelings were purely selfish – Zaboleff knew too much.

But the Count was speaking again. A faint sneer was on his face; he had read the other's mind like an open book.

'And so,' he continued, 'did the Black Gang. They removed Zaboleff and our friend Waldock from under the very noses of the police, and, like the twenty others, they have disappeared.'

'My God!' There was no doubt now about Mr Latter's state of mind. 'And now they've threatened me.'

'And now they've threatened you,' agreed the Count. 'And you, I am glad to say, have done exactly what I should have told you to do, had I seen you sooner. You have gone to the police.'

'But – but,' stammered Latter, 'the police were no good to Zaboleff last night.'

'And it is quite possible,' returned the other calmly, 'that they will be equally futile in your case. Candidly, Mr Latter, I am completely indifferent on the subject of your future. You have served our purpose, and all that matters is that you happen to be the bone over which the dogs are going to fight. Until last night the dogs hadn't met – officially; and in the rencontre last night, the police dog, unless I'm greatly mistaken, was caught by surprise. McIver doesn't let that happen twice. In your case he'll be ready. With luck this cursed Black Gang, who are infinitely more nuisance to me than the police have been or ever will be, will get bitten badly.'

Mr Latter was breathing heavily.

'But what do you want me to do, Count?'

'Nothing at all, except what you were going to do normally,' answered the other. He glanced at a notebook on his desk. 'You were going to Lady Manton's near Sheffield, I see. Don't alter your plans – go. In all probability it will take place at her house.' He glanced contemptuously at the other's somewhat green face, and his manner changed abruptly. 'You understand, Mr Latter,' his voice was deadly smooth and quiet, 'you understand, don't you, what I say? You will go to Lady Manton's house as arranged, and you will carry on exactly as if you had never received this note. Because if you don't, if you attempt any tricks with me, whatever the Black Gang may do or may not do to you – however much the police may protect you or may not protect you – you will have us to reckon with. And you know what that means.'

'Supposing the gang gets me and foils the police,' muttered Latter through dry lips. 'What then?'

'I shall deal with them personally. They annoy me.'

There was something so supremely confident in the tone of the Count's voice, that the other man looked at him quickly.

'But have you any idea who they are?' he asked eagerly.

'None – at present. Their leader is clever – but so am I. They have deliberately elected to fight me, and now I have had enough. It will save trouble if the police catch them for me: but if not . . . '

The Count shrugged his shoulders, and with a gesture of his hand dismissed the matter. Then he picked up a piece of paper from the desk and glanced at it.

'I will now give you your orders for Sheffield,' he continued. 'It has been reported to me that in Sir John Manton's works there is a red-hot madman named Delmorlick. He has a good job himself, but he spends most of his spare time inciting the unemployed – of which I am glad to say there are large numbers in the town – to absurd deeds of violence. He is a very valuable man to us, and appears to be one of those extraordinary beings who really believe in the doctrines of Communism. He can lash a mob, they tell me, into an absolute frenzy with his tongue. I want you to seek him out, and give him fifty pounds to carry on with. Tell him, of course, that it comes from the Great Master in Russia, and spur him on to renewed activity.

'You will also employ him, and two or three others whom you must leave him to choose, to carry out a little scheme of which you will find full details in this letter.' He handed an envelope to Latter, who took it with a trembling hand. 'You personally will make arrangements about the necessary explosives. I calculate that, if successful, it should throw at least three thousand more men out of work. Moreover, Mr Latter, if it is successful your fee will be a thousand pounds.'

'A thousand!' muttered Latter. 'Is there much danger?'

The Count smiled contemptuously. 'Not if you do your work properly. Hullo! What's up?'

From a little electric bell at his elbow came four shrill rings, repeated again and again.

The Count rose and with systematic thoroughness swept every piece of paper off the desk into his pocket. Then he shut down the top and locked it, while the bell, a little muffled, still rang inside.

'What's the fool doing?' he cried angrily, stepping over to the big safe let into the wall, while Latter, his face white and terrified, followed at his side. And then abruptly the bell stopped.

Very deliberately the Count pressed two concealed knobs, so sunk into the wall as to be invisible to a stranger, and the door of the safe swung open. And only then was it obvious that the safe was not a safe, but a second exit leading to a flight of stairs. For a moment or two he stood motionless, listening intently, while Latter fidgeted at his side. One hand was on a master switch which controlled all the lights, the other on a knob inside the second passage which, when turned, would close the great steel door noiselessly behind them.

He was frowning angrily, but gradually the frown was replaced by a look of puzzled surprise. Four rings from the shop below was the recognised signal for urgent danger, and everybody's plan of action was cut and dried for such an emergency. In the other rooms every book and paper in the slightest degree incriminating was hurled pell-mell into secret recesses in the floor which had been specially constructed under every table. In their place appeared books carefully and very skilfully faked, purporting to record the business transactions of Mr William Atkinson. And in the event of surprise being expressed at the size of Mr Atkinson's business considering the sort of office he possessed below, and the type of his clientele, it would soon be seen that Hoxton was but one of several irons which that versatile gentleman had in the fire. There were indisputable proofs in indisputable ledgers that Mr Atkinson had organised similar enterprises in several of the big towns of England and Scotland, to say nothing of a large West End branch run under the name of Lewer Brothers. And surely he had the perfect right, if he so wished, to establish his central office in Hoxton . . . Or Timbuctoo . . . What the devil did it matter to anyone except himself?

In the big room at the end the procedure was even simpler. The Count merely passed through the safe door and vanished through his private bolt-hole, leaving everything in darkness. And should inconvenient visitors ask inconvenient questions – well, it was Mr Atkinson's private office, and a very nice office too, though at the moment he was away.

Thus the procedure – simple and sound; but on this occasion something seemed to have gone wrong. Instead of the industrious silence of clerks working overtime on affairs of financial import in Edinburgh and Manchester, a perfect babel of voices became audible in the passage. And then there came an agitated knocking on the door.

'Who is it?' cried the Count sharply. It may be mentioned that even the most influential members of his staff knew better than to come into the room without previously obtaining permission.

'It's me, sir – Cohen,' came an agitated voice from outside.

For a moment the Count paused: then with a turn of the knob he closed the safe door silently. With an imperious hand he waved Latter to a chair, and resumed his former position at the desk.

'Come in,' he snapped.

It was a strange and unwholesome object that obeyed the order, and the Count sat back in his chair.

'What the devil have you been doing?'

A pair of rich blue-black eyes, and a nose from which traces of blood still trickled had not improved the general appearance of the assistant downstairs. In one hand he carried a pair of hobnail boots, in the other a piece of paper, and he brandished them alternately while a flood of incoherent frenzy burst from his lips.

For a minute or two the Count listened, until his first look of surprise gave way to one of black anger.

'Am I to understand, you wretched little worm,' he snarled, 'that you gave the urgency danger signal, not once but half a dozen times, merely because a man hit you over the nose?'

'But he knocked me silly, sir,' quavered the other. 'And when I came to, and saw the boots lying beside me and the till opened, I kind of lost my head. I didn't know what had happened, sir – and I thought I'd better ring the bell – in case of trouble.'

He retreated a step or two towards the door, terrified out of his wits by the look of diabolical fury in the hunchback's eyes. Three or four clerks, who had been surreptitiously peeping through the open door, melted rapidly away, while from his chair Mr Latter watched the scene fascinated. He was reminded of a bird and a snake, and suddenly he gave a little shudder as he realised that his own position was in reality much the same as that of the unfortunate Cohen.

And then just as the tension was becoming unbearable there came the interruption. Outside in the passage, clear and distinct, there sounded twice the hoot of an owl. To Mr Latter it meant nothing; to the frightened little Jew it meant nothing; but on the Count the effect was electrical. With a quickness incredible in one so deformed he was at the door, and into the passage, hurling Cohen out of his way into a corner. His powerful fists were clenched by his side: the veins in his neck were standing out like whipcord. But to Mr Latter's surprise he made no movement, and rising from his chair he too peered round the door along the passage, only to stagger back after a second or two with a feeling of sick fear in his soul, and a sudden dryness in the throat. For twenty yards away, framed in the doorway at the head of the stairs leading down to the office below, he had seen a huge, motionless figure. For a perceptible time he had stared at it, and it had seemed to stare at him. Then the door had shut, and on the other side a key had turned. And the figure had been draped from head to foot in black . . .

Chapter 5

In which Charles Latter, M.P., goes mad

Drummond arrived at Drayton House just as the house-party was sitting down to tea in the hall. A rapid survey of the guests as the footman helped him out of his coat convinced him that, with the exception of Latter, he didn't know a soul: a second glance indicated that he could contemplate the fact with equanimity. They were a stodgy-looking crowd, and after a brief look he turned his attention to his hostess.

'Where is Lady Manton?' he asked the footman.

'Pouring out tea, sir,' returned the man surprised.

'Great Scott!' said Drummond, aghast. 'I've come to the wrong house.'

'The wrong house, sir?' echoed the footman, and the sound of their voices made Lady Manton look up.

In an instant that astute woman spotted what had happened. The writer of the strange letter she had received at lunch-time had arrived, and had realised his mistake. Moreover, this was the moment for which she had been waiting ever since, and now to add joy to joy it had occurred when her whole party was assembled to hear every word of her conversation with Drummond. With suitable gratitude she realised that such opportunities are rare.

With a charming smile she advanced towards him, as he stood hesitating by the door.

'Mr Drummond?' she inquired.

'Yes,' he murmured, with a puzzled frown. 'But – but I seem to have made some absurd mistake.'

She laughed, and drew him into the hall.

'A perfectly natural one, I assure you,' she replied, speaking so that her guests could hear. 'It must have been my sister-in-law that you met at Wiltshire Towers. My husband was not very fit at the time and so I had to refuse the Duchess's invitation.' She was handing him a cup of tea as she spoke. 'But, of course, I know your cousin, Lord Staveley, well. So we really know one another after all, don't we?'

'Charming of you to put it that way, Lady Manton,' answered Drummond, with his infectious grin. 'At the same time I feel a bit of an interloper – what! Sort of case of fools toddling in where angels fear to tread.'

'A somewhat infelicitous quotation,' remarked an unctuous-looking man with side-whiskers, deprecatingly.

'Catches you too, does it, old bird?' boomed Hugh, putting down his empty cup.

'It was the second part of your quotation that I was alluding to,' returned the other acidly, when Lady Manton intervened.

'Of course, Mr Drummond, my husband and I insist on your re-maining with us until you have completed your business in Sheffield.'

'Extraordinarily kind of you both, Lady Manton,' answered Hugh. 'How long do you think you will be?'

'Three or four days. Perhaps a little more.' As he spoke he looked quite casually at Latter. For some minutes that worthy pillar of Parlia-ment had been staring at him with a puzzled frown: now he gave a slight start as recognition came to him. This was the enormous indiv-idual who had snored in Sir Bryan Johnstone's office the previous afternoon. Evidently somebody connected with the police, reflected Mr Latter, and glancing at Drummond's vast size he began to feel more reassured than he had for some time. A comforting sort of individual to have about the premises in the event of a brawl: good man – Sir Bryan. This man looked large enough to cope even with that monstrous black apparition, the thought of which still brought a shudder to his spine.

Drummond was still looking at him, but there was no trace of recognition in his eyes. Evidently they were to meet as strangers before the house-party: quite right too, when some of the guests themselves might even be members of this vile gang.

'It depends on circumstances outside my control,' Drummond was saying. 'But if you can do with me for a few days . . . '

'As long as you like, Mr Drummond,' answered Lady Manton. 'And now let me introduce you to my guests.'

* * *

It was not until just before dinner that Mr Latter had an opportunity of a few private words with Drummond. They met in the hall, and for the moment no-one else was within earshot.

'You were in Sir Bryan Johnstone's office yesterday,' said the M.P. hoarsely. 'Are you connected with the police?'

'Intimately,' answered Hugh. 'Even now, Mr Latter, you are completely surrounded by devoted men who are watching and guarding you.'

A gratified smile spread over the other's face, though Drummond's remained absolutely expressionless.

'And how did you get here, Mr Drummond?'

'By car,' returned Hugh gravely.

'I mean into the house-party,' said Mr Latter stiffly.

'Ah!' Hugh looked mysterious. 'That is between you and me, Mr Latter.'

'Quite: quite. I am discretion itself.'

'Until two hours ago I thought I was the biggest liar in the world: now I know I'm not. Our hostess has me beat to a frazzle.'

'What on earth are you talking about?' cried Latter, amazed.

'There are wheels within wheels, Mr Latter,' continued Hugh still more mysteriously. 'A network of intrigue surrounds us. But do not be afraid. My orders are never to leave your side.'

'Good God, Mr Drummond, do you mean to say . . . ?'

'I mean to say nothing. Only this one thing I will mention.' He laid an impressive hand on Latter's arm. 'Be very careful what you say to that man with the mutton-chop whiskers and the face like a sheep.'

And the startled M.P. was too occupied staring suspiciously at the worthy Sheffield magnate and pillar of nonconformity who had just descended the stairs with his hostess to notice a sudden peculiar shaking in Drummond's shoulders as he turned away.

* * *

Mr Charles Latter was not a pleasant specimen of humanity even at the best of times, and that evening he was not at his best. He was frightened to the core of his rotten little soul, and when a constitutional coward is frightened the result is not pretty. His conversational efforts at dinner would have shamed a boy of ten, and though he made one or two feeble efforts to pull himself together, it was no good. Try as he would his mind kept reverting to his own position. Over and over again he went on weighing up the points of the case until his brain was whirling. He tried to make out a mental balance sheet where the stock was represented by his own personal safety, but there was always that one unknown factor which he came up against – the real power of this mysterious gang.

Coming up in the train he had decided to curtail his visit as much as possible. He would carry through what he had been told to do, and then, having pocketed his thousand, he would leave the country for a few months. By that time the police should have settled matters. And he had been very lucky. It had proved easy to find the man Delmorlick, and once he had been found, the other more serious matter had proved easy too.

Delmorlick had arranged everything, and had brought three other men to meet him in a private room at one of the smaller hotels. Like all the Count's schemes, every detail was perfect, and once or twice exclamations of amazement interrupted him as he read on. Every possible eventuality was legislated for, and by the time he had finished reading Delmorlick's eyes were glowing with the enthusiasm of a fanatic.

'Magnificent,' he had cried, rising and going to the window. 'Another nail in the coffin of Capital. And, by heaven! a big one.'

He had stood there, his head covered with a shock of untidy hair, staring with sombre eyes at the street below. And beside him had stood one of the other men. After a while Latter joined them, and he too for a moment had looked down into the street where little knots of men lounged round doorways with their hands in their pockets, and the apathy of despair on their faces. A few women here and there mingled with them, but there was no laughing or jesting – only the sullenness of lost hope. The hope that had once been theirs of work and plenty was dead; there was nothing for them to do – they were just units in the vast army of unemployed. Occasionally a man better dressed and more prosperous than the others would detach himself from one group and go to another, where he would hold forth long and earnestly. And his listeners would nod their heads vigorously or laugh sheepishly as he passed on.

For a few moments Delmorlick had watched in silence. Then with a grave earnestness in his voice he had turned to Latter.

'We shall win, Mr Latter, I tell you. That,' with a lean forefinger he pointed to the man outside, 'is going on all over England, Scotland and Ireland. And the fools in London prate of economic laws and inflated currencies. What does an abstract cause matter to those men? They want food.'

He had glanced at Delmorlick, to find the eyes of the other man fixed on him gravely. He had hardly noticed it at the time – he had been too anxious to get away; now, as he sat at dinner, he found strangely enough that it was the other man's face which seemed to have made the biggest impression on his mind. A new arrival in the place, so Delmorlick had told him – but red-hot for the cause of freedom and anarchy.

He made some vague remark to his neighbour and once more relapsed into moody silence. So far, so good; his job was done – he could leave tomorrow. He would have left that afternoon but for the fact that he had sent his baggage up to Drayton House, and it would have looked strange. But he had already arranged for a wire to be sent to him from London the following morning, and for the night – well, there were Drummond and the police. Decidedly, on points he appeared to be in a winning position – quite a comfortable position. And yet – that unknown factor . . . Still, there was always Drummond; the only trouble was that he couldn't quite place him. What on earth had he meant before dinner? He glanced across the table at him now: he was eating salted almonds and making love to his hostess.

'A fool,' reflected Mr Latter, 'but a powerful fool. If it was necessary, he'd swallow anything I told him.'

And so, towards the end of dinner, aided possibly by his host's very excellent vintage port, Mr Charles Latter had more or less soothed his fears. Surely he was safe in the house, and nothing would induce him to leave it until he went to the station next morning. No thought of the abominable crime he had planned only that afternoon disturbed his equanimity; as has been said, he was not a pleasant specimen of humanity.

Charles Latter was unmoral rather than immoral: he was a constitutional coward with a strong liking for underhand intrigue, and he was utterly and entirely selfish. In his way he was ambitious: he wanted power, but, though in many respects he was distinctly able, he lacked that essential factor – the ability to work for it. He hated work: he wanted easy results. And to obtain lasting results is not easy, as Mr Latter gradually discovered. A capability for making flashy speeches covered with a veneer of cleverness is an undoubted asset, but it is an asset the value of which has been gauged to a nicety by the men who count. And so as time went on, and the epoch-making day when he had been returned to Parliament faded into the past, Mr Latter realised himself for what he was – a thing of no account. And the realisation was as gall and wormwood to his soul. It is a realisation which comes to many men, and it takes them different ways. Some become resigned – some make new and even more futile efforts: some see the humour of it, and some don't. Mr Latter didn't: he became spiteful. And a spiteful coward is a nasty thing.

It was just about that time that he met Count Zadowa. It was at dinner at a friend's house, and after the ladies had left he found himself sitting next to the hunchback with the strange, piercing eyes. He wasn't conscious of having said very much: he would have been amazed had he been told that within ten minutes this charming foreigner had read his unpleasant little mind like a book, and had reached a certain and quite definite decision. In fact, looking back on the past few months, Mr Latter was at a loss to account as to how things had reached their present pass. Had he been told when he stood for Parliament, flaunting all the old hackneyed formulae, that within two years he would be secretly engaged in red-hot Communist work, he would have laughed the idea to scorn. Anarchy, too: a nasty word, but the only one that fitted the bomb outrage in Manchester, which he had himself organised. Sometimes in the night, he used to wake and lie sweating as he thought of that episode . . .

And gradually it had become worse and worse. Little by little the charming Count Zadowa, realising that Mr Latter possessed just those gifts which he could utilise to advantage, had ceased to be charming. There were many advantages in having a Member of Parliament as chief liaison officer.

There had been that first small slip when he signed a receipt for money paid him to address a revolutionary meeting in South Wales during the coal strike. And the receipt specified the service rendered. An unpleasant document in view of the fact that his principal supporters in his constituency were coal-owners. And after that the descent had been rapid.

Not that even now Mr Latter felt any twinges of conscience: all he felt was occasional twinges of fear that he might be found out. He was running with the hare and hunting with the hounds with a vengeance, and at times his cowardly little soul grew sick within him. And then, like a dreaded bolt from the blue, had come the letter of warning from the Black Gang.

Anyway, he reflected, as he turned out his light after getting into bed that night, the police knew nothing of his double life. They were all round him, and there was this big fool in the house . . . For a moment his heart stopped beating: was it his imagination or was that the figure of a man standing at the foot of the bed?

The sweat poured off his forehead as he tried to speak: then he sat up in bed, plucking with trembling hands at the collar of his pyjamas. Still the shape stood motionless: he could swear there was something there now – he could see it outlined against the dim light of the window. He reached out fearfully for the switch: fumbled a little, and then with a click the light went on. His sudden scream of fear died half-strangled in his throat: a livid anger took the place of terror. Leaning over the foot of the bed and regarding him with solicitous interest, lounged Hugh Drummond.

'All tucked up and comfy, old bean,' cried Drummond cheerfully. 'Bedsocks full of feet and all that sort of thing?'

'How dare you,' spluttered Latter, 'how dare you come into my room like this . . .'

'Tush, tush,' murmured Drummond, 'don't forget my orders, old Latter, my lad. To watch over you as a crooning mother crooneth over the last batch of twins. By the way, my boy, you skimped your teeth pretty badly tonight. You'll have to do better tomorrow. Most of your molars must be sitting up and begging for Kolynos if that's your normal effort.'

'Do you mean to tell me that you were in here while I was undressing,' said Latter angrily. 'You exceed your instructions, sir: and I shall report your unwarrantable impertinence to Sir Bryan Johnstone when I return to London.'

'Exactly, Mr Latter. But when will you return to London?' Drummond regarded him dispassionately. 'To put some, if not all, of the cards on the table, the anonymous letter of warning which you received was not quite so anonymous as you would have liked. In other words, you know exactly whom it came from.'

'I don't,' replied the other. 'I know that it came from an abominable gang who have been committing a series of outrages lately. And that is why I applied for police protection.'

'Quite so, Mr Latter. And as – er – Fate would have it, I am here to help carry out that rôle.'

'What did you mean when you gave me that warning before dinner? That man is one of the leading citizens of Sheffield.'

'That was just a little jest, Mr Latter, to amuse you during the evening. The danger does not lie there.'

'Where does it lie?'

'Probably where you least expect it,' returned Drummond with an enigmatic smile.

'I shall be going tomorrow,' said Latter with attempted nonchalance. 'Until then I rely on you.'

'Precisely,' murmured Drummond. 'So you have completed your business here quicker than you anticipated.'

'Yes. To be exact, this afternoon before you arrived.'

'And was that the business which brought you to Sheffield?'

'Principally. Though I really don't understand this catechism, Mr Drummond. And now I wish to go to sleep . . . '

'I'm afraid you can't, Mr Latter. Not quite yet.' For a moment or two Charles Latter stared at the imperturbable face at the foot of his bed: it seemed to him that a strange tension was creeping into the conversation – a something he could not place which made him vaguely alarmed.

'Do you think this mysterious Black Gang would approve of your business this afternoon?' asked Drummond quietly.

Mr Latter started violently.

'How should I know of what the scoundrels would approve?' he cried angrily. 'And anyway, they can know nothing about it.'

'You feel quite confident in Mr Delmorlick's discretion with regard to the friends he selects?'

And now a pulse was beginning to hammer in Mr Latter's throat, and his voice when he spoke was thick and unnatural.

'How do you know anything about Delmorlick?'

Drummond smiled.

'May I reply by asking a similar question, Mr Latter? How do you?'

'I met him this afternoon on political business,' stammered the other, staring fascinated at the man opposite, from whose face all trace of buffoonery seemed to have vanished, to be replaced by a grim sternness the more terrifying because it was so utterly unexpected. And he had thought Drummond a fool . . .

'Would it be indiscreet to inquire the nature of the business?'

'Yes,' muttered Latter. 'It was private.'

'That I can quite imagine,' returned Drummond grimly. 'But since you're so reticent I will tell you. This afternoon you made arrangements, perfect in every detail, to blow up the main power station of the Greystone works.' The man in the bed started violently. 'The result of that would have been to throw some three thousand men out of work for at least a couple of months.'

'It's a lie,' said Latter thickly.

'Your object in so doing was obvious,' continued Drummond. 'Money. I don't know how much, and I didn't know who from – until last night.' And now Latter was swallowing hard, and clutching the bedclothes with hands that shook like leaves.

'You saw me last night, Mr Latter, didn't you? And I found out your headquarters . . . '

'In God's name – who are you?' His voice rose almost to a scream. 'Aren't you the police?'

'No – I am not.' He was coming nearer, and Latter cowered back, mouthing. 'I am not the police, you wretched thing: I am the leader of the Black Gang.'

Latter felt the other's huge hands on him, and struggled like a puny child, whimpering, half sobbing. He writhed and squirmed as a gag was forced into his mouth: then he felt a rope cut his wrists as they were lashed behind his back. And all the while the other went on speaking in a calm, leisurely voice.

'The leader of the Black Gang, Mr Latter: the gang that came into existence to exterminate things like you. Ever since the war you poisonous reptiles have been at work stirring up internal trouble in this country. Not one in ten of you believe what you preach: your driving force is money and your own advancement. And as for your miserable dupes – those priceless fellows who follow you blindly because (God help them) they're hungry and their wives are hungry – what do you care for them, Mr Latter? You just laugh in your sleeve and pocket the cash.'

With a heave he jerked the other on to the floor, and proceeded to lash him to the foot of the bed.

'I have had my eye on you, Mr Latter, since the Manchester effort when ten men were killed, and you were the murderer. But other and more important matters have occupied my time. You see, my information is very good – better than Delmorlick's selection of friends. The new devoted adherent to your cause this afternoon happens to be an intimate, personal friend of mine.'

He was busying himself with something that he had taken from his pocket – a thick, square slab with a hole in the centre.

'I admit that your going to the police with my note surprised me. And it really was extraordinarily lucky that I happened to be in the office at the time. But it necessitated a slight change of plan on my part. If dear old McIver and his minions are outside the house, it's much simpler for me to be in. And now, Mr Latter – to come to business.'

He stood in front of the bound man, whose eyes were rolling horribly.

'We believe in making the punishment fit the crime. This afternoon you planned to destroy the livelihood of several thousand men with explosive, simply that you might make money. Here,' he held up the square slab, 'is a pound of the actual gun-cotton, which was removed from Delmorlick himself before he started on a journey to join my other specimens. I propose to place this slab under you, Mr Latter, and to light this piece of fuse which is attached to it. The fuse will take about three minutes to burn. During that three minutes if you can get free, so much the better for you; if not – well, it would be a pity not to have any explosion at all in Sheffield, wouldn't it?'

For a moment or two Drummond watched the struggling, terrified man, and his eyes were hard and merciless. Then he went to the door, and Latter heard it opened and shut and moaned horribly. His impotent struggles increased: out of the corner of his eye he could see the fire burning nearer and nearer. And then all of a sudden something seemed to snap in his brain . . .

Four minutes later Drummond came out from the screen behind which he had been standing. He picked up the burnt-out fuse and the block of wood to which it had been attached. Then he undid the ropes that bound the other man, removed the gag and put him back into bed. And after a while he nodded thoughtfully.

'Poetic justice,' he murmured. 'And it saves a lot of trouble.'

Then, after one searching look round the room, he turned out the light and stepped quietly into the passage.

* * *

'An extraordinary thing, McIver,' said Sir Bryan Johnstone, late on the afternoon of the following day. 'You say that when you saw Mr Latter this morning he was mad.'

'Mad as a hatter, sir,' answered McIver, turning for confirmation to Drummond, who was sprawling in a chair.

'Absolutely up the pole, Tum-tum,' agreed Drummond.

'Gibbered like a fool,' said McIver, 'and struggled wildly whenever he got near the foot of the bed. Seemed terrified of it, somehow. Did you notice that, Mr Drummond?'

'My dear old lad, it was only ten o'clock, and I was barely conscious,' yawned that worthy, lighting a cigarette.

'Well, anyway, you had no trouble with the gang, McIver,' said his chief.

'None, sir,' agreed the Inspector. 'I thought they wouldn't try it on with me twice. I heard some fool story just before I caught the train, about one of the nightwatchmen at a big works who swears he saw a sort of court-martial – he was an old soldier – being held on three men by a lot of black-masked figures. But a lot of these people have got this yarn on the brain, Sir Bryan. It's spread a good deal farther than I thought.'

Sir Bryan nodded thoughtfully.

'I must say I'd like to know what sent Charles Latter mad!'

Drummond sat up lazily.

'Good heavens! Tumkins, don't you know? The house-party, old son – the house-party; they had to be seen to be believed.'

Chapter 6

In which an effusion is sent to the newspapers

Take a garrulous nightwatchman and an enterprising journalist; mix them together over one, or even two glasses of beer, and a hard-worked editor feels safe for a column every time. And since the nightwatchman at Greystone's Steel Works was very garrulous, and the journalist was young and ambitious, the result produced several columns of the sort of stuff that everybody likes to read, and pretends he doesn't.

Mr Day was the nightwatchman's name, and Mr Day was prepared to tell his story at a pint a time to anyone who cared to listen. It differed in detail, the difference depending entirely on the number of payments received during the day, but the essential part remained the same. And it was that essential part that was first published in one of the local Sheffield papers, and from there found its way into the London Press.

Mr Day, it appeared, had, according to his usual custom, been making his hourly tour of the works. It was about midnight, or perhaps a little after, that he thought he heard the sound of voices coming from the central power-station. As he approached, it had seemed to him that it was more lit up than it had been on his previous round, when only one electric light had been burning. He was on the point of opening the door to go in and investigate, when he heard at least half a dozen voices speaking angrily, and one in particular had stood out above the others. It was loud and convulsed with passion, and on hearing it Mr Day, remembering his wife and four children, had paused.

'You damned traitor, as sure as there's a God above, I'll kill you for this some day.'

Such were the words which it appeared had given Mr Day cause for reflection. At any time, and in any place, they would be apt to stand out from the ordinary level of bright chat; but as Mr Day remarked succinctly, 'they fair gave me the creeps, coming out o' that there place, which was hempty, mind you, not 'alf an hour before.'

And there are few, I think, who can blame him for his decision not to open the door, but to substitute for such a course a strategic move to a flank. There was an outside flight of steps leading to a door which opened on to the upstairs platform where stood the indicator board. And half-way up that flight of stairs was a window – a window through which Mr Day was peering a few seconds afterwards.

It was at this point in the narrative that Mr Day was wont to pause, while his listeners drew closer. Standing between the four huge dynamos which supplied the whole of the power necessary for the works were ten or a dozen men. Three of them had their hands lashed behind their backs, and these were the only three whose faces he could see. The others – and here came a still more impressive pause – were completely covered in black from head to foot. Black masks – black cloaks, the only difference between them being in height. He couldn't hear what was being said: ever since the Boer War Mr Day had been a little hard of hearing. But what it reminded him of was a drumhead court-martial. The three men whose hands were lashed behind them were the prisoners; the men in black, standing motionless round them, their judges. He heard vaguely the sound of a voice which went on speaking for some time. And since the three bound men seemed to be staring at one of the masked figures, he concluded that that must be the speaker. Then he saw the masked men surround the other three closely, and when they stood back again Mr Day noticed that the prisoners had been gagged as well as bound. It was at this moment, apparently, that a hazy idea of going for the police penetrated his brain for the first time, but it was too late. Powerless in the hands of their captors, the three men were forced to the door, and shortly afterwards Mr Day affirmed that he heard the sound of a car driving off. But he was unable to swear to it; he was still flattening a fascinated nose against the window; for two of the masked men had remained behind, and Mr Day wasn't going to miss anything.

These two gathered together into bundles a lot of things that looked like wooden slabs – also some stuff that looked like black cord. Then they walked carefully round the whole power station, as if to make sure that nothing had been left behind. Apparently satisfied with their inspection, they went to the door, carrying the bundles they had collected. They turned out all the lights except the one which had originally been burning, took one final look round to make certain that everything was as it should be, and then they, too, vanished into the night, leaving Mr Day to scratch his head and wonder if he had been dreaming.

In fact, but for one indisputable certainty, it is very doubtful whether Mr Day's story would have been received with the respect which it undoubtedly deserved. When he first recounted it there were scoffers of the most incredulous type; scoffers who cast the most libellous reflections on the manner in which Mr Day had spent the evening before going on duty, and it was not until the fact became established two or three days later that three men who should have come to work the next morning at their different jobs not only failed to appear, but had completely disappeared, leaving no trace behind them, that the scoffers became silent. Moreover, the enterprising journalist came on the scene, and Mr Day became famous, and Mr Day developed an infinite capacity for beer. Was not he, wildly improbable though his story might be, the only person who could throw any light at all on the mysterious disappearance of three workmen from Sheffield? Certainly the journalist considered he was, and proceeded to write a column of the most convincing journalese to proclaim his belief to the world at large, and Sheffield in particular.

Thus was the ball started. And no sooner had it commenced to move than it received astonishing impetus from all sorts of unexpected directions. The journalist, in his search for copy to keep his infant alive, discovered to his astonishment that he had unearthed a full-grown child. The activities of the Black Gang were not such a profound mystery as he had at first thought. And though he failed to get the slightest clue as to the identity of the men composing it, he was soon absolutely convinced of the truth of Mr Day's story. But there he stuck; the whole matter became one of conjecture in his mind. That there was a Black Gang, he was certain; but why or wherefore was beyond him.

Men he encountered in odd places were noncommittal. Some obviously knew nothing about it; others shrugged their shoulders and looked wise.

There was one group of youngish men he approached on the matter. They were standing at the corner of the long street which led from Greystone's Works, muttering together, and their conversation ceased abruptly as he sauntered up.

'Journalist, are you?' said one. 'Want to know about this 'ere Black Gang? Well, look 'ere, mister, I'll tell you one thing. See them furnaces over there?'

He pointed to the ruddy, orange light of Greystone's huge furnaces, glowing fiercely against the evening sky.

'Well, if me and my mates ever catch the leader of that there gang, or anybody wot's connected with it, they goes in them furnaces alive.'

'Shut up, yer blasted fool!' cried one of the others.

'Think I'm afraid of that bunch!' snarled the first speaker. 'A bunch wot's frightened to show their faces . . . '

But the journalist had passed on.

'Don't you pay no attention to them young fools, mate,' said an elderly, quiet-looking man, who was standing smoking in a doorway a few yards on. 'They talks too much and they does too little.'

'I was asking them about this so-called Black Gang,' said the searcher after news.

'Ah!' The elderly man spat thoughtfully. 'Don't profess to know nothing about them myself; but if wot I've 'eard is true, we could do with a few more like 'em.'

And once more the journalist passed on.

The police refused point-blank to make any communication on the matter at all. They had heard Mr Day's story, and while not disposed to dismiss it entirely, they would not say that they were prepared to accept it completely; and since it was a jolly day outside, and they were rather busy, the door was along the passage to the left.

Such were the ingredients, then, with which one, and sometimes two columns daily were made up for the edification of the inhabitants of Sheffield. Brief notices appeared in one or two of the London dailies, coupled with the announcement that Mr Charles Latter had suffered a nervous breakdown, and that this well-known M.P. had gone into a nursing-home for some weeks. But beyond that the matter was too local to be of importance, until a sudden dramatic development revived the flagging interest in Sheffield, and brought the matter into the national limelight.

It was nothing more nor less than an announcement purporting to come from the leader of the Black Gang himself, and sent to the editor of the Sheffield paper. It occupied a prominent position in the centre page, and was introduced to the public in the following words:

The following communication has been received by the editor. The original, which he has handed over to the proper authorities, was typewritten; the postmark was a London one. The editor offers no comment on the genuineness of the document, beyond stating that it is printed exactly as it was received.

The document ran as follows:

In view of the conflicting rumours started by the story of Mr Day, the nightwatchman at Greystone's Works, it may be of interest to the public to know that his story is true in every detail. The three men whom he saw bound were engaged at the instigation of others in an attempt to wreck the main power station, thereby largely increasing unemployment in Sheffield, and fomenting more unrest. The driving force behind this, as behind other similar activities, is international. The source of it all lies in other countries; the object is the complete ruin of the great sober majority of workers in England by a loud-voiced, money-seeking minority which is composed of unscrupulous scoundrels and fanatical madmen. For these apostles of anarchy a home has been prepared, where the doctrines of Communism are strictly enforced. The three men who have disappeared from Sheffield have gone to that home, but there is still plenty of room for others. Mr Charles Latter has gone mad, otherwise he would have accompanied them. The more intelligent the man, the more vile the scoundrel. Charles Latter was intelligent. There are others more intelligent than he. It is expressly for their benefit that the Black Gang came into being.

(Signed) THE LEADER OF THE GANG

The reception of this remarkable document was mixed. On the strength of the first sentence Mr Day's price rose to two pints; but it was the rest of the communication which aroused public interest. For the first time some tangible reason had been advanced to account for the presence of the three bound men and their masked captors in the power-station at Greystone's. Inquiries revealed the fact that all three of them were men educated above the average, and of very advanced Socialistic views. And to that extent the document seemed credible. But it was the concluding sentences that baffled the public.

True, Mr Charles Latter, M.P., had been staying on the night in question at Lady Manton's house a few miles out of the town. Equally true he had had a nervous breakdown which necessitated his removal to a nursing-home in London. But what connection there could possibly be between him and the three men it was difficult to see. It was most positively asserted that the well-known Member of Parliament had not left Drayton House during the night on which the affair took place; and yet, if credence was to be attached to the document, there was an intimate connection between him and the affair at the steel works. Callers at the nursing-home came away none the wiser; his doctor had positively forbidden a soul to be admitted save his brother, who came away frowning after the first visit, and returned no more. For Charles Latter not only had not recognised him, but had shrunk away, babbling nonsense, while continually his eyes had sought the foot of the bed with a look of dreadful terror in them.

And so speculation continued. No further communication emanated from the mysterious Black Gang. Mr Latter was insane; the three men had disappeared, and Mr Day, even at two pints, could say no more than he had said already. There were people who dismissed the entire thing as an impudent and impertinent hoax, and stated that the editor of the Sheffield paper should be prosecuted for libel. It was obvious, they explained, what had occurred. Some irresponsible practical joker had, for reasons of his own, connected together the two acts, whose only real connection was that they had occurred about the same time, and had maliciously sent the letter to the paper.

But there were others who were not so sure – people who nodded wisely at one another from the corners of trains, and claimed inside knowledge of strange happenings unknown to the mere public. They affirmed darkly that there was more in it than met the eye, and relapsed into confidential mutterings.

And then, when nothing further happened, the matter died out of the papers, and speculation ceased amongst the public. The general impression left behind favoured a hoax; and at that it was allowed to remain until the events occurred which were to prove that it was a very grim reality.

*   *   *

But whatever the general public may have thought about the matter, there were two people in London who viewed the sudden newspaper notoriety with rage and anger. And it is, perhaps, needless to say that neither of them concurred in the impression that it was a hoax; only too well did they know that it was nothing of the kind.

The first of these was Count Zadowa, alias Mr William Atkinson. He had duly received from Latter a telegram in code stating that everything was well – a telegram dispatched from Sheffield after the meeting with Delmorlick in the afternoon. And from that moment he had heard nothing. The early editions of the evening papers on the following day had contained no reference to any explosion at Sheffield; the later ones had announced Mr Latter's nervous breakdown. And the Count, reading between the lines, had wondered, though at that time he was far from guessing the real truth. Then had come strange rumours – rumours which resulted in the summoning post-haste from Sheffield of a man who was alluded to in the archives at 5, Green Street, as John Smith, commission agent. And, though he may have fully deserved the description of commission agent, a glance at his face gave one to wonder at his right to the name of John Smith.

'Tell me exactly what has happened,' said the Count quietly, pointing to a chair in his inner office. 'Up to date I have only heard rumours.'

And John Smith, with the accent of a Polish Jew, told. Mr Latter had called on him early in the afternoon, and, in accordance with his instructions, he had arranged a meeting between Mr Latter and Delmorlick at an hotel. Delmorlick had taken three other men with him, and he presumed everything had been arranged at that meeting. No; he had not been present himself. For two of Delmorlick's companions he could vouch; in fact – and then, for the first time, Count Zadowa heard the story so ably spread abroad by Mr Day. For it was those two men and Delmorlick who had disappeared.

'Then it was the fourth man who gave it away,' snapped the Count. 'Who was he?'

'He called himself Jackson,' faltered the other. 'But I haven't seen him since.'

Thoughtfully the Count beat a tattoo with his fingers on the desk in front of him; no-one looking at him would have guessed for an instant the rage that was seething in his brain. For the first time he realised fully that, perfect though his own organisation might be, he had come up against one that was still better.

'And what about this nervous breakdown of Mr Latter's?' he demanded at length.

But on that subject John Smith knew nothing. He had no ideas on the subject, and, after a few searching questions, he found himself curtly dismissed, leaving the Count to ponder over the knotty point as to the connection between Latter's breakdown and the affair at the power-station. And he was still pondering over it three days later when the bombshell exploded in the form of the document to the Press. That the concluding sentences were evidently directed against him did not worry him nearly as much as the publicity afforded to activities in which secrecy was essential. And what worried him even more was the fact that others on the Continent – men whose names were never mentioned, but who regarded him almost as he regarded

Latter – would see the English papers, and would form their own conclusions. Already some peremptory letters had reached him, stating that the activities of the Black Gang must cease – how, it was immaterial. And he had replied stating that he had the thing well in hand. On top of which had come this damnable document, which was published in practically every paper in the country, and had produced a sort of silly-season discussion from 'Retired Colonel' and 'Maiden Lady'. Of no importance to him that 'Common Sense' decreed that it was a stupid hoax: he knew it was not. And so did those others, as he very soon found out. Two days after the appearance of the document, he received a letter which bore the postmark of Amsterdam. It stated merely: 'I am coming', and was signed X. And had anyone been present when Count Zadowa opened that letter in his private office, he would have seen an unexpected sight. He would have seen him tear the letter into a thousand pieces, and then wipe his forehead with a hand that trembled a little. For Count Zadowa, who terrified most men, was frightened himself.

The second person who viewed this sudden notoriety with dislike was Inspector McIver. And in his case, too, the reason was largely personal. He was caught on the horns of a dilemma, as Sir Bryan Johnstone, who was not too pleased with the turn of events, pointed out to him a little caustically. Either the entire thing was a hoax, in which case why had McIver himself taken such elaborate precautions to prevent anything happening? Or it was not a hoax, in which case McIver had been made a complete fool of.

'I'll stake my reputation on the fact that no-one got into or left the house that night, Sir Bryan,' he reiterated again and again. 'That the Black Gang was at work in the town, I admit; but I do not believe that Mr Latter's condition is anything more that a strange coincidence.'

It was an interview that he had with Mr Latter's brother that caused him to go round to Drummond's house in Brook Street. Much as he disliked having to do so, he felt he must leave no stone unturned if he was to get to the bottom of the affair, and Mr Latter's brother had said one or two things which he thought might be worth following up. If only Hugh Drummond wasn't such a confounded fool, he reflected savagely, as he turned into Bond Street, it would have been possible to get some sane information. But that was his chief's fault; he entirely washed his hands of the responsibility of roping in such a vast idiot. And it was at that stage in his meditations that a Rolls-Royce drew silently up beside him, and the cheerful voice of the subject of his thoughts hailed him delightedly.

'The very man, and the very spot!'

'McIver turned round and nodded briefly.'

'Morning, Captain Drummond! I was just going round to your house to see you.'

'But, my dear old top,' cried Hugh, 'don't you see where you are? The portals of the Regency positively beckon us. Behind those portals a cocktail apiece, and you shall tell me all your troubles.'

He gently propelled the Inspector through the doors of the celebrated club, still babbling cheerfully.

'After profound experience, old lad,' he remarked, coming to anchor by the bar, 'I have come to the conclusion that there is only one thing in this world better than having a cocktail at twelve o'clock.'

'What's that?' said McIver perfunctorily.

'Having two,' answered Drummond triumphantly.

The Inspector smiled wanly. After his profound experience he had come to the conclusion that there could exist no bigger ass in the world than Drummond, but he followed a trade where at times it is necessary to suffer fools gladly. And this was one of them.

'Is there any place where we could have a little private talk, Captain Drummond?' he asked, as the other pushed a Martini towards him.

'What about that corner over there?' said Drummond, after glancing round the room.

'Excellent!' agreed the Inspector, and, picking up his cocktail, he crossed over to it and sat down. It took his host nearly five minutes to do the same short journey, and McIver chafed irritably at the delay. He was a busy man, and it seemed to him that Drummond knew everyone in the room. Moreover, he insisted on talking to them at length. And once again a feeling of anger against his chief filled his mind. What had Drummond except his great strength to distinguish him from this futile crowd of cocktail-drinking men? All of them built on the same pattern; all of them fashioned along the same lines. Talking a strange jargon of their own – idle, perfectly groomed, bored. As far as they were concerned, he was non-existent save as the man who was with Drummond. He smiled a little grimly; he, who did more man's work in a week than the whole lot of them put together got through in a year. A strange caste, he reflected, as he sipped his drink: a caste which does not aim at, because it essentially is, good form; a caste which knows only one fetish – the absolute repression of all visible emotion; a caste which incidentally pulled considerably more than its own weight in the war. McIver gave them credit for that.

'Sorry to be so long.' Drummond lowered himself into a chair. 'The place is always crowded at this hour. Now, what's the little worry?'

'It's about the affair up at Sheffield,' said the Inspector. 'I suppose you've seen this communication in the papers, purporting to come from the leader of the Black Gang.'

'Rather, old lad,' answered Drummond. 'Waded through it over the eggs the other morning. Pretty useful effort, I thought.'

'The public at large regard it as a hoax,' continued McIver. 'Now, I know it isn't! The typewriter used in the original document is the same as was used in their previous communications.'

'By Jove, that's quick!' said Drummond admiringly. 'Deuced quick.' McIver frowned.

'Now please concentrate, Captain Drummond. The concluding sentence of the letter would lead one to suppose that there was some connection between the activities of this gang and Mr Charles Latter's present condition. I, personally, don't believe it. I think it was mere coincidence. But whichever way it is, I would give a great deal to know what sent him mad.'

'Is he absolutely up the pole?' demanded Drummond.

'Absolutely! His brother has seen him, and after he had seen him he came to me. He tells me that the one marked symptom is an overmastering terror of something which he seems to see at the foot of the bed. He follows this thing round with his eyes – I suppose he thinks it's coming towards him – and then he screams. His brother believes that someone or something must have been in his room that night – a something so terrifying that it sent him mad. To my mind, of course, the idea is wildly improbable, but strange things do occur.'

'Undoubtedly!' agreed Drummond.

'Now you were in the house,' went on the Inspector; 'you even examined his room, as you told Sir Bryan. Now, did you examine it closely?'

'Even to looking under the bed,' answered Drummond brightly.

'And there was nothing there? No place where anybody or anything could hide?'

'Not a vestige of a spot. In fact, my dear old police hound,' continued Drummond, draining his glass, 'if the genial brother is correct in his supposition, the only conclusion we can come to is that I sent him mad myself.'

McIver frowned again.

'I wish you'd be serious, Captain Drummond. There are other

things in life beside cocktails and – this.' He waved an expressive hand round the room. 'The matter is an important one. You can give me no further information? You heard no sounds during the night?'

'Only the sheep-faced man snoring,' answered Drummond with a grin. And then, of a sudden, he became serious and, leaning across the table, he stared fixedly at the Inspector.

'I think we must conclude, McIver, that the madness of Mr Latter is due to the ghosts of the past, and perhaps the spectres of the present. A punishment, McIver, for things done which it is not good to do – a punishment which came to him in the night. That's when the ghosts are abroad.' He noted McIver's astonished face and gradually his own relaxed into a smile. 'Pretty good, that – wasn't it, after only one cocktail. You ought to hear me after my third.'

'Thanks very much, Captain Drummond,' laughed the Inspector, 'but that was quite good enough for me. We don't deal in ghosts in my service.'

'Well, I've done my best,' sighed Drummond, waving languidly at a waiter to repeat the dose. 'It's either that or me. I know my face is pretty bad, but – '

'I don't think we need worry about either alternative,' said McIver, rising.

'Right oh, old lad,' answered Drummond. 'You know best. You'll have another?'

'No more, thanks. I have to work sometimes.'

The inspector picked up his hat and stick, and Drummond strolled across the room with him.

'Give my love to Tum-tum.'

'Sir Bryan is not at the office today, Captain Drummond,' answered McIver coldly. 'Good morning.'

With a faint smile Drummond watched the square, sturdy figure swing through the doors into Bond Street, then he turned and thoughtfully made his way back to the table.

'Make it seven, instead of two,' he told the waiter, who was hovering round.

And had McIver returned at that moment he would have seen six of these imperturbable, bored men rise unobtrusively from different parts of the room, and saunter idly across to the corner where he had recently been sitting. It would probably not have struck him as an unusual sight – Drummond and six of his pals having a second drink; in fact, it would have struck him as being very usual. He was an unimaginative man was the Inspector.

'Well,' said Peter Darrell, lighting a cigarette. 'And what had he got to say?'

'Nothing of interest,' answered Drummond. 'I told him the truth, and he wouldn't believe me. Algy back yet?'

'This morning,' said Ted Jerningham. 'He's coming round here. Had a bit of trouble, I gather. And, talk of the devil – here he is.'

Algy Longworth, his right arm in a sling, was threading his way towards them.

'What's happened, Algy?' said Hugh as he came up.

'That firebrand Delmorlick stuck a knife into me,' grinned Algy. 'We put him on a rope and dropped him overboard, and towed him for three hundred yards. Cooled his ardour. I think he'll live all right.'

'And how are all the specimens?'

'Prime, old son – prime! If we leave 'em long enough, they'll all have murdered one another.'

Drummond put down his empty glass with a laugh.

'The first British Soviet. Long life to 'em! Incidentally, ten o'clock tonight. Usual rendezvous. In view of your arm, Algy – transfer your instructions to Ted. You've got 'em?'

'In my pocket here. But, Hugh, I can easily – '

'Transfer to Ted, please. No argument! We've got a nice little job – possibly some sport. Read 'em, Ted – and business as usual. So long, boys! Phyllis and I are lunching with some awe-inspiring relatives.'

The group broke up as casually as it had formed, only Ted Jerningham remaining behind. And he was reading what looked like an ordinary letter. He read it through carefully six or seven times; then he placed it in the fire, watching it until it was reduced to ashes. A few minutes later he was sitting down to lunch with his father, Sir Patrick Jerningham, Bart., at the latter's club in Pall Mall. And it is possible that that worthy and conscientious gentleman would not have eaten such a hearty meal had he known that his only son was detailed for a job that very night which, in the event of failure, would mean either prison or a knife in the back – probably the latter.

Chapter 7

In which a bomb bursts at unpleasantly close quarters

It was perhaps because the thought of failure never entered Hugh Drummond's head that such a considerable measure of success had been possible up to date – that, and the absolute, unquestioning obedience which he demanded of his pals, and which they accorded him willingly. As they knew, he laid no claims to brilliance; but as they also knew, he hid a very shrewd common sense beneath his frivolous manner. And having once accepted the sound military truism that one indifferent general is better than two good ones, they accepted his leadership with unswerving loyalty. What was going to be the end of their self-imposed fight against the pests of society did not worry them greatly; all that mattered was that there should be a certain amount of sport in the collection of the specimens. Granted the promise of that, they willingly sacrificed any engagements and carried out Hugh's orders to the letter. Up to date, however, the campaign, though far from being dull, had not produced any really big results. A number of sprats and a few moderate-sized fish had duly been caught in the landing-net, and been sent to the private pool to meditate at leisure. But nothing really large had come their way. Zaboleff was a good haul, and the madness of Mr Latter was all for the national welfare. But the Black Gang, which aimed merely at the repression of terrorism by terrorism, had found it too easy. The nauseating cowardice of the majority of their opponents was becoming monotonous, their strong aversion to soap and water, insanitary. They wanted big game – not the rats that emerged from the sewers.

Even Drummond had begun to feel that patriotism might be carried too far until the moment when the address in Hoxton had fallen into his hands. Then, with the optimism that lives eternal in the hunter's breast, fresh hope had arisen in his mind. It had been held in abeyance temporarily owing to the little affair at Sheffield. Yet now that that was over he had determined on a bigger game. If it failed – if they drew blank – he had almost decided to chuck the thing up altogether. Phyllis, he knew, would be over-joyed if he did.

'Just this one final coup, old girl,' he said, as they sat waiting in the Carlton for the awe-inspiring relatives. 'I've got it cut and dried, and it comes off tonight. If it's a dud, we'll dissolve ourselves – at any rate, for the present. If only – '

He sighed, and his wife looked at him reproachfully.

'I know you want another fight with Petersen, you old goat,' she remarked. 'But you'll never see him again, or that horrible girl.'

'Don't you think I shall, Phyl?' He stared despondently at his shoes. 'I can't help feeling myself that somewhere or other behind all this that cheery bird is lurking. My dear, it would be too ghastly if I never saw him again.'

'The next time you see him, Hugh,' she answered quietly, 'he won't take any chances with you.'

'But, my angel child,' he boomed cheerfully. 'I don't want him to. Not on your life! Nor shall I. Good Lord! Here they are. Uncle Timothy looks more like a mangel-wurzel than ever.'

And so at nine-thirty that evening, a party of five men sat waiting in a small sitting-room of a house situated in a remote corner of South Kensington. Some easels stood round the walls covered with half-finished sketches, as befitted a room belonging to a budding artist such as Toby Sinclair. Not that he was an artist or even a budding one, but he felt that a man must have some excuse for living in South Kensington. And so he had bought the sketches and put them round the room, principally to deceive the landlady. The fact that he was never there except at strange hours merely confirmed that excellent woman's opinion that all artists were dissolute rascals. But he paid his rent regularly, and times were hard, especially in South Kensington. Had the worthy soul known that her second best sitting-room was the rendezvous of this Black Gang whose letter to the paper she and her husband had discussed over the matutinal kipper, it is doubtful if she would have been so complacent. But she didn't know, and continued her weekly dusting of the sketches with characteristic zeal.

'Ted should be here soon,' said Drummond, glancing at his watch. 'I hope he's got the bird all right.'

'You didn't get into the inner room, did you, Hugh?' said Peter Darrell.

'No. But I saw enough to know that it's beyond our form, old lad. We've got to have a skilled cracksman to deal with one of the doors – and almost certainly anything important will be in a safe inside.'

'Just run over the orders again.' Toby Sinclair came back from drawing the blinds even more closely together.

'Perfectly simple,' said Hugh. 'Ted and I and Ginger Martin – if he's got him – will go straight into the house through the front door. I know the geography of the place all right, and I've already laid out the caretaker clerk fellow once. Then we must trust to luck. There shouldn't be anybody there except the little blighter of a clerk. The rest of you will hang about outside in case of any trouble. Don't bunch together, keep on the move; but keep the doors in sight. When you see us come out again, make your own way home. Can't give you any more detailed instructions because I don't know what may turn up. I shall rig myself out here, after Ted arrives. You had better go to your own rooms and do it, but wait first to make sure that he's roped in Ginger Martin.'

He glanced up as the door opened and Jerry Seymour – sometime of the R.A.F. – put his head into the room.

'Ted's here, and he got the bird all right. Unpleasant-looking bloke with a flattened face.'

'Right.' Drummond rose, and crossed to a cupboard. 'Clear off, you fellows. Zero – twelve midnight.'

From the cupboard he pulled a long black cloak and mask, which he proceeded to put on, while the others disappeared, with the exception of Jerry Seymour, who came into the room. He was dressed in livery like a chauffeur, and he had, in fact, been driving the car in which Ted had brought Ginger Martin.

'Any trouble?' asked Drummond.

'No. Once he was certain Ted was nothing to do with the police he came like a bird,' said Jerry. 'The fifty quid did it.' Then he grinned. 'You know, Ted's a marvel. I'll defy anybody to recognise him.'

Drummond nodded, and sat down at the table facing the door.

'Tell Ted to bring him up. And I don't want him to see you, Jerry, so keep out of the light.'

Undoubtedly Jerry Seymour was right with regard to Jerningham's make-up. As he and Martin came into the room, it was only the sudden start and cry on the part of the crook that made Drummond certain as to which was which.

'Blimey!' muttered the man, shrinking back as he saw the huge figure in black confronting him. 'Wot's the game, guv'nor?'

'There's no game, Martin,' said Drummond reassuringly. 'You've been told what you're wanted for, haven't you? A little professional assistance tonight, for which you will be paid fifty pounds, is all we ask of you.'

But Ginger Martin still seemed far from easy in his mind. Like most of the underworld he had heard strange stories of the Black Gang long before they had attained the notoriety of print. Many of them were exaggerated, doubtless, but the general impression left in his mind was one of fear. The police were always with him: the police he understood. But this strange gang was beyond his comprehension, and that in itself was sufficient to frighten him.

'You're one of this 'ere Black Gang,' he said sullenly, glancing at the door in front of which Jerningham was standing Should he chance it and make a dash to get away? Fifty pounds are fifty pounds, but – He gave a little shiver as his eyes came round again to the motionless figure on the other side of the table.

'Quite correct, Martin,' said the same reassuring voice. 'And it's only because I don't want you to recognise me that I'm dressed up like this. We don't mean you any harm.' The voice paused for a moment, and then went on again. 'You understand that, Martin. We don't mean you any harm, unless' – and once again there came a pause – 'unless you try any monkey tricks. You are to do exactly as I tell you, without question and at once. If you do you will receive fifty pounds. If you don't – well, Martin, I have ways of dealing with people who don't do what I tell them.'

There was silence while Ginger Martin fidgeted about, looking like a trapped animal. How he wished now that he'd had nothing to do with the thing at all. But it was too late to bother about that; here he was, utterly ignorant of his whereabouts – trapped.

'What do yer want me to do, guv'nor?' he said at last.

'Open a safe amongst other things,' answered Drummond. 'Have you brought your tools and things?'

'Yus – I've brought the outfit,' muttered the other. 'Where is the safe? 'Ere?'

'No, Martin, not here. Some distance away in fact. We shall start in about an hour. Until then you will stop in this room. You can have a whisky-and-soda, and my friend here will stay with you. He has a gun, Martin, so remember what I said. No monkey tricks.'

With fascinated eyes the crook watched the speaker rise and cross to an inner door. Standing he seemed more huge than ever, and Martin gave a sigh of relief as the door closed behind him.

'I reckon 'e wouldn't win a prize as a blinking dwarf,' he remarked hoarsely to Jerningham. 'I say, mister, wot abaht that there whisky-and-soda?'

* * *

The entrance to Number 5, Green Street, proved easier than Drummond had expected – so easy as to be almost suspicious. No lights shone in the windows above: the house seemed completely deserted. Moreover, the door into the street was unbolted, and without a moment's hesitation Drummond opened it and stepped inside, followed by Martin and Ted Jerningham. The long black cloak had been discarded; only the black mask concealed his face, as the three men stood inside the door, listening intently. Not a sound was audible, and after a moment or two Drummond felt his way cautiously through the downstairs office towards the flight of stairs that led to the rooms above. And it was just as his foot was on the first stair that a sudden noise behind made him draw back sharply into the darkness behind the counter, with a warning whisper to the other two to follow his example.

The front door had opened again; someone else had come in. They could see nothing, and the only sound seemed to be the slightly quickened breathing of Ted Jerningham, whose nerve was not quite as good as the others at affairs of this sort. Then came the sound of bolts being shot home, and footsteps coming into the office.

With a whispered 'Stay there', Drummond glided across towards the door like a shadow, moving with uncanny silence for such a big man. And a moment or two afterwards someone came into the office. Jerningham, crouching against the crook behind the counter, could see the outline of a figure framed in the faint light that filtered in from a street lamp through the fanlight over the door. Then there was a click, and the electric light was switched on.

For a second the newcomer failed to see them; then, with a sudden gasp he stiffened, and stood staring at them rigidly. It was Cohen, the unpleasant little clerk, returning from an evening out, which accounted for the front door having been unbolted. And undoubtedly his luck was out. Because, having seen the two of them there behind the counter, he somewhat naturally failed to look for anybody else. It would not have made any great difference if he had, but the expression on his face as he felt two enormous hands close gently but firmly round his throat from behind caused even the phlegmatic Ginger to chuckle grimly.

'Out with the light,' snapped Drummond, 'then help me lash him up and gag him.'

It was done quickly and deftly, and for the second time in a week the wretched Cohen was laid under his own counter to cool. It had been carried out as noiselessly as possible, but it was five minutes before Drummond again led the way cautiously up the stairs. And during that five minutes the three men listened with every sense alert, striving to differentiate between the ordinary street noises and anything unusual in the house above them. But not even Drummond's ears, trained as they had been for many nights in No Man's Land, could detect anything. All seemed as quiet as the grave.

'It probably is empty except for that little rat,' he whispered to Jerningham. 'But we'll take no chances.'

In single file they crept up the stairs, Drummond leading. The door at the top was ajar, and for a while they stood in the carpeted passage above listening again.

'Along this passage are the clerks' offices,' he explained in a low voice to the other two. 'At the far end is another door which we shall probably find locked. Beyond that is the inner office, which we want.'

'Well, let's get on wiv it, guv'nor,' muttered Ginger Martin hoarsely. 'There's no good in 'anging abaht.'

Drummond switched on his electric torch, and flashed it cautiously round. Doors leading off the passage were open in most cases, and all the rooms were empty; it was obvious that none of the staff were about. And yet he felt an indefinable sense of danger, which he tried in vain to shake off. Somehow or other, he felt certain that they were not alone – that there were other people in the house, besides the trussed-up clerk below. But Ginger Martin had no such presentiments, and was rapidly becoming impatient. To open the door at the end of the passage, if it should prove to be locked, was such child's play as to be absolutely contemptible. He wanted to get on with the safe, which might take time, instead of fooling round in a passage listening for mice.

At last Drummond moved slowly forward with the other two just behind him. Whatever he may have thought, he had every intention of going through with the job, and delay in such cases only tends to turn vague fears into certain realities. Gently he tried the door at the end of the passage; as he had anticipated it was locked.

' 'Old the light, guv'nor, so that it shines on the blinkin' key-'ole!'

said Ginger Martin impatiently. 'I'll get this open as easy as kiss yer 'and.'

Without a sound, the cracksman set to work, his coarse features outlined in the circle of the torch, his ill-kept fingers handling his instruments as deftly as any surgeon. A little oil here and there; a steady pressure with a short pointed steel tool; a faint click.

'There you are, guv'nor,' he muttered, straightening up. 'Easy as kiss yer 'and. And if yer waits till I find me glove I'll open it for yer; but Ginger Martin's fingerprints are too well known to run any risks.'

Still no sound came from anywhere, though the click as the lock shot back had seemed horribly loud in the silence. And then, just as Martin cautiously turned the handle and pushed open the door, Drummond stiffened suddenly and switched off his torch. He could have sworn that he heard the sound of voices close by.

Only for a second – they were instantly silenced; but just for that fraction of time as the door opened he felt certain he had heard men speaking.

'Wot's the matter?' he heard Martin's hoarse whisper come out of the darkness.

'Did you hear voices?' he breathed in reply. 'I thought I did as you opened the door.'

Once again the three men stood motionless, listening intently, but the sound was not repeated. Absolute silence reigned, broken only by the noise of their own breathing. And at last, after what seemed an interminable pause, Drummond switched on his torch again. The passage was empty; the door of the inner office was just in front of them. Almost he was persuaded that he must have made a mistake – that it had been his imagination. He peered through the keyhole: the room was in darkness. He turned the handle cautiously; the door gave to him; and still with his torch held well in front of him, he stepped into the room, turning the light into every corner. Not a trace of anyone; the inner office was absolutely empty. He flashed the light all round the walls, as far as he could see there was no other door – not even a window. Consequently the only way out was by the door through which they had just entered, which was obviously impossible for anyone to have done without his knowledge.

'It's all right!' he muttered, turning round to the other two. 'Must have been my mistake. Let's get on with it.'

'There's a mighty strong smell of cigar smoke,' said Jerningham dubiously.

'No ventilation, old man,' returned Drummond. 'Hangs about for hours. No other door, no window. Now then, Ginger, let's tackle the big desk first. It looks pretty easy, even to me.'

As he spoke he moved into the centre of the room, his torch lighting up the big roll-top desk.

'Right-ho, guv'nor. Keep the beam on the keyhole – '

The crook bent over his task, only to straighten up suddenly as all the lights went on.

'Yer damned fool!' he snarled. 'Switch 'em off! It ain't safe.'

'I didn't put 'em on!' snapped Drummond.

'Nor I,' said Jerningham.

For a moment or two no-one spoke; then Ginger Martin made a wild dive for the door. But the door which had opened so easily a few moments before now refused to budge, though he tugged at it, cursing horribly. And after a while he gave it up, and turned on Drummond like a wild beast.

'You've trapped me, yer – swine. I'll get even with you over this if I swing for it!'

But Drummond, to whom the presence of actual danger was as meat and drink, took not the slightest notice. His brain, ice-cold and clear, was moving rapidly. It had not been a mistake, he *had* heard voices – voices which came from that very room in which they now were. Men had been there – men who had got out by some other way. And Ginger Martin was trapped – all of them. More out of thoughtlessness than anything else, he brushed the swearing crook aside with the back of his hand – much as one brushes away a troublesome fly. And Martin, feeling as if he'd been kicked in the mouth by a horse, ceased to swear . . .

It was uncanny – devilish. The room was empty, save for them, suddenly flooded with light. But by whom? Drummond felt they were being watched. But by whom? And then suddenly he heard Ted Jerningham's voice, low and tense.

'There's a man watching us, Hugh. I can see his eyes. In that big safe door.'

Like a flash, Drummond swung round, and looked at the safe. Ted was right; he could see the eyes himself, and they were fixed on him with an expression of malignant fury through a kind of opening that looked like the slit in a letter box. For a moment or two they remained there, staring at him, then they disappeared, and the opening through which he had seen them disappeared also, and seemed to become part of the door. And it was just as he was moving towards this mysterious safe to examine it closer that with a sudden clang, another opening appeared – one much larger than the first. He stopped involuntarily as something was thrown through into the room – something which hissed and spluttered.

For a moment he gazed at it uncomprehendingly as it lay on the floor; then he gave a sudden, tense order.

'On your faces – for your lives!' His voice cut through the room like a knife. 'Behind the desk, you fools! It's a bomb!'

Chapter 8

In which the Bag of Nuts is Found by Accident

It was the desk that saved Drummond, and with him Ted Jerning-ham. Flat on their faces, their arms covering their heads, they lay on the floor waiting, as in days gone by they had waited for the bursting of a too-near crump. They heard Ginger Martin, as he blundered round the room, and then – suddenly it came.

There was a deafening roar, and a sheet of flame which seemed to fill the room. Great lumps of the ceiling rained down and the big roll-top desk, cracked in pieces and splintered into matchwood, fell over on top of them. But it had done its work: it had borne the full force of the explosion in their direction. As a desk its day was past; it had become a series of holes roughly held together by fragments of wood.

So much Drummond could see by the aid of his torch. With the explosion all the lights had gone out, and for a while he lay pressed against Ted Jerningham trying to recover his wits. His head was singing like a bursting kettle: his back felt as if it was broken where a vast lump of ceiling had hit him. But after moving his legs cautiously and then his arms, he decided that he was still alive. And having arrived at that momentous conclusion, the necessity for prompt action became evident. A bomb bursting in London is not exactly a private affair.

'Are you all right, Ted?' he muttered hoarsely, his mouth full of plaster and dust.

'I think so, old man,' answered Jerningham, and Drummond heaved a sigh of relief. 'I got a whack on the back of the head from something.'

Drummond scrambled to his feet, and switched on his torch. The wreckage was complete, but it was for the third member of the party that he was looking. And after a moment or two he found him, and cursed with a vigorous fury that boded ill for the person who had thrown the bomb, if he ever met him.

For Ginger Martin, being either too frightened or too ignorant, had not done as he was told. There had been no desk between him and the bomb when it burst, and what was left of him adorned a corner. There was nothing to be done: the unfortunate crook would never again burgle a safe. And the only comfort to Drummond was that death must have been absolutely instantaneous.

'Poor devil,' he muttered. 'Someone is going to pay for this.'

And then he felt Ted Jerningham clutching his arm.

'It's blown a hole in the wall, man. Look.'

It was true: he could see the light of a street lamp shining through a great jagged hole.

'Some bomb,' he muttered. 'Let's clear.'

He gave a final flash of his torch round the floor, as they moved towards the shattered wall, and then suddenly stopped.

'What's that?'

Right in the centre of the beam, lying in the middle of the floor, was a small chamois-leather bag. It seemed unhurt, and, without thinking, Hugh picked it up and put it in his pocket. Then, switching off the torch, they both clambered through the hole, dropped on to a lean-to roof, and reached the ground.

They were at the back of the house in some deserted mews, and rapidity of movement was clearly indicated. Already a crowd was hurrying to the scene of the explosion, and slipping quietly out of the dark alley, they joined in themselves.

'Go home, Ted,' said Drummond. 'I must get the others.'

'Right, old man.' He made no demur, but just vanished quietly, while his leader slouched on towards the front door of Number 5, Green Street. The police were already beating on it, while a large knot of interested spectators giving gratuitous advice stood around them. And in the crowd Drummond could see six of his gang: six anxious men who had determined – police or no police – to get upstairs and see what had happened. In one and all their minds was a sickening fear, that the man they followed had at last bitten off more than he could chew – that they'd find him blown to pieces in the mysterious room upstairs.

And then, quite clear and distinct above the excited comments of the crowd, came the hooting of an owl. A strange sound to hear in a London street, but no-one paid any attention. Other more engrossing matters were on hand, more engrossing that is to all except the six men who instantaneously swung half round as they heard it. For just a second they had a glimpse of a huge figure standing in the light of a lamp-post on the other side of the street – then it disappeared. And with astonishing celerity they followed its example. Whoever had been hurt it was not Drummond; and that, at the moment, was all they were concerned with.

By devious routes they left the scene of the explosion – each with the same goal in his mind. The owl had only hooted once, which meant that they were to reassemble as soon as possible: the second call, which meant disperse, had not been given. And so within an hour six young men, shorn of all disguise and clad in immaculate evening clothes, were admitted to Drummond's house in Brook Street by a somewhat sleepy Denny.

They found Hugh arrayed in a gorgeous dressing-gown with a large tankard of beer beside him, and his wife sitting on the arm of his chair.

'Beer, souls,' he grunted. 'In the corner, as usual.'

'What happened, old lad?' asked Peter Darrell.

'I got handed the frozen mitten. I asked for bread, and they put across a half-brick. To be absolutely accurate we got into the room all right, and having got in we found we couldn't get out. Then someone switched on the light, and bunged a bomb at us through a hole in the door. Quite O.K., old girl' – he put a reassuring arm round Phyllis's waist – 'I think we'd be still there if they hadn't.'

'Is Ted all right?' asked Toby Sinclair.

'Yes. Ted's all right. Got a young load of bricks in his back when the ceiling came down – but he's all right. It's the other poor devil – Ginger Martin.' His face was grim and stern, and the others waited in silence for him to continue.

'There was a big desk in the room, and the bomb fell on one side of it. Ted and I gave our well-known impersonation of an earthworm on the other, which saved us. Unfortunately, Ginger Martin elected to run round in small circles and curse. And he will curse no more.'

'Dead?' Peter Darrell's voice was low.

'Very,' answered Drummond quietly. 'In fact, he's now giving his well-known impersonation of a wallpaper. The poor blighter was blown to pieces. If he'd done what I told him he wouldn't have been, but that's beside the point. He was working for me, and he was killed while he was doing so. And I don't like that happening.'

'Oh! my dear,' said Phyllis. 'I do wish you'd give it up. You've escaped this time, but sooner or later they'll get you. It isn't worth it.'

Drummond shook his head, and again encircled his wife's waist with his arm.

'You wouldn't like me to let that poor devil's death go unavenged, would you?' He looked up at her, and she shrugged her shoulders resignedly. A year of marriage with this vast husband of hers had convinced her of the futility of arguing with him once his mind was made up. 'Not that the country will be appreciably worse off for his departure, but that's not the point. He was doing a job for me when it happened, and I don't stand for that at all.'

'What do you propose to do?' demanded Jerry Seymour, thoughtfully refilling his glass.

'Well, there, old son, at the moment you have me beat,' conceded Hugh. 'I sort of figured it out this way. Whoever the bird is who bunged that bomb, he recognised me as being the leader of our little bunch. I mean it was me he was staring at through the door, with eyes bubbling over with tenderness and love. It was me that bally bomb was intended for – not Ginger Martin, though he was actually doing the work. And if this cove is prepared to wreck his own office just to get me out of the way – I guess I must be somewhat unpopular.'

'The reasoning seems extraordinarily profound,' murmured Peter.

'Now the great point is – does he know who I am?' continued Hugh. 'Is the little treasure now saying to himself, what time he lowers the evening cup of bread-and-milk, "That has settled the hash of one Hugh Drummond", or is he merely saying, "I have nastily disintegrated the leader of the Black Gang"?'

'But what's it matter anyway?' demanded Toby. 'He hasn't disintegrated you, and he's smashed up his own office – so I fail to see where he wins the grand piano.'

'That, old Toby, is where you show yourself incapable of grasping the finer points of the situation.' Hugh thoughtfully lit a cigarette. 'Our great difficulty before Zaboleff was kind enough to present us with the address of their headquarters was to get in touch with the man at the top. And now the headquarters are no more. No man can work in an office with periodical boulders falling on his head from the roof, and a large hole in the wall just behind him. I mean there's no privacy about it. And so – unless he knows me – he won't be able to carry on the good work when he finds that neither of my boots has reached the top of St. Paul's. We shall be parted again – which is dreadful to think of. There's no cheery little meeting-ground where we can foregather for the matutinal Martini or even Manhattan. Why, we might even pass one another in the street as complete strangers.'

'I get you,' said Peter. 'And you don't know him.'

'Not well enough to call him Bertie. There's a humpbacked blighter up there who calls himself a Count, and on whom I focused the old optic for about two seconds the other evening. But whether he's the humorist who bunged the bomb or not is a different matter.' He glanced up as the door opened. 'What is it, Denny?'

'I found this bag, sir, in the pocket of the coat you were wearing tonight.'

His servant came into the room carrying the chamois-leather bag, which he handed to Drummond.

'Will you be wanting anything more tonight, sir?'

'No, thank you, Denny. You toddle off to bye-bye. And give Mrs Denny a chaste salute from Mr Darrell.'

'Very good, sir!'

The door closed behind him, and Hugh stared thoughtfully at the bag in his hand.

'I'd forgotten about this. Saw it lying on the floor, just before we hopped it. Hullo! it's sealed.'

'For goodness' sake be careful, boy!' cried Phyllis. 'It may be another bomb.'

Hugh laughed and ripped open the bag; then his eyes slowly widened in amazement as he saw the contents.

'Great Scott!' he cried. 'What the devil have we got here?'

He emptied the bag out on to the table, and for a moment or two the others stared silently at half a dozen objects that flashed and glittered with a thousand fires. Five of them were white; but the sixth – appreciably larger than the others, and they were the size of walnuts – was a wonderful rose pink.

'What on earth are they? Lumps of glass?'

With a hand that shook a little, Toby Sinclair picked one of them up and examined it.

'No, you fellows,' he muttered. 'they're diamonds!'

'Rot!' cried Hugh incredulously.

'They're diamonds,' repeated Toby. 'I happen to know something about precious stones. These are diamonds.'

'But they must be worth a lot,' said Phyllis, picking up the pink one.

'Worth a lot,' said Toby dazedly. 'Worth a lot! Why, Mrs Hugh, they are literally worth untold gold in the right market. They are absolutely priceless. I've never even thought of such stones. That one that you're holding in your hand would be worth over a quarter of a million pounds, if you could get the right buyer.'

For a moment no-one spoke; then Hugh laughed cheerily.

'Bang goes next month's dress allowance, old thing!' He swept them all into the bag, and stood up. 'I'm laying even money that the bomb-thrower is coughing some and then again over his bread-and-milk. This bag must have been in the desk.' His shoulders began to shake. 'How frightfully funny!'

Chapter 9

In which there is a stormy supper party at the Ritz

It was just about the time that Ginger Martin's wife became, all unconsciously, a widow, that the sitting-room bell of a certain private suite in the Ritz was rung. The occupants of the room were two in number – a man and a woman – and they had arrived only that morning from the Continent. The man, whose signature in the register announced him to be the Reverend Theodosius Long-moor – looked a splendid specimen of the right sort of clergyman. Tall, broad-shouldered, with a pair of shrewd, kindly eyes and a great mass of snow-white hair, he was the type of man who attracted attention wherever he went, and in whatever society he found himself. A faint twang in his speech betrayed his nationality, and, indeed, he made no secret of it. He was an American born and bred, who had been seeing first-hand for himself some of the dreadful horrors of the famine which was ravaging Central Europe.

And with him had gone his daughter Janet – that faithful, constant companion of his, who since her mother's death had never left him. She was a good-looking girl, too – though perhaps unkind people might have said girlhood's happy days had receded somewhat into the past. Thirty, perhaps – even thirty-five – though her father always alluded to her as 'My little girl'.

There was something very sweet and touching about their relationship; his pride in her and her simple, loving adoration for Dad. Only that evening before dinner they had got into conversation in the lounge with a party of American globe-trotters, who had unanimously voted them quite charming.

'I feel,' had said the Reverend Theodosius, 'that it is almost wicked our staying in such an hotel as this, after the dreadful things we've seen. How my little girl stood it at all I don't know.' He took his daughter's hand and patted it lovingly.

'I guess,' said Janet with her faint, sweet smile. 'I guess that Dad deserves it. Why, he nearly worked himself ill doing relief work and things out there in Vienna and places.'

'Is there any lack of funds, Mr Longmoor?' asked one lady. 'One feels one ought to do something to help.'

The Reverend Theodosius gave her one of his rare sweet smiles.

'There was when I left,' he murmured. 'You'd never believe how money goes out there, and really the poor children have very little to show for it.'

'Too bad – too bad.' A square-jawed man who was a member of the party beckoned to a passing waiter. 'Say, Mr Longmoor, will you drink a cocktail with me? And your daughter, too?'

'It is very good of you, sir,' answered the clergyman, with a courteous bow. 'My little girl has never even tasted one and I think perhaps she had better not. What do you think, my child?'

'I'd love to try, Daddy, dear,' she said coaxingly. 'Do you think I might? Or would it make my head go funny?'

They all laughed.

'That settles it, Miss Longmoor,' cried the man. 'I've ordered one for you, and if you don't drink it your father will have to drink two.'

Undoubtedly a charming couple, had been the verdict of these chance acquaintances – so simple, so fresh, so unassuming in these days of complexity and double-dealing. The only pity of it was, as the square-jawed man remarked to his wife at dinner, that the very quality of childlike simplicity which made them so charming was the one which laid them open to the most barefaced swindling if they ever came up against blackguards.

After dinner they had all drunk coffee together, and then, because his little Janet was tired, the Reverend Theodore and his daughter had retired after accepting an invitation to dinner the next day.

'Who are they?' asked Janet, as they entered their sitting room.

'That square-jawed man is John Pendel,' answered her father, thoughtfully lighting a cigar. 'Worth about three million. He's good for dining with, though I'm not over here on any sideshows.'

And then for two hours until he got up and rang the bell, the Reverend Theodosius remained engrossed in work while his little Janet, lying on the sofa, displayed considerably more leg than one would have expected a vicar's daughter even to possess. And occasional gurgles of laughter seemed to prove that Guy de Maupassant appeals to a more catholic audience than he would have suspected.

She was knitting decorously when the waiter came in, and her father ordered a little supper to be sent up.

'Some chicken, please, and a little foie gras. I am expecting a friend very soon – so lay for three. Some champagne – yes. Perrier Jouet '04 will do. I'm afraid I don't know much about wine. And a little Vichy water for my daughter.'

The waiter withdrew, and the Reverend Theodosius chuckled.

'There's a very good bath you can empty it down, my dear,' he said. 'But I don't think my little Janet should drink champagne so late. It might make her head go funny.'

She smiled and then grew serious.

'What time do you expect Zadowa?'

'He should have been here by now. I don't know why he's late.'

'Did you see him this afternoon?'

'No. I was down at the office, but only for a short while.'

The sound of voices outside the door caused Janet to resume her knitting, and the next moment Count Zadowa was announced. For an appreciable time after the waiter had withdrawn he stood staring at them: then a smile crossed his face.

'Magnificent,' he murmured. 'Superb. Madame, I felicitate you. Well though I know your powers, this time you have excelled yourself.'

'Cut that out, and get to business,' returned little Janet shortly, 'I'm tired.'

'But should we be interrupted,' remarked the Reverend Theodosius, 'we have just returned from an extensive tour in the famine-stricken area round Vienna.'

The Count bowed and smiled again.

'*C'est entendu*,' he said quietly. 'And now we will certainly get to business. For I have the most wonderful news for you, *mes amis*.'

A warning gesture from the girl announced the arrival of supper, and for a while the conversation turned on the rival merits of different types of soup kitchen. And it was not until the outer door finally closed behind the waiter, that the Reverend Theodosius bit the end off another cigar and stared at his visitor with eyes from which every trace of kindliness had vanished.

'It's about time you did have some good news, Zadowa,' he snapped. 'Anything more damned disgraceful than the way you've let this so-called Black Gang do you in, I've never heard of.'

But the other merely smiled quietly.

'I admit it,' he murmured. 'Up to date they have scored a faint measure of success – exaggerated, my friends, greatly exaggerated by the papers. Tonight came the reckoning, which incidentally is the reason why I am a little late. Tonight' – he leaned forward impressively – 'the leader of the gang himself honoured me with a visit. And the leader will lead no more.'

'You killed him,' said the girl, helping herself to champagne.

'I did,' answered the Count. 'And without the leader I think we can ignore the gang.'

'That's all right as far as it goes,' said the Reverend Theodosius in a slightly mollified tone. 'But have you covered all your traces? In this country the police get peevish over murder.'

The Count gave a self-satisfied smile.

'Not only that,' he remarked, 'but I have made it appear as if he had killed himself. Listen, my friends, and I will give you a brief statement of the events of the past few days. It was the day before the affair at Sheffield which caused such a commotion in the papers that I suddenly found out that the leader of this gang had discovered my headquarters in Hoxton. I was actually talking to that wretched man Latter in my office at the time, when I heard outside the call of an owl. Now from information I had received, that was the rallying call of their gang, and I dashed into the passage. Sure enough, standing by the door at the end was a huge man covered from head to foot in black. Whether it was bravado that made him give the cry, or whether it was a ruse to enable him to see me, is immaterial now. As I say – he is dead. But – and this is the point – it made me decide that the office there, convenient though it was, would have to be given up. There were far too many incriminating documents to allow me to run the risk of a police raid; and since I frankly admit now that I was not at all sure what were the relations between this gang and the police, I decided to move my headquarters.'

Count Zadowa helped himself to a sandwich before continuing, with a pleasant feeling that the motionless attention of the Reverend Theodosius was a compliment to his powers as a raconteur. And as the hunchback reflected complacently, there was no falling off in this story – no anticlimax.

'Tonight,' he continued, sipping his glass, 'I was completing the final sorting out of my papers with my secretary, when the electric warning disc on my desk glowed red. Now the office was empty, and the red light meant that someone had opened the door outside. I heard nothing, which only made it all the more suspicious. So between us we gathered up every important paper, switched off all lights, and went out through the secret door. Then we waited.'

He turned to the clergyman, still motionless save for a ceaseless tapping of his left knee with his hand.

'As you know, monsieur,' he proceeded, 'there is an opening in that door through which one can see into the room. And through that opening I watched developments. After a while a torch was switched on at the farther door, and I heard voices. And then the man holding the torch came cautiously in. He was turning it into every corner, but finally he focused it on the desk. I heard him speak to one of his companions, who came into the beam of light and started to pick the lock. And it was then that I switched on every light, and closed the door electrically. They were caught – caught like rats in a trap.'

The hunchback paused dramatically, and drained his champagne. If he was expecting any laudatory remarks on the part of his audience he was disappointed. But the Reverend Theodosius and his little Janet might have been carved out of marble, save for that ceaseless tapping by the man of his left knee. In fact, had Count Zadowa been less pleased with himself and less sure of the effect he was about to cause he might have had a premonition of coming danger. There was something almost terrifying in the big clergyman's immobility.

'Like rats in a trap,' repeated the hunchback gloatingly. 'Two men I didn't know, and – well, you know who the other was. True he had his mask on by way of disguise, but I recognised him at once. That huge figure couldn't be mistaken – it was the leader of the Black Gang himself.'

'And what did you do, Zadowa?'

The Reverend Theodosius's voice was very soft.

'How did you dispose of one or all those men so that no suspicion is likely to rest on you?'

The hunchback rubbed his hands together gleefully.

'By an act which, I think you will agree, is very nearly worthy of yourself, monsieur. To shoot was impossible – because I am not sufficiently expert with a revolver to be sure of killing them. No – nothing so ordinary as that. They saw me watching them: "I can see his eyes, Hugh," said one of them to the leader, and I remember suddenly that in the passage not far from where I stood were half a dozen bombs – What is it, monsieur?'

He paused in alarm at the look on the clergyman's face as he slowly rose.

'Bombs!' he snarled. 'Bombs! Tell me what you did, you dreg!'

'Why,' stammered the frightened hunchback, 'I threw one into the room. I no longer wanted it as an office, and . . . Ah, heaven, don't murder me! . . . What have I done?'

His words died away in a dreadful gurgle, as the clergyman, his face diabolical with fury, sprang on him and gripped him by the throat. He shook the hunchback as a terrier shakes a rat, cursing horribly under his breath – and for a moment or two it seemed as if the other's fear was justified. There was murder in the big man's face, until the touch of the girl's hand on his arm steadied him and brought him to his senses. With a last spasm of fury he hurled the wretched Zadowa into a corner, and left him lying there; then his iron self-control came back to him.

'Get up,' he ordered tensely, 'and answer some questions.'

Trembling all over, the hunchback staggered to his feet, and came into the centre of the room.

'Monsieur,' he whined, 'I do not understand. What have I done?'

'You don't need to understand!' snarled the clergyman. 'Tell me exactly what happened when the bomb burst.'

'It killed the three men, monsieur,' stammered the other.

'Curse the three men!' He lifted his clenched fist, and Zadowa shrank back. 'What happened to the room?'

'It was wrecked utterly. A great hole was blown in the wall.'

'And what happened to the desk?'

'I don't know exactly, monsieur,' stammered the other. 'I didn't go back to see. But it must have been blown to match-wood. Only as there was nothing inside of importance it makes no odds.'

'Did you look in the secret drawer at the back of the centre opening? You didn't know there was one, did you? Only I knew of its existence, and short of taking the desk to pieces no-one would be able to find it. And you took the desk to pieces, Zadowa, didn't you? You blew it to pieces, Zadowa, didn't you? Just to kill the leader of this trumpery gang, Zadowa, you cursed fool!'

Step by step the hunchback was retreating before the other, terror convulsing his face, until the wall brought him to an abrupt stop.

'You blew the desk to pieces, Zadowa,' continued the Reverend Theodosius, standing in front of him, 'a desk that contained the six most perfect diamonds in the world, Zadowa. With your wretched bomb, you worm, you destroyed a fortune. What have you got to say?'

'I didn't know, monsieur,' cringed the other. 'How could I know? When were they put there?'

'I put them there this afternoon for safety. Not in my wildest imagination did I dream that you would start throwing bombs about the place.'

'Perhaps they are not destroyed,' stammered the hunchback hopefully.

'In which case they are now in the hands of the police. You have one chance, Zadowa, and only one. It *is* that those diamonds are in the hands of the police. If they are and you can get them – I will say no more.'

'But if they have been destroyed, monsieur?' muttered the other.

'Then, Zadowa, I am afraid you will share their fate.'

Almost indifferently the clergyman turned back into the room, taking no notice whatever of the wretched man who followed him on his knees begging for mercy. And then after a while the hunchback pulled himself together and stood up.

'It was a mistake, monsieur,' he said quietly, 'which I deeply regret. It was, however, you must admit, hardly my fault. I will do my best.'

'Let us hope, then, for your sake, Zadowa, that your best will be successful. Now go.'

He pointed to the door, and without another word the hunchback went.

'I'm glad you were here tonight, my dear,' remarked the Reverend Theodosius. 'I don't often lose my temper, but I very nearly killed that man this evening.' The girl rose and came over to where he was standing.

'I don't understand, *mon chéri*,' she said quietly. 'What diamonds are these you talk about?'

The man gave a short, hard laugh.

'I didn't tell you,' he answered. 'There was no object in your knowing for a time. I know your weakness where jewels are concerned too well, my dear; I got them the night before last in Amsterdam. Do you remember that Russian – Stanovitch? That wasn't his real name. He was the eldest son of the Grand Duke Georgius, and he had just arrived from Russia.'

'The man who took that overdose of his sleeping-draught?' whispered the girl barely above her breath.

The Reverend Theodosius smiled grimly.

'So they decided,' he remarked. 'He confided in me the night before he came to his sad end what he had been doing in Russia. His father had hidden the family heirlooms from the Bolshevists, and our young friend went over to retrieve them. Most ingenious – the way he got them out of Russia. Such a pity he had a lapse with his sleep dope.'

And now the Reverend Theodosius was snarling like a mad dog.

'By heavens, girl – do you wonder that I nearly killed that fool Zadowa? The coup of a lifetime – safely brought off. Not a trace of suspicion on me – not a trace. I know I said I wasn't over here on sideshows, but I couldn't have been expected to let such a chance slip by. And then, after having got them safely into his country to lose them like that. Why, do you know that one of them was the rose diamond of the Russian Crown jewels?'

The girl's eyes glistened, then she shrugged her shoulders.

'They would have been unsaleable, *mon ami*,' she said quietly.

'Don't you believe it,' snapped the other. 'There are markets for anything in the world, if one takes the trouble to look for them.'

He was pacing up and down the room, and for a while she stood watching him in silence.

'I'm glad I didn't know about them till now,' she said at length. 'I might not have stopped you killing him, if I had. And it would have been rather awkward.'

He gave a short laugh, and threw the end of his cigar into the grate.

'No good crying over spilt milk, my dear. Let's go to bed.'

But little Janet still stood by the table watching him thoughtfully.

'What are you thinking about?'

'I was thinking about a rather peculiar coincidence,' she answered quietly. 'You were too worried over the diamonds to notice it – but it struck me instantly. The leader of this gang – this huge man whom Zadowa killed tonight. Did you notice what his Christian name was?'

The Reverend Theodosius shook his head.

'It was Hugh – Zadowa heard one of the others call him by name. Hugh, *mon ami*; Hugh – and a huge man. A coincidence, I think.'

The man gave a short laugh.

'A very long one, my dear. Too long to bother about.'

'It would be a pity if he was dead,' she went on thoughtfully. 'I would have liked to see my Hugh Drummond again.'

'If he has been killed, if your supposition is correct,' returned the man, 'it will do something towards reconciling me to the loss of the diamonds. But I don't think it's likely. And incidentally he is the only sideshow I am going to allow myself during this trip.'

Little Janet laughed softly.

'I wonder,' she said, 'I wonder. Let us, as you say, go to bed.'

Chapter 10

In which Hugh Drummond makes a discovery

The prospect in front of Count Zadowa *alias* Mr Atkinson was not a very alluring one, and the more he thought about it the less he liked it. Either the diamonds were blown to dust, or they were in the hands of the authorities. In the first event he had the Reverend Theodosius to reckon with; in the second the police. And for preference the police won in a canter.

He was under no delusions was the hunchback. This mysterious man who signed all his communications by the enigmatic letter X, and whose real appearance was known probably only to the girl who was his constant companion, so wonderful and varied were his disguises, was not a person whom it paid to have any delusions about. He paid magnificently, even lavishly, for work well done: for failure he took no excuse. Even long association did not mitigate the offence. With a shudder Count Zadowa remembered the fate of certain men he had known in the past, men who had been employed, even as he was now employed, on one of the innumerable schemes of their chief. No project, from the restoration of a monarchy to the downfall of a business combine, was too great for the man who now called himself the Reverend Theodosius Longmoor. All that mattered was that there should be money in it. Why he should be interesting himself in the spread of Communism in England it was not for Count Zadowa to inquire, even though he was the head of that particular activity. Presumably he was being paid for it by others; it was no business of Count Zadowa's.

And as he undressed that night in the quiet hotel in Bloomsbury where he lived the hunchback cursed bitterly under his breath. It was such a cruel stroke of luck. How much he had dreaded that first interview with his chief he had hardly admitted even to himself. And then had come the heaven-sent opportunity of killing the leader of the Black Gang in perfect safety; of making it appear that the three men inside the room, and who had no business to be inside the room, had blown themselves up by mistake. How was he to know about the diamonds: how could he possibly be expected to know? And once again he cursed, while the sweat glistened on his forehead as he realised his predicament.

He had already decided that his only method lay in going down to the office next morning as usual. He would find it, of course, in the possession of the police, and would be told what had happened. And then he would have to trust to luck to discover what he could. Perhaps – and at the thought of it he almost started to dress again – perhaps the desk was not utterly ruined. Perhaps the diamonds were there, even now, in the secret drawer. And then he realised that if he went to his office at two o'clock in the morning, it must look suspicious. No; waiting was the only possibility, and Count Zadowa waited. He even went so far as to get into bed, but Count Zadowa did not sleep.

Punctually at half-past nine the next morning he arrived at 5, Green Street. As he had expected, a constable was standing at the door.

'Who are you, sir?' The policeman was barring his entrance.

'My name is Atkinson,' said the Count, with well-feigned surprise. 'May I ask what you're doing here?'

'Haven't you heard, sir?' said the constable. 'There was a bomb outrage here last night. In your office upstairs.'

'A bomb outrage?' Mr Atkinson gazed at the constable in amazement, and a loafer standing by began to laugh.

'Not 'arf, guv'nor,' he remarked cheerfully. 'The 'ole ruddy place is gone to blazes.'

'You dry up,' admonished the policeman. 'Move along, can't you?'

'Orl rite, orl rite,' grumbled the other, shambling off. 'Not allowed to live soon, we won't be.'

'You'd better go up, sir,' continued the constable. 'The Inspector is upstairs.'

Mr Atkinson needed no second invitation. Taking no notice of the half-dozen clerks who had gathered in a little group discussing the affair, he passed along the passage into his own room. And the scene that met his eyes reflected credit on the manufacturer of the bomb. Viewed by the light of day which came streaming in through the great hole in the wall the ruin was complete. In the centre – and it was there Mr Atkinson's eyes strayed continuously even while he was acknowledging the greetings of the Inspector – stood the remnants of the desk. And as he looked at it any faint hope he may have cherished vanished completely. It was literally split to pieces in every direction; there was not left a hiding-place for a pea, much less a bag of diamonds.

'Not much in the office, sir, which was lucky for you.'

The Inspector was speaking and Mr Atkinson pulled himself together. He had a part to play, and whatever happened no suspicions must be aroused.

'I feel quite staggered, Inspector.' His glance travelled to a sinister-looking heap in the corner – a heap roughly covered with an old rug. The wall above it was stained a dull red, and from under the rug stretched out two long streams of the same colour – streams which were not yet dry.

'What on earth has happened?'

'There seems very little doubt about that, sir,' remarked the Inspector. 'I have reconstructed the whole thing with the help of your clerk here, Mr Cohen. It appears that last night about twelve o'clock three men entered your office downstairs. They bound and gagged Cohen – and then they came on up here. Evidently their idea was burglary. What happened, then, of course, it is hard to say exactly. Presumably they started using explosive to force your safe, and explosive is funny stuff even for the expert.'

The Inspector waved a hand at the heap in the corner.

'And he – poor devil, was quite an expert in his way. One of the three men, Mr Atkinson – or what's left of him, Ginger Martin – an old friend of mine.'

For a moment Mr Atkinson's heart stood still. One of the three men! Then, where in Heaven's name, were the other two?

'One of the three, Inspector,' he said at length, steadying his voice. 'But what happened to the others?'

'That is the amazing thing, sir,' answered the Inspector. 'I can but think that though three men entered the office downstairs, only Martin can have been in here at the time of the explosion.' He pulled back the bloodstained rug, and with a shudder Mr Atkinson contemplated what was underneath. He recognised the face; sure enough it was the man who had run round the room when he found himself trapped. But there was no trace of anyone else. The mangled remnants had formed one man and one man only. Then what, he reflected again – what had become of the other two? He knew they had been in there at the time of the explosion, and as he vaguely listened to the Inspector's voice his mind was busy with this new development.

They had been in there – the leader of the Black Gang and one of his pals. There was no trace of them now. Wherefore, somehow, by some miraculous means they must have escaped, and the soul of Count Zadowa grew sick within him. Not only had the whole thing been useless and unnecessary; not only had he incurred the wrath of his own leader, and unwelcome attention from the police, but, in addition, this mysterious being whom he had thought to kill was not dead but very much alive. He had two people up against him now, and he wasn't quite sure which of the two he feared most.

Suddenly he became aware that the Inspector was asking him a question.

'Why, yes,' he said, pulling himself together, 'that is so. I was leaving this office here, and had removed almost everything of value. Only some diamonds were left, Inspector – and they were in that desk. I have somewhat extensive dealings in precious stones. Was there any trace of them found?'

The Inspector laughed grimly.

'You see the room for yourself, sir. But that perhaps supplies us with the motive for the crime. I am afraid your diamonds are either blown to pieces, or in the hands of the other two men, whom I have every hope of laying my hands on shortly. There is no trace of them here.'

In the hands of the other two men! The idea was a new one, which had not yet come into his calculations, so convinced had he been that all three men were dead. And suddenly he felt a sort of blinding certainty that the Inspector – though in ignorance of the real facts of the case – was right in his surmise. Diamonds are not blown to pieces by an explosion; scattered they might be – disintegrated, no. He felt he must get away to consider this new development. Where did he stand if the diamonds were indeed in the possession of the Black Gang? Would it help him or would it not, with regard to that implacable man at the Ritz?

He crossed over to the jagged hole in the wall and looked out.

'This has rather upset me, Inspector,' he said, after a while. 'The South Surrey Hotel in Bloomsbury will always find me.'

'Right, sir!' The Inspector made a note, and then leaned out through the hole, with a frown. 'Get out of this, you there! Go on, or I'll have you locked up as a vagrant!'

'Orl rite, orl rite! Can't a bloke 'ave a bit o' fun when 'e ain't doing no 'arm?'

The loafer, who had been ignominiously moved on from the front door, scrambled down from the lean-to roof behind, and slouched away, muttering darkly. And he was still muttering to himself as he opened the door of a taxi a few minutes later, into which Mr Atkinson hurried stepped. For a moment or two he stood on the pavement until it had disappeared from view; then his prowling propensities seemed to disappear as if by magic. Still with the same shambling gait, but apparently now with some definite object in his mind, he disappeared down a side street, finally coming to a halt before a public telephone-box. He gave one rapid look round, then he stepped inside.

'Mayfair 12345.' He waited, beating a tattoo with his pennies on the box. Things had gone well that morning – very well.

'Hullo, is that you, Hugh? Yes, Peter speaking. The man Atkinson is the hunchback. Stopping South Surrey Hotel, Bloomsbury. He's just got into a taxi and gone off to the Ritz. He seemed peeved to me . . . Yes, he inquired lovingly about the whatnots . . . What's that? You'll toddle round to the Ritz yourself. Right ho! I'll come, too. Cocktail time. Give you full details then.'

The loafer stepped out of the box and shut the door. Then, still sucking a filthy clay pipe, he shambled off in the direction of the nearest Tube station. A slight change of attire before lining up at the Ritz seemed indicated.

And it would, indeed, have been a shrewd observer who would have identified the immaculately-dressed young gentleman who strolled into the Ritz shortly before twelve o'clock with the dissolute-looking object who had so aroused the wrath of the police a few hours previously in Hoxton. The first person he saw sprawling contentedly in an easy chair was Hugh Drummond, who waved his stick in greeting.

'Draw up, Peter, old lad,' he boomed, 'and put your nose inside a wet.'

Peter Darrell took the next chair, and his eyes glanced quickly round the lounge.

'Have you seen him, Hugh?' he said, lowering his voice. 'I don't see anything answering to the bird growing about the place here.'

'No,' answered Hugh. 'But from discreet inquiries made from old pimply-face yonder I find that he arrived here about ten o'clock. He was at once shown up to the rooms of a gent calling himself the Reverend Theodosius Longmoor, where, as far as I can make out, he has remained ever since. Anyway, I haven't seen him trotting up and down the hall, calling to his young; nor have either of the beadles at the door reported his departure. So here I remain like a bird in the wilderness until the blighter and his padre pal break covert. I want to see the Reverend Theodosius Longmoor, Peter.'

A ball of wool rolled to his feet, and Hugh stooped to pick it up. The owner was a girl sitting close by, busily engaged in knitting some obscure garment, and Hugh handed her the wool with a bow.

'Thank you so much!' she said, with a pleasant smile. 'I'm afraid I'm always dropping my wool all over the place.'

'Don't mention it,' remarked Hugh politely. 'Deuced agile little thing – a ball of wool. Spend my life picking up my wife's. Everybody seems to be knitting these jumper effects now.'

'Oh, this isn't a jumper,' answered the girl a little sadly. 'I've no time for such frivolities as that. You see, I've just come back from the famine-stricken parts of Austria – and not only are the poor things hungry, but they can't get proper clothes. So just a few of us are knitting things for them – stock sizes, you know – big, medium, and small.'

'How fearfully jolly of you!' said Hugh admiringly. 'Dashed sporting thing to do. Awful affair, though, when the small size shrinks in the wash. The proud proprietor will burst out in all directions. Most disconcerting for all concerned.'

The girl blushed faintly and Hugh subsided abashed in his chair.

'I must tell my wife about it,' he murmured in confusion. 'She's coming here to lunch, and she ought to turn 'em out like bullets from a machine-gun – what?'

The girl smiled faintly as she rose.

'It would be very good of her if she would help,' she remarked gently, and then, with a slight bow, she walked away in the direction of the lift.

'You know, old son,' remarked Hugh, as he watched her disappearing, 'it's an amazing affair when you really come to think of it. There's that girl with a face far superior to a patched boot and positively oozing virtue from every pore. And yet, would you leave your happy home for her? Look at her skirts – five inches too long; and yet she'd make a man an excellent wife. A heart of gold probably, hidden beneath innumerable strata of multi-coloured wools.'

Completely exhausted he drained his cocktail, and leaned back in his chair, while Peter digested the profound utterance in silence. A slight feeling of lassitude was beginning to weigh on him owing to the atrocious hour at which he had been compelled to rise, and he felt quite unable to contribute any suitable addition to the conversation. Not that it was required: the ferocious frown on Drummond's face indicated that he was in the throes of thought and might be expected to give tongue in the near future.

'I ought to have a bit of paper to write it all down on, Peter,' he remarked at length. 'I was getting it fairly clear when that sweet maiden put me completely in the soup again. In fact, I was just going to run over the whole affair with you when I had to start chasing wool all over London. Where are we, Peter? That is the question. Point one: we have the diamonds – more by luck than good management. Point two: the hunchback gentleman who has a sufficiently strong constitution to live at the South Surrey Hotel in Bloomsbury has not got the diamonds. Point three: he, at the present moment, is closeted with the Reverend Theodosius Longmoor upstairs. Point four: we are about to consume another cocktail downstairs. Well – bearing that little lot in mind, what happens when we all meet?'

'Yes, what!' said Peter, coming out of a short sleep.

'A policy of masterly inactivity seems indicated,' continued Hugh thoughtfully, 'We may even have to see them eat. But I can't button-hole Snooks, or whatever the blighter's name is, and ask him if he bunged a bomb at me last night, can I? It would be so deuced awkward if he hadn't. As I said before, a brief survey of the devil-dodger's face might help. And, on the other hand, it might not. In fact, it is all very obscure, Peter – very obscure.'

A slight snore was his only answer, and Hugh continued to ponder on the obscurity of the situation in silence. That several rays of light might have been thrown on it by a conversation then proceeding upstairs was of no help to him: nor could he have been expected to know that the fog of war was about to lift in a most unpleasantly drastic manner.

'Coincidence? Bosh!' the girl with the heart of gold was remarking at that very moment. 'It's a certainty. Whether he's got the diamonds or not, I can't say, but your big friend of last night, Zadowa, is sitting downstairs now drinking a cocktail in the lounge.

'And your big friend of last night is a gentleman with whom he and I' – she smiled thoughtfully at the Reverend Theodosius – 'have a little account to settle.'

'My account is not a little one,' said the hunchback viciously.

'Amazing though it is, it certainly looks as if you were right, my dear,' answered her father thoughtfully.

'Of course I'm right!' cried the girl. 'Why, the darned thing is sticking out and barking at you. A big man, Christian name Hugh, was in Zadowa's office last night. Hugh Drummond is downstairs at the moment, having actually tracked Zadowa here. Of course they're the same; an infant in arms could see it.'

'Granted you're right,' said the Reverend Theodosius, 'I confess at the moment that I am a little doubtful as to how to turn the fact to our advantage. The fact is an interesting one, my dear, more than interesting; but it don't seem to me to come within the range of practical politics just at present.'

'I wonder,' said the girl. 'His wife is coming here to lunch. You remember her – that silly little fool Phyllis Benton? And they live in Brook Street. It might be worth trying. If by any chance he has got the diamonds – well, she'll be very useful. And if he hasn't' – she shrugged her shoulders – 'we can easily return her if we don't want her.'

The Reverend Theodosius smiled. Long-winded explanations between the two of them were seldom necessary. Then he looked at his watch.

'Short notice,' he remarked; 'but we'll try. No harm done if we fail.'

He stepped over to the telephone, and put through a call. And having given two or three curt orders he came slowly back into the room.

'Chances of success very small, I'm afraid; but as you say, my dear, worth trying. And now I think I'll renew my acquaintance with Drummond. It would be wiser if you had your lunch sent up here, Janet; just for the time our friend had better not connect us together in any way. And as for you, Zadowa' – his tone became curt – 'you can go. Let us hope for your sake that Drummond has really got them.'

'There's only one point,' put in the girl; 'his departure will be reported at once to Drummond. He's tipped both the men at the doors.'

'Then in that case you'd better stop here,' said the Reverend Theodosius. 'I shall probably come up to lunch, but I might have it in the restaurant. I might' – he paused by the door – 'I might even have it with Drummond and his friend.'

With a short chuckle he left the room, and a minute or two later a benevolent clergyman, reading the *Church Times*, was sitting in the lounge just opposite Hugh and Peter. Through half-closed eyes Hugh took stock of him, wondering casually if this was the Reverend Theodosius Longmoor. If so, assuredly nothing more benevolent in the line of sky-pilots could be well imagined. And when a few minutes

later the clergyman took a cigarette out of his case, and then commenced to fumble in his pockets for matches which he had evidently
forgotten, Hugh rose and offered him one.

'Allow me, sir,' he murmured, holding it out.

'I thank you, sir,' said the clergyman, with a charming smile. 'I'm
so terribly forgetful over matches. As a matter of fact I don't generally smoke before lunch, but I've had such a distressing morning that
I felt I must have a cigarette just to soothe my nerves.'

'By Jove! That's bad,' remarked Hugh. 'Bath water cold, and all
that?'

'Nothing so trivial, I fear,' said the other. 'No; a poor man who has
been with me since ten has just suffered the most terrible blow. I
could hardly have believed it possible here in London, but the whole
of his business premises were wrecked by a bomb last night.'

'You don't say so,' murmured Hugh, sinking into a chair, and at
the table opposite Peter Darrell opened one eye.

'All his papers – everything – gone. And it has hit me, too. Quite a
respectable little sum of money – over a hundred pounds, gathered
together for the restoration of the old oak chancel in my church –
blown to pieces by this unknown miscreant. It's hard, sir, it's hard.
But this poor fellow's loss is greater than mine, so I must not complain. To the best of my poor ability I have been helping him to bear
his misfortune with fortitude and strength.'

The clergyman took off his spectacles and wiped them, and Drummond stole a lightning glance at Darrell. The faintest shrug of his
shoulders indicated that the latter had heard, and was as much
in the dark as Hugh. That this was the Reverend Theodosius
Longmoor was now obvious, but what a charming, courteous old
gentleman! It seemed impossible to associate guilt with such a
delightful person, and, if so, they had made a bad mistake. It was
not the hunchback who had thrown the bomb; they were up another
blind alley.

For a while Hugh chatted with him about the outrage, then he
glanced at his watch.

'Nearly time for lunch, I think,' said the clergyman. 'Perhaps you
would give a lonely old man the pleasure of your company.'

'Very nice of you, but I'm expecting my wife,' said Hugh. 'She said
she'd be here at one, and now it's a quarter past. Perhaps you'll lunch
with us?'

'Charmed,' said the clergyman, taking a note which a page-boy
was handing to him on a tray. 'Charmed.' He glanced through the

note and placed it in his pocket. 'The ladies, bless them! so often keep us waiting.'

'I'll just go and ring up,' said Drummond. 'She may have changed her mind.'

'Another prerogative of their sex,' beamed his companion, as Drummond left him. He polished his spectacles and once more resumed his perusal of the *Church Times*, bowing in old-world fashion to two or three acquaintances who passed. And more and more was Peter Darrell becoming convinced that a big mistake had been made somewhere, when Hugh returned looking a little worried.

'Can't make it out, Peter,' he said anxiously. 'Just got through to Denny, and Phyllis left half an hour ago to come here.'

'Probably doing a bit of shopping, old man,' answered Peter reassuringly. 'I say, Hugh, we've bloomered over this show.'

Hugh glanced across at the table where the clergyman was sitting, and suddenly Peter found his arm gripped with a force that made him cry out. He glanced at Hugh, and that worthy was staring at the clergyman with a look of speechless amazement on his face. Then he swung round, and his eyes were blazing.

'Peter!' he said tensely. 'Look at him. The one trick that gives him away every time! Bloomered, have we? Great heavens above, man, it's Carl Peterson!'

A little dazedly Darrell glanced at the clergyman. He was still reading the *Church Times*, but with his left hand he was drumming a ceaseless tattoo on his knee.

Chapter 11

*In which Hugh Drummond and the Reverend
Theodosius Longmoor take lunch together*

'Rot, Hugh!' Peter turned a little irritably from his covert inspection of the Reverend Theodosius Longmoor. 'You've got Peterson on the brain. Why, that old bird is no more like him than my boot.'

'Nevertheless, it's Peterson,' answered Drummond doggedly. 'Don't look at him, Peter; don't let him think we're talking about him on any account. I admit he bears not the slightest resemblance to our one and only Carl, but he's no more unlike him than the Comte de Guy was that time in Paris. It's just that one little trick he can never shake off – that tapping with his left hand on his knee – that made me spot him.'

'Well, granted you're right,' conceded Darrell grudgingly, 'what do we do now, sergeant-major?'

Drummond lit a cigarette thoughtfully before he replied. Half-hidden by a large luncheon party which was just preparing to move into the restaurant, he stole another look at the object of their remarks. With an expression of intense benevolence the Reverend Theodosius was chatting with an elderly lady, and on Drummond's face, as he turned back, was a faint grin of admiration. Truly in the matter of disguises the man was a living marvel.

'I don't know, Peter,' he answered after a while. 'I've got to think this out. It's been so sudden that it's got me guessing. I know it's what we've been hoping for; it's what we wrote that letter to the paper for – to draw the badger. And by the Lord! we've drawn him, and the badger is Peterson. But somehow or other I didn't expect to find him disguised as a Mormon missionary residing at the Ritz.'

'You're perfectly certain, Hugh?' said Peter, who was still far from convinced.

'Absolutely, old man,' answered Drummond gravely. 'The clergy-man over there is Carl Peterson, late of the Elms, Godalming. And the game has begun again.'

Darrell gave a short laugh as he noted the gleam in his leader's eyes.

'I'm thinking,' he remarked soberly, 'that this time the game is going to make us go all out.'

'So much the better,' grinned Hugh. 'We'll add him to our collection, Peter, and then we'll present the whole damned bunch to the Zoo. And, in the meantime, he shall lunch with us when Phyllis arrives, and prattle on theology to an appreciative audience. Incidentally it will appeal to his sense of humour; there's no difficulty about recognising us.'

'Yes,' agreed Peter, 'we start one up there. He doesn't know that we've spotted him. I wonder where the diamonds come in, Hugh?'

'Darned intimately, from what I know of the gentleman. But that's only one of several little points that require clearing up. And in the next few days, Peter, my boy – we will clear them up.'

'Or be cleared up ourselves,' laughed Darrell. 'Look out, he's coming over.'

They turned as the clergyman crossed the lounge towards them.

'Jolly old tum-tum beginning to shout for nourishment,' said Hugh with an affable smile as he joined them. 'My wife should be here at any moment now, Mr – er – '

'Longmoor is my name,' said the clergyman, beaming on them. 'It is very charming of you to take such compassion on a lonely old man.'

'Staying here all by yourself?' asked Drummond politely.

'No; my daughter is with me. The dear child has been my constant companion ever since my beloved wife's death some years ago.'

He polished his glasses, which had become a little misty, and Drummond made noises indicative of sympathy.

'You wouldn't believe the comfort she has been to me. In these days, when it seems to me that the modern girl thinks of nothing but dancing and frivolity, it is indeed a blessing to find one who, while preserving her sinsome sense of humour, devotes her life to the things that really matter. In our recent tour in Austria – I beg your pardon, you said – '

'Nothing,' answered Drummond quietly. 'You have been to Austria, you say?'

'Yes; we have just returned from a visit to the famine-stricken area,' replied the clergyman. 'Most interesting – but most terribly sad. You know – I don't think I caught your name.'

'Drummond, Captain Drummond,' answered Hugh mechanically. 'And this is Mr Darrell. I think I have had the pleasure of making your daughter's acquaintance already. She was manufacturing woollen garments for the Austrians down here, and I retrieved an elusive ball of wool for her.'

'That is just my daughter all over, Captain Drummond,' beamed the Reverend Theodosius. 'Never wasting her time, always doing something for the good of humanity.'

But at the moment it is to be regretted that Hugh was not worrying his head over the good of humanity. Inconceivable though it was, judged on the mere matter of appearance, that the Reverend Theodosius was Carl Peterson, it was still more inconceivable that the wool-knitter with the heart of gold could be Irma. Of course Peterson might have changed his daughter – but if he hadn't, what then? What had he said to Peter Darrell when the girl, recognising him all the time, was sitting in the next chair? How much had she overheard? And suddenly Hugh began to feel that he was floundering in deep waters. How many cards did the other side hold? And, what was even more important, how many of his own cards had they placed correctly? And glancing up he found the reverend gentleman's blue eyes fixed on him and glinting with a certain quizzical humour. Assuredly, reflected Drummond, it was up to him to find out, and that as soon as possible, exactly how matters stood. The trouble was how to set about it. To greet the Reverend Theodosius as a long-lost friend and ask him whether the disguise was donned to amuse the children would certainly precipitate affairs, but it would also throw one of his best cards on the table. And Carl Peterson was not a gentleman with whom it was advisable to weaken one's hand unnecessarily. So it all boiled down to a policy of waiting for the other side to play first, which, in view of the fact that he was getting distinctly peckish, seemed to Hugh to be an eminently sound decision.

He glanced at his watch and turned to Darrell.

'Confound the girl, Peter! She's nearly forty minutes late.'

'Picked up a pal, old boy,' answered that worthy. 'Picked up a pal and they're masticating a Bath bun somewhere. Why not leave a message at the door, and let's get on with it? I'm darned hungry.'

The Reverend Theodosius beamed from behind his spectacles.

' 'Tis ever the same,' he murmured gently. 'But it is the prerogative of their sex.'

'Well, let's toddle in and take nourishment,' said Hugh, taking hold of the clergyman's arm with his hand and pushing him towards the restaurant. 'Jove! Mr Longmoor – you've got some pretty useful biceps on you.'

The other smiled as if pleased with the compliment.

'Nothing to you, Captain Drummond, to judge by your size, but I think I may say I'm a match for most men. My ministry has led me into some very rough corners, and I have often found that where gentle persuasion fails, force will succeed.'

'Quite so,' murmured Drummond, gazing at the menu. 'Nothing like a good one straight on the point of the jaw for producing a devout manner of living in the recipient. Often found that out myself. By the way, what about the daughter? Isn't she going to honour us?'

'Not today,' answered the Reverend Theodosius. 'She is lunching upstairs with the poor fellow I told you about, whose office was wrecked last night. He is sadly in need of comfort.'

'I'll bet he is,' agreed Hugh. 'But if he put on one of those jolly little things she's knitting and trotted up and down Piccadilly he'd soon get all the money back for your chancel steps. The man I'm sorry for is the poor devil who was found adhering to the wall.'

The Reverend Theodosius glanced at him thoughtfully, and Drummond realised he had made a slip.

'You seem to know quite a lot about it, Captain Drummond,' murmured the other, dissecting a sardine.

'It's in the early editions of the evening papers,' returned Hugh calmly. 'Pictures and everything. The only thing they've left out is that reference to your little lump of dough.'

'In such a dreadful thing as this, a trifle like that might well be overlooked,' said the Reverend Theodosius. 'But I understand from my poor friend upstairs that the police are satisfied that three scoundrels were involved in the crime. And two of them have escaped.'

'Dirty dogs,' said Hugh, frowning. 'Now if all three had been found adhering to the furniture it might have reconciled you to the loss of those hundred acid drops.'

'In fact,' continued the clergyman, helping himself to some fish, 'the whole thing is very mysterious. However, the police have every hope of laying their hands on the two others very shortly.'

'They're always optimistic, aren't they?' returned Hugh. 'Pity no-one saw these blighters running round and throwing bombs about the house.'

'That is just the fortunate thing, Captain Drummond,' said the other mildly. 'Far be it from me to desire vengeance on any man, but in this case I feel it is deserved. The unfortunate clerk downstairs who was brutally assaulted by them has confided to his employer that he believes he knows who one of the other two was. A huge man, Captain Drummond, of enormous strength: a man – well, really, do you know? – a man I should imagine just like you, and a man, who, popular rumour has it, is the head of a mysterious body calling itself the Black Gang. So that should prove a valuable clue for the police when they hear of it.'

Not by the flicker of an eyelid did Drummond's face change as he listened with polite attention to the clergyman's remarks. But now once again his brain was moving quickly as he took in this new development. One card, at any rate, was down on the table: his identity as leader of the Black Gang was known to Peterson. It was the girl who had found him out: that was obvious. The point was how did it affect matters.

'An elusive person, I believe,' he remarked quietly. 'We've heard quite a lot of him in the papers recently. In fact, I was actually in Sir Bryan Johnstone's office when a gentleman of the name of Charles Latter came and demanded protection from the Black Gang.'

For a moment a gleam of amazement shone in the other's eye.

'You surprise me,' he murmured. 'I trust it was afforded him.'

Hugh waved a vast hand. 'Do you doubt it, Mr Longmoor? I personally accompanied him to a house-party to ensure his safety. But as I told old Tum-tum afterwards – that's Sir Bryan Johnstone, you know, a great pal of mine – nothing that I could do could avert the catastrophe. I prattled to him gently, but it was no good. He went mad, Mr Longmoor – quite, quite mad. The boredom of that house-party unhinged his brain. Have another chop?'

'How very extraordinary!' remarked the clergyman. 'And what did your friend – er – Tum-tum say when he heard of the results of your supervision?'

'Well, quite unofficially, Mr Longmoor, I think he was rather pleased. Latter was an unpleasant man, engaged in unpleasant work, and he does less harm when insane. A merciful thing, wasn't it, that we found such a suitable gathering of guests at our disposal?'

'And yet,' pursued the Reverend Theodosius, 'it struck me from an English paper I happened to pick up in Paris a little while ago, that the leader of this obscure gang claimed in some way to be responsible for the condition of Mr Latter. He issued a ridiculous sort of manifesto to the Press, didn't he?'

'I believe he did,' answered Drummond, draining his glass. 'An effusion which ended with a threat to the people at the back of men like Latter. As if it would have any effect! Scum like that, Mr Longmoor, remain hidden. They blush unseen. I do wish you'd have another chop.'

'Thank you – no.' The Reverend Theodosius waved away the waiter and leaned back in his chair. 'Doubtless you are right, Captain Drummond, in championing this person; but if what this wretched, ill-treated clerk says is correct, I am afraid I can look on him as nothing less than a common thief. Of course, he may have made a mistake, but he seems very positive that one of the miscreants last night was the leader of the Black Gang himself.'

'I see,' said Drummond, with the air of a man on whom a great truth had dawned. 'That hundred thick 'uns still rankling in the grey matter what time the vestry collapses.'

'Hardly that,' returned the clergyman severely. 'My friend, whose office was wrecked, was amongst other things a dealer in precious stones. Last night in his desk were six magnificent diamonds – entrusted to him for sale by a – well, I will be discreet – by a well-known Russian nobleman. This morning he finds them gone – vanished – his room wrecked. Why, my heart bleeds for him.'

'I'll bet it does,' answered Drummond sympathetically. 'Darned careless, isn't it, the way some of these people drop bombs about the place? Still, if your pal circulates an exact description of the diamonds to the police, he'll probably get 'em back in time. I suppose,' he added by way of an afterthought, 'I suppose he *can* go to the police about it?'

'I don't quite understand you, Captain Drummond.' The Reverend Theodosius stared at his host in surprise.

'One never knows, these days, does one?' said Hugh mildly. 'Dreadful thing to get a nice little bunch of diamonds shot at one's head, and then find you've got stolen property. It puts the next fellow who pinches them rather on velvet. A cup of coffee, won't you?'

'Fortunately nothing of that sort exists in this case. Yes, thank you, I would like some coffee.'

'Good,' said Hugh, giving the order to the waiter. 'So that all you've got to do – or rather your pal – is to tell the police that the office was blown up by the leader of the Black Gang, and that the diamonds were pinched by the leader of the Black Gang, and that you would like his head on a silver salver by Wednesday week. It seems too easy to me. Cigarette? Turkish this side – gaspers the other.'

'Thank you.' The Reverend Theodosius helped himself from the case Hugh was holding out. 'It certainly does seem easy, the way you put it.'

'The only small trifle which seems to jut out from an otherwise clear-cut horizon is too ridiculous to worry about.'

'And that is?'

'Why – who is the leader of the Black Gang? It would be a dreadful affair if they brought the wrong bird's head on a charger. No diamonds; no Bradburys; no nothing.'

'I don't anticipate that it should be hard to discover that, Captain Drummond,' said the clergyman mildly. 'Surely with your marvellous police system . . . '

'And yet, Mr Longmoor,' said Hugh gravely, 'even though lately I have been reinforcing that system – literally helping them myself – they are still completely in the dark as to his identity.'

'Incredible,' cried the other. 'Still, we can only hope for the best. By the way, I'm afraid your wife has finally deserted you for lunch.' He pushed back his chair. 'I shall hope to have the pleasure of making her acquaintance some other day. And now if you will excuse me, I must run away. My correspondence at the moment with regard to the relief funds for destitute Austrians is very voluminous. A thousand thanks for a most enjoyable meal.'

He bowed with a courteous smile, and threaded his way through the crowded restaurant towards the door. And it was not until he had finally disappeared from sight that Hugh turned to Peter Darrell with a thoughtful expression on his face.

'Deuced interesting position of affairs, Peter,' he remarked, lighting another cigarette. 'He knows I'm the leader of our bunch, and doesn't know I know it; I know he's Peterson, and he doesn't know I know it. I wonder how long it will be before the gloves come off.'

'Supposing he keeps out of it himself, and gives you away to the police,' said Peter. 'It'll be rather awkward, old son.'

'Supposing he does, it would be,' grinned Hugh. 'I'd love to see Tum-tum's face. But, my dear old Peter, hasn't your vast brain grasped the one essential fact, that that is precisely what he can't do until he's certain I haven't got the diamonds? Apart altogether from a variety of very awkward disclosures about Number 5, Green Street – he, or his hunchback friend, would have to explain how they gained possession in the first place of those stones. I made discreet inquiries this morning, Peter, and that rose-pink diamond was one of the Russian Crown jewels. Awkward – very.'

He smiled and ordered two brandies.

'Very, very awkward, Peter – but with distinct elements of humour. And I'm inclined to think the time is approaching when the seconds get out of the ring.'

Chapter 12

In which Count Zadowa is introduced to Alice in Wonderland

A quarter of an hour later the two young men stepped into Picca-dilly. Evidently Phyllis was not proposing to turn up, and nothing was to be gained by remaining. The next move lay with the other side, and until it was played it was merely a question of marking time. At the entrance to the Ritz they separated, Peter turning eastwards to keep some mysterious date with a female minor star of theatrical London, while Hugh strolled along Berkeley Street towards his house. At times a faint smile crossed his face at the thought of Peterson devoting his young brain to the matter of starving Austrians, but for the most part a portentous frown indicated thought. For the life of him he couldn't see what was going to happen next. It appeared to him that the air wanted clearing; that in military parlance the situation was involved. And it was just as he was standing in Berkeley Square, waving his stick vaguely as a material aid to thought, that he felt a touch on his arm.

'Excuse me, sir,' said a voice at his elbow, 'but I would like a few words with you.'

He looked down, and his eyes narrowed suddenly. Standing beside him was the hunchback, Mr Atkinson, and for a moment Hugh regarded him in silence. Then, dismissing a strong inclination to throw this unexpected apparition under a passing furniture van, he raised his eyebrows slightly and removed his cigar from his mouth. Evidently the next move had begun, and he felt curious as to what form it would take.

'My powers as a conversationalist are well known,' he remarked, 'amongst a large and varied circle. I was not, however, aware that you belonged to it. In other words, sir, who the deuce are you and what the dickens do you want to talk to me about?'

'Something which concerns us both very intimately,' returned the other. 'And with regard to the first part of your question – do you think it necessary to keep up the pretence, especially as there are no witnesses present? I suggest, however, that as our conversation may be a trifle prolonged, and this spot is somewhat draughty, we should adjourn to your house; Brook Street, I believe, is where you live, Captain Drummond.'

Hugh removed his cigar, and stared at the hunchback thoughtfully.

'I haven't the slightest wish to have a prolonged conversation with you in any place, draughty or otherwise,' he remarked at length. 'However, if you are prepared to run the risk of being slung out of the window if you bore me, I'll give you ten minutes.'

He turned on his heel and strolled slowly on towards his house, while the hunchback, shooting venomous glances at him from time to time, walked by his side in silence. And it was not until some five minutes later when they were both in Drummond's study that any further remark was made.

It was Hugh who spoke, standing with his back to the fireplace, and looking down on the misshapen little man who sat in an armchair facing the light. An unpleasant customer, he reflected, now that he saw him close to for the first time: a dangerous, vindictive little devil – but able, distinctly able. Just such a type as Peterson would choose for a tool.

'What is it you wish to say to me?' he said curtly.

'A few things, Captain Drummond,' returned the other, 'that may help to clear the air. In the first place may I say how pleased I am to make your acquaintance in the flesh, so to speak? I have long wanted a little talk with the leader of the Black Gang.'

'I trust,' murmured Hugh solicitously, 'that the sun hasn't proved too much for you.'

'Shall we drop this beating about the bush,' snapped the other.

'I shall drop you down the stairs if you talk to me like that, you damned little microbe,' said Hugh coldly, and the other got to his feet with a snarl. His eyes, glaring like those of an angry cat, were fixed on Drummond, who suddenly put out a vast hand to screen the lower part of the hunchback's face. With a cry of fear he recoiled, and Hugh smiled grimly. So it had been Mr Atkinson himself who had flung the bomb the night before: the eyes that had glared at him through the crack in the door were unmistakably the same as those he had just looked into over his own hand. With the rest of the face blotted out to prevent distraction there could be no doubt about it, and he was still smiling grimly as he lowered his hand.

'So you think I'm the leader of the Black Gang, do you?' he remarked. 'I don't know that I'm very interested in your thoughts.'

'I don't think: I know,' said the hunchback viciously. 'I found it out today.'

'Indeed,' murmured Hugh politely. 'Would it be indiscreet to ask how you found out this interesting fact?'

'Do you deny it?' demanded the other furiously.

'My dear little man,' said Hugh, 'if you said I was the Pope I wouldn't deny it. All I ask is that now you've afflicted me with your presence you should amuse me. What are your grounds for this somewhat startling statement?'

'My grounds are these,' said the hunchback, recovering his self-control: 'last night my office in Hoxton was wrecked by a bomb.'

'Good Lord!' interrupted Hugh mildly, 'it must be old Theodosius Longmoor and his hundred quid. I thought he looked at me suspiciously during lunch.'

'It was wrecked by a bomb, Captain Drummond,' continued the other, not heeding the interruption. 'That bomb also killed a man.'

'It did,' agreed Hugh grimly.

'One of the three men who broke in. The other two escaped – how I don't know. But one of them was recognised by the clerk downstairs.'

'I gathered that was the story,' said Hugh.

'He was recognised as the leader of the Black Gang,' continued the hunchback. 'And that was all until today. Just the leader of the Black Gang – an unknown person. But today – at the Ritz, Captain Drummond – my clerk, who had brought me a message, recognised him again, without his disguise. No longer an unknown man, you understand – but you.'

Drummond smiled, and selected a cigarette from his case.

'Very pretty,' he answered, 'but a trifle crude. As I understand you, I gather that your shrewd and intelligent clerk states that the leader of the Black Gang broke into your office last night in order to indulge in the doubtful pastime of throwing bombs about the premises. He further states that I am the humorist in question. Allowing for the moment that your clerk is sane, what do you propose to do about it?'

'In certain eventualities, Captain Drummond, I propose to send an anonymous letter to Scotland Yard. Surprised though they would be to get it, it might help them to clear up the mystery of Mr Latter's insanity. It may prove rather unpleasant for you, of course, but that can't be helped.'

'It's kind of you to give me a loophole of escape,' said Drummond pleasantly. 'What are the eventualities to which you allude?'

'The non-return to me of a little bag containing diamonds,' remarked the hunchback quietly. 'They were in the desk which was wrecked by the bomb.'

'Dear, dear,' said Hugh. 'Am I supposed to have them in my possession?'

'I can only hope most sincerely for your sake that you have,' returned the other. 'Otherwise I'm afraid that letter will go to the police.'

For a while Drummond smoked in silence: then, with a lazy smile on his face, he sat down in an armchair facing the hunchback.

'Most interesting,' he drawled. 'Most interesting and entertaining. I'm not very quick, Mr – I've forgotten under what name you inflict yourself on a long-suffering world, but I shall call you Snooks – I'm not, as I say, very quick, Snooks, but as far as my brain can grapple with the problem it stands thus. If I give you back a packet of diamonds which I may, or may not, possess you will refrain from informing the police that I am the leader of the Black Gang. If, on the contrary, I do not give them back to you, you will send them that interesting piece of information by means of an anonymous letter.' The smile grew even lazier. 'Well, you damned little excrescence, I call your bluff. Get on with it.'

With a snarl of rage the hunchback snatched up his hat and rose to his feet.

'You call it bluff, do you?' – and his voice was shaking with fury. 'Very good, you fool – I accept. And you'll be sorry when you see my cards.'

'Sit down, Snooks: I haven't finished with you yet.' There was still the same maddening smile on Drummond's face, which disappeared suddenly as the hunchback moved towards the door. In two strides Hugh had him by the collar, and with a force that made his teeth rattle Mr Atkinson found himself back in his chair.

'I said sit down, Snooks,' said Drummond pleasantly. 'Don't let me have to speak to you again, or I might hurt you. There are one or two things I have to say to you before depriving myself of the pleasure of your company. By the post following the one which carries your interesting disclosure will go another letter addressed to Sir Bryan Johnstone himself. I shall be in the office when he opens it – and we shall both be roaring with laughter over the extraordinary delusion that I – quite the biggest fool of his acquaintance – could possibly be the leader of the Black Gang. And, as if to prove the utter absurdity of the suggestion, this second letter will be from the leader of the Black Gang himself. In it he will state that he was present at 5, Green Street, Hoxton, last night in an endeavour to obtain possession of the anarchist and Bolshevist literature stored there. That he took with him a professional burglar to assist him in opening the safe and other things which might be there, and that while engaged in this eminently virtuous proceeding he found that he was trapped in the room by some mechanical device. And then, Snooks, will come a very interesting disclosure. He will state how suddenly he saw through a crack in the door a pair of eyes looking at him. And their colour – see, what is the colour of your eyes, Snooks? – grey-blue, very noticeable. Much the same as old Longmoor's – though his are a little bluer. And then the owner of the eyes, Snooks, was so inconsiderate as to throw a bomb in the room; a bomb which killed one of the men, and wrecked the desk. So that the owner of the eyes, Snooks, grey-blue eyes just like yours, is a murderer – a common murderer. And we hang men in England for murder.' He paused and stared at the hunchback. 'This is a jolly game, isn't it?'

'And you really imagine,' said the hunchback contemptuously, 'that even your police would believe such a story that a man would wreck his own office, when on your own showing he had the men trapped inside it.'

'Probably not,' said Drummond affably. 'Any more than that they would believe that I was the leader of the Black Gang. So since they're such a wretched crowd of unbelievers I don't think it's much good playing that game, Snooks. Waste of time, isn't it? So I vote we play another one, all on our own – a little game of make-believe – like we used to play in the nursery.'

'I haven't an idea what you're talking about, Captain Drummond,' said the hunchback, shifting uneasily in his chair. For all trace of affability had vanished from the face of the man opposite him, to be replaced by an expression which made Mr Atkinson pass his tongue once or twice over lips that had suddenly gone dry.

'Haven't you, you rat?' said Drummond quietly. 'Then I'll tell you. Just for the next five minutes we're going to pretend that these two astonishing statements which the police – stupid fellows – won't believe are true. We're going to pretend – only pretend, mind you, Snooks – that I am the leader of the Black Gang; and we're going to pretend that you are the man who flung the bomb last night. Just for five minutes only, then we go back to reality and unbelieving policemen.'

And if during the following five minutes strange sounds were heard by Denny in the room below, he was far too accustomed to the sounds of breaking furniture to worry. It wasn't until the hunchback pulled a knife that Drummond warmed to his work, but from that moment he lost his temper. And because the hunchback was a hunchback – though endowed withal by Nature with singular strength – it jarred on Drummond to fight him as if he had been a normal man. So he flogged him with a rhinoceros-hide whip till his arm ached, and then he flung him into a chair, gasping, cursing, and scarcely human.

'You shouldn't be so realistic in your stories, Snooks,' he remarked affably, though his eyes were still merciless as he looked at the writhing figure. 'And I feel quite sure that that is what the leader of the Black Gang would have done if he had met the peculiar humorist who threw that bomb last night. Bad habit – throwing bombs.'

With a final curse the hunchback staggered to his feet, and his face was diabolical in its fury.

'You shall pay for that, Captain Drummond, stroke by stroke, and lash by lash,' he said in a shaking voice.

Drummond laughed shortly.

'All the same, old patter,' he remarked. 'Tell old Longmoor with my love – ' He paused and grinned. 'No, on second thoughts I think I'll tell his reverence myself – at the appointed time.'

'What will you tell him?' sneered the hunchback.

'Why, that his church isn't the only place where dry rot has set in. It's prevalent amongst his pals as well. Must you go? Straight down the stairs, and the card tray in the hall is only electric-plate – so you might leave it.'

With a great effort Mr Atkinson pulled himself together. His shoulders were still aching abominably from the hiding Drummond had given him, but his loss of self-control had been due more to mental than to physical causes. Immensely powerful though Drummond was, his clothes had largely broken the force of the blows for the hunchback. And now as he stood by the door the uppermost thought in his mind was that he had failed utterly and completely in the main object of his interview. He had come, if possible, to get the diamonds, and failing that, to find out for certain whether Drummond had them in his possession or not. And the net result had been a flogging and nothing more. Too late he realised that in dealing with men of the type of Hugh Drummond anything in the nature of a threat is the surest guarantee of a thick ear obtainable: but then Mr Atkinson was not used to dealing with men of that type. And the uppermost thought in his mind at the moment was not how he could best revenge himself on this vast brute who had flogged him, but what he was going to say to the Reverend Theodosius Longmoor when he got back to the Ritz. The question of revenge could wait till later.

'Can we come to an understanding, Captain Drummond?' he remarked quietly. 'I can assure you, of course, that you have made a terrible mistake in thinking that it was I who threw that bomb at you last night.'

'At me?' Drummond laughed shortly. 'Who said you'd thrown it at me? That wasn't the game at all, Snooks. You threw it at the leader of the Black Gang.'

'Can't we put our cards on the table?' returned the other with studied moderation. 'I know that you are that leader, you know it – though it is possible that no-one else would believe it. I was wrong to threaten you – I should have known better; I apologise. But if I may say so I have had my punishment. Now as man to man – can we come to terms?'

'I am waiting,' said Hugh briefly. 'Kindly be as concise as possible.'

'Those diamonds, Captain Drummond. Rightly or wrongly I feel tolerably certain that you either have them in your possession, or that you know where they are. Now those diamonds were not mine – did you speak? No. Well – to resume. The diamonds were not mine; they had been deposited in the desk in my office unknown to me. Then this fool – whom you foolishly think was myself – threw the bomb into the office to kill you. I admit it; he told me all about it. He did not kill you, for which fact, if I may say so, I am very glad. You're a sportsman, and you've fought like a sportsman – but our fight, Captain Drummond, has been over other matters. The diamonds are a sideshow and hardly concern you and me. I'll be frank with you; they are the sole wealth saved by a Russian nobleman from the Bolshevist outrages. He deposited them in my office during my absence, with the idea of my selling them for him – and now he and his family must starve. And so what I propose is – '

'I don't think I want to hear your proposal, Snooks,' said Drummond kindly. 'Doubtless I look a fool; doubtless I am a fool, but I like to think that I'm not a congenital idiot. I'm glad you have discovered that it's not much use threatening me; but to tell you the strict truth, I prefer threats to nauseating hypocrisy. So much so in fact that the thought of that starving nobleman impels me to take more exercise. Ever read *Alice in Wonderland*, Snooks? A charming book – a masterpiece of English literature. And there is one singularly touching, not to say fruity, bit which concerns Father William – and a genteel young man.'

With a look of complete bewilderment on his face Mr Atkinson felt himself propelled through the door, until he came to a halt at the top of the stairs.

'It's a little poem, Snooks, and some day I will recite it to you. Just now I can only remember the one singularly beautiful line which has suggested my new form of exercise.'

Mr Atkinson became aware of a boot in the lower portion of his back, and then the stairs seemed to rise up and hit him. He finally came to rest in the hall against an old oak chest of the pointed-corner type, and for a moment or two he lay there dazed. Then he scrambled to his feet to find three young men, who had emerged from a lower room during his flight, gazing at him impassively: while standing at the top of the stairs down which he had just descended and outlined against a window was the huge, motionless figure of Drummond. Half cursing, half sobbing, he staggered to the front door and opened it. Once more he looked back – not one of the four men had moved. They were just staring at him in absolute silence, and, with a sudden feeling of pure terror, Count Zadowa, *alias* Mr Atkinson, shut the door behind him and staggered into the sunlit street.

Chapter 13

In which Hugh Drummond and the Reverend Theodosius have a little chat

'Come up, boys,' laughed Hugh. 'The fog of war is lifting slowly.'

He led the way back into the study, and the other three followed him.

'That object, Ted, you will be pleased to hear, is the humorist who threw the bomb at us last night.'

'The devil it was,' cried Jerningham. 'I hope you gave him something for me. Incidentally, how did he run you to earth here?'

'Things have moved within the last two or three hours,' answered Drummond slowly. 'Who do you think is stopping at the Ritz at the present moment? Who do you think lunched with Peter and me today? Why – Peterson, my buckos – no more and no less.'

'Rot!' said Toby Sinclair incredulously.

'No more and no less. Peterson himself – disguised as a clergyman called Longmoor. And with him is dear Irma encased in woollen garments. And it was Irma who spotted the whole thing. I never recognised her, and she was sitting next to Peter and me in the lounge when we were discussing things. Of course, they're mixed up with that swab I've just kicked down the stairs – in fact, we've bolted the fox. The nuisance of it is that by putting two and two together they've spotted me as the leader of our bunch. How I don't quite know, but they indubitably have. They also think I've got those diamonds: hence the visit of the hunchback, who did not know they were in the desk when he bunged the bomb. In fact, things are becoming clearer all the way round.'

'I'm glad you think so,' remarked Algy. 'I'm dashed if I see it.'

Drummond thoughtfully filled himself a glass of beer from the cask in the corner.

'Clearer, Algy – though not yet fully luminous with the light of day. Between Peterson and those diamonds there is, or was, a close and tender connection. I'll eat my hat on that. Between Peterson and the hunchback there is also a close connection – though I have my doubts if it's tender. And then there's me tripping lightly like the good fairy . . . Hullo! What's this?'

He had opened his desk as he spoke, and was now staring fixedly at the lock.

'It's been forced,' he said grimly. 'Forced since this morning. They've been over this desk while I've been out. Push the bell, Ted.'

They waited in silence till Denny appeared in answer to the ring.

'Someone has been in this room, Denny,' said Drummond. 'Someone has forced this desk since half-past eleven this morning.'

'There's been no-one in the house, sir,' answered Denny, 'except the man who came about the electric light.'

'Electric grandmother,' snapped his master. 'You paralytic idiot, why did you leave him alone?'

'Well, sir, Mrs Drummond was in the house at the time – and the servants were all round the place.' Denny looked and felt aggrieved, and after a while Drummond smiled.

'What sort of a man was it, you old fathead?'

'A very respectable sort of man,' returned Denny with dignity. 'I remarked to Mrs Denny how respectable he was, sir. Why, he actually went some distance down the street to call a taxi for Mrs Drummond to go to the Ritz . . . '

His words died away, as he stared in amazement at the expression on his master's face.

'What the devil is it, Hugh?' cried Ted Jerningham.

'He called a taxi, you say?' muttered Drummond. 'The man who came here called a taxi?'

'Yes, sir,' answered Denny. 'He was leaving the house at the same time, and as there was none in sight he said he'd send one along at once.'

'And Mrs Drummond went in the taxi he sent?'

'Certainly, sir,' said Denny in surprise. 'To the Ritz, to join you. I gave the order myself to the driver.'

The veins were standing out on Drummond's forehead, and for a moment it seemed as if he was going to hit his servant. Then with an effort he controlled himself, and sank back in his chair with a groan.

'It's all right, Denny,' he said hoarsely. 'It's not your fault: you couldn't have known. But – what a fool I've been! All this time wasted, when I might have been doing something.'

'But what on earth's happened?' cried Algy.

'She never turned up at the Ritz, Algy: Phyllis never turned up for lunch. At first I thought she was late, and we waited. Then I thought she'd run into some pal and had gone to feed somewhere else. And then, what with talking to Peterson, and later that hunchback, I forgot all about her.'

'But, good heavens, Hugh, what do you mean?' said Ted. 'You don't think that – '

'Of course I think it. I know it. They've got her: they've kidnapped her. Right under my nose.' He rose and began to pace up and down the room with long, uneven strides, while the others watched him anxiously.

'That damned girl heard me say that she was coming to lunch, and just after that she went upstairs. And Peterson, being Peterson, took a chance – and he's pulled it off.'

'Ring up Scotland Yard, man,' cried Toby Sinclair.

'What the devil am I to tell them? They'd think I was off my head. And I've got no proof that Peterson is at the bottom of it. I haven't even got any proof that would convince them that Longmoor is Peterson.'

Algy Longworth stood up, serious for once in a way.

'There's no time now to beat about the bush, Hugh. If they've got Phyllis there's only one possible thing that you can do. Go straight to Bryan Johnstone and put all your cards on the table. Tell him the whole thing from A to Z – conceal nothing. And then leave the matter in his hands. He won't let you down.'

For a moment or two Hugh faced them undecided. The sudden danger to Phyllis seemed to have robbed him temporarily of his power of initiative; for the time he had ceased to be the leader.

'Algy's right,' said Jerningham quietly. 'It doesn't matter a damn what happens to us, you've got to think about Phyllis. We'll get it in the neck – but there was always that risk.'

'I believe you're right,' muttered Hugh, looking round for his hat. 'My brain's all buzzing, I can't think – '

And at that moment the telephone bell rang on his desk.

'Answer it, Ted,' said Hugh.

Jerningham picked up the receiver.

'Yes – this is Captain Drummond's house. No – it's not him speaking. Yes – I'll give him any message you like. Who are you? Who? Mr Longmoor at the Ritz. I see. Yes – he told me you had lunched with him today. Oh! yes, certainly.'

For a while Ted Jerningham stood holding the receiver to his ear, and only the thin, metallic voice of the speaker at the other end broke the silence of the room. It went on, maddeningly indistinct to the three men crowding round the instrument, broken only by an occasional monosyllable from Jerningham. Then with a final – 'I will certainly tell him,' Ted laid down the instrument.

'What did he say, Ted?' demanded Hugh agitatedly.

'He sent a message to you, old man. It was approximately to this effect – that he was feeling very uneasy because your wife had not turned up at lunch, and that he hoped there had been no accident. He further went on to say that since he had parted from you a most peculiar piece of information had come to his knowledge, which, incredible though it might appear, seemed to bear on her failure to turn up at the Ritz. He most earnestly begged that you should go round and see him at once – because if his information was correct any delay might prove most dangerous for her. And lastly, on no account were you to go to the police until you had seen him.'

For a while there was silence in the room. Drummond, frowning heavily, was staring out of the window; the others, not knowing what to say, were waiting for him to speak. And after a while he swung round, and they saw that the air of indecision had gone.

'That simplifies matters considerably,' he said quietly. 'It reduces it to the old odds of Peterson and me.'

'But you'll go to the police, old man,' cried Algy. 'You won't pay any attention to that message. He'll never know that you haven't come straight to him.'

Drummond laughed shortly.

'Have you forgotten the rules so much, Algy, that you think that? Look out of the window, man, only don't be seen. There's a fellow watching the house now – I couldn't go a yard without Peterson knowing. Moreover I'm open to a small bet that he knew I was in the house when he was talking to Ted. Good heavens, no. Peterson is not the sort of man to play those monkey-tricks with. He's got Phyllis, the whole thing is his show. And if I went to the police, long before they could bring it home to him, or get her back – she'd be – why – ' and once again the veins stood out on his forehead – 'Lord knows what the swine wouldn't have done to her. It's just a barter at the present moment – the diamonds against her. And there's going to be no haggling. They win the first round – but there are a few more on the horizon.'

'What are you going to do?' said Ted.

'Exactly what he suggests,' answered Hugh. 'Go round and see him at the Ritz – now, at once. I shan't take the diamonds with me, but there will be no worry over the exchange as far as I'm concerned. It's just like his dirty method of fighting to go for a girl,' he finished savagely.'

'You don't think they've hurt Mrs Drummond, sir,' said Denny anxiously.

'If they have, they'll find the remains of an elderly parson in Piccadilly,' returned Hugh, as he slipped a small revolver into his pocket. 'But I don't think so. Carl is far too wise to do anything so stupid as that. He's tried with the hunchback and failed, now he's trying this. And he wins.'

He crossed to the door and opened it.

'In case I don't come back by six, the diamonds are in my sponge bag in the bathroom – and go straight to Scotland Yard. Tell Tum-tum the whole yarn.'

With a brief nod he was gone, and a moment later he was in the street. It was almost deserted, and he waited on the pavement for the loitering gentleman who came obsequiously forward.

'Taxi, sir?'

A convenient one – an almost too convenient one – came to a standstill beside them, and Hugh noticed a quick look flash between the driver and the other man. Then he took stock of the taxi, and behold it was not quite as other taxis. And in his mind arose an unholy desire. As has been said, the street was nearly deserted, and it was destined to become even more deserted. There was a crash of breaking glass and the loiterer disappeared through one window of the machine.

Hugh stared at the astounded driver.

'If you say one word, you appalling warthog,' he remarked gently, 'I'll throw you through the other.'

It was a happy omen, and he felt better as he walked towards the Ritz. Simple and direct – that was the game. No more tortuous intrigues for him; hit first and apologise afterwards. And he was still in the same mood when he was shown into the sitting-room where the Reverend Theodosius Longmoor was busily working on Austrian famine accounts. He rose as Hugh entered, and his daughter, still knitting busily, gave him a charming girlish smile.

'Ah! my dear young friend,' began Mr Longmoor, 'I see you've had my message.'

'Yes,' answered Hugh affably, 'I was standing next door to the fellow you were talking to. But before we come to business, so to speak – I must really ask you not to send Snooks round again. I don't like him. Why, my dear Carl, I preferred our late lamented Henry Lakington.'

There was a moment of dead silence, during which the Reverend Theodosius stared at him speechlessly and the busy knitter ceased to knit. The shock was so complete and sudden that even Carl Peterson seemed at a loss, and Drummond laughed gently as he took a chair.

'I'm tired of this dressing-up business, Carl,' he remarked in the same affable voice. 'And it's so stupid to go on pretending when everybody knows. So I thought we might as well have all the cards on the table. Makes the game much easier.'

He selected a cigarette with care, and offered his case to the girl.

'My most hearty congratulations, mademoiselle,' he continued. 'I may say that it was not you I recognised, but your dear – it is father still, isn't it? And now that we've all met again you must tell me some time how you got away last year.'

But by this time the clergyman had found his voice.

'Are you mad, sir?' he spluttered. 'Are you insane? How dare you come into this room and insult my daughter and myself? I shall ring the bell, sir, and have you removed.'

He strode across the room, and Drummond watched him calmly.

'I've just called one bluff this afternoon, Carl,' he said lazily. 'Now I'll call another. Go on, push the bell. Send for the police and say I've insulted you. Go and see dear old Tum-tum yourself: he'll be most awfully braced at meeting you.'

The other's hand fell slowly to his side, and he looked at his daughter with a resigned expression in his face.

'Really, my dear, I think that the heat – or perhaps – ' He paused expressively, and Drummond laughed.

'You were always a good actor, Carl, but is it worth while? There are no witnesses here, and I'm rather pressed for time. There's no good pretending that it's the heat or that I'm tight, because I'm the only member of the audience, and you can't deceive me, you really can't. Through a series of accidents you have become aware of the fact that I am the leader of the Black Gang. You can go and tell the police if you like – in fact, that horrible little man who came round to see me threatened to do so. But, if you do so, I shall tell them who you are, and I shall also inform them of the secret history of the bomb. So that, though it will be awkward for me, Carl, it will be far more awkward for you and Mademoiselle Irma; and it will be positively unhealthy for Snooks. You take me so far, don't you? Up to date I have been dealing in certainties; now we come to contingencies. It strikes me that there are two doubtful points, old friend of my youth – just two. And those two points are the whereabouts respectively of my wife and your diamonds. Now, Carl, do we talk business or not?'

'My dear young man,' said the other resignedly, 'I intended to talk business with you when you arrived if you had given me a chance. But as you've done nothing but talk the most unmitigated drivel since you've come into the room I haven't had a chance. You appear obsessed with this absurd delusion that I am some person called Carl, and – But where are you going?'

Drummond paused at the door.

'I am going straight to Scotland Yard. I shall there tell Sir Bryan Johnstone the whole story from A to Z, at the same time handing him a little bag containing diamonds which has recently come into my possession.'

'You admit you've got them,' snapped the other, letting the mask drop for a moment.

'That's better, Carl – much better.' Drummond came back into the room. 'I admit I've got them – but they're in a place where you can never find them, and they will remain there until six o'clock tonight, when they go straight to Scotland Yard – unless, Carl – unless my wife is returned to me absolutely unscathed and unhurt before that hour. It is five o'clock now.'

'And if she is returned – what then?'

'You shall have the diamonds.'

For a space the two men stared at one another in silence, and it was the girl who finally spoke.

'What proof have we that you'll keep your word?'

'Common sense,' said Hugh quietly. 'My wife is somewhat more valuable to me than a bagful of diamonds. In addition, you know me well enough to know that I do not break my word. Anyway, those are my terms – take them or leave them. But I warn you that should anything happen to her – nothing will prevent me going straight to the police. No consideration of unpleasant results for me will count even for half a second. Well, do you accept?'

'There is just one point, Captain Drummond,' remarked the clergyman mildly. 'Supposing that I am able to persuade certain people to – er – expedite the return of Mrs Drummond in exchange for that little bag, where do you and I stand after the bargain is transacted. Do you still intend to tell the police of your extraordinary delusions with regard to me?'

'Not unless they should happen to become acquainted with the ridiculous hallucination that I am the leader of the Black Gang,' answered Drummond. 'That was for your ears alone, my little one, and as you knew it already, you won't get fat on it, will you? No, my intentions – since we are having a heart-to-heart talk – are as follows. Once the exchange is effected we will start quite fair and square – just like last time, Carl. It doesn't pay you to go to the police: it doesn't pay me, so we'll have a single on our own. I am frightfully anxious to add you to my collection of specimens, and I can't believe you are burning with zeal to go. But we'll see, Carl, we'll see. Only – no more monkey-tricks with my wife. Don't let there be any misunderstanding on that point.'

The clergyman smiled benevolently.

'How aptly you put things!' he murmured. 'I accept your terms, and I shall look forward afterwards to the single on our own that you speak about. And now – as to details. You must bear in mind that just as Mrs Drummond is more valuable to you than diamonds, she is also somewhat larger. In other words, it will be obvious at once whether those whom I represent have kept their side of the bargain by producing your wife. It will not be obvious whether you have kept yours. The diamonds may or may not be in your pocket, and once you have your wife in your arms again the incentive to return the diamonds would be diminished. So I suggest, Captain Drummond, that you should bring the diamonds to me – here in this room, before six o'clock as a proof of good faith. You may keep them in your possession; all that I require is to see them. I will then engage on my side to produce Mrs Drummond within a quarter of an hour.'

For a moment Drummond hesitated, fearing a trick. And yet it was a perfectly reasonable request, as he admitted to himself. From their point of view it was quite true that they could have no proof that he would keep his word, and once Phyllis was in the room there would be nothing to prevent the two of them quietly walking out through the door and telling the Reverend Theodosius to go to hell.

'Nothing can very well happen at the Ritz, can it?' continued the clergyman suavely. 'And you see I am even trusting you to the extent that I do not actually ask you to hand over the diamonds until your wife comes. I have no guarantee that even then you will not get up and leave the room with them still in your possession. You are too big and strong a man, Captain Drummond, to allow of any horseplay – especially – er – in a clergyman's suite of rooms.'

Drummond laughed. 'Cut it out, Carl!' he exclaimed. 'Cut it out, for heaven's sake! All right. I agree. I'll go round and get the stones now.'

He rose and went to the door.

'But don't forget, Carl – if there are any monkey-tricks, heaven help you.'

The door closed behind him, and with a snarl the clergyman spun round on the girl.

'How the devil has he spotted us?' His face was convulsed with rage. 'He's the biggest fool in the world, and yet he spots me every time. However, there's no time to worry about that now; we must think.'

He took one turn up and down the room, then he nodded his head as if he had come to a satisfactory decision. And when he spoke to the girl, who sat waiting expectantly on the sofa, he might have been the head of a big business firm giving orders to his managers for the day.

'Ring up headquarters of A Branch,' he said quietly. 'Tell them to send round Number 13 to this room at once. He must be here within a quarter of an hour.'

'Number 13,' repeated the girl, making a note. 'That's the man who is such a wonderful mimic, isn't it? Well?'

'Number 10 and the Italian are to come with him, and they are to wait below for further orders.'

'That all?' She rose to her feet as the Reverend Theodosius crossed rapidly to the door which led to the bathroom. 'What about that silly little fool – his wife?'

For a moment the man paused, genuine amazement on his face.

'My dear girl, you don't really imagine I ever intended to produce her, do you? And any lingering doubt I might have had on the matter disappeared the moment I found Drummond knew us. There's going to be no mistake this time over that young gentleman, believe me.'

With a slight laugh he disappeared into the bathroom, and as little Janet put through her call a tinkling of bottles seemed to show that the Reverend Theodosius was not wasting time.

Chapter 14

In which a Rolls-Royce runs amok

Some ten minutes later he emerged from the bathroom carefully carrying a saucer in his hand. The girl's announcement that Number 13 had started at once had been received with a satisfied grunt, but he had spoken no word. And the girl, glancing through the door, saw him, with his shirt sleeves rolled up above his elbows, carefully mixing two liquids together and stirring the result gently with a glass rod. He was completely absorbed in his task, and with a faint smile on her face she went back to the sofa and waited. She knew too well the futility of speaking to him on such occasions. Even when he came in, carrying the result of his labours with a pair of india-rubber gloves on his hands, she made no remark, but waited for him to relieve her curiosity.

He placed the mixture on the table and glanced round the room. Then he pulled up one of the ordinary stuff armchairs to the table and removed the linen headrest, which he carefully soaked with the contents of the saucer, dabbing the liquid on with a sponge, so as not to crumple the linen in any way. He used up all the liquid, and then, still with the same meticulous care, he replaced the headrest on the chair, and stood back and surveyed his handiwork.

'Look all right?' he asked briefly.

'Quite,' answered the girl. 'What's the game?'

'Drummond has got to sit in that chair,' he returned, removing the saucer and the sponge to the bathroom, and carefully peeling off his gloves. 'He's got to sit in that chair, my dear, and afterwards that linen affair has got to be burnt. And whatever happens' – he paused for a moment in front of her – 'don't you touch it.'

Quietly and methodically, he continued his preparations, as if the most usual occurrence in the world was in progress. He picked up two other chairs, and carried them through into the bedroom; then he returned and placed an open dispatch-case with a sheaf of loose papers on another one.

'That more or less limits the seating accommodation,' he remarked, glancing round the room. 'Now if you, *cara mia*, will spread some of your atrocious woollen garments on the sofa beside you, I think we can guarantee the desired result.'

But apparently his preparations were not over yet. He crossed to the sideboard and extracted a new and undecanted bottle of whisky. From this he withdrew about a dessertspoonful of the spirit, and replaced it with the contents of a small phial which he took out of his waistcoat pocket. Then he forced back the cork until it was right home, and with the greatest care replaced the cap of tinfoil round the top of the bottle. And the girl, coming over to where he was working, saw that the bottle was again as new.

'What a consummate artist you are, *chéri*!' she said, laying a hand on his shoulder.

The Reverend Theodosius smiled and passed his arm round her waist.

'One of the earliest essentials of our – er – occupation, my little one, is to learn how to insert dope into an apparently untouched bottle.'

'But do you think you will get him to drink even out of a new bottle?'

'I hope so. I shall drink myself. But even if he doesn't, the preparation on the chair is the essential thing. Once his neck touches that – '

With an expressive wave of his hand he vanished once more into the bathroom, returning with his coat.

'Don't you remember that Italian toxicologist – Fransioli?' he remarked. 'We met him in Naples three years ago, and he obligingly told me that he had in his possession the secret of one of the real Borgia poisons. I remember I had a most interesting discussion with him on the subject. The internal application is harmless; the external application is what matters. That acts alone, but if the victim can be induced to take it internally as well it acts very much better.'

'Fransioli?' She frowned thoughtfully. 'Wasn't that the name of the man who had the fatal accident on Vesuvius?'

'That's the fellow,' answered the Reverend Theodosius, arranging a siphon and some glasses on a tray. 'He persuaded met to ascend it with him, and on the way up he was foolish enough to tell me that the bottles containing this poison had been stolen from his laboratory. I don't know whether he suspected me or not – I was an Austrian Baron at the time, if I remember aright – but when he proceeded to peer over the edge of the crater at a most dangerous point I thought it better to take no risks. So – er – the accident occurred. And I gathered he was really a great loss to science.'

He glanced at his watch, and the girl laughed delightedly.

'It will be interesting to see if his claims for it are true,' he continued thoughtfully. 'I have only used it once, but on that occasion I inadvertently put too much into the wine, and the patient died. But with the right quantities it produces – so he stated, and I saw him experiment on a dog – a type of partial paralysis, not only of the body, but of the mind. You can see, you can hear, but you can't speak and you can't move. What ultimately happens with a human being I don't know. but the dog recovered.'

A quick double knock came at the door, and with one final glance round the room the Reverend Theodosius crossed to his desk and sat down.

'Come in,' he called, and a small dapper-looking man entered.

'Number 13, sir,' said the newcomer briefly, and the other nodded.

'I am expecting a man here shortly, 13,' remarked the clergyman, 'whose voice I shall want you to imitate over the telephone.

'Only over the telephone, sir?'

'Only over the telephone. You will not be able to be in this room, but there is a bathroom adjoining in which you can hear every word that is spoken.' The other nodded as if satisfied. 'For how long will you require to hear him talk?'

'Five or ten minutes, sir, will be ample.'

'Good. You shall have that. There's the bathroom. Go in, and don't make a sound.'

'Very good, sir.'

'And wait. Have Giuseppi and Number 10 come yet?'

'They left headquarters, sir, just after I did. They should be here by now.'

The man disappeared into the bathroom, closing the door behind him, and once again the Reverend Theodosius glanced at his watch.

'Our young friend should be here shortly,' he murmured. 'And then the single which he seems so anxious to play can begin in earnest.'

The benign expression which he had adopted as part of his rôle disappeared for an instant to be replaced by a look of cold fury.

'The single will begin in earnest,' he repeated softly, 'and it's the last one he will ever play.'

The girl shrugged her shoulders.

'He has certainly asked for it,' she remarked, 'but it strikes me that you had better be careful. You may bet on one thing – that he hasn't kept his knowledge about you and me to himself. Half those young idiots that run about behind him know everything by this time, and if they go to Scotland Yard it will be very unpleasant for us, *mon chéri*. And that they certainly will do if anything should happen to dear Hugh.'

The clergyman smiled resignedly.

'After all these years, you think it necessary to say that to me! My dear, you pain me – you positively wound me to the quick. I will guarantee that all Drummond's friends sleep soundly in their beds tonight, harbouring none but the sweetest thoughts of the kindly and much-maligned old clergyman at the Ritz.'

'And what of Drummond himself?' continued the girl.

'It may be tonight, or it may be tomorrow. But accidents happen at all times – and one is going to happen to him.' He smiled sweetly, and lit a cigar. 'A nasty, sticky accident which will deprive us of his presence. I haven't worried over the details yet – but doubtless the inspiration will come. And here, if I mistake not, is our hero himself.'

The door swung open and Drummond entered.

'Well, Carl, old lad,' he remarked breezily, 'here I am on the stroke of time with the bag of nuts all complete.'

'Excellent,' murmured the clergyman, waving a benevolent hand towards the only free chair. 'But if you must call me by my Christian name, why not make it Theo?'

Drummond grinned delightedly.

'As you wish, my little one. Theo it shall be in future, and Janet.' He bowed to the girl as he sat down. 'There's just one little point I want to mention, Theo, before we come to the laughter and games. Peter Darrell, whom you may remember of old, and who lunched with us today, is sitting on the telephone in my house. And eight o'clock is the time limit. Should his childish fears for my safety and my wife's not be assuaged by that hour, he will feel compelled to interrupt Tum-tum at his dinner. I trust I make myself perfectly clear.'

'You are the soul of lucidity,' beamed the clergyman.

'Good! Then first of all, there are the diamonds. No, don't come too near, please; you can count them quite easily from where you are.' He tumbled them out of the bag, and they lay on the table like great pools of liquid light. The girl's breath came quickly as she saw them, and Drummond turned on her with a smile.

'To one given up to good works and knitting, Janet, doubtless, such things do not appeal. Tell me, Theo,' he remarked as he swept them back into the bag – 'who was the idiot who put them in Snooks' desk? Don't answer if you'd rather not give away your maidenly secrets; but it was a pretty full-sized bloomer on his part, wasn't it – pooping off the old bomb?'

He leaned back in his chair, and for a moment a gleam shone in the other's eyes, for the nape of Drummond's neck came exactly against the centre of the impregnated linen cover.

'Doubtless, Captain Drummond, doubtless,' he murmured politely. 'But if you will persist in talking in riddles, don't you think we might choose a different subject until Mrs Drummond arrives?'

'Anything you like, Theo,' said Drummond. 'I'm perfectly happy talking about you. How the devil do you do it?' He sat up and stared at the other man with genuine wonder on his face. 'Eyes different – nose – voice – figure – everything different. You're a marvel – but for that one small failing of yours.'

'You interest me profoundly,' said the clergyman. 'What is this one small failing that makes you think I am other than what I profess to be?'

Drummond laughed genially.

'Good heavens, don't you know what it is? Hasn't Janet told you? It's that dainty little trick of yours of tickling the left ear with the right big toe that marks you every time. No man can do that, Theo, and blush unseen.'

He leaned back again in his chair, and passed his hand over his forehead.

'By Jove, it's pretty hot in here, isn't it?'

'It is close everywhere today,' answered the other easily, though his eyes behind the spectacles were fixed intently on Drummond. 'Would you care for a drink?'

Drummond smiled; the sudden fit of muzziness seemed to have passed as quickly as it had come.

'Thank you – no,' he answered politely. 'In your last incarnation, Theo, you may remember that I did not drink with you. There is an element of doubt about your liquor which renders it a dangerous proceeding.'

'As you will,' said the clergyman indifferently, at the same time placing the bottle of whisky and the glasses on the table. 'If you imagine that I am capable of interfering with an unopened bottle of Johnny Walker, obtained from the cellars of the Ritz, it would be well not to join me.' He was carefully removing the tinfoil as he spoke, and once again the strange muzzy feeling swept over Drummond. He felt as if things had suddenly become unreal – as if he was dreaming. His vision seemed blurred, and then for the second time it passed away, leaving only a strange mental confusion. What was he doing in this room? Who was this benevolent old clergyman drawing the cork out of a bottle of whisky?

With an effort he pulled himself together. It must be the heat or something, he reflected, and he must keep his brain clear. Perhaps a whisky-and-soda *would* help. After all, there could be no danger in drinking from a bottle which he had seen opened under his very eyes.

'Do you know, Theo,' he remarked, 'I think I will change my mind and have a whisky-and-soda.'

His voice sounded strange to his ears; and he wondered if the others noticed anything. But apparently not; the clergyman merely nodded briefly, and remarked, 'Say when.'

'When,' said Drummond, with a foolish sort of laugh. It was a most extraordinary thing, but he couldn't focus his eyes; there were two glasses on the table and two clergymen splashing in soda from two siphons. Surely he wasn't going to faint; bad thing to faint when he was alone with Peterson.

He took a gulp at his drink and suddenly began to talk – foolishly and idiotically.

'Nice room, Carl, old lad . . . Never expected meet you again: certainly not in nice room . . . Wrote letter paper after poor old Latter went mad. Drew you – drew badger. Send badger mad too.'

His voice trailed away, and he sat there blinking stupidly. Everything was confused, and his tongue seemed weighted with lead. He reached out again for his glass – or tried to – and his arm refused to move. And suddenly out of the jumble of thoughts in his brain there emerged the one damning certainty that somehow or other he had been trapped and drugged. He gave a hoarse, inarticulate cry, and struggled to rise to his feet, but it was useless; his legs and arms felt as if they were bound to the chair by iron bands. And in the mist that swam before his eyes he saw the mocking faces of the clergyman and his daughter.

'It seems to have acted most excellently,' remarked the Reverend Theodosius, and Drummond found he could hear quite normally; also his sight was improving; things in the room seemed steadier. And his mind was becoming less confused – he could think again. But to move or to speak was utterly impossible; all he could do was to sit and watch and rage inwardly at having been such a fool as to trust Peterson.

But that gentleman appeared in no hurry. He was writing with a gold pencil on a letter pad, and every now and then he paused and smiled thoughtfully. At length he seemed satisfied, and crossed to the bathroom door.

'We are ready now,' Drummond heard him say, and he wondered what was going to happen next. To turn his head was impossible; his range of vision was limited by the amount he could turn his eyes. And then, to his amazement, he heard his own voice speaking from somewhere behind him – not, perhaps, quite so deep, but an extraordinary good imitation which would have deceived nine people out of ten when they could not see the speaker. And then he heard Peterson's voice again mentioning the telephone, and he realised what they were going to do.

'I want you,' Peterson was saying, 'to send this message that I have written down to that number – using this gentleman's voice.'

They came into his line of vision, and the new arrival stared at him curiously. But he asked no questions – merely took the paper and read it through carefully. Then he stepped over to the telephone, and took off the receiver. And, helplessly impotent, Drummond sat in his chair and heard the following message spoken in his own voice:

'Is that you, Peter, old bird? I've made the most unholy bloomer. This old bloke Theodosius isn't Carl at all. He's a perfectly respectable pillar of the Church.'

And then apparently Darrell said something, and Peterson, who was listening through the second earpiece, whispered urgently to the man.

'Phyllis,' he went on – 'she's as right as rain! The whole thing is a boss shot of the first order . . . '

Drummond made another stupendous effort to rise, and for a moment everything went blank. Dimly he heard his own voice still talking into the instrument, but he only caught a word here and there, and then it ceased, and he realised that the man had left the room. It was Peterson's voice close by him that cleared his brain again.

'I trust you approve of the way our single has started, Captain Drummond,' he remarked pleasantly. 'Your friend Peter, I am glad to say, is more than satisfied, and has announced his intention of dining with some female charmer. Also he quite understands why your wife has gone into the country – you heard that bit, I hope, about her sick cousin? – and he realises that you are joining her.'

And suddenly the pleasant voice ceased, and the clergyman continued in a tone of cold, malignant fury.

'You rat! You damned interfering young swine! Now that you're helpless I don't mind admitting that I am the man you knew as Carl Peterson, but I'm not going to make the mistake he made a second time. I underestimated you, Captain Drummond. I left things to that fool Lakington. I treated you as a blundering young ass, and I realised too late that you weren't such a fool as you looked. This time I am paying you the compliment of treating you as a dangerous enemy, and a clever man. I trust you are flattered.'

He turned as the door opened, and the man who had telephoned came in with two others. One was a great, powerful-looking man who might have been a prize-fighter; the other was a lean, swarthy-skinned foreigner, and both of them looked unpleasant customers. And Hugh wondered what was going to happen next, while his eyes rolled wildly from side to side as if in search of some way of escape. It was like some ghastly nightmare when one is powerless to move before some dreadful figment of the brain, only to be saved at the last moment by waking up. Only in Hugh's case he was awake already, and the dream was reality.

He saw the men leave the room, and then Peterson came over to him again. First he took the little bag of diamonds out of his pocket, and it struck Hugh that though he had seen the other's hand go into his pocket, he had felt nothing. He watched Peterson and the girl as they examined the stones; he watched Peterson as he locked them up in a steel dispatch-case. And then Peterson disappeared out of his range of vision. He was conscious that he was near him – just behind him – and the horror of the nightmare increased. It had been better when they were talking; at least then he could see them. But now, with both of them out of sight – hovering round the back of his chair, perhaps – and without a sound in the room save the faint hum of the traffic outside, the strain was getting unbearable.

And then another thought came to add to his misery. If they killed him – and they intended to, he was certain – what would happen to Phyllis? They'd got her too, somewhere; what were they going to do to her? Again he made a superhuman effort to rise; again he failed so much as to move his finger. And for a while he raved and blasphemed mentally.

It was hopeless, utterly hopeless; he was caught like a rat in a trap.

And then he began to think coherently again. After all, they couldn't kill him here in the Ritz. You can't have dead men lying about in your room in an hotel. And they would have to move him some time; they couldn't leave him sitting there. How were they going to get him out? He couldn't walk, and to carry him out as he was would be impossible. Too many of the staff below knew him by sight.

Suddenly Peterson came into view again. He was in his shirt-sleeves and was smoking a cigar, and Hugh watched him sorting out papers. He seemed engrossed in the matter, and paid no more attention to the helpless figure at the table than he did to the fly on the window. At length he completed his task, and having closed the dispatch-case with a snap, he rose and stood facing Hugh.

'Enjoying yourself?' he remarked. 'Wondering what is going to happen? Wondering where dear Phyllis is?'

He gave a short laugh.

'Excellent drug that, isn't it? The first man I tried it on died – so you're lucky. You never felt me put a pin into the back of your arm, did you?'

He laughed again; in fact, the Reverend Theodosius seemed in an excellent temper.

'Well, my friend, you really asked for it this time, and I'm afraid you're going to get it. I cannot have someone continually worrying me like this, so I'm going to kill you, as I always intended to some day. It's a pity, and in many ways I regret it, but you must admit yourself that you really leave me no alternative. It will appear to be accidental, so you need entertain no bitter sorrow that I shall suffer in any way. And it will take place very soon – so soon, in fact, that I doubt if you will recover from the effects of the drug. I wouldn't guarantee it: you might. As I say, you are only the second person on whom I have tried it. And with regard to your wife – our little Phyllis – it may interest you to know that I have not yet made up my mind. I may find it necessary for her to share in your accident – or even to have one all on her own: I may not.'

The raving fury in Drummond's mind as his tormentor talked on showed clearly in his eyes, and Peterson laughed.

'Our friend is getting quite agitated, my dear,' he remarked, and the girl came into sight. She was smoking a cigarette, and for a while they stared at their helpless victim much as if he was a specimen in a museum.

'You're an awful idiot, my Hugh, aren't you?' she said at length. 'And you have given us such a lot of trouble. But I shall quite miss you, and all our happy little times together.'

She laughed gently, and glanced at the clock.

'They ought to be here fairly soon,' she remarked. 'Hadn't we better get him out of sight?'

Peterson nodded, and between them they pushed Drummond into the bathroom.

'You see, my friend,' remarked Peterson affably, 'it is necessary to get you out of the hotel without arousing suspicion. A simple little matter, but it is often the case that one trips up more over simple matters than over complicated ones.'

He was carefully inserting a pin into his victim's leg as he spoke, and watching intently for any sign of feeling.

'Why, I remember once,' he continued conversationally, 'that I was so incredibly foolish as to replace the cork in a bottle of prussic acid after I had – er – compelled a gentleman to drink the contents. He was in bed at the time, and everything pointed to suicide, except that confounded cork. I mean, would any man, after he's drunk sufficient prussic acid to poison a regiment, go and cork up the empty bottle? It only shows how careful one must be over these little matters.'

The girl put her head round the door.

'They're here,' she remarked abruptly, and Peterson went into the other room, half closing the door. And Drummond, writhing impotently, heard the well-modulated voice of the Reverend Theodosius.

'Ah, my dear friend, my very dear old friend! What joy it is to see you again. I am greatly obliged to you for escorting this gentleman up personally.'

'Not at all, sir, not at all! Would you care for dinner to be served up here?'

Someone to do with the hotel, thought Drummond, and he made one final despairing effort to move. He felt it was his last chance, and it failed – as the others had done before. And it seemed to him that the mental groan he gave must have been audible, so utterly beyond hope did he feel. But it wasn't; no sound came from the bathroom to the ears of the courteous sub-manager.

'I will ring later if I require it,' Peterson was saying in his gentle, kindly voice. 'My friend, you understand, is still on a very strict diet, and he comes to me more for spiritual comfort than for bodily. But I will ring should I find he would like to stay.'

'Very good, sir.'

And Drummond heard the door close, and knew that his last hope had gone.

Then he heard Peterson's voice again, sharp and incisive.

'Lock the door. You two – get Drummond. He's in the bathroom.'

The two men he had previously seen entered, and carried him back into the sitting-room, where the whole scheme was obvious at a glance. Just getting out of an ordinary invalid's chair was a big man of more or less the same build as himself. A thick silk muffler partially disguised his face; a soft hat was pulled well down over his eyes, and Drummond realised that the gentleman who had been wheeled in for spiritual comfort would not be wheeled out.

The two men pulled him out of his chair, and then, forgetting his condition, they let him go, and he collapsed like a sack of potatoes on the floor, his legs and arms sprawling in grotesque attitudes.

They picked him up again, and not without difficulty they got him into the other man's overcoat; and finally they deposited him in the invalid's chair, and tucked him up with the rug.

'We'll give it half an hour,' remarked Peterson, who had been watching the operation. 'By that time our friend will have had sufficient spiritual solace; and until then you two can wait outside. I will give you your full instructions later.'

'Will you want me any more, sir?' The man whose place Drummond had taken was speaking.

'No,' said Peterson curtly. 'Get out as unostentatiously as you can. Go down by the stairs and not by the lift.'

With a nod he dismissed them all, and once again Drummond was alone with his two chief enemies.

'Simple, isn't it, my friend?' remarked Peterson. 'An invalid arrives, and an invalid will shortly go. And once you've passed the hotel doors you will cease to be an invalid. You will become again that well-known young man about town – Captain Hugh Drummond – driving out of London in his car – a very nice Rolls, that new one of yours – bought, I think, since we last met. Your chauffeur would have been most uneasy when he missed it but for the note you've left him, saying you'll be away for three days.' Peterson laughed gently as he stared at his victim.

'You must forgive me if I seem to gloat a little, won't you?' he continued. 'I've got such a large score to settle with you, and I very much fear I shan't be in at the death. I have an engagement to dine with an American millionaire, whose wife is touched to the heart over the sufferings of the starving poor in Austria. And when the wives of millionaires are touched to the heart, my experience is that the husbands are generally touched in the pocket.'

He laughed again even more gently and leaned across the table towards the man who sat motionless in the chair. He seemed to be striving to see some sign of fear in Drummond's eyes, some appeal for mercy. But if there was any expression at all it was only a faint mocking boredom, such as Drummond had been wont to infuriate him with during their first encounter a year before. Then he had expressed it in words and actions; now only his eyes were left to him, but it was there all the same. And after a while Peterson snarled at him viciously.

'No, I shan't be in at the death, Drummond, but I will explain to you the exact programme. You will be driven out of London in your own car, but when the final accident occurs you will be alone. It is a most excellent place for an accident, Drummond – most excellent. One or two have already taken place there, and the bodies are generally recovered some two or three days later – more or less unrecognisable. Then when the news comes out in the evening papers tomorrow I shall be able to tell the police the whole sad story. How you took compassion on an old clergyman and asked him to lunch, and then went out of London after your charming young wife – only to meet with this dreadful end. I think I'll even offer to take part in the funeral service. And yet – no, that is a pleasure I shall have to deny myself. Having done what I came over to do, Drummond, rather more expeditiously than I thought likely, I shall return to my starving children in Vienna. And, do you know what I came over to do, Drummond? I came over to smash the Black Gang – and I came over to kill you – though the latter could have waited.'

Peterson's eyes were hard and merciless, but the expression of faint boredom still lingered in Drummond's. Only too well did he realise now that he had played straight into his enemy's hands, but he was a gambler through and through, and not by the quiver of an eyelid did he show what he felt. Right from the very start the dice had been loaded in Peterson's favour owing to that one astounding piece of luck in getting hold of Phyllis. It hadn't even been a fight – it had been a walk-over. And the cruel part of it was that it was not through any mistake of Drummond's. It was a fluke pure and simple – an astounding fluke – a fluke which had come off better than many a carefully-thought-out scheme. If it hadn't been for that he would never have come to Peterson's sitting-room at all; he would never have been doped; he wouldn't have been sitting helpless as a log while Peterson put down his cards one after the other in cold triumph.

'Yes, it could have waited, Captain Drummond – that second object of mine. I assure you that it was a great surprise to me when I realised who the leader of the Black Gang was – a great surprise and a great pleasure. To kill two birds, so to speak, with one stone, saves trouble; to accomplish two objects in one accident is much more artistic. So the Black Gang loses its leader, the leader loses his life, and I regain my diamonds. Eminently satisfactory, my friend, eminently. And when your dear wife returns from the country – if she does, well, Captain Drummond, it will be a very astute member of Scotland Yard who will associate her little adventure with that benevolent old clergyman, the Reverend Theodosius Longmoor, who recently spent two or three days at the Ritz. Especially in view of your kindly telephone message to Mr – what's his name? – Mr Peter Darrell?'

He glanced at his watch and rose to his feet.

'I fear that that is all the spiritual consolation that I can give you this evening, my dear fellow,' he remarked benignly. 'You will understand, I'm sure, that there are many calls on my time. Janet, my love' – he raised his voice – 'our young friend is leaving us now. I feel sure you'd like to say goodbye to him.'

She came into the room, walking a little slowly and for a while she stared in silence at Hugh. And it seemed to him that in her eyes there was a gleam of genuine pity. Once again he made a frantic effort to speak – to beg, beseech, and implore them not to hurt Phyllis – but it was useless. And then he saw her turn to Peterson.

'I suppose,' she said regretfully, 'that it is absolutely necessary.'

'Absolutely,' he answered curtly. 'He knows too much, and he worries us too much.'

She shrugged her shoulders and came over to Drummond.

'Well, goodbye, *mon ami*,' she remarked gently. 'I really am sorry that I shan't see you again. You are one of the few people that make this atrocious country bearable.'

She patted him on his cheek, and again the feeling that he was dreaming came over Drummond. It couldn't be real – this monstrous nightmare. He would wake up in a minute and find Denny standing beside him, and he registered a vow that he would go to an indigestion specialist. And then he realised that the two men had come back into the room, and that it wasn't a dream, but hard, sober fact. The Italian was putting a hat on his head and wrapping the scarf round his neck while Peterson gave a series of curt instructions to the other man. And then he was being wheeled along the passage towards the lift, while the Reverend Theodosius walked solicitously beside him, murmuring affectionately in his ear.

'Goodbye, my dear friend – goodbye,' he remarked, after the chair had been wheeled into the lift. 'It was good of you to come. Be careful, liftman, won't you?'

He waved a kindly hand, and the last vision Drummond had of him before the doors closed was of a benevolent old clergyman beaming at him solicitously from behind a pair of horn-rimmed spectacles.

And now came his only chance. Surely there would be someone who would recognise him below; surely the hall porter, who in the past had received many a tip from him, must realise who he was in spite of the hat pulled down over his eyes. But even that hope failed. The elderly party in the invalid's chair who had come half an hour ago was now going, and there was no reason why the hall porter should suspect anything. He gave the two men a hand lifting the chair into a big and very roomy limousine car which Drummond knew was certainly not his, and the next instant they were off.

He could see nothing – the hat was too far over his eyes. For a time he tried to follow where they were going by noting the turns, but he soon gave that up as hopeless. And then, after driving for about half an hour, the car stopped and the two men got out, leaving him alone. He could hear a lot of talking going on, but he didn't try to listen. He was resigned by this time – utterly indifferent; his only feeling was a mild curiosity as to what was going to happen next.

The voices came nearer, and he found himself being lifted out of the car. In doing so his hat was pulled back a little so that he could see, and the first thing he noticed was his own new Rolls-Royce. They couldn't have brought it to the Ritz, he reflected, where it might have been recognised – and an unwilling admiration for the master brain that had thought out every detail, and the wonderful organisation that allowed of them being carried out, took hold of his mind.

The men wheeled him alongside his own car; then they lifted him out of his chair and deposited him on the back seat. Then the Italian and the other man who had been at the Ritz sat down one on each side of him, while a third man took the wheel.

'Look slippy, Bill,' said the big man beside him. 'A boat will be coming through about half-past nine.'

A boat! What was that about a boat? Were they going to send him out to sea, then, and let him drown? If so, what was the object of getting his own car? The hat slipped forward again; but he guessed by some of the flaring lights he could dimly see that they were going through slums. Going eastward Essex way, or perhaps the south side of the river towards Woolwich. But after a time he gave it up: it was no good wondering – he'd know for certain soon enough. And now the speed was increasing as they left London behind them. The headlights were on, and Hugh judged that they were going about thirty-five miles an hour. And he also guessed that it was about forty-five minutes before they pulled up, and the engine and lights were switched off. The men beside him got out, and he promptly rolled over into a corner, where they left him lying.

'This is the place to wait,' he heard the Italian say. 'You go on, Franz, to the corner, and when it's ready flash your torch. You'll have to stand on the running-board, Bill, and steer till he's round the corner into the straight. Then jump off – no-one will see you behind the headlights. I'm going back to Maybrick Tower.'

And then he heard a sentence which drove him impotent with fury, and again set him struggling madly to move.

'The girl's there. We'll get orders about her in the morning.'

There was silence for a while; then he heard Bill's voice.

'Let's get on with it. There's Franz signalling. We'll have to prop him up on the steering-wheel somehow.'

They pulled Drummond out of the back of the car, and put him in the driver's seat.

'Doesn't matter if he does fall over at the last moment. It will look as if he'd fainted, and make the accident more probable,' said the Italian, and Bill grunted.

'Seems a crime,' he muttered, 'to smash up this peach of a car.' He started the engine and switched on the headlights; then he slipped her straight into third speed and started. He was on the running-board beside the wheel, steering with one hand and holding on to Drummond with the other. As they rounded the corner he straightened the car up and opened the throttle. Then he jumped off, and Drummond realised the game at last.

A river was in front – a river spanned by a bridge which swung open to let boats go through. And it was open now. He had a dim vision of a man waving wildly; he heard the crash as the car took the guarding gate, and then he saw the bonnet dip suddenly; there was a rending, scraping noise underneath him as the framework hit the edge; an appalling splash – and silence.

Chapter 15

In which Hugh Drummond arrives at Maybrick Hall

Two things saved Drummond from what was practically certain death – the heavy coat he was wearing, and the fact that he rolled sideways clear of the steering-wheel as soon as the man let go of him with his hand. Had he remained behind the wheel he must infallibly have gone to the bottom with the car, and at that point where the river narrowed to come through the piers of the bridge the water was over twenty feet deep. He had sufficient presence of mind to take a deep breath as the car shot downwards; then he felt the water close over his head. And if before his struggles to move had been fierce – now that the end seemed at hand they became desperate. The desire to get clear – to give one kick with his legs and come to the surface – roused him to one superhuman effort. He felt as if the huge heave he gave with his legs against the floorboards must send him flying to the top; afterwards he realised that this vast effort had been purely mental – the actual physical result had been practically negligible. But not quite, it had done something, and the coat did the rest.

With that one last supreme throw for his life his mind had overcome the effects of the poison to the extent of forcing his legs to give one spasmodic little kick. He floated clear of the car, and slowly – how slowly only his bursting lungs could testify – the big coat brought him to the surface. For a moment or two he could do nothing save draw in deep gulps of air; then he realised that the danger was not yet past. For he couldn't shout, he could do nothing save float and drift, and the current had carried him clear of the bridge out of sight of those on top. And his mind was quite clear enough to realise that the coat which had saved him, once it became sodden would just as surely drown him.

He could see men with lanterns on the bridge; he could hear them shouting and talking. And then he saw a boat come back from the ship that had passed through just before he went over the edge in his car. Surely they'd pull downstream to look for him, he thought in an agony of futile anger; surely they couldn't be such fools as to go on pulling about just by the bridge when it was obvious he wasn't there. But since they thought that he was at the bottom in his car, and blasphemous language was already being wafted at them by the skipper of the vessel for the useless delay, with a sinking heart Drummond saw the boat turn round and disappear upstream into the darkness. Men with lanterns still stood on the bridge, but he was far beyond the range of their lights, and he was drifting farther every minute. It was just a question of time now – and it couldn't be very long either. He could see that his legs had gone down well below the surface, and only the air that still remained in the buttoned-up part of his overcoat kept his head out and his shoulders near the top. And when that was gone – the end. He had done all he could; there was nothing for it now but to wait for the inevitable finish. And though he had been credibly informed that under such circumstances the whole of a man's life passes in rapid review before him, his sole and only thought was an intense desire to get his hands on Peterson again.

For a while he pictured the scene with a wealth of pleasant detail, until a sudden change in his immediate surroundings began to take place. At first he could not realise what had happened; then little by little it began to dawn on him what had occurred. Up to date the water in which he floated had seemed motionless to him; he had been drifting in it at exactly the same velocity as the current. And now, suddenly, he saw that the water was going past him. For a moment or two he failed to understand the significance of the fact; then wild hope surged up in his mind. For a time he stared fixedly at the bridge, and the hope became a certainty. He was not drifting any farther from it; he was stationary; he was aground. He could feel nothing; he could see nothing – but the one stupendous fact remained that he was aground. Life took on another lease – anything might happen now. If only he could remain there till the morning they would see him from the bridge, and there seemed no reason why he shouldn't. The water still flowed sluggishly past him, broken with the faintest ripple close to his head. So he reasoned that it must be very shallow where he was, and being an incurable optimist, he resumed, with even fuller details, his next meeting with Peterson.

But not for long. Starting from his waist and spreading downwards to his feet and outwards through his shoulders to his hands there slowly began to creep the most agonising cramp. The torture was indescribable, and the sweat dripped off his forehead into his eyes. And gradually it dawned on him that the effects of the poison were wearing off. Sensation was returning to his limbs; even through his agony he could feel that he was resting against something under the water. Then he heard a strange noise, and realised that it was he himself groaning with the pain. The use of his voice had come back. He spoke a sentence aloud, and made certain.

And then Drummond deliberately decided on doing one of those things which Peterson had always failed to legislate for in the past. Ninety-nine men out of a hundred would have shouted themselves hoarse under such circumstances; not so Drummond. Had he done so a message would have reached Peterson in just so long as it took a trunk call to get through; the man called Franz was still assiduously helping the gate-keeper on the bridge. And the Reverend Theodosius Longmoor and his little Janet would have vanished into the night, leaving no traces behind them.

Which all flashed through Drummond's mind as the cramp took and racked him, and the impulse to shout grew stronger and stronger. Twice he opened his mouth to hail the men he could see not three hundred yards away – to give a cry that would bring a boat post-haste to his rescue; twice he stopped himself with the shout unuttered. A more powerful force was at work within him than mere pain – a cold, bitter resolve to get even with Carl Peterson. And it required no great effort of brain to see that that would be more easily done if Peterson believed he had succeeded. Moreover if he shouted there would be questions asked. The police would inevitably come into the matter, demanding to know why he adopted such peculiar forms of amusement as going into twenty feet of water in a perfectly good motor-car. And all that would mean delay, which was the last thing he wanted. He felt tolerably certain that, for all his apparent confidence, Peterson was not going to stop one minute longer in the country than was absolutely necessary.

So he stayed where he was, in silence – and gradually the cramp passed away. He could turn his head now, and with eyes that had grown accustomed to the darkness he saw what had happened. On each side of him the river flowed past smoothly, and he realised that by a wonderful stroke of luck he had struck a small shoal. Had he missed it – had he floated by on either side – well, Peterson's plan would have succeeded.

Following the extraordinary motor accident reported in our previous issue, we are now informed that the body of the unfortunate driver has been discovered some three miles from the scene of the tragedy. He was drowned, and had evidently been dead some hours.

Drummond smiled grimly to himself as he imagined the paragraphs in the papers. His nerves were far too hardened to let his narrow escape worry him for an instant, and he felt an unholy satisfaction in thinking of Peterson searching the early specials and the late extras for that little item of news.

'I'd hate you to be disappointed, my friend,' he muttered to himself, 'but you'll have to be content with the coat and hat. The body has doubtless drifted farther on and will be recovered later.'

He took off his hat, and let it drift away; he unbuttoned his overcoat and sent it after the hat. Then letting himself down into the deep water, he swam noiselessly towards the bank.

A little to his surprise he found that his legs and arms felt perfectly normal – a trifle stiff perhaps, but beyond that the effects of the poison seemed to have worn off completely. Beyond being very wet he appeared to have suffered no evil results at all, and after he'd done 'knees up' on the bank for five minutes to restore his circulation he sat down to consider his plan of action.

First, Phyllis at Maybrick Hall. He must get at her somehow, and, even if he couldn't get her away, he must let her know that she would be all right. After that things must look after themselves; everything would depend on circumstances. Always provided that those circumstances led to the one great goal – Peterson. Once Phyllis was safe, everything was subservient to that.

A church clock nearby began to toll the hour, and Drummond counted the strokes. Eleven o'clock – not two hours since he had gone over the bridge – and it felt like six. So much the better; it gave him so many more hours of darkness, and he wanted darkness for his explorations at Maybrick Hall. And it suddenly dawned on him that he hadn't the faintest idea where the house was.

It might have deterred some men; it merely made Drummond laugh. If he didn't know, he'd find out – even if it became necessary to pull someone out of bed and ask. The first thing to do was to get back to the spot where the car had halted, and to do that he must go across country. Activity was diminishing on the bridge, but he could still see lanterns dancing about, and the sudden appearance of a very wet man might lead to awkward questions. So he struck off in the direction he judged to be right – moving with that strange, cat-like silence which was a never-ceasing source of wonderment even to those who knew him best.

No man ever heard Drummond coming, and very few ever saw him until it was too late, if he didn't intend that they should. And now, in utterly unknown country, with he knew not how many undesirable gentlemen about, he was taking no risks. Mercifully for him it was a dark night – just such a night in fact as he would have chosen, and as he passed like a huge shadow from tree to tree, only to vanish silently behind a hedge, and reappear two hundred yards farther on, he began to feel that life was good. The joy of action was in his veins; he was going to get his hands on somebody soon, preferably the Italian or the man who called himself Franz. For Bill he had a sneaking regard; Bill at any rate could appreciate a good car when he saw one. The only trouble was that he was unarmed, and an unarmed man can't afford to stop and admire the view in a mix-up. Not that the point deterred him for a moment, it only made him doubly cautious. He must see without being seen; he must act without being heard. Afterwards would be a different matter.

Suddenly he stiffened and crouched motionless behind a bush. He had heard voices and the sound of footsteps crunching on the gravel.

'No good waiting any more,' said the man whom he recognised as Franz. 'He's dead for a certainty, and they can't pull him out till tomorrow. Couldn't have gone better. He swayed right over just as the car took the gates, and the bridge-keeper saw it. Think he fainted – '

Their voices died away in the distance, and Drummond came out from behind the bush. He stepped forward cautiously and found himself confronted with a high wire fence. Through it he could see a road along which the two men must have been walking. And then through a gap in the trees he saw a light in the window of a house. So his first difficulty was solved. The man called Franz and his companion could have but one destination in all probability – Maybrick Hall. And that must be the house he could see through the trees, while the road on the other side of the fence was the drive leading up to it.

He gave them half a minute or so; then he climbed through the fence. It was a fence with horizontal strands of thick wire, about a foot apart, and the top strand was two feet above Drummond's head. An expensive fence, he reflected; an unusual fence to put round any property of such a sort. An admirable fence for cattle in a corral because of its strength, but for a house and grounds – peculiar, to say the least. It was not a thing of beauty; it afforded no concealment, and it was perfectly simple to climb through. And because Drummond had been trained in the school which notices details, even apparently trivial ones, he stood for a moment or two staring at the fence, after he had clambered through. It was the expense of the thing more than anything else that puzzled him. It was new – that was obvious, and after a while he proceeded to walk along it for a short way. And another peculiar thing struck him when he came to the first upright. It was an iron T-shaped post, and each strand of wire passed through a hole in the bottom part of the T. A perfectly simple and sound arrangement, and, but for one little point, just the type of upright one would have expected to find in such a fence. Round every hole was a small white collar, through which each strand of wire passed, so that the wires rested on the collars, and not on the holes in the iron uprights. Truly a most remarkable fence, he reflected again – in fact, a thoroughly eccentric fence. But he got no farther than that in his thoughts; the knowledge which would have supplied him with the one clue necessary to account for that fence's eccentricity of appearance was not his. The facts he could notice; the reason for the facts was beyond him. And after a further examination he shrugged his shoulders and gave it up. There were bigger things ahead of him than a mere question of fencing, and, keeping in the shadow of the shrubs which fringed each side of the drive, he crept silently towards the house.

It was a low, rambling type of building covered as far as he could see with ivy and creepers. There were only two storeys, and Hugh nodded his satisfaction. It made things simpler when outside work was more than likely. For a long time he stood in the shadow of a big rhodo-dendron bush, carefully surveying every possible line of approach and flight, and it was while he was balancing up chances that he gradually became aware of a peculiar noise proceeding from the house. It sounded like the very faint hum of an aeroplane in the far distance, except that every two or three seconds there came a slight thud. It was quite regular, and during the four or five minutes whilst he stood there listening there was no variation in the monotonous rhythm. Thud: thud: thud – faint, but very distinct; and all the time the gentle whirring of some smooth-running, powerful engine.

The house was in darkness save for one room on the ground floor, from which the light was streaming. It was empty, and appeared to be an ordinary sitting-room. And, as a last resort, Hugh decided he would go in that way, if outside methods failed. But to start with he had no intention of entering the house; it struck him that the odds against him were unnecessarily large.

He retreated still farther into the shadow, and then quite clear and distinct the hoot of an owl was heard in the silent garden. He knew that Phyllis would recognise the call if she heard it; he knew that she would give him some sign if she could. And so he stood and waited, eagerly watching the house for any sign of movement. But none came, and after a pause of half a minute he hooted again. Of course it was possible that she was a room facing the other way, and he had already planned his line of advance round to the back of the house. And then, just as he was preparing to skirt round and investigate he saw the curtains of one of the upper rooms shake and open slightly. Very faintly he repeated the call, and to his joy he saw a head poked through between them. But he was taking no chances, and it was impossible to tell to whom the head belonged. It might be Phyllis, and on the other hand it might not. So once again he repeated the call, barely above his breath, and then he waited for some answer.

It came almost at once; his own name called very gently, and he hesitated no more. He was across the lawn in a flash and standing under her window, and once again he heard her voice tense with anxiety.

'Is that you, Hugh?'

'Yes, darling, it's me right enough,' he whispered back. 'But there's no time to talk now. I want you to jump on to the flower-bed. It's soft landing, and it won't hurt you.'

'But I can't, old man,' she said, with a little catch in her breath. 'They've got me lashed up with a steel chain.'

'They've got you lashed up with a steel chain,' repeated Hugh stupidly. 'The devil they have; the devil they have!'

And his voice was shaking a little with cold, concentrated fury.

'All right, kid,' he went on after a moment; 'if you can't come to me, I must come to you. We'll soon deal with that chain.'

He glanced into the room underneath hers and saw that it looked like a drawing-room. The windows seemed easy to force if necessary, but he decided first of all to try the ivy outside. But it was useless for a man of his weight. Just at the bottom it supported him, but as soon as he started to climb it gave way at once. Twice he got up about six feet, twice he fell back again as the ivy broke away from the wall. And after the second attempt he looked up at the anxious face of his wife above.

'No go, darling,' he muttered. 'And I'm afraid of making too much noise. I'm going to try and force this window.'

By a stroke of luck they had not taken his clasp-knife, and by a still greater stroke of luck he found that the catch on the window had been broken, and that it proved even easier to open than he had thought. He stepped back and looked up.

'I'm coming in, kid,' he whispered. 'Do you know where the stairs are?'

'Just about the middle of the house, old man. And listen. I can't quite reach the door to open it, but I've got my parasol and I can tap on it so that you'll know which it is.'

'Right,' he answered. 'Keep your tail up.'

The next moment he had vanished into the drawing-room. And now he noticed that that strange noise which he had heard while standing on the lawn was much louder. As he cautiously opened the door and peered into the passage the very faint hum became a steady drone, while with each successive thud the floor-boards shook a little.

The passage was in darkness, though light was shining from under some of the doors. And as he crept along in search of the stairs he heard voices proceeding from one of the rooms he passed. Evidently a fairly populous household, it struck him, as he tested the bottom stair with his weight to see if it creaked. But the staircase was old and solid, and the stair carpet was thick, and at the moment Hugh was not disposed to linger. Afterwards the house seemed to promise a fairly fruitful field for investigation; at present Phyllis was all that mattered. So he vanished upwards with the uncanny certainty of all his movements at night, and a moment later he was standing on the landing above.

It was a long, straight corridor, a replica of the one below, and he turned in the direction in which he knew her room must lie. And he had only taken a couple of steps when he stopped abruptly, peering ahead with eyes that strove to pierce the darkness. For it seemed to him that there was something in the passage – something darker than its surroundings. He pressed against the wall absolutely motionless, and as he stood there with every sense alert, and his arms hanging loosely forward ready for any emergency, he heard a tapping on one of the doors just ahead of him. It was Phyllis signalling with her parasol as she had said, and he took a step forward. And at that moment something sprang out of the darkness, and he found himself fighting for his life.

For a second or two he was at a disadvantage, so completely had he been taken by surprise; then the old habits returned. And not a moment too soon; he was up against an antagonist who was worthy of him. Two hands like iron hooks were round his neck, and the man who gets that grip first wins more often than not. His own hands shot out into the darkness, and then for the first time in his life he felt a stab of fear. For he couldn't reach the other man: long though his arms were, the other man's were far longer, and as his hands went along them he could feel the muscles standing out like steel bars. He made one supreme effort to force through to his opponent's throat and it failed; with his superior reach he could keep his distance. Already Drummond's head was beginning to feel like bursting with the awful pressure round his throat, and he knew he must do something at once or lose. And just in time he remembered his clasp-knife. It went against his grain to use it; never before had he fought an unarmed man with a weapon – and as far as he could tell this man was unarmed. But it had to be done and done quickly.

With all his force he stabbed sideways at the man's left arm. He heard a snarl of pain, and the grip of one of the hands round his throat relaxed. And now the one urgent thing was to prevent him shouting for help. Like a flash Drummond was on him, one hand on his mouth and the other gripping his throat with the grip he had learned from Osaki the Jap in days gone by, and had never forgotten. And because he was fighting to kill now he wasted no time. The grip tightened; there was a dreadful worrying noise as the man bit into his thumb – then it was over. The man slipped downwards on to the floor, and Drummond stood drawing in great mouthfuls of air.

But he knew there was no time to lose. Though they had fought in silence, and he could still hear the monotonous thud and the beat of the engine, at any moment someone might come upstairs. And to be found with a dead man at one's feet in a strange house is not the best way of securing a hospitable welcome. What to do with the body – that was the first insistent point. There was no time for intricate schemes; it was a question of taking risks and chancing it. So for a moment or two he listened at the door of the room opposite that on which he had heard Phyllis tapping, and from which the man had sprung at him – then he gently opened it. It was a bedroom and empty, and without further hesitation he dragged his late opponent in, and left him lying on the floor. By the dim light from the un-curtained window, he could see that the man was almost deformed, so enormous was the length of his arms. They must have been six inches longer than those of an average man, and were almost as powerful as his own. And as he saw the snarling, ferocious face upturned to his, he uttered a little prayer of thanksgiving for the presence of his clasp-knife. It had been altogether too near a thing for his liking.

He closed the door and stepped across the passage, and the next moment Phyllis was in his arms.

'I thought you were never coming, old man,' she whispered. 'I was afraid the brutes had caught you.'

'I had a slight difference of opinion with a warrior outside your door,' said Hugh, grinning. 'Quite like old times.'

'But, my dear,' she said, with sudden anxiety in her voice, 'you're sopping wet.'

'Much water has flowed under the bridge, my angel child, since I last saw you, and I've flowed with it.' He kissed her on the right side of her mouth, then on the left for symmetry, and finally in the middle for luck. Then he grew serious. 'No time for hot air now, old thing; let's have a look at this jolly old chain effect of yours. Once we're out of here, you shall tell me everything and I'll eat several pounds of mud for having been such an unmitigated idiot as to let these swine get hold of you.'

He was examining the steel chain as he spoke, and gradually his face grew grave. He didn't seem to have gained much after all by breaking in; Phyllis was just as much a prisoner as ever. The chain, which was about six feet long, was fastened at one end to a big staple in the wall and at the other to a bracelet which encircled his wife's right wrist. And the bracelet could only be opened with a key. Any idea of breaking the chain or pulling out the staple was so preposterous as not to be worth even a moment's thought; so everything depended on the bracelet. And when he came to examine it more carefully he found that it had a Yale lock.

He sat down on the edge of the bed, and she watched him anxiously.

'Can't you get it undone, boy?' she whispered.

'Not if I stopped here till next Christmas, darling,' he answered heavily.

'Well, get out of the window and go for the police,' she implored.

'My dear,' he said still more heavily, 'I had, as I told you, a little difference of opinion with the gentleman outside the door – and he's very dead.' She caught her breath sharply. 'A nasty man with long arms who attacked me. It might be all right, of course – but I somehow feel that this matter is beyond the local constable, even if I could find him. You see, I don't even know where we are.' He checked the exclamation of surprise that rose to her lips. 'I'll explain after, darling; let's think of this now. If only I could get the key; if only I knew where it was even.'

'A foreigner came in about an hour ago,' answered his wife. 'He had it then. And he said he'd come again tonight.'

'He did, did he?' said Hugh slowly. 'I wonder if it's my friend the Italian. Anyway, kid, it's the only chance. Did he come alone last time?'

'Yes: I don't think there was anyone with him. I'm sure there wasn't.'

'Then we must chance it,' said Hugh. 'Say something; get him into the room and then leave him to me. And if for any reason he doesn't come I'll have to leave you here and raise the gang.'

'Wouldn't it be safer, boy, to do that now?' she said imploringly. 'Suppose anything happened to you.'

'Anything further that happens to me tonight, old thing,' he remarked grimly, 'will be as flat as a squashed pancake compared to what's happened already.'

And then because she saw his mind was made up, and she knew the futility of arguing under those conditions, she sat on the bed beside him to wait. For a while they sat in silence listening to the monotonous thudding noise which went ceaselessly on; then because he wanted to distract her mind he made her tell him what had happened to her. And in disjointed whispers, with his arm round her waist, she pieced together the gaps in the story. How the man had come about the electric light, and then had offered to fetch her a taxi he knew already from Denny. She had got in, never suspecting anything, and told him to drive to the Ritz – and almost at once she had begun to feel faint. Still she suspected nothing, until she tried to open one of the windows. But it wouldn't open, and the last thing she remembered before she actually fainted was tapping on the glass to try to draw the driver's attention. Then when she came to, she found to her horror that she was not alone. A man was in the car with her, and they were out of London in the country. Both windows were wide open, and she asked him furiously what he was doing in her car. He smiled, and remarked that so far he was not aware he had sold it, but he was always open to an offer. And it was then that she realised for the first time exactly what had happened.

The man told her quite frankly that she hadn't fainted at all, but had been rendered unconscious by a discharge of gas down the speaking-tube; that acting under orders he was taking her to a house in the country where she would have to remain for how long he was unable to say, and further if she made a sound or gave any trouble he would gag her on the spot.

Hugh's arm tightened round her waist, and he cursed fluently under his breath.

'And what happened when you got here, darling?' he asked as she paused.

'They brought me straight up here, and tied me up,' she answered. 'They haven't hurt me – and they've given me food, but I've been terrified – simply terrified – as to what they were going to do next.' She clung to him, and he kissed her reassuringly. 'There's a man below with red hair and a straggling beard, who came and stared at me in the most horrible way. He was in his shirtsleeves and his arms were all covered with chemical stains.'

'Did he touch you?' asked Hugh grimly.

'No – he just looked horrible,' she said, with a shudder. 'And then he repeated the other man's threat – the one who had been in the car – that if I shouted or made any fuss he'd lash me up and gag me. He spoke in a sort of broken English – and his voice never seemed to rise above a whisper.'

She was trembling now, and Hugh made a mental note of another gentleman on whom he proposed to lay hands in the near future. Red hair and a straggling beard should not prove hard to recognise.

He glanced at the watch on Phyllis's wrist, and saw that it was very nearly one o'clock. The noise of the engine was still going monotonously on; except for that the house seemed absolutely silent. And he began to wonder how long it would be wise to continue the vigil. Supposing no-one did come; supposing somebody came who hadn't got the key; supposing two or three of them came at the same time. Would it be better, even now, to drop through the window – and try to find a telephone or the police? If only he knew where he was; it might take him hours to find either at that time of night. And his whole being revolted at the idea of leaving Phyllis absolutely defenceless in such a house.

He rose and paced softly up and down the room trying to think what was the best thing to do. It was a maddening circle whichever way he looked at it, and his fists clenched and unclenched as he tried to make up his mind. To go or to wait; to go at once or to stop in the hope that one man would come up and have the key on him. Common sense suggested the first course; something far more powerful than common sense prompted the latter. He could not and would not leave Phyllis alone. And so he decided on a compromise. If when daylight came no-one had been up to the room, he would go; but he would wait till then. She'd feel safer once the night was over, and in the dawn he would be able to find his way outside more easily.

And he was just going to tell Phyllis what he had decided, when he heard a sound that killed the words on his lips. A door had opened below, and men's voices came floating up the stairs.

'Lie down, darling,' he breathed in her ear, 'and pretend to be asleep.'

Without a word she did as he told her, while Hugh tiptoed over towards the door. There were steps coming up the stairs, and he flattened himself against the wall – waiting. The period of indecision was passed; unless he was very much mistaken the time of action had arrived. How it would pan out – whether luck would be in, or whether luck would fail – was on the lap of the gods. All he could do was to hit hard and if necessary hit often, and a tingle of pure joy spread over him. Even Phyllis was almost forgotten at the moment; he had room in his mind for one thought only – the man whose steps he could hear coming along the passage.

There was only one of them, he noted with a sigh of relief – but for all that silence would be essential. It would take time to find the key; it would take even longer to get Phyllis free and out of the house. So there must be no risk of an alarm whatever happened.

The steps paused outside the door, and he heard a muttered ejaculation in Italian. It was his own particular friend of the motor right enough, and he grinned gently to himself. Apparently he was concerned over something, and it suddenly dawned on Drummond that it was the absence from duty of the long-armed bird that was causing the surprise. In the excitement of the moment he had forgotten all about him, and for one awful second his heart stood still. Suppose the Italian discovered the body before he entered the room, then the game was up with a vengeance. Once the alarm was given he'd have to run the gauntlet of the whole crowd over ground he didn't know.

But his fears were groundless; the non-discovery of the watcher by the door took the Italian the other way. His first thought was to make sure that the girl was safe, and he flung open the door and came in. He gave a grunt of satisfaction as he saw her lying on the bed; then like a spitting cat he swung round as he felt Drummond's hand on his shoulder.

'*E pericoloso sporgersi*,' muttered Hugh pleasantly, recalling the only Italian words he knew.

'*Dio mio!*' stammered the other, with trembling lips. Like most southerners he was superstitious, and to be told that it was dangerous to lean out of the window by a man whom he knew to be drowned was too much for him. It was a ghost; it could be nothing else, and his knees suddenly felt strangely weak.

'You didn't know I was a linguist, did you?' continued Hugh, still more pleasantly; and with every ounce of weight in his body behind the blow, he hit the Italian on the point of the jaw. Without a sound the man crumpled up and pitched on his face.

And now there was not a moment to be lost. At any moment one of his pals might come upstairs, and everything depended on speed and finding the key. Hugh shut the door and locked it; then feverishly he started to search through the Italian's pockets. Everything up to date had panned out so wonderfully that he refused to believe that luck was going to fail him now, and sure enough he discovered the bunch in one of the unconscious man's waistcoat pockets. There were four of them, and the second he tried was the right one. Phyllis was free, and he heard her give a little sob of pure excitement.

'You perfectly wonderful boy!' she whispered, and Hugh grinned.

'We'll hurl floral decorations afterwards, my angel,' he remarked. 'Just at the moment it seems a pity not to replace you with someone.'

He heaved the Italian on to the bed, and snapped the steel bracelet on to his arm. Then he slipped the keys into his own pocket, and crossed to the window. The engine was still humming gently; the thudding noise was still going on; nothing seemed in any way different. No light came from the room below them, everything had worked better than he had dared to hope. He had only to lower Phyllis out of the window, and let her drop on to the flower-bed and then follow himself. After that it was easy.

'Come along, darling,' he said urgently, 'I'm going to lower you out first – then I'll follow. And once we're down, you've got to trice up your skirts and run like a stag across the lawn till we're under cover of those bushes. We aren't quite out of the wood yet.'

They were not indeed. It was just as Phyllis let go, and he saw her pick herself up and dart across the lawn, that he heard a terrific uproar in the house below, and several men came pounding up the stairs. There were excited voices in the passage outside, and for a moment he hesitated, wondering what on earth had caused the sudden alarm. Then realising that this was no time for guessing acrostics, he vaulted over the window-sill himself, and lowered himself to the full extent of his arms. Then he too let go and dropped on to the flower-bed below. And it was as he was picking himself up, preparatory to following Phyllis – whom he could see faintly across the lawn waiting for him, that he heard someone in the house shout an order in a hoarse voice.

'Switch on the power at once, you damned fool; switch it on at once!'

Chapter 16

In which things happen at Maybrick Hall

Had the Italian come up five minutes sooner – a minute even – all would have been well. As it was, at the very moment when Drummond's crashing blow took him on the point of the jaw with mathematical precision, another mathematical law began to operate elsewhere – the law of gravity. Something fell from a ceiling on to a table in the room below that ceiling, even as in days gone by an apple descended into the eye of the discoverer of that law.

The two men seated in the room below the ceiling in question failed to notice it at first. They were not interested in mathematics but they were interested in their conversation. One was the red-headed man of whom Phyllis had spoken: the other was a nonde-script type of individual who looked like an ordinary middle-class professional man.

'Our organisation has, of course, grown immensely,' he was say-ing. 'Our Socialist Sunday Schools, as you may know, were started twenty-five years ago. A very small beginning, my friend, but the result now would stagger you. And wishy-washy stuff was taught to start with too; now I think even you would be satisfied.'

Something splashed on the table beside him, but he took no notice.

'Blasphemy, of course – or rather what the Bourgeois call blas-phemy – is instilled at once. We teach them to fear no God; we drive into them each week that the so-called God is merely a weapon of the Capitalist class to keep them quiet, and that if it had not that effect they would see what a machine-gun could do. And, Yulowski, it is having its effect. Get at the children has always been my motto – for they are the next generation. They can be moulded like plastic clay; their parents, so often, are set in a groove. We preach class hatred – and nothing but class hatred. We give them songs to sing – songs with a real catchy tune. There's one very good one in which the chorus goes:

'Come, workers, sing a rebel song, a song of love and hate,
　Of love unto the lowly and of hatred to the great.'

He paused to let the full effect of the sublime stanza sink in, and again something splashed on to the table.

Yulowski nodded his head indifferently.

'I admit its value, my friend,' he remarked in a curious husky whisper. 'And in your country I suppose you must go slowly. I fear my inclinations lead towards something more rapid and – er – drastic. Sooner or later the Bourgeois must be exterminated all the world over. On that we are agreed. Why not make it sooner as we did in Russia? The best treatment for any of the Capitalist class is a bayonet in the stomach and a rifle butt on the head.'

He smiled reminiscently, a thin, cruel smile, and once again there came an unheeded splash.

'I have heard it said,' remarked the other man, with the faintest hesitation, 'that you yourself were responsible in Russia for a good many of them.'

The smile grew more pronounced and cruel.

'It was I, my friend, who battered out the brains of two members of the Arch Tyrant's family. Yes, I – I who sit here.' His voice rose to a sort of throaty shout and his eyes gleamed. 'You can guess who I mean, can't you?'

'Two girls,' muttered the other, recoiling a little in spite of himself.

'Two – ' The foul epithet went unuttered; Yulowski was staring fascinated at the table. 'Holy Mother! What's that?'

His companion swung round, and every vestige of colour left his face. On the table was a big red pool, and even as he watched it there came another splash and a big drop fell into it.

'Blood!' he stammered, and his lips were shaking. 'It's blood.' And then he heard the Russian's voice, low and tense.

'Look at the ceiling, man; look at the ceiling.'

He stared upwards and gave a little cry of horror. Slowly spreading over the white plaster was a great crimson stain, whilst from a crack in the middle the steady drip fell on to the table.

It was Yulowski who recovered himself first; he was more used to such sights than his companion.

'There's been murder done,' he shouted hoarsely, and dashed out of the room. Doors were flung open, and half a dozen men rushed up the stairs after him. There was no doubt which the room was, and headed by Yulowski they crowded in – only to stop and stare at what lay on the floor.

'It's the Greek,' muttered one of them. 'He was guarding the girl. And someone has severed the main artery in his arm.'

With one accord they dashed across the passage to the room where Phyllis had been. In a second the door was broken in, and they saw the unconscious Italian lying on the bed.

'The Black Gang,' muttered someone fearfully, and Yulowski cursed him for a cowardly swine. And it was his hoarse voice that Drummond heard shouting for the power to be switched on, as he turned and darted across the lawn.

Completely ignorant of what had taken place, he was just as ignorant of what was meant by switching on the power. His one thought now was to get away with Phyllis. A start meant everything, and at the best he couldn't hope for a long one. With his arm through hers he urged her forward, while behind him he heard a confused shouting which gradually died away under the peremptory orders of someone who seemed to be in command. And almost subconsciously he noticed that the thudding noise had ceased; only the faint humming of the engine broke the silence.

Suddenly in front of him he saw the fence which had caused him to wonder earlier in the evening. It was just the same in this part as it had been in the other, but he wasn't concerned with speculations about it now. The only thing he was thankful for was that it was easy to get through.

He was not five feet from it, when it happened – the amazing and at the moment inexplicable thing. For months after he used to wake in the night and lie sweating with horror at the nearness of the escape. For it would have been Phyllis who would have gone through first; it would have been Phyllis, who – But it did happen – just in time.

He saw a dark shape dart across the open towards the fence, an animal carrying something in its mouth. It reached the fence, and the next instant it bounded an incredible height in the air, only to fall backwards on to the ground and lie motionless almost at Drummond's feet. It was so utterly unexpected that he paused instinctively and stared at it. It was a fox, and the fowl it had been carrying lay a yard away. It lay there rigid and motionless, and completely bewildered he bent and touched it, only to draw back his hand as if he'd been stung. A sharp stabbing pain shot up his arm, as if he'd had an electric shock – and suddenly he understood, and with a cry of fear he dragged Phyllis back just in time.

The brain moves rapidly at times; the inherent connection of things takes place in a flash. And the words he had used to the Italian, '*E pericoloso sporgersi*,' took him back to Switzerland, where the phrase is written on every railway carriage. And in Switzerland, you may see those heavy steel pylons with curved pointed hooks to prevent people climbing up, and red bands painted with the words *Danger de mort*. Live wires there are at the top, carried on insulators – even as the fence wires were carried through insulators in the uprights.

Danger de mort. And the fox had been electrocuted. That was what the man had meant by shouting for the power to be switched on. And as he stood there still clutching Phyllis's arm, and shaken for the moment out of his usual calm, there came from the direction of the house, the deep-throated baying of a big hound.

'What is it, Hugh?' said Phyllis in an agonised whisper.

With terrified eyes she was staring at the body of the fox, stiff and rigid in death, and with its jaws parted in a hideous snarl. And again there came from the direction of the house a deep-throated bay.

Then suddenly she realised that her husband was speaking – quietly, insistently. Only too well did he know the danger: only too well did he know that never before in his life had the situation been so tight. But no sign of it showed on his face: not a trace of indecision appeared in his voice. The position was desperate, the remedy must be desperate too.

'We can't climb through the fence, dear,' he was saying calmly. 'You see they've switched an electric current through the wires, and if you touch one you'll be electrocuted. Also they seem to have turned an unpleasant little animal into the garden, so we can't stay here. At least – you can't. So I'm going to throw you over the top.'

In an agony of fear she clung to him for a moment: then as she saw his quiet, set face she pulled herself together and smiled. There was no time for argument now: there was no time for anything except instant action. And being a thoroughbred, she was not going to hinder him by any weakness on her part. Of fear for herself she felt no trace: her faith and trust in her husband was absolute. And so she stood there silently waiting while he measured height and distance with his eye.

Of his ability to get her over he felt no doubt: but when a mistake means death to the woman he loves a man does not take risks.

'Come, dear,' he said after a moment's pause. 'Put your knees close up to your chin, and try to keep like a ball until you feel yourself falling.'

She doubled herself up and he picked her up. One hand held both her feet – the other gripped the waistband at the back of her skirt. Once he lifted her above his head to the full extent of his arms to free his muscles: then he took a little run and threw her up and forward with all his strength. And she cleared the top strand by two feet . . .

She landed unhurt in some bushes, and when she had scrambled to her feet she realised he was speaking again – imperatively, urgently.

'Get the gang, darling: somehow or other get the gang. I'll try and get you a good start. But – hurry.'

The next instant he had disappeared into the undergrowth, and only just in time. A huge hound running mute had dashed into the clearing where a second or two before they had been standing, and was cautiously approaching the dead fox. She stared at it fascinated, and then with a little cry of terror she pulled herself together and ran. She had forgotten the fence that was between them: for the moment she had forgotten everything except this huge brute that looked the size of a calf. And the hound, seeing the flutter of her dress, forgot things too. A dead fox could wait, a living human was better fun by far. He bounded forward: gave one agonised roar as he hit the fence, and turning a complete somersault lay still. And as Phyllis stumbled blindly on, she suddenly heard Hugh's cheerful voice from the darkness behind her, apparently addressing the world at large.

'Roll up! Roll up! Roll up! One fox: one Pomeranian: one fowl. No charge for admittance. Visitors are requested not to touch the exhibits.'

And then loud and clear the hoot of an owl thrice repeated. It was a message for her, she knew – not a senseless piece of bravado: a message to tell her that he was all right. But the call at the end was the urgent call of the gang, and though he was safe at the moment she knew there was no time to be lost. And, with a little prayer that she would choose the right direction, she broke into the steady run of the girl who beagles when she goes beagling, and doesn't sit on the top of a hill and watch. Hugh had never let her down yet: it was her turn now.

To what extent it was her turn, perhaps it was as well that she did not realise. Even Drummond, hidden in the undergrowth just by the clearing where lay the body of the hound, was ignorant of the nature of the odds against him. He had not the slightest idea how many men there were in the house – and while it remained dark he didn't much care. In the dark he felt confident of dealing with any number, or at any rate of eluding them. It was the thing of all others that his soul loved – that grim fighting at night, when a man looks like a trunk of a tree, and the trunk of a tree looks like a man. It was in that that he was unequalled – superb: and the inmates of Maybrick Hall would have been well advised to have stayed their hands till the light came. Then the position, in military parlance, could have been taken without loss. An unarmed man is helpless when he can be seen.

But since the inmates were ignorant of what they were up against, they somewhat foolishly decided on instant action. They came streaming across in a body in the track of the dead hound, and by so doing they played straight into the hands of the man who crouched in the shadows close by them. He listened for one moment to the babel of tongues of every nationality, and decided that a little more English might adjust the average. So without a sound he faded away from his hiding-place, and emerged from the undergrowth ten yards nearer the house. Then with his collar turned up, and his shoulders hunched together, he joined the group. And a man-eating tiger in their midst would have been a safer addition to the party.

Certain it is that the next quarter of an hour proved a period of such terror for the inmates of Maybrick Hall that at the end of that time they reassembled at the house and flatly refused to budge, despite the threats and curses of the red-headed Russian. For Drummond had heard the original orders – to form a line of beaters and shoot on sight – and had smiled gently to himself in the darkness. There is always an element of humour in stalking the stalkers, and when the line formed up at intervals of two or three yards the quarry was behind it. Moreover the quarry was angry, with the cold, steady rage of a powerful man who realises exactly what he is up against. Shoot on sight was the order, and Drummond accepted the terms.

Slowly the line of shadowy men moved forward through the undergrowth, and creeping behind them came the man they were out to kill. And gradually he edged nearer and nearer to the wire fence, until he was following the outside man of the line. He saw him pause for a moment peering round a bush, with his revolver ready in his hand. And then the terror started. The beater next to the victim had a fleeting vision of a huge black object springing through the darkness: a muttered curse and a gurgle – and a dreadful strangled scream. And the outside beater was no more. He had been hurled against the live-wire fence as if he was a child – and the exhibits had been increased by one.

With a hoarse cry of fear the man who had been next to him turned and ran towards the house, only to find himself seized from behind with a grip of iron. It was Franz, and as he stared into the face of the man whom he knew to be drowned he gave a squawk like a trapped rabbit. But there was nothing ghostly about the hands round his neck, and as he felt himself being rushed towards the fence of death he began to struggle furiously. But Drummond was mad at the moment, and though Franz was a powerful man he might have saved himself the trouble. A terrific blow hit him on the face, and with a grunt he fell back against the fence. The exhibits were increased by two, and through the darkness rang a cheerful laugh, followed by the hooting of an owl.

And now the line was broken, and men were crashing about in all directions shouting hoarsely. Experts of the Red Terror they might be – butcherers of women and children whose sole fault lay in the fact that they washed: that night they found themselves up against a terror far worse than even their victims had ever experienced. For they, poor wretches, knew what was coming: the men who ran shouting through the undergrowth did not. Here, there, and everywhere they heard the hooting of an owl: they formed into bunches of twos and threes for protection, they blazed away with compressed-air revolvers at harmless rhododendron bushes, and sometimes at their own pals. And every now and then a great black figure would leap silently out of the darkness on to some straggler: there would be a bellow of fear and pain – followed by an ominous silence, which was broken a second or two later by the hooting of an owl twenty yards away.

Occasionally they saw him – a dim, fleeting shadow, and once four of them fired at him simultaneously. But luck was with him, and though two holes were drilled in his coat Drummond was not hit himself. His quiet laugh came suddenly from behind them, and even as they swung round cursing, one of them collapsed choking with a bullet through his chest. It was the first time he had used his first victim's revolver, but the target was too tempting to be let off. And at last they could stand it no longer. They had no idea how many men they were up against, and a complete panic set in. With one accord they rushed for the house, and a mocking peal of laughter followed them as they ran. For Drummond had gambled on that, and he had won. In the position of knowing that every man was his enemy, he had been at an advantage over the others, who were never sure who was a friend. For a while he listened to the flood of lurid blasphemy which came from the open windows of the room into which they had crowded: then he dodged along the bushes and looked in. For a moment he was sorely tempted to fire: in fact he went so far as to draw a bead on the red-headed Russian, who was gesticulating furiously. Then his hand dropped to his side: shooting into the brown was not his idea of the game. And at the same moment, the lights were switched off in the room: it had evidently struck someone inside that the position was a trifle insecure. The talking ceased abruptly, and with a faint grin on his face Drummond swung round and vanished into the deepest part of the undergrowth. It was necessary to do some thinking.

He had got the start he wanted for Phyllis, which was all to the good, but he was as far as ever himself from getting out. There was still the fence to be negotiated if he was to escape, and common sense told him that there wasn't the remotest chance of the current having been switched off. And incidentally it didn't much matter whether it had been or not, since the only way of finding out for certain was to touch one of the wires – a thing he had not the faintest intention of doing. He could still hear the steady thrumming of the engine, and so the fence was out of the question.

Delving into memories of the past, when he had sat at the feet of the stinks master at his school, he tried to remember some of the gems of wisdom, anent electricity, which had fallen from his lips. But since his sole occupation during such lectures had been the surreptitious manufacture of sulphuretted hydrogen from a retort concealed below his desk, he finally gave up the attempt in despair. One thing was certain; the fence must be continuous. From knowledge gained from the sparking plugs of his car, he knew that a break in the circuit was fatal. Therefore, there could be no break in the fence which encircled the house. And if that was so – how about the drive? How did the drive pass through the fence? There must be a break there, or something capable of forming a break. A motor-car will not go over an eight-foot fence, and he had seen the wheel tracks of a car quite clearly on the drive earlier in the evening.

Yes – he would try the gate. It was imperative to get away, and that as soon as possible. When dawn came, and the first faint streaks were already beginning to show in the east, he realised that he would be at a hopeless disadvantage. Moreover the absolute silence which now reigned after the turmoil and shouting of the last few minutes struck him as ominous. And Drummond was far too clever a man to underrate his opponents. The panic had been but a temporary affair; and the panic was now over.

He began to thread his way swiftly and silently in the direction of the drive. Not for a second did he relax his caution, though he felt tolerably certain that all his opponents were still inside the house. Only too well did he know that the greatest danger often lies when things seem safest. But he reached the edge of the drive without incident, and started to skirt along it away from the house. At last he saw the gate, and turned deeper into the undergrowth. He wanted to examine it at leisure, before making up his mind as to what he would do. As far as he could see from the outline he could make out against the road, it was an ordinary heavy wooden gate, such as may be seen frequently at the entrance to small country houses.

A tiny lodge lay on one side: the usual uncared-for undergrowth on the other. He could see the wire fence coming to the gatepost on each side; he could see that the strands were bunched together at the gate as telegraph wires are bunched when they pass underneath a bridge on a railway line. And it was while he was cogitating on the matter that he saw a man approaching from the other side. He came up to the gate, climbed over it with the utmost nonchalance, and turned into the little lodge. And Hugh noticed that as he climbed he was careful to avoid the second horizontal from the ground. At last it seemed to him that everything was clear. Contact was made through the latch; the current passed along the wires which were laid on the top of the second horizontal from the ground, and thence to the continuation of the fence on the other side. Anyway, whatever the electrical device, if this man could climb the gate in safety – so could he. There was a risk – a grave risk. It meant going out into the open; it meant exposing himself for a considerable period. But every moment he delayed the light grew better, and the risk became worse. And it was either that or waiting in the garden till daylight made his escape impossible. And still he hung back.

Men who knew Hugh Drummond well often said that he had a strange sixth sense which enabled him to anticipate danger, when to others with him everything seemed perfectly safe. Well-nigh fantastic stories were told of him by men who had accompanied him on those unofficial patrols he had carried out in No Man's Land whenever his battalion was in the line, and frequently when it wasn't. And as he stood there motionless as a statue, with only the ceaseless movement of his eyes to show his strained attention, that sixth sense of his warned him, and continued warning him insistently. There was danger: he felt it, he knew it – though where it lay he couldn't tell.

And then suddenly he again saw a man approaching from the other side – a man who climbed the gate with the utmost nonchalance and turned into the little lodge. He, too, carefully avoided the second horizontal from the ground, but Drummond was not paying any attention to the gate now. Once again his sixth sense had saved him, for it was the same man who had climbed over the first time. And why should a man adopt such a peculiar form of amusement, unless he was deliberately acting as a decoy? He had disappeared into the lodge, only to leave it again by a back entrance – and in an instant the whole thing was clear. They had gambled on his going to the gate: they had gambled on his having a dart for it when he saw the gate was safe to climb. And he smiled grimly when he realised how nearly they had won their bet.

Suddenly his eyes riveted themselves on the little hedge in front of the lodge. Something had stirred there: a twig had snapped. And the smile grew more grim as he stared at the shadow. Up to date it was the gate that had occupied his attention – now he saw that the hedge was alive with men. And after a while he began to shake gently with laughter. The idea of the perspiring sportsman trotting in and out of the back door, to show off his particular line in gates, while a grim bunch of bandits lay on their stomachs in the dew, hoping for the best, appealed to his sense of humour. For the moment the fact that he was now hopelessly trapped did not trouble him: his whole soul went out to the painstaking gate-hopper. If only he would do it again – that was his one prayer. And sure enough about five minutes later he hove in sight again, stepping merrily and brightly along the road.

His nonchalance was superb: he even hummed gently to show his complete disdain for gates in general and this one in particular. And then Drummond plugged him through the leg. He felt that it would have been a crime to end the career of such a bright disposition: so he plugged him through the fleshy part of the leg. And the man's howl of pain and Drummond's raucous bellow of laughter broke the silence simultaneously.

Not the least merry interlude, he reflected, in an evening devoted to fun and games, as he took cover rapidly behind a big tree. For bullets were whistling through the undergrowth in all directions, as the men who had been lying under cover of the hedge rose and let fly. And then quite abruptly the shooting died away, and Drummond became aware that a car was approaching. The headlights were throwing fantastic shadows through the bushes, and outlined against the glare he could see the figures of his opponents. Now was his chance, and with the quickness of the born soldier he acted on it. If the car was to come in they must open the gate; and since nothing blinds anyone so completely as the dazzle of strong headlights, he might be able to slip out unseen, just after the car had passed through. He skirted rapidly to one side out of the direct beam: then he made his way towards the lodge, keeping well out on the flank. And from a concealed position under the cover of the little house he awaited developments.

The man he had shot through the leg was unceremoniously bundled on to the grass beside the drive, whilst another man climbed the gate and went up to the car, which had come to a standstill ten yards or so away. Drummond heard the sound of a window being lowered, and an excited conversation: then the man who had approached the car stepped back again into the glare of the headlights.

'Open the gate,' he said curtly, and there was a sardonic grin on his face.

And now Drummond was waiting tensely. If he was to bring it off it would be a matter of seconds and half-seconds. Little by little he edged nearer to the drive, as a man with what appeared to be a huge glove on his hand approached the gate. There was a bright flash as he pressed down the catch and the circuit was broken, and at the same moment the headlights on the car went out, while an inside light was switched on.

And Drummond stopped dead – frozen in his tracks. The car was moving forward slowly, and he could see the people inside clearly. One was Count Zadowa – *alias* Mr Atkinson; one was the Reverend Theodosius Longmoor. But the other – and it was the third person on whom his eyes were fixed with a hopeless feeling of impotent rage – the other was Phyllis herself. The two men were holding her in front of them, so that to fire was an impossibility, and Peterson was smiling out of the window with the utmost benevolence. Then they were past him, and he watched the red tail-lamp disappearing up the drive, while the gate was shut behind them. Another flashing spark stabbed the darkness: the circuit was complete again. And with a feeling of sick, helpless fury, Drummond realised that it had all been useless. He was exactly where he had been half an hour before, with the vital difference that the events of the last half-hour could not be repeated. He was caught: it was the finish. Somehow or other the poor girl must have blundered right into the car, and probably asked the occupants for help. She wouldn't have known who they were; she'd just stopped the car on spec, and . . . He shook his fists impotently, and at that moment he heard a loud, powerful voice which he recognised at once speaking from the direction of the house.

'Unless Captain Drummond comes into the house within five minutes, I shall personally kill Mrs Drummond.'

And the voice was the voice of Carl Peterson.

Chapter 17

In which a murderer is murdered at Maybrick Hall

'You appear to have a wonderful faculty for remaining alive, my young friend,' remarked Peterson two minutes later, gazing benevolently at Drummond over his clerical collar.

'Principally, Theo, my pet, because you've got such a wonderful faculty for making bloomers,' answered Drummond affably.

No trace of the impotent rage he had given way to in the garden showed in his face as he spoke; and yet, in all conscience, the situation was desperate enough. He was unarmed – his revolver had been removed from him as he entered the house – and behind his chair stood two men, each with the muzzle of a gun an inch off his neck. In another corner sat Phyllis, and behind her stood an armed man also. Every now and then his eyes stole round to her, and once he smiled reassuringly – an assurance he was far from feeling. But principally his eyes were fixed on the three men who were sitting at the table opposite him. In the centre was Carl Peterson, smoking the inevitable cigar; and, one on each side of him, sat Count Zadowa and the red-headed Russian Yulowski.

'You can't imagine the pleasant surprise it gave me,' Peterson continued gently, 'when your charming wife hailed my car. So unexpected: so delightful. And when I realised that you were running about in our grounds here instead of being drowned as that fool No. 10 told me over the telephone . . . By the way, where is No. 10?'

He turned snarling on the Russian, but it was one of the men behind Drummond's chair who answered.

'He's dead. This guy threw him on the live wires.'

'Is that little Franz?' murmured Hugh Drummond, lighting a cigarette. 'Yes – I regret to state that he and I had words, and my impression is that he has passed away. Do you mind standing a little farther away?' he continued, addressing the men behind him. 'You're tickling the back of my neck, and it makes me go all goosey.'

'Do you mean to say,' said the Russian in his harsh voice, 'that it was you and only you outside there?'

'You have guessed it, Adolph,' answered Drummond, speaking mechanically. It had seemed to him, suddenly, that, unseen by the others, Phyllis was trying to convey some message. 'Alone I did it, to say nothing of that squib-faced bird upstairs with the long arms. In fact, without wishing to exaggerate, I think the total bag is five – with dear old "pericoloso sporgersi" as an "also ran".'

What was she trying to make him understand?

And then suddenly she began to laugh hysterically, and he half rose from his seat, only to sit down again abruptly as he felt the cold ring of a revolver pressed into the nape of his neck.

'Three and two make five,' said Phyllis, half laughing and half crying, 'and one makes six. I worked it out tonight, and it all came right.'

She went on aimlessly for a while in the same strain, till the Russian swung round on her with a snarl, and told her to shut her mouth. He was talking in low tones to Peterson, and, with one searching look at Hugh, she relapsed into silence. There was no hysteria in that look, and his heart began to pound suddenly in his excitement. For 3256 Mayfair was the number of Peter Darrell's telephone, and she could only mean one thing – that she had got through to Peter before she stopped the car. And if that was so there was still hope, if only he could gain time. Time was the essential factor: time he must have somehow. And how was he to get it? Not by the quiver of an eyelid did the expression on his face change: he still smoked placidly on, looking with resigned boredom at the three men who were now conferring earnestly together. But his mind was racing madly, as he turned things over this way and that. Time: he must gain time.

If his supposition was right, Carl Peterson was in ignorance of the fact that a message had been got through. And in that lay the only chance. Just as in Bridge there comes a time when to win the game one must place a certain card with one of the opponents and play accordingly – so that card must be placed in Peterson's hand. If the placing has been done correctly, you take your only chance of winning: if the placing is wrong, you lose anyway. And so, starting with that as a foundation, he tried to work out the play of the hand. Peter Darrell knew, and Peterson was in ignorance of the fact.

First – how long did he want? Two hours at least: three if possible. To round up all the gang and get cars in the middle of the night would take time – two hours at the very least. Secondly – and there was the crux – how was he going to get such a respite? For this time he could not hope for another mistake. It was the end, and he knew it.

No trace of mercy showed in the faces of the three men opposite him. He caught occasional remarks, and after a while he realised what the matter under discussion was. Evidently the red-headed Russian was in favour of killing him violently, and at once – and it was Count Zadowa who was advocating caution, while Peterson sat between them listening impassively, with his eyes fixed on Drummond.

'Bayonet the pair of them,' snarled Yulowski at length, as if tired of arguing the point. 'I'll do the job if you're too squeamish, and will bury 'em both with the rest of the bodies in the grounds somewhere. Who's to know: who's to find out?'

But Count Zadowa shook his head vigorously.

'That's just where you're wrong, my friend. No-one would see you do it more willingly than I – but you've got to remember the rest of his gang.'

His voice died away to a whisper, and Drummond could only catch disjointed fragments.

'I know the Black Gang,' Zadowa was saying. 'You don't. And they know me.' Then he heard the word 'accident' repeated several times, and at length Yulowski shrugged his shoulders and leaned back in his chair.

'Have it your own way,' he remarked. 'I don't care how they're killed, as long as they are killed. If you think it's necessary to pretend there has been an accident, we'll have an accident. The only point is what sort of an accident.'

But Count Zadowa had apparently not got as far as that, and relapsed into silence. His powers of imagination were not sufficiently great to supply the necessary details, and it was left to Carl Peterson to decide matters.

'Nothing is easier,' he remarked suavely, and his eyes were still fixed on Drummond. 'We are discussing, my young friend,' he continued, raising his voice slightly, 'the best way of getting rid of you and your charming wife. I regret that she must share your fate, but I see no way out of it. To keep her permanently about the premises would be too great an inconvenience; and since we can't let her go without involving ourselves in unpleasant notoriety, I fear – as I said – that she must join you. My friend Yulowski wishes to bayonet you both, and bury you in the grounds. He has done a lot of that sort of thing in his time, and I believe I am right in stating that his hand has not lost its cunning since leaving Russia. A little out of practice, perhaps: but the result is the same. On the other hand, Count Zadowa, whom you know of old, quite rightly points out that there are the members of your ridiculous gang who know about him, and might very easily find out about me. And when in a few days your motor-car is hoisted out of the water, and is traced by the registration number as being yours, he fears that not only may he find things very awkward, but that a certain amount of unenviable and undesirable limelight may be thrown on this part of the country, and incidentally on this house. You follow our difficulties so far?'

'With the utmost clarity, Theo,' answered Drummond pleasantly.

'It's always such a pleasure talking to you,' continued Peterson. 'You're so unexpectedly quick on the uptake. Well then – to proceed. Though it will not interfere with me personally – as I leave England in four hours – it will interfere considerably with my plans if the police come poking their noses into this house. We like to hide our light under a bushel, Captain Drummond: we prefer to do our little bit unnoticed. So I feel sure that you will be only too ready to help us in any way you can, and fall in with my suggestion for your decease with goodwill. I have a very warm regard for you in so many ways, and I should hate to think that there was any bad blood between us at the end.'

'Carl – my pet – you'll make me cry in a minute,' said Drummond quietly. To all outward appearances he was in the same mocking vein as his principal enemy, but a little pulse was beginning to hammer in his throat, and his mouth felt strangely dry. He knew he was being played with as a mouse is played with by a cat, and it was all he could do to stop himself from demanding outright to know what was coming. Out of the corner of his eye he could see Phyllis sitting very white and still, but he didn't dare to look at her direct for fear he might break down.

And then, still in the same tone, Peterson went on: 'I knew I could rely on you to meet me. I shall tell Irma when I see her, and she will be very touched by your kindness, Drummond – very touched. But to come back to the point. As my friend Zadowa most justly observed – we want an accident: a real good *bona-fide* accident, which will relieve the world of your presence and will bring no scorching glare of publicity upon this house or any of my confrères who remain in England. You may recall that that was my original idea, only you seem in the most extraordinary way to have escaped from being drowned. Still, as far as it goes, we have a very good foundation to build on.

Your car – duly perceived by the gentleman of limited intelligence who works the bridge – went over the edge. You were duly perceived in it. Strangely enough, his eyesight must have been defective – or else he was so flustered by your amazing action that he was incapable of noticing everything at such a moment. Because he actually failed to see that your charming wife was seated beside you. In the moment of panic when she realised you had fainted, she leant forward – doubtless to try and throw out the clutch. Yes' – his eyes, cold and expressionless, were turned momentarily on Phyllis – 'I think that is what she must have done. That accounts for the not very intelligent gate-opener failing to see her. But that she was there is certain. Because, Captain Drummond, both bodies will be recovered from the river the day after tomorrow, shall we say? some two or three miles downstream.'

'Your efforts at drowning have not been vastly successful up to date, Carl, have they?' said Drummond genially. 'Do I understand that we are both to be taken out and held under the water, or are you going to use the bath here? That is to say' – and he glanced pointedly at Yulowski – 'if such a commodity exists. Or are you again going to experiment with that dope of yours?'

'Wrong on all counts,' answered Peterson. 'You are far too large and strong, my dear Drummond, to be drowned by such rudimentary methods. And it is more than likely that even if we attempted to do it, the fact that you struggled would be revealed in a post-mortem examination. And that would spoil everything, wouldn't it? No longer would it appear to be an accident: Count Zadowa's masterly argument would all have been wasted. Why – I might as well agree at once to Yulowski's suggestion of the bayonet. Pray give me credit, my dear young friend, for a little more brains than that.'

'I do, Theo: I assure you I do,' said Drummond earnestly. 'It's only my terrible fear that you'll again go and make a hash of it that inspires my remarks.'

'Thank you a thousand times,' murmured the clergyman gently. He was leaning forward, his elbows on the table – and for the first time Drummond understood something of the diabolical hatred which Peterson felt for him. He had never shown it before: he was far too big a man ever to betray his feeling unnecessarily. But now, as he sat facing him, gently rubbing his big white hands together, Drummond understood.

'Thank you a thousand times,' he repeated in the same gentle voice. 'And since you are so concerned about the matter, I will tell you my plan in some detail. I need hardly say that any suggestions you make on any points that may strike you will receive my most careful attention. When the car crashed into the water it carried you and your wife with it. We have got as far as that, haven't we? As it plunged downwards you – still unconscious from your dreadful and sudden fainting fit – were hurled out. Your wife, in a magnificent endeavour to save you, rose in her seat and was hurled out too. I think we can safely say that, don't you, seeing that the not too intelligent gatekeeper could not have seen the car as it fell?'

'Go on,' said Drummond quietly.

'Interested, I hope,' murmured Peterson. 'But don't hesitate to stop me if anything is at all obscure. I feel that you have a perfect right to suggest any small alterations you like. Well – to proceed. You were both hurled out as the car plunged into the water, and somewhat naturally you were both thrown forward. Head foremost, you will note, Drummond, you left the car – and your heads struck the stonework of the opposite pier with sickening force, just before you reached the water. In fact, a marked feature of the case, when this dreadful accident is reported in the papers, will be the force with which you both struck that pier. Your two heads were terribly battered. In fact, I have but little doubt that the coroner will decide, when your bodies are recovered some few miles downstream – that you were not in reality drowned, but that the terrific impact on the stone pier killed you instantly. Do you think it's sound up to date?'

'I think it's damned unsound,' remarked Drummond languidly. 'If you propose to take me and endeavour to make my head impinge on a stone wall, someone is going to get a thick ear. Besides, the bridge isn't open, and even your pal, the not too intelligent gatekeeper, might stick in his toes a bit. Of course' – he added hopefully – 'you might say you were doing it for the movies. Tell him you're Charlie Chaplin, but that you dressed in such a hurry you've forgotten your moustache.'

The red-headed Russian was snarling venomously.

'Let me get at him, chief. He won't try being funny again.'

'No. I shall be too occupied sprinkling myself with insect powder,' retorted Drummond vulgarly. 'Why, you lousy brute, if you got at me, as you call it, and there wasn't half a battalion of infantry holding guns in my head, I'd break your neck with one hand strapped behind my back.'

The Russian half rose to his feet, his teeth bared, and Peterson pulled him back into his chair.

'You'll get your chance in a moment or two, Yulowski,' he remarked savagely. Then he turned once more on Drummond, and the genial look had vanished from his face. 'Doubtless your humour appeals to some people; it does not to me. Moreover, I am in rather a hurry. I do not propose, Captain Drummond, to take you to the bridge and endeavour to make your head impinge on a wall, as you call it. There is another far simpler method of producing the same result. The impinging will take place in this house. As a soldier you should know the result of a blow over the head with the butt of a rifle. And I can assure you that there will be no bungling this time. Yulowski is an expert in such matters, and I shall stay personally to see that it is done. I think we can give a very creditable imitation of what would have happened had my little story been true, and tomorrow night – I see that it is getting a little too light now for the purpose – your two bodies will be carried over and dropped in the river. The length of time you will both have been dead will be quite correct, within an hour or so – and everything will be most satisfactory for all concerned.'

Drummond passed his tongue over his lips, and despite himself his voice shook a little.

'Am I to understand,' he said after a moment, 'that you propose to let that man butcher us here – in this house – with a rifle?'

'Just so,' answered Peterson. 'That is exactly what you are to understand.'

'You are going to let him bash my wife over the head with a rifle butt?'

'I am going to order him to do so,' said Peterson mildly. 'And very shortly at that. We must not have any mistakes over the length of time you've both been dead. I confess it sounds drastic, but I can assure you it will be quite sudden. Yulowski, as I told you, is an expert. He had a lot of experience in Russia.'

'You inhuman devil!' muttered Drummond dazedly. 'You can do what you like to me, but for Heaven's sake let her off.'

He was staring fascinated at the Russian, who had risen and crossed to a cupboard in the wall. There was something almost maniacal in the look on his face – the look of a savage, brute beast, confronted with the prey it desires.

'Impossible, my dear young friend,' murmured Peterson regretfully. 'It affords me no pleasure to have her killed, but I have no alternative. To see you dead, I would cross two continents,' he snarled suddenly, 'but' – and his voice became normal again – 'only bitter necessity compels me to adopt such measures with Phyllis. You see, she knows too much.' He whispered in Count Zadowa's ear, who rose and left the room, to return shortly with half a dozen more men.

'Yes, she knows too much, and so I fear I cannot let her off. She would be able to tell such a lot of most inconvenient things to the police. This house is so admirably adapted for certain of our activities that it would be a world of pities to draw undesirable attention to it. Especially now that Count Zadowa has been compelled to leave his own office, owing entirely to your reprehensible curiosity.'

But Drummond was paying no attention to him. His eyes were fixed on the Russian, who had come back slowly into the centre of the room, carrying a rifle in his hand. It was an ordinary Russian service rifle, and a bayonet was fixed in position. Yulowski handled it lovingly, as he stood beside Peterson – and suddenly Count Zadowa turned white and began to tremble. To throw a bomb into a room and run for your life is one thing: to sit at a table in cold blood and witness a double execution is another. Even Peterson's iron nerves seemed a little shaken, and his hand trembled as he removed his cigar. But there was no sign of relenting on his face; no sign of faltering in his voice as he spoke to the men who had just come into the room.

'In the interests of us all,' he remarked steadily, 'I have decided that it is necessary to kill both the prisoners.' He made a sign, and Drummond, sitting almost paralysed in his chair, found both his arms gripped, with three men hanging on to each.

'The man,' continued Peterson, 'has been interfering with our work in England – the work of the Red International. He is the leader of the Black Gang, as you probably know; and as you probably do *not* know, it is he and his gang who have been responsible for the mysterious disappearance of some of our most trusted workers. Therefore with regard to him there can be no second thought: he deserves death, and he must die. With regard to the woman, the case is a little different. She has done us no active harm – but she is a member of the bourgeois class, and she in his wife. Moreover she knows too much. And so it becomes necessary that she should die too. The reason why I am adopting this method of putting them both out of the way, is – as I have already explained to all save you newcomers – that, when the bodies are discovered, the cause of death will appear to be accidental. They will both of them seem to the police to have gone over the edge of the bridge in the car, and hit their heads on the pier opposite. And tomorrow night you will carry the bodies to the river and drop them in. And that' – he resumed his cigar – 'I think is all.'

Yulowski handled his rifle lovingly, and once again his teeth showed in a wolfish grin.

'Which shall I take first, chief?' he said carelessly.

'The point is immaterial,' returned Peterson. 'I think perhaps the woman.'

Drummond tried to speak and failed. His tongue was clinging to the roof of his mouth: everything in the room was dancing before his eyes. Dimly he saw the red-headed brute Yulowski swinging his rifle to test it: dimly he saw Phyllis sitting bolt upright, with a calm, scornful expression on her face, while two men held her by the arms so that she would not move. And suddenly he croaked horribly.

Then he saw Yulowski put down the rifle and listen intently for a moment.

'What's the matter?' snapped Peterson irritably.

'Do you hear the different note to that dynamo?' said Yulowski.

'What the hell's that got to do with it?' roared Peterson. 'Get on with it, damn you – and attend to the dynamo afterwards.'

Yulowski nodded, and picked up his rifle again.

'The last time,' he said, turning on Drummond with a dreadful look of evil in his face, 'that this rifle was used by me was in a cellar in Russia – on even more exalted people than you. I brought it especially with me as a memento, never thinking I should have the pleasure of using it again.'

He swung it over his head, and Drummond shut his eyes – to open them again a moment later, as the door was flung open and a man distraught with terror dashed in.

'The Black Gang!' he shouted wildly. 'Hundreds of them – all round the house. They've cut the wires.'

With a fearful curse Peterson leaped to his feet, and the men holding Drummond, dumbfounded at the sudden turning of the tables, let go his arms. Yulowski stood staring foolishly at the door, and what happened then was so quick that none of the stupefied onlookers raised a finger to prevent it.

With the howl of an enraged beast, Drummond hurled himself on the Russian – blind mad with fury. And when two seconds later a dozen black-cowled, black-hooded figures came swarming in through the door, for one instant they paused in sheer horror.

Pinned to the wall with his own bayonet which stuck out six inches beyond his back, was a red-headed, red-bearded man gibbering horribly in a strange language; whilst creeping towards a benevolent-looking clergyman, who crouched in a corner, was a man they scarce recognised as their leader, so appalling was the look of malignant fury on his face.

Carl Peterson was no coward. In the world in which he moved, there were many strange stories told of his iron nerve and his complete disregard of danger. Moreover Nature had endowed him with physical strength far above the average. But now, for perhaps the first time in his life, he knew the meaning of stark, abject terror.

The sinister men in black – members of that very gang he had come over to England to destroy – seemed to fill the room. Silently, as if they had been drilled to it, they disarmed everyone: then they stood round the walls – waiting. No-one spoke: only the horrible imprecations of the dying Russian broke the silence, as he strove feebly to pull out the rifle and bayonet from his chest, which had fixed him to the wall as a dead butterfly is fixed in a collection with a pin.

Peterson had a fleeting vision of a girl with white face and wide, staring eyes, beside whom were standing two of the motionless black figures as guards – the girl whom he had just sentenced to a dreadful and horrible death, and then his eyes came back again as if fascinated to the man who was coming towards him. He tried to shrink farther into his corner, plucking with nerveless fingers at his clerical collar – while the sweat poured off his face in a stream. For there was no mercy in Hugh Drummond's eyes: no mercy in the great arms that hung loosely forward. And Peterson realised he deserved none.

And then it came. No word was spoken – Drummond was beyond speech. His hands shot out and Peterson felt himself drawn relentlessly towards the man he had planned to kill, not two minutes before. It was his turn now to wonder desperately if it was some hideous nightmare, even while he struggled impotently in his final frenzy with a man whose strength seemed equal to the strength of ten. He was choking: the grip on his throat was not human in its ferocity. There was a great roaring in his ears, and suddenly he ceased to struggle. The glare in Drummond's eyes hypnotised him, and for the only time in his life he gave up hope.

The room was spinning round: the silent black figures, the dying Yulowski, the girl – all seemed merged in one vast jumble of colour growing darker and darker, out of which one thing and one thing only stood out clear and distinct on his dying consciousness – the blazing eyes of the man who was throttling him. And then, as he felt himself sinking into utter blackness, some dim sense less paralysed than the rest seemed to tell him that a change had taken place in the room. Something new had come into that whirling nightmare that spun round him: dimly he heard a voice – loud and agonised – a voice he recognised. It was a woman's voice, and after a while the grip on his throat relaxed. He staggered back against the wall gasping and spluttering, and gradually the room ceased to whirl round – the iron bands ceased to press upon his heart and lungs.

It was Irma who stood there: Irma whose piteous cry had pierced through to his brain: Irma who had caused those awful hands to relax their grip just before it was too late. Little by little everything steadied down: he found he could see again – could hear. He still crouched shaking against the wall, but he had got a respite anyway – a breathing-space. And that was all that mattered for the moment – that and the fact that the madness was gone from Hugh Drummond's eyes.

The black figures were still standing there motionless round the walls; the Russian was lolling forward – dead; Phyllis was lying back in her chair unconscious. But Peterson had eyes for none of these things: Count Zadowa shivering in a corner – the huddled group of his own men standing in the centre of the room he passed by without a glance. It was on Drummond his gaze was fixed: Drummond, who stood facing Irma with an almost dazed expression on his face, whilst she pleaded with him in an agony of supplication.

'He ordered that man to brain my wife with a rifle butt,' said Drummond hoarsely. 'And yet you ask for mercy.'

He passed his hand two or three times over his forehead as Irma once again broke into wild pleadings; then he turned and stared at Peterson. She stopped at last, and still he stared at the gasping clergyman as if making up his mind. And, in truth, that was precisely what he was doing. Like most big men he was slow to anger, but once his temper was roused it did not cool easily. And never before in his life had he been in the grip of such cold, maniacal fury as had held him during the last few minutes. Right from the start had Peterson deceived him: from the very moment when he had entered his sitting-room at the Ritz. He had done his best to murder him, and not content with that he had given orders for Phyllis and him to be butchered in cold blood. If the Black Gang had not arrived – had they been half a minute later – it would have been over. Phyllis – his Phyllis – would have been killed by that arch-devil whom he had skewered to the wall with his own rifle. And as the thought took hold of him, his great fists clenched once more, and the madness again gleamed in his eyes. For Peterson was the real culprit: Peterson was the leader. To kill the servant and not the master was unjust.

He swung round on the cowering clergyman and gripped him once again by the throat, shaking him as a terrier shakes a rat. He felt the girl Irma plucking feebly at his arm, but he took no notice. In his mind there was room for no thought save the fixed determination to rid the world for ever of this monstrous blackguard. And still the motionless black figures round the wall gave no sign, even when the girl rushed wildly from one to the other imploring their aid. They knew their leader, and though they knew not what had happened to cause his dreadful rage they trusted him utterly and implicitly. Whether it was lawful or not was beside the point: it was just or Hugh Drummond would not have done it. And so they watched and waited, while Drummond, his face blazing, forced the clergyman to his knees, and the girl Irma sank half-fainting by the table.

But once again Fate was to intervene on Peterson's behalf, through the instrumentality of a woman. And mercifully for him the inter- vention came from the only woman – from the only human being – who could have influenced Drummond at that moment. It was Phyllis who opened her eyes suddenly, and, half-dazed still with the horror of the last few minutes, gazed round the room. She saw the huddled group of men in the centre: she saw the Russian lolling grotesquely forward supported on his own rifle: she saw the Black Gang silent and motionless like avenging judges round the walls. And then she saw her husband bending Carl Peterson's neck farther and farther back, till at any moment it seemed as if it must crack.

For a second she stared at Hugh's face, and saw on it a look which she had never seen before – a look so terrible, that she gave a sharp, convulsive cry.

'Let him go, Hugh: let him go. Don't do it.'

Her voice pierced his brain, though for a moment it made no impression on the muscles of his arms. A slightly bewildered look came into his eyes: he felt as a dog must feel who is called off his lawful prey by his master.

Let him go – let Carl Peterson go! That was what Phyllis was asking him to do – Phyllis who had stood at death's door not five minutes before. Let him go! And suddenly the madness faded from his eyes: his hands relaxed their grip, and Carl Peterson slipped unconscious to the floor – unconscious but still breathing. He had let him go, and after a while he stepped back and glanced slowly round the room. His eyes lingered for a moment on the dead Russian, they travelled thoughtfully on along the line of black figures. And gradually a smile began to appear on his face – a smile which broadened into a grin.

'Perfectly sound advice, old thing,' he remarked at length. 'Straight from the stable. I really believe I'd almost lost my temper.'

Chapter 18

In which the Home Secretary is taught the foxtrot

It was a week later. In Sir Bryan Johnstone's office two men were seated, the features of one of whom, at any rate, were well known to the public. Sir Bryan encouraged no notoriety: the man in the street passed him by without recognition every time. In fact it is doubtful if many of the general public so much as knew his name. But with his companion it was different: as a member of several successive Cabinets, his face was almost as well known as one or two of the lesser lights in the film industry. And it is safe to say that never in the course of a life devoted to the peculiar vagaries of politics had his face worn such an expression of complete bewilderment.

'But it's incredible, Johnstone,' he remarked for the fiftieth time. 'Simply incredible.'

'Nevertheless, Sir John,' returned the other, 'it is true. I have absolute indisputable proof of the whole thing. And if you may remember, I have long drawn the Government's attention to the spread of these activities in England.'

'Yes, yes, I know,' said Sir John Haverton a little testily, 'but you have never given us chapter and verse like this before.'

'To be perfectly frank with you,' answered Sir Bryan, 'I didn't realise it fully myself until now. Had it not been for the Black Gang stumbling upon this house in Essex – Maybrick Hall – overpowering the owners and putting me on their track, much of this would never have come to light.'

'But who are the members of this Black Gang?' demanded the Cabinet Minister.

Sir Bryan Johnstone gave an enigmatic smile.

'At the moment, perhaps,' he murmured, 'that point had better remain in abeyance. I may say that in the whole of my official career I have never received such a profound surprise as when I found out who the leader of the gang was. In due course, Sir John, it may be necessary to communicate to you his name; but in the meantime

I suggest that we should concentrate on the information he has provided us with, and treat him as anonymous. I think you will agree that he has deserved well of his country.'

'Damned well,' grunted the other, with a smile. 'He can have a seat in the Cabinet if this is his usual form.'

'I hardly think,' returned Sir Bryan, smiling even more enigmatically, 'that he would help you very much in your proceedings, though he might enliven them.'

But the Cabinet Minister was once more engrossed in the report he was holding in his hand.

'Incredible,' he muttered again. 'Incredible.'

'And yet, as I said before – the truth,' said the other. 'That there is an organised and well-financed conspiracy to preach Bolshevism in England we have known for some time: how well organised it is we did not realise. But as you will see from that paper, there is not a single manufacturing town or city in Great Britain that has not got a branch of the organisation installed, which can if need be draw plentifully on funds from headquarters. Where those funds come from is at the present moment doubtful: in my own mind I have no doubt that Russia supplies the greater portion. You have in front of you there, Sir John' – he spoke with sudden passion – 'the definite proofs of a gigantic attempt at world revolution on the Russian plan. You have in front of you there the proofs of the appalling spread of the Proletarian Sunday Schools, with their abominable propaganda and their avowed attempt to convert the children who attend them to a creed whose beginning is destruction and whose end is chaotic anarchy. You have in front of you there the definite proofs that 80 per cent of the men engaged in this plot are not visionaries, swayed by some grandiloquent scheme of world reform – are not martyrs sacrificing their lives for what seems to them the good of the community – but criminals, and in many cases murderers. You have there before you the definite proofs that 80 per cent of these men think only of one thing – the lining of their own pockets, and to carry out that object they are prepared utterly to destroy sound labour in this and every other country. It's not as difficult as it looks; it's not such a big proposition as it seems. Cancer is a small growth compared to the full body of the victim it kills: the cancer of one man's tongue will kill a crowd of a thousand. We're a free country, Sir John; but the time is coming when freedom as we understood it in the past will have to cease. We can't go on as the cesspit of Europe, sheltering microbes who infect us as soon as they are here. We want disinfecting: we want

it badly. And then we want sound teaching, with the best representatives of the employers and the best representatives of the employed
as the teachers. Otherwise you'll get this.'

With his finger he flicked a paper towards the Cabinet Minister.

' "To teach the children the ideal of Revolution – that should be
the primary aim of a Proletarian school." '

'Printed at Maybrick Hall,' said Sir Bryan grimly. 'And listen to
this – a couple of the Ten Proletarian Maxims.

' "Thou shalt demand on behalf of your class the *Complete Surrender
of the Capitalist Class*." '

'And another: "Thou shalt teach *Revolution*, for revolution means
the abolition of the present political state, the end of *Capitalism*." '

He gave a short laugh.

'That's what they're teaching the children. Destruction: destruction: destruction – and not a syllable devoted to *con*struction. What
are they going to put in its place? They don't know – and they don't
care – as long as they get paid for the teaching.'

Sir John Haverton nodded thoughtfully.

'I must go into all this in detail,' he remarked. 'But in the meantime you have raised my curiosity most infernally about this Black
Gang of yours. I seem to remember some extraordinary manifesto in
the paper – something to do with that damned blackguard Latter,
wasn't it?'

Sir Bryan leaned back in his chair and lit a cigarette.

'There are one or two gaps I haven't filled in myself at the moment,'
he answered. 'But I can tell you very briefly what led us to our
discoveries at that house in Essex of which I spoke to you – Maybrick
Hall. About six days ago I received a typewritten communication of a
similar type to one or two which I had seen before. A certain defect in
the typewriter made it clear that the source was the same, and that
source was the leader of the Black Gang. Here is the communication.'

He opened a drawer in his desk, and passed a sheet of paper across
to the Cabinet Minister.

If [it ran] jolly old McIver will take his morning constitutional to
Maybrick Hall in Essex, he will find much to interest him in that
delightful and rural spot. Many specimens, both dead and alive,
will be found there, all in a splendid state of preservation. He will
also find a great many interesting devices in the house. Above all,
let him be careful of an elderly clergyman of beneficent aspect,
whose beauty is only marred by a stiff and somewhat swollen neck,

accompanied by a charming lady who answers to the name of Janet. They form the peerless gems of the collection, and were on the point of leaving the country with the enclosed packet which I removed from them for safe keeping. My modesty forbids me to tell an unmarried man like you in what portion of dear Janet's garments this little bag was found, but there's no harm in your guessing.

'What the devil?' spluttered Sir John. 'Is it a practical joke?'
'Far from it,' answered the other. 'Read to the end.'

After McIver has done this little job, [Sir John read out] he might like a trip to the North. There was an uninhabited island off the West coast of Mull, which is uninhabited no longer. He may have everything he finds there, with my love. –

THE LEADER OF THE BLACK GANG

Sir John laid down the paper and stared at the Director of Criminal Investigation.

'Is this the rambling of a partially diseased intellect?' he inquired with mild sarcasm.

'Nothing of the sort,' returned the other shortly. 'McIver and ten plain-clothes men went immediately to Maybrick Hall. And they found it a very peculiar place. There were some fifteen men there – trussed up like so many fowls, and alive. They were laid out in a row in the hall.

'Enthroned in state, in two chairs at the end, and also trussed hand and foot, were the beneficent clergyman and Miss Janet. So much for the living ones, with the exception of an Italian, who was found peacefully sleeping upstairs, with his right wrist padlocked to the wall by a long chain. I've mentioned him last, because he was destined to play a very important part in the mater.' He frowned suddenly. 'A very important part, confound him,' he repeated. 'However, we will now pass to the other specimens. In the grounds were discovered – 'a dead fowl, a dead fox, a dead hound the size of a calf – and three dead men.'

Sir John ejaculated explosively, sitting up in his chair.

'They had all died from the same cause,' continued the other imperturbably – 'electrocution. But that was nothing compared to what they found inside. In an upstairs room was a dreadful-looking specimen, more like an ape than a man, whose neck was broken. In addition, the main artery of his left arm had been severed with a knife. And even that was mild to what they found downstairs. Supported against the wall was a red-headed man stone dead. A bayonet fixed to a rifle had been driven clean through his chest, and stuck six inches into the wall behind him. And on that the body was supported.'

'Good heavens!' said Sir John, aghast. 'Who had done it?'

'The leader of the Black Gang had done it all, fighting desperately for his own life and that of his wife. One of the men lashed up in the hall turned King's Evidence and told us everything. I'm not going to weary you with the entire story, because you wouldn't believe it. This man had heard everything: had been present through it all. He heard how this leader – a man of gigantic strength – had thrown his wife over the high live-wire fence, just as the hound was on top of them, and the hound dashing after her had electrocuted itself. He heard how the girl, rushing blindly through the night in an unknown country, had stumbled by luck on the local post office, and managed to get a telephone call through to London, where she found the rest of the gang assembled and waiting – their suspicions aroused over some message received that evening from the Ritz. Then she left the post office and was wandering aimlessly along the road, when a car pulled up suddenly in front of her. Inside was a clergyman accompanied by another man – neither of whom she recognised. They offered her a lift, and the next thing she knew was that she'd been trapped again, and was back at Maybrick Hall. So much this man heard: the rest he saw. The leader of the Black Gang and his wife were sentenced to death by the clergyman . . . Clergyman!' Sir Bryan shook his fist in the air. 'I'd give a year's screw to have laid my hands on that clergyman.'

'He escaped?' cried the other.

'All in due course,' said Sir Bryan. 'They were sentenced to death by having their brains bashed out with the butt of a rifle – after which they were to be thrown in the river. It was to be made to appear an accident. And the man who was to do it was a Russian called Yulowski – one of the men who butchered the Russian Royal family . . . A devil of the most inhuman description. He literally had the rifle raised to kill the girl, when the Black Gang, having cut the wire fence, arrived in the nick of time. And it was then that the leader of that gang, who had thought he was on the point of seeing his wife's brains dashed out, took advantage of the utter confusion and sprang on the Russian with a roar of rage. The man who told us stated that he had never dreamed such a blow was possible as the rifle thrust which pierced clean through the Russian. It split him like a rotten cabbage, and he died in three minutes.'

'But, my dear fellow,' spluttered the Cabinet Minister, 'you can't expect me to believe all this. You're pulling my leg.'

'Never farther from it in my life, Haverton,' said the other. 'I admit it seems a bit over the odds, but every word I've told you is gospel. To return to the discoveries. McIver found that the house was the headquarters of a vast criminal organisation. There were schemes of the most fantastic description cut and dried in every detail. Some of them were stupid: some were not. I have them all here. This one' – he glanced through some papers on his desk – 'concerns the blowing of a large gap in one of the retaining walls of the big reservoir at Staines. This one concerns a perfectly-thought-out plot on your life when you go to Beauchamp Hall next week. You were to be found dead in your railway carriage.'

'What!' roared Sir John, springing to his feet.

'It would very likely have failed,' said Sir Bryan calmly, 'but they would have tried again. They don't like you or your views at all – these gentlemen. But those are the least important. From time immemorial wild, fanatical youths have done similar things: the danger was far greater and more subtle. And perhaps the most dangerous activity of all was what I have spoken about already – Maybrick Hall was the headquarters of these poisonous Proletarian Sunday Schools. But in addition to that there was forgery going on there on a big scale: money is necessary for their activities. There were also long lists of their agents in different parts of the country, and detailed instructions for fomenting industrial unrest. But you have it all there – you can read it at your leisure for yourself. Particularly I commend to your notice, the series of pamphlets on Ireland, and the methods suggested for promoting discord between England and France, and England and America.'

Sir Bryan lit a cigarette.

'To return to the personal side of it. McIver, engrossed in his search, paid very little attention to the row of mummies in the hall. They certainly seemed extraordinarily safe, and one can hardly blame him. But the fact remains that, at some period during the morning, the Italian, who, if you remember, was padlocked in a bedroom upstairs, escaped. How I can't tell you: he must have had a key in his pocket. They found the padlock open, and the room empty. And going downstairs they found the chairs recently occupied by the clergyman and Miss Janet empty also. Moreover from that moment no trace of any of them has been found. It is as if the earth had opened and swallowed them. Which brings us to the packet enclosed with the letter from the leader of the Black Gang.'

He crossed to a safe and took out the little chamois-leather bag of diamonds.

'Nice stones,' he remarked quietly. 'Worth literally a king's ransom. The pink one is part of the Russian crown jewels: the remainder belonged to the Grand Duke Georgius, who was murdered by the Bolshevists. His son, who had these in his possession, died ten days ago of an overdose of a sleeping-draught in Amsterdam. At least that is what I understood until I received these. Now I am not so sure. I would go further, and say I am quite sure that even if he did die of an overdose, it was administered by the beneficent clergyman calling himself the Reverend Theodosius Longmoor – the most amazing international criminal of this or any other age – the man who, with Miss Janet and the Italian, has vanished into thin air, right under McIver's nose.'

'And you mean to say this man has been in England and you haven't laid him by the heels?' said Sir John incredulously.

'Unfortunately that is what I mean,' answered the other. 'The police of four continents know about him, but that's a very different thing from proof. This time we had proof – these diamonds: and the man has vanished – utterly and completely. He is the master mind who controls and directs, but very rarely actually does anything himself. That's why he's so devilishly difficult to catch. But we'll do it sooner or later.'

The Cabinet Minister was once more studying the typewritten communication from the leader of the Black Gang.

'It's the most astounding affair, this, Johnstone,' he said at length. 'Most astounding. And what's all this about the island off the coast of Mull?'

Sir Bryan laughed.

'Not the least astounding part of the whole show, I assure you. But for you to understand it better I must go back two or three months, to the time when we first became aware of the existence of the Black Gang. A series of very strange disappearances were taking place: men were being spirited away, without leaving a trace behind them. Of course we knew about it, but in view of the fact that our assistance was never asked to find them, and still more in view of the fact that in every case they were people whose room we preferred to their company, we lay low and said nothing.

'From unofficial inquiries I had carried out we came to the conclusion that this mysterious Black Gang was a reality, and that, further, it was intimately connected with these disappearances. But we also came to the conclusion that the ideals and objects of this gang were in every way desirable. Such a thing, of course, could not be admitted officially: the abduction of anyone is a criminal offence. But we came to the conclusion that the Black Gang was undoubtedly an extremely powerful and ably led organisation whose object was simply and solely to fight the Red element in England. The means they adopted were undoubtedly illegal – but the results were excellent. Whenever a man appeared preaching Bolshevism, after a few days he simply disappeared. In short, a reign of terror was established amongst the terrorists. And it was to put that right, I have no doubt, that the Reverend Theodosius Longmoor arrived in this country.'

Sir Bryan thoughtfully lit another cigarette.

'To return to the island. McIver went there, and after some little difficulty located it, out of the twenty or thirty to which the description might apply. He found it far from uninhabited, just as that letter says. He found it occupied by some fifty or sixty rabid anarchists – the gentlemen who had so mysteriously disappeared – who were presided over by twenty large demobilised soldiers commanded by an ex-sergeant-major of the Guards. The sixty frenzied anarchists, he gathered, were running a state on communist lines, as interpreted by the ex-sergeant-major. And the interpretation moved even McIver to tears of laughter. It appeared that once every three hours they were all drawn up in a row, and the sergeant-major, with a voice like a bull, would bellow:

' "Should the ruling classes have money?"'

'Then they answered in unison – "No".'

' "Should anyone have money?" Again they answered "No".'

' "Should everyone work for the common good for love?" "Yes".'

'Whereat he would roar: "Well, in this 'ere island there ain't no ruling classes, and there ain't no money, and there's dam' little love, so go and plant more potatoes, you lop-eared sons of Beelzebub." '

'At which point the parade broke up in disorder.'

Sir John was shaking helplessly.

'This is a jest, Johnstone. You're joking.'

'I'm not,' answered the other. 'But I think you'll admit that the man who started the whole show – the leader of the Black Gang – is a humorist, to put it mildly, who cannot well be spared.'

'My dear fellow, as I said before, the Cabinet is the only place for him. If only he'd export two or three of my colleagues to this island and let 'em plant potatoes I'd take off my hat to him. Tell me – do I know him?'

Sir Bryan smiled.

'I'm not certain: you may. But the point, Haverton, is this. We must take cognisance of the whole thing, if we acknowledge it at all. Therefore shall we assume that everything I have been telling you is a fairy story: that the Black Gang is non-existent – I may say that it will be shortly – and that what has already appeared in the papers is just a hoax by some irresponsible person? Unless we do that there will be a *cause célèbre* fought out on class prejudice – a most injudicious thing at the present moment. I may say that the island is shut down, and the sixty pioneers have departed to other countries. Also quite a number of those agents whose names are on the list you have have left our shores during the past few days. It is merely up to us to see that they don't come back. But nothing has come out in the papers: and I don't want anything to come out either.'

He paused suddenly, as a cheerful voice was heard in the office outside.

'Ah! Here is one Captain Drummond, whom I asked to come round this morning,' he continued, with a faint smile. 'I wonder if you know him.'

'Drummond?' repeated the other. 'Is he a vast fellow with an ugly face?'

'That's the man,' said Sir Bryan.

'I've seen him at his aunt's – old Lady Meltrose. She says he's the biggest fool in London.'

Sir Bryan's smile grew more pronounced as the door opened and Hugh came in.

'Morning, Tum-tum,' he boomed genially. 'How's the liver and all that?'

'Morning, Hugh. Do you know Sir John Haverton?'

'Morning, Sir John. Jolly old Cabinet merry and bright? Or did you all go down on Purple Polly at Goodwood yesterday?'

Sir John rose a little grimly.

'We have other things to do besides backing horses, Captain Drummond. I think we have met at Lady Meltrose's house, haven't we?'

'More than likely,' said Hugh affably. 'I don't often dine there: she ropes in such a ghastly crowd of bores, don't you know.'

'I feel sure, Captain Drummond, that you're an admirable judge.'

Sir John turned to Sir Bryan Johnstone and held out his hand. 'Well, I must be off. Good morning, Johnstone – and you've thoroughly roused my curiosity. I'd very much like to know who the gentleman is whom we've been discussing. And in the meantime I'll look through these papers and let you know my decision in due course.'

He bustled out of the office, and Hugh sank into a chair with a sigh of relief.

'The old boy's clothes seem full of body this morning, Tum-tum,' he remarked as the door closed. 'Indigestion – or don't the elastic-sided boots fit?'

'Do you know what we have been discussing, Hugh?' said the other quietly.

'Not an earthly, old man. Was it that new one about the girl in the grocer's shop?'

'We've been discussing the leader of the Black Gang,' said Sir Bryan, with his eyes fixed on the man sprawling in the chair opposite.

Not by the twitch of a muscle did Drummond's face change: he seemed engrossed in the task of selecting a cigarette.

'You've been in Deauville, haven't you, Hugh – the last few days?'

'Quite right, old man. All among the fairies.'

'You don't know that a burglary has taken place at your house in London?'

'A burglary!' Drummond sat up with a jerk. 'Why the deuce hasn't Denny told me?'

'A very small one,' said Sir Bryan, 'committed by myself, and perhaps he doesn't know. I took – your typewriter.'

For a few moments Hugh Drummond stared at him in silence: then his lips began to twitch.

'I see,' he said at length. 'I meant to have that defective 's' repaired.'

'You took me in, old boy,' continued Sir Bryan, 'utterly and absolutely. If it hadn't been for one of the men at Maybrick Hall turning King's evidence, I don't believe I should have found out now.'

'Well, what are you going to do about it?' asked Drummond after a pause.

'Nothing. I was discussing the matter with Sir John this morning, and we both agreed that you either deserved penal servitude or a seat in the Cabinet. And since neither course commends itself to us, we have decided to do nothing. There are reasons, which you will appreciate, against any publicity at the moment. But, Hugh, the Black Gang must cease.'

Drummond nodded.

'Carried, *nem. con.*, Tum-tum. It shall automatically dissolve today.'

'And further,' continued Sir Bryan, 'will you relieve my curiosity and tell me what sent Charles Latter mad?'

'I did,' said Drummond grimly, 'as I told that ass McIver over a cocktail at the Regency. He was plotting to blow up three thousand men's employment, Tum-tum, with gun-cotton. It was at his instigation that four men were killed in Manchester as the result of another outrage. So I lashed him to his bed, and underneath him I put what he thought was a slab of gun-cotton with fuse attached. It wasn't gun-cotton: it was wood. And he went mad.' He paused for a moment, and then continued. 'Now, one for you. Why did you let Carl Peterson escape? I nearly killed him that night, after I'd bayoneted the Russian.'

'How did you know he had escaped?' demanded Sir Bryan.

Hugh felt in his pocket and produced a note.

'Read it,' he said, passing it across the desk.

It was a pity you forgot that there might be another key to the padlock, Captain Drummond. [it ran] And Giuseppi is an old friend of mine. I quite enjoyed our single.

Sir Bryan returned the note without a word, and Drummond replaced it in his pocket.

'That's twice,' he said quietly, and suddenly the Director of Criminal Investigation, than whom no shrewder judge of men lived, saw and understood the real Drummond below the surface of inanity – the real Drummond, cool, resourceful, and inflexible of will – the real Drummond who was capable of organising and carrying through anything and everything once he had set his mind to it.

'That's twice,' he repeated, still in the same quiet tone. 'Next time – I win.'

'But no more Black Gang, Hugh,' said the other warningly.

Drummond waved a huge hand. 'I have spoken, Tum-tum. A rose by any other name, perhaps – but no more Black Gang.'

He rose and grinned at his friend.

'It's deuced good of you, old man, and all that . . . '

The eyes of the two men met.

'If it was found out, I should be looking for another job,' remarked Sir Bryan dryly. 'And perhaps I should not get the two thousand pounds which I understand the widow of the late lamented Ginger Martin has received anonymously.'

'Shut up,' said Drummond awkwardly.

'Delighted, old man,' returned the other. 'But the police in that district are demanding a rise of pay. She has been drunk and disorderly five times in the last week.'

*   *   *

To those strong-minded individuals who habitually read the entrancing chit-chat of Mrs Tattle in *The Daily Observer*, there appeared the following morning a delightful description of the last big fancy-dress ball of the season held at the Albert Hall the preceding night. Much of it may be passed over as unworthy of perpetuation, but the concluding paragraph had its points of interest.

Half-way through the evening, [she wrote in her breezy way] just as I was consuming an ice in one hand with the Duchess of Sussex, and nibbling the last of the asparagus in the other with the Princess of Montevideo, tastefully disguised as an umbrella stand, we were treated to the thrill of the evening. It seemed as if suddenly there sprang up all round the room a mass of mysterious figures clothed from head to foot in black. The dear Princess grew quite hysterical, and began to wonder if it was a 'hold-up' as she so graphically described it. In fact, for safety, she secreted the glass-headed parasol – the only remaining heirloom of the Royal House – and which formed a prominent part of her costume, behind a neighbouring palm. Whispers of the mysterious Black Gang were heard on all sides, but we were soon reassured. Belovd'st, they all carried champagne bottles! Wasn't it too, too thrilling! And after a while they all formed up in a row, and at a word from the leader – a huge man, my dears, puffectly 'uge – they discharged the corks in a volley at one of the boxes, which sheltered no less than two celebrities – Sir Bryan Johnstone, the chief of all the policemen, and Sir John Haverton, the Home Secretary. It is rumoured that one of the corks became embedded in Sir John's right eye – but rumour is a lying jade, is not she? Anyway loud sounds of revelry and mirth were heard proceeding from the box, and going a little later to powder my nose I distinctly saw Sir John being taught the intricacies of the fox-trot by the huge man in the passage. Presumably the cork had by then been removed from his eye, but one never knows, does one? Anything can happen at an Albert Hall ball, especially at the end of the season.

THE END

THE THIRD ROUND

Chapter 1

In which the Metropolitan Diamond Syndicate holds converse with Mr Edward Blackton

With a sigh of pleasure Mr Edward Blackton opened the windows of his balcony and leaned out, staring over the lake. Opposite, the mountains of Savoy rose steeply from the water; away to the left the Dent du Midi raised its crown of snow above the morning haze.

Below him the waters of the lake glittered and scintillated with a thousand fires. A steamer, with much blowing of sirens and reversing of paddle-wheels, had come to rest at a landing-stage hard by, and was taking on board a bevy of tourists, while the gulls circled round shrieking discordantly. For a while he watched them idly, noting the quickness with which the birds swooped and caught the bread as it was thrown into the air, long before it reached the water. He noted also how nearly all the food was secured by half a dozen of the gulls, whilst the others said a lot but got nothing. And suddenly Mr Edward Blackton smiled.

'Like life, my dear,' he said, slipping his arm round the waist of a girl who had just joined him at the window. 'It's the fool who shouts in this world: the wise man says nothing and acts.'

The girl lit a cigarette thoughtfully, and sat down on the ledge of the balcony. For a while her eyes followed the steamer puffing fussily away with its load of sightseers and its attendant retinue of gulls: then she looked at the man standing beside her. Point by point she took him in: the clear blue eyes under the deep forehead, the aquiline nose, the firm mouth and chin. Calmly, dispassionately, she noted the thick brown hair greying a little over the temples, the great depth of chest, and the strong, powerful hands: then she turned and looked once again at the disappearing steamer. But to the man's surprise she gave a little sigh.

'What is it, my dear?' he said solicitously. 'Bored?'

'No, not bored,' she answered. 'Whatever may be your failings, *mon ami*, boring me is not one of them. I was just wondering what it would feel like if you and I were content to go on a paddle-wheel steamer with a Baedeker and a Kodak, and a paper bag full of bananas.'

'We will try tomorrow,' said the man, gravely lighting a cigar.

'It wouldn't be any good,' laughed the girl. 'Just once in a way we should probably love it. I meant I wonder what it would feel like if that was our life.'

Her companion nodded.

'I know, *carissima*,' he answered gently. 'I have sometimes wondered the same thing. I suppose there must be compensations in respectability, otherwise so many people wouldn't be respectable. But I'm afraid it is one of those things that we shall never know.'

'I think it's that,' said the girl, waving her hand towards the mountains opposite – 'that has caused my mood. It's all so perfectly lovely: the sky is just so wonderfully blue. And look at that sailing boat.'

She pointed to one of the big lake barges, with its two huge lateen sails, creeping gently along in the centre of the lake. 'It's all so peaceful, and sometimes one wants peace.'

'True,' agreed the man; 'one does. It's just reaction, and we've been busy lately.' He rose and began to pace slowly up and down the balcony. 'To be quite honest, I myself have once or twice thought recently that if I could pull off some really big coup – something, I mean, that ran into the millions – I would give things up.'

The girl smiled and shook her head.

'Don't misunderstand me, my dear,' he went on. 'I do not suggest for a moment that we should settle down to a life of toping and ease. We could neither of us exist without employing our brains. But with really big money behind one, we should be in a position to employ our brains a little more legitimately, shall I say, than we are able to at present, and still get all the excitement we require.

'Take Drakshoff: that man controls three of the principal Governments of Europe. The general public don't know it; the Governments themselves won't admit it: but it's true for all that. As you know, that little job I carried out for him in Germany averted a second revolution. He didn't want one at the time, and so he called me in. And it cost him in all five million pounds. What was that to him?'

He shrugged his shoulders contemptuously.

'A mere fleabite – a bagatelle. Why, with that man an odd million or two one way or the other wouldn't be noticed in his passbook.'

He paused and stared over the sunlit lake, while the girl watched him in silence.

'Given money as big as that, and a man can rule the world. More-over, he can rule it without fear of consequences. He can have all the excitement he requires; he can wield all the power he desires – and have special posses of police to guard him. I'm afraid we don't have many to guard us.'

The girl laughed and lit another cigarette.

'You are right, *mon ami*, we do not. Hullo! Who can that be?'

Inside the sitting-room the telephone bell was ringing, and with a slight frown Mr Edward Blackton took off the receiver.

'What is it?'

From the other end came the voice of the manager, suitably defer-ential as befitted a client of such obvious wealth installed in the most palatial suite of the Palace Hotel.

'Two gentlemen are here, Mr Blackton,' said the manager, 'who wish to know when they can have the pleasure of seeing you. Their names are Sir Raymond Blantyre and Mr Jabez Leibhaus. They arrived this morning from England by the Simplon Orient express, and they say that their business is most urgent.'

A sudden gleam had come into Mr Blackton's eyes as he listened, but his voice as he answered was almost bored.

'I shall be pleased to see both gentlemen at eleven o'clock up here. Kindly have champagne and sandwiches sent to my sitting-room at that hour.'

He replaced the receiver, and stood for a moment thinking deeply.

'Who was it?' called the girl from the balcony.

'Blantyre and Leibhaus, my dear,' answered the man. 'Now, what the deuce can they want with me so urgently?'

'Aren't they both big diamond men?' said the girl, coming into the room.

'They are,' said Blackton. 'In romantic fiction they would be described as two diamond kings. Anyway, it won't do them any harm to wait for half an hour.'

'How did they find out your address? I thought you had left strict instructions that you were not to be disturbed.'

There was regret in the girl's voice, and with a faint smile the man tilted back her head and kissed her.

'In our profession, *cara mia*,' he said gently, 'there are times when the strictest instructions have to be disobeyed. Freyder would never have dreamed of worrying me over a little thing, but unless I am much mistaken this isn't going to be little. It's going to be big: those two below don't go chasing half across Europe because they've mislaid a collar stud. Why – who knows? – it might prove to be the big coup we were discussing a few minutes ago.'

He kissed her again; then he turned abruptly away and the girl gave a little sigh. For the look had come into those grey-blue eyes that she knew so well: the alert, keen look which meant business. He crossed the room, and unlocked a heavy leather dispatch-case. From it he took out a biggish book which he laid on the table. Then having made himself comfortable on the balcony, he lit another cigar, and began to turn over the pages.

It was of the loose-leaf variety, and every page had entries on it in Blackton's small, neat handwriting. It was what he called his 'Who's Who', but it differed from that excellent production in one marked respect. The people in Mr Edward Blackton's production had not compiled their own notices, which rendered it considerably more truthful even if less complimentary than the orthodox volume.

It was arranged alphabetically, and it contained an astounding wealth of information. In fact in his lighter moments the author was wont to say that when he retired from active life he would publish it, and die in luxury on the large sums paid him to suppress it. Mentioned in it were the names of practically every man and woman possessed of real wealth – as Blackton regarded wealth – in Europe and America.

There were, of course, many omissions, but in the course of years an extraordinary amount of strange and useful information had been collected. In many cases just the bare details of the person were given: these were the uninteresting ones, and consisted of people who passed the test as far as money was concerned but about whom the author had no personal knowledge.

In others, however, the entries were far more human. After the name would be recorded certain details, frequently of a most scurrilous description. And these details had one object and one object only – to assist at the proper time and place in parting the victim from his money.

Not that Mr Edward Blackton was a common blackmailer – far from it. Blackmailing pure and simple was a form of amusement which revolted his feelings as an artist. But to make use of certain privately gained information about a man when dealing with him was a different matter altogether.

It was a great assistance in estimating character when meeting a man for the first time to know that his previous wife had divorced him for carrying on with the housemaid, and that he had then failed to marry the housemaid. Nothing of blackmail in that: just a pointer as to character.

In the immense ramifications of Mr Blackton's activities it was of course impossible for him to keep all these details in his head. And so little by little the book had grown until it now comprised over three hundred pages. Information obtained first-hand or from absolutely certain sources was entered in red; items not quite so reliable in black. And under Sir Raymond Blantyre's name the entry was in red.

> Blantyre, Raymond. Born 1858. Vice-President Metropolitan Diamond Syndicate. Married daughter of John Perkins, wool merchant in London. Knighted 1904. Something shady about him in South Africa – probably I.D.B. Races a lot. Wife a snob. Living up to the limit of his income. 5.13.

Mr Blackton laid the book on his knee and looked thoughtfully over the lake. The last three figures showed that the entry had been made in May 1913, and if he was living up to the limit of his income then, he must have had to retrench considerably now. And wives who are snobs dislike that particularly.

He picked up the book again and turned up the dossier of his other visitor, to find nothing of interest. Mr Leibhaus had only bare details after his name, with the solitary piece of information that he, too, was a Vice-President of the Metropolitan Diamond Syndicate.

He closed the book and relocked it in the dispatch-case; then he glanced at his watch.

'I think, my dear,' he said, turning to the girl, 'that our interview had better be apparently private. Could you make yourself comfortable in your bedroom, so that you will be able to hear everything and give me your opinion afterwards?' He opened the door for her and she passed through. 'I confess,' he continued, 'that I'm a little puzzled. I cannot think what they want to see me about so urgently.'

But there was no trace of it on his face as five minutes later his two visitors were ushered in by the sub-manager.

'See that the sandwiches and champagne are sent at once, please,' he remarked, and the hotel official bustled away.

'We shall be undisturbed, gentlemen,' he said, 'after the waiter brings the tray. Until then we might enjoy the view over the lake. It is rare, I am told, that one can see the Dent du Midi quite so clearly.'

The three men strolled on to the balcony and leaned out. And it struck that exceptionally quick observer of human nature, Mr Blackton, that both his visitors were a little nervous. Sir Raymond

Blantyre especially was not at his ease, answering the casual remarks of his host at random. He was a short, stocky little man with a white moustache and a gold-rimmed eyeglass, which he had an irritating habit of taking in and out of his eye, and he gave a sigh of relief as the door finally closed behind the waiter.

'Now perhaps we can come to business, Count – er – I beg your pardon, Mr Blackton.'

'The mistake is a natural one,' said his host suavely. 'Shall we go inside the room to avoid any risk of being overheard?'

'I had better begin at the beginning,' said Sir Raymond, waving away his host's offer of champagne. 'And when I've finished, you will see, I have no doubt, our reasons for disturbing you in this way. Nothing short of the desperate position in which we find ourselves would have induced us to seek you out after what Mr Freyder told my friend Leibhaus. But that situation is so desperate that we had no alternative.'

Mr Blackton's face remained quite expressionless, and the other, after a little pause, went on: 'Doubtless you know who we are, Mr Blackton. I am the President of the Metropolitan Diamond Syndicate and Mr Leibhaus is the senior Vice-President. In the event of my absence at any time, he deputises for me. I mention these facts to emphasise the point that we are the heads of that combine, and that you are therefore dealing with the absolute principals, and not with subordinates.

'Now, I may further mention that although the Metropolitan is our particular Syndicate, we are both of us considerably interested in other diamond enterprises. In fact our entire fortune is bound up irretrievably in the diamond industry – as are the fortunes of several other men, for whom, Mr Blackton, I am authorised to speak.

'So that I am in a position to say that not only am I here as representative of the Metropolitan Syndicate, but I am here as representative of the whole diamond industry and the enormous capital locked up in that industry.'

'You make yourself perfectly clear, Sir Raymond,' said Mr Blackton quietly. His face was as masklike as ever, but he wondered more and more what could be coming.

Sir Raymond took out his eyeglass and polished it; then he took a sip of the champagne which, despite his refusal, his host had poured out for him.

'That being so, Mr Blackton, and my position in the matter

being fully understood, I will come to the object of our visit. One day about a fortnight ago I was dining at the house of a certain Professor Goodman. You may perhaps have heard of him by name? No?

'Well, he is, I understand, one of the foremost chemists of the day. He and I have not got much in common, but my wife and his became acquainted during the war, and we still occasionally dine with one another. There were six of us at dinner – our four selves, his daughter, and an extraordinarily inane young man with an eyeglass – who, I gathered, was engaged to the daughter.

'It was during dinner that my attention was caught by a rather peculiar ornament that the daughter was wearing. It looked to me like a piece of ordinary cut glass mounted in a claw of gold, and she was using it as a brooch. The piece of glass was about the size of a large marble, and it scintillated so brilliantly as she moved that I could not help noticing it.

'I may say that it struck me as a distinctly vulgar ornament – the sort of thing that a housemaid might be expected to wear when she was out. It surprised me, since the Goodmans are the last people one would expect to allow such a thing. And, of course, I should have said nothing about it had not the vapid youth opposite noticed me.

' "Looking at the monkey nut?" he said, or something equally foolish. "Pretty sound bit of work on the part of the old paternal parent."

'Professor Goodman looked up and smiled, and the girl took it off and handed it to me.

' "What do you think of it, Sir Raymond?" she asked. "I put it on especially for your benefit tonight."

'I glanced at it, and to my amazement I found that it was a perfectly flawless diamond, worth certainly ten to twelve thousand pounds, and possibly more. I suppose my surprise must have been obvious, because they all began to laugh.

' "Well, what is your verdict, Blantyre?" said the Professor.

' "I will be perfectly frank," I answered. "I cannot understand how you can have placed such a really wonderful stone in such an unworthy setting."

'And then the Professor laughed still more.

' "What would you say was the value of that stone?" he inquired.

' "I should be delighted to give Miss Goodman a cheque for ten thousand pounds for it here and now," I said.

'And then he really roared with laughter.

' "What about it, Brenda?" he cried. "Do you know what that stone cost me, Blantyre? Five pounds ten shillings and sixpence – and two burnt fingers." '

Blackton leaned forward in his chair and stared at the speaker.

'Well – what then?' he said quietly.

Sir Raymond mopped his forehead and took another sip of champagne.

'You've guessed it, Mr Blackton. It was false – or when I say false, it was not false in the sense that Tecla pearls are false, But it had been made by a chemical process in Professor Goodman's laboratory. Otherwise it was indistinguishable from the genuine article: in fact' – in his agitation he thumped the table with his fist – 'it *was* the genuine article!'

Blackton carefully lit another cigar.

'And what did you do?' he inquired. 'I presume that you have tested the matter fully since.'

'Of course,' answered the other. 'I will tell you exactly what has happened. That evening after dinner I sat on talking with the Professor. Somewhat naturally I allowed no hint of my agitation to show on my face.

'As you probably know, Mr Blackton, artificial diamonds have been manufactured in the past – real diamonds indistinguishable from those found in nature. But they have been small, and their cost has been greater when made artificially than if they had been found. And so the process has never been economically worth while. But this was altogether different.

'If what Professor Goodman told me was the truth – if he had indeed manufactured that diamond for five pounds in his laboratory, we were confronted with the possibility of an appalling crisis. And since he was the last person to tell a stupid and gratuitous lie, you may imagine my feelings.

'I need hardly point out to you that the whole diamond market is an artificial one. The output of stones from the mines has to be limited to prevent a slump – to keep prices up. And what would happen if the market was swamped with stones worth a king's ransom each as prices go today and costing a fiver to produce was too impossible to contemplate. It meant, of course, absolute ruin to me and others in my position – to say nothing of hundreds of big jewellers and dealers.

'I pointed this out to Professor Goodman, but' – and once again Sir Raymond mopped his forehead – 'would you believe it, the wretched man seemed completely uninterested. All he was concerned about was his miserable chemistry.

' "An unique discovery, my dear Blantyre," he remarked complacently. "And two years ago I bet Professor – " I forget the fool's name, but, at any rate, he had bet this Professor a fiver that he'd do it.'

Sir Raymond rose and walked up and down the room in his agitation.

'A fiver, Mr Blackton – a fiver! I asked him what he was going to do, and he said he was going to read a paper on it, and give a demonstration at the next meeting of the Royal Society. And that takes place in a fortnight. I tried to dissuade him; I'm afraid I was foolish enough to threaten him.

'At any rate, he rose abruptly from the table, and I cursed myself for a fool. But towards the end of the evening he recovered himself sufficiently to agree to give me and the other members of my Syndicate a private demonstration. His daughter also allowed me to take away her brooch, so that I could subject it to more searching tests the next day.'

He again sat down and stared at the man opposite him, who seemed more intent on how long he could get the ash of his cigar before it dropped than on anything else.

'Next day, Mr Blackton, my worst fears were confirmed. I subjected that stone to every known test – but it was useless. *It was a diamond* – perfect, flawless; and it had cost five pounds to make. I called together my Syndicate, and at first they were inclined to be incredulous.

'They suggested fraud – as you know, there have been in the past several attempts made to obtain money by men who pretended they had discovered the secret of making diamonds in the laboratory. And in every case, up till now, sleight-of-hand has been proved. The big uncut diamond was not produced by the chemical reaction, but was introduced at some period during the experiment.

'Of course the idea was to obtain hush-money to suppress the supposed secret. I pointed out to my friends how impossible such a supposition was in the case of a man like Professor Goodman; and finally – to cut things short – they agreed to come round with me the following afternoon to see the demonstration.

'The Professor had forgotten all about the appointment – he is that sort of man – and we waited in an agony of impatience while his secretary telephoned for him all over London. At last she got him, and the Professor arrived profuse in his apologies.

' "I have just been watching a most interesting experiment with some blue cheese-mould," he told me, "and I quite forgot the time. Now, what is it you gentlemen want to see?" '

For the first time a very faint smile flickered on Mr Blackton's lips, but he said nothing.

'I told him,' continued Sir Raymond, 'and we at once adjourned to the laboratory. We had most of us attended similar demonstrations before, and we expected to find the usual apparatus of a mould and a furnace. Nothing of the sort, however, could we see. There was an electric furnace: a sort of bowl made of some opaque material, and a variety of chemical salts in bottles.

' "You will forgive me, gentlemen," he remarked, "if I don't give you my process in detail. I don't want to run any risk of my discovery leaking out before I address the Royal Society."

'He beamed at us through his spectacles; and – serious though it was – I really could not help smiling. That he should make such a remark to us of all people!

' "You are, of course, at liberty to examine everything that I put into this retort," he went on, "and the retort itself."

'He was fumbling in his pocket as he spoke, and he finally produced two or three dirty sheets of paper, at which he peered.

' "Dear me!" he exclaimed, "I've got the wrong notes. These are the ones about my new albumen food for infants and adults. Where can I have left them?"

' "I hope," I remarked as calmly as I could, "that you haven't left them lying about where anyone could get at them, Professor."

'He shook his head vaguely, though his reply was reassuring.

' "No-one could understand them even if I had," he answered. "Ah! here they are." With a little cry of triumph he produced some even dirtier scraps which he laid on the desk in front of him.

' "I have to refer to my notes," he said, "as the process – though the essence of simplicity, once the correct mixture of the ingredients is obtained – is a difficult one to remember. There are no fewer than thirty-nine salts used in the operation. Now would you gentlemen come closer, so that you can see everything I do?"

'He produced a balance which he proceeded to adjust with mathematical precision, while we crowded round as close as we could.

' "While I think of it," he said, looking up suddenly, "is there any particular colour you would like me to make?"

' "Rose pink," grunted someone, and he nodded.

' "Certainly," he answered. "That will necessitate the addition of a somewhat rare strontium salt – making forty in all."

'He beamed at us and then he commenced. To say that we watched him closely would hardly convey our attitude: we watched him without movement, without speech, almost without breathing. He weighed his salts, and he mixed them – and that part of the process took an hour at least.

'Then he took up the bowl and we examined that. It was obviously some form of metal, but that was as far as we could get. And it was empty.

' "Without that retort, gentlemen," he remarked, "the process would be impossible. There is no secret as to its composition. It is made of a blend of tungsten and osmium, and is the only thing known to science today which could resist the immense heat to which this mixture will be subjected in the electric furnace. Now possibly one of you would like to pour this mixture into the retort, place the retort in the furnace, and shut the furnace doors. Then I will switch on the current."

'I personally did what he suggested, Mr Blackton. I poured the mixture of fine powders into the empty bowl; I placed the bowl into the furnace, having first examined the furnace; and then I closed the doors. And I knew, and every man there knew, that there had been no suspicion of fraud. Then he switched on the current, and we sat down to wait.

'Gradually the heat grew intense – but no-one thought of moving. At first the Professor rambled on, but I doubt if anyone paid any attention to him. Amongst other things he told us that from the very start of his experiments he had worked on different lines from the usual ones, which consisted of dissolving carbon in molten iron and then cooling the mass suddenly with cold water.

' "That sets up gigantic pressure," he remarked, "but it is too quick. Only small stones are the result. My process was arrived at by totally different methods, as you see."

'The sweat poured off us, and still we sat there silent – each of us busy with his own thoughts. I think even then we realised that there was no hope; we knew that his claims were justified. But we had to see it through, and make sure. The Professor was absorbed in some profound calculations on his new albumen food; the furnace glowed white in the corner; and, Mr Blackton, men worth tens of millions sat and dripped with perspiration in order to make definitely certain that they were not worth as many farthings.

'I suppose it was about two hours later that the Professor, having looked at his watch, rose and switched off the current.

'"In about an hour, gentlemen," he remarked, "the retort will be cool enough to take out. I suggest that you should take it with you, and having cut out the clinker you should carry out your own tests on it. Inside that clinker will be your rose-pink diamond – uncut, of course. I make you a present of it: all I ask is that you should return me my retort."

'He blinked at us through his spectacles.

'"You will forgive me if I leave you now, but I have to deliver my address to some students on the catalytic influence of chromous chloride. I fear I am already an hour and a half late, but that is nothing new."

'And with that he bustled out of the room.'

Sir Raymond paused and lit a cigarette.

'You may perhaps think, Mr Blackton, that I have been unnecessarily verbose over details that are unimportant,' he continued after a moment. 'But my object has been to try to show you the type of man Professor Goodman is.'

'You have succeeded admirably, Sir Raymond,' said Blackton quietly.

'Good, Then now I will go quicker. We took his retort home, and we cut out the clinker. No-one touched it except ourselves. We chipped off the outside scale, and we came to the diamond. Under our own eyes we had it cut – roughly, of course, because time was urgent. Here are the results.'

He handed over a small box to Blackton, who opened it. Inside, resting on some cotton-wool, were two large rose-pink diamonds and three smaller ones – worth in all, to that expert's shrewd eye, anything up to twenty-five thousand pounds. He took out a pocket lens and examined the largest, and Sir Raymond gave a short, hard laugh.

'Believe me,' he said harshly, 'they're genuine right enough. I wish to Heaven I could detect even the trace of a flaw. There isn't one, I tell you: they're perfect stones – and that's why we've come to you.'

Blackton laid the box on the table and renewed the contemplation of his cigar.

'At the moment,' he remarked, 'the connection is a little obscure. However, pray continue. I assume that you have interviewed the Professor again.'

'The very next morning,' said Sir Raymond. 'I went round, ostensibly to return his metal bowl, and then once again I put the whole matter before him. I pointed out to him that if this discovery of his was made known, it would involve thousands of people in utter ruin.

'I pointed out to him that after all no-one could say that it was a discovery which could benefit the world generally, profoundly wonderful though it was. Its sole result, so far as I could see, would be to put diamond tiaras within the range of the average scullery-maid. In short, I invoked every argument I could think of to try to persuade him to change his mind. Useless, utterly useless. To do him justice, I do not believe it is simply pigheadedness. He is honestly unable to understand our point of view.

'To him it is a scientific discovery concerning carbon, and according to him carbon is so vitally important, so essentially at the root of all life, that to suppress the results of an experiment such as this would be a crime against science. He sees no harm in diamonds being as plentiful as marbles; in fact, the financial side of the affair is literally meaningless to him.

'Meaningless, Mr Blackton, as I found when I played my last card. In the name of my Syndicate I offered him two hundred and fifty thousand pounds to suppress it. He rang the bell – apologised for leaving me so abruptly – and the servant showed me out. And that is how the matter stands today. In a fortnight from now his secret will be given to the world, unless . . . '

Sir Raymond paused, and glanced at Mr Leibhaus.

'Precisely,' he agreed. 'Unless, as you say . . . '

Mr Blackton said nothing. It was not his business to help them out, though the object of their journey was now obvious.

'Unless, Mr Blackton,' Sir Raymond took the plunge, 'we can induce you to interest yourself in the matter.'

Mr Blackton raised his eyebrows slightly.

'I rather fail to see,' he remarked, 'how I can hope to succeed where you have failed. You appear to have exhausted every possible argument.'

And now Sir Raymond was beginning to look visibly agitated. Unscrupulous businessman though he was, the thing he had to say stuck in his throat. It seemed so cold-blooded, so horrible – especially in that room looking on to the sparkling lake with the peaceful, snow-tipped mountains opposite.

'It was Baron Vanderton,' he stammered, 'who mentioned the Comte de Guy to me. He said that in a certain matter connected, I believe, with one of the big European banking firms, the Comte de Guy had been called in. And that as a result – er – a rather troublesome international financier had – er – disappeared.'

He paused abruptly as he saw Blackton's face. It was hard and merciless, and the grey-blue eyes seemed to be boring into his brain.

'Am I to understand, Sir Raymond,' he remarked, 'that you are trying to threaten me into helping you?'

He seemed to be carved out of stone, save for the fingers of his left hand, which played a ceaseless tattoo on his knee.

'Good heavens! no, Mr Blackton,' cried the other. 'Nothing of the sort, believe me. I merely mentioned the Baron to show you how we got on your trail. He told us that you were the only man in the world who would be able to help us, and then only if you were convinced the matter was sufficiently big.

'I trust that now you have heard what we have to say you will consider – like Mr Freyder – that the matter is sufficiently big to warrant your attention. You must, Mr Blackton; you really must.' He leaned forward in his excitement. 'Think of it: millions and millions of money depending on the caprice of an old fool, who is really far more interested in his wretched albumen food. Why – it's intolerable.'

For a while there was silence, broken at length by Blackton.

'And so,' he remarked calmly, 'if I understand you aright, Sir Raymond, your proposal is that I should interest myself in the – shall we say – removal of Professor Goodman? Or, not to mince words, in his death.'

Sir Raymond shivered, and into Blackton's eyes there stole a faint contempt.

'Precisely, Mr Blackton,' he muttered. 'Precisely. In such a way of course that no shadow of suspicion can rest on us, or on – or on – anyone.'

Mr Blackton rose: the interview was over.

'I will let you know my decision after lunch,' he remarked. 'Shall we drink coffee together here at two o'clock? I expect my daughter will be in by then.'

He opened the door and bowed them out; then he returned to the table and picked up the bottle of champagne. It was empty, as was the plate of sandwiches. He looked at his own unused glass, and with a faint shrug of his shoulders he crossed to his dispatch-case and opened it. But when the girl came in he was making a couple of entries in his book.

The first was under the heading 'Blantyre' and consisted of a line drawn through the word 'Vice'; the second was under the heading

'Leibhaus,' and consisted of the one word 'Glutton' written in red. He was thorough in his ways.

'You heard?' he said, as he replaced the book.

'Every word,' she answered, lighting a cigarette. 'What do you propose to do?'

'There is only one possible thing to do,' he remarked. 'Don't you realise, my dear, that had I heard of this discovery I should have been compelled to interfere, even if they had not asked me to. In my position I could not allow a diamond slump; as you know, we have quite a few ourselves. But there is no reason why they shouldn't pay me for it . . . ' He smiled gently. 'I shall cross to England by the Orient express tonight.'

'But surely,' cried the girl, 'over such a simple matter you needn't go yourself.'

He smiled even more gently, and slipped his arm round her shoulders.

'Do you remember what we were talking about this morning?' he said. 'The big coup? Don't you see that even if this is not quite it, it will fill in the time?'

She looked a little puzzled.

'I'm damned if I do,' she cried tersely. 'You can't ask 'em more than half a million.'

'Funnily enough, that is the exact figure I intended to ask them,' he replied. 'But you've missed the point, my love – and I'm surprised at you. Everything that Blantyre said this morning was correct with regard to the impossibility of letting such a discovery become known to the world at large.

'I have no intention of letting it become known; but I have still less intention of letting it be lost. That would be an act of almost suicidal folly. Spread abroad, the knowledge would wreck everything; retained by one individual, it places that individual in a position of supreme power. And needless to say, I propose to be that individual.'

He was staring thoughtfully over the lake, and suddenly she seized his left hand.

'Ted – stop it.'

For a moment he looked at her in surprise; then he laughed.

'Was I doing it again?' he asked. 'It's a good thing you spotted that trick of mine, my dear. If there ever is a next time with Drummond' – his eyes blazed suddenly – 'if there ever is – well, we will see. Just at the moment, however, let us concentrate on Professor Goodman.

'A telling picture that – wasn't it? Can't you see the old man, blinking behind his spectacles, absorbed in calculations on proteins for infants, with a ring of men around him not one of whom but would have murdered him then and there if he had dared!'

'But I still don't see how this is going to be anything out of the ordinary,' persisted the girl.

'My dear, I'm afraid that the balmy air of the Lake of Geneva has had a bad effect on you.' Mr Blackton looked at her in genuine surprise. 'I confess that I haven't worked out the details yet, but one point is quite obvious. Before Professor Goodman departs this life he is going to make several hundred diamonds for me, though it would never do to let the two anxious gentlemen downstairs know it. They might say that I wasn't earning my half-million.

'Those diamonds I shall unload with care and discretion during the years to come, so as not to cause a slump in prices. So it really boils down to the fact that the Metropolitan Diamond Syndicate will be paying me half a million for the express purpose of putting some five or ten million pounds' worth of stones in my pocket. My dear! it's a gift; it's one of those things which make strong men consult a doctor for fear they may be imagining things.'

The girl laughed.

'Where do I come in?'

'At the moment I'm not sure. So much will depend on circumstances. At any rate, for the present you had better stop on here, and I will send for you when things are a little more advanced.'

A waiter knocked and began to lay the table for lunch; and when at two o'clock the coffee and liqueurs arrived, closely followed by his two visitors, Mr Blackton was in a genial mood. An excellent bottle of Marcobrunner followed by a glass of his own particular old brandy had mellowed him to such an extent that he very nearly produced the bottle for them, but sanity prevailed.

It was true that they were going to pay him half a million for swindling them soundly, but there were only three bottles of that brandy left in the world.

The two men looked curiously at the girl as Blackton introduced them – Baron Vanderton had told them about the beauty of this so-called daughter who was his constant and invariable companion. Only she, so he had affirmed, knew what the man who now called himself Blackton really looked like when shorn of his innumerable disguises into which he fitted himself so marvellously.

But there were more important matters at stake than that, and Sir

Raymond Blantyre's hand shook a little as he helped himself to a cigarette from the box on the table.

'Well, Mr Blackton,' he said as the door closed behind the waiter. 'Have you decided?'

'I have,' returned the other calmly. 'Professor Goodman's discovery will not be made public. He will not speak or give a demonstration at the Royal Society.'

With a vast sigh of relief Sir Raymond sank into a chair.

'And your – er – fee?'

'Half a million pounds. Two hundred and fifty thousand paid by cheque made out to Self – now; the remainder when you receive indisputable proof that I have carried out the job.'

It was significant that Sir Raymond made no attempt to haggle. Without a word he drew his cheque-book from his pocket, and going over to the writing-table he filled in the required amount.

'I would be glad if it was not presented for two or three days,' he remarked, 'as it is drawn on my private account, and I shall have to put in funds to meet it on my return to England.'

Mr Blackton bowed.

'You return tonight?' he asked.

'By the Orient Express. And you?'

Mr Blackton shrugged his shoulders.

'The view here is delightful,' he murmured.

And with that the representatives of the Metropolitan Diamond Syndicate had to rest content for the time – until, in fact, the train was approaching the Swiss frontier. They had just finished their dinner, their zest for which, though considerably greater than on the previous night in view of the success of their mission, had been greatly impaired by the manners of an elderly German sitting at the next table.

He was a bent and withered old man with a long hook nose and white hair, who, in the intervals of querulously swearing at the attendant, deposited his dinner on his waistcoat.

At length he rose, and having pressed ten centimes into the out-raged hand of the head waiter, he stood for a moment by their table, swaying with the motion of the train. And suddenly he bent down and spoke to Sir Raymond.

'Two or three days, I think you said, Sir Raymond.'

With a dry chuckle he was gone, tottering and lurching down the carriage, leaving the President of the Metropolitan Diamond Syndicate gasping audibly.

Chapter 2

*In which Professor Goodman realises that there
are more things in life than chemistry*

When Brenda Goodman, in a moment of mental aberration, consented to marry Algy Longworth, she little guessed the result. From being just an ordinary, partially wanting specimen he became a raving imbecile. Presumably she must have thought it was natural as she showed no signs of terror, at any rate in public, but it was otherwise with his friends.

Men who had been wont to forgather with him to consume the matutinal cocktail now fled with shouts of alarm whenever he hove in sight. Only the baser members of that celebrated society, the main object of which is to cultivate the muscles of the left arm when consuming liquid refreshment, clung to him in his fall from grace. They found that his mental fog was so opaque that he habitually forgot the only rule and raised his glass to his lips with his right hand.

And since that immediately necessitated a further round at his expense, they gave great glory to Allah for such an eminently satisfactory state of affairs. And when it is further added that he was actually discovered by Peter Darrell reading the poems of Ella Wheeler Wilcox on the morning of the Derby, it will be readily conceded that matters looked black.

That the state of affairs was only temporary was, of course, recognised; but while it lasted it became necessary for him to leave the councils of men. A fellow who wants to trot back to the club-house from the ninth green in the middle of a four-ball foursome to blow his fiancée a kiss through the telephone is a truly hideous spectacle.

And so the sudden action of Hugh Drummond, one fine morning in June, is quite understandable. He had been standing by the window of his room staring into the street, and playing Beaver to himself, when with a wild yell he darted to the bell. He pealed it several times; then he rushed to the door and shouted: 'Denny! Where the devil are you, Denny?'

'Here, sir.'

His trusted body-servant and erstwhile batman appeared from the nether regions of the house, and regarded his master in some surprise.

'The door, Denny – the front door. Go and bolt and bar it; put the chain up; turn all the latchkeys. Don't stand there blinking, you fool. Mr Longworth is tacking up the street, and I know he's coming here. Blow at him through the letter-box, and tell him to go away. I will not have him about the house at this hour of the morning. Tell him I'm in bed with housemaid's knee. Not *the* housemaid's knee, you ass: it's a malady, not a dissecting-room in a hospital.'

With a sigh of relief he watched Denny bar the door; then he returned to his own room and sank into an armchair.

'Heavens!' he muttered, 'what an escape! Poor old Algy!'

He sighed again profoundly, and then, feeling in need of support, he rose and crossed to a cask of beer which adorned one corner of the room. And he was just preparing to enjoy the fruits of his labours, when the door opened and Denny came in.

'He won't go, sir – says he must see you, before you dine with his young lady tonight.'

'Great Scott! Denny – isn't that enough?' said Drummond wildly. 'Not that one minds dining with her, but it's watching him that is so painful. Have you inspected him this morning?'

'I kept the door on the chain, sir, and glanced at him. He seems to me to be a little worried.'

Drummond crossed to the window and looked out. Standing on the pavement outside was the unfortunate Algy, who waved his stick wildly as soon as he saw him.

'Your man Denny has gone mad,' he cried. 'He kept the door on the chain and gibbered like a monkey. I want to see you.'

'I know you do, Algy: I saw you coming up Brook Street. And it was I who told Denny to bar the door. Have you come to talk to me about love?'

'No, old man, I swear I haven't,' said Algy earnestly. 'I won't mention the word, I promise you. And it's really most frightfully important.'

'All right,' said Drummond cautiously. 'Denny shall let you in; but at the first word of poetry – out you go through the window.'

He nodded to his servant, and a moment or two later Algy Long-worth came into the room. The newcomer was arrayed in a faultless morning coat, and Hugh Drummond eyed him noncommittally. He certainly looked a little worried, though his immaculate topper and white spats seemed to show that he was bearing up with credit.

'Going to Ranelagh, old bird,' said Algy. 'Hence the bathing suit. Lunching first, don't you know, and all that – so I thought I'd drop in this morning to make sure of catching you. You and Phyllis are dining, aren't you, this evening?'

'We are,' said Hugh.

'Well, the most awful thing has happened, old boy. My prospective father-in-law to be – Brenda's dear old male parent – has gone mad. He's touched; he's wanting; he's up the pole.'

He lit a cigarette impressively, and Drummond stared at him.

'What's the matter with the old thing?' he demanded. 'I met him outside his club yesterday and he didn't seem to me to be any worse than usual.'

'My dear boy, I didn't know anything about it till last night,' cried Algy. 'He sprang it on us at dinner, and I tell you I nearly swooned. I tried to register mirth, but I failed, Hugh – I failed. I shudder to think what my face must have looked like.' He was pacing up and down the room in his agitation.

'You know, don't you, old man, that he ain't what you'd call rolling in boodle. I mean, with the best will in the world you couldn't call him a financial noise. And though, of course, it doesn't matter to me what Brenda has – if we can't manage, I shall have to do a job of work or something – yet, I feel sort of responsible for the old parent.

'And when he goes and makes a prize ass of himself, it struck me that I ought to sit up and take notice. I thought it over all last night, and decided to come and tell you this morning, so that we could all have a go at him tonight.'

'What has he done?' demanded Hugh with some interest.

'You know he's got a laboratory,' continued Algy, 'where he goes and plays games. It's a perfect factory of extraordinary smells, but the old dear seems to enjoy himself. He'll probably try his new albumenised chicken food on you tonight, but that's a detail. To get to the point – have you ever noticed that big diamond Brenda wears as a brooch?'

'Yes, I have. Phyllis was speaking about it the other night.'

'You know he made it,' said Algy quietly, and Hugh stared at him. 'It is still supposed to be a secret: it was to be kept dark till the next meeting of the Royal Society – but after what has happened I decided to tell you. About a fortnight ago a peculiar-looking bloke called Sir Raymond Blantyre came and dined.

'He's made his money in diamonds, and he was on to that diamond like a terrier on to a rat. And when he heard old Goodman had made it, I thought he was going to expire from a rush of blood to the head. He'd just offered Brenda a cheque for ten thousand for it, when he was told it had cost a little over a fiver to make.

'As I say, he turned a deep magenta and dropped his eyeglass in the sauce *tartare*. That was the first spasm; the next we heard last night. Apparently the old man agreed to give a demonstration to this bloke and some of his pals, and the result of the show was – great heavens! when I think of it, my brain comes out in a rash – the result, Hugh, was that they offered him a quarter of a million pounds to suppress his discovery.

'Two hundred and fifty thousand acidulated tablets – and he refused. One supreme glorious burst on fifty thousand of the best, and an income from the remaining two hundred for the rest of his life. We worked it out after dinner, my boy – Brenda and I. Two hundred thousand at five per cent. We couldn't quite make out what it would come to, but whatever it is he has cast it from him. And then you wonder at my anguish.'

With a hollow groan Algy helped himself to beer and sank into a chair.

'Look here, Algy,' said Hugh, after a pause, 'you aren't playing the fool, are you? You literally mean that Professor Goodman has discovered a method by which diamonds can be made artificially?'

'Exactly; that is what I literally mean. And I further literally mean that he has turned down an offer of a quarter of a million thick 'uns to keep dark about it. And what I want you and Phyllis to do this evening . . . '

'Dry up,' interrupted Hugh. He was staring out of the window, and his usual look of inane good temper had completely vanished. He was thinking deeply, and after a few moments he swung round on the disconsolate Algy.

'This is a pretty serious affair, Algy,' he remarked.

'You bet your life it is,' agreed his friend. 'Quarter . . . '

'Cut it out about the boodle. That's bad, I admit – but it's not that I'm thinking of.'

'I don't know what the deuce else there is to think about, Just because he wants to spout out his footling discovery to a bunch of old geysers at the Royal Society . . . '

Hugh regarded him dispassionately.

'I have often wondered why they ever let you leave school,' he remarked. 'Your brain is even smaller than the ten-bob helping of caviare they gave me at the Majestic last night. You don't really think it's a footling discovery, do you? You don't really think people run about the streets of London pressing two hundred and fifty thousand pounds on comparative strangers for fun?'

'Oh! I suppose the old bean has spotted a winner right enough,' conceded Algy grudgingly.

'Now, look here,' said Drummond quietly. 'I don't profess to know anything about diamonds or the diamond market. But if what you say is correct – if the Professor can manufacture a stone worth at current prices ten thousand pounds for a fiver – you don't require to know much about markets to see that diamonds will be on a par with bananas as soon as the process is known.

'Further, you don't require to know much about markets to see that such a state of affairs would be deuced unpopular with quite a lot of people. If you've got all your money in diamonds and wake up one bright morning to read in the paper that a diamond weighing half a ton has just been manufactured for three and sixpence, it's going to make the breakfast kipper look a bit jaded.'

'I know all that, old boy,' said Algy a bit wearily. 'But they're just additional reasons for the old ass taking the money. Then everyone would be happy. Only he's so confoundedly pigheaded. Why, when I sort of suggested after dinner last night during the nut-mastication period that he could do a lot with the boodle – help him no end with his albumenised chicken seed, and all that – he got quite stuffy.'

' "My dear boy," he said, "you don't understand. To offer a scientist money to suppress a discovery of possibly far-reaching importance is not only an insult to him, but it is also an insult to science. I would not suppress this for a million pounds."

'Then he forgot to pass the port, and the meeting broke up in disorder.'

Hugh nodded thoughtfully.

'I'm afraid they will suppress it for him,' he said gravely.

Algy stared at him.

'How do you mean, suppress it for him?' he demanded at length.

'I haven't an idea,' answered Drummond. 'Not even the beginning of one. But people have fallen in front of tube trains before now; people have been accidentally killed by a passing car – '

'But, good heavens, man,' cried Algy dazedly, 'you don't mean to say that you think someone will murder the poor old fruit.'

Drummond shrugged his shoulders. 'Your future father-in-law

has it in his power to completely ruin large numbers of extremely wealthy men. Apparently with the best will in the world he proposes to do so. He has butted into a huge vested interest, and, as far as I can make out from what you've told me, he quite fails to realise the fact.' He lit a cigarette thoughtfully.

'But what the devil are we to do, Hugh?' said Algy, now very serious himself. 'I tell you it will be impossible to make him accept that money. He's as docile as a sheep in some ways, but once he does stick his toes in over anything, a bag of gunpowder won't shift him.'

'Well, if he really is determined to go through with it, it may be necessary to get him away and keep a watchful eye on him till he gets it off his chest at the Royal Society. That's to say if he'll come. Once it's out – it's out, and the reasons for doing away with him will largely have disappeared.'

'Yes; but I say, old man – murder!' Algy harked back to his original point. 'Don't you think that's a bit over the odds?'

Hugh laughed grimly. 'You've lived the quiet life too long, Algy. There are stakes at issue now which strike me as being a deuced sight bigger than anything we played for with dear old Carl Peterson. Bigger at any rate financially.'

An almost dreamy look came into his eyes, and he sighed deeply. 'Those were the days, Algy – those were the days. I'm afraid we shall never have them again. Still – if what I'm afraid of is correct, we might have a bit of fun, looking after the old man. Dull, of course, but better than nothing.' He sighed again, and helped himself to more beer.

'Now you trot off, and lunch with Brenda. Don't tell her anything about what I've said. I shall make one or two discreet inquiries this afternoon, and this evening I will bring the brain to bear over the fish and chips.'

'Right, old man,' cried Algy, rising with alacrity. 'Deuced good of you and all that. I'd hate the dear old bird to take it in the neck. His port is pretty putrid, I admit – but still – '

He waved his stick cheerfully, and a few seconds later Hugh watched him walking at speed down Brook Street. And long after Algy had disappeared he was still standing at the window staring into the street.

Hugh Drummond laid no claim to being brilliant. His brain, as he frequently remarked, was of the 'also-ran' variety. But he was undoubtedly the possessor of a very shrewd common sense, which generally enabled him to arrive at the same result as a far more brilliant man and, incidentally, by a much more direct route.

He was, it may be said, engaged in trying to arrive at what he called in military parlance, the general idea. He did it by a process of reasoning which at any rate had the merit of being easy to follow.

First, Algy, though a fool and partially demented, was not a liar. Therefore the story he had just listened to was true.

Second, the bloke who had turned a deep magenta, though possibly a liar, was certainly not a fool. If he had made his money in diamonds, he couldn't be, at any rate, as far as diamonds were concerned.

Third, since he had offered Professor Goodman no less than a quarter of a million to suppress the secret, he had evidently got a jolt in a tender spot.

Fourth, here was the great query: just how tender was that spot?

He had spoken glibly about markets to Algy, but he realised only too well that he actually knew nothing about diamonds. He recalled dimly that they were found in mines near Kimberley; beyond that his knowledge of the subject was limited to the diamond engagement ring he had bought for Phyllis. And having reached that point in his deliberations, he decided that before coming to any definite conclusion it would be well to take some expert advice on the matter.

He rose and pressed the bell: Toby Sinclair was the very man. In the intervals of backing losers, that bright particular star graced a city firm with his presence – a firm which dealt in precious stones on the wholesale side.

'Denny,' he said, as his servant came in, 'ring up Mr Sinclair in the city and ask him to come and lunch with me at the club today. Tell him it's very important.'

And five minutes later he was strolling in the same direction as that taken by Algy, but at a more leisurely rate. His face was still contorted with thought; he periodically stopped abruptly and glared into space. How big was the jolt? Was it really big enough to justify the fears he had expressed to Algy, or was he exaggerating things in his own mind? He ruminated on the point over a cocktail in the Regency; he was still ruminating as he passed into St. James's Square on the way to his club.

To reach it he had to pass the doors of Professor Goodman's club, and as he walked slowly on the cause of all his profound mental activity – the worthy Professor himself – hove into sight. Drummond paused: it seemed to him that something had happened. For the Professor was muttering wildly to himself, while periodically he shook his fist in the air.

'Morning, Professor,' he remarked affably. 'Been stung by a bee, or what?'

The Professor stopped abruptly and stared at him.

'It's you, Drummond, is it,' he said. 'I've just received a most scandalous letter – perfectly scandalous. A threat, sir – an anonymous threat. Read it.'

He held out a common-looking envelope which he handed to Drummond. But that worthy only took it mechanically; his eyes – shrewd and thoughtful – were looking over the Professor's shoulder. A man had come hurriedly round King Street, only to pause with equal suddenness and stare into an area below.

'I suppose, Professor,' he remarked quietly, still holding the letter in his hand, 'that you know you're being followed.'

'I know I'm being what?' barked the Professor. 'Who is following me?'

Drummond slightly raised his voice.

'If you turn round you will see an unpleasant specimen of humanity gazing into the basement of that house. I allude to the bird with the large ears, who is beginning to go a little red about the tonsils.'

With a snarl the man swung on his heel and came towards them. 'Are you talking about me, damn you?' he said, addressing Drummond.

'I am,' remarked Drummond dispassionately. 'Mushrooms growing well down below there?' The man looked somewhat disconcerted. 'Now, who told you to follow Professor Goodman?'

'I don't know what you're talking about,' said the man surlily.

'Dear me!' remarked Drummond mildly. 'I should have thought the question was sufficiently clear even to a person of your limited intelligence. However, if it will save you any bother, the Professor is lunching with me at my club – that one over there with the warrior in uniform outside the door – and will probably be leaving about three. So you can either run away and play marbles till then, or you can stay here and watch the door.'

He put his hand through the Professor's arm, and gently propelled him towards the club, leaving the man scratching his head foolishly.

'But, my dear fellow,' mildly protested the Professor, 'this is very kind of you. I'd no idea I was lunching with you.'

'No more had I,' answered Hugh genially. 'But I think it's a jolly sort of idea, don't you? We'll get a table in the window and watch our friend earning his pay outside, while we toy with a bit of elusive Stilton.'

'But how do you know the man was following me, Drummond?' said the Professor excitedly. 'And if he was, don't you think I ought to tell the police?'

Gently but firmly Drummond piloted him up the steps of his club. 'I have an unerring instinct in such matters, Professor,' he remarked. 'And he was very bad at it – very bad. Now we will lower a Martini apiece, and I will read this threatening missive of yours.'

The Professor sank into a chair and blinked at Hugh through his spectacles. He had had a trying morning, and there was something very reassuring about this large and imperturbable young man who he knew was his future son-in-law's greatest friend. And as he watched him reading the typewritten piece of paper, strange stories which he had heard of some of Drummond's feats in the past came back to him. They had been told him by Algy and one or two by Brenda, but he had not paid any great attention to them at the time. They were not very much in his line, but now he felt distinctly comforted as he recalled them. To have his life threatened was a new experience for the worthy Professor, and one not at all to his liking. It had interfered considerably with his work that morning, and produced a lack of mental concentration which he found most disturbing.

The letter was short and to the point.

Unless you accept the two hundred and fifty thousand pounds recently offered to you, you will be killed.

The Professor leaned forward as Drummond laid the sheet of paper on the table.

'I must explain, Drummond,' he began, but the other interrupted him.

'No need to, Professor. Algy came round to see me this morning, and he told me about your discovery.'

He again picked up the paper and glanced at it.

'You have no idea, I suppose, who can have sent this?'

'None,' said the Professor. 'It is utterly inconceivable that Sir Raymond Blantyre should have stooped to such a thing. He, as Algy probably told you, is the man who originally offered me this sum to suppress my discovery. But I refuse to believe for a moment that he would ever have been guilty of such a vulgar threat.'

Drummond regarded him thoughtfully.

'Look here, Professor,' he said at length, 'it seems to me that you are getting into pretty deep water. How deep I don't quite know. I tell you frankly I can't understand this letter. If, as you say, it is merely a vulgar threat, it is a very stupid and dangerous thing to put on paper. If, on the other hand, it is more than a threat – if it is an actual statement of fact – it is even more incredibly stupid and dangerous.'

'A statement of fact,' gasped the Professor. 'That I shall be killed if I don't suppress my discovery!'

He was blinking rapidly behind his spectacles, and Drummond smiled.

'A statement of fact as far as the writer of this epistle is concerned,' he remarked. 'No more than that, Professor, I hope. In fact we must take steps to ensure that it is no more than that. But this letter, on top of your being followed, shows that you're in the public eye, so to speak.'

'But I don't understand, Drummond,' said the Professor feebly.

'No more do I,' answered Hugh. 'However, that will make it all the jollier when we do. And it is possible that we may get a bit nearer the mark today at lunch. A fellow of the name of Sinclair is joining us – he's a pal of Algy's too – and he's in a big diamond merchant's office down in the city. He's a knowledgeable sort of bird, and we'll pump him. I don't want you to say a word as to your discovery – not a word. We'll just put the case to him as an academic one, and we'll get his actual opinion on it.'

'But I know their opinion about it already,' said the Professor peevishly. 'And I tell you that nothing is going to stop me announcing my discovery in ten days' time before the Royal Society.'

Drummond drained his cocktail.

'That's the spirit, Professor,' he cried cheerily. 'But for all that we may just as well see where we are. Here is Sinclair now: don't forget – not a word.'

He rose as Toby Sinclair came up.

'Morning, Toby. Do you know, Professor Goodman? He is the misguided man who is allowing Algy to marry into his family.'

'Morning, sir,' said Sinclair with a grin. 'Well, old man – a cocktail, a rapid lunch, and I must buzz back. I tell you things are moving with some celerity in our line, at present. And as the bright boy of the firm, my time is fully occupied.'

He lit a cigarette and Hugh laughed.

'With a *Lunar Guide* and the *Sportsman*. Quite so, old boy – I know.'

'No, really, Hugh,' said Toby seriously, 'the old office has not been the usual rest-cure just lately. Strong men have rushed in and out and conferred behind locked doors, and the strain has been enormous. Made one quite dizzy to see them. However, it's been better the last two or three days, ever since old Blantyre came back from Switzerland.'

Drummond adroitly kicked the Professor's leg.

'And who is old Blantyre?' he remarked carelessly, 'and why does he go to Switzerland?'

'Sir Raymond Blantyre is the head of the syndicate to which our firm belongs, though why he went to Switzerland I haven't any idea. All I can tell you is that he went out there looking like nothing on earth, and came back two days later smiling all over his face.'

'Speaks well for the Swiss air,' said Hugh dryly. 'However, let's go and inspect the menu.'

He led the way towards the dining-room, and his expression was thoughtful. If, as he had been given to understand, Sir Raymond Blantyre was now facing immediate ruin, it was a little difficult to see why he should be smiling all over his face. It showed, at any rate, a resignation to Fate which was beyond all praise. Unless, of course, something had happened in Switzerland . . . But, then, what could have happened? Had he gone over there to dispose of his stock before the crash came? He felt very vague as to whether it would be possible to do such a thing. Anyway, it mightn't be a bad idea to find out where he had been to in Switzerland. Just for future reference; in case anything happened.

'Yes – a deuced good advertisement for the Swiss air, old man,' he repeated, after they had sat down. 'Where did he go to?'

'You seem very interested in his wanderings,' said Toby with a laugh. 'As a matter of fact, I believe he went to Montreux, but since he was only there a day, the air can't have had much to do with it.'

Hugh glanced through the window; the man who had been following the Professor was still loitering about the corner of the square. And the frown on his face grew more pronounced. It beat him – the whole thing beat him completely. Especially the threatening letter . . .

'You're marvellously merry and bright this morning, old boy.' Toby broke off his desultory conversation with the Professor and regarded Hugh with the eye of an expert. 'I don't think you can have been mother's angel-boy last night. Anyway, what is this important thing you wanted to see me about?'

With an effort his host pulled himself together.

'I was thinking, Toby,' he remarked, 'and you know what an awful effect that always has on my system. Look here, diamonds are a pretty good thing, aren't they, as a birthday present for Phyllis?'

Toby stared at him.

'I think they're a very good thing,' he remarked. 'Why?'

'No danger of them losing their value?'

'None whatever. The output is far too carefully controlled for that.'

'But supposing someone came along and manufactured them cheap?'

Toby laughed. 'You needn't worry about that, old man. It has been done in the past and the results cost more than the genuine article.'

'Yes, but supposing it did happen,' persisted Hugh. 'Supposing a process was discovered by which big stones – really big stones – could be made for a mere song – what then?'

Toby shrugged his shoulders.

'The discoverer of the process could ask practically what he liked to suppress it,' he answered.

'And if it wasn't suppressed – if it became known?'

'If it became widely known it would mean absolute ruin to thousands of people. You may take it from me, old man, that in the first place such a process is never likely to be found, and, if it ever was, that it would never come out.'

Hugh flashed a warning glace at the Professor.

'There are hundreds of millions of pounds involved directly or indirectly in the diamond business,' went on Toby. 'So I think you can safely invest in a few if you want to, for Phyllis.'

He glanced at his watch and rose.

'Look here, I must be toddling. Another conference on this afternoon. If you want any advice on choosing them, old boy, I'm always in the office from eleven-thirty to twelve.'

Hugh watched him cross the room; then he turned thoughtfully to the Professor.

'So that's that,' he said. 'Now, what about a bit of Stilton and a glass of light port while we consider the matter.'

'But I knew all that before, and it has no influence on me, Drummond. None at all.' The Professor was snorting angrily. 'I will not be intimidated into the suppression of a far-reaching chemical discovery by any considerations whatever.'

'Quite so,' murmured Hugh soothingly. 'I thought you'd probably feel like that about it. But it's really Algy I'm thinking about. As you know, he's a dear old pal of mine; his wedding is fixed in about a month, and since that is the only thing that can possibly restore him to sanity, we none of us want it postponed.'

'Why should it be postponed?' cried the Professor.

'Mourning in the bride's family,' said Drummond. 'The betting is a tenner to a dried banana that you expire within a week. Have some more cheese?'

'Don't be absurd, Drummond. If you think you are going to persuade me – you're wrong. I suppose that foolish boy Algy has been trying to enlist you on his side.'

'Now look here, Professor,' said Hugh quietly. 'Will you listen to me for a moment or two? It is perfectly true that Algy did suggest to me this morning that I should try to persuade you to accept the offer Sir Raymond made you. But I am not going to do anything of the sort. I may say that even this morning it struck me that far more serious things were at stake than your acceptance or refusal of two hundred and fifty thousand pounds. I am not at all certain in my own mind that if you accepted the money you would even then be safe. You are the owner of far too dangerous a piece of knowledge. However, as I say, it struck me this morning that things were serious – now I'm sure of it, after what Toby said. He evidently knows nothing about it, so the big men are keeping it dark. More-over, the biggest man of all, according to him, seems perfectly pleased with life at the present moment. Yet it's not due to anything that you have done; you haven't told them that you will accept their offer. Then why is he pleased? Most people wouldn't be full of happiness when they were facing immediate ruin. Professor, you may take it from me – and I am not an alarmist by any means – that the jolly old situation has just about as many unpleasant snags sticking out of it as any that I have ever contemplated. And I've contemplated quite a few in my life.'

He sat back in his chair and drained his port, and the Professor, impressed in spite of himself, looked at him in perplexity.

'Then what do you suggest that I should do, Drummond?' he said. 'These sort of things are not at all in my line.'

Hugh smiled. 'No, I suppose they're not. Well, I'll tell you what I would suggest your doing. If you are determined to go through with this, I would first of all take that threatening letter to Scotland Yard. Ask for Sir Bryan Johnstone, tell him you're a pal of mine, call him Tum-tum, and he'll eat out of your hand. If you can't see him, round up Inspector McIver, and tell him – well, as much or as little as you like. Of course, it's a little difficult. You can hardly accuse Sir Raymond Blantyre of having sent it. But still it seems the only thing to do. Then I propose that you and your wife and your daughter should all come away, and Algy too, and stop with my wife and me, for a little house-warming party at a new place I've just bought down in Sussex. I'll rope in a few of Algy's pals and mine to stop there too and we'll keep an eye on you, until the meeting of the Royal Society.'

'It's very good of you, Drummond,' said the Professor uncertainly. 'I hardly know what to say. This letter, for instance.'

He fumbled in his pocket and drew out a bunch of papers, which he turned over in his hands.

'To think that there's all this trouble over that,' he continued, holding out two or three sheets of notepaper. 'Whereas nobody worries over these notes on albumenised proteins.'

Hugh stared at him in amazement.

'You don't mean to say that those are the notes of your diamond process,' he gasped. 'Carried loose in your pocket.'

'Yes – why not?' said the Professor mildly. 'I always carry everything loose like that, otherwise I lose them. And I should be helpless without these.'

'Good heavens! man, you must be mad,' cried Hugh. 'Do you mean to say that you couldn't carry on without those notes? And yet you carry them like that!'

'I should have to do it all over again, and it would take me months to arrive at the right proportions once more.' He was peering through the scattered sheets. 'Even now I believe I've lost one – oh! no, here it is. You see, it doesn't make much odds, because no-one could understand them except me.'

Hugh looked at him speechlessly for a while: then he passed his hand dazedly across his forehead.

'My dear Professor,' he murmured, 'you astound me. You positively stagger my brain. The only remaining thing which I feel certain you have not omitted to do is to ensure that Sir Raymond and his friends know that you carry your notes about in your pocket like that. You haven't forgotten to tell them that, have you?'

'Well, as a matter of fact, Drummond,' said the Professor apologetically, 'I'm afraid they must guess that I do. You see, when I did my demonstration before them I pulled my notes out of my pocket just as I did a moment or two ago. I suppose it is foolish of me, but until now I haven't thought any more about the matter. It all comes as such a complete shock, that I really don't know where I am. What do you think I'd better do with them?'

'Deposit them at your bank the very instant you leave here,' said Hugh. 'I will come round with you, and – well, what's the matter now, Professor?'

The Professor had risen to his feet, blinking rapidly in his agitation.

'Good heavens! Drummond, I had completely forgotten. All this bother put it quite out of my head. Professor Scheidstrun – a celebrated German geologist – made an appointment with me at my house for this afternoon. He has brought several specimens of carboniferous quartz which he claims will completely refute a paper I have just written on the subject of crystalline deposits. I must get home at once, or I shall be late.'

'Not quite so fast, Professor,' said Hugh with a smile. 'I don't know anything about carboniferous quartz, but there's one thing I do know. Not for one minute longer do you walk about the streets of London with those notes in your pocket. Come into the smoking-room and we'll seal them up in an envelope. Then I'll take charge of them, at any rate until tonight when I'm coming to dine at your house. And after dinner we can discuss matters further.'

He led the agitated savant into the smoking-room, and stood over him while he placed various well-thumbed pieces of paper into an envelope. Then he sealed the envelope and placed it in his pocket, and with a sigh of relief the Professor rose. But Drummond had not finished yet.

'What about that letter and the police?' he said, holding out a detaining hand.

'My dear boy, I really haven't got the time now,' cried the old man. 'You've no idea of the importance of this interview this afternoon. Why' – he laid his hand impressively on Drummond's arm – 'if what Scheidstrun claims is correct, it may cause a complete revolution in our present ideas on the atomic theory. Think of that, my friend, think of that.'

Drummond suppressed a strong desire to laugh.

'I'm thinking, Professor,' he murmured gravely. 'And even though he does all that you say and more, I still think that you ought to go to the police with that letter.'

'Tomorrow, Drummond – I will.' Like a rabbit between a line of beaters he was dodging towards the door, with Drummond after him.

'You shall come with me yourself tomorrow, I promise you. And we'll discuss matters again tonight. But the atomic theory – think of it.'

With a gasp of relief he dashed into a waiting taxi, leaving Hugh partially stupefied on the pavement.

'Tell him where to go, there's a good fellow,' cried the Professor. 'And if you could possibly lend me half-a-crown, I'd be very grateful. I've left all my money at home, as usual.'

Drummond smiled and produced the necessary coin. Then a sudden thought struck him.

'I suppose you know this German bloke, don't you?'

'Yes, yes,' cried the Professor testily. 'Of course I know him. I met him ten years ago in Geneva. For goodness' sake, my boy, tell the man to drive on.'

Drummond watched the taxi swing round into King Street; then somewhat thoughtfully he went back into his club. Discussing the atomic theory with a German Professor he knew, seemed a comparatively safe form of amusement, calculated, in fact, to keep him out of mischief, but he still felt vaguely uneasy. The man who had followed him seemed to have disappeared; St. James's Square was warm and peaceful. From one point of view, it was hard to believe that any real danger could threaten the old man: he felt he could understand his surprised incredulity. As he had said, such things were out of his line. But as Drummond might have answered, they were not out of his, and no man living knew better that strange things took place daily in London, things which would tax the credulity of the most hardened reader of sensational fiction. And the one great dominant point which stuck out, and refused to be argued away, was this. What was the life of one old man compared to the total loss of hundreds of millions of pounds, when viewed from the standpoint of the losers? He glanced at the envelope he still held in his hand, and slipped it into his pocket. Then he went into the telephone box and rang up his chauffeur to bring round his car.

He felt he wanted some fresh air to clear his brain, and all the way down to Ranelagh the same question kept clouding it. Why had that threatening letter been sent? If the intention was indeed to kill Professor Goodman, why, in the name of all that was marvellous, be so incredibly foolish as not only to warn him, but also to put that warning on paper? And if it was merely a bluff, again why put it on paper when the writer must have known that in all probability it would be taken straight to the police? Or was the whole thing just a silly jest, and was he, personally, making an appalling fool of himself by taking it seriously?

But the last alternative was untenable. The offer of a quarter of a million pounds was no jest; not even the most spritely humorist could possibly consider it one. And so he found himself back at the beginning again, and he was still there when he saw Algy and his girl having tea.

He deposited himself in a vacant chair beside Brenda, and having assured her of his continued devotion, he consumed the last sugar-cake.

'The male parent has just lunched with me,' he remarked genially. 'And as a result I am in the throes of brain-fever. He borrowed half-a-crown, and went off in Admiral Ferguson's hat, as I subsequently discovered. I left the worthy seaman running round in small circles snorting like a bull. You should discourage your father, Brenda, from keeping pieces of paper written on with copying ink in the lining of his head-piece. Old Ferguson, who put the hat on by mistake, has a chemistry lecture written all over his forehead.'

'Did you persuade Dad not to be such an unmitigated idiot, Hugh?' asked the girl eagerly.

'I regret to state that I did not,' answered Hugh. 'In fact, honesty compels me to admit, Brenda, that I no longer wonder at his allowing you to marry Algy. He may be the outside size in chemistry, but beyond that he wants lessons. Will you believe it, that at lunch today he suddenly removed from his pocket the notes of this bally discovery of his? He has been carrying them loose along with some peppermint bull's-eyes and bits of string!'

'Oh! but he always carries everything like that,' laughed the girl. 'What is the old dear doing now?'

'He rushed away to commune with a German professor on carboniferous quartz and the atomic theory. Seemed immensely excited about it, so I suppose it means something. But to come to rather more important matters, I have invited him and Mrs Goodman and you to come down and spend a few days with us in Sussex. We might even include Algy.'

'What's the notion, old man?' murmured Algy. 'Think he's more likely to see reason if we take him bird-nesting.'

'It's no good, Hugh,' said Brenda decisively. 'Besides, he wouldn't go.'

She turned to speak to a passing acquaintance, and Hugh bent over to Algy.

'He's damn well got to go,' he said in a low voice. 'He was being followed this morning when I met him outside the club, and he's had a letter threatening his life.'

'The devil he has!' muttered Algy.

'If we can make him see reason and suppress his discovery, so much the better,' went on Hugh. 'Personally, I think he's a pigheaded old ass, and that it undoubtedly ought to be suppressed, but there's no good telling him that at present. But if he won't, it's up to us anyway to look after him, because he's utterly incapable of doing it himself. Not a word to Brenda, mind, about the letter or his being followed. He's all right for this afternoon, and we'll fix things up this evening definitely.'

And since the afternoon was all that an afternoon should be, and no-one may ask for more than that and Ranelagh combined, it was just as well for the peace of mind of all concerned that no power of second sight enabled them to see what was happening in Professor Goodman's laboratory, where he was discussing carboniferous quartz and the atomic theory with a celebrated German geologist.

Chapter 3

*In which strange things happen in Professor
Goodman's laboratory*

At just about the same time that Algy Longworth was dancing on
the pavement in Brook Street and demanding admission to Drummond's house, Sir Raymond Blantyre was holding a conference with
the other members of the Metropolitan Diamond Syndicate. The
proceedings were taking place behind locked doors, and had an onlooker been present he would have noticed that there was a general air
of tension in the room. For good or ill the die was cast, and try as
they would the seven eminently respectable city magnates assembled
round the table could not rid themselves of the thought that they had
deliberately hired a man to commit murder for them. Not that they
admitted it even to themselves – at any rate, not as crudely as that.
Mr Blackton's services had been secured to arrange matters for them
with Professor Goodman – to negotiate for the suppression of his
discovery. How he did it was, of course, his concern, and nothing
whatever to do with them. Even Sir Raymond himself tried to lull his
conscience by reflecting that perhaps the drastic measures alluded to
in his interview at the Palace Hotel would not be necessary. And
if they were – well, only a weak man wavered and hesitated once he
was definitely committed to a particular line of action. After all, the
responsibility was not his alone; he had merely been the spokesman
for the combined opinions of the Syndicate reached after mature
reflection. And if Professor Goodman was so pigheaded and obstinate, he must take the consequences. There were others to be considered – all those who would be ruined.

Just at first after his return from Switzerland such specious arguments had served their purpose; but during the last two days they
seemed to have lost some of their soothing power. He had found
himself feverishly snatching at every fresh edition of the evening
paper to see if anything had happened. He had even found himself
wondering whether it was too late to stop things even now, but he

didn't know where the man who called himself Blackton could be found. From the moment when he had realised in the restaurant wagon that the old German professor and Mr Edward Blackton were one and the same person, he had not set eyes on him again. There had been no trace of him in Paris, and no trace on the boat. He had no idea where he was; he did not even know if he was in London.

His cheque had been presented in Paris, so he had discovered from his bank only that morning. And that was the last trace of the man he had interviewed at Montreux.

'I suppose there's no chance of this man double-crossing us.' A dark sallow man was speaking and Sir Raymond glanced up quickly. 'When all is said and done he has had a quarter of a million, and we're hardly in a position to claim it back.'

'That was one of the risks we discussed before we approached him,' said Sir Raymond. 'Of course there's a chance; that is obvious on the face of it. My impression is, however, that he will not, apart from the fact that another quarter of a million is at stake. He struck me, in a very marked degree, as being a man of his word.'

There was silence for a while, a silence which was broken suddenly by a mild-looking middle-aged man.

'It's driving me mad, this – absolutely mad,' he cried, mopping the sweat from his forehead. 'I fell asleep last night after dinner, and I tell you, I woke up shouting. Dreams – the most awful dreams, with that poor old devil stabbed in the back and looking at me with great staring eyes. He was calling me a murderer, and I couldn't stand it any more. I know I agreed to it originally, but I can't go on with it – I can't.'

There was a moment's tense silence, and then Sir Raymond spoke.

'I don't understand you, Mr Lewisham,' he said coldly. 'It is quite impossible for you to back out of it now, without betraying us all. And anyway, I would be greatly obliged if you would lower your voice.'

With a great effort Mr Lewisham controlled himself.

'Can't we think of some other method, gentlemen?' he said. 'This seems so horribly cold-blooded.'

'What other possible method is there?' snarled Leibhaus. 'We've tried everything.'

The telephone in front of Sir Raymond rang suddenly and everyone started. It showed the condition of their nerves, and for an appreciable time the President tried to steady his hand before he picked up the receiver. And when after a few seconds he laid it down again he moistened his lips with his tongue before he trusted himself to speak.

'Mr Blackton will be with us in a quarter of an hour, gentlemen,' he remarked, and his voice was shaking a little. 'I have no idea what he wants, and I am somewhat surprised at his coming here, since I laid especial stress on the fact that we were not to be implicated in any way with his – er – visit to England.'

He gave a brief order through a speaking-tube; then he rose and walked wearily up and down the room. The prospect of meeting Blackton again was not at all to his taste, though his dislike was not in any way due to a belated access of better feeling and remorse. It was due to the fact that Blackton as a man thoroughly frightened him, and as he paced up and down glancing at his watch every half-minute or so he felt exactly as he had felt in years long gone by when he had been told that the headmaster was awaiting him in his study. It was useless to try to bolster up his courage by reflecting that Blackton was, after all, merely the paid servant of his syndicate. He knew perfectly well that Blackton was nothing of the sort, any more than a doctor can be regarded as the paid servant of his patient. The situation in brief was that Mr Blackton for a suitable fee had agreed to assist them professionally, and any other interpretation of the position would be exceedingly unwise.

He started nervously as he heard the sound of voices on the stairs, but it was with a very creditable imitation of being at ease that he went forward as the door opened and Mr Blackton was shown in. He had discarded the disguise he had worn in the train, and appeared as he had done at their first meeting in Switzerland. He nodded briefly to Sir Raymond; then coming a few steps into the room, he favoured each man present with a penetrating stare. Then he laid his gloves on the table and sat down.

'On receiving your message, I was not quite sure in which guise we were to expect you,' said Sir Raymond, breaking the silence.

'The absurd passport regulations,' said Mr Blackton suavely, 'necessitate one's altering one's appearance at times. However, to get to business. You are doubtless wondering at my action in coming round to see you. I may say that I had no intention of so doing until this morning. I have been in London for two days, and my plans were complete – when a sudden and most unexpected hitch occurred.'

He paused and fixed his eyes on Sir Raymond.

'How many people are there who know of this discovery of Professor Goodman's?'

'His family and our syndicate,' answered the President.

'No-one else in the diamond world except the gentlemen in this room knows anything about it?'

'No-one,' cried Sir Raymond. 'We have most sedulously kept it dark. I feel sure I may speak for my friends.'

He glanced round the room and there was a murmur of assent.

'Then I am forced to the conclusion,' continued Mr Blackton, 'that the writer of an anonymous letter received by the Professor this morning is amongst us at the moment.'

His eyes travelled slowly round the faces of his audience, to stop and fasten on Mr Lewisham, whose tell-tale start had given him away.

'I am informed,' went on Mr Blackton – 'and my informant, who was cleaning the windows amongst other things at the Professor's house, is a very reliable man – I am informed, I say, that this morning the Professor received a letter stating that unless he accepted the money you had offered him, he would be killed. Now, who can have been so incredibly foolish as to send that letter?'

Mr Lewisham fidgeted in his chair, until at length everyone in the room, noting the direction of Blackton's glance, was staring at him.

'Was it you, Lewisham?' snapped Leibhaus. Mr Lewisham swallowed once or twice; then he stood up, clutching the edge of the table.

'Yes – it was,' he said defiantly. 'It seemed to me that we ought to neglect no possible chance of getting him to agree to our terms. I typed it, and posted it myself last night.'

Smothered curses came from all sides; only Mr Blackton seemed unmoved.

'You have realised, of course, what will happen should Professor Goodman take that letter to the police,' he remarked quietly. 'The fact that it was your syndicate that offered him the money will make it a little unpleasant for you all.'

But behind the impassive mask of his face Mr Blackton's brain was busy. The thing – the only thing – with which even the most perfectly laid schemes were unable to cope had happened here. And that thing was having a chicken-hearted confederate, or, worse still, one who became suddenly smitten with conscience. Against such a person nothing could be done. He introduced an incalculable factor into any situation with which even a master-craftsman was unable to deal.

Not that he had the remotest intention of giving up the scheme – that was not Mr Blackton's way at all. A further priceless idea had come to him since the interview at Montreux, which would render this coup even more wonderful than he had at first thought. Not only would he amass a large store of diamonds himself, but after that had been done and any further necessity for the continued existence of Professor Goodman had ceased, he would still have the secret of the process in his possession. And this secret he proposed to sell for a price considerably in excess of the two hundred and fifty thousand pounds offered to its original discoverer. After which he would decide what to do with the copy he had kept.

In fact Mr Blackton fully realised that, in the hands of a master-expert like himself, the affair presented promises of such boundless wealth that at times it almost staggered even him. And now, at the last moment, this new factor had been introduced into the situation which might possibly jeopardise his whole carefully-thought-out scheme. And the problem was to turn it to the best advantage.

'I don't care,' Mr Lewisham was saying obstinately to the little group of men who were standing round him. 'I don't care if that letter of mine does stop it all. I'd sooner be ruined than go through the rest of my life feeling that I was a murderer.'

'Mr Lewisham seems a little excited,' said Blackton suavely. 'Who, may I ask, has said anything about murder?'

They fell silent, and stared at him.

'When Sir Raymond Blantyre came to me in Montreux, his request to me was to prevent the publication of this secret process of Professor Goodman's. I stated that I would. I stated that the Professor would not give his lecture before the Royal Society. I believe that the word "murder" occurred in the conversation' – he gave a somewhat pained smile – 'but do you really imagine, gentlemen, that my methods are as crude as that?'

He carefully lit a cigar, while his audience waited breathlessly for him to continue.

'Since I find, however, that this gentleman has been so incredibly foolish and has lost his head so pitiably, I regret to state that in all probability I shall have to wash my hands of the entire business.'

Cries of anger and dismay greeted this announcement, though the anger was entirely directed against the author of the letter.

'But, really – ' stammered Mr Lewisham, plucking nervously at his collar.

'You have behaved like an hysterical schoolgirl, sir,' snapped Blackton. 'You have jeopardised the success of my entire plan, and apart altogether from the sending of this letter you have shown yourself to be totally unfitted to be mixed up in an affair of this description. Even if the police did treat it as a stupid hoax – even, in fact, if we were able to prevent the letter being shown to the police at all – you are still totally unfit to be trusted. You would probably proclaim your sin through a megaphone in Trafalgar Square, taking special care to incriminate all these other gentlemen. And so I think, since you have decided to act on your own initiative in this way, you had better undertake the affair yourself.'

He rose as if to leave, only to be, at once, surrounded by the other members of the syndicate, imploring him to reconsider his decision. And at length Mr Blackton allowed himself to be persuaded to resume his chair. His indifference was sublime; to all outward intents and purposes he was utterly bored with the whole proceedings.

'Really, Mr Blackton – I implore of you, we all implore of you, not to desert us like this.' Sir Raymond's eyeglass was dreadfully agitated. 'Can nothing be done to counteract Mr Lewisham's inconceivable stupidity?'

Mr Blackton affected to consider the point. Not for him to say that he had already decided exactly what was going to be done; not for him to say that the sole object of his recent remarks had been to produce the exact atmosphere that now existed – an atmosphere of combined antagonism to Lewisham, and an uncomfortable feeling on the part of that unfortunate man that he really had made a fool of himself. And certainly not for him to say what he had decided was a meet and fit punishment for Mr Lewisham.

He shrugged his shoulders indifferently.

'Since Mr Lewisham has caused all this trouble,' he said carelessly, 'it is up to Mr Lewisham to endeavour to rectify it.'

A chorus of approval greeted the remark, and Lewisham leaned forward a little in his chair.

'I suggest therefore that this afternoon he should pay a visit to Professor Goodman, and find out what has happened to his letter. Should it have been handed over to the police, he must endeavour to convince the Professor that it was a stupid practical joke on his part, and persuade the Professor to ring up Scotland Yard and explain things. There will be no need for Mr Lewisham's name to be mentioned, if he handles the Professor tactfully. On the other hand, if the note has not been handed over to the police, Mr Lewisham must endeavour to regain possession of it. And according to Mr Lewisham's report, I will decide whether I can continue in this matter or not.'

'That is tantamount to an avowal that the letter was sent by a member of our syndicate,' said Sir Raymond doubtfully. 'You don't think that perhaps it might be advisable to say that he had just discovered that some clerk had played a foolish practical joke.'

'The point seems really immaterial,' returned Mr Blackton indifferently. 'But if Mr Lewisham prefers to say that, by all means let him do so.'

'You will go, of course, Lewisham,' said Sir Raymond, and the other nodded.

'I will go and see what I can do,' he answered. 'And I can take it from you, Mr Blackton, that there will be no question of – of – killing Professor Goodman?'

For a brief moment there came into Mr Blackton's grey-blue eyes a faint gleam as if some delicate inward jest was tickling his sense of humour.

'You may take it from me,' he answered gravely, 'that nothing so unpleasant is likely to happen to Professor Goodman.'

Mr Lewisham gave a sigh of relief.

'What time shall I go?' he asked.

Mr Blackton paused in the act of drawing on his gloves.

'The Professor, I am told,' he remarked, 'has an appointment at three o'clock this afternoon. I would suggest therefore that you should call about two-thirty.'

'And where shall I communicate with you?'

'You can leave that entirely to me, Mr Lewisham,' murmured the other, with an almost benevolent smile. 'I will take all the necessary steps to get in touch with you. Well, gentlemen' – he turned to the others – 'that is all, I think, for the present. I will report further in due course. By the way, Mr Lewisham, I wouldn't give your name to the servant, if I were you.'

With a slight bow he opened the door and passed down the stairs. He paused as he reached the crowded pavement and spoke two words to a man who was staring into a shop-window; then he deliberated whether he should call a taxi, and decided to walk. And as he strolled along – slowly, so as not to destroy the aroma of his cigar, his reflections were eminently satisfactory. If the police had not received the note, he was in clover; if they had, a little care would be necessary. But in either case the one detail which had previously been, if not lacking, at any rate not entirely satisfactory, was now supplied. It gratified his intellect; it pleased his artistic sense. Just as the sudden and unexpected acquisition of a tube of some rare pigment completes a painter's joy, so this one detail completed Mr Blackton's. That it consisted of a singularly cold-blooded murder is beside the point: all artists are a little peculiar. And if fool men write fool letters, they must expect to suffer small annoyances of that sort. After all, reflected Mr Blackton with commendable thoughtfulness, the world would endure Mr Lewisham's departure with almost callous fortitude.

He realised suddenly that he had reached his destination, and throwing away his cigar he produced his latchkey and entered the house. It was situated in one of those quiet squares which lie, like placid backwaters, off the seething rivers of London. And its chief point of interest lay in the fact that it formed the invariable *pied-à-terre* of Mr Blackton when visiting England in whatever character he might at the moment be assuming. It appeared in the telephone-book as belonging to William Anderson, a gentleman who spent much of his time abroad. And it was to William Anderson that the Inland Revenue were wont yearly to address their friendly reminders as to the duties of British citizens. Ever mindful of those duties, Mr Anderson had declared his income at nineteen hundred and fifty pounds per annum, and had opened a special account at a branch bank to cope with the situation. He drew the line at admitting his liability to super-tax; but after mature reflection he decided that his method of life rendered it advisable to state that his income was unearned.

He placed his gloves and stick on the table in the hall, and slowly ascended the stairs. A few little details still required polishing up in connection with his afternoon's work, and he was still deep in thought as he entered a room on the first landing.

A man was seated at a desk, who rose as he entered – a man whose face was well-nigh as inscrutable as his chief's. He was Mr Blackton's confidential secretary, Freyder, a man with a salary of ten thousand a year plus commission. He was as completely unscrupulous as his employer, but he lacked the wonderful organising brain of the other. Given a certain specific job to do, he could carry it out to perfection; and for making arrangements in detail he was unrivalled. Which made him an ideal staff officer – a fact which the other had very soon recognised. And because Edward Blackton, like all big men, was not such a fool as to underpay an almost invaluable subordinate, he took care that Freyder's salary should be such that he would have no temptation to go. For it he demanded implicit obedience, no mistakes, and at times twenty-four hours' work out of twenty-four.

'What did you find out, Chief?' he asked curiously.

'It was sent by one of them, as I suspected,' answered Blackton, seating himself at his desk. 'A stupid little man called Lewisham, who appears to have lost his head completely. However, on my assuring him that I had no intention of killing the excellent Goodman, he agreed to go round this afternoon and talk to the Professor about the matter.'

'Go round this afternoon?' echoed Freyder, surprised. 'What do you want him there for, this afternoon?'

Blackton smiled gently.

'He happens to be about the same size as our worthy Professor,' he murmured, 'so it struck me he would come in very handy. By the way, make a note, will you, to obtain a specimen of his writing and signature. Find out if he's married, and, if so, draft a letter to his wife from him saying that he's gone to Valparaiso for the good of his health. Have it sent out to Number 13, and posted there.'

He stared thoughtfully out of the window, and Freyder waited for any further instructions.

'Anything more to be settled about the house?'

'Everything fixed, Chief; it's ready to move straight into this afternoon.'

The telephone bell rang on Freyder's table.

'Good,' he remarked a few moments later, replacing the receiver. 'Number 10 reports that he followed Goodman to St. James's Square; that he is now having lunch at the Junior Sports Club, and that he has not communicated verbally with the police.'

'And since the letter was in his pocket when he left his house, presumably he has not communicated in writing. He must be a frivolous old man, Freyder, to lunch at such a club. Anyway, I trust he will have a substantial meal, as I'm afraid his constitution may be tried a little during the next few hours.'

He glanced at his watch. 'The box and the men are ready?'

'Loaded up on the car at the garage.'

'Excellent. Then I think a pint of champagne and a little caviare – and after that I must get to work. And we will drink a silent toast to the worthy Mr Lewisham for his kindly forethought in being much the same size as the Professor, and wish him *bon voyage* to – what did I say? – oh yes, Valparaiso.'

'I don't quite get Mr Lewisham's part in this show, Chief,' remarked Freyder.

Mr Blackton positively chuckled.

'No more does he, my good Freyder – no more does he. But I can positively assure you of one thing – he is not going to Valparaiso.'

And he was still chuckling ten minutes later when he rose and passed into an inner room at the back. It was a strange place – this inner sanctum of Mr Edward Blackton. The window was extra large, and was made of frosted glass which effectually prevented any inquisitive neighbour from seeing in. Around the walls full-length mirrors set at different angles enabled him to see himself from every position – an indispensable adjunct to making up on the scale he found necessary. A huge cupboard filled one wall of the room, a cupboard crammed with clothes and boots of all sorts and descriptions; whilst on a shelf at the top, each in its separate pigeon-hole, were half a dozen wigs. But the real interest of the room lay in the small dressing-table which he proceeded to unlock. A score of little bottles containing strange liquids, brushes, instruments, lumps of a peculiar putty-like substance, were all most carefully arranged on shelves. And it was the contents of this table far more than any change of clothes that enabled him to make such extraordinary alterations in his personal appearance. Literally, when seated at that table, he could build himself a new face. He could change the colour of his eyes, he could alter the shape of his nose. A judicious stain could turn his normally perfect teeth into unpleasant, badly kept ones; whilst on the subject of dyes for hair and eyebrows he could have written a text-book.

It was three-quarters of an hour before the door opened again and the snuffling old German of the restaurant wagon emerged. Professor Scheidstrun was ready to discuss the atomic theory with Professor Goodman with special reference to carboniferous quartz. Outside the door a motor-car was standing with a large box on board containing his specimens; while by its side were two men who were to lift the box off the car, and in due course lift it on again. And the only other thing of interest which might be mentioned in passing is that if Frau Scheidstrun had happened to see him getting into the car wheezing peevishly in German, she would undoubtedly have wondered what on earth her husband was doing in London – so perfect was the make-up. But since that excellent woman was chasing the elusive mark in Dresden at the moment, there was but little fear of such an unfortunate contretemps.

It was at twenty past two that he arrived at Professor Goodman's house. As he stepped out of the car a man walked quietly towards him, a man who stopped to watch the big box being carefully lowered to the ground. He stopped just long enough to say, 'No-one in the house except the servants', and then he strolled on.

With great care the two men carried the box up the steps and, considering the contents were lumps of carboniferous quartz, the intense respect with which they handled it might have struck an onlooker as strange. But the parlourmaid, grown used through long experience to the sudden appearance of strange individuals at odd hours, merely led the way to the laboratory, and having remarked that the Professor might be back at three, or possibly not till six, according to whether he had remembered the appointment or not, she returned to her interrupted dinner.

'Get the box undone,' said Blackton curtly. 'But don't take anything out.'

The two men set to work, while he walked quickly round every corner of the room. Of necessity a little had had to be left to chance, and though he was perfectly capable of dealing with the unexpected when it arrived, he preferred to have things as far as possible cut and dried beforehand. And at the moment what he wanted to find was a cupboard large enough to accommodate a man. Not that it was absolutely necessary, but it would assist matters, especially in the event of the Professor bringing a friend with him. That was a possibility always present in his mind, and one which he had been unable to guard against without running the risk of raising the Professor's suspicions.

He found what he wanted in a corner – a big recess under the working bench screened by a curtain, and used for old retorts and test-tubes. It was ideal for his purpose, and with a nod of satisfaction he went over to the door. All was well – the key was on the inside; and with one final glance round the room the exponent of the new atomic theory sat down to wait.

Before him lay the riskiest thing he had ever done in all his risky career, but had anyone felt his pulse he would have found it normal. And it wasn't of the next hour that Mr Blackton was thinking so much, but of the future, when his coup had succeeded. That it would succeed was certain; no thought of failure was ever allowed to enter his mind.

Five minutes passed – ten – when the ringing of the front-door bell brought him back from dreams of the future. This must be Mr Lewisham, and with his arrival came the time for action. Blackton listened intently – would he be shown into the laboratory or into some other room? If the latter, it would necessitate getting him in on some pretext; but steps coming along the passage settled that point. Once more the door was flung open by the parlourmaid; once more she returned to better things in the servants' hall.

Lewisham paused, and glanced a little doubtfully at the old German in his dirty black clothes. Some chemical friend of the Professor's evidently; possibly it would be better to wait somewhere else. He half turned to the door as if to go out again, when suddenly he felt two hands like bars of steel around his throat. For a moment or two he struggled impotently; then he grew still. And after a while the limp body slipped to the floor and lay still.

'Underneath that bench with him,' snapped Blackton. 'Quick.'

He had opened the door an inch or two and was peering out. The passage was empty, and faint sounds were coming up the stairs from the servants' quarters.

'Stay where you are,' he said to the two men. 'I shall be back in a minute.'

He walked along the passage towards the front door, which he opened. Then he deliberately rang the bell, and stood for a few seconds peering out. And it was not until he heard the footsteps of the parlourmaid that he shut the door again with a bang, and advanced towards her, gesticulating wildly.

'Where is your master?' he cried. 'I must to my business get; I cannot here the whole day wait. That other gentleman – he does not wait. He go. I too – I follow him.' He glanced at the girl. 'Speak, woman.' He waved his arms at her, and she retreated in alarm. 'I will take my specimens, and I will go – like him.'

Still muttering horribly under his breath, he walked up and down the hall, while the parlourmaid endeavoured to soothe him.

'I expect the Professor will be back soon, sir,' she murmured.

'Soon,' he raved. 'I who have come from Germany him to see, and then I wait. He write to me: I write to him – and then I come with my specimens. And you say soon. *Nein* – I go. I go like that other.'

It was at that moment that the front door opened and Professor Goodman entered.

'A thousand apologies, my dear Professor,' he cried, hurrying forward. 'I fear I am late – very late. I hope I have not kept you waiting.'

He led the other towards the laboratory, and the parlourmaid made hurried tracks for safety.

'No wonder that there other one wouldn't wait,' she remarked to the cook. 'He's a holy terror – that German. Dirty old beast, with egg all over his coat, waving his arms at me. Old Goodman is a pretty fair freak, but he does wash. I 'opes he enjoys himself.'

Which was a kindly thought on the part of the parlourmaid. And the fact that it was expressed at the exact moment that Professor Goodman went fully under the influence of an anaesthetic may be regarded as a strange coincidence. For there was no time wasted in the laboratory that afternoon. Much had to be done, and hardly had the door closed behind the master of the house when he found himself seized and pinioned. One feeble cry was all he gave; then a pad soaked in ether was pressed over his nose and mouth, and the subsequent proceedings ceased to interest him.

Very interesting proceedings they were too – that went on behind the locked door. Bursts of German loquacity with intervals of a voice astonishingly like Professor Goodman's would have convinced any inquisitive person listening outside the door that the two savants were in full blast. Not that anyone was likely to listen, but Blackton was not a man who took chances. And it takes time to change completely two men's clothes when one is dead and the other is unconscious. One hour it was, to be exact, before the body of Mr Lewisham dressed in Professor Goodman's clothes, even down to his boots, was propped up in a chair against the bench, with various bottles and retorts in front of him. One hour and a quarter it was before a number of small packets had been taken from the big wooden case and stacked carefully on the bench so that they touched the dead man's chest. One hour and a half it was before the still unconscious Professor Goodman was placed as comfortably as possible – Mr Blackton had no wish to run any chances with *his* health – in the big wooden case, and nailed up. And during the whole of that hour and a half the discussion on carboniferous quartz had continued with unabated zest.

At last, however, everything was finished, and Blackton took from his pocket a little instrument which he handled very gingerly. He first of all wound it up rather as a Bee clock is wound, and when it was ticking gently he placed it in the centre of the heap of small packets. Then he unlocked the door.

'Put the box on the car,' he ordered. 'Then pick up Freyder, and go straight to the house.'

Once again the two men staggered down the passage with their load, while Blackton glanced at his watch. Just a quarter of an hour to get through – before things happened. He closed the door again, and once more his guttural voice was raised in wordy argument for the benefit of any possible audience. And in the intervals when he ceased only the faint ticking broke the silence. Everything had gone without a hitch, but there were still one or two small things to be done. And the first of these showed the amazing attention to detail which characterised all his actions. He took the key from the door and put it on the desk; a master-key of his own would enable him to lock the door from outside, whereas the presence of the key in the room would make it appear that it had been locked from within. And it was precisely that appearance which he wished given.

Once more he looked at his watch: ten minutes to go. Nervous work, that waiting; and even he began to feel the strain. But he daren't go too soon; he daren't leave too long a space of time between the moment he left the house and the moment when the ticking would cease. And he didn't want to go too late, because the last thing he desired was to be on, or even too near, the premises when the ticking ceased. Moreover, there was always the possibility of a flaw in the mechanism. Morelli was a wonderful craftsman, and he had staked his reputation on it taking exactly a quarter of an hour. But even so – it was nervous work, waiting.

Precisely five minutes later – and they were the longest five minutes Mr Blackton had ever spent in his life – he pressed the bell. His guttural voice was raised in expostulation and argument as the parlourmaid knocked at the door. Still talking, he opened it himself, and over his shoulder the girl got a fleeting glance of Professor Goodman engaged in one of his experiments to the exclusion of all else.

'My hat, girl,' cried the German, waving his arms at her. She went to get it, and from behind her back came the noise of a key turning. 'Ach! my friend – no-one will disturb you,' rumbled the German. 'No need to your door lock.' Mechanically he took the hat the parlourmaid was holding out, while he still continued muttering to himself. 'What is the good? One mistake, and you will experiment no more. You and your house will go sky-high.'

Still waving his arms, he shambled off down the street, and the girl stood watching him. And it was just after he had turned the corner and she was expressing her opinion of his appearance to the cook, who was taking a breather in the area below, that she was hurled forward flat on her face. A terrific explosion shook the house; windows broke; plaster and pictures came crashing down. And if it was bad in the front, it was immeasurably worse at the back. A huge hole had been blown in the outside wall of what had once been the Professor's laboratory; the three inside walls had collapsed, and the ceiling had descended, bringing with it a bed, two wardrobes, and a washing-stand complete.

In fact there was every justification for the remark of the parlour-maid as she picked herself up.

'Lumme! What's the old fool done now? I suppose he'll ring the bell in a minute and ask me to sweep up the mess.'

An hour later Edward Blackton was seated at his desk in the house in the quiet square. Up to date his scheme had gone even more smoothly than he had expected, though there were still one or two small points to be attended to before he could retire from observation and devote himself to the Professor. There was bound to be an inquest, for instance, and he was far too big a man not to realise that it might be fatal for him not to attend it. Moreover, there was the little matter of that extra quarter of a million from the Metropolitan Syndicate.

But just at the moment Lewisham was occupying his mind. A note in cipher on the table in front of him from Freyder informed him that Henry Lewisham was a married man, and that he lived in South Kensington. And since the appearance of the late Mr Lewisham betokened his immense respectability, there was but little doubt that Mrs Lewisham would become seriously alarmed if her spouse absented himself for the night from the conjugal roof without any word to her.

Blackton pressed a bell on his desk twice, and a moment or two later the man who had been staring into the shop-window, and to whom he had spoken as he left the Metropolitan Syndicate earlier in the day, entered.

'That man you followed this morning – Lewisham: did he go home to lunch?'

'No, Chief. He had a chop in a restaurant in the city.'

'Did he use the telephone as far as you know?'

'I know he didn't use it. He was never out of my sight from the time he came into the street till he went into Goodman's house.'

Blackton nodded as if satisfied.

'Go to Euston, and send a wire to this address. "Called North on urgent business, Henry." Then go to the Plough Inn in Liverpool, and wait there for further orders. Draw fifty pounds for expenses' – he scribbled his signature on a slip of paper – 'and it is possible you will have to start for South America at a moment's notice. If you do, it will be necessary for you to make yourself up to an approximate resemblance of Henry Lewisham, and your berth will be taken in his name.'

'I didn't have a chance of studying his face very closely, Chief,' said the man doubtfully.

Blackton waved his hand in dismissal.

'Approximate resemblance, I said,' he remarked curtly. 'You will receive full instructions later. Go.'

He lay back in his chair as the door closed behind the man, and pulled thoughtfully at his cigar. A merciful fact, he reflected, that it is not a police offence for a man to run away from his wife. In fact if Mrs Lewisham was anything like Mr Lewisham, it could hardly be regarded as an offence at all by any disinterested person, but rather as an example of praiseworthy discretion. A letter in due course from Liverpool stating his intention; a resemblance sufficient to cope with a wireless description in case the lady should think of such a thing – and finally complete disappearance in South America. An easy place to disappear in, South America, reflected Mr Blackton; a fact he had made use of on several occasions, when the circumstances had been similar. And it was better for sorrowing relatives to picture their dear one alive and wandering through primeval forests in Brazil, or dallying with nitrates in Chile, than for them to realise that the dear one was very, very dead. It was also better for Mr Blackton.

He dismissed the unfortunate Lewisham from his mind, and produced from his pocket the papers he had taken from Professor Goodman before removing his clothes. The first thing he saw, to his intense satisfaction, was the warning typewritten letter, and holding a match under one corner of it he reduced it to ashes and finally to powder. Two or three private letters he treated similarly, and then he came to a dozen loose sheets of paper covered with incomprehensible scrawling hieroglyphics. These he carefully pinned together and put in his pocket, reflecting yet again on the extreme goodness of fate. And then for the second time he took from the drawer where he had placed it for safety the metal retort which apparently played such an important part in the process. He had found it standing on the electric furnace in the Professor's laboratory, and now he examined it curiously. It was about double the size of an ordinary tumbler, and was made of some dull opaque substance which resembled dirty pewter. And as Blackton looked at it and realised the incredible fortune that was soon to come to him out of that uninteresting-looking pot, his hand shook uncontrollably.

He replaced it in the drawer, as someone knocked on the door. It was the man who had spoken to him outside the Professor's house.

'They're all humming like a hive of bees, Chief,' he remarked. 'The police are in, and they've cleared away the débris. I managed to get in and have a look – and it's all right.'

'You're certain of that,' said Blackton quietly.

'There's nothing left of him, Chief, except a boot in one corner.'

Blackton rubbed his hands together.

'Excellent – excellent! You've done very well: cash this downstairs.'

Again he scribbled his initials on a slip of paper, and pushing it across the table dismissed the man. Assuredly luck was in, though as a general rule Blackton refused to allow the existence of such a thing. The big man, according to him, made allowance for every possible contingency; only the fool ever trusted to luck if anything of importance was at stake. And in this case he only regarded his luck as being in because he would be able, as far as he could see, to carry on with the simplest of the three schemes which he had worked out to meet different emergencies should they arise. And though he had employed enough explosive to shatter ten men, no man knew better than he did how capricious it was in its action.

Now he was only waiting for one thing more – a telephone call from Freyder. He glanced at his watch: hardly time as yet, perhaps, for him to have reached his destination and to get through to London. In fact it was twenty minutes before the bell rang at his side.

'Everything gone without a hitch.'

Freyder was speaking, and with a gentle sigh of pure joy for work well and truly done Mr Blackton laid down the receiver.

Half an hour later he was strolling along Pall Mall towards his club. A newsboy passed him shouting ''Orrible explosion in 'Ampstead', and he paused to buy a copy. It had occurred to him that it is always a good thing to have something to read in the cooler rooms of a Turkish bath. And he never went into the hotter ones; there were peculiarities about Mr Edward Blackton's face which rendered great heat a trifle ill-advised.

Chapter 4

In which Mr William Robinson arrives at his country seat

The report made to Mr Blackton on the condition of the Professor's house was certainly justified. It looked just as if a heavy aeroplane bomb had registered a direct hit on the back of the premises. And the damage was continually increasing. The whole fabric of the house had been undermined, and it was only at considerable personal risk that the police pursued their investigations. Frequent crashes followed by clouds of choking dust betokened that more and more of the house was collapsing, and at length the Inspector in charge gave the order to cease work for the time. Half a dozen policemen kept the curious crowd away, whilst the Inspector retired to the front of the house, which had escaped the damage, to await the arrival of some member of the Professor's family. It was not a task that he relished, but it was his duty to make what inquiries he could.

In his own mind he felt pretty clear as to what had happened. The parlourmaid, who appeared a sensible sort of girl, had told him all she knew – particularly mentioning the German Professor's remark as he left the house. And it seemed quite obvious that Professor Goodman had been experimenting with some form of violent explosive, and that, regrettable to say, the explosive had not behaved itself. When the débris had ceased to fall and it was safe to resume work, it might be possible to discover something more definite, but up to date the sole thing they had found of interest was one of the unfortunate savant's boots. And since that had already been identified by the parlourmaid as belonging to Professor Goodman, all the identification necessary for the inquest was there. Which from a professional point of view was just as well, since there was nothing else left to identify.

An open Rolls-Royce drew up outside, and the Inspector went to the window and looked out. From the driver's seat there descended a large young man, who said something to the two other occupants of the car, and then came rapidly up the short drive to the front door, where the Inspector met him.

'What on earth has happened?' he demanded.

'May I ask if you are a relative of Professor Goodman's?' said the Inspector.

'No; I'm not. My name is Drummond, Captain Drummond. But if you'll cast your eye on the back of my car you'll see his daughter, Miss Goodman.'

'Well,' said the Inspector gravely, 'I fear that I have some very bad news for Miss Goodman. There has been an accident, Captain Drummond – an appalling accident. The whole of the back of the house has been blown to pieces, and with it, I regret to say, Professor Goodman. There is literally nothing left of the unfortunate gentleman.'

'Good God!' gasped Algy, who had come up in time to hear the last part of the remark. 'Have you caught the swine . . . '

Hugh's hand gripped his arm in warning.

'How did it happen?' he asked quietly. 'Have you any ideas?'

The Inspector shrugged his shoulders.

'There is no doubt whatever as to how it happened,' he answered. 'The whole thing will, of course, be gone into thoroughly at the inquest, but it is all so obvious that there is no need for any secrecy. The unfortunate gentleman was experimenting with some form of high explosive, and he blew himself up and the house as well.'

'I see,' said Drummond thoughtfully. 'Look here, Algy – take Brenda back to my place, and tell the poor kid there. Turn her over to Phyllis.'

'Right you are, Hugh,' said Algy soberly. 'By God!' he exploded again, and once more Drummond's warning hand silenced him.

Without another word he turned and walked away. Brenda, in an agony of suspense, met him at the gateway and her sudden little pitiful cry showed that she had already guessed the truth. But she followed Algy back into the car, and it was not until it had disappeared that Drummond spoke again.

'You have no suspicions of foul play, I suppose?'

The Inspector looked at him quickly.

'Foul play, Captain Drummond? What possible reason could there be for foul play in the case of such a man as Professor Goodman? Oh! no. He was seen by the parlourmaid immersed in an experiment as she was letting some German Professor out – a scientific acquaintance of the unfortunate gentleman. They had been having a discussion all the afternoon, and not five minutes after his visitor left the explosion took place.'

Drummond nodded thoughtfully.

'Deuced agile fellow – the Boche. Did the hundred at precisely the right psychological moment. Would there be any objection, Inspector – as a friend of the family and all that – to my having a look at the scene of the accident? You see, there are only his wife and daughter left – two women alone; and Miss Goodman's fiancé – the man who took her off in the car – not being here, perhaps I might take it on myself to give them what information I can.'

'Certainly, Captain Drummond. But I warn you that there's nothing to see. And you'd better be careful that you don't get a fall of bricks on your head. I'll come with you, if you like.'

The two men walked round to the back of the house. The crowd, which by now had largely increased in size, surged forward expectantly as they disappeared through the shattered wall, and the Inspector gave an order to one of the constables.

'Move them along,' he said. 'There's nothing to be seen.'

'Good heavens!' remarked Drummond, staring round in amazement. 'This is what one used to expect in France. In fact I've slept in many worse. But in Hampstead . . . '

'I found this, sir, on the remains of the table,' said a sergeant, coming up to the Inspector with a key in his hand. 'It belongs to the door.'

The Inspector took the key and tried it himself.

'That confirms what the maid said.' He turned to Drummond. 'The door was locked on the inside. The maid heard him lock it as she showed the German out, which, of course, was a few minutes before the accident took place.'

Drummond frowned thoughtfully and lit a cigarette. That was a complication, and a very unexpected complication. In fact at one blow it completely shattered the idea that was already more than half formed in his mind – an idea which, needless to say, differed somewhat radically from the worthy Inspector's notion of what had happened.

'And what of the Professor himself?' he asked after a moment or two. 'Is the body much damaged?'

'There is nothing left of the body,' said the Inspector gravely. 'At least practically nothing.'

He crossed to the corner of the room by the door, where the damage was least, and removed a cloth which covered some object on the floor.

'This is all we have found at present.'

'Poor old chap,' said Drummond quietly, staring at the boot. There was a patch on it – a rather conspicuous patch which he had noticed at lunch that day.

'It has been identified already by the parlourmaid as the Professor's boot,' said the Inspector, replacing the cloth. 'Not that there is much need for identification in this case. But it is always necessary at the inquest as a matter of form.'

'Of course,' answered Drummond absently, and once more fell to staring round the wrecked room. Three plain-clothes men were carefully turning over heaps of débris, searching for further traces of the dead scientist. But the task seemed hopeless, and after a while he said goodbye to the Inspector and started to walk back to Brook Street.

The whole thing had come with such startling suddenness that he felt shaken. It seemed incredible that the dear, absentminded old man who had lunched with him only that day was dead and blown to pieces. Over and over again in his mind there arose the one dominant question – was it foul play, or was it not? If it wasn't, it was assuredly one of the most fortunate accidents for a good many people that could possibly have taken place. No longer any need to stump up a quarter of a million for the suppression of the Professor's discovery – no longer any need to worry. And suddenly Hugh stopped short in his tracks, and a thoughtful look came into his eyes.

'Great Scott!' he muttered to himself, 'I'd almost forgotten.'

His hand went to his breast-pocket, and a grim smile hovered for a moment or two round his mouth as he strolled on. Professor Goodman might be dead, but his secret wasn't. And if by any chance it had *not* been an accident . . . if by any chance this diamond syndicate had deliberately caused the poor defenceless old man's death, the presence of those papers in his pocket would help matters considerably. They would form an admirable introduction to the gentlemen in question – and he was neither old nor defenceless. In fact there dawned on his mind the possibility that there might be something doing in the near future. And the very thought of such a possibility came with the refreshing balm of a shower on parched ground. It produced in him a feeling of joy comparable only to that with which the hungry young view the advent of indigestible food. It radiated from his face; it enveloped him in a beatific glow. And he was still looking like a man who has spotted a winner at twenty to one as he entered his house.

His wife met him in the hall.

'Hugh, for goodness' sake, compose your face,' she said severely. 'Poor Mrs Goodman is here, and Brenda, and you come in roaring with laughter.'

'Good Lord! I'd forgotten all about 'em,' he murmured, endeavouring to assume a mournful expression. 'Where are they?'

'Upstairs. They're going to stop here tonight. Brenda telephoned through to her mother. Hugh – what an awful thing to have happened.'

'You're right, my dear,' he answered seriously. 'It is awful. The only comfort about it is that it must have been absolutely instantaneous. Where's Algy?'

'He's in your room. He's most frightfully upset, poor old thing, principally on Brenda's account.' She laid her hand on his arm. 'Hugh – he said something to me about it not being any accident. What did he mean?'

'Algy is a talkative ass,' answered her husband quietly. 'Pay no attention to him, and don't under any circumstances even hint at such a thing to Mrs Goodman or Brenda.'

'But you don't mean he killed himself?' said Phyllis in a horrified whisper.

'Good heavens! no,' answered Hugh. 'But there is a possibility, my dear, and more than a possibility that he was murdered. Now – not a word to a soul. The police think it was an accident; let it remain at that for the present.'

'But who on earth would want to murder the dear old man?' gasped his wife.

'The Professor had made a discovery, darling,' said Hugh gravely, 'which threatened to ruin everyone who was concerned in the diamond industry. He had found out a method of making diamonds artificially at a very low cost. To show you how seriously the trade regarded it, he was offered two hundred and fifty thousand pounds to suppress it. That he refused to do. This morning he received a letter threatening his life. This afternoon he died, apparently as the result of a ghastly accident. But – I wonder.'

'Does anybody know all this?' said Phyllis.

'A few very interested people who won't talk about it, and you and Algy and I who won't talk about it either – yet. Later on we might all have a chat on the subject, but just at present there's rather too much of the fog of war about. In fact the only really definite fact that emerges from the gloom, except for the poor old chap's death, is this.'

He held out an envelope in his hand, and his wife looked at it, puzzled.

'That is the discovery which has caused all the trouble,' went on Hugh. 'And the few very interested people I was telling you about don't know that I've got it. And they won't know that I've got it either – yet.'

'So that's why you were looking like that as you came in.'

His wife looked at him accusingly, and Hugh grinned.

'Truly your understanding is great, my angel,' he murmured.

'But how did you get it?' she persisted.

'He gave it to me at lunch today,' said her husband. 'And in the near future it's going to prove very useful – very useful indeed. Why, I almost believe that if I advertised that I'd got it, it would draw old Peterson himself. Seconds out of the ring; third and last round: time.'

'Hugh – you're incorrigible. And don't do that in the hall – someone will see.'

So he kissed her again, and went slowly up the stairs to his own room. Most of the really brilliant ideas in life come in flashes, and he had had many worse than that last. There were times when his soul positively hankered for another little turn-up with Carl Peterson – something with a real bit of zip in it, something to vary his present stagnation. But he fully realised that a gentleman of Peterson's eminence had many other calls on his time, and that he must not be greedy. After all, he'd had two of the brightest and best, and that was more than most people could say. And perhaps there might be something in this present show which would help to keep his hand in. Sir Raymond Blantyre, the bird with the agitated eyeglass, for instance. He didn't sound much class – a bit of a rabbit at the game probably, but still, something might come of him.

He opened the door of his room, and Algy looked up from his chair.

'You don't think it was an accident, do you, Hugh?' he remarked quietly.

'I don't know what to think, old man,' answered Drummond. 'If it was an accident, it was a very remarkable and fortunate one for a good many people. But there is one point which is a little difficult to explain unless it was: Hannah, or Mary, or whatever that sweet woman's name is who used to breathe down one's neck when she handed you things at dinner, saw the old man at work through the open door. She heard him lock the door. Moreover, the key was found in the room – on the floor or somewhere; it was found while I was there. From that moment no-one else entered the room until the explosion. Now, *you* haven't seen the appalling mess that explosion made. There must have been an immense amount of explosive used. The darned place looks as if it had had a direct hit with a big shell. Well, what I'm getting at is that it is quite out of the question that the amount of explosive necessary to produce such a result could have been placed there unknown to old Goodman. And that rules out of court this German bloke who spent the afternoon with him.'

'He might have left a bomb behind him,' said Algy.

'My dear boy,' exclaimed Hugh, 'you'd have wanted a bomb the size of a wheelbarrow. That's the point I've been trying to force into your skull. You can't carry a thing that size about in your waistcoat pocket. No – it won't work. Either the maid is talking through the back of her neck, or she isn't. And if she isn't, the old chap was dancing about in the room after the German left. Not only that, but he locked himself in. Well, even you wouldn't lock yourself in with a land-mine, would you? Especially one you'd just seen carefully arranged to explode in five minutes. Besides, he knew this German; he told me so at lunch today.'

'I suppose you're right,' grunted Algy. 'And yet it seems so deuced suspicious.'

'Precisely: it is deuced suspicious. But don't forget one thing, old boy. It is only suspicious to us because we've got inside information. It is not a bit suspicious to the police.'

'It would be if you told 'em about that letter he got.'

Hugh lit a cigarette and stared out of the window.

'Perhaps,' he agreed. 'But do we want to rouse their suspicions, old boy? If we're wrong – if it was a bona-fide accident – there's no use in doing so; if we're right, we might have a little game all on our own. I mean I was all in favour of the old boy going to the police about it while he was alive, but now that he's dead it seems a bit late in the day.'

'And how do you propose to make the other side play?' demanded Algy.

'Good Lord! I haven't got as far as that,' said Hugh vaguely. 'One might biff your pal with the eyeglass on the jaw, or something like that. Or one might get in touch with them through these notes on the Professor's discovery, and see what happens. If they then tried to murder me, we should have a bit of a pointer as to which way the wind was blowing. Might have quite a bit of fun, Algy; you never know. Anyway, I think we'll attend the inquest tomorrow; we might spot something if we're in luck. We will sit modestly at the back of the court, and see without being seen.'

But the inquest failed to reveal very much. It was a depressing scene, and more in the nature of a formality than anything else. The two young men arrived early, and wedged themselves in the back row, whence they commanded a good view of the court. And suddenly Algy caught Hugh's arm.

'See that little bird with the white moustache and the eyeglass in the second row,' he whispered. 'That's the fellow I was telling you about, who put up the offer of a quarter of a million.'

Hugh grunted noncommittally; seen from that distance he seemed a harmless sort of specimen. And then the proceedings started. The police gave their formal evidence, and after that the parlourmaid was put into the box. She described in detail the events of the afternoon, and the only new point which came to light was the fact that another man beside the German Professor had been to the house for a short time and left almost at once. First the German had arrived. No, she did not know his name – but his appearance was peculiar. Pressed for details, it appeared that his clothes were dirty, and his hands stained with chemicals. Oh! yes – she would certainly know him again if she saw him. A box had come with him which was carried into the laboratory by two men. They had brought it in a car, and had waited outside part of the time the German was there. Yes – she had talked to them. Had they said anything about the German? Surely they must have mentioned his name. No – they didn't even know it. The witness paused, and having been duly encouraged by the Coroner was understood to say that the only thing they had said about him was that he was a bit dippy.

The laughter in court having been instantly quelled, the witness proceeded. Just after the German had arrived another visitor came. No – she didn't know his name either. But he was English, and she showed him into the laboratory too. Then she went down to finish her dinner.

About ten minutes later the front-door bell rang again. She went upstairs to find the German dancing about in the hall in his excitement. He wanted to know when Professor Goodman was returning. Said he had made an appointment, and that unless the Professor returned shortly he would go as the other visitor had gone.

Pressed on this point by the Coroner – she knew the second visitor had gone, as the only people in the laboratory as she passed it were the two men already alluded to. And just then Professor Goodman came in, apologised for having kept the German waiting, and they disappeared into the laboratory. For the next hour and a half she heard them talking whenever she passed the door; then the laboratory bell rang. She went up to find that the German was leaving. Through the open door she saw Professor Goodman bending over his bench hard at work; then just as she was halfway across the hall she heard the key turn in the door. And the German had waved his arms in the air, and said something about the house going sky-high. The motor had gone by that time, and the box and the two men. It was just before then that she'd spoken to them. And it was about four or five minutes later after the German had disappeared down the road that the explosion took place.

The witness paused, and stared into the court.

'There he is,' she cried. 'That's him – just come in.'

Drummond swung round in time to see the tall, ungainly figure of Professor Scheidstrun go shambling up the court. He was waving his arms, and peering shortsightedly from side to side.

'I hof just heard the dreadful news,' he cried, pausing in front of the Coroner. 'I hof it read in the newspaper. My poor friendt has himself blown up. But that I had gone he would myself have blown also.'

After a short delay he was piloted into the witness-box. His evidence, which was understood with difficulty, did, however, elucidate the one main fact which was of importance – namely, the nature of the explosive which had caused the disaster. It appeared that Professor Goodman had been experimenting for some time with a new form of blasting powder which would be perfectly harmless unless exploded by a detonator containing fulminate of mercury. No blow, no heat would cause it to explode. And when he left the house the Professor had in front of him numerous specimens of this blasting powder of varying quality. One only was the perfected article – the rest were the failures. But all were high explosive of different degrees of power. And then some accident must have happened.

He waved his arms violently in the air, and mopped his forehead with a handkerchief that had once been white. Then like a momentarily dammed stream the flood of verbosity broke forth again. The partially stunned court gathered that it was his profound regret that he had only yesterday afternoon called the deceased man a fool. He still considered that his views on the atomic theory were utterly wrong, but he was not a fool. He wished publicly to retract the statement, and to add further that as a result of this deplorable accident not only England but the world had lost one of its most distinguished men. And with that he sat down again, mopping his forehead.

It was then the Coroner's turn. He said that he was sure the bereaved family would be grateful for the kind words of appreciation from the distinguished scientist who had just given evidence – words with which he would humbly like to associate himself also. It was unnecessary, he considered, to subject Mrs Goodman to the very painful ordeal of identifying the remains, as sufficient evidence had already been given on that point. He wished to express his profound sympathy with the widow and daughter, and to remind them that 'Peace hath its victories no less renowned than War.'

And so with a verdict of 'Accidental Death caused by the explosion of blasting powder during the course of experimental work', the proceedings terminated. The court arose, and with the court rose Algy, to discover, to his surprise, that Hugh had already disappeared. He hadn't seen him go, but that was nothing new. For as Algy and everyone else connected with Hugh Drummond had discovered long ago, he had a power of rapid and silent movement which was almost incredible in such a big man. Presumably he had got bored and left. And sure enough when Algy got outside he saw Drummond on the opposite side of the street staring into the window of a tobacconist's. He sauntered across to join him.

'Well – that's that,' he remarked. 'Don't seem to have advanced things much.'

'Get out of sight,' snapped Drummond. 'Go inside and stop there. Buy matches or something.'

With a feeling of complete bewilderment Algy did as he was told. He went inside and he stopped there, until the proprietor began to eye him suspiciously. There had been two or three cases of hold-ups in the papers recently, and after he had bought several packets of unprepossessing cigarettes and half a dozen boxes of matches the atmosphere became strained. In desperation he went to the door and peered out, thereby confirming the shopman's suspicions to such good effect that he ostentatiously produced a dangerous-looking life-preserver.

Hugh had completely disappeared. Not a trace of him was to be seen, and feeling more bewildered than ever Algy hailed a passing taxi and drove off to Brook Street. Presumably Hugh would return there in due course, and until then he would have to possess his soul in patience.

It was two hours before he came in, and sank into a chair without a word.

'What's all the excitement?' demanded Algy eagerly.

'I don't know that there is any,' grunted Hugh. 'I'm not certain the whole thing isn't a false alarm. What did you think of the inquest?'

'Not very helpful,' said Algy. 'Seems pretty conclusive that it really was an accident.'

Once again Hugh grunted.

'I suppose you didn't notice the rather significant little point that your diamond pal Blantyre knew the old German.'

Algy stared at him.

'I happened to be looking at him as the German appeared, and I saw him give a most violent start. And all through the Boche's evidence he was as nervous as a cat with kittens. Of course there was no reason why he shouldn't have known him – but in view of what we know it seemed a bit suspicious to me. So I waited for them to come out of court. Sir Raymond came first and hung about a bit. Then came the old German, who got into a waiting taxi. And as he got in he spoke to Sir Raymond – just one brief sentence. What it was I don't know, of course, but it confirmed the fact that they knew one another. It also confirmed the fact that for some reason or other they did not wish to have their acquaintance advertised abroad. Now – why? That, old boy, is the question I asked myself all the way down to Bloomsbury in a taxi. I had one waiting too, and I followed the German. Why this mystery? Why should they be thus bashful of letting it be known that they had met before?'

'Did you find out anything?' asked Algy.

'I found out where the old German is staying. But beyond that nothing. He is stopping at a house belonging to a Mr Anderson – William Anderson, who, I gathered from discreet inquiries, is a gentleman of roving disposition. He uses the house as a sort of *pied-à-terre* when he is in London, which is not very often. Presumably he made the German's acquaintance abroad, and invited him to make use of his house.'

'Don't seem to be much to go on, does there?' said Algy disconsolately.

'Dam' little,' agreed Hugh cheerfully. 'In fact if you boil down to it, nothing at all. But you never can tell, old boy. I saw a baby with a squint this morning and passed under two ladders, so all may yet be well. Though I greatly fear nothing will come of it. I thought vaguely yesterday that we might get some fun by means of these notes of the old man's, but 'pon my soul – I don't know how. In the first place, they're indecipherable; and even if they weren't, I couldn't make a diamond in a thousand years. In the second place, they don't belong to us; and in the third it would look remarkably like blackmail. Of course, they're our only hope, but I'm afraid they won't amount to much in our young lives.'

He sighed profoundly, and replaced the envelope in his pocket.

'Oh for the touch of a vanished hand,' he murmured. 'Carl – my Carl – it cannot be that we shall never meet again. I feel, Algy, that if only he could know the position of affairs he would burst into tears and fly to our assistance. He'd chance the notes being unintelligible if he knew what they were about. Once again would he try to murder me with all his well-known zest. What fun it would all be!'

'Not a hope,' said Algy. 'Though I must say I do rather wonder what the blighter is doing now.'

To be exact, he was just putting the last final touch on the aquiline nose of Edward Blackton, and remarking to himself that everything was for the best in the best of all possible worlds. Replaced carefully on their respective pegs were the egg-stained garments of Professor Scheidstrun; the grey wig carefully combed out occupied its usual head-rest.

And not without reason did Edward Blackton – alias Carl Peterson – alias the Comte du Guy, etc. – feel pleased with himself. Never in the course of his long and brilliant career had a coup gone with such wonderful success. It almost staggered him when he thought about it. Not a hitch anywhere; not even the suspicion of a check. Everything had gone like clockwork from beginning to end, thereby once again bearing out the main theory of his life, which was that the bigger the coup the safer it was. It is the bank clerk with his petty defalcations who gets found out every time; the big man does it in millions and entertains Royalty on the proceeds. But in his line of business, as in every other, to get big results the original outlay must be big. And it was on that point that Mr Blackton felt so particularly pleased. For the original outlay in this case had not only been quite small, but, in addition, had been generously found by the Metropolitan Diamond Syndicate. Which tickled his sense of humour to such an extent that once or twice it had quite interfered with the delicate operation of face-building.

But at last he had finished, and with his Corona drawing to his entire satisfaction he locked up his inner sanctuary and stepped into the room which served him as an office. At three o'clock he was to meet Sir Raymond Blantyre and receive from him the remaining quarter of a million in notes; at three-fifteen he would be on his way to the house Freyder had acquired for him to begin business in earnest. A note from Freyder received that morning had stated that Professor Goodman, though a little dazed, seemed in no way to have suffered from his uncomfortable journey, which was eminently satisfactory. For it was certainly no part of his play to treat his prisoner with anything but the utmost care and consideration, unless, of course, he should prove foolish. For a moment Blackton's eyes narrowed at the thought; then he gave the faintest possible shrug of his shoulders. Sufficient unto the day, and he had dealt with such cases before.

So after a final look round the room he carefully pulled down the blinds and went downstairs. Mr William Anderson was leaving London for another of his prolonged visits abroad.

His anticipations that there would be no trouble over the second payment were justified. Sir Raymond Blantyre and three other members of the syndicate were awaiting his arrival, and the expressions on their faces reminded him of young girls being introduced to a man who mother has told them is very wicked and not at all a nice person to know.

'Well, gentlemen,' he remarked affably, 'I trust you are satisfied. This – er – fortunate accident has settled things very pleasantly for all concerned, has it not?'

'It really was an accident?' said Sir Raymond, and his voice shook a little.

'Surely, Sir Raymond, your pitiable agitation in court this morning was not so great as to prevent your hearing the verdict? And that, I think, is all that concerns any of us; that, and the fact that Professor Goodman will not deliver his address to the Royal Society which was the *raison d'être* of our meeting. And so shall we terminate the business?'

In silence Sir Raymond handed over the notes which Blackton carefully folded and placed in his pocket-book.

'Delightful weather, is it not?' he said courteously. 'My – ah – daughter tells me that Montreux has never been more lovely.'

'You are going back to Switzerland at once?' said Sir Raymond.

'Who knows?' answered the other. 'I am a man of moods.' He picked up his hat, and a faint smile hovered round his lips. 'But I certainly feel that I have earned a holiday. Well, gentlemen – I will say goodbye. Possibly we may meet again, though I doubt if I shall still be Mr Blackton. A pity, because I rather fancy myself like this. It is quite my best-looking rôle, so I am informed by competent judges. But change and novelty are essential in my work, as doubtless you can understand.'

He strolled towards the door, still smiling gently.

'One moment, Mr Blackton,' cried Sir Raymond. 'What about Mr Lewisham? His wife rang me up on the telephone this morning to say that he had not returned last night, and that she'd had a wire from Euston saying he'd been called North on business.'

Blackton studied the ash on his cigar.

'Really,' he murmured. 'You don't say so. However, I don't know that I'm greatly interested. He wasn't very entertaining, was he?'

'But that note,' cried Leibhaus – 'the threatening note.'

'Destroyed by me personally. You may rest assured of that. And when you next see Mr Lewisham, please give him my kind regards. Doubtless an excellent man, though I thought him very quiet the last time I saw him. Dull – and overburdened with conscience. A depressing mixture. Well, gentlemen, once again – goodbye. Or shall I say – *au revoir*?'

The door closed behind him a little abruptly. Just at the moment the topic of Mr Lewisham was not one he wished to go into in detail. Once he was on his way to Valparaiso it wouldn't matter so much – but at the moment, no. The subject failed to commend itself to him, and he dismissed it from his mind as he entered his waiting motor-car. It still remained the one weak link in the whole business, but nothing more could be done to strengthen it than he had already done. And that being the case, there was no object in bothering about it further. There were other things of more immediate importance in the near future to be decided, and it was of those he was thinking as the car spun smoothly along towards the luxurious house Freyder had acquired for him on the borders of the New Forest.

After mature thought he had decided to add a completely new character to his repertoire. At first he had considered the possibilities of being an ordinary English country gentleman, but he had very soon dismissed the idea. The gentleman part he could do – none better; even the English, but not the country. And he was far too clever not to realise his own limitations. Yet it was a pity, since no type is more inconspicuous in its proper place, and to be inconspicuous was his object in life. But it was too risky a rôle to play in the middle of the genuine article, and so he had reluctantly decided against it. And his intention now was to assume the character of an elderly recluse of eccentric habits and great wealth devoted to all sorts of scientific research work – particularly electrical and chemical. Most of his life had been spent abroad, and now, in his declining years, he had come back to the country of his birth partially from feelings of sentiment, but more particularly to look after his only brother, whose health and brain had been failing for some time. A part of the house was set apart for this brother, who was subject to delusions and saw no-one.

Six months was the period he gave it before – in a last despairing effort to restore his brother's health – he took him for a cruise on a private yacht, and buried him quietly at sea. Possibly less; a great deal would depend on the rapidity with which the invalid produced the diamonds. For though he had no doubt as to his ability to learn the process in a very short time, the thought of mixing chemicals and getting electric shocks bored him excessively. Having got the dog, he had no intention of barking himself. No – six months was the period he had in his mind; after which the real game would begin. Again would an eminent savant approach Sir Raymond Blantyre and his syndicate and make diamonds artificially; again would the services of Mr Edward Blackton be requisitioned to deal with the situation. And as the gorgeous possibility of being paid a vast sum to kill himself dawned on him, as the endless vista of money, money, all the time stretched out before his imagination in all its wonderful simplicity, the charm of the countryside took on an added beauty. A glow of sublime benevolence flooded his soul; for one brief moment he took up the speaking-tube to stop the car. He felt he wanted to hear the birds sing, to put buttercups in his hair and dance with the chauffeur on the green sward. And since such a performance might have perplexed that worthy mechanic more than it enthralled him, it was just as well that at that moment the car swung through some massive gates and entered the drive of a largish house, which could be seen in the distance through the trees.

Mr William Robinson had reached his destination. For, quite rightly realising that shibboleth of our country life which concerns itself with whether a stranger belongs to the Leicestershire or the Warwickshire branch of the family, he had decided against calling himself De Vere Molyneux.

Chapter 5

In which Mr William Robinson loses his self-control

He was met at the front door by Freyder, who led him at once to the room which he had set apart for his Chief's own particular and private use. In every house taken by Mr William Robinson – to adopt, at once, his new name – there was one such room into which no-one, under any pretext whatever, might enter without his permission, once he was in residence. Freyder himself would not have dreamed of doing so; and even the girl, who was still enjoying the sunshine at Montreux, invariably knocked before she went into the holy of holies.

'Capital, Freyder,' he remarked, glancing round the room with a critical eye. 'And how is our friend?'

'Getting damned angry, Chief,' answered the other. 'Talking about legal proceedings and infamous conduct. The poor old bloke was wedged up against a nail in the packing-case, and it's made him as mad as the devil.'

'A pity,' murmured Mr Robinson. 'Still, I don't know that it matters very much. It would have been pleasanter, of course, if we could have kept the proceedings on an amicable basis, but I always had grave doubts. A pigheaded old man, Freyder; but there are ways of over-coming pigheadedness.' He smiled genially; he still felt he wanted to hear the birds sing. 'And now I will just make one or two alterations in my personal appearance. Then I will interview our friend.'

'Very good, Chief. By the way – the dynamo is installed, also the most modern brand of electric furnace. But, of course, I haven't been able to do anything with regard to the chemicals as yet.'

'Of course not. You've done extremely well, my dear fellow – extremely well. He will have to tell me what chemicals he requires this evening, and you will go up to London first thing tomorrow and obtain them.'

With a wave of his hand he dismissed his subordinate, and then for over an hour he occupied himself in front of a mirror. Mr

William Robinson was being created. It was his first appearance in public, and so a little licence was allowable. There would be no-one to point an accusing finger at his nose and say it had grown larger in the night or anything awkward of that sort. This was creation, pure and simple, giving scope to the creator's artistic mind. He could make what he would. Once made, a series of the most minute measurements with gauges recording to the hundredth of an inch would be necessary. Each would be entered up with mathematical precision in a book kept specially for the purpose, along with other details concerning the character. But that came later, and was merely the uninteresting routine work. The soul of the artist need not be troubled by such trifles.

And since the soul of the artist was gay within him, he fashioned a genial old man with twinkling eyes and mutton-chop whiskers. His nose was rather hooked; his horn spectacles reposed on his forehead as if they had been absentmindedly pushed up from their proper position. His scanty grey hair was brushed back untidily (it was the ruthless thinning out of his normal crop with a razor that he disliked most); his clothes were those of a man who buys good ones and takes no care of them. And, finally, his hands were covered with the stains of the chemist.

At length he had finished, and having surveyed himself from every angle he rang the bell for Freyder, who paused in genuine amazement at the door. Accustomed as he was to these complete metamorphoses of his Chief, he never ceased to marvel at them.

'How's that, Freyder?' demanded Mr Robinson.

'Wonderful, Chief,' said the other. 'Simply wonderful. I congratulate you.'

'Then I think I'll go and see our friend – my dear, dear brother. Doubtless a little chat will clear the air.'

With a curious shambling gait he followed Freyder up the stairs to the top of the house. Then rubbing his hands together genially, he entered the room which Freyder had pointed to and closed the door behind him.

Professor Goodman rose as he came in and took a step forward.

'Are you the owner of this house, sir?' he demanded angrily.

'Yes,' said the other. 'I am. I hope my servants have made you comfortable.'

'Then I demand to know by what right you dare to keep me a prisoner. How dare you, sir – how dare you? And where am I, anyway?'

With a sudden little gesture of weakness Professor Goodman sat down. He was still bewildered and shaken at his treatment, and Mr Robinson smiled affably.

'That's better,' he remarked. 'Let us both sit down and have a friendly talk. I feel that one or two words of explanation are due to you, which I trust, my dear Professor, you will receive in a friendly and – er – brotherly spirit. Brotherly, because you are my brother.'

'What the devil do you mean, sir?' snapped the Professor. 'I haven't got a brother; I've never had a brother.'

'I know,' murmured the other sadly. 'A most regrettable oversight on your parents' part. But isn't it nice to have one now? One, moreover, who will surround you with every care and attention in your illness.'

'But, damn you!' roared the unhappy man, 'I'm not ill.'

Mr Robinson waved a deprecating hand.

'I implore of you, do not excite yourself. In your weak mental state it would be most injurious. I assure you that you are my partially insane brother, and that I have taken this house entirely on your account. Could altruism go farther?'

Professor Goodman was swallowing hard, and clutching the arms of his chair.

'Perhaps you'll say what you really do mean,' he muttered at length.

'Certainly,' cried Mr Robinson benevolently. 'It is for that express purpose that we are having this interview. It is essential that you should understand exactly where you are. Now, perhaps you are unaware of the fact that you died yesterday.'

'I did – what?' stammered the other.

'Died,' said Mr Robinson genially. 'I thought you might find that bit a little hard to follow, so I've brought you a copy of one of the early evening papers. In it you will find a brief account of the inquest – your inquest.'

With a trembling hand the Professor took the paper.

'But I don't understand,' he said after he had read it. 'For Heaven's sake, sir, won't you explain? I remember nothing from the time when I was chloroformed in my laboratory till I came to in a packing-case. It wasn't I who was blown up?'

'Obviously,' returned the other. 'But the great point is, Professor, that everyone thinks it was. The cream of the scientific world, in fact, will attend the burial of somebody else's foot, in the firm belief that they are honouring your memory. Whose foot it is you needn't worry about; I assure you he was a person of tedious disposition,'

'But I must go at once and telephone.' He rose in his agitation. 'It's the most dreadful thing. Think of my poor wife.'

'I know,' said Mr Robinson sadly. 'Though not exactly married myself, I can guess your feelings. But I'm afraid, my dear brother, that your wife must remain in ignorance of the fact that she is not a widow.'

Professor Goodman's face went grey. He knew now what he had only suspected before – that he was in danger.

'Possibly things are becoming clearer to you,' went on the other. 'The world thinks you are dead. No hue-and-cry will be raised to find you. But you are not dead – far from it. You are, as I explained, my partially insane brother, whom no-one is allowed to see. I admit that you are not insane nor are you my brother – but qu'importe. It is not the truth that counts, but what people think is the truth. I trust I make myself clear?'

Professor Goodman said nothing; he was staring at the speaker with fear in his eyes. For the mask of benevolence had slipped a little from Mr Robinson's face: the real man was showing through the assumed rôle.

'From your silence I take it that I do,' he continued. 'No-one will look for you as Professor Goodman; no-one will be permitted to see you as my brother. So – er – you will not be very much disturbed.'

'In plain language, you mean I'm a prisoner,' said the Professor. 'Why? What is your object?'

'You have recently, my dear Professor,' began Mr Robinson, 'made a most remarkable discovery.'

'I knew it,' groaned the other. 'I knew it was that. Well, let me tell you one thing, sir. If this infamous outrage has been perpetrated on me in order to make me keep silent about it – I still refuse utterly. You may detain me here in your power until after the meeting of the Society, but I shall give my discovery to the world all the same.'

Mr Robinson gently stroked his side whiskers.

'A most remarkable discovery,' he repeated as if the other had not spoken. 'I congratulate you upon it, Professor. And being a chemist in a small way myself, I am overcome with curiosity on the subject. I have therefore gone to no little inconvenience to bring you to a place where, undisturbed by mundane trifles, you will be able to impart your discovery to me, and at the same time manufacture diamonds to your heart's content. I should like you to make hundreds of diamonds during the period of your retirement; in fact, that will be your daily task . . . '

'You want me to make them,' said the bewildered man. 'But that's the very thing Blantyre and those others didn't want me to do.'

Mr Robinson stroked his whiskers even more caressingly.

'How fortunate it is,' he murmured, 'that we don't all think alike!'

'And if I refuse?' said the other.

Mr Robinson ceased stroking his whiskers.

'You would be unwise, Professor Goodman – most unwise. I have methods of dealing with people who refuse to do what I tell them to do which have always succeeded up to date.'

His eyes were suddenly merciless, and with a sick feeling of fear the Professor sat back in his chair.

'A dynamo has been installed,' went on Mr Robinson after a moment or two. 'Also the most modern type of electric furnace. Here I have the retort which you use in your process' – he placed it on the table beside him – 'and all that now remains are the necessary chemicals. Your notes are a trifle difficult to follow, so you will have to prepare a list yourself of those chemicals and they will be obtained for you tomorrow.'

He took the papers from his pocket and handed them to the Professor.

'Just one word of warning. Should anything go wrong with your process, should you pretend out of stupid obstinacy that you are unable to make diamonds – may God help you! If there is anything wrong with the apparatus, let me know, and it will be rectified. But don't, I beg of you, try any tricks.'

He rose, and his voice became genial again.

'I am sure my warning is unnecessary,' he said gently. 'Now I will leave you to prepare the list of the salts you require.'

'But these are the wrong notes,' said Professor Goodman, staring at them dazedly. 'These are my notes on peptonised proteins.'

Mr Robinson stood very still.

'What do you mean?' he said at length. 'Are those not the notes on your process of making diamonds?'

'Good gracious – no,' said the Professor. 'These have got nothing to do with it.'

'Are the notes necessary?'

'Absolutely. Why, I can't even remember all the salts without them – let alone the proportions in which they are used.'

'Do you know where they are?'

The Professor passed his hand wearily across his forehead.

'Whom was I lunching with?' he murmured. 'It was just before I went to meet Professor Scheidstrun, and I gave them to him to take care of. And by the way – what has happened to Scheidstrun? Surely it wasn't he who was killed.'

'Don't worry about Scheidstrun,' snarled Mr Robinson. 'Whom were you lunching with, you damned old fool?'

'I know – I remember now. It was Captain Drummond. I lunched at his club. He's got them. Good God! Why are you looking like that?'

For perhaps the first time in his life every vestige of self-control had left the master-criminal's face and he looked like a wild beast.

'Drummond!' he shouted savagely. 'Not Captain Hugh Drummond, who lives in Brook Street?'

'That's the man,' said the Professor. 'Such a nice fellow, though rather stupid. Do you know him by any chance?'

How near Professor Goodman was to a violent death at that moment it is perhaps as well he did not know. In mild perplexity he watched the other man's face, diabolical with its expression of animal rage and fury, and wondered vaguely why the mention of Hugh Drummond's name should have produced such a result. And it was a full minute before Mr Robinson had recovered himself sufficiently to sit down and continue the conversation. Drummond again – always Drummond. How, in the name of everything conceivable and inconceivable, had *he* got mixed up in this affair? All his carefully worked out and brilliantly executed plan frustrated and brought to nothing by one miserable fact which he could not possibly have foreseen, and which, even now, he could hardly believe.

'What induced you to give the notes to him ?' he snarled at length.

'He said he didn't think it was safe for me to carry them about with me,' said the other mildly. 'You see, I had received a threatening letter in the morning – a letter threatening my life . . . ' He blinked apologetically.

So it was Lewisham's letter that had done it, and the only ray of comfort in the situation lay in the fact that at any rate he'd killed Lewisham.

'Did you give him any special instructions ?' he demanded.

'No – I don't think so,' answered the Professor. 'I think he said something about handing them over to the bank.'

Mr Robinson rose and started to pace up and down the room. The blow was so staggering in its unexpectedness that his brain almost refused to work. That Drummond of all people should again have crossed his path was as far as his thoughts would go. The fact that Drummond was blissfully unaware that he had done so was beside the point; it seemed almost like the hand of Fate. And incredible though it may seem, for a short time he was conscious of a feeling of genuine superstitious fear.

But not for long. The prize, in this case, was too enormous for any weakness of that sort. If Captain Drummond had the notes, steps would have to be taken to make him give them up. The question was – what were those steps to be?

With an effort he concentrated on the problem. The thing must be done with every appearance of legality; it must be done naturally. From Drummond's point of view, which was the important one to consider, the situation would be a simple one. He was in the possession of valuable papers belonging to a dead man – papers to which he had no right; but papers to which he – being the type of person he was – would continue to stick if he had the faintest suspicion of foul play. And since he had seen the threatening letter, those suspicions must be latent in his mind already. To keep them latent and not arouse them was essential.

And the second and no less important part of the problem was to ensure that once the notes had left Drummond's hands they should pass with a minimum of delay into his. The thought of anything happening to them or of someone else obtaining possession of them turned him cold all over.

He paused in his restless pacing up and down, and thoughtfully lit a cigar. His self-control was completely recovered; Mr William Robinson was himself again. A hitch had occurred in an otherwise perfect plan – that was all. And hitches were made to be unhitched.

'What is the name of your lawyer?' he said quietly.

'Mr Tootem of Tootem, Price & Tootem,' answered Professor Goodman in mild surprise. 'Why do you want to know?'

'Never mind why. Now here's a pen and some paper. Write as I dictate. And don't let there be any mistake about the writing, my friend.

'DEAR DRUMMOND,
'I have been discussing things with my friend Scheidstrun this afternoon, and he agrees with you that it is better that I should not carry about the notes I gave you. So will you send them to Tootem, Price & Tootem . . .

'What's the address? Austin Friars. Well – put it in.

' . . . They will keep them for me until the meeting of the Royal Society. And if, as Scheidstrun humorously says, I shall have blown myself up before then with my new blasting powder, it is my wish that he should be given the notes. He is immensely interested in my discovery, and I know of no-one to whom I would sooner bequeath it. But that, my dear Drummond, is not likely to occur.

'Yours sincerely,

'Now sign your name.'

The Professor laid down his pen with a sigh.

'It is all very confusing,' he murmured. 'And I do hope I'm not going to get blood poisoning where that nail in the packing-case ran into my leg.'

But Mr Robinson evinced no interest in such an eventuality. He stood with the letter in his hand, pulling thoughtfully at his cigar, and striving to take into account every possible development which might arise. For perhaps a minute he remained motionless while Professor Goodman rubbed his injured limb; then he made a decisive little gesture oddly out of keeping with his benevolent appearance. His mind was made up; his plan was clear.

'Address an envelope,' he said curtly, 'to Captain Drummond.'

He took the envelope and slipped the letter inside. There was no time to be lost; every moment was valuable.

'Now, Professor Goodman,' he remarked, 'I want you to pay close attention to what I am going to say. The fact that you have not got the notes of your process constitutes a slight check in my plans. However, I am about to obtain those notes, and while I am doing so you will remain here. You will be well looked after, and well fed. A delightful bedroom will be placed at your disposal, and I believe, though I have not personally verified the fact, that there is a very good library below. Please make free use of it. But I must give you one word of warning. Should you make any attempt to escape, should you make the slightest endeavour even to communicate with the outside world you will be gagged and put in irons in a dark room.'

Professor Goodman's hands shook uncontrollably; he looked what at the moment he was, a badly frightened old man.

'But, sir,' he quavered pitifully, 'won't you tell me where I am, and why all this is happening to me?'

'Finding the answer should give you some interesting mental recreation during my absence,' said Mr Robinson suavely.

'And my poor wife,' moaned the unhappy man.

'The pangs of widowhood are hard to bear,' agreed the other. 'But doubtless time will soften the blow. And anyway, my dear Professor, you died in the cause of duty. I can assure you that Professor Scheid-strun's peroration over your sole remaining boot brought tears to the eyes of all who heard it. Well, I will say *au revoir*. Ask for anything you require, but don't, I beg of you, try any stupid tricks. My servants are rough fellows – some of them.'

With a genial smile he left the room and went downstairs. Whatever may have been his thoughts, only the most perfect equanimity showed on his face. He possessed that most priceless asset of any great leader – the power of concealing bad news from his staff. In fact the tighter the corner the more calmly confident did this man always look. Nothing is more fatal to any enterprise than the knowledge on the part of subordinates that the man in charge is shaken. And though he would hardly admit it to himself, Mr William Robinson was badly shaken. In fact when he reached his own private sanctum he did a thing which in his whole long career of crimes he had done but twice before. From a small locked cabinet he took a bottle containing a white powder, and calmly and methodically he measured out a dose which he sniffed up his nose. And had anyone seen this secret operation, he would have realised that the man was the master and not the drug. Only one man in a million may employ cocaine as a servant and keep it in that position: Mr William Robinson was that one.

Deliberately he sat down to await the drug's action; then with a faint smile he rose and replaced the bottle in the cabinet. The nerve crisis had passed; the master-criminal was himself again.

'Freyder,' he remarked as that worthy entered the room in answer to the bell, 'a slight hitch has occurred in my scheme. The indecipherable notes which I so carefully extracted from our friend's pocket yesterday refer apparently to the prolongation of the lives of rabbits and other fauna. The ones we require are – er – elsewhere. I, naturally, propose to obtain them forthwith, but it will be necessary to proceed with a certain amount of discretion. Incredible to relate, they are in the possession of a young gentleman whom we have come across before – one Drummond.'

Freyder's breath came in a sharp whistle.

'I see that you recall the name,' went on the other quietly. 'And I must say that when Professor Goodman informed me of the fact, I felt for the moment unreasonably annoyed. One cannot legislate for everything, and how any man out of an asylum could give that vast fool anything of importance to look after is one of those things which I confess baffles me completely. However, all that concerns us is that he has them at the moment: the problem is to remove them from his keeping as rapidly as possible. Under normal circumstances the solution of that problem would have presented no difficulties, but Drummond, I am bound to admit, is not normal. In fact, Freyder, as you may remember, I have twice made the unforgivable mistake of underestimating him. This time, however, I have decided on a little scheme which, though a trifle complicated at first sight, is, in reality, profoundly simple. Moreover, it appeals to my sense of humour, which is a great point in its favour. You have your notebook? Then I will give you my instructions.'

They were clear and concise with no possibility of a misunderstanding, and, as Mr Robinson had said, they contained in them a touch of humour that was akin to genius. In fact, despite the seriousness of the situation, on two or three occasions Freyder broke into uncontrollable chuckles of laughter. The whole thing was so gloriously simple that it seemed there must be a flaw somewhere, and yet, try as he would, he could discover none.

'The essence of the whole thing is speed, Freyder,' said his Chief, rising at length. 'It is impossible to say what Drummond will do with those notes if he's left too long in undisturbed possession of them. He must know their value, but for all that he's quite capable of using them for shaving paper. The one thing, knowing him, which I don't think he will do is to take them to Scotland Yard. But I don't want to run any risks. To have to be content with a miserable half-million for this little affair would deprive me of my reason. I should totter to an early grave, as a grey-headed old man. So speed, don't forget – speed is absolutely essential.'

'I can make all arrangements tonight, Chief,' said Freyder, rising, 'and start at dawn tomorrow morning. Back tomorrow evening, and the whole thing can be done the day after.'

'Good,' answered the other. 'Then send for the car at once and we'll get off.'

And thus it happened that two hours after Mr Edward Blackton had arrived at his house on the borders of the New Forest, Mr William Robinson left it again. But on the return journey it is to be regretted that he no longer wished to hear the birds sing or put buttercups in his hair. He sat in his corner sunk in silence while the powerful limousine ate up the miles to London. And his companion Freyder knew better than to break that silence.

It was not until the tramlines at Hounslow were reached that he spoke.

'If I fail to settle accounts with Drummond this time, Freyder, I'll do as he once recommended and take to growing tomatoes.'

Freyder grunted.

'The notes first, Chief, and after that the man. You'll win this time.' He spoke down the speaking-tube and the car slowed up. 'I'll get out here; our man is close to. And I'll be back tomorrow evening.'

He gave the chauffeur the name of a residential hotel in a quiet part of Bayswater, and stood for a moment watching the car drive away. Then he turned and disappeared down a side-street, while Mr Robinson continued his journey alone. There was nothing more to be done now until Freyder returned, and so, in accordance with his invariable custom, he dismissed the matter from his mind.

To do in Rome as the Romans was another rule of his. And so after dinner at the quiet residential hotel Mr Robinson joined heartily in a merry round game which lacked much of its charm as two cards were missing from the pack. Then refusing with becoming modesty a challenge to take on the hotel champion at halma, he retired to his room and was asleep almost at once. And he was still peacefully sleeping at five o'clock the next morning, when Freyder, shivering a little in the morning air, drew his thick leather coat more closely around his throat. Below him lay the grey sea – hazy still, for the sun had no warmth as yet. In front the pilot was sitting motionless, and after a while the steady roar of the engine lulled him into a gentle doze. The aeroplane flew steadily on towards the east . . . and Germany.

Chapter 6

In which Hugh Drummond loses his self-control

It must be admitted that there was an air of gloom over Hugh Drummond's house on the day following the inquest. Mrs Goodman and Brenda had not left their rooms, and somewhat naturally Phyllis was principally occupied in seeing what she could do for them in their terrible sorrow; while Algy Longworth, faced with the necessity of postponing the wedding, had relapsed into a condition of complete imbecility and refused to be comforted. In fact it was not an atmosphere conducive to thought, and Hugh was trying to think.

On the next day was the funeral. The whole thing had already dropped out of the public eye, Professor Goodman, having been neither a pugilist, film star, nor criminal, but merely a gentle old man of science, could lay no claim whatever to the slightest popular interest. But to Hugh he was something more than a gentle old man of science. He was a man who to all intents and purposes had appealed to him for help – a man whose life had been threatened, and who, within a few hours of receiving that threat, had died.

True, according to the verdict at the inquest, he would have died whether he had received that threat or not. But Hugh was still dissatisfied with that verdict. The proofs, the evidence, all pointed that way – but he was still dissatisfied. And coupled with his dissatisfaction was an uneasy feeling, which only grew stronger with time, that he had been wrong to suppress his knowledge of that letter from the police.

Now it was impossible to put it forward, but that made things no better. The only result in fact as far as he was concerned was that it hardened his resolve not to let the matter drop where it was. Until after the funeral he would say nothing; then he'd begin some inquiries on his own. And for those inquiries two obvious avenues suggested themselves: the first was Professor Scheidstrun, the second Sir Raymond Blantyre.

Once again he took the Professor's notes out of his pocket-book and studied them. He had already shown one sheet to a chemist in a neighbouring street in the hope that he might be able to decipher it, but with no result. The atrocious handwriting, coupled with the fact that, according to the chemist, it was written in a sort of code, made them completely incomprehensible to anyone save the man who wrote them. And he was dead . . .

With a sigh he replaced the papers in his notecase and strolled over to the window. Brook Street presented a quiescent appearance due to the warmth of the day and the recent consumption by its dwellers of lunch. And Hugh was just wondering what form of exercise he could most decently take in view of Mrs Goodman's presence in the house, when he straightened up and his eyes became suddenly watchful. A wild, excited figure whom he recognised instantly was tacking up the street, peering with shortsighted eyes at the numbers of the houses.

'Algy!'

'What is it?' grunted Longworth, coming out of a melancholy reverie.

'Old Scheidstrun is blowing up the street. He's looking for a house. Surely he can't be coming here?'

Algy Longworth sat up in his chair.

'You mean the old bloke who gave evidence at the inquest?'

Hugh nodded.

'By Jove! He *is* coming here.' His voice held traces of excitement. 'Now, why the deuce should he want to see me?'

He went quickly to the door.

'Denny,' he called, and his servant, who was already on his way to the front door, paused and looked up. 'Show the gentleman outside straight up here to my room.'

He came back frowning thoughtfully.

'How on earth does he connect me with it, Algy?'

'It's more than likely, old man,' answered Longworth, 'that he may have heard that Mrs Goodman is here, and has come to shoot a card. Anyway, we'll soon know.'

A moment later Denny ushered Professor Scheidstrun into the room. Seen from close to, he seemed more untidy and egg-stained than ever, as he stood by the door peering at the two young men.

'Captain Drummond?' he demanded in his hoarse, guttural voice.

'That's me,' said Hugh, who was standing with his back to the fireplace regarding his visitor curiously. 'What can I do for you, sir?'

The Professor waved his arms like an agitated semaphore and sank into a chair.

'Doubtless you wonder who I may be,' he remarked, 'and what for I come you to see.'

'I know perfectly well who you are,' said Drummond quietly, 'but I confess I'm beat as to why you want to see me. However, the pleasure is entirely mine.'

'So.' The German stared at him. 'You know who I am?'

'You are Professor Scheidstrun,' remarked Drummond. 'I was present at the inquest yesterday and saw you.'

'Goot.' The Professor nodded his head as if satisfied, though his brain was busy with this very unexpected item of news. 'Then I will proceed at once to the business. In the excitement of all this dreadful accident I haf forgotten it until this moment. Then I remember and come to you at once.' He was fumbling in his pocket as he spoke. 'A letter, Captain Drummond, which my poor friend give to me to post – and I forget it till an hour ago. And I say at once, I will go round myself and see this gentleman and explain.'

Drummond took the envelope and glanced at it thoughtfully, while Algy looked over his shoulder.

'That's Professor Goodman's writing.'

'Since he the letter wrote presumably it is,' remarked the German with ponderous sarcasm.

'You know the contents of this letter, Professor?' asked Drummond, as he slit open the envelope.

'He it read to me,' answered the other. 'Ach! it is almost incredible that what my dear friend should have said to me in jest – indeed that which he has written there in jest – should have proved true. Even now I can hardly believe that he is dead. It is a loss, gentlemen, to the world of science which can never be replaced.'

He rambled on while Drummond, having read the letter in silence, handed it to Algy. And if for one fleeting second there showed in the German's eyes a gleam of almost maniacal hatred as they rested on the owner of the house, it was gone as suddenly as it came. The look on his face was benevolent, even sad, as befitted a man who had recently lost a confrère and friend, when Drummond turned and spoke again.

'The letter is a request, Professor, that certain notes now in my possession should be handed over to you.'

'That is so,' assented the other. 'He to me explained all. He told me of his astounding discovery – a discovery which even now I can hardly believe. But he assured me that it was the truth. And on my shoulders he laid the sacred duty of giving that discovery to the world, if anything should happen to him.'

'Astounding coincidence that on the very afternoon he wrote this something did happen to him,' remarked Drummond quietly.

'As I haf said, even now I can hardly believe it,' agreed the Professor. 'But it is so, and there is no more to be said.'

'Rather astounding also that you did not mention this at the inquest,' pursued Drummond.

'Till one hour ago, my young friend, I forget I had the letter. I forget about his discovery – about the diamonds – about all. My mind was stunned by the dreadful tragedy. And think – five, ten minutes more and I also to pieces would have been blown. *Mein Gott!* it makes me sweat.'

He took out a handkerchief and mopped his forehead.

'By the way, Professor,' said Drummond suddenly, 'do you know Sir Raymond Blantyre?'

For the fraction of a second Professor Scheidstrun hesitated. It was not a question he had been expecting and he realised that a lot might hinge on the answer. And then like a flash he remembered that on leaving the inquest he had spoken two or three words to Sir Raymond. Moreover, Drummond had been there himself.

'Sir Raymond Blantyre,' he murmured. 'He has a grey moustache and an eyeglass. Slightly I know him. He was – *ja*! he was at the inquest himself.'

It was glib, it was quick. It would have passed muster nine times out of ten as a spontaneous reply to a perfectly ordinary question. But it was made to a man who was already suspicious, and it was made to a man whose lazy eyes missed nothing. Drummond had noticed that almost imperceptible pause; what was more to the point, he had noticed the sudden look of wariness on the other's face. More a fleeting shadow than a look, but it had not escaped the lynx-eyed man lounging against the mantelpiece. And it had not tended to allay his suspicions, though his face was still perfectly impassive.

'I assume from what he has written here that Professor Goodman discussed with you the threatening letter he received,' he went on placidly.

'He mentioned it, of course.' The German shrugged his shoulders. 'But for me it seems a stupid joke. Absurd! Ridiculous! Who would be so foolish as to write such a thing if it was a genuine threat? It was – how do you say it – it was a hoax? *Nein – nein* – to that I paid no attention. It was not for that he this letter wrote. He told me of his discovery, and I who know him well, I say, "Where are the notes? It is not safe for you to carry them. You who lose everything – you will lose them. Or more likely still someone will your pocket pick. There are people in London who would like those notes." '

'There undoubtedly are,' agreed Drummond mildly.

'He tells me he give them to you. I say, "This young man – he too may lose them. Tell him to send them to your men of business." He says, "Goot – I will." And he write the letter there. Then he add, as he thinks, his little joke. My poor friend! My poor, poor friend! For now the joke is not a joke. And on me there falls the sacred trust he has left. But his shall be the glory; all the credit will I give to him. And the world of science shall remember his name for ever by this discovery.'

Overcome by his emotion the Professor lay back in his chair breathing stertorously, while once again he dabbed at his forehead with his handkerchief.

'Very praiseworthy and all that,' murmured Drummond. 'Then I take it that your proposal is, sir, that I should hand these notes over to you here and now?'

The German sat up and shrugged his shoulders.

'It would save trouble, Captain Drummond. For me I wish to return to Germany after my poor friend's funeral tomorrow. Naturally I must with me take the notes. But if for any reason you would prefer to hand them to the good Mr Tootem of Austin Friars, then perhaps we could arrange to meet there some time tomorrow morning.'

He leaned back in his chair as if the matter was of no account, and Drummond, his hands in his pocket, strolled over to the window. On the face of it everything was perfectly above board – and yet, try as he would, he could not rid himself of the feeling that something was wrong. Later, when he recalled that interview and realised that for half an hour on that warm summer's afternoon he had been in his own house with the man he knew as Carl Peterson sitting in his best chair, he used to shake with laughter at the humour of it. But at the time no thought of such a wildly amazing thing was in his mind; no suspicion that Professor Scheidstrun was not Professor Scheidstrun had even entered his head. It was not the German's identity that worried him, but his goodwill. Was he what he professed to be – a friend of the late Professor Goodman's? Did he intend to give this scientific discovery to the world as he had promised to do? Or had he deceived Professor Goodman? And if so, why? Could it be possible that this man was being employed by Sir Raymond Blantyre, and that he too was engaged in the conspiracy to destroy the results of the discovery for ever?

He turned and stared at the German, who, overcome by the heat, was apparently asleep. But only apparently. Behind that coarse face and heavy forehead the brain was very wide awake. And it would have staggered Drummond could he have realised how exactly his thoughts were being read. Not very extraordinary either, since the whole interview had been planned to produce those thoughts by a master of psychology.

Suddenly the German sat up with a start.

'It is warm; I sleep.' He extracted a huge watch from his pocket and gave an exclamation as he saw the time. 'I must go,' he said, scrambling to his feet. 'Well – how say you, Captain Drummond? Will you give me now the notes, or do we meet at the good Mr Tootem's?'

'I think, Professor,' said Drummond slowly, 'that I would sooner we met at the lawyer's. These notes were handed to me personally, and I should feel easier in my mind if I handed them over personally to the lawyer. Then my responsibility will end.'

'As you will,' remarked the German indifferently. 'Then we will say eleven o'clock tomorrow morning, unless I let you know to the contrary.'

He shambled from the room, and Drummond escorted him to the front door. Then, having watched him down the steps, he returned to his room.

'Seems a bona-fide show, Algy,' he remarked, lighting a cigarette.

'Will you give up the notes?' demanded his friend.

'My dear old thing, I must,' answered Hugh. 'You've seen the Professor's distinct instructions that jolly old Tootem & Tootem are to have 'em. I can't go against that. What the legal wallah does with them afterwards is nothing to do with me. Still, I wish I could feel more certain in my own mind. You see, the devil of it is, Algy, that even if that bloke is a stumer, our hands are tied. There are old Goodman's instructions, and the only thing I can do is to throw the responsibility on the lawyer's shoulders.'

He paced thoughtfully up and down the room, to stop suddenly and pick up his hat.

'It's worth trying,' he remarked half to himself and the next moment Algy was alone. From the window he saw Hugh hail a taxi and disappear, and with a shrug of his shoulders he resumed his study of *Ruff's Guide*. At times the vagaries of his host were apt to be a little wearing.

And when some four hours later Hugh returned just in time for dinner, it certainly seemed as if he'd wasted his time.

'I've been watching Mr Atkinson's house, Algy,' he said despondently, 'you know the one I spotted after the inquest, where Scheidstrun is living. Went to ground in a house opposite. Said I was a doctor looking for rooms. Thank heavens! the servant developed no symptoms requiring medical attention, because all I could have conscientiously recommended for anybody with a face like hers was a lethal chamber. However, as I say, I took cover in the parlour behind a bowl of stuffed fruit, and there I waited. Devil a thing for hours. Atkinson's house was evidently occupied; in fact, I saw him look out of the window once. A benevolent-looking old chap with mutton-chop whiskers. However, I stuck it out, and at last, just as I was on the point of giving it up, something did happen, though not much. A closed car drove up, and from it there descended old Scheidstrun, a youngish man, and an elderly woman. Couldn't see her very well – but she looked a typical Boche. Probably his wife, I should think.'

He relapsed into silence and lit a cigarette.

'An afternoon wasted,' he grunted after a while. 'I'm fed up with the whole dam' show, Algy. Why the devil didn't I give him the notes and be done with it when he was here? As it is, I've got to waste tomorrow morning as well fooling round in the city; and with the funeral in the afternoon the old brain will cease to function. Mix me a cocktail, like a good fellow. Everything is in the cupboard.'

And thus it came about that whilst two cocktails were being lowered in gloomy silence in Brook Street, a cheerful-looking old gentleman with mutton-chop whiskers entered his quiet residential hotel in Bayswater. There were no signs of gloomy silence about the old gentleman; in fact, he was almost chatty with the lounge-waiter.

'I think – yes, I think,' he remarked, 'that I will have a small cocktail. Not a thing I often do – but this evening I will indulge.'

'Spotted a winner, sir?' said the waiter, responding to the old gentleman's mood.

'Something of that sort, my lad,' he replied genially – 'something of that sort.' And Mr William Robinson's smile was enigmatic.

He seldom remembered an afternoon when in a quiet way he had enjoyed himself so much. In fact, he was almost glad that Drummond had refused to hand over the notes: it would have been so inartistic – so crude. Of course it would have saved bother, but where is the true artist who thinks of that? And he had never really imagined that Drummond would; he knew that young gentleman far too well for that. Naturally he was suspicious: well, he would be more suspicious tomorrow morning. He would be so suspicious, in fact, that in all probability the worthy Mr Tootem would get the shock of his life. He chuckled consumedly, and departed so far from his established custom as to order a second Martini. And as he lifted it to his lips he drank a silent toast: he drank to the shrewd powers of observation of a beautiful girl who was even then watching orange change to pink on the snow-capped Dent du Midi from the balcony of her room in the Palace Hotel.

And so it is unnecessary to emphasise the fact that there were wheels destined to rotate within wheels in the comfortable room in Austin Friars where Mr Tootem senior discharged his affairs, though that pillar of the legal profession was supremely unaware of the fact. With his usual courtly grace he had risen to greet the eminent German savant Professor Scheidstrun who had arrived at about ten minutes to eleven on the following morning. Somewhat to Mr Tootem's surprise, the Professor had been accompanied by his wife, and Frau Scheidstrun was now waiting in the next room for the business to be concluded.

'Most sad, Professor,' murmured Mr Tootem. 'An irreparable loss, as you say, to the scientific world – and to his friends.' He glanced at the clock. 'This young man – Captain Drummond – will be here, you say, at eleven.'

'That is the arrangement that I haf with him made,' answered the German. 'He would not to me quite rightly the notes hand over yesterday; but as you see from the letter, it was my dear friend's wish that I should haf them, and carry on with the great discovery he has made.'

'Quite so,' murmured Mr Tootem benevolently, wishing profoundly that Drummond would hasten his arrival. The morning was warm; the Professor's egg-stained garments scandalised his British soul to the core; and in addition, Mr Tootem senior had arrived at that ripe age when office hours were made to be relaxed. He particularly wished to be at Lord's in time to see Middlesex open their innings against Yorkshire, and only the fact that Professor Goodman had been a personal friend of his had brought him to the city at all that day.

At length with a sigh of relief he looked up. Sounds of voices outside betokened someone's arrival, and the business would be a short one.

'Is this the young man?' he said, rubbing his hands together.

But the Professor made no reply: he was watching the door which opened at that moment to admit Drummond. And since Mr Tootem rose at once to greet him, the fact that he had not answered escaped the lawyer's attention. He also failed to notice that an unaccountable expression of uneasiness showed for a moment on the German's face, as he contemplated Drummond's vast bulk.

'Ah! Captain Drummond, I'm glad you've come,' remarked Mr Tootem. 'Let me see – you know Professor Scheidstrun, don't you?'

He waved Drummond to a chair.

'Yes, we had a little pow-wow yesterday afternoon,' said Drummond, seating himself.

The strained look had vanished from the Professor's face: he beamed cheerfully.

'In which I found him most suspicious,' he said in his guttural voice. 'But quite rightly so.'

'Exactly,' murmured Mr Tootem, again glancing at the clock. It would take him at least twenty minutes to get to Lord's. 'But I am sure he will not be suspicious of me. And since I have one or two important – er – business engagements, perhaps we can conduct this little matter through expeditiously.' He beamed benevolently on Drummond, who was leaning back in his chair regarding the Professor through half-closed lids.

'Now, I understand that my dear friend and client, the late Professor Goodman, handed over to you some very valuable papers, Captain Drummond,' continued Mr Tootem. 'A great compliment, I may say, showing what faith he placed in your judgment and trustworthiness. I have here – and I gather you have seen this letter – instructions that those papers should be handed over to me. You have them with you, I trust?'

'Oh yes, I've got them with me,' said Drummond quietly, though his eyes never left the German's face.

'Excellent,' murmured Mr Tootem. At a pinch he might do Lord's in a quarter of an hour. 'Then if you would kindly let me have them, that will – ah – conclude the matter. I may say that I quite appreciate your reluctance to hand them to anyone but me . . . ' The worthy lawyer broke off abruptly. 'Good heavens! Captain Drummond, what is the matter?'

For Drummond had risen from his chair, and was standing in front of the Professor.

'You're not the man who came to see me yesterday,' he said quietly. 'You're not Professor Scheidstrun at all.'

'But the man is mad,' gasped the German. 'You say I am not Scheidstrun – me.'

'You're made up to look exactly like him – but you're not Scheidstrun! I tell you, Mr Tootem' – he turned to the lawyer, who was staring at him aghast – 'that that man is no more Scheidstrun than I am. The disguise is wonderful – but his hair is a slightly different colour. Ever since I came in I've been wondering what it was.'

'This young man is mad,' said the German angrily. 'The reason that it is a slightly different colour is that I wear a wig. I haf two: this morning I wear the other one to what I wear yesterday.'

But Drummond wasn't even listening. Like a bird fascinated by a snake he was staring at the Professor's left hand, beating an agitated tattoo on his knee. For a moment or two he was dazed, as the stupendous reality burst on his mind. Before him sat Carl Peterson himself, given away once again by that one trick which he could never get rid of, that ceaseless nervous movement of the left hand. It was incredible; the suddenness of the thing took his breath away. And then the whole thing became clear to him. Somehow or other Peterson had heard of the discovery; perhaps employed by Sir Raymond Blantyre himself. He had found out that the notes of the process were to be handed to Scheidstrun, and with his usual consummate daring had decided to impersonate the German. And the woman he had seen arriving the night before was Irma.

His thoughts were chaotic: only the one great thing stuck out. The man in front of him was Peterson: he knew it. And with one wild hoot of utter joy he leapt upon him.

'My little Carl,' he murmured ecstatically, 'the pitcher has come to the well once too often.' Possibly it had; but the scene which followed beggared description. Peterson or not Peterson, his confession as to wearing a wig was the truth. It came off with a slight sucking noise, revealing a domelike cranium completely devoid of hair. With a wild yell of terror the unfortunate German sprang from his chair, and darted behind the portly form of Mr Tootem, while Drummond, brandishing the wig, advanced on him.

'Damn it, sir,' spluttered Mr Tootem, 'I'll send for the police, sir; you must be mad.'

'Out of the way, Tootles,' said Drummond happily. 'You'll scream with laughter when I tell you the truth. Though we'd best make certain the swab hasn't got a gun.'

With a quick heave he jerked the cowering man out from behind the lawyer, who immediately rushed to the door shouting for help.

'A madman,' he bellowed to his amazed staff. 'Send for a keeper, and a straitjacket.'

He turned round, for a sudden silence had settled on the room behind. Drummond was standing motionless gripping both the Professor's arms, with a look of amazement slowly dawning on his face. Surely he couldn't be mistaken, and yet – unless Peterson had suffered from some wasting disease – what on earth had happened to the man? The arms he felt under the coat-sleeve were thin as match-sticks, whereas Peterson as he remembered of old was almost as strong as he was.

He stared at Professor Scheidstrun's face. Yes – surely that nose was too good to be true. He pulled it thoughtfully and methodically – first this way then that – while the unhappy victim screamed with agony, and the junior clerk upset the ink in his excitement at the untoward spectacle.

It was real right enough – that nose. At least nothing had come off so far, and a little dazedly Drummond backed away, still staring at him. Surely he hadn't made a mistake: the gesture – that movement of the left hand had been quite unmistakable. And the next instant a terrific blow on the right ear turned his attention to other things.

He swung round to find a monumental woman regarding him with the light of battle in her eyes.

'How dare you,' she boomed, 'the nose of my Heinrich pull?'

With great agility Drummond dodged a heavy second to the jaw, and it was now his turn to flee for safety. And it took a bit of doing. The lady was out for blood, as a heavy volume on the intricacies of Real Estate which missed Drummond's head by half an inch and broke a flower-vase clearly proved.

'He seize my wig; he try to pull off my nose,' wailed the Professor, as Mr Tootem junior, attracted by the din, rushed in.

'And if I the coward catch,' bellowed his spouse, picking up a companion volume on Probate and Divorce, 'I will not try – I will succeed with his.'

'Three to one on the filly,' murmured young Tootem gracelessly, as with a heavy crash Probate and Divorce shot through the window.

But mercifully for all concerned, especially the reputation of Tootem, Price & Tootem, it proved to be the lady's dying gasp. Completely exhausted she sank into a chair, and Drummond caut-iously emerged from behind a table. He was feeling a little faint himself; the need for alcohol was pressing. One thing even to his whirling brain was beyond dispute. Impossible though it was that Peterson should have shrunk, it was even more impossible that Irma should have swollen. By no conceivable art of disguise could that beautiful and graceful girl have turned herself into the human monstrosity who was now regarding him balefully from her chair. Her arms were twice the size of his own, and unless Irma had developed elephantiasis the thing simply could not be. Of course she might have covered herself with india-rubber and blown herself out in some way; he didn't put anything beyond Peterson. But the thought of pricking her with a pin to make sure was beyond even his nerve. It was too early in the day to ask any woman to burst with a slow whistling noise. And if she was real . . . He trembled violently at the mere thought of what would happen.

No; incredible though it was, he had made a ghastly mistake. Moreover, the next move was clearly with him.

'I'm afraid I've made a bloomer,' he murmured, mopping his forehead. 'What about a small spot all round, and – er – I'll try to explain.'

It cannot be said that he found the process of explaining an easy one. The lady in particular, having got her second wind, seemed only too ready to cut the cackle and get down to it again; and, as Drummond had to admit even to himself, the explanation sounded a bit lame. To assault unmercifully an elderly German savant in a lawyer's office merely because he was drumming with his left hand on his knee was, as Mr Tootem junior put it, a shade over the odds. And his excuse for so doing – his description of the inconceivable villainies of Carl Peterson in the past – was received coldly.

In fact Hugh Drummond proceeded to spend an extremely unpleasant twenty minutes, which might have been considerably prolonged but for Mr Tootem senior remembering that the umpires were just about coming out at Lord's.

He rose from his chair pontifically.

'I think we must assume,' he remarked, 'that this misguided young man was actuated by worthy motives, even though his actions left much to be desired. His keenness to safeguard the valuable notes of my late lamented client no doubt inspired his amazing outburst. And since he has apologised so profusely to you, Professor – and also, my dear Madam, to you – I would suggest that you might see your way to accepting that apology, and that we – ah – might terminate the interview. I have no doubt that now that Captain Drummond has satisfied himself so – ah – practically that you are not – I forget his friend's name – he will have no hesitation in handing over the notes to me. Should he still refuse, I shall, of course, have no other alternative but to send for the police – which would cause a most unpleasant contretemps for all concerned. Especially on the very day of the – er – funeral.'

Drummond fumbled in his pocket.

'I'll hand 'em over right enough,' he remarked wearily. 'I wish I'd never seen the blamed things.'

He passed the sheets of paper across the desk to Mr Tootem.

'If I don't get outside a pint of beer soon,' he continued, reaching for his hat, 'there will be a double event in the funeral line.'

Once again he apologised profusely to the German, and staggered slightly in his tracks as he gazed at the lady. Then blindly he made his way to the door, and twenty minutes later he entered his house a comparatively broken man. Even Algy awoke from his lethargy and gazed at him appalled.

'You mean to say you pulled the old bean's nose?' he gasped.

'This way and that,' sighed Hugh. 'And very, very hard. Only nothing like as hard as his wife hit me. She's got a sweeping left, Algy, like the kick of a mule. Good Lord! What an unholy box-up. I must say if it hadn't been for old Tootem, it might have been deuced serious. The office looked like the morning after a wet night.'

'So you've handed over the notes?'

'I have,' said Hugh savagely. 'And as I told old Tootem in his office, I wish to heavens I'd never seen the bally things. Old Scheid-strun's got 'em, and he can keep 'em.'

Which was where the error occurred. Professor Scheidstrun had certainly got them – Mr Tootem senior had pressed them into his hands with almost indecent brevity the instant Drummond left the office – but Professor Scheidstrun was not going to keep them. At that very moment, in fact, he was handing them over to a bene-volent-looking old gentleman with mutton-chop whiskers in a room in Mr Atkinson's house in the quiet square.

'Tell me all about it,' murmured the old gentleman, with a smile. 'You've no idea how interested I am in it. I would have given quite a lot to have been present myself.'

'*Mein Gott!*' grunted the Professor. 'He is a holy terror, that man. He tear off my wig; he try to tear off my nose.'

'And then I him on the ear hit,' boomed his wife.

'Splendid,' chuckled the other. 'Quite splendid. He is a violent young man at times is Captain Drummond.'

'It was that the colour of my wig was different that first made him suspect,' went on the German. 'And then I do what you tell me – I tap with my left hand so upon my knee. The next moment he jumps upon me like a madman.'

'I thought he probably would,' said the old gentleman. 'A very amusing little experiment in psychology. You might make a note of it, Professor. The surest way of allaying suspicions is to arouse them thoroughly, and then prove that they are groundless. Hence your somewhat sudden summons by aeroplane from Germany. I have arranged that you should return in the same manner tomorrow after the funeral – which you will attend this afternoon.'

'It was inconvenient – that summons,' said his wife heavily. 'And my husband has been assaulted . . . '

Her words died away as she looked at the benevolent old man. For no trace of benevolence remained on his face, and she shuddered uncontrollably.

'People who do inconvenient things, Frau,' he said quietly, 'and get found out must expect inconvenient calls to be made upon them.'

'How long is this to continue?' she demanded. 'How long are we to remain in your power? This is the second time that you have impersonated my husband. I tell you when I heard that young man speaking this morning, and knew how near he was to the truth – almost did I tell him.'

'But not quite. Not quite, Frau Scheidstrun. You are no fool; you know what would have happened if you had. I still hold the proofs of your husband's unfortunate slip a year or two ago.'

His eyes were boring into her, and once again she shuddered.

'I shall impersonate your husband when and where I please,' he continued, 'if it suits my convenience. I regard him as one of my most successful character-studies.'

His tone changed; he was the benevolent old gentleman again.

'Come, come, my dear Frau Scheidstrun,' he remarked affably, 'you take an exaggerated view of things. After all, the damage to your husband's nose is slight, considering the far-reaching results obtained by letting that young man pull it. All his suspicions are allayed; he merely thinks he's made a profound ass of himself. Which is just as it should be. Moreover, with the mark in its present depreciated state, I think the cheque I propose to hand to your husband for the trouble he has taken will ease matters in the house-keeping line.'

He rose from his chair chuckling.

'Well, I think that is all. As I said before, you will attend the funeral this afternoon. Such a performance does not call for conversation, and so it will not be necessary for me to prime you with anything more than you know already. Your brother-scientists, who will doubtless be there in force, you will know how to deal with far better than I, seeing that I should undoubtedly fail to recognise any of them. And should Drummond be there – well, my dear fellow, I leave it to your sense of Christian decency as to how you treat him. In the presence of – ah – death' – the old gentleman blew his nose – 'a policy of kindly charity is, I think, indicated. Anyway, don't I beg of you, so far forget yourself as to pull *his* nose. For without your wife to protect you I shudder to think what the results might be.'

He smiled genially as he lit a cigar.

'And you,' said the German, 'you do not the funeral attend?'

'My dear Professor,' murmured the other, 'you surprise me. In what capacity do you suggest that I should attend this melancholy function? Even the mourners might be a trifle surprised if they saw two of us there. And as Mr William Robinson – my present rôle – I had not the pleasure of the deceased gentleman's acquaintance. No; I am going into the country to join my brother – the poor fellow is failing a little mentally. Freyder will make all arrangements for your departure tomorrow, and so I will say goodbye. You have committed to memory – have you not? – the hours and days when you did things in London before you arrived? And destroyed the paper? Good; a document of that sort is dangerous. Finally, Professor, don't forget your well-known reputation for absentmindedness and eccentricity. Should anyone ask you a question about your doings in London which you find difficult to answer, just give your celebrated imitation of a windmill and say nothing. I may remark that if Freyder's telephone report to me is satisfactory this evening, I shall have no hesitation in doubling the amount I suggested as your fee.'

With a wave of his hand he was gone, and Professor Scheidstrun and his wife watched the big car drive away from the door.

'*Gott in Himmel*,' muttered the German. 'But the man is a devil.'

'His money is far from the devil,' replied his wife prosaically. 'If he doubles it, we shall have five hundred pounds. And five hundred pounds will be very useful just now.'

But her husband was not to be comforted.

'I am frightened, Minna,' he said tremulously. 'We know not what we are mixed up in. He has told us nothing as to why he is doing all this.'

'He has told us all that he wishes us to know,' answered his wife. 'That is his way.'

'Why is he dressed up like that?' continued the Professor. 'And how did Goodman really die?' He stared fearfully at his wife. 'Blown up? Yes. But – by whom?'

'Be silent, Heinrich,' said his wife, but fear was in her eyes too. 'It is not good to think of these things. Let us have lunch, and then you must go to the funeral. And after that he will send us the money, as he did last time, and we will go back to Dresden. Then we will pray the good God that he will leave us alone.'

'What frightens me, Minna, is that it is I who am supposed to have been with Goodman on the afternoon it happened. And if the police should find out things, what am I to say? Already there are people who suspect – that big man this morning, for instance. How am I to prove that it was not I, but that devil made up to look like me? *Mein Gott*, but he is clever. I should not have hidden myself away as he told me to do in his letter.'

'He would have found out if you hadn't,' said his wife. 'He knows everything.'

'There was no-one who saw us start,' went on the German excitedly. 'At least no-one who saw me start. You they saw – but me, I was smuggled into the aeroplane. Everything is accounted for by that devil. It is impossible for me to prove an alibi. For four days I have concealed myself; our friends all think, as you told them, that I have gone to England. They think you follow, and they will see us return. Would anyone believe us if now we said it was all a lie? They would say – why did you remain hidden? What was the object of all this deceit? And I – what can I say? That I am in the power of someone whom, to save my life, I cannot describe. No-one would believe me; it would make my position worse.'

He grew almost hysterical in his agitation.

'There is one comfort, my dear,' said his wife soothingly. 'As long as everyone believes that it was you who was with Professor Goodman they are not likely to suspect very much. For foul play there must be a motive, and there could be no motive in your case. No, Heinrich, that devil has foreseen everything. No-one was suspicious except the big man this morning, and now he is suspicious no longer. All that we have to do is just what we are told, and we shall be safe. But, *mein Gott*, I wish that we were on board that foul machine again, even though I shall assuredly be sick the whole way.'

The worthy woman rose and placed a hand like a leg of mutton on her husband's shoulder.

'Lunch,' she continued. 'And then you must go to the funeral, while I await you here.'

And so an hour later Professor Scheidstrun, fortified by a most excellent meal, chartered a taxi and drove off to attend the ceremony. After all, his wife was a woman of sound common sense, and there was much in what she said. Moreover, five hundred pounds was not obtained every day. With his usual diabolical cleverness that man, whose real name even he did not know, had so arranged things that his scheme would succeed. He always did succeed; this would be no exception. And provided the scheme was successful, he personally would be safe.

He stepped out at the church door and paid his fare. A celebrated Scotch chemist whom he knew, and who was entering the church at the same moment, stopped and spoke a few words with him, and for a while they stood chatting on the pavement outside. Then the Scotchman moved away, and the Professor was about to enter the church when someone touched him on the arm.

He turned to find a young man, wearing an eyeglass, whom he had never seen before in his life.

'Afternoon, Professor,' said the young man.

The Professor grunted. Who on earth was this? Some relative presumably of the dead man.

'You don't seem to remember me,' went on the young man slowly.

The fact was hardly surprising, but mindful of his instructions the German waved his arms vaguely and endeavoured to escape into the church. But the young man, whose eyes had narrowed suddenly, was not to be shaken off quite so easily.

'One moment, Professor,' he said quietly. '*Do* you remember me?'

Again the German grunted unintelligibly, but his brain was working quickly. Obviously this young man knew him; therefore he ought obviously to know the young man.

'Ja,' he grunted, 'I haf met you, but I know not where.'

'Don't you remember coming round to Captain Drummond's house yesterday afternoon?' went on the other.

'Of course,' said the Professor, beginning to feel firm ground again. 'It was there that we did meet.'

'That's it,' said the young man cheerfully. 'I was one of the four fellows there with Drummond.'

'It vos stupid of me to haf forgotten,' remarked the German, breathing an inward sigh of relief. 'But so many were there, that must be my excuse.'

He escaped into the church, and Algy Longworth made no further attempt to detain him. Without thought, and as a mere matter of politeness, he had spoken to the Professor on seeing him, to be greeted with the blank stare of complete non-recognition. And now the German had concurred in his statement that there had been five of them in the room during the interview, whereas only Hugh and he himself had been present. The short service was drawing to a close, and Algy, who had not heard a word, still stared thoughtfully at the back of the Professor's head, two pews in front. He had noted the nods of greeting from several distinguished-looking old gentlemen as the German had entered the church; but five instead of two! Surely it was incredible that any man, however absentminded and engrossed in other things, should have made such a mistake as that. Even poor old Goodman himself had not been as bad as that. Besides, he personally had spoken not once but several times to the German during the interview. He couldn't have forgotten so completely.

But the fact remained that after the service was over, Professor Scheidstrun chatted for some time with several other elderly men, who apparently had no doubts as to his identity. In fact it was impossible to believe that the man was not what he professed to be, especially as he too, remembering what Hugh had said, had laid his hand on the German's arm outside the church and felt it. It was skinny and thin – and yet five instead of two! That was the thing that stuck in his gizzard.

If only he could think of some test question which would settle the matter! But he couldn't, and even if he had been able to there was no further chance of asking it. Professor Scheidstrun completely ignored his existence, and finally drove away without speaking to him again.

And it was a very puzzled young man who finally returned to Brook Street to find Hugh Drummond sunk in the depths of depression. He listened in silence to what Algy had to say, and then he shook his head.

'My dear old man,' he said at length, 'it cuts no ice. It's funny, I know. If you or I went round to have a buck with a fellow, we should remember whether the isolation was complete or whether we were crushed to death in the mob. But with these scientific blokes it's altogether different. He probably has completely forgotten the entire incident. And yet, Algy, the conviction is growing on me that I've been had for a mug. Somehow or other they've handed us the dirty end. I confess it's difficult to follow. I'm convinced that the man today in Tootem's office is the genuine article. And if he is it's almost impossible to believe that poor old Goodman's death was anything but an accident. Then where's the catch? That's what I've been try-ing to puzzle out for the last three hours, and I'm just where I was when I started.'

'You think that German is going to do what he said? Go back and carry on with Goodman's discovery?'

'I don't know what else to think.'

'Then I'll tell you one thing, Hugh,' said Algy thoughtfully. 'You'd have a death from heat-apoplexy if old Blantyre knew it. And he was showing no signs of a rush of blood to the face at the funeral today.'

Drummond sat up and stared at his friend.

'Which means either that he doesn't know anything about it and believes that the secret died with Goodman; or else, Algy, he's got at Scheidstrun. Somehow or other he's found out about that letter, and he's induced the German to part with the notes.'

He rose and paced up and down the room.

'Or else – Great Scott! Algy, can it be possible that the whole thing has been carefully worked from beginning to end? Blantyre went over to Switzerland – Toby told me that. He went over looking like a sick headache and came back bursting with himself.'

Drummond's face was hard.

'If I thought that that swine had deliberately hired the German to murder poor old Goodman . . . '

His great hands were clenched by his side, as he stared grimly out of the window.

'I made a fool of myself this morning,' he went on after a while. 'I suppose I've got Carl Peterson on the brain. But there are other swine in the world, Algy, beside him. And if I could prove . . . '

'Quite,' remarked Algy. 'But how the devil can you prove anything?'

Suddenly Drummond swung round.

'I'm going round to see Blantyre now,' he said decisively. 'Will you come?'

Chapter 7

In which Drummond takes a telephone call and regrets it

Half an hour later Algy and he walked through the unpretentious door that led to the office of the Metropolitan Diamond Syndicate, to be greeted with a shout of joy from Toby Sinclair emerging from an inner room.

'You have come to ask me to consume nourishment at your expense,' he cried. 'I know it. I accept. I will also dine this evening.'

'Dry up, Toby,' grunted Hugh. 'Is your boss in?'

'Sir Raymond? Yes – why?'

'I want to see him,' said Hugh quietly.

'My dear old man, I'm sorry, but it's quite out of the question,' answered Toby. 'There's a meeting of the whole syndicate on at the present moment upstairs, and . . .'

'I want to see Sir Raymond Blantyre,' interrupted Hugh. 'And, Toby, I'm going to see Sir Raymond Blantyre. And if his darned syndicate is there, I'll see his syndicate as well.'

'But, Hugh, old man,' spluttered Toby, 'be reasonable. It's an important business meeting, and . . .'

Hugh laid his hands on Toby's shoulders and grinned.

'Toby, don't waste time. Trot along upstairs – bow nicely, and say "Captain Drummond craves audience". And when he asks what for, just say, "In connection with an explosion which took place at Hampstead".'

And of a sudden it seemed as if a strange tension had come into Toby Sinclair's room. For Toby was one of those who had hunted with Hugh in days gone by, and he recognised the look in the big man's eyes. Something was up – something serious, that he knew at once. And certain nebulous, half-formed suspicions which he had vigorously suppressed in his own mind stirred into being.

'What is it, old man?' he asked quietly.

'I'll know better after the interview, Toby,' answered the other. 'But one thing I will tell you now. It's either nothing at all, or else your boss is one of the most blackguardly villains alive in London today. Now go up and tell him.'

And without another word Toby Sinclair went. Probably not for another living man would he have interrupted the meeting upstairs. But the habits of other days held; when Hugh Drummond gave an order, it was carried out.

A minute later he was down again.

'Sir Raymond will see you at once, Hugh,' and for Toby Sinclair his expression was thoughtful. For the sudden silence that had settled on the room of directors as he gave the message had not escaped his attention. And the air of carefully suppressed nervous expectancy on the part of the Metropolitan Diamond Syndicate did not escape Drummond's attention either as he entered, followed by Algy Longworth.

'Captain Drummond?' Sir Raymond Blantyre rose, and indicated a chair with his hand. 'Ah! and Mr Longworth surely. Please sit down. I think I saw you in the distance at the funeral today. Now, Captain Drummond, perhaps you will tell us what you want as quickly as possible, as we are in the middle of a rather important meeting.'

'I will try to be as short as possible, Sir Raymond,' said Drummond quietly. 'It concerns, as you have probably guessed, the sad death of Professor Goodman, in which I, personally, am very interested. You see, the Professor lunched with me at my club on the day of his death.'

'Indeed,' murmured Sir Raymond politely.

'Yes – I met him in St. James's Square, where he'd been followed.'

'Followed,' said one of the directors. 'What do you mean?'

'Exactly what I say. He was being followed. He was also in a very excited condition owing to the fact that he had just received a letter threatening his life, unless he consented to accept two hundred and fifty thousand pounds as the price for suppressing his discovery for manufacturing diamonds cheaply. But you know all this part, don't you?'

'I know nothing whatever about a threatening letter,' said Sir Raymond. 'It's the first I've heard of it. Of his process, of course, I know. I think Mr Longworth was present at the dinner on the night I examined the ornament Miss Goodman was wearing. And believing then that the process was indeed capable of producing genuine diamonds, I did offer Professor Goodman a quarter of a million pounds to suppress it.'

'Believing *then*?' said Drummond, staring at him.

'Yes; for a time I and my colleagues here did really believe that the discovery had been made,' answered Sir Raymond easily. 'And I will go as far as to say that even as it stands the process – now so unfortunately lost to science – produced most marvellous imitations. In fact' – he gave a deprecatory laugh – 'it produced such marvellous imitations that it deceived us. But they will not stand the test of time. In some samples he made for us at a demonstration minute flaws are already beginning to show themselves – flaws which only the expert would notice, but they're there.'

'I see,' murmured Drummond quietly, and Sir Raymond shifted a little in his chair. Ridiculous though it was, this vast young man facing him had a peculiarly direct stare which he found almost disconcerting.

'I see,' repeated Drummond. 'So the system was a dud.'

'Precisely, Captain Drummond. The system was of no use. A gigantic advance, you will understand, on anything that has ever been done before in that line – but still, of no use. And if one may extract some little ray of comfort from the appalling tragedy which caused Professor Goodman's death, it surely is that he was at any rate spared from the laughter of the scientific world whose good opinion he valued so greatly.'

Sir Raymond leaned back in his chair, and a murmur of sympathetic approval for words well and truly uttered passed round the room. And feeling considerably more sure of himself, it dawned on the mind of the chairman that up to date he had done most of the talking, and that so far his visitor's principal contribution had been confined to monosyllables. Who was he, anyway, this Captain Drummond? Some friend of the idiotic youth with the eyeglass, presumably. He began to wonder why he had ever consented to see him.

'However, Captain Drummond,' he continued with a trace of asperity, 'you doubtless came round to speak to me about something. And since we are rather busy this evening . . . '

He broke off and waited.

'I did wish to speak to you,' said Drummond, carefully selecting a cigarette. 'But since the process is no good, I don't think it matters very much.'

'It is certainly no good,' answered Sir Raymond.

'So I'm afraid old Scheidstrun will only be wasting his time.'

For a moment it almost seemed as if the clock had stopped, so intense was the sudden silence.

'I don't quite understand what you mean,' said Sir Raymond, in a voice which, strive as he would, he could not make quite steady.

'No?' murmured Drummond placidly. 'You didn't know of Professor Goodman's last instructions? However, since the whole thing is a dud, I won't worry you.'

'What do you know of Scheidstrun,' asked Sir Raymond.

'Just a funny old Boche. He came to see me yesterday afternoon with the Professor's last will, so to speak. And then I interviewed him this morning in the office of the excellent Mr Tootem, and pulled his nose – poor old dear!'

'Professor Scheidstrun came to see you?' cried Sir Raymond, standing up suddenly. 'What for?'

'Why, to get the notes of the diamond process, which the Professor gave me at lunch on the day of his death.'

Drummond thoughtfully lit his cigarette, apparently oblivious of the fact that every man in the room was glaring at him speechlessly.

'But since it's a dud – I'm afraid he'll waste his time.'

'But the notes were destroyed.' Every vestige of control had left Sir Raymond's voice; his agitation was obvious.

'How do you know?' snapped Drummond, and the President of the Metropolitan Diamond Syndicate found himself staring almost fascinated at a pair of eyes from which every trace of laziness had vanished.

'He always carried them with him,' he stammered. 'And I – er – assumed . . . '

'Then you assumed wrong. Professor Goodman handed me those notes at lunch the day he died.'

'Where are they now?' It was Mr Leibhaus who asked the question in his guttural voice.

'Since they are of no use, what does it matter?' answered Drummond indifferently.

'Gentlemen!' Sir Raymond's peremptory voice checked the sudden buzz of conversation. 'Captain Drummond,' he remarked, 'I must confess that what you have told me this afternoon has given me a slight shock. As I say, I had assumed that the notes of the process had perished with the Professor. You now tell us that he handed them to you. Well, I make no bones about it that though – from a purely scientific point of view the process fails – yet – er – from a business point of view it is not one that any of us would care to have noised abroad. You will understand that if diamonds can be made cheaply which except to the eye of the most practical expert are real, it will –

er – not be a good thing for those who are interested in the diamond market? You can understand that, can't you?'

'I tell you what I can understand, Sir Raymond,' said Drummond quietly. 'And that is that you're a damned bad poker-player. If flaws – as you say – have appeared in the diamonds manufactured by this process, you and your pals here would not now be giving the finest example of a vertical typhoon that I've ever seen.'

Sir Raymond subsided in his chair a little foolishly; he felt at a complete loss as to where he stood with this astonishing young man. And it was left to Mr Leibhaus to make the next move.

'Let us leave that point for the moment,' he remarked. 'Where are these notes now?'

'I've already told you,' replied Drummond casually. 'The worthy Scheidstrun has them. And in accordance with Professor Goodman's written instructions he proposes to give the secret to the world of science at an early date. In fact he is going back to Germany tomorrow to do so.'

'But the thing is impossible,' cried Sir Raymond, recovering his speech. 'You mean to say that Professor Goodman left written instructions that the notes of his process were to be handed over to – to Scheidstrun?'

'I do,' returned Drummond. 'And if you want confirmation, you can ring up Mr Tootem of Austin Friars – Professor Goodman's lawyer. He saw the letter, and it was in his office the notes were handed over.'

'You will excuse me, Captain Drummond, if I confer for a few moments with my friends,' said Sir Raymond, rising.

The directors of the Metropolitan Diamond Syndicate withdrew to the farther end of the long room, leaving Drummond still sitting at the table. And to that gentleman's shrewd eye it was soon apparent that his chance arrow had hit the mark, though exactly what mark it was, was still beyond him. But the agitation displayed by the group of men in the window was too obvious to miss, and had he known all the facts he would have found it hardly surprising. The directors were faced unexpectedly with as thorny a problem as could well be devised.

Believing as they had that the notes had been destroyed – had not Mr Edward Blackton assured them of that fact? – they had unanimously decided to adopt the rôle that the process had proved useless, thereby removing any possible suspicion that might attach itself to them. And now they found that not only had the notes not been destroyed, but that they were in the possession of Blackton himself. And it needed but little imagination to realise that dangerous though the knowledge of the process had been in the hands of Professor Goodman, it was twenty times more so in the hands of Blackton if he meant to double-cross them.

That was the point: did he? Or had he discovered somehow or other that Drummond held the notes and taken these steps in order to get them?

And the second little matter which had to be solved was how much this man Drummond knew. If he knew nothing at all, why had he bothered to come round and see them? It was out of the question, surely, that he could have any inkling of the real truth concerning the bogus Professor Scheidstrun. Had not the impersonation deceived even London scientists who knew the real man at the funeral that afternoon?

For a while the directors conferred together in whispers; then Sir Raymond advanced towards the table. The first thing was to get rid of Drummond.

'I am sure we are all very much obliged to you, Captain Drummond, for taking so much trouble and coming round to see us, but I don't think there is anything more you can do. Should an opportunity arise I will take steps to let Professor Scheidstrun know what we think – '

He held out a cordial hand to terminate the interview.

But it takes two people to terminate an interview, and Drummond had no intention of being the second. He realised that he was on delicate ground and that it behoved him to walk warily. But his conviction that something was wrong somewhere was stronger than ever, and he was determined to try to get to the bottom of it.

'It might perhaps be as well, Sir Raymond,' he remarked, 'to go round and tell him now. I know where he is stopping.'

Was it his imagination, or did the men in the window look at one another uneasily?

'As I told you, I pulled the poor old bean's nose this morning, and it seems a good way of making amends.'

Sir Raymond stared at him.

'May I ask why you pulled his nose?'

And Drummond decided on a bold move.

'Because, Sir Raymond, I came to the conclusion that Professor Scheidstrun was not Professor Scheidstrun, but somebody else.' There was no mistaking the air of tension now. 'I may say that I was mistaken.'

'Who did you think he was?' Sir Raymond gave a forced laugh.

'A gentleman of international reputation,' said Drummond quietly, 'who masquerades under a variety of names. I knew him first as Carl Peterson, but he answers to a lot of titles. The Comte de Guy is one of them.'

And now the atmosphere was electric, a fact which did not escape Drummond. His eyes had narrowed; he was sitting very still. In the language of the old nursery game, he was getting warm.

'But I conclusively proved, gentlemen,' he continued, 'that the man to whom I handed those notes this morning was not the Comte de Guy. The Comte, gentlemen, has arms as big as mine. His physical strength is very great. This man had arms like walking-sticks, and he couldn't have strangled a mouse.'

One by one the men at the window had returned to their seats, and now they sat in perfect silence staring at Drummond. What on earth was this new complication, or was this man deliberately deceiving them?

'Do you know the Comte de Guy well?' said Sir Raymond after a pause.

'Very well,' remarked Drummond. 'Do you?'

'I have heard of him,' answered the other.

'Then, as you probably know, his power of disguising himself is so miraculous as to be uncanny. He has one little mannerism, however, which he sometimes shows in moments of excitement, whatever his disguise. And it has enabled me to spot him on one or two occasions. When therefore I saw that little trick of his in the lawyer's office this morning, I jumped to the conclusion that my old friend was on the warpath again. So I leaped upon him, and the subsequent scene was dreadful. It was not my old friend at all, but a complete stranger with a vast wife who nearly felled me with a blow on the ear.'

He selected another cigarette with care.

'However,' he continued casually, 'it's a very good thing for you that the process is a dud. Because I am sure nothing would induce him to disregard Professor Goodman's wishes on the subject if it hadn't been.'

'You say you know where he is stopping?' said Sir Raymond.

'I do,' answered Drummond.

'Then I think perhaps that it would be a good thing to do as you suggest, and go round and see him now.' He had been thinking rapidly while Drummond was speaking, and one or two points were clear. In some miraculous way this young man had blundered on to the truth. That the man Drummond had met in the lawyer's office that morning was any other than Blackton he did not for a moment believe. But Blackton had bluffed him somehow, and for the time had thrown him off the scent. The one vital thing was to prevent him getting on to it again. And since there was no way of telling what Drummond would find when he went round to the house, it was imperative that he should be there himself. For if there was one person whom Sir Raymond did not expect to meet there, it was Professor Scheidstrun. And in that event he must be on hand to see what happened.

'Shall we go at once? My car is here.'

'By all means,' said Drummond. 'And if there's room we might take Algy as well. He gets into mischief if he's left lying about.'

On one point at any rate Sir Raymond's expectations were not realised. Professor Scheidstrun was at the house right enough; in fact he and his wife had just finished their tea. And neither the worthy Teuton nor his spouse evinced the slightest pleasure on seeing their visitors. With the termination of the funeral they had believed their troubles to be over, and now this extremely powerful and objectionable young man had come to worry them again, to say nothing of his friend who had spoken to the Professor at the funeral. And what did Sir Raymond Blantyre want? Scheidstrun had been coached carefully as to who and what Sir Raymond was, but what on earth had he come round about? Especially with Drummond?

It was the latter who stated the reason of their visit.

'I've come about those notes, Professor,' he remarked cheerfully. 'You know – the ones that caused that slight breeze in old Tootem's office this morning.'

'So,' grunted the Professor, blinking uneasily behind his spectacles. It struck him that the ground was getting dangerous.

'I feel,' went on Drummond affably, 'that after our unfortunate little contretemps I ought to try to make some amends. And as I know you're a busy man I shouldn't like you to waste your time needlessly. Now, you propose, don't you, to carry on with Professor Goodman's process, and demonstrate it to the world at large?'

'That is so,' said the German.

Out of the corner of his eye Drummond looked at Sir Raymond, but the President of the Metropolitan Diamond Syndicate was staring impassively out of the window.

'Well, I'm sorry to say the process is a dud; a failure; no bally earthly. You get me, I trust.'

'A failure. Ach! is dot so?' rumbled Scheidstrun, who was by this time completely out of his depth.

'And that being the case, Professor,' murmured Sir Raymond, 'it would be better to destroy the notes at once, don't you think? I was under the impression' – he added pointedly – 'that they had already been destroyed in the accident.'

Strangely enough, the presence of Drummond gave him a feeling of confidence with Mr Edward Blackton which he had never experienced before. And this was a golden opportunity for securing the destruction of those accursed papers, and thus preventing any possibility of his being double-crossed.

'Shall we therefóre destroy them at once?' he repeated quietly.

The German fidgeted in his chair. Willingly would he have destroyed them on the spot if they had still been in his possession. Anything to be rid of his visitors. He glanced from one to the other of them. Drummond was apparently staring at the flies on the ceiling; Sir Raymond was staring at him, and his stare was full of some hidden meaning. But since it was manifestly impossible for him to do as Sir Raymond suggested, the only thing to do was to temporise.

'I fear that to destroy them I cannot,' he murmured. 'At least – not yet. My duty to my dear friend . . . '

'Duty be damned!' snarled Sir Raymond, forgetting Drummond's presence in his rage. This swine *was* trying to double-cross him after all.

'You'll destroy those notes here and now, or . . . '

With a great effort he pulled himself together.

'Or what?' asked Drummond mildly. 'You seem strangely determined, Sir Raymond, that Professor Scheidstrun shouldn't waste his time. Deuced praiseworthy, I call it, on your part . . . Interests of science and all that . . . '

Sir Raymond smothered a curse, and glared still more furiously at the German. And suddenly Drummond rose to his feet, and strolled over to the open window.

'Well, I don't think there's much good our waiting here,' he remarked in a bored voice. 'If he wants to fool round with the process, he must. Coming, Sir Raymond?'

'In a moment or two, Captain Drummond. Don't you wait.'

'Right. Come on, Algy. Apologies again about the nose, Professor. So long.'

He opened the door, and paused outside for Algy to join him. And every trace of boredom had vanished from his face.

'Go downstairs noisily,' he whispered. 'Make a remark as if I was with you. Go out and slam the front door. Then hang about and wait for me.'

'Right,' answered the other. 'But what are you going to do?'

'Listen to their conversation, old man. I have an idea it may be interesting.'

Without a sound he opened the door of the next room and went in. It was a bedroom and it was empty, and Drummond heaved a sigh of relief. The window, he knew, would be open – he had seen that as he looked out in the other room. Moreover, the square was a quiet one; he could hear easily what was being said next door by leaning out.

And for the next five minutes he leaned out, and he heard. And so engrossed was he in what he heard that he quite failed to notice a dark-skinned, sturdy man who paused abruptly on the pavement a few houses away, and disappeared as suddenly as he had come. So engrossed was he in what he heard that he even failed to hear a faint click from the door behind him a few moments later.

All he noticed was that the voices in the next room suddenly ceased, but he had heard quite enough. There was not one Scheid-strun, but two Scheidstruns, and he had assaulted the wrong one. Of Mr Edward Blackton he had never heard; but there was only one man living who could have suggested that unmistakable trick with his hand – the man he knew as Carl Peterson. Somehow or other he had found out this mannerism of his and had used it deliberately to bluff Drummond, even as he had deliberately double-crossed the Metropolitan Diamond Syndicate. It was just the sort of thing that would appeal to his sense of humour.

So be it: they would crack a jest together over it later. At the moment he wanted a word or two with Sir Raymond Blantyre. He crossed to the door and tried to open it. But the door was locked, and the key was on the outside.

For a moment or two he stood staring at it. His mind was still busy with the staggering conversation he had been listening to, which had almost, if not quite, explained everything. Facts, disconnected before, now joined themselves together in a more or less logical sequence. Sir Raymond Blantyre's visit to Montreux to enlist the aid of this Mr Edward Blackton; the arrival in England of the spurious Professor Scheidstrun; the accident at Hampstead – all that part was clear now. And with regard to that accident, Drummond's face was grim. Cold-blooded murder it must have been, in spite of all Sir Raymond's guarded utterances on the subject.

For it had taken that gentleman ten minutes before he finally realised that the Scheidstrun he was talking to was the genuine article, and during that ten minutes he had spoken with some freedom. And then when he had finally realised it, and grasped the fact that he and his syndicate had been double-crossed, his rage had been terrible. Moreover, he had then said things which made matters even clearer to the man who was listening in the next room. Out of his own mouth he stood condemned as the instigator of an abominable crime.

But Sir Raymond could wait; there would be plenty of time later to deal with that gentleman and his syndicate. The man who called himself Edward Blackton was the immediate necessity, and Drummond had no illusions now as to his identity. It *was* Carl Peterson again, and with the faintest flicker of a smile he acknowledged the touch of genius that had caused him to pass on his little mannerism to the genuine Scheidstrun. It had had exactly the intended effect: certainty that they had again met in the lawyer's office, followed immediately by a crushing proof to the contrary – a proof so overwhelming that but for vague suspicion engendered by the Professor's non-recognition of Algy at the funeral he would have let the whole thing drop.

It was just like Peterson to bluff to the limit of his hand; moreover, it would have appealed to his sense of humour. And the point which was not clear to either Sir Raymond or the German was very clear to him. To them it had seemed an unnecessary complication to bring over the genuine Scheidstrun – but there Drummond could supply the missing link. And that link was his previous acquaintance with the arch-criminal. The combination of shrewd insight and consummate nerve which deliberately banked on that previous acquaintance and turned it to gain was Peterson all over – or rather Blackton, to give him his present name. Moreover, the advantage of having the genuine article at the funeral where he was bound to run into many friends and acquaintances was obvious. Most assuredly the touch of the master-hand was in evidence again, but where was the hand itself? It was that question which Sir Raymond, almost inarticulate with rage, had asked again and again; and it was the answer to that question which Professor Scheidstrun would not or could not give. Listening intently, Drummond had inclined to the latter alternative, though not being able to see the speaker's face, he had had to rely on inflection of voice. But it had seemed to him as if he was speaking the truth when he absolutely denied any knowledge whatever of

Blackton's whereabouts. An old gentleman with mutton-chop whiskers – that was all he could say. But where he was, or what he was doing, he knew no more than Sir Raymond. He had left that morning with the notes in his possession, and that was all he could tell his infuriated questioner.

And then a sudden silence had fallen while Drummond still craned out of the window listening – a silence which endured so long that finally he stepped back into the room, only to discover that he was locked in. For a moment or two, as has been said, he stood staring at the door; then with a grunt he charged it with his shoulders. But the door was strong, and it took him three minutes before, with a final splintering crash, the door burst open, almost throwing him on his face. For a while he stood listening: the house was silent. And since in ordinary respectable houses the bursting open of a door is not greeted with absolute silence, Drummond's hand went automatically to his hip-pocket. Past association with Peterson accounted for the involuntary movement, but much water had flowed under the bridge since those happy days, and with a sigh he realised that he was unarmed. With his back to the wall he took careful stock of his surroundings. Every nerve was alert for possible eventualities; his arms, hanging a little forward, were tingling at the prospect of action.

Still there was no sound. The passage was deserted; all the doors were shut. And yet keys do not turn by themselves. Someone had locked him in: the question was, who had done it? And where was he? Or could it be a she? Could it be that monumental woman who had assaulted him only that morning. He turned a little pale at the thought; but with the knowledge that he now possessed of her husband's complicity in the affair he felt he could meet her on rather more level terms. And there was comfort in the knowledge that everyone in the house was so confoundedly crooked. The likelihood of their sending for the police to eject him from the premises was, to put it mildly, remote.

Silently as a cat, he took a quick step along the passage and flung open the door of the room in which he had left Sir Raymond Blantyre and the German. It was empty; there was no sign of either man. He crossed to one of the heavy curtains which was drawn back in the window behind the desk, and hit it a heavy blow with his fist. But the folds went back unresistingly; there was no-one hiding behind it. And then swiftly and methodically he went from room to room, moving with that strange, silent tread which was one of his most marked peculiarities. No-one ever heard Drummond coming; in the darkness no-one ever saw him, if he didn't wish him to. The first thing he knew of his presence was a pair of great hands which seemed to materialise out of the night, forcing his head backwards and farther back. And sometimes that was the last thing he knew as well . . .

But there was no darkness in the house as he searched it from top to bottom – only silence. Once he thought he heard the sound of a step above him as he stood downstairs in the dining-room, but it was not repeated, and he decided it was only imagination – a board creaking, perhaps. He went into the kitchen and the scullery; the fire was lit in the range, but of cook or servant there was no sign.

And finally, he returned thoughtfully to the hall. There was no doubt about it, the house was empty save for himself. Sir Raymond and the German had gone during the period that he was locked in the room upstairs. And during that period the other occupants of the house, if any, had gone also.

He carefully selected a cigarette and lit it. The situation required reviewing.

Item one. Sir Raymond Blantyre was a consummate swine who had, by the grace of Allah, been stung on the raw by a hornet. Moreover, before Drummond had finished with him the hornets would have swarmed. But he could wait.

Item two. The genuine Professor Scheidstrun appeared to be a harmless old poop, who was more sinned against than sinning. And he certainly could wait.

Item three. The other Professor Scheidstrun – alias Blackton, alias Peterson, present address unknown – had got away with the goods. He was in full and firm possession of the momentous secret, which Blantyre had paid him half a million to destroy. And involuntarily Drummond smiled. How like him! How completely Peterson to the life! And then the smile faded. To get it, he had murdered a harmless old man in cold blood.

Item four. He himself was in undisputed possession of an empty house in which Peterson had been only that morning.

Could he turn item four to advantage in solving the address question in item three? Everything else was subservient to that essential fact: where was Peterson now? And from his knowledge of the gentleman it was unlikely that he had left directions for forwarding letters pasted conspicuously on the wall. He was one of those shy flowers that prefer to blush unseen. At the same time it was possible that an exhaustive search of the desk upstairs might reveal some clue. And if it didn't presumably the bird who had locked him in would return in due course to find out how he was getting on. Everything therefore pointed to a policy of masterly inactivity in the hopes that something or somebody would turn up.

He slowly ascended the stairs, and again entered the room where the interview had taken place. Time was of no particular object, and for a while he stood by the door turning over the problem in his mind. Then suddenly his eyes became alert: there was a door let into the wall which, by some strange oversight, he had not seen before. And in a flash he remembered the step which he thought he had heard while he was below. Was there someone in that room? and if so, who? Could it be possible – and a glow of wild excitement began to tingle in his veins at the mere thought – could it be possible that the solution of the problem lay close at hand? That here, practically in the same room with him, was Peterson himself?

With one bound he was across the room, and the door was open. One glance was sufficient to dash the dawning hope to the ground: the room was empty, like all the rest had been. But though it was empty it was not devoid of interest, and a faint smile came on Drummond's face as he surveyed the contents. Wigs, clothes, mirrors filled the place to overflowing, though there was no trace of untidiness. And he realised that he was in the inner sanctum where Peterson carried out his marvellous changes of appearance. And with a sudden grim amusement he recognised on a chair the identical egg-stained coat that the spurious Professor Scheidstrun had worn on his visit to him the preceding afternoon. In fact he was so interested in that and other things that he failed to notice a rather curious phenomenon in the room behind him. The heavy curtain which he had hit with his fist moved slightly as if blown by the wind. And there was no wind.

With genuine interest he examined the exhibits – as he called them in his own mind. It was the first time he had ever penetrated into one of Peterson's holy of holies, and though the proprietor was not there himself to act as showman, he was quite able to appreciate the museum without the services of a guide. The wigs – each one on its own head-rest – particularly appealed to him. In fact he went so far as to try some of them on. And after a time a feeling of genuine admiration for the wonderful thoroughness of the man filled his mind. Murderer, thief, forger, and blackguard generally – but what a brain! After all, he fought a lone hand, deliberately pitting himself against the whole of the organised resources of the world. With only the girl to help him he had fought mankind, and up to date he had won through. For both their previous battles had been drawn, and now that the third round was under way – or soon would be – he saluted his adversary in spirit as a foeman worthy of his steel. It was a good thing, after all, that he had not brought in the police. Peterson fought alone: so would he. As it had been in the past, so let it be this time. Their own particular pals on each side could join in the battle if and when occasion arose; but the principal combat must be between Peterson and him – no mercy given, no mercy asked. And this time he had a presentiment that it would be a fight to a finish. It required no stretch of imagination on his part to realise the enormous plum which the criminal had got hold of; it required no stretch of imagination to realise that he would fight as he had never fought before to retain it.

And once again there came up the unanswered question – where was he? It was even impossible to say if he was still in England.

Another thing occurred to Drummond also, as he strolled back into the other room and sat down at the desk. On this occasion the dice would be loaded more heavily in Peterson's favour than before. In the past the only method by which he had ever recognised him was by his strange but unmistakable little mannerism when excited – the mannerism which was innate and had persisted through all his disguises. And now he had discovered what it was; had actually told another man to employ the very trick to fool Drummond. And if he had discovered it, he would take very good care not to use it himself. He would keep his hand in his pocket or something of that sort.

Drummond lay back in his chair and stared at the ceiling, with his head almost touching the heavy curtains behind him. Life undoubtedly was good; but for the murder of Professor Goodman it would have been very good – very good indeed. And at that moment the telephone on the desk in front of him began to ring.

With a jerk Drummond sat up and looked at it – his mind recalled to the circumstances of the moment. Should he let it go on ringing till the operator gave up in despair, or should he take the call? One thing was obvious on the face of it: the call could not be for him. But that was no conclusive reason why he shouldn't take it. Monotonously, insistently, the instrument went on sounding in the silent room, and at last Drummond leaned forward and took the receiver from the hook. And as he did so the curtain behind him stirred again and then was still. But whereas before it had hung in even, regular folds, now it did not. Outlined against it was the figure of a man – a man who inch by inch was pulling the curtain back, a man who held in his right hand a short, villainous-looking iron bar. And as

Drummond leaned forward to be ready to speak into the mouth-piece, Freyder's hard eyes concentrated on the nape of his neck. He was an expert with a life-preserver . . .

Julius Freyder had been anticipating that telephone call, which was why he had concealed himself behind the curtain. From the room which Drummond had overlooked until the end he had watched him strike that curtain with his fist, and had gambled on his not doing so again. Rarely had he received such a shock as when, rounding the corner of the street below, he had seen Drummond of all men leaning out of the window. For it showed conclusively that this accursed *bête noire* was on their heels again, though how he had managed to get there was a mystery. And when on entering the house he had heard, even before he mounted the stairs, the furious utterances of Sir Raymond Blantyre and had realised that Drummond must have heard them too, the need for instant action was obvious.

Julius Freyder was no fool, or he would not have occupied the position he did. And not only was he no fool, but he was also an extremely powerful and dangerous man. It was the work of a second to lock Drummond in, and rush the two excited gentlemen and everyone else in the house through a bolt-hole at the back into some old mews and thus away. But he had no delusions as to the efficacy of a mere bolt against Drummond, and the door was already beginning to crack and splinter as he hid himself amongst the clothes in the inner sanctum. What to do: that was the question. Powerful though he was, he would no more have dreamed of tackling Drummond single-handed than he would have thought of challenging the entire London police force. He would have lasted five seconds with luck. At the same time it was manifestly impossible to leave him in the house alone. Apart from the telephone call which he expected from the Chief at any moment, there might be incriminating documents in the desk. But it was the call that worried him most. Once Drummond got that, even if he didn't recognise the voice at the other end, he would be sure to ask exchange where it came from. And from that, to going down to the New Forest to investigate for himself, probably supported by a bunch of his damned friends, would only be a question of hours. Which was the very last thing to be desired. Just as speed had been the essence of the game before, now it was secrecy. At all costs Drummond must be prevented from finding out the whereabouts of Mr William Robinson.

Perhaps he'd go – leave the house when he found it empty. But no such luck, and Freyder, ensconced behind the curtain, cursed savagely under his breath, as Drummond sat down not two feet from him. Once he was sorely tempted to use his life-preserver then and there, but caution prevailed. Perhaps the call would be delayed; perhaps he would get tired of waiting and go. That was all Freyder wanted – to get him out of the house. A stunned or wounded man at that stage of the proceedings would complicate matters terribly, and when that man was Drummond it could only be done as a last resource. But if it was done it would have to be done properly – no bungling, no faltering.

And then came the ring. Freyder gripped his life-preserver a little tighter and waited. He heard the click of the receiver being taken off the hook; he heard Drummond's preliminary 'Hullo'. And the next moment he struck. It was an easy mark, and, as has been said, he was an expert. With a little sighing grunt Drummond pitched forward and lay motionless, and Freyder picked up the receiver. From it came the Chief's voice vibrant with suspicion.

'What's happened? What was that I heard?'

'It's Freyder speaking, Chief. Drummond is here.'

'What?' It was almost a shout from the other end of the wire.

'He is asleep.' There was a peculiar inflection in Freyder's voice, and he smiled grimly as he heard the long-drawn sigh of relief. 'But I don't think it would be wise in his present condition of health to leave him here.'

'What does he know?'

'That it is impossible to say at present. But Sir Raymond Blantyre has found out a lot.'

The voice at the other end cursed thoughtfully.

'I *must* have at least twenty-four hours, Freyder; if possible more. I'd like three days, but two might do.' There was a pause. 'Will our friend sleep for long?'

'Quite a time, I think,' said Freyder. 'But I think he should be under supervision when he wakes. He might have concussion or be suffering from loss of memory.'

'Ah!' Again came that long-drawn sigh of relief. 'Then a sea voyage, Freyder, is clearly indicated. We will have two invalids instead of one. So bring our young friend here tonight.'

With a faint smile Freyder replaced the receiver on its hook and bent over the unconscious figure of Drummond as it sprawled over the desk.

'I trust you'll enjoy the trip, you young devil,' he snarled.

Chapter 8

In which Drummond plays a little game of trains

The blow that Drummond had received would have broken the neck of any ordinary man. But not being an ordinary man he was only badly stunned. And he was still unconscious when he was carried out of a motor-car at Mr William Robinson's house in the New Forest. That his arrival was regarded as an important affair was evident from the fact that his host came himself to the front door to greet him. But from that moment it is to be feared that Mr Robinson's knowledge of those excellent books on etiquette which deal with the whole duty of a host towards those who honour his roof with their presence went under a slight eclipse. Regrettable to state, he did not escort his guest personally to the old oak bedroom complete with lavender-scented sheets; in fact, he even forgot himself so far as to leave him lying in the hall with his head in the coal-scuttle. But it is pleasant to state that not for long was he so remiss. At a sign from him two men picked up Drummond and carried him into his own private room, where they dropped him on the floor.

'I will make arrangements for the night later,' he remarked. 'Just at present I would like to look at him from time to time, so leave him here.'

The two men went out, leaving Freyder alone with his Chief. And though he had much to tell him of importance, for a while Freyder said nothing. For there was an expression of such incredible ferocity on the benign countenance of Mr Robinson as he stared at the motionless body on the floor that Freyder realised his presence was forgotten. For perhaps two minutes Mr Robinson's eyes never left Drummond's face; then he turned to his subordinate.

'I don't think I should ever have forgiven you, my dear Freyder,' he said softly, 'if you'd had the misfortune to kill him. That supreme joy must be mine and mine alone.'

With almost an effort he obliterated Drummond from his mind, and sat down at his desk.

'Business first; pleasure afterwards. Things have evidently been happening in London. Tell me everything.'

Clearly and concisely Freyder told him what had occurred, while Mr Robinson smoked his cigar in silence. Once or twice he frowned slightly, but otherwise he gave no sign of his feelings.

'You have no idea, then, as to how Drummond and Sir Raymond Blantyre found the house?' he asked as Freyder finished.

'Not the slightest, Chief,' he answered. 'All I know is that it was Drummond who found it, and not Blantyre. Sir Raymond told me that much as I was rushing him out of the house.'

'Did he make any objections to going?'

'Not the slightest. In fact, when he realised that what he had been saying to Scheidstrun had been overheard by Drummond, his one desire was to get away as fast as he could. He apparently thought Drummond had left the house a quarter of an hour before.'

Mr Robinson shrugged his shoulders.

'The point really is immaterial,' he murmured. 'That fool Blantyre dare not speak; Drummond can't. By the way, what has become of Scheidstrun?'

'I sent him and his wife off this evening' said Freyder. 'The pilot said he could make Brussels tonight, and finish the journey tomorrow.'

'Excellent, Freyder – excellent,' said Mr Robinson. 'And the slight inconvenience of Blantyre knowing that I have not destroyed the notes is amply compensated for by the possession of our young friend here.'

'But it will mean altering our plans somewhat,' remarked Freyder doubtfully.

For a while Mr Robinson smoked in silence, gently stroking his mutton-chop whiskers.

'Yes,' he remarked at length, 'it will. Not the plans so much as the timetable. The advent of Drummond at this stage of the proceedings I must confess I did not contemplate. And since I am under no delusions as to his infinite capacity for making a nuisance of himself, the sooner he is finally disposed of the better.'

Freyder shrugged his shoulders.

'Well, Chief,' he said callously, 'there he is. And there's no time like the present.'

Mr Robinson raised a deprecating hand.

'How coarse, my dear Freyder! – How almost vulgar! My feelings against this young man are of a purely personal type. And I assure you they would not be gratified in the smallest degree by disposing of him when he was in the condition he is in now. One might just as well assault a carcase in a butcher's shop. No, no. It will be my earnest endeavour to restore Captain Drummond to perfect health before disposing of him. Or at any rate to such a condition that he realises what is taking place. But from my knowledge of him it is a matter that cannot be postponed indefinitely. As I said before, his capacity for making trouble when confined in any ordinary house is well-nigh unbelievable.'

'Then what do you propose to do, Chief?' asked Freyder.

Given his own way now that Drummond was safely out of London and in their power, he would have finished him off then and there. To his mind Drummond was one of those unpleasant individuals who can be regarded as really safe only when they're dead. And once granted that he was going to be killed in the near future, Freyder would have wasted no further time about it. But he knew the absolute futility of arguing with his Chief once the latter's mind was made up, so he resigned himself at once to the inevitable.

'You are certain that you were not followed here,' said Mr Robinson.

'As certain as anyone can ever be,' answered Freyder. 'Twice I stopped the car at the end of a long, straight stretch of road and turned into a lane. There was no sign of anyone. I didn't bother to change the tyres, since most of the road is tar macadam and there's been no rain. And really there are so many Dunlop Magnums about now, that it's only a waste of time.'

'And as far as I could make out, the telephone operator had no suspicions,' went on his Chief. 'You did it extremely skilfully and silently. So I think, Freyder, we can assume on twenty-four hours for certain before anyone even begins to take any notice. Drummond is a man of peculiar habits, and, somewhat naturally, when I realised he was coming here, I sent a letter in his writing to that inconceivable poop Longworth. A friend of his,' he explained, seeing the look of mystification on the other's face, 'who is engaged to Miss Goodman. It states that he is hot on the trail and the postmark will be Birmingham. So I think we can certainly rely on twenty-four hours, or even forty-eight before his friends begin to move. And that will give me plenty of time to ensure that our friend upstairs has not forgotten his process. Once I am assured of that, and he has written out in a legible hand the ingredients he uses, we will delay no longer. It's a nuisance – for I detest manual labour and smells in a laboratory. And but for Drummond, as you know, we would have remained on here for six months or so, and let the old fool make the stones himself, before disposing of him finally. But since this slight contretemps has occurred, I shall have, much as I regret it, to dispense with that part of the programme. Once I know for certain that I can do it myself – and I shall devote tomorrow to that exclusively – we will give up this house forthwith and go on board the yacht. A good idea of mine, that yacht, Freyder. There is nothing like dying convincingly to enable one to live in comfort.'

Freyder grinned, as he watched Mr Robinson help himself to a mild whisky and soda: undoubtedly the Chief was in an excellent humour.

'We've run a pretty big risk this time, my dear fellow,' he went on thoughtfully. 'And sometimes it almost staggers me when I think how wonderfully we've succeeded. But I am under no delusions as to the abilities of the English police. Once they get on to a thing they never let go – and sooner or later they are bound to get on to this. Probably they will do it through Drummond's disappearance, and Scheidstrun. Sooner or later they will track our connection with this house, and the good ship *Gadfly*. And then when they find that the *Gadfly* left England and has never been heard of again, with true British phlegm they will assume that she has sunk with all hands. And Sir Raymond Blantyre will breathe again – unless they've put the scoundrel in prison for having suggested such an abominable crime to me; in fact, everyone will breathe again except Drummond and our friend upstairs. Oh! and Mr Lewisham. Did you attend the obsequies on Mr Lewisham, Freyder?'

'I did not,' laughed Freyder; and Mr Robinson, contrary to his usual custom, helped himself to another whisky and soda.

'Yes,' he continued dreamily. 'it's a wonderful end to what I may claim without conceit has been a wonderful career. Henceforward, Freyder, my life will be one of blameless virtue.'

The other shook his head doubtfully.

'You'll find it a bit monotonous, Chief,' he said.

Mr Robinson smiled.

'Perhaps so – but I shall give it a trial. And whenever it becomes too monotonous, I shall merely remove more money from the pockets of those two villainous men Blantyre and Leibhaus. It almost makes one despair of human nature when one realises that such cold-blooded scoundrels exist.'

'And Drummond! Have you made up your mind yet as to how you intend to dispose of him?'

'Quite simply,' replied Mr Robinson genially. 'I shall merely attach some heavy weights to his feet and drop him overboard. I am not anxious that his body should be recovered, any more than that of our other friend. That part of the affair presents no difficulties.' His eyes, grown suddenly hard and cruel, fastened on the motionless figure of Drummond, still sprawling on the floor. And suddenly he rose and bent over him with a look of anxiety on his face which changed to relief.

'For a moment I thought he was dead,' he remarked, resuming his seat. 'And that would have been a real grief to me. For him to die without knowing would rob this final coup of its crown. It is the one thing needed, Freyder, to make it perfect.'

The other looked at him curiously.

'How you must hate him, Chief!'

A strange look came into Mr Robinson's eyes, and involuntarily Freyder shuddered. Anger, rage, passion, he had seen on many men's faces, but never before such cold-blooded ferocity as that which showed on the face of the man opposite.

'We all have our weaknesses, Freyder, and I confess that Drummond is mine. And incredible though it may sound to you, if such a thing were possible as for me to have to choose between revenge on him and getting away with Professor Goodman's secret, I believe I would choose the former.'

For a while he sat silent; then with a short laugh he rose. Mr Robinson was his benevolent self once more.

'Happily the alternative is not likely to arise. We have both, my dear fellow – thanks largely to your quickness and skill. And now I think I will go upstairs and see how our friend is getting on. By this time he should be very nearly ready to show me the result of his afternoon's labours.'

'And what about Drummond?' said Freyder, eyeing him professionally. 'I don't think he's likely to give us any trouble for the present, but it's just as well to be on the safe side.'

Mr Robinson turned the unconscious man over with his foot.

'Have him carried upstairs,' he ordered, 'and put in one of the bedrooms. And tell off someone to look after him.' He paused by the door as a thought struck him. 'And by the way – let me know the instant he recovers consciousness. I'd hate to postpone my first interview with the gentleman for one instant longer than necessary.'

'Well, if I'm any judge of such matters, Chief, you'll have to postpone it till tomorrow.'

'Then it will be a refreshing interlude in my period of tuition.'

And with a cheerful wave of his hand Mr Robinson made his way up the stairs. It was six hours since Professor Goodman had started, and by now the clinker in the metal retort should be quite cold enough to handle. Just at first the obstinate old fool had given a little trouble; in fact, he had even gone so far as to categorically refuse to carry out the experiment. But not for long – two minutes to be exact. At the end of that period a whimpering and badly hurt old man had started mixing the necessary ingredients under the watchful eye of Mr Robinson himself. And not till they were mixed and the retort placed in the electric furnace did he leave the room.

Twice during the two hours that followed did he come back again, unexpectedly. But the old scientist's feeble resistance was broken and the visits were unnecessary. Bent almost double he sat in his chair, with the white light from the glowing furnace falling on his face. And he was still in the same position when Mr Robinson opened the door and went in.

The heat in the room was stifling, though the furnace had now been out for two or three hours, and he left the door open. Then without a glance at the huddled figure he strode over to the table, his eyes gleaming with suppressed excitement. For there was the retort, and after cautiously testing it with his hand to discover the temperature, he picked it up and examined it curiously.

Though he had heard the experiment described in detail by Sir Raymond Blantyre, it was the first time he had actually seen it done. The retort, still warm, was full of an opaque, shaly substance which he realised was the clinker. And inside that, like the stone inside a cherry, was the diamond. For a moment his hands shook uncontrollably; then with feverish excitement he started to chip the clinker away with a small chisel.

It broke up easily, coming off in great flakes. And as he got down deeper and deeper his excitement increased. Amongst his other accomplishments Mr Robinson was no bad judge of diamonds in the rough; in fact, if pushed to it, he could even cut and polish a stone for himself. Not, of course, with the wonderful accuracy of the expert, but sufficient to alter the appearance of any well-known historical diamond should it come into his possession. And in the past, it may be mentioned that many had. But in this case he had no intention of bothering over such trifles. Once satisfied that the diamond was there, and that Professor Goodman had forgotten nothing, he proposed to waste no time over that particular stone. Certainly he would put it aside for future use – but what was one paltry diamond to him? It was the process he wanted – and the certainty that he could carry out that process himself.

Deeper and deeper went the chisel, and gradually a dreadful suspicion began to grip him. Surely by now he ought to have struck the stone itself? More than half of the clinker had come away, and still there was no sign of it. Could it be possible that the accursed old fool had made a mistake?

Feverishly he went on chipping, and at length the suspicion became a certainty. There was no diamond in the retort; nothing but valueless grey powder. The experiment had failed.

For a moment or two Mr Robinson stood motionless, staring at the now empty retort This was the one thing for which he had not legislated. That owing to the unusual conditions, and the strain to which Professor Goodman had been subjected, the stones might prove indifferent, he had been prepared for. But not total failure. His eyes rested thoughtfully on the huddled figure in the chair, but in them there was no trace of mercy. He cared not one whit for the obvious exhaustion of the weary old man; his sole thought was blind, overmastering rage at this further hitch in his scheme. Especially now that time had again become a dominant factor.

'This seems an unfortunate little effort on your part, my dear brother,' he remarked softly.

Professor Goodman sat up with a start.

'I beg your pardon,' he mumbled. 'I'm afraid I was asleep.'

'Then you would be well advised to wake up.' He crossed and stood in front of the Professor. 'Are you aware that your experiment has failed, and that there is no diamond in that retort?'

The old man sat up blinking.

'It is not my fault,' he said querulously. 'How can I be expected to carry out a delicate process under such conditions, and after the abominable way I have been treated?'

'May I point out,' pursued Mr Robinson, still in the same soft tone, 'that you assured me yourself that the conditions were in every way favourable? Further that you told me yourself, as you put the retort into the furnace, that everything was all right. Since then you have had to do nothing save regulate the heat of the electric furnace.' He paused, and a new note crept into his voice. 'Can it be, my dear brother, that you were lying to me?'

'It may be that the heat in the furnace was different from the one to which I have been accustomed,' answered the other, scrambling to his feet.

'May I point out that you assured me that the furnace was if anything better than your own? Further, you have a thermometer there by which to regulate the heat. So once again, dear brother, can it be that you were lying to me?' With a snarl he gripped the Professor by the arm, and shook him roughly. 'Speak, you miserable old fool – speak. And if you don't speak the truth, I'll torture you till you pray for death.'

He let go suddenly, and the Professor collapsed in his chair, only to stand up again and face the other bravely.

'A man can only die once,' he said simply. 'And men have been tortured in vain for other things besides religion. To me my science is my religion. I knew you would find no diamond in the retort – and you never will. You may torture me to death, you vile scoundrel – but never, never, never will I tell you my secret.'

Gently, almost caressingly Mr Robinson stroked his mutton-chop whiskers.

'Is that so?' he murmured. 'Most interesting, my dear brother – most interesting.' With a benevolent smile he walked over to the bell and rang it.

'Most interesting,' he continued, returning to the other man, who was watching him with fear in his eyes. 'Brave words, in fact – but we will see. I think you remarked before you told me the truth, that it was possibly the fault of the electric furnace. A naughty fib, dear brother – and naughty fibs should always be punished. One presses this switch, I think, to start it. Yes – why, I feel the warmth already. And I see that the maximum temperature registered this evening was 2000° Centigrade. Is that you, Freyder?' he continued without turning his head, as someone entered the room.

'It is, Chief. What's the trouble?'

'The trouble, Freyder, is that this incredibly stupid old man refuses to carry out his process for me. He has wasted six valuable hours producing a nasty-looking mess of grey powder. He has also wasted a lot of expensive electric current. And we are now going to waste a little more. I can only hope that my experiment will prove more satisfactory than his, though I greatly fear, my dear brother, that you will find it rather more painful.'

'What are you going to do?' Professor Goodman's voice was shaking, as he looked first at his tormentor, and then at the furnace which was already glowing a dull red.

'I'm going to make quite certain,' remarked Mr Robinson affably, 'that these thermometers register correctly. I imagine that there must be a difference in the feeling of metal at 1000° and metal at 2000°, though both, I should think, would be most unpleasant. However, my dear Professor, you will know for certain very shortly. I see that it is just about 1000° now. The left arm, I think, Freyder – if you would be so good. And perhaps you had better turn up his sleeve: burning cloth gives such an unpleasant smell.'

A dreadful scream rang through the house, and Professor Goodman fell back in his chair almost fainting.

'Only half a second,' murmured Mr Robinson. 'And it will only be half a second at 2000° – this time. Then, dear brother, you will again carry out your process. If it succeeds – well and good. If it should fail again – I fear we shall have to make it a full second. And a second is a long time under certain conditions.'

Moaning pitifully, Professor Goodman lay back in his chair with his eyes closed.

'I won't,' he muttered again and again through clenched teeth, while the heat from the furnace grew greater and greater, and the dull red changed to white.

'Foolish fellow,' sighed Mr Robinson. 'However,' he added hopefully, 'it's only half a second this time. And as a special concession I'll let you off with only 1900°. Now, Freyder – we are quite ready.'

Freyder took a step forward, and at that moment it happened. He gave one agonised shout of terror, and then scream after scream of agony rang through the house. For it was not Professor Goodman's arm which touched the white-hot furnace, but Freyder's face – and to his Chief's horrified eyes it had seemed as if he had dived straight at it.

'My God!' he muttered foolishly, as Freyder, moaning horribly, dashed from the room. 'How did it happen?'

The words died away on his lips and he stood staring into the shadows beyond the light thrown by the furnace. Drummond was sitting on the floor grinning vacantly at space.

'Gug, gug, gug,' he burbled foolishly. 'Pretty light.'

Then, apparently bored with life in general, he returned with interest to his occupation.

'Puff – puff!' he cried happily. 'Puff – puff! Naughty man kicked train.'

And the train which he was busily pushing along the floor consisted of his own shoes.

Once again Mr Robinson dashed to the bell and pealed it. His momentary shock at Freyder's ghastly accident had passed; his sole thought was that Drummond was no longer unconscious. And Drummond in full possession of his physical powers was a dangerous person to have about the place, even if his mind was wandering. But was it? That was the point. Or was he shamming? Such a possibility at once suggested itself to Mr Robinson's tortuous brain, and he was not a gentleman who took any unnecessary risks.

He had watched Professor Goodman totter from his chair with a look of wild hope in his face as he realised the unexpected presence of a friend; he had watched him sink back into it again with a groan as his cry for help was greeted with a vacuous grin from the man so happily playing on the floor. But still he was not satisfied, and a revolver gleamed ominously in his hand as he watched his enemy. His mind was made up on one point. Shamming or not shamming – mad or sane – at the slightest hint of trouble on Drummond's part he would kill him and be done with it. In fact he was sorely tempted to do so at once: it would save a lot of bother in the long run.

His finger tightened on the trigger, and he raised his revolver till it was pointing direct at Drummond's heart.

'I'm going to kill you, Drummond,' he said quietly.

But if he expected to discover anything by such a test he was doomed to disappointment. Still the same vacuous grin, still the same lolling head, and a jumble of incoherent words was all the result; and very slowly he lowered his weapon, as one of his men came rushing into the room, to stop abruptly at the door as his eyes fell on the figure on the floor.

He gave a sigh of relief.

'So there you are, my beauty,' he muttered.

'Was it you who was told off to look after Captain Drummond?' said Mr Robinson softly.

The man looked at the speaker with fear in his eyes.

'I put him on the bed, Chief,' he said sullenly, 'and he was unconscious. And I hadn't had any supper, so . . . '

'You went downstairs to get some,' Mr Robinson concluded his sentence for him. 'You went downstairs, you miserable fool, leaving him alone.' His eyes bored into the man's brain, and he shrank back against the wall. 'I will deal with you later,' continued Mr Robinson, 'and until then you will continue to look after him. If nothing further of this sort happens, it is possible that I may overlook your fault – so you had better see to it.'

'I'll swear it won't happen again, Chief,' said the man eagerly. 'It was only because I thought the young swine was stunned . . . '

With a gesture Mr Robinson cut him short.

'You're not paid to think, you're paid to do what you're told,' he remarked coldly. 'Go, now, and get one of the others. And bring some rope when you return.'

The man departed with alacrity, and once more Mr Robinson fell to staring at the man sitting on the floor. To Professor Goodman he paid not the slightest attention; all his thoughts were concentrated on Drummond. Was he shamming, or was he not? Had Freyder's blow on the head deprived him of his reason – or was it a wonderful piece of acting? And finally he decided on yet another test.

Still watching Drummond narrowly, he walked over to the door and affected to give an order to someone in the passage outside.

'Bring the girl Phyllis in here.'

Now surely there would be some tell-tale start if he was shamming – some little movement that would give him away. But there was nothing – absolutely nothing – to show that Drummond had even heard. He was engrossed in some intricate shunting operations with his shoes, and after a time Mr Robinson came back into the room. Almost, if not quite, his mind was made up – Drummond was insane. Only temporarily possibly – but insane. The blow on the back of his head had caused something in his brain to snap, and the man he hated most on earth was just a babbling lunatic. Almost, if not quite, he was sure of it; for certain proof he would have to wait until he could examine him – and especially his eyes – more closely. And Mr Robinson had no intention of examining Drummond, sane or insane, closely until Drummond's arms were very securely lashed together.

'You'd better be very careful of him,' he remarked as the two men came in with rope. 'I am almost certain that he's got very bad concussion, but if you handle him roughly he may get angry. I shall be covering him the whole time with a revolver, but I want you to lash his wrists behind his back.'

They approached him cautiously, and Drummond smiled at them vacantly.

'All right, old chap,' murmured the first man ingratiatingly. 'Pretty train you've got there. Won't you shake hands?'

'Gumph,' remarked Drummond brightly, busily pushing his shoe.

'Get hold of his other hand,' said the first man tersely to his companion. 'Then we'll get them both behind his back, and I'll slip a running noose over them.'

Which was excellent in theory, but poor in execution. A loud crack was heard and the two men staggered back holding their heads, which had impinged with violence.

'Gumph,' again remarked Drummond. 'Puff – puff – puff.'

'Damn the swine!' snarled the man who had originally been told off to look after him, and Mr Robinson smiled gently. It was very obvious that, whatever his mental condition might be, Drummond's physical strength was unimpaired.

'I think, Chief,' said the second man, 'that we should do it better if we lashed his wrists in front of him to start with. It's being man-handled that he doesn't take to, and we might be able to slip the noose over his wrists without his realising what the game is.'

'Do it how you like,' snapped Mr Robinson, 'but do it quickly.'

Which again proved excellent in theory, but poor in execution. For it soon transpired that Drummond was far too happy playing trains on the floor to realise the desirability of having his hands lashed together. In fact the proceeding appeared to annoy him considerably. And it was not until another man had been summoned and Mr Robinson himself had joined in the fray that they finally got the noose over his wrists and drew it tight. And in the course of doing so two of the men had crashed heavily into the furnace, which, though cooling, was still unpleasantly hot.

But at last it was done, and four panting men stood round in a ring regarding him triumphantly as he rolled on the floor. And then after a while he lay still, with a foolish grin on his face.

'Gug-gug,' he burbled. 'Where's my train?'

'I'll gug-gug him,' snarled one of the men, kicking him heavily in the ribs. 'The young devil's a homicidal maniac.'

'Stop that!' said Mr Robinson savagely. 'All accounts with this young man are settled by me. Now stand by in case he struggles. I'm going to examine his eyes.'

They approached him cautiously, but for the moment the trouble seemed over. Like so many madmen, and people temporarily insane, his frenzied struggles of the last ten minutes had completely exhausted Drummond. And even when Mr Robinson raised his eyelids and stared into his eyes he made no attempt to move, but just lay there smiling stupidly. For a long while Mr Robinson examined him, and then with a nod of satisfaction he rose to his feet.

'Take him to his room, and see that he doesn't escape again. He's mad, but for how long he'll remain so I can't tell. If you see the faintest sign of his recovering his reason, come and tell me at once.'

He watched them pick up Drummond and carry him out. They took him into the next room and threw him on the bed, and Mr Robinson followed. For a moment or two he moved restlessly on the pillows – then he gave a strangled grunt and a snore.

'He's asleep, Chief,' said one of the men, bending over him.

'Good,' answered Mr Robinson. 'Let us trust he remains so for some time.'

Then with a look of cold determination on his face he returned to the room where Professor Goodman still sat huddled in his chair.

Chapter 9

In which Professor Goodman has a trying time

'And now, dear brother' he remarked, gently closing the door, 'we will resume our little discussion where we left off. I was, if you remember, just about to ask you to sample the temperature of the furnace at 2000° when the interruption occurred. Is it necessary that I should repeat that request, or was your experience at the lower temperature sufficient for you?'

Professor Goodman raised his haggard face and stared at his tormentor.

'What have you done to that poor young man, you devil?'

Mr Robinson smiled and stroked his whiskers.

'Well, really,' he answered mildly, 'I think the boot is on the other leg. The question is more what has he done to my unfortunate staff? Poor Mr Freyder I feel almost certain must be in great pain with his face, judging by the noise he made, and two of my other servants have very nasty burns.'

'I know all that,' said the other. 'But what has sent him insane?'

Mr Robinson smiled even more gently.

'As a scientist, dear brother, you should know the tiny dividing line between sanity and madness. One little link wrong in that marvellous mechanism of the brain, and the greatest thinker becomes but a babbling fool. Not that his best friends could ever have called poor Drummond a great thinker, but' – he paused to emphasise his words – 'but, dear brother, he serves as a very good example of what might happen to one who is a great thinker.'

Professor Goodman shivered; there had been no need to emphasise the meaning underlying the words.

'You see,' continued Mr Robinson, 'Drummond very foolishly and very unfortunately for himself has again crossed my path. This time, as a matter of fact, it was by pure accident. Had you not lunched with him on the day of your death and given him the notes of your process, you may take it from me that this little interlude would never have occurred. But you did – and, well, you see what has happened to Drummond. The silly young fellow is quite mad.'

'You have done something to him to make him so,' said the other dully.

'Of course,' agreed Mr Robinson. 'Or to be strictly accurate, Freyder has.'

And suddenly Professor Goodman rose to his feet with a pitiful little cry.

'Oh! my God! I don't understand. I think I'm going mad myself.'

For a moment or two Mr Robinson looked at him narrowly. If such an appalling eventuality as that happened, the whole of his scheme would be frustrated. True, it was a common figure of speech, but Professor Goodman was a frail old man, accustomed to a sedentary life. And during the past two or three days his life had been far from sedentary. Supposing under the strain the old man's reason did snap . . . Mr Robinson drew a deep breath: the mere thought of such a thing was too impossible to contemplate.

But it had to be contemplated, and it had to be taken into account in his immediate course of action. Whatever happened, Professor Goodman's intellect must be preserved at all costs. Even a nervous breakdown would constitute a well-nigh insuperable obstacle to his plans. And in spite of the seriousness of the position, Mr Robinson could hardly help smiling at the irony of the thing.

Here was he with the greatest prize of his career waiting to be picked up – almost, but not quite, within his grasp. All the difficult practical details, all that part of his scheme concerned solely with organisation, had gone without a hitch. And now he was confronted by something far smaller in comparison, and yet almost as important as all the rest put together – the state of the mind of an elderly scientist. It was a problem in psychology which in the whole of his career he had never had to face under exactly similar conditions.

There had been occasions when men's reasons had snapped under the somewhat drastic treatment with which Mr Robinson was wont to enforce his wishes. But on all those occasions a remarkable aptitude with the pen had enabled him to dispense with the formality of their signature. This time, however, his wonderful gifts as a forger were wasted. Knowledge of ancient cuneiform writing might have been of some use in enabling him to decipher the notes, he reflected grimly – but as it was they were hopelessly and utterly unintelligible. Only Professor Goodman could do it, and that was the problem which had just come home to him more acutely than ever. What was the best line to adopt with the old man? How far would it be safe to go in a policy of threats and force? Or would apparent kindness do the trick better and quicker? Especially quicker – that was the important thing. It was a ticklish point to decide; but it was essential that it should be decided, and at once.

He glanced at the haggard, staring eyes of the man confronting him; he noted the twitching hands, and he made up his mind. After all, it was easy to go from kindness to threats, whereas the converse was difficult. And though he had reluctantly to admit to himself that burning a man's arm on red-hot metal can hardly be regarded as the act of a personal friend, there was no good worrying about it. It had been done, and could not be undone. All that he could do now was to try to efface the recollection of it as far as possible.

'Sit down, Professor,' he said gently. 'I feel that I owe you some explanation.'

With a groan the other sank back into his chair.

'Will you have a cigar?' went on Mr Robinson easily, holding out his case. 'You don't smoke? You should. Most soothing to the nerves. In the first place I must apologise for not having made things clearer to you before, but this slight contretemps with Drummond has kept me rather fully occupied. Now I want you to recall to your mind the interviews that you had with Sir Raymond Blantyre.'

'I recall them perfectly,' answered the Professor, and Mr Robinson noted with quiet satisfaction that he seemed to be less agitated.

'He offered you, did he not, a large sum of money for the suppression of your secret, which you refused – and very rightly refused. But, my dear Professor, do you really imagine for a moment that an unscrupulous blackguard of his type was going to lie down and accept your refusal? If you chose to refuse the money, so much the better for him; but whether you refused or accepted, he intended to suppress you. And but for me' – he paused impressively – 'he would have done.'

Professor Goodman passed a bewildered hand across his forehead.

'But for me,' repeated Mr Robinson, 'you would now be dead – foully murdered. You have never in your life – and I trust you never will again – been in such deadly peril as you were in a few days ago. Indeed, if it were known now that you were alive, I fear that even I would be powerless to save you.'

He drew carefully at his cigar; then he leaned forward and touched the Professor on the knee.

'Have you ever heard of a man called Peterson?'

'Never,' returned the other.

'No – probably not. You and he hardly move in the same circles. Peterson, of course, is only one of the many names by which that arch-devil is known. He is a King of Criminals – a man without mercy – a black-hearted villain.' Mr Robinson's voice shook with the intensity of his emotion. 'And to that man Sir Raymond Blantyre went with a certain proposal. Do you know what that proposal was? It concerned you and your death. You were to be murdered before you gave your secret to the world.'

'The villain!' cried Professor Goodman, in a shaking voice. 'To think that I've had him to dinner, and that his wife is a friend of ours.'

Mr Robinson smiled pityingly.

'My dear Professor,' he said, 'I'm afraid that your life has been lived far apart from the realities of the world. Do you really suppose that such a trifle as that would have weighed for one instant with Sir Raymond Blantyre? However, I will get on with my explanation. It matters not how I discovered these things: I will merely say that for twenty years now I have dogged this man Peterson as his shadow. He did me the greatest wrong one man can do another: I won't say any more.'

Mr Robinson choked slightly.

'I have dogged him, Professor,' he went on after a while, 'as I say, for twenty years, hoping – always hoping – that the time would come for my revenge. I have lived for nothing else; I have thought of nothing else. But one thing I was determined on – that my revenge when it did come should be a worthy one. A dozen times could I have given him away to the police, but I stayed my hand. When it came, I wanted the thing to be more personal. And at last the opportunity did come. It came with you.'

'With me?' echoed Professor Goodman. 'How can I have had anything to do with your revenge on this man?'

'That is what I am just going to explain to you,' continued Mr Robinson. 'In this man Peterson, Sir Raymond Blantyre had encountered a blackguard far more subtle than himself. Peterson was perfectly prepared to murder you – but he had no intention of murdering the secret of your process. That he proposed to keep for himself – so that he could continue blackmailing Sir Raymond. You see the manner of blackguard he is. It was a scheme after his own heart, and I made up my mind to strike at last. Apart from frustrating the monstrous crime of murdering you, I should achieve an artistic revenge.'

He again pulled thoughtfully at his cigar.

'Now pay close attention, Professor. Scheidstrun the German scientist made an appointment to see you, didn't he?'

'He was with me when I was chloroformed,' cried the other.

Mr Robinson smiled.

'No, he wasn't. A man you thought was Scheidstrun was with you.'

'But – good heavens!' gasped the Professor. 'I met him in the hall. I was late, I remember . . .'

'And, as you say, you met him in the hall talking to your maidservant.'

'But how on earth did you know that?'

'Because the man you met in the hall was not Scheidstrun – but me.' He laughed genially at the amazement on the other's face. 'It's a shame to keep you mystified any further; I will explain everything. It was Peterson who made the original appointment with you, writing in Scheidstrun's hand. What he intended to do I know not; how he intended to murder you I am not prepared to say. But the instant I discovered about it, I realised that there was not a moment to be lost. So I took the liberty, my dear Professor, of posing over the telephone as your secretary. I rang up Peterson, and speaking in an assumed voice I postponed his appointment with you until the following day. And then I took his place. I may say that I am not unskilled in the art of disguise, and I knew I could make myself up to resemble Scheidstrun quite sufficiently well to deceive you.'

'But why on earth didn't you tell me at the time?' said Professor Goodman, peering at the speaker suspiciously.

Once again the other laughed.

'My dear fellow, surely Mrs Goodman must, during the course of your married life, have let you into the secret of one of your characteristics. Or has she been too tactful? You are, as I think you must admit yourself, a little obstinate, aren't you?' He dropped his tone of light banter, and became serious. 'I don't think – in fact, I know you don't realise the deadly peril you were in. Even had I succeeded in convincing you on the matter, and you had agreed to come away and hide yourself, you would not have consented to the destruction of your laboratory. And that was essential. As long as Peterson thought you were alive he would have found you wherever you had hidden yourself. It was therefore of vital importance that he should think you dead – as he does now. Big issues, my dear Professor, require big treatments.'

Mr Robinson, having delivered himself of this profound utterance, leaned back in his chair and gazed at his listener. Bland assurance radiated from his mutton-chop whiskers, but his mind was busy. How was the old fool taking it? He still had his trump card to play, but he wanted that to win the game without possibility of failure. And as his mental metaphors grew a little mixed, he realised that it must fall on carefully prepared soil.

Professor Goodman stirred uneasily in his chair.

'I really can hardly believe all this,' he said at length. 'Why is all this deception necessary? Why have I to pose as your brother? And why, above all, have you tortured me?'

'Let me answer your last point first if I can,' said Mr Robinson. 'And yet I can't. Even if I can persuade you to forgive me, I never shall be able to forgive myself. Sudden anger, Professor, makes men do strange things – dreadful things. And I was furious with rage when I found that you had deliberately failed in the experiment. I realise now that I should have explained everything to you to start with. But I suppose my hatred of Peterson and my wish for revenge blinded me to other things. Everything, as I have told you, is subservient to that in my mind. Bringing you here, making you pose as my brother – what was all that done for except to throw that devil off the scent should he by any chance suspect? And at present he does not. He believes that the secret for which he would have given untold gold has perished with you. He is angry, naturally, at what he considers a buffet of fate, but that is no use to me as a revenge. He must know that it was not fate – but I who wrecked his scheme. He must know that not only has he lost the secret for ever – but that I have got it. There will be my revenge for which I have waited twenty years.' His eyes glistened, and he shook his fists in the air. 'And then and not till then will it be safe for you to go back and join your wife.'

Professor Goodman leapt from his chair.

'You mean that?' he cried. 'You will let me go?'

Mr Robinson gazed at him in pained surprise; then he bowed his head.

'I deserve it,' he said in a low voice. 'I deserve your bad opinion of me, firstly for not having told you, but especially for my vile and inexcusable loss of temper. But surely you can never have believed I was going to keep you here for good. Why' – he gave a little pained laugh – 'it's almost as if you thought I was a murderer. Foolish I may have been, obsessed with one idea, but I never thought that you would think quite as badly of me as that. After all, believe me or not as you like, I saved your life.'

He rose from his chair and paced thoughtfully up and down the room.

'No, no, my dear fellow – please reassure yourself on that point. The very instant it is safe for you to do so, you shall return to your wife.'

'But when will it be safe?' cried the Professor excitedly.

'When Peterson knows that your secret is in my possession, and that therefore murdering you will avail him nothing,' answered Mr Robinson calmly.

'But how do I know you will keep your word?'

'You don't,' said the other frankly. 'You've got to trust me. At the same time I beg of you to use your common sense. Of what possible advantage is it to me to keep you here? I shall have to trust you to take no steps to incriminate me, and that I am fully prepared to do. My quarrel is not with you, Professor; nor is it with that young man Drummond. But quite by accident he got between me and my life's object – and he had to be removed. So is it fair to Mrs Goodman to keep her in this dreadful sorrow for one moment longer than is necessary? The very instant you have given me your secret, and your word of honour that you will say nothing to the police, you have my word of honour that you are free to go.'

'But what do you propose to do with my secret when you've got it?' asked the Professor. He was watching his captor with troubled eyes, wondering what to believe.

'Do with it?' cried the other exultantly. 'I propose to seek out Peterson and let him know that I have got what he has missed. And if you but knew the man, you would realise that no more wonderful revenge could be thought of.'

'Yes, yes – I see all that,' said the Professor irritably. 'But in the event of my giving the secret to the world – what then?'

Mr Robinson curbed a rising desire to throttle the old man in the chair. Never had his self-control been so severely tried as it was now; precious moments were flying when every one was of value. But true to his new policy he kept every hint of irritation out of his voice as he answered.

'I shall have to have your promise also on that point, Professor. For one year you will have to keep your discovery to yourself. That will be sufficient for my revenge.'

He realised that had he made no proviso of that sort it would have been enough to raise the other's suspicions, for Professor Goodman was no fool. He also realised that if he made the period too long the other's inherent pigheadedness might tempt him to refuse. So he compromised on a year, and to his intense relief it looked as if the old man was inclined to consider it favourably. He still sat motionless, but his brow was wrinkled in thought, and he drummed incessantly with his fingers on the arms of his chair.

'One year,' he said at length. 'For I warn you, sir, that all the Petersons in the world will not prevent me publishing my discovery then.'

'One year will be sufficient,' said Mr Robinson quietly.

'And will you on your side,' continued the Professor, 'promise not to publish it before that date?'

Mr Robinson concealed a smile.

'I undoubtedly will promise that,' he answered.

'And the instant you possess the secret I may go to my wife?'

Mr Robinson's pulse was beating a little quicker than normal. Could it be that he had succeeded in bluffing him?

'As soon as Peterson knows that the secret of the process is mine – and that will be very soon – you may go. Before that it would not be safe.'

'And if I refuse?'

For a moment or two Mr Robinson did not reply; he seemed to be weighing his words with care.

'Need we discuss that, Professor?' he said at length. 'I have already told you the main – almost the sole – object of my life: revenge on this man Peterson. Rightly or wrongly, I have decided that this is my opportunity for obtaining it. I have gone to an immensity of trouble and risk to achieve my object, and though, as I said, I have no quarrel with you, yet, Professor, you are an essential part of my scheme. Without you I must fail; I make no bones about it. And I do not want to fail. So should you still refuse, your wife will go on thinking herself a widow until you change your mind. It rests with you and you alone.'

His eyes, shrewd and penetrating, searched the old man's face. Had he said enough, or had he said too much? Like an open book he read the other's mind: saw doubt, indecision, despair, succeed one another in rapid succession. And then suddenly he almost stopped breathing. For the Professor had risen to his feet, and Mr Robinson knew that one way or the other he had come to a decision.

'Very well, sir,' said the old man wearily. 'I give in. It seems that the only way of setting my poor wife's mind at rest as soon as possible is for me to trust you. I will tell you my process.'

Mr Robinson drew in his breath in a little whistling hiss, but his voice was quite steady as he answered.

'You have decided very wisely,' he remarked. 'And since there is no time like the present, I think we will have a bottle of champagne and some sandwiches to fortify us, and then get on with the experiment at once.'

'As you will,' said the Professor. 'And then perhaps tomorrow you will let me go.'

Mr Robinson glanced at his watch.

'Today, Professor,' he remarked jovially. 'It is past midnight. And I can promise you that should your experiment succeed, you will leave this house today.'

He watched the champagne bring back some colour to the other's cheeks, and then he produced his notebook.

'To save time,' he said, 'I propose to write down the name of each salt as you take it, and the amount you use. Does it make any difference in what order the salts are mixed?'

'None whatever,' answered the Professor. 'Provided they are all mixed properly. No chemical reaction takes place until the heat is applied.'

'And to make it perfectly certain, you had better give me the formula for each salt at the same time,' continued Mr Robinson.

At first the old man's fingers trembled so much that he could hardly use the balance, but Mr Robinson betrayed no impatience. And after a while the enthusiasm of the scientist supplanted everything else, and the Professor became absorbed in his task. Entry after entry was made in Mr Robinson's neat handwriting, and gradually the look of triumph deepened in his eyes. Success had come at last.

Of pity for the poor old man opposite he felt no trace; pity was a word unknown in his vocabulary. And so for an hour in the silent house the murderer and his victim worked on steadily, until, at length, the last salt was mixed, the last entry made. The secret was in Mr Robinson's possession. Not for another four hours would he be absolutely certain; the test of the electric furnace would furnish the only conclusive proof. But short of that he felt as sure as a man may feel that there had been no mistake this time, and his eyes were gleaming as he rose from the table.

'Excellent, my dear Professor,' he murmured. 'You have been lucidity itself. Now all that remains is to start up our current and await results.'

'The results will be there,' answered the other. 'That I know.'

He opened the furnace door and placed the retort inside; then, switching on the current, he sank wearily into his chair.

'You don't think it will be long, do you, before you can convince this man Peterson?' he said with a pathetic sort of eagerness.

'I can assure you that it won't be,' returned the other, with an enigmatic smile. 'I keep in very close touch with him.'

'Because I would be prepared to run any risk in order to let my dear wife know that I am alive as soon as possible.'

Mr Robinson nodded sympathetically.

'Of course you would, my dear fellow. I quite understand that. But I feel that I must safeguard you even against your own inclinations. The instant, however, that I consider it safe, you shall go back.'

'Can't I even write to her?' queried the other.

Mr Robinson affected to consider the point; then regretfully he shook his head.

'No – not even that,' he answered. 'I know this man Peterson too well. In fact, Professor, I am not even going to allow you to return to your wife from this house. It is better and safer for you that you should remain in ignorance of where you have been, and so I propose to take you for a short sea-voyage in my yacht and land you on another part of the coast. From the boat you will be able to radio to your wife, so that her mind will be set at rest. And then when you finally rejoin her, I would suggest your pleading sudden loss of memory to account for your mysterious disappearance.'

'But what on earth am I to say about the man who was buried?' And suddenly the full realisation of all that the question implied came home to him and he stood up. 'Who was that man?'

'An uninteresting fellow,' remarked Mr Robinson genially.

'But if you were the man I thought was Scheidstrun, you must – you must have murdered him.' The old man's voice rose almost to a scream. 'My God! I'd forgotten all about that.'

He shrank back staring at Mr Robinson, who was watching him narrowly.

'My dear Professor,' he said coldly, 'pray do not excite yourself unnecessarily. I have often thought that a society of murderers run on sound conservative lines would prove an admirable institution. After all, it is the majority who should be considered, and there are so many people who are better out of the way. However, to set your mind at rest,' he continued, 'it may interest you to know that the foot which was buried in your boot did not belong to a living man. There are methods of obtaining these things, as you are doubtless aware, for experimental purposes, if you possess a degree.'

There was no object, he reflected, in unnecessarily alarming the old man; it saves bother to get an animal to walk to the slaughter-house rather than having to drag it there. And he was likely to have all the dragging he wanted with Drummond, even though he was insane.

Professor Goodman, only half satisfied, sank back in his chair. Already the sweat was running down both their faces from the heat of the furnace, but Mr Robinson had no intention of leaving the room. He was taking no chances this time; not until the current was turned off and the furnace was cool enough to handle did he propose to go and rest. Then, once he was satisfied that the retort did contain diamonds, he would have some badly needed sleep in preparation for the work next night.

The yacht *Gadfly* was lying in Southampton Water, and he had decided to go on board in the late afternoon. His two invalids would be carried on stretchers; an ambulance was even now in readiness below to take them to the coast. They would both be unconscious – a matter which presented but little difficulty to Mr Robinson. And the Professor would never regain consciousness. He had served his purpose, and all that mattered as far as he was concerned was to dispose of him as expeditiously as possible. With Drummond things were a little different. In spite of what he had said to Freyder downstairs, the scheme was too big to run any unnecessary risks, and though it went against his grain to kill him in his present condition, he quite saw that he might have to. Drummond might remain in his present condition for months, and it was manifestly impossible to wait for that length of time to obtain his revenge. It might be, of course, that when he woke up he would have recovered his reason, and, if so . . . Mr Robinson's eyes gleamed at the thought. In anticipation he lived through the minute when he would watch Drummond, bound and weighted, slip off the deck into the sea.

Then with an effort he came back to the present. Was there anything left undone in his plans which would cause a check? Point by point he ran over them, and point by point he found them good. Their strength lay in their simplicity, and he could see nothing which was likely to go wrong before he was on board the *Gadfly*. Up to date no mention of Mr Lewisham's sudden disappearance had found its way into the papers; presumably, whatever Mrs Lewisham might think of the matter, she had not consulted the police. Similarly with regard to Drummond. No questions were likely to be asked in his case until long after he was safely out of the country. And after that, as he had said to Freyder, nothing mattered. The s.y. *Gadfly* would founder with all hands somewhere off the coast of Africa, but not too far from the shore to prevent Freyder and himself reaching it. That the crew, drugged and helpless, would go down in her he did not propose to tell them when he went on board. After all, there were not many of them, and it would be a pity to spoil their last voyage.

The heat from the furnace was growing almost insupportable, and he glanced at his watch. There was another hour to go, and with a sigh of impatience he sat back in his chair. Opposite him Professor Goodman was nodding in a kind of heavy doze, though every now and then he sat up with a jerk and stared about him with frightened eyes. He was muttering to himself, and once he sprang out of his chair with a stifled scream, only to sink back again as he saw the motionless figure opposite.

'I was dreaming,' he muttered foolishly. 'I thought I saw a man standing by the door.'

Mr Robinson swung round and peered into the passage; there was no-one there. Absolute silence still reigned in the house. And then suddenly he rose and went to the door: it seemed to him as if something had stirred outside. But the passage was empty, and he resumed his seat. He felt angry with himself because his own nerves were not quite under their usual iron control. After all, what could possibly happen? It must be the strain of the last few days, he decided.

Slowly the minutes ticked on, and had anyone been there to see, it must have seemed like some ceremony of black magic. The furnace glowing white hot, and in the circle of light thrown by it two elderly men sitting in chairs – one gently stroking his mutton-chop whiskers, the other muttering restlessly to himself. And then outside the ring of light – darkness. Every now and then a sizzling hiss came from inside the furnace, as the chemical process advanced another stage towards completion – that completion which meant all power to one of the two who watched and waited, and death to the other. The sweat dripped down their faces; breathing was hard in the dried-up air. But to Mr Robinson nothing mattered: such things were trifles. Whatever might be the material discomfort, it was the crowning moment of his life – the moment when the greatest coup of his career had come to a successful conclusion.

And suddenly he shut his watch with a snap.

'Two hours,' he cried, and strive as he would he could not keep the exultation out of his voice. 'The time is up.'

With a start Professor Goodman scrambled to his feet, and mumbling foolishly he switched off the current. It was over; he had given away his secret. And all he wanted to do now was to get home as soon as possible. Two hours more to let it cool . . .

He paused, motionless, his lips twitching. Great heavens! What was that in the door – that great dark shape. It was moving, and he screamed. It was coming into the circle of light, and as he screamed again, Mr Robinson leapt to his feet.

Once more the thing moved, and now the light from the furnace shone on it. It was Drummond, his arms still lashed in front of him. His face was covered with blood, but his eyes were fixed on Professor Goodman. And they were the eyes of a homicidal maniac.

For a moment or two Mr Robinson stood motionless, staring at him. Drummond's appearance was so utterly unexpected and terrifying that his brain refused to work, and before he realised what had happened, Drummond sprang. But not at him. It was Professor Goodman who had evidently incurred the madman's wrath, and the reason was soon obvious. Insane though he was, the one dominant idea of his life was still a ruling factor in his actions, though now it was uncontrolled by any reason. And that idea was Peterson.

Why he should imagine that Professor Goodman was Peterson it was impossible to say, but he undoubtedly did. Again and again he grunted the name as he shook the unfortunate scientist backwards and forwards, and for a while Mr Robinson wondered cynically whether he should let him go on in his delusion and await results. He was almost certain to kill the old man, which might save trouble. At the same time there was still the possibility of some mistake in the process, which rendered it inadvisable to dispense with him for good quite yet.

An uproar in the passage outside took him to the door. Two of the three men who had been told off to guard Drummond were running towards him, and he cursed them savagely.

'Pull him off,' he roared. 'He'll murder the old man.'

They hurled themselves on Drummond, who had forced the Professor to his knees. And this time, strangely enough, he gave no trouble. He looked at them with a vacant stare, and then grinned placidly.

'Chief!' cried one of the men, 'he's murdered Simpson. He's lying there with his neck broken.'

Mr Robinson darted from the room, to return almost at once. It was only too true. The third man was lying across the bed dead.

'Where were you two imbeciles?' he snarled savagely.

'We were taking it in turns, boss,' said the one who had spoken, sullenly. 'The swine was asleep and his arms were bound . . .'

He turned vindictively on Drummond, who grinned vacantly again.

'So you left him alone with only one of you,' Mr Robinson remarked coldly. 'You fools! – You triple-distilled damned fools. And then I suppose he woke and Simpson went to tuck him up. And Drummond just took him by the throat, and killed him, as he'd kill you or anyone else he got his hands on – bound or not.'

'Gug-gug,' said Drummond, sitting down and beaming at them. 'That man in there hit me in the face, when I took his throat in my hands.'

And suddenly the madness returned to his eyes, and his huge hands strained and wrestled with the rope that bound them. He grunted and cursed, and the two men instinctively backed away. Only Mr Robinson remained where he was, and the light from the still glowing furnace glinted on the revolver which he held in his hand. This was no time for half-measures; there was no telling what this powerful madman might do next. If necessary, though he did not want to have to do it, he would shoot him where he sat. But the spasm passed, and he lowered his revolver.

'Just so,' he remarked. 'You might as well hit a steam-roller as hit Drummond, once he's got hold. And judging by his face, Simpson must have hit him hard and often before he died. Take him away; lash him up; and unless you want to join that fool Simpson, don't take it in turns to guard him – and don't get within range of his hands.'

The two men closed in warily on their prisoner, but he gave no further bother. Babbling happily he walked between them out of the room, and Mr Robinson suddenly remembered the unfortunate Professor.

'A powerful and dangerous young man,' he remarked suavely. 'I trust he hasn't hurt you, my dear Professor.'

'No,' said the other dazedly; 'he hasn't hurt me.'

'An extraordinary delusion of his,' pursued Mr Robinson. 'Fancy thinking that you, of all people, were that villain Peterson.'

'Most extraordinary!' muttered the Professor.

'And it's really quite amazing that he should have allowed himself to be separated from you so easily. His friends, I believe, call him

Bulldog, and he has many of the attributes of that noble animal.' He peered at the Professor's throat. 'Why, he's hardly marked you. You can count yourself very lucky, believe me. Even when sane he's a terror – but in his present condition . . . However, such a regrettable contretemps will not occur again, I trust.'

He glanced at the furnace.

'Another hour, I suppose, before it will be cool enough to see the result of our experiment?'

'Another hour,' agreed the Professor mechanically.

And during that hour the two men sat in silence. Each was busy with his own thoughts, and it would be hard to say which would have received the greater shock had he been able to read the other's mind.

For Mr Robinson was thinking, amongst other things, of the approaching death of the Professor, which would scarcely have been comforting to the principal actor in the performance. And Professor Goodman – who might have been expected to be thinking of nothing but his approaching reunion with his wife – had, sad to relate, completely forgotten the lady's existence. His mind was engrossed with something quite different. For when a man who is undoubtedly mad – so mad, in fact, that in a fit of homicidal mania he has just throttled a man – gets you by the throat, you expect to experience a certain discomfort. But you do not expect to be pushed backwards and forwards as a child is pushed when you play with it – without discomfort or hurt. And above all you do not expect that madman to mutter urgently in your ear, 'For God's sake – don't give your secret away. Delay him – at all costs. You're in the most deadly peril. Burn the house down. Do anything.'

Unless, of course, the madman was not mad.

Chapter 10

In which Drummond goes on board the s.y. 'Gadfly'

But however chaotic Professor Goodman's thoughts, they were like a placid pool compared to Drummond's. He had first recovered consciousness as he lay on the floor in the room below, and with that instinctive caution which was second nature to him, he had remained motionless. Two men were talking, and the sound of his own name instinctively put him on his guard. At first he listened vaguely – his head was still aching infernally – while he tried to piece together in his mind what had happened. He remembered taking the receiver off the telephone in the deserted house; he remembered a stunning blow on the back of his head; and after that he remembered nothing more. And since he realised that he was now lying on the floor, it was obvious that an overwhelming desire for his comfort was not a matter of great importance with the floor's owner. The first point, therefore, to be decided was the identity of that gentleman.

On that score he was not left long in doubt, and it needed all his marvellous self-control to go on lying doggo when he realised who it was. It was Peterson – and as he listened to the thoughtful arrangements for his future it was evident that Peterson's feelings for him were still not characterised by warm regard. He heard the other man pleasantly suggest finishing him off then and there; he heard Peterson's refusal and the reasons for it. And though his head was still swimming, and thinking was difficult, his subconscious mind dictated the obvious course. As long as he remained unconscious, Peterson's insensate hatred for him would keep him safe. So far, so good – but it wasn't very far. However, they couldn't sit there talking the whole night, and once they left him alone, or even with some man to guard him, he had ample faith in his ability to get away. And once out of the house he and Peterson would be on level terms again.

Once again he turned his attention to the conversation. Yacht – what was this about a yacht? With every sense alert he strove to make his throbbing brain take in what they were saying. And gradually as he listened the main outline of the whole diabolical scheme grew clear in all its magnificent simplicity. But who on earth was the man upstairs to whom Peterson kept alluding? Whoever he was, he was presumably completely unconscious of the fate in store for him. And it struck Drummond that he was going to complicate matters. It would mean intense rapidity of action on his part once he was out of the house if he was going to save the poor devil's life.

For one brief instant, as Peterson bent over him, he had a wild thought of bringing matters to a head then and there. To get his hands on the swine once more was an almost overmastering temptation, but he resisted it successfully. It would mean a fight and an unholy fight at that, and Drummond realised that conditions were all against him. His head, for one thing – and total ignorance of the house. And then, to his relief, Peterson sat down again. No – there was nothing for it but to go on shamming and take his chance later.

Up to date he had not dared to open his eyes for even the fraction of a second, so he had no idea in what guise Peterson was at present masquerading. Nor had he a notion as to what the second man looked like. All he knew about that sportsman was that he was the dealer of the blow that had stunned him. And Drummond had a rooted dislike for men who stunned him. His name he gathered was Freyder, so he added Mr Freyder to his mental black-list.

At last, to his relief, the conversation had ended, and he heard the orders given about his disposal for the night. Inert and sagging, he had allowed himself to be carried upstairs, and thrown on the bed. And then in very truth nature had asserted herself. He ceased to sham and fell asleep. For how long he remained asleep he had no idea, but he awoke to find himself alone in the room. The door was open, and from outside there came the sound of voices. It seemed to him that it was now or never, and the next instant he was off the bed. He slipped off his shoes and stole into the passage.

The voices were coming from the next room, and the door of that was also open. He recognised Peterson and the man called Freyder, and without further delay he turned and went in the opposite direction, only to stop short in his tracks as a terrible scream rang out. It came from the room where Peterson was.

Like a shadow he stole back and looked in, and the sight he saw almost made him wonder if he wasn't delirious. For there, moaning pitifully in a chair, was Professor Goodman. That was the staggering fact which drummed in his brain – Professor Goodman was not dead, but alive. But – what to do: that was the point. They were going to torture the poor old man again, and he already heard steps in the hall.

And like a flash there came the only possible solution. Downstairs they had mentioned concussion: so be it – he would be concussed. It was the only hope, and the ease with which Freyder's face made contact with the electric furnace was a happy augury.

But he was under no delusions. From being a helpless log, he had suddenly become an obstreperous madman. It was going to make things considerably more difficult. And one thing it had definitely done – it had lessened any chance he had of escaping from the house. They would be certain to tie him up. Still, now that he had discovered the amazing fact about Professor Goodman, it would have been impossible for him to leave the house in any case, unless he could take the old man with him.

With his hands lashed together on the bed, and this time feigning sleep, he tried to see the way out. Three men were in the room with him now, and for a time he was inclined to curse himself for a fool. Better almost to have let the old man be burnt again – and got away himself for help. But no man – certainly not Drummond – could have allowed such a thing to take place if it was in his power to prevent it. Besides, Freyder's face was an immense compensation.

Why were they torturing him? There could only be one reason – to compel him to do something which he didn't wish to. And what could that be except reveal to Peterson the secret of his process? The more he thought about it, the clearer it became. Once Peterson was in possession of the secret, any further necessity for keeping Goodman alive would have departed. Obviously he had deceived Peterson once – but would he have the pluck to do it again? That he was an obstinate old man at times, Drummond knew – but torture has a way of overcoming obstinacy. Especially Peterson's brand of torture.

For all that, however, torture would be better than death, and to give Peterson the secret would be signing his death-warrant. For hours he lay there trying to see a ray of light. That Peterson would try to restore him to sanity before killing him he knew, but, at the same time, it was not safe to bank on it absolutely. That Peterson would kill Goodman at the first moment possible he also knew. And that was the fact which tied his hands so completely.

If only he could get at Goodman – if only he could warn him not to give away his secret, whatever happened – there was hope. The

Professor's life was safe till then; they might hurt him – but his life was safe. And if only he could get away, he might pull it off even now. The process, he knew, took six hours; if the Professor had the nerve to bluff Peterson twice more – twelve hours, say fourteen . . . A lot could be done in fourteen hours.

And suddenly he lay very still – two of the men were leaving the room. Was this his chance? He stirred uneasily on the bed, as a sick man does who is asleep. Then he rolled over on his back breathing stertorously. It was all perfectly natural, and roused no suspicions in the mind of the remaining man. But it brought Drummond's hands into the position in which he wanted them.

Contemptuously the man came over and stared at him as he lay. It was a foolish thing to do, and it was still more foolish to lean down a little to see the patient better. For the next moment a pair of hands with fingers like steel hooks had fastened on his throat, and the sleeper was asleep no more. Gasping and choking, he beat impotently at the big man's face, striking it again and again, but he might as well have hit the wall for all the good he did. And gradually his struggles grew fainter and fainter till they ceased altogether.

Thus had Drummond got his message through to Professor Goodman. On the spur of the moment it had occurred to him that by pretending to believe he was Peterson not only would it increase his chances of speaking to the Professor, but it would also tend to strengthen the belief that he was insane. An unexpected and additional help towards that end had been his appearance, though that he couldn't be expected to know. And now as once again he lay on the bed – bound this time hand and foot – he wondered desperately if he had succeeded.

Professor Goodman had got his whispered message – that he knew. But had he been in time? In addition, so far as he could tell, he had, up to the present, successfully bluffed Peterson and everyone else in the house as to his mental condition. But could he keep it up? And, anyway, trussed up as he now was, and as common sense told him he would continue to be until he was taken on board the yacht, what good would it do even if he could? It might save his life for the time being, but it wouldn't help his ultimate hopes of getting away. Nor the Professor's. Once they were on board he had to admit to himself that their chance of coming out alive was small. Anything can happen on a boat where the whole crew are unscrupulous. And even if the possibility arose of his getting away by going overboard and swimming, it was out of the question for the Professor. The chances were that the old man couldn't swim a stroke, and Drummond, powerful though he was in the water, was not such a fool as to imagine that he could support a non-swimmer for possibly several hours. Besides, it was not a matter of great difficulty to lower a boat, and an oar is a nasty thing to be hit on the head with, when swimming. No, the only hope seemed to be that Professor Goodman should hold out, and that by some fluke he should get away. Or send a message. But whom to? And how? He didn't even know where he was.

And at that very moment the principal part of that forlorn hope was being dashed to the ground in the next room. Once again the benevolent Mr Robinson was chiselling out the clinker from the metal retort, while the Professor watched him wearily from his chair. There was no mistake this time; Drummond's warning had come too late. And with a cry of triumph Mr Robinson felt his chisel hit something hard: the diamond was there. He dug on feverishly, and the next minute a big uncut diamond – dirty still with the fragments of clinker adhering to it – lay in his hand. He gazed at it triumphantly, and for a moment or two felt almost unable to speak. Success at last: assured and beyond doubt. In his notebook was the process; there was no need for further delay.

And then he realised that Professor Goodman was saying something.

'I have shown you as I promised.' His voice seemed very weary. 'That is the method of making the ordinary white diamond. To-morrow, after I have rested for a while, I will show you how to make one that is rose-pink.'

Mr Robinson hesitated. 'Is there much difference in the system?' he remarked thoughtfully.

The Professor's voice shook a little – but then it was hardly to be wondered at. He had had a trying evening.

'It will mean obtaining a somewhat rare strontium salt,' he answered. 'Also it has to be added to the other salts in minute doses from time to time to ensure perfect mixing. The heat also has to be regulated a little differently.'

His eyes searched the other's face anxiously. Delay him – at all costs. Drummond's urgent words still rang in his ears, and this seemed the only chance of doing so. The main secret he had already given away; there was nothing he could do or say to alter that. Only with Drummond's warning had he realised finally that he had been fooled; that in all probability the promise of rejoining his wife had been a lie from beginning to end. And the realisation had roused every atom of fight he had in him.

He was a shrewd old man for all his absentmindedness, and during the hour he had sat there while the furnace cooled his mind had been busy. How Drummond had got there he didn't know, but in Drummond lay his only hope. And if Drummond said delay, he would do his best to carry out instructions. Moreover, Drummond had said something else too, and he was a chemist.

'Where can you obtain this strontium salt?' asked Mr Robinson at length.

'From any big chemist in London,' replied the other.

Mr Robinson fingered the diamond in his hand. It would mean additional delay, but did that matter very much? Now that he was in possession of the secret he had half decided to get away early in the morning. The yacht was ready; he could step on board when he liked. But there were undoubted advantages in being able to make rose-pink diamonds as well as the ordinary brand, and it struck him that, after all, he might just as well adhere to his original plan. Drummond was safe; there was nothing to fear from the old fool in the chair. So why not?

'Give me the name of the salt and it shall be sent for tomorrow,' he remarked.

'If you're sending,' said the Professor mildly, 'you might get some other salts too. By my process I can make them blue, green, black, or yellow, as well as red. Each requires a separate salt, though the process is basically the same.'

Once again Mr Robinson frowned thoughtfully, and once again he decided – why not? Blue diamonds were immensely valuable, and he might as well have the process complete.

'Make a list of everything you want,' he snapped, 'and I will get the whole lot tomorrow. And now, after you've done that, go to bed.'

He watched the old man go shambling along the passage to his room; then, slipping the diamond into his pocket, he went in to have a look at Drummond. He was apparently asleep, and for a while Mr Robinson stood beside him with a look of malignant satisfaction on his face. That his revenge on the man lying bound and helpless on the bed added to the risk of his plans, he knew; but no power on earth would have made him forego it. In the eyes of the world Professor Goodman was already dead; in his case he would merely be confirming an already established fact. But with Drummond it was different. There would be a hue and cry: there was bound to be. But what did it matter? Was he not going to die himself – officially? And dead men are uninteresting people to pursue.

'Don't relax your guard for an instant,' he said to the two men. 'We shall be leaving here tomorrow afternoon.'

He left the room and went down to his own particular sanctum. He had made up his mind as to what he would do, and it seemed to solve all the difficulties in the most satisfactory way. These special salts should be sent direct to the yacht, and Professor Goodman should initiate him into their mysteries on board. He would have the electric furnace taken from the house, and the experiments could be carried out just as easily at sea. And when finally he felt confident of making all the various colours, and not till then, he would drop the old fool overboard. Drummond also; the extra few days would increase the chance of his becoming sane again.

He suddenly bethought him of Freyder, and went into his room. His face, even his eyes, were completely hidden by bandages, and Mr Robinson expressed his sympathy. In fact after Freyder had exhausted his vocabulary on the subject of Drummond, Mr Robinson even went so far as to promise his subordinate a special private chance of getting some of his own back.

'You may do anything you like to him, my dear fellow,' he said soothingly, 'save actually kill him. I shall watch it all with the greatest pleasure. I only reserve to myself the actual *coup de grâce*.'

He closed the door and, returning to his study, took the diamond out of his pocket. The tools at his disposal were not very delicate, but he determined, even at the risk of damaging the diamond, to work with them. He wanted to make assurance doubly sure, and it was not until the first faint streaks of dawn were coming through the window that he rose from his work with a sigh of satisfaction. On the table in front of him lay diamonds to the value of some six or seven thousand pounds; there had been no mistake this time. And with a sigh of satisfaction he placed them in his safe.

He felt suddenly tired, and glancing at his watch he found that it was already half-past three. A little rest was essential, and Mr Robinson went upstairs. He stopped by the Professor's room and looked in: the old man was fast asleep in bed. Then he went to see Drummond once more, and found him muttering uneasily under the watchful eyes of his two guards. Everything was correct and in order, and with another sigh of satisfaction he retired to his room for a little well-earned repose.

It was one of his assets that he could do with a very small amount of sleep, and eight o'clock the following morning found him up and about again. His first care was his two prisoners, and to his surprise he found the Professor already up and pottering about in the room where he had been working the night before. He seemed in the best of spirits, and for a moment or two Mr Robinson eyed him suspiciously. He quite failed to see what the old man had to be pleased about.

'One day nearer rejoining my dear wife,' he remarked as he saw the other standing in the doorway. 'You can't think how excited I feel about it.'

'Not being married myself,' agreed Mr Robinson pleasantly, 'I admit that I cannot enter into your joy. You're up early this morning.'

'I couldn't sleep after six,' explained the Professor. 'And so I decided to rise.'

Mr Robinson grunted.

'Your breakfast will be brought to you shortly,' he remarked. 'I would advise you to eat a good one, as we shall be starting shortly afterwards.'

'Starting?' stammered the Professor. 'But I thought you wished me to show you how to make blue diamonds. And the other colours too.'

'I do,' answered the other. 'But you will show me, Professor, on board my yacht. I trust that you are a good sailor, though at this time of year the sea should be calm.'

Professor Goodman stood by the electric furnace plucking nervously at his collar. It seemed as if the news of this early departure had given him a bit of a shock.

'I see,' he said at length. 'I did not understand that we were starting so soon.'

'You have no objections, I hope,' murmured Mr Robinson politely. 'The sooner we start, the sooner will come that delirious moment when you once more clasp Mrs Goodman in your arms. And now I will leave you, if you will excuse me. I have one or two things to attend to – amongst them our obstreperous young friend of last night.'

He strolled along the passage into the room where Drummond was. And though he realised that the idea was absurd, he felt a little throb of relief when he saw him still lying bound on the bed. Ridiculous, of course, that he should find anything else, and yet Drummond, in the past, had extricated himself from such seemingly impossible situations that the sight of him bound and helpless was reassuring. Drummond smiled at him vacantly, and with a shrug of his shoulders he turned to the two men.

'Has he given any trouble?' he asked.

'Not a bit, guv'nor,' answered one of them. 'He's as balmy as he can be. Grins and smiles all over his face, except when that old bloke next door comes near him.'

Mr Robinson stared at the speaker.

'What do you mean?' he said. 'Has the old man been in here this morning?'

'He came in about half an hour ago,' answered the other. 'Said he wanted to see how the poor fellow was getting on. And as soon as Drummond saw him he started snarling and cursing and trying to get at him. I tell you we had the devil's own job with him – and then after a while he lay quiet again. Thinks he's some bloke of the name of Peterson.'

'How long was the old man here?' said Mr Robinson abruptly.

'About half a minute. Then we turned him out.'

'Under no circumstances is he to be allowed in here again.'

Mr Robinson again bent over Drummond and stared into his eyes. But no sign of reason showed on his face: the half-open mouth still grinned its vacant grin. And after a while Mr Robinson straightened up again. He had allowed himself to be alarmed unnecessarily: Drummond was still off his head.

'We are leaving at once after breakfast,' he remarked. 'He is to be put in the ambulance as he is. And if he makes any noise – gag him.'

'Very good, guv'nor. Is he to have anything to eat?'

'No – let the swine starve.'

Mr Robinson left the room without a backward glance, and the sudden desperate glint in Drummond's eyes passed unnoticed. For now indeed things did look utterly hopeless. The Professor's plan passed to him on a piece of paper and which he had conveyed to his mouth and swallowed as soon as read, even if it was a plan of despair, had in it the germ of success. It was nothing more nor less than to set fire to the house with chemicals that would burn furiously, and trust to something happening in the confusion. At any rate it might have brought in outside people – the police, the fire-brigade. And Peterson could hardly have left him bound upstairs with the house on fire. Not from any kindly motives – but expediency would have prevented it. Only the chemicals had to come from London, and if they were starting at once after breakfast it was obvious that the stuff couldn't arrive in time.

The dear old Professor he took his hat off to. Tortured and abominably treated, he had kept his head and his nerve in the most wonderful way. For a man of his age and sedentary method of life not to have broken down completely under the strain was nothing short of marvellous. And not only had he not broken down, but he'd thought out a scheme and got it to Drummond wrapped round a Gillette razor-blade. It had taken a bit of doing to get the blade into his waistcoat pocket, and had his arms been bound to his body he couldn't have done it. But fortunately only his wrists were lashed together, and he had managed it. And now it all seemed wasted.

He debated in his mind whether he would try to cut the ropes, and chance everything in one wild fight at once. But the two men eating their breakfast near the foot of his bed were burly brutes. And even if by twisting himself up he had been able to cut the cord round his legs without their noticing he would be at a terrible disadvantage, cramped after his confinement as he was. Besides, there was the Professor. Nothing now would have induced him to leave the old man. Whatever happened, he must stay beside him in the hopes of being able to help him. Because one thing was clear. Even if he personally escaped, unless he could get help before the yacht started – the Professor was doomed. The yacht was going down with all hands: there lay the devilish ingenuity of the scheme.

And even if he could have prevented the yacht sailing, he knew Peterson quite well enough to realise that he would merely change his plans at the last moment. As he had so often done in the past, he would disappear, with the secret – having first killed Professor Goodman.

No; the only possible chance lay in his going on the yacht himself and trusting to luck to find a way out. Incidentally it was perhaps as well that the only possible chance did lie in that direction, since, as far as Drummond could see, his prospects of not going on board were even remoter than his prospects of getting any breakfast.

A sudden shuffling step in the passage outside brought his two guards to their feet. They dashed to the door just as Professor Goodman appeared, and then they stopped with a laugh. For the old man was swaying backwards and forwards and his eyes were rolling horribly.

'I've been drugged,' he muttered, and pitched forward on his face. The men sat down again, leaving him where he lay.

'That'll keep him quiet,' said one of them. 'It was in his tea.'

'If I had my way I'd put a bucket of it into the swab on the bed,' answered the other. 'It's him that wants keeping quiet.'

The first speaker laughed brutally.

'He won't give much trouble. Once we've got him on board, it'll be just pure joy to watch the fun. Freyder's like a man that's sat on a hornet's nest this morning.'

And at that moment Freyder himself entered the room. His face was still swathed in bandages, and Drummond beamed happily at him. The sight of him provided the one bright spot in an otherwise gloomy horizon, though the horrible blow which he received on the mouth rather obscured the brightness, and gave him a foretaste of what he could expect from the gentleman. But true to his rôle, Drummond still grinned on, though he turned his head away to hide the smouldering fury in his eyes. In the past he had been fairly successful with Peterson's lieutenants, and he registered a mental vow that Mr Julius Freyder would not be an exception.

He watched him go from the room kicking the sprawling body of the Professor contemptuously as he passed, and once again he was left to his gloomy thoughts. It was all very well to register vows of vengeance, but to carry them out first of all entailed getting free. And then a sudden ray of hope dawned in his mind. How were they going to be got on board? Stretchers presumably, and that would be bound to attract attention if the yacht was lying in any harbour. But was she? She might be lying out to sea somewhere, and send a boat ashore for them in some deserted stretch of coast. That was the devil of it, he hadn't the faintest idea where he was. He might be in Essex; he might be on the South Coast; he might even be down on the Bristol Channel.

A little wearily he gave it up; after all, what was the good of worrying? He was bound and the Professor was drugged, and as far as he could see any self-respecting life insurance would hesitate at a ninety-five per cent. premium for either of them. His principal desire at the moment was for breakfast, and as that was evidently not in the programme, all he could do was to inhale the aroma of eggs and bacon, and wonder why he'd been such a damned fool as to take that telephone call.

The tramp of footsteps on the stairs roused him from his lethargy, and he half-turned his head to look at the door. Two men were there with a stretcher, on which they were placing the Professor. Then they disappeared, to return again a few moments later with another, which they put down beside his bed. It was evidently his turn now, but, even bound as he was, they showed no inclination to treat him as unceremoniously as the Professor. His reputation seemed to have got abroad, and, though he smiled at them inanely and burbled foolishly, they invoked the assistance of the other two men, who had just finished their breakfast, before lifting him up and putting him on the stretcher.

In the hall stood Mr Robinson, who again peered at him intently as he passed, and then Drummond found himself hoisted into the back of a car which seemed to be a cross between an ambulance and a caravan. The back consisted of two doors instead of the conventional ambulance curtains, and on each side was a window covered with a muslin blind. Two bunks, one on each side, stretched the full length of the car and a central gangway, which had a little wash-basin at the end nearest the engine, separated them.

On one of these bunks lay Professor Goodman, breathing with the heavy, stertorous sounds of the drugged. The men pitched him on to the other, as Mr Robinson, who had followed them out, appeared.

'You have your orders,' he remarked curtly. 'If Drummond makes a sound – gag him. I shall be on board myself in about two hours.'

He closed the doors, leaving the two men inside, and the car started. It was impossible to see out of either window owing to the curtains, and the ostentatious production of a revolver by one of the men removed any thought Drummond might have had of trying to use the razor-blade. 'Mad or not, take no chances' was the motto of his two guards, and when on top of everything else, though he hadn't made a sound, they crammed a handkerchief half down his throat, he almost laughed.

He judged they had been going for about an hour, when the diminished speed of the car and the increased sounds of traffic indicated a town. It felt as if they were travelling over cobbles, and once they stopped at what was evidently a level crossing, for he heard a train go by. And then came the sound of a steamer's siren, to be followed by another and yet a third.

A seaport town obviously, he reflected, though that didn't help much. The only comfort was that a seaport town meant a well-used waterway outside. And if he could get free, if he could go overboard with the Professor, there might be a shade more of a chance of being picked up. Also there would almost certainly be curious loungers about as they were carried on board.

The car had stopped; he could hear the driver talking to someone. Then it ran forward a little and stopped again. And a moment or two later a curious swaying motion almost pitched him off the bunk. Surely they couldn't be at sea yet. The car dropped suddenly, and with a sick feeling of despair he realised what had happened. The car had been hoisted bodily on board; his faint hope of being able to communicate with some onlooker had gone.

Once again the car became stationary, save for a very faint and almost imperceptible movement. From outside came the sounds of men heaving on ropes, and the car steadied again. They were actually on board, and the car was being made fast.

Still the two men sat there with the doors tight shut, and the windows hermetically sealed by the blinds of them. They seemed to be waiting for something, and suddenly, with a sigh of relief, one spoke.

'She's off.'

It was true: Drummond could feel the faint throb of the propeller.

'The specimens are aboard,' laughed the other man, 'and I guess it will be safe to open the doors in about a quarter of an hour or so, and get a bit of air. This damned thing is like a Turkish bath.'

He rose and peered cautiously through a slit in the curtain, but he made no movement to open the door until the throbbing of the propeller had ceased, and the harsh rattle of a chain showed that they were anchoring. Then and not till then did he open the doors with a sigh of relief.

Cautiously Drummond raised his head, and stared out. Where were they? He had followed every movement in his mind since he had come on board, but he was still as far as ever from knowing where they were. And luckily one glance was enough. It didn't even need the glimpse he got of a huge Cunarder about a half-mile away: he recognised the shore. They were in Southampton Water, and though the knowledge didn't seem to help very much, at any rate it was something to have one definite fact to start from.

Southampton Water! He managed to shift the sodden pocket-handkerchief into a more comfortable position, and his train of thought grew pessimistic. Why would men invent processes for making diamonds? he reflected morosely. If only the dear old blitherer still peacefully sleeping in the opposite bunk had stuck to albumenised food, he wouldn't have been lying trussed up like a Christmas turkey. Far from it: he would have been disporting himself on Ted Jerningham's governor's yacht at Cowes. Had not Ted expressly invited him – Ted, who had hunted Peterson with him in the past, and asked for nothing better than to hunt him again?

The irony of it! To think that Ted might even see the yacht go by; might remark on the benevolence of the appearance of mutton-chop whiskers, if by chance he should be on deck. And he would never know. In all ignorance he would return to one of his habitual spasms of love, which always assailed him when afloat, with anyone who happened to be handy.

It was a distressing thought, and, after a while, he resolutely tried to banish it from his mind. But it refused to be banished. Absurd, of course, but suppose – just suppose he could communicate with Ted. Things were so desperate that he could not afford to neglect even the wildest chance. Ted's father's yacht generally lay, as he knew, not far from the outgoing waterway; he remembered sitting on deck with Phyllis and watching a Union Castle boat go by so close that he could see the passengers' faces on deck. What if he could shout or something? But Ted might not be on deck.

Eagerly he turned the problem over in his mind, and the more he thought of it the more it seemed to him to be the only possible way out. How to do it, he hadn't an idea – but at any rate it was something to occupy his thoughts. And when the benevolent face of Mr Robinson appeared at the door some hours later, he was still wrestling with the problem, though the vacant look in his eyes left nothing to be desired.

'Any difficulty getting on board?' asked Mr Robinson.

'None at all, boss,' answered the man who was still on guard. 'We gagged the madman to be on the safe side.'

Mr Robinson beamed.

'Take the old man below,' he remarked. 'He'll be coming round soon. I will stay with our friend here till you return.'

Thoughtfully he pulled the handkerchief out of Drummond's mouth and sat down on the opposite bunk.

'Still suffering from concussion,' he said gently. 'Still, we have plenty of time, Captain Drummond – plenty of time.'

'Gug-gug,' answered Drummond happily.

'Precisely,' murmured the other. 'I believe that men frequently say that when they drown. But I promise you we won't drown you at once. As I say – there is plenty of time.'

Chapter 11

In which Drummond leaves the s.y. 'Gadfly'

Still smiling benevolently, Mr Robinson strolled away, and shortly afterwards a series of sharp orders followed by a faint throbbing announced that the voyage of the s.y. *Gadfly* had commenced. The Cunarder receded into the distance, and still Drummond lay on the bunk wrestling with the problem of what to do. He judged the time as being about six, so they would pass Ted Jerningham's yacht in daylight.

Apparently no guard was considered necessary for him now that the yacht was under way; after all, to watch a completely bound madman is a boring and uninteresting pastime. And with a feeling of impotent rage Drummond realised how easy it would be to cut the ropes and go quietly overboard. A swim of a mile or so meant nothing to him. If only it hadn't been for the Professor! . . .

No; the last hope – the only hope – lay in Ted Jerningham. Once that failed, it seemed to Drummond that nothing could save them. And it was perfectly clear that by no possibility could he hope to communicate with Ted from his present position. He must be free to use his limbs. And during the next ten minutes he discovered that the blade of a safety-razor is an unpleasant implement with which to cut half-inch rope, especially when one's wrists are bound.

But at last it was done, and he was free. No-one had interrupted him, though once some footsteps outside had made him sweat with fear. But he was still no nearer to the solution of the problem. At any moment someone might come in and find him, and there would be no mistake about binding him the second time. Moreover, it would prove fairly conclusively that he was not as mad as he pretended.

Quickly he arranged the ropes with the cut ends underneath, so that to a cursory glance they appeared intact. Then he again lay still. That the glance would have to be very cursory for anyone to be deceived he realised, but it was the best he could do. And anyway he was free, even if only for the time. If the worst came to the worst he had no doubt as to his ability to fight his way to the side and go overboard; gun work is impossible in Southampton Water. But unless he did it near another ship, he feared that the delay before he could do anything would be fatal to the Professor. Peterson would take no chances in this case; he would murder the old man out of hand, instead of postponing the event.

And then, suddenly, came the idea – Ted's motor-boat. How it was going to help he didn't see; he had no coherent plan. But with a sort of subconscious certainty he felt that in Ted's motor-boat lay the key to the problem. She was a wonderful machine, capable of doing her forty knots with ease, and she was the darling of Ted's heart. Her method of progress in the slightest swell resembled a continuous rush down the water-chute at Earl's Court; and her owner was wont to take whoever occupied his heart for the moment for what he termed 'a bit of a breather' on most evenings after dinner.

Ted's motor-boat was their hope, he decided; but how? How to get at Ted, how to tell him, was the problem. Methodically he thought things out; now that he had something definite in his mind to go on, his brain was cool and collected. And it seemed to him that the only way would be to go overboard as they passed Ted's yacht, and then follow the *Gadfly* at once while she was still close to land. There would be men on Ted's yacht, and they could board the *Gadfly* and hold her up. That there were difficulties he realised. It meant leaving the Professor for at least an hour even under the most favourable conditions. Further it would be getting dark when they overtook the *Gadfly*, and to board a yacht steaming her twelve to fifteen knots is not a simple matter when the crew of the yacht do not desire your presence, and await you with marlin-spikes on deck. Besides, the guests on Ted's yacht might feel that as an evening's amusement 'hunt the slipper' won on points. Still, it seemed the only chance, and he decided on it unless something better turned up. Anyway, it was a plan with a chance of success, which was something.

He glanced through the open door to try to spot his position, and estimated that another half-hour at the rate they were going would just about bring them opposite Ted's yacht. Still no-one came near him, though periodically he could see one of the sailors moving about the deck. As far as he could tell, he had been slung just aft of the funnel, though he dared not raise himself too much for fear of being seen.

The minutes passed, and his hopes began to rise. Could it be that luck was going to be on his side? Could it be that no-one would come, and that in the failing light he might be able to slip over the side unperceived? If so, he might gain an invaluable half-hour; more – he might be able to get the motor-boat alongside the *Gadfly* later without the crew suspecting anything. It seemed too good to be true, and yet a quarter of an hour, twenty minutes, passed, and he was still alone.

He peered out again; they were getting very close. The deck was deserted, and suddenly he felt he could bear the strain no longer. He rose from the bunk and cautiously peered out of the door. And the sight he saw almost staggered him with his good fortune. If he had been walking about the deck instead of being cooped up under cover he could not have timed it more exactly. Not a hundred yards away to port lay Jerningham's yacht, with the motor-boat alongside the gangway.

Drummond glanced round; he could see no-one. The structure in which he had been hoisted on board effectively screened him from the bridge; the sailors were apparently having their evening meal. And taking a quick breath he prepared to make a sprint for the side when he saw something which completely altered his plans. Leaning over the side of the yacht he was watching were a man and a woman. And the man was Ted Jerningham himself.

Drummond saw him focus a pair of field-glasses and turn them on the *Gadfly*. And then clear and distinct across the water he heard the amazed shout of 'Hugh'. Jerningham had seen him; the supreme chance had come, if only he wasn't interrupted. And it is safe to say that during the next minute a very astonished girl stood beside a man whom she almost failed to recognise as the Ted Jerningham of normal life.

'A pencil,' he snapped. 'Write as I spell out. Get a move on. Look out: he's beginning. D.A.N.G.E.R. F.O.L.L.O.W. I.N. M.O.T.O.R. B.O.A.T. P.E.T.E.R.S.O.N. U.R.G.E.N.T. That's all.'

She looked up: the huge man on board the passing yacht who had been standing outlined against the sky waving his arms had disappeared.

'What on earth was he doing?' she cried.

'Semaphoring,' answered Jerningham briefly.

'But I don't understand,' she said.

'Nor do I,' returned her companion. 'But that was Hugh Drummond. And what Hugh says – goes, if we follow for the whole night. Coming?'

'Rather. Who's Peterson?'

'A very dear old friend,' said Jerningham with a grim smile. 'But how the deuce . . . ' He broke off, and stared after the retreating yacht. 'He loves me, because I emptied the entire sauce-boat over his shirt-front one night in Paris, when disguised as a waiter at the Ritz.'

'My dear Ted, are you mad?' laughed the girl, following him down the gangway into the waiting motor-boat.

'Oh no – just fun and laughter. You wouldn't believe what a humorist old man Peterson is.'

A terrific explosion rent the air, followed by a cloud of blue exhaust smoke, and Jerningham took the tiller.

'Warm enough, Pat?' he asked. 'It may be a long show.'

'Quite, thanks,' she answered. 'Ted, why do you look so grave?'

'I'm just wondering, my dear, if I ought to take you.' His hand was still on the gangway, and he looked at her irresolutely.

'Why on earth not?'

'Because there may be very grave danger.'

The girl laughed.

'Get on with it while the going's good,' she said. 'That yacht will be past the Needles if you delay much longer.'

And so it came about that Drummond, watching feverishly from his bunk in the *Gadfly*, saw with a sigh of intense relief the motor-boat shoot out across the water. It was nearly a mile astern, but a mile was nothing to a boat of its great speed. Moreover, the distance was lessening, and he breathed a prayer that Ted wouldn't come too close. With the amount of traffic round and about Cowes at that time of year an odd motor-boat could raise no suspicion, but if he settled down to follow steadily at a hundred yards or so astern he would be bound to draw attention to himself.

He had not dared to send a longer message, and, of necessity, it had left a good deal to Ted's imagination. But of all the men who had followed him unhesitatingly in the past, Ted Jerningham had been always the quickest on the uptake, and he soon saw that his confidence had not been misplaced. Ted had evidently realised that to follow steadily would arouse suspicion, and was laying his plans accordingly. He overhauled them like an express train, passed forty yards to starboard, circled across their bow, and came dashing back. Then away at a tangent for half a mile or so, only to shoot back and stop apparently with engine trouble.

The sea was like a millpond, and as the *Gadfly* passed the now silent motor-boat the sounds of a gramophone were plainly audible from it. Obviously someone with a racing motor-boat joy-riding with a girl, reflected the skipper as he paced the bridge; and forth-with dismissed the matter from his mind. He had other more important things to think of, and the first was the exact object of this trip. That the benevolent Mr Robinson had hired the *Gadfly* from its owner to take two invalids to Madeira he knew, but he wasn't quite satisfied. The method of bringing the invalids on board had seemed so unnecessarily secretive. However, as is the way of men who go down to the sea in ships, his nature was not curious. He was there to carry out orders, and mind his own busi-ness – not other people's. Still, he couldn't help wondering. And had he seen the occupation of one of those invalids at the moment he would have wondered still more. For Drummond, having found a cake of soap on the basin beside his bunk, was carefully cutting it into small cubes with the blade of a safety-razor. Though perhaps that is what one would expect from a madman.

A sudden hoarse scream of fear some five minutes later made the Captain jump to the side of the bridge. Two sailors were rushing along the deck as if pursued by the devil, and he roared an order at them. But they took no notice of him, and dashed below. For a moment the worthy skipper stood there dumbfounded; then, cursing fluently, he dashed after them, only to stop with a strange pricking feeling in his scalp as a huge and ghastly figure confronted him. A great mass of foam was round its mouth, and it was brandishing a marlin-spike and bellowing. A terrifying spectacle in the half-light of dusk – a spectacle to put the fear of God into any man. And then as suddenly as it appeared it was gone.

Terror is an infectious thing, and the infection spread in the good ship *Gadfly*. Within two minutes men were running in all directions, shouting that a homicidal maniac was loose on board. Below an appalling crash of breaking crockery and the sudden appearance on deck of a terrified steward told its own tale. The Captain was powerless; things had gone beyond him. He roared a futile order or two: no-one paid the slightest attention to him. And then, quite suddenly, the pandemonium ceased – and men held their breath. How he had got there no-one could say – but they all saw him outlined against the darkening sky.

The madman was in the stern, and in his arms he held the body of a man.

'At last,' they heard him shout, 'at last I've got you, Peterson. We die together – you devil . . .'

'Stop them,' howled Mr Robinson, who had just dashed on deck, holding a limp right arm; but no man moved. Only a loud splash broke the silence, and the stern was empty.

'Man overboard. Lower a boat. Stop the yacht, you cursed fool,' snarled Mr Robinson to the Captain, and then he rushed to the stern. Dimly in the failing light he thought he could see two heads in the water, but it was a couple of minutes before a boat was lowered, and in that couple of minutes he heard the roar of an engine coming nearer. Then the engine ceased, and he saw the outline of a motor-boat.

'That boat may have picked 'em up, sir,' said the Captain, as Mr Robinson ran down the gangway into the waiting cutter.

'Give way all,' came the second officer's curt order. 'With a will, boys.'

The motor-boat, still motionless, loomed rapidly up, and Mr Robinson stood up.

'Ahoy there! Did you pick up those two men who fell overboard?'

'Two!' Ted Jerningham, a conspicuous figure in white flannels, stood up also. 'I heard the most infernal shindy on board your yacht and then a splash. Do you mean to say two men have fallen overboard?'

The yacht's boat was close to, the sailors resting on their oars.

'Yes. Have you seen 'em?' asked the second officer.

'Not a sign. And the water's like a duckpond too.'

The girl with him shuddered.

'How dreadful! You don't mean the poor fellows are drowned?'

'Afraid it looks like it, miss,' said the officer, staring round the water. 'Even in this light we'd see them with the sea as calm as it is.'

Mr Robinson whispered something in his ear, which he seemed to resent.

'Do what you're told,' snarled his master, and with a shrug he gave an order.

'Give way.'

The oars dipped into the water, and they passed astern of the motor boat. And had Mr Robinson been watching Ted Jerningham instead of the water he might have seen a sudden strained look appear on that young gentleman's face, and his hand move instinctively towards the starting-switch. He might even have wondered why the girl, who had seemed so calm and unperturbed in the face of this dreadful tragedy, should suddenly give vent to a loud and hysterical outburst.

'It's dreadful,' she sobbed – 'too dreadful! To think of those two poor men being drowned like that.'

But Mr Robinson was not concerned with the dreadfulness of the situation; all that mattered to him was whether it was true or not. From the moment when Drummond, foaming at the mouth, had dashed into the dining-saloon, Mr Robinson's brain had been working furiously. An attempt to intercept himself between Drummond and Professor Goodman had resulted in an appalling blow on his arm with a marlin-spike. And then, accustomed though he was to the rapidity of Drummond's movements, even he for a few seconds had been nonplussed. There had been something so diabolical about this huge man, bellowing hoarsely, who had, after that first blow, paid no more attention to him, but had hurled himself straight on the dazed Professor. And even when the Professor, squealing like a rabbit, had dashed on deck with Drummond after him, for an appreciable time Mr Robinson had remained staring stupidly at the door. Drummond sane was dangerous; Drummond mad was nerve-shattering. And then he had pulled himself together just in time to dash on deck and see them both go overboard.

Thoughtfully his eyes searched the water again; there was no trace of either man. Of a suspicious nature, he had examined both sides of the motor-boat; moreover, he had seen inside the motor-boat. And now as the girl's sobs died away he turned to the officer beside him.

'There can be no doubt about it, I fear,' he remarked with a suitable inflection of sorrow in his voice.

'None, sir, I'm afraid. Even if we couldn't see them, we could hear them. I'm afraid the madman's done the poor old gentleman in.'

'Sink in a brace of shakes with a holy terror like that 'anging round yer neck,' said one of the sailors, and a mutter of agreement came from the others.

'Yes, I'm afraid there can be no possibility of saving them now.' Ted Jerningham took out his cigarette-case, only to replace it hurriedly as he remembered the dreadful tragedy they had just witnessed. 'Doubtless, however, their bodies will be washed ashore in time.'

'Er – doubtless,' murmured Mr Robinson. That aspect of the case had already struck him, and had not pleased him in the slightest degree. Had he been able to conform with his original plan, neither body would have ever been seen again. However, he had not been able to conform to that plan, so there was no more to be said about it. The main point was that both of them were drowned.

'Doubtless,' he repeated. 'Poor fellows! – Poor fellows! Two neurasthenic patients of mine, sir . . . How sad! – How terribly sad! However, I fear there is no good wasting any more time. I can only thank you for your prompt assistance, and regret that, through no fault of yours, it was not more effective.'

Jerningham bowed.

'Don't mention it, sir – don't mention it,' he murmured. 'But I think, as I can do no more, that I will now get back. The tragedy, as you will understand, has somewhat upset this lady.'

He put his finger on the starting-switch, and the quiet of the night was broken by the roar of the engine. And as the sailors dipped in their oars to row back to the yacht, the motor-boat circled slowly round.

'Good night, sir.' Mr Robinson waved a courteous hand. 'And again a thousand thanks.'

'And again don't mention it,' returned Jerningham, sitting down by the tiller. 'You can take your wrap off his hand now, Pat,' he whispered. 'They can't see.'

A vast hand grasping the gunwale was revealed as she did so, and an agonised whisper came from the water.

'Hurry, old man, for the love of Pete. Unless we can hold the old man upside-down soon to drain the water out of him, he'll drown.'

'Right-oh! Hugh. Can you hold on for a couple of hundred yards. I'll go slow. But they may have a searchlight on the yacht, and we're still very close to her.'

'All right, Ted. I leave it to you.'

'I'll still keep broadside on, old man; though I don't think he had any suspicions.'

He nosed the motor-boat through the water, and a few moments later the necessity of his precaution was justified. A blinding light flickered across the water, found them, and held steady: it was the *Gadfly's* searchlight. Jerningham rose and waved his hand, and after a while the beam passed on searching the sea. One final attempt evidently to try to spot the victims of the tragedy, rewarded by empty water. And at last the light went out; all hope had been abandoned.

'Quick, Hugh,' cried Jerningham. 'Get the old boy on board.'

With a heave the almost unconscious form of Professor Goodman was hoisted into the boat, to be followed immediately by Drummond himself.

'Lie down, old man – lie down in case they use that searchlight again.'

The engine roared and spluttered, and two black mountains of water swirled past the bows.

'Forty-five on her head, Hugh,' shouted Ted. 'Incidentally, what's this particular brand of round game?'

'The largest drink in the shortest time, old son,' laughed the other. 'And for the Professor – bed, quick.'

He turned to the girl.

'My dear soul,' he said, 'you were magnificent. If you hadn't had hysteria when I began to sneeze it was all up.'

'But what could he have done?' cried the girl. 'And he looked such a nice old man.'

Drummond laughed grimly.

'Did you recognise him, Ted?' Once again he turned to the girl. 'If he'd known that we were in the water, that nice old man would have had no more compunction in shooting you and Ted and dropping your bodies overboard than I shall have in drinking that drink. It's been the biggest coup of his life, Ted – but it's failed. But, by Jove, old man, it's been touch and go, believe me.'

The roar of the engine made conversation difficult, and after covering the dripping form of the Professor with a dry rug they fell silent. Astern the lights of the *Gadfly* were growing fainter and fainter in the distance; ahead lay Cowes and safety. But Drummond's mind, now that the immediate danger was over, had jumped ahead to the future. To restore the Professor to the bosom of his family was obviously the first thing to be done; but – after that?

The engine ceased abruptly, and he realised they had reached the yacht. Leaning over the side were some of the guests, and as he and Ted lifted the body of the Professor up the gangway a chorus of excited questioning broke out, a chorus which was interrupted by the amazed ejaculation of an elderly man.

'God bless my soul,' he cried incredulously, as the light fell on the Professor's face, 'it's old Goodman's double!'

'Not exactly,' answered Drummond. 'It's Professor Goodman himself.'

'Damme, sir,' spluttered the other, 'I was at his funeral a week ago. He was blown up in his house in Hampstead doing some fool experiment.'

'So we all thought,' remarked Drummond quietly. 'And as it happened we thought wrong. Get him below, Ted – and get him to bed, or we really shall be attending his funeral. He's swallowed most of the English Channel as it is. Though I can assure you, sir,' he addressed the elderly man again, 'that he possesses a vitality which turns Kruschen salts a pale pink. Within the last week he's been blown up; his remains, consisting of one boot, have been buried; he's been bounced on a white-hot electric furnace to keep his circulation going; he's had his breakfast doped; and last, but not least, he's gone backwards and forwards under Ted's motor-boat. And now if someone will lead me to a whisky-and-soda of vast dimensions, I'll – My God! What's that?'

It was very faint, like the boom of a distant heavy gun, but he happened to be looking towards the Needles. And he had seen a sudden deep orange flash, in the water against the sky – the flash such as in old days an aeroplane bomb had made on bursting. The others swung round and stared seawards, but there was nothing more to be seen.

'It sounded like a shell,' said one of the men. 'What did you think it was?'

He turned to Drummond, but he had disappeared, only to dash on deck a moment or two later with Ted behind him.

'Every ounce you can get out of her, Ted. Rip her to pieces if necessary – but get there. That infernal devil has blown up the yacht.'

The motor-boat spun round, and like a living beast gathered speed. The bow waves rose higher and higher, till they stood four feet above the gunwales, to fall away astern into a mass of seething white.

'I'll never forgive myself,' shouted Drummond in Ted's ear. 'I knew he was going to blow her up, but I never thought he'd do it so soon.'

Quivering like a thing possessed, the boat rushed towards the scene of the explosion. The speedometer needle touched – went back – touched again – and then remained steady at fifty.

'Go to the bows,' howled Ted. 'Wreckage.' With a nod Drummond scrambled forward, and lying between the two black walls of water, he slowly swung the headlight backwards and forwards over the sea in front. To hit a piece of floating wreckage at the speed they were travelling would have ripped them open from stem to stern. Other craft attracted to the spot loomed up and dropped back as if stationary, and then suddenly Drummond held up his hand. In front was a large dark object with two or three men clinging to it, and as he focused the headlight on them he could see them waving. The roar of the engine died away, and timing it perfectly Jerningham went full speed astern.

The thing in the water was one of the large wooden lockers used for storing life-belts, and they drew alongside just in time. It was waterlogged, and the weight of the men clinging to it was more than it could stand. Even as the last of them stepped into the boat, with a sullen splash the locker turned over and drifted away only just awash.

'Yer'd better mind out,' said one of the men. 'There's a lot of that about.'

'Go slow, Ted,' cried Drummond. Then he turned to the men. 'What happened?'

'Strike me pink, governor, I'm damned if I know. We've had a wonderful trip, we 'ave – you can take my word. Fust a ruddy madman jumps overboard with another bloke – and they both drowns. Then half an hour later there comes the devil of an explosion from below; the 'ole deck goes sky 'igh, and the skipper he yells, "We're sinking." It didn't require for 'im to say that; we all knew we was. We 'eeled right over, and in 'alf a minute she sank.'

'Anybody else saved?' asked Drummond.

'I dunno, governor,' answered the man. 'There wasn't no women and children on board, so I reckons it was everyone for himself.'

'Any idea what caused the explosion?'

'I 'aven't, governor – that's strite. But I knew as no good was a-going to come of this trip, as soon as that there madman went and drowned hisself.'

Drummond stared silently ahead. In the dim light he had no fear of being recognised, even if any of the three men they had saved had seen him. And his mind was busy. He had not the slightest doubt that Peterson had caused the explosion; he had even less doubt that Peterson, at any rate, was not drowned. But why had he taken the appalling risk of doing such a thing in so populous a waterway?

He went back to the stern and sat down beside Ted, who was nosing the boat gently through the water. Masses of débris surrounded them, and it was necessary to move with the utmost caution.

'What made him risk it here, Ted?' he whispered.

'Obvious, old man,' returned the other in a low voice. 'He thought your bodies would be washed ashore; he had no means of telling when. He knew they would be identified; he further knew that I would at once say what had happened. From that moment he would be in deadly danger; wireless would put every ship at sea wise. And to do a little stunt of this sort, if he was to escape, it was imperative he should be near land. So, as Peterson would do, he didn't hesitate for a moment, but put the job through at once.'

Drummond nodded thoughtfully.

'You're right, Ted – perfectly right.'

'And unless I'm very much surprised, our friend at the present moment is stepping out of his life-belt somewhere on the beach in Colwell Bay. Tomorrow, I should imagine, he will cross to Lymington – and after that you possibly know what his moves will be. I certainly don't – for I'm completely in the dark over the whole stunt.'

'It's too long a story to tell you now, old man,' said Drummond. 'But one thing I do know. Whoever else may be picked up, our friend will not be amongst the survivors. He's run unheard-of risks to pull this thing off, including a cold-blooded murder. And now officially he's going to die himself in order to throw everyone off the scent.' He laughed grimly. 'Moreover, he'd have done what he set out to do if you hadn't been leaning over the side of your governor's yacht.'

'But what's the prize this time?'

'Old Goodman's secret for making artificial diamonds – that was the prize, and Peterson has got it.'

Ted whistled softly.

'I heard something about it from Algy,' he remarked. 'But it seems to me, Hugh, that if that is the case, he's won.'

Drummond laughed.

'You were a bit surprised, Ted, when I refused to allow you to pull us on board your boat. Of course I knew as well as you did that with your speed we could have got clean away from them. But don't you see, old man, the folly of doing so? He would have spotted at once that we were not drowned; he would further have spotted that I was not as mad as I made out. Chawing soap is the hell of a game,' he added inconsequently. Then he went on again, emphasising each point on his fingers.

'Get me so far? Once he knew we were alive, it would have necessitated a complete alteration of his plans. He'd probably have put straight into some place on the south coast; gone ashore himself and never returned. And then he'd have disappeared into the blue. Maybe he'd have had another shot at murdering old Goodman; however, that point doesn't arise. The thing is he'd have disappeared.'

'Which is what he seems to have done now,' remarked Ted.

Again Drummond laughed.

'But I think I know where he'll turn up again. In what form or guise remains to be seen: our one and only Carl is never monotonous, to give him his due. You see, Ted, you don't seem to realise the intense advantage of being dead. I didn't till I heard him discussing it one night in his study. And now I'm dead, and the

Professor's dead, and dear Carl is dead. That's why I bumped the poor old man's head on the barnacles underneath your boat, as we changed sides. It's a gorgeous situation.'

'Doubtless, old man,' murmured the other. 'Though you must remember it's all a little dark and confusing to me. And anyway, where do you think he'll turn up again so that you can recognise him?'

'My dear man, our little Irma, or Janet, or whatever name the sweet thing is masquerading under this time, is a powerful magnet. And I am open to a small bet that at the moment she is taking the air in Switzerland: Montreux to be exact. What more natural, then, that believing himself perfectly safe, our one and only Carl will return to the arms of his lady – if only for a time.'

'And you propose to fly there also?'

'Exactly. I want the notes of that process, and I also want a final reckoning with the gentleman.'

'Final?' said Ted, glancing at Drummond thoughtfully.

'Definitely final,' answered Drummond quietly. 'This time our friend has gone too far.'

Jerningham looked at the numerous other boats which, by this time, had arrived at the scene of the disaster. Then he swung his helm hard round.

'That being so,' he remarked, 'since our presence is no longer needed here, I suggest that we get a move on. From my knowledge of Montreux, old man, it is getting uncomfortably hot just now. Deauville will be more in Irma's line. If I were you, I'd get out there, and do it quick. Joking apart, you may be right and, of course, I don't know all the facts of the case. But from what I've guessed, I think friend Peterson will cover all his tracks at the first possible moment.'

'He may,' agreed Drummond. 'And yet – believing that the Professor and I are both dead – he may not. You see,' he repeated once again, 'he thinks he's safe. Therein lies the maggot in the Stilton.'

With which profound simile he relapsed into silence, only broken as once more the boat drew up alongside the yacht.

'He thinks he's safe, which is where he goes into the mulligatawny up to his neck. Put these fellows on shore, Ted, give me a change of clothes, and then run me over to Lymington.'

Chapter 12

In which he samples Mr Blackton's Napoleon brandy

That Drummond was no fool his intimate friends knew well. He had a strange faculty for hitting the nail on the head far more often than not. Possibly his peculiarly direct method of argument enabled him to reach more correct conclusions than someone subtler-minded and cleverer could achieve. His habit of going for essentials and discarding side issues was merely the mental equivalent of those physical attributes which had made him a holy terror in the ring. Moreover, he had the invaluable gift of being able to put himself in the other man's place.

But it may be doubted if in any of his duels with Peterson he had ever been more unerringly right than in his diagnosis of the immediate future. It was not a fluke; it was in no sense guesswork. He merely put himself in Peterson's place, and decided what he would do under similar circumstances. And having decided on that, he went straight ahead with his own plans, which, like all he made, were simple and to the point. They necessitated taking a chance, but, after all, what plan doesn't?

He had made up his mind to kill Peterson, but he wanted to do it in such a manner that it would appeal to his sense of art in after-life. And with Drummond the sense of art was synonymous with the sense of fair play. He would give Peterson a fair chance to fight for his life. But in addition to that his ambition went a little farther. He felt that this culminating duel should be worthy of them both. The mental atmosphere must be correct, as well as the mundane surroundings. That that was largely beyond his control he realised, but he hoped for the best. The sudden plunging of Peterson from the dizzy heights of success into the valley of utter failure must not be a hurried affair, but a leisurely business in which each word would tell. How dizzy were the heights to which Peterson thought he had attained was, of course, known only to Peterson. But, on that point, he need not have worried.

For Mr Edward Blackton, as he stepped out of the train at Montreux station at nine o'clock on a glorious summer's evening, was in a condition in which even a request for one of his three remaining bottles of Napoleon brandy might have been acceded to. True, his right arm pained him somewhat; true, he was supremely unaware that at seven o'clock that morning Drummond had descended from the Orient express on to the same platform. What he was aware of was that in his pocket reposed the secret which would make him allpowerful; and in his handbag reposed an English morning paper giving the eminently satisfactory news that only six survivors had been rescued from the s.y. *Gadfly*, which had mysteriously blown up off the Needles. Moreover, all six had combined in saying that the temporary owner of the yacht – a Mr Robinson – must be amongst those drowned.

The hotel 'bus drew up at the door of the Palace Hotel, and Mr Blackton descended. He smiled a genial welcome at the manager, and strolled into the luxurious lounge. In the ballroom leading out of it a few couples were dancing, but his shrewd glance at once found whom he was looking for. In a corner sat Irma talking to a young Roumanian of great wealth, and a benevolent glow spread over him. No more would the dear child have to do these fatiguing things from necessity. If she chose to continue parting men from their money as a hobby it would be quite a different thing. There is a vast difference between pleasure and business.

He sauntered across the lounge towards her, and realised at once that there was something of importance she wished to say to him. For a minute or two, however, they remained there chatting; then with a courteous goodnight they left the Roumanian and ascended in the lift to their suite.

'What is it, my dearest?' he remarked, as he shut the sitting-room door.

'That man Blantyre is here, Ted,' said the girl. 'He's been asking to see you.'

He sat down and pulled her on to his knee.

'Blantyre,' he laughed. 'Sir Raymond! I thought it possible he might come. And is he very angry?'

'When he saw me he was nearly speechless with rage.'

'Dear fellow! It must have been a dreadful shock to him.'

'But, Ted,' she cried anxiously, 'is it all right?'

'Righter even than that, *carissima*. Blantyre simply doesn't come into the picture. All I trust is that he won't have a fit in the room or anything, because I think that Sir Raymond in a fit would be a disquieting spectacle.'

There was a knock at the door, and the girl got quickly up.

'Come in.'

Mr Blackton regarded the infuriated man who entered with a tolerant smile.

'Sir Raymond Blantyre, surely. A delightful surprise. Please shut the door, and tell us to what we are indebted for the pleasure of this visit.'

The President of the Metropolitan Diamond Syndicate advanced slowly across the room. His usually florid face was white with rage, and his voice, when he spoke, shook uncontrollably.

'You scoundrel – you infernal, damned scoundrel!'

Mr Blackton thoughtfully lit a cigar; then, leaning back in his chair, he surveyed his visitor benignly.

'Tush, tush!' he murmured. 'I must beg of you to remember that there is a lady present.'

Sir Raymond muttered something under his breath; then, controlling himself with an effort, he sat down.

'I presume it is unnecessary for me to explain why I am here,' he remarked at length.

'I had imagined through a desire to broaden our comparatively slight acquaintance into something deeper and more intimate,' said Mr Blackton hopefully.

'Quit this fooling,' snarled the other. 'Do you deny that you have the papers containing Goodman's process?'

'I never deny anything till I'm asked, and not always then.'

'Have you got them, or have you not?' cried Sir Raymond furiously.

'Now I put it to you, my dear fellow, am I a fool or am I not?' Mr Blackton seemed almost pained. 'Of course I have the papers of the process. What on earth do you suppose I put myself to the trouble and inconvenience of coming over to England for? Moreover, if it is of any interest to you, the notes are no longer in the somewhat difficult calligraphy of our lamented Professor, but in my own perfectly legible writing.'

'You scoundrel!' spluttered Sir Raymond. 'You took our money – half a million pounds – on the clear understanding that the process was to be suppressed.'

Mr Blackton blew out a large cloud of smoke.

'The point is a small one,' he murmured, 'but that is not my recollection of what transpired. You and your syndicate offered me half a million pounds to prevent Professor Goodman revealing his secret to the world. Well, Professor Goodman hasn't done so – nor will he do so. So I quite fail to see any cause for complaint.'

The veins stood out on Sir Raymond's forehead.

'You have the brazen effrontery to sit there and maintain that our offer to you did not include the destruction of the secret? Do you imagine we should have been so incredibly foolish as to pay you a large sum of money merely to transfer those papers from his pocket to yours?'

Mr Blackton shrugged his shoulders.

'The longer I live, my dear Sir Raymond, the more profoundly do I become impressed with how incredibly foolish a lot of people are. But, in this case, do not let us call it foolishness. A kinder word is surely more appropriate to express your magnanimity. There are people who say that businessmen are hard. No – a thousand times, no. To present me with the secret was charming; but to force upon me half a million pounds sterling as well was almost extravagant.'

'Hand it over – or I'll kill you like a dog.'

Mr Blackton's eyes narrowed a little; then he smiled.

'Really, Sir Raymond – don't be so crude. I must beg of you to put that absurd weapon away. Why, my dear fellow, it might go off. And though I believe capital punishment has been abolished in most of the cantons in Switzerland, I don't think imprisonment for life would appeal to you.'

Slowly the other man lowered his revolver.

'That's better – much better,' said Mr Blackton approvingly. 'And now, have we anything further to discuss?'

'What do you propose to do?' asked Sir Raymond dully.

'Really, my dear fellow, I should have thought it was fairly obvious. One thing you may be quite sure about: I do not propose to inform the Royal Society about the matter.'

'No, but you propose to make use of your knowledge yourself?'

'Naturally. In fact I propose to become a millionaire many times over by means of it.'

'That means the ruin of all of us.'

'My dear Sir Raymond, your naturally brilliant brain seems amazingly obtuse this evening. Please give me the credit of knowing something about the diamond market. I shall place these stones with such care that even you will have no fault to find. It will do me no good to deflate the price of diamonds. Really, if you look into it, you know, your half-million has not been wasted. You would have been ruined without doubt if Professor Goodman had broadcasted his discovery to the world at large. Every little chemist would have had genuine diamonds the size of tomatoes in his front window. Now nothing of the sort will happen. And though I admit that it is unpleasant for you to realise that at any moment a stone worth many thousands may be put on the market at the cost of a fiver, it's not as bad as it would have been if you hadn't called me in. And one thing I do promise you: I will make no attempt to undersell you. My stones will be sold at the current market price.'

Sir Raymond stirred restlessly in his chair. It was perfectly true what this arch-scoundrel said: it was better that the secret should be in the hands of a man who knew how to use it than in those of an unpractical old chemist.

'You see, Sir Raymond,' went on Mr Blackton, 'the whole matter is so simple. The only living people who know anything about this process are you and your syndicate – and I. One can really pay no attention to that inconceivable poop – I forget his name. I mean the one with the eyeglass.'

'There's his friend,' grunted Sir Raymond – 'that vast man.'

'You allude to Drummond,' said Mr Blackton softly.

'That's his name. I don't know how much he *knows*, but he suspects a good deal. And he struck me as being a dangerous young man.'

Mr Blackton smiled sadly.

'Drummond! Dear fellow! My darling,' he turned to the girl, 'I have some sad news for you. In the excitement of Sir Raymond's visit, I quite forgot to tell you. Poor Drummond is no more.'

The girl sat up quickly.

'Dead! Drummond dead! Good heavens! How?'

'It was all very sad, and rather complicated. The poor dear chap went mad. In his own charming phraseology he got kittens in the granary. But all through his terrible affliction, one spark of his old life remained: his rooted aversion to me. The only trouble was that he mistook someone else for your obedient servant, and at last his feelings overcame him. I took him for a short sea-voyage, with the gentleman he believed was me, and he rewarded me by frothing at the mouth, and jumping overboard in a fit of frenzy, clutching this unfortunate gentleman in the grip of a maniac. They were both drowned. Too sad, is it not?'

'But I don't understand,' cried the girl. 'Good heavens! What's that?'

From a large cupboard occupying most of one wall came the sound of a cork being extracted. It was unmistakable, and a sudden deadly silence settled on the room. The occupants seemed temporarily paralysed: corks do not extract themselves. And then a strange pallor spread over Mr Blackton's face, as if some ghastly premonition of the truth had dawned on him.

He tottered rather than walked to the cupboard and flung it open. Comfortably settled in the corner was Drummond. In one hand he held a corkscrew, in the other a full bottle of Napoleonic brandy, which he was sniffing with deep appreciation.

'I pass this, Carl,' he remarked, 'as a very sound liqueur brandy. And if you would oblige me with a glass, I will decide if the taste comes up to the bouquet. A tooth-tumbler will do excellently, if you have no other.'

The pallor grew more sickly on Blackton's face as he stared at the speaker. He had a sudden sense of unreality; the room was spinning round. It was untrue, of course; it was a dream. Drummond was drowned: he knew it. So how could he be sitting in the cupboard? Manifestly the thing was impossible.

'Well, well,' said the apparition, stretching out his legs comfortably, 'this is undoubtedly a moment fraught with emotion and, I trust I may say, tender memories.' He bowed to the girl, who, with her hands locked together, was staring at him with unfathomable eyes. 'Before proceeding, may I ask the correct method of addressing you? I like to pander to your foibles, Carl, in any way I can, and I gather that neither Mr Robinson nor Professor Scheidstrun is technically accurate at the moment.'

'How did you get here?' said Blackton in a voice he hardly recognised as his own.

'By the Orient express this morning,' returned Drummond, emerging languidly from the cupboard.

'My God! You're not human.'

The words seemed to be wrung from Blackton by a force greater than his own, and Drummond looked at him thoughtfully. There was no doubt about it – Peterson's nerve had gone. And Drummond would indeed not have been human if a very real thrill of triumph had not run through him at that moment. But no trace showed on his face as he opened his cigarette-case.

'On the contrary – very human indeed,' he murmured. 'Even as you, Carl – you'll excuse me if I return to our original nomenclature: it's so much less confusing. To err is human – and you erred once.

It's bad luck, because I may frankly say that in all the pleasant *rencontres* we've had together nothing has filled me with such profound admiration for your ability as this meeting. There are one or two details lacking in my mind – one in particular; but on what I do know, I congratulate you. And possessing, as I think you must admit, a sense of sportsmanship, I feel almost sorry for that one big error of yours, though it is a delightful compliment to my histrionic abilities. How's Freyder's face?'

'So you hadn't got concussion?' said the other. His voice was steadier now; he was thinking desperately.

'You've hit it, Carl. I recovered from my concussion on the floor of your room, and listened with interest to your plans for my future. And having a certain natural gift for lying doggo, I utilised it. But if it's any gratification to you, I can assure you that I very nearly gave myself away when I found who it was you had upstairs. You will doubtless be glad to hear that by this time Professor Goodman is restored to the bosom of his family.'

A strangled noise came from behind him, and he turned round to find Sir Raymond Blantyre in a partially choking condition.

'Who did you say?' he demanded thickly.

'Professor Goodman,' repeated Drummond, and his voice was icy. 'I haven't got much to say to you, Sir Raymond – except that you're a nasty piece of work. Few things in my life have afforded me so much pleasure as the fact that you were swindled out of half a million. I wish it had been more. For the man who carried this coup through one can feel a certain unwilling admiration; for you, one can feel only the most unmitigated contempt.'

'How dare you speak like that!' spluttered the other, but Drummond was taking no further notice of him.

'That was your second error, Carl. You ought to have come into the motor-boat. I assure you I had a dreadful time dragging that poor old chap underneath it, as you crossed our stern. His knowledge of swimming is rudimentary.'

'So that was it, was it?' said Blackton slowly. His nerve had completely recovered, and he lit a cigar with ease. 'I really think it is for me to congratulate you, my dear Drummond. Apart, however, from this exchange of pleasantries – er – what do we do now?'

'You say that Professor Goodman is still alive?' Sir Raymond had found his voice again. 'Then who – who was buried?'

'Precisely,' murmured Drummond. 'The one detail in particular in which I am interested. Who was the owner of the boot? Or shall I say who was the owner of the foot inside the boot, because the boot was undoubtedly the Professor's?'

'The point seems to me to be of but academic interest,' remarked Mr Blackton in a bored voice. '*Nil nisi bonum* – you know the old tag. And I can assure you that the foot's proprietor was a tedious individual. No loss to the community whatever.'

And suddenly a light dawned on Sir Raymond Blantyre.

'Great heavens! It was poor Lewisham.'

Absorbed as he had been by other things, the strange disappearance of his indiscreet fellow-director, the peculiar radiogram from mid-Atlantic and subsequent silence, had slipped from his mind. Now it came back, and he stared at Blackton with a sort of fascinated horror. The reason for Lewisham's visit to Professor Goodman was clear, and he shuddered uncontrollably.

'It was Lewisham,' he repeated dully.

'I rather believe it was,' murmured Blackton, dismissing the matter with a wave of his hand. 'As I said before, the point is of but academic interest.' He turned again to Drummond. 'So Professor Goodman is restored to his family once more. I trust he has suffered no ill-effects from his prolonged immersion.'

'None at all, thank you,' answered Drummond. 'Somewhat naturally, he is angry. In fact, for a mild and gentle old man, he is in what might be described as the devil of a temper.'

'But if he's back in London,' broke in Sir Raymond excitedly, 'what about his secret? It will be given to the world, and all this will have been in vain.'

Mr Blackton thoughtfully studied the ash on his cigar, while Drummond stared at the speaker. And then for one fleeting instant their eyes met. Sworn enemies though they were, for that brief moment they stood on common ground – unmitigated contempt for the man who had just spoken.

'From many points of view, Sir Raymond, I wish it could be given to the world,' said Drummond. 'I can think of no better punishment for you, or one more richly deserved. Unfortunately, however, you can set your mind at rest on that point. Professor Goodman no longer possesses his notes on the process.'

'Precisely,' murmured Mr Blackton. 'It struck me that one copy was ample. So I destroyed his.'

'But for all that,' continued Drummond, noting the look of relief that spread over Sir Raymond's face, 'I don't think you're going to have a fearfully jolly time when you return to London.

In fact, if I may offer you a word of advice, I wouldn't return at all.'

'What do you mean?' stammered the other.

'Exactly what I say, you damned swine,' snapped Drummond. 'Do you imagine you can instigate murder and sudden death, and then go trotting into the Berkeley as if nothing had happened? You're for it, Blantyre; you're for it – good and strong. And you're going to get it. As I say, the Professor is angry and he's obstinate – and he wants your blood. My own impression is that if you get off with fifteen years, you can think yourself lucky.'

Sir Raymond plucked at his collar feverishly.

'Fifteen years! My God!' Then his voice rose to a scream. 'But it was this villain who did it all, I tell you, who murdered Lewisham, who . . . '

With a crash he fell back in the chair where Drummond had thrown him, and though his shaking lips still framed words, no sound came from them. Blackton was still critically regarding the ash on his cigar; Drummond had turned his back and was speaking again.

'Yes, Carl,' he was saying, 'the Professor and I will deal with Sir Raymond. Or if anything should happen to me, then the Professor is quite capable of doing it himself.'

'And what do you anticipate should happen to you?' asked Blackton politely.

'Nothing, I trust. But there is one thing which I have never done in the past during all our games of fun and laughter. I have never made the mistake of underrating you.'

Blackton glanced at him thoughtfully.

'We appear,' he murmured, 'to be approaching the sixpence in the plum-pudding.'

'We are,' returned Drummond quietly. 'Sir Raymond is the Professor's portion; you are mine.'

A silence settled on the room – a silence broken at length by Blackton. His blue eyes never left Drummond's face; the smoke from his cigar rose into the air undisturbed by any tremor of his hand.

'I am all attention,' he remarked.

'There is not much to say,' said Drummond. 'But what there is, I hope may interest you. If my memory serves me aright, there was one unfailing jest between us in the old days. Henry Lakington did his best to make it stale before he met with his sad end; that unpleasant Count Zadowa let it trip from his tongue on occasions; in fact, Carl, you yourself have used it more than once. I allude to the determination expressed by you all at one time or another to kill me.'

Blackton nodded thoughtfully.

'Now you speak of it, I do recall something of the sort.'

'Good,' continued Drummond. 'And since no-one could call me grudging in praise, I will admit that you made several exceedingly creditable attempts. This time, however, the boot is on the other leg: it's my turn to say – snap. In other words, I am going to kill you, Carl. At least, lest I should seem to boast, I'm going to have a damned good attempt – one that I trust will be even more creditable than yours.'

Once again a silence settled, broken this time by an amused laugh from the girl.

'Adorable as ever, my Hugh,' she murmured. 'And where shall I send the wreath?'

'Mademoiselle,' answered Drummond gravely, 'I propose to be far more original than that. To do your – er – father – well, we won't press that point – to do Carl justice, his attempts were most original. You were not, of course, present on the evening at Maybrick Hall, when that exceedingly unpleasant Russian came to an untimely end. But for the arrival of the Black Gang, I fear that I should have been the victim – and Phyllis. However, let me assure you that I have no intention whatever of doing you any harm. But I should like you to listen – even as Phyllis had to listen – while I outline my proposals. Carl ran over his that night for my benefit, and I feel sure he would have fallen in with any proposals I had to make. Similarly, believe me, I shall be only too charmed to do the same for him.'

Sir Raymond Blantyre sat up and pinched himself. Was this some strange jest staged for his special benefit? Was this large young man who spoke with a twinkle in his eyes the jester? And glancing at the two men, he saw that there was no longer any twinkle, and that Blackton's face had become strangely drawn and anxious. But his voice when he spoke was calm.

'We appear to be in for an entertaining chat,' he murmured.

'I hope you will find it so,' returned Drummond gravely. 'But before we come to my actual proposal, I would like you to understand quite clearly what will happen if you refuse to fall in with it. Outside in the passage, Carl, are two large, stolid Swiss gendarmes: men of sterling worth, and quite unbribable. They don't know why they are there at present; but it will not take long to enlighten them. Should you decide, therefore, to decline my suggestion. I shall be under the painful necessity of requesting them to step in here, when I will inform them of just so much of your past history as to ensure your sleeping for the next few nights in rather less comfortable quarters. Until, in fact, extradition papers arrive from England. Do I make myself clear?'

'Perfectly,' answered the other. 'That will occur if I do not fall in with your suggestion. So let us hear the suggestion.'

'It took a bit of thinking out,' admitted Drummond. 'I haven't got your fertile brain, Carl, over these little matters. Still, I flatter myself it's not bad for a first attempt. I realised somewhat naturally the drawbacks to shooting you on sight – besides, it's so bad for the carpet. At the same time I have come to the unalterable conclusion that the world is not big enough for both of us. I might – you will justly observe – hand you over anyway to those stolid warriors outside. And since you would undoubtedly be hanged, the problem would be solved. But unsatisfactorily, Carl – most unsatisfactorily.'

'We are certainly in agreement on that point,' said the other.

'We have fought in the past without the police; we'll finish without them. And having made up my mind to that, it became necessary to think of some scheme by which the survivor should not suffer. If it's you – well, you'll get caught sooner or later; if it's me, I certainly don't propose to suffer in any way. Apart from having just bought weight-carrying hunters for next winter, it would be grossly unfair that I should.'

He selected a cigarette with care and lit it.

'It was you, Carl, who put the idea into my head,' he continued, 'so much of the credit is really yours. Your notion of making my death appear accidental that night at Maybrick Hall struck me as excellent. Worthy undoubtedly of an encore. Your death, Carl – or mine – will appear accidental, which makes everything easy for the survivor. I hope I'm not boring you.'

'Get down to it,' snarled Blackton. 'Don't play the fool, damn you!'

'As you did, Carl, that night at Maybrick Hall.' For a moment the veins stood out on Drummond's neck as the remembrance of that hideous scene came back to him; then he controlled himself and went on. 'At first sight it may seem absurd – even fanciful – this scheme of mine; but don't judge it hastily, I beg you. Know anything about glaciers, Carl?'

He smiled at the look of blank amazement on the other's face.

'Jolly little things, my dear fellow, if you treat 'em the right way. But dangerous things to play tricks with. There are great cracks in them, you know – deep cracks with walls of solid ice. If a man falls down one of those cracks, unless help is forthcoming at once, he doesn't live long, Carl; in fact, he dies astonishingly quickly.'

Blackton moistened his lips with his tongue.

'People fall down these cracks accidentally sometimes,' continued Drummond thoughtfully. 'In fact there was a case once – I won't vouch for its truth – but I'm sure you'd like to hear the story. It occurred on the glacier not far from Grindelwald – and it's always tickled me to death. It appears that one of the local celebrities went out to pick edelweiss or feed the chamois or something equally jolly, and failed to return. He'd gone out alone, and after a time his pals began to get uneasy. So they instituted a search-party, and in due course they found him. Or rather they saw him. He had slipped on the edge of one of the deepest crevasses in the whole glacier, and there he was about fifty feet below them wedged between the two walls of ice. He was dead, of course – though they yodelled at him hopefully for the rest of the day. A poor story, isn't it, Carl? – but it's not quite finished. They decided to leave him there for the night, and return next day and extract him. Will you believe it, Mademoiselle, when they arrived the following morning, they couldn't get at him. The old glacier had taken a heave forward in the night, and there he was wedged. Short of blasting him out with dynamite he was there for keeps. A terrible position for a self-respecting community, don't you think? To have the leading citizen on full view in a block of ice gives visitors an impression of carelessness. Of course, they tried to keep it dark; but it was useless. People came flocking from all over the place. Scientists came and made mathematical calculations as to when he'd come out at the bottom. Every year he moved on a few more yards; every year his widow – a person now of some consequence – took her children to see father, and later on her grandchildren to see grandfather. Forty years was the official time – and I believe he passed the winning-post in forty-one years three months: a wonderful example of pertinacity and dogged endurance.' Drummond paused hopefully. 'That's a pretty original idea, Carl, don't you think?'

Sir Raymond gave a short, almost hysterical laugh, but there was no sign of mirth on the faces of the other two.

'Am I to understand,' said Blackton harshly, 'that you propose that one or other of us should fall down a crevasse in a glacier? I've never heard anything so ridiculous in my life.'

'Don't say that,' answered Drummond. 'It's no more ridiculous than braining me with a rifle butt, as you intended to do once. And a great deal less messy. Anyway, that is my proposal. You and I, Carl, will go unarmed to a glacier. We will there find a suitably deep crevasse. And on the edge of that crevasse' – his voice changed suddenly – 'we will fight for the last time, with our bare hands. It will be slippery, which is to your advantage, though the fact that I am stronger than you cannot be adjusted at this late hour. It's that – or the police, Peterson: one gives you a chance, the other gives you none. And if, as I hope, you lose – why, think of your triumph. The leading detectives of four continents will be dancing with rage on the top of the ice watching you safely embalmed underneath their feet.'

'I refuse utterly,' snarled the other. 'It's murder – nothing more nor less.'

'A form of amusement you should be used to,' said Drummond. 'However, you refuse. Very good. I will now send for the police.'

He rose and went to the door, and Blackton looked round desperately.

'Wait,' he cried. 'Can't we – can't we come to some arrangement?'

'None. Those are my terms. And there is one other that I have not mentioned. You said that two copies of the Professor's notes were excessive. I agree – but I go farther: one is too much; that process is altogether too dangerous. If the police take you – it doesn't matter; but if you accept my terms, you've got to hand that copy over to me now. And I shall burn it. I don't mind running the risk of being killed; but if I am, you're not going to get away with the other thing too.' Drummond glanced at his watch. 'I give you half a minute to decide.'

The seconds dragged by and Blackton stared in front of him. Plan after plan flashed through his mind, only to be dismissed as impossible. He was caught – and he knew it. Once the police had him, he was done for utterly and completely. They could hang him ten times over in England alone. Moreover, anything in the nature of personal violence under present circumstances was out of the question. Powerful though he was, at no time was he a match for Drummond in the matter of physical strength; but here in the Palace Hotel it was too impossible even to think of. Almost as impossible as any idea of bribery.

He was caught: not only had this, his greatest coup, failed, but his life was forfeit as well. For he was under no delusions as to what would be the result of the fight on the glacier.

He heard the snap of a watch closing.

'Your half-minute is up, Peterson.' Drummond's hand was on the door. 'And I must say – I thought better of you.'

'Stop,' said the other sullenly. 'I accept.'

Drummond came back into the room slowly.

'That is good,' he remarked. 'Then – first of all – the notes of Professor Goodman's process.'

Without a word Blackton handed over two sheets of paper, though in his eyes was a look of smouldering fury.

'You fool!' he snarled, as he watched them burn to ashes. 'You damned fool!'

'Opinions differ,' murmured Drummond, powdering the ash on the table. 'And now to discuss arrangements. We start early to-morrow morning by car. I have been to some pains to examine the timetable – I mention this in case you should try to bolt. There is nothing that will do you any good either in the Lausanne direction or towards Italy. Behind you have the mountain railways, which don't run trains at night; in front you have the lake. Below two very good friends of mine are waiting to assist if necessary – though I can promise you they will take no part in our little scrap. But you're such an elusive person, Peterson, that I felt I could take no chances. To the best of my ability I've hemmed you in for the few hours that remain before we start. And then you and I will sit on the back seat and discuss the view. I feel the precautions seem excessive, but I have not the advantage of a specially prepared house – like you have always had in the past.'

'And until we start?' said Blackton quietly.

'We remain in this room,' answered Drummond. 'At least – you and I do. Mademoiselle must please herself.'

The girl looked at him languidly.

'You don't mind if I leave you?' she remarked. 'To tell you the truth, *mon ami*, you're being a little tedious this evening. And since I am going to Evian-les-Bains for the waters tomorrow, I think I'll retire to bed. Do you know Evian?'

'Never heard of it, I'm afraid,' said Drummond. 'My geography was always rotten.'

He was lighting a cigarette, more to conceal his thoughts than for any desire to smoke. That she was a perfect actress he knew, and yet it seemed impossible to believe that her composure was anything but natural. He glanced at Peterson, who was still sitting motionless, his chin sunk on his chest. He glanced at the girl, and she was patting a stray tendril of hair in front of a mirror. He even glanced at Sir

Raymond, but there was nothing to be learned from that gentleman. He still resembled a man only partially recovered from a drugged sleep. Was it conceivable that he had left a loophole in his scheme? Or could it be that she had ceased to care for Peterson?

She had turned and was regarding him with a faint smile.

'I fear I shan't be up before you go tomorrow,' she murmured. 'But whoever does not go into cold storage must come and tell me about it. And there are a lot of other things, too, I want to hear about. Why Carl, for instance, ought to have looked in the motor-boat, and how you got concussion.'

Drummond looked at her steadily.

'I find you a little difficult to understand, Mademoiselle. I trust you are under no delusions as to whether I am bluffing or not. You can, at any rate, settle one point in your mind by glancing outside the door.'

'To see the two large policemen,' laughed the girl. 'La, la, my dear man – they would give me what you call a nightmare. I will take your word for it.'

'And any appeal for help will result somewhat unfortunately for Carl.'

She shrugged her shoulders irritably.

'I know when the game is up,' she remarked. Then abruptly she turned on the man who had been her companion for years. 'Bah! You damned fool!' she stormed. 'Every time this great idiot here does you down. Not once, but half a dozen times have you told me "Drummond is dead", and every time he bobs up again like a jack-in-the-box. And now – this time – when you had everything – everything – everything, you go and let him beat you again. You tire me. It is good that we end our partnership. You are imbecile.'

She raged out of the room, and Carl Peterson raised his haggard eyes as the door closed. His lips had set in a twisted smile, and after a while his head sank forward again, and he sat motionless, staring at the table in front of him. His cigar had long gone out; he seemed to have aged suddenly. And into Drummond's mind there stole a faint feeling of pity.

'I'm sorry about that, Peterson,' he said quietly. 'She might at least have seen the game out to the end.'

The other made no reply – only by a slight shake of his shoulders did he show that he had heard. And Drummond's feeling of pity increased. Scoundrel, murderer, unmitigated blackguard though he knew this man to be, yet when all was said and done he was no weakling. And it wasn't difficult to read his thoughts at the moment –

to realise the bitterness and the fury that must be possessing him. Half an hour ago he had believed himself successful beyond his wildest dreams; now – And then for the girl to go back on him at the finish.

Drummond pulled himself together; such thoughts were dangerous. He forced himself to remember that night when it had been the question of seconds between life and death for Phyllis; he recalled to his mind the words he had listened to as he lay on the floor in the house to which Freyder had brought him while still unconscious.

'I think if it was a question between getting away with the process and killing Drummond – it would be the latter.'

If the positions were reversed, would one thought of mercy have softened the man he now held in his power? No-one knew better than Drummond himself that it would not. He was a fool even to think about it. The man who hated him so bitterly was in his power. He deserved, no man more so, to die; he was going to die. Moreover he was going to have a sporting chance for his life into the bargain. And that was a thing he had never given Drummond. And yet he could have wished the girl had not proved herself so rotten.

The lights went out on the long terrace fronting the lake, and he glanced at his watch. It was twelve o'clock: in another three hours it would be light enough to start. Through Château d'Oex to Interlaken – he knew the way quite well. And then up either by train or car to Grindelwald. It would depend on what time they arrived as to the rest of the programme. And as he saw in his mind's eye the grim struggle that would be the finish one way or the other – for Peterson was no mean antagonist physically – Drummond's fists tightened instinctively and his breathing came a little quicker. Up above the snow-line they would fight, in the dusk when the light was bad, and there would be no wandering peasant to spread awkward stories.

Peterson's voice cut in on his thoughts.

'You are quite determined to go through with this?'

'Quite,' answered Drummond. 'As I told you, I have definitely come to the conclusion that the world is not big enough for both of us.'

Peterson said no more, but after a while he rose and walked into the glassed-in balcony. The windows were open, and with his hands in his pockets he stood staring out over the lake.

'I advise you to try nothing foolish,' said Drummond, joining him. 'The Swiss police are remarkably efficient, and communication with the frontiers by telephone is rapid.'

'You think of everything,' murmured Peterson. 'But there are no trains, and it takes time to order a car at midnight. And since it is beyond my powers to swim the lake, there doesn't seem much more to be said.' He turned and faced Drummond thoughtfully. 'How on earth do you do it, my young friend? Are you aware that you are the only man in the world who has ever succeeded in doing me down? And you have done it not once – but three times. I wonder what your secret is.' He gave a short laugh, then once again stared intently out of the window. 'Yes, I wonder very much. In fact I shall really have to find out. Good God! Look at that fool Blantyre.'

Drummond swung round, and even as he did so Peterson hit him with all his force under the jaw. The blow caught him off his balance, and he crashed backwards, striking the back of his head against the side of the balcony as he fell. For a moment or two he lay there half-stunned. Dimly he saw that Peterson had disappeared, then, dazed and sick, he scrambled to his feet and tottered to the window. And all he saw was the figure of a man which showed up for a second in the light of a street-lamp and then disappeared amongst the trees which led to the edge of the lake.

Desperately he pulled himself together. The police outside; the telephone; there was still time. He could hear the engine of a motor-boat now, but even so there was time. He rushed across the room to the door; outside in the passage were the two gendarmes.

They listened as he poured out the story, and then one of them shook his head a little doubtfully.

'It is perfectly true, Monsieur,' he remarked, 'that we can communicate with the gendarmes of all the Swiss towns *au bord du lac* – and at once. But with the French towns it is different.'

'French?' said Drummond, staring at him. 'Isn't this bally lake Swiss?'

'*Mais non, monsieur*. Most of it is. But the southern shore from St Gingolph to Hermance is French. Evian-les-Bains is a well-known French watering-place.'

'Evian-les-Bains!' shouted Drummond – 'Evian-les-Bains! Stung! – Utterly, absolutely, completely stung! And to think that that girl fixed the whole thing under my very nose.'

For a moment he stood undecided; then at a run he started along the corridor.

'After 'em, *mes braves*. Another motor-boat is the only chance.'

There was another moored close in-shore, and into it they all tumbled, followed by Ted Jerningham and Algy Longworth, whom they had roused from their slumbers in the lounge. Ted, as the authority, took charge of the engine – only to peer at it once and start laughing.

'What's the matter?' snapped Drummond.

'Nothing much, old man,' said his pal. 'Only that there are difficulties in the way of making a petrol engine go when both sparking-plugs have long been removed.'

And it seemed to Drummond that, at that moment, there came a faint, mocking shout from far out on the darkness of the lake.

'Mind you wear hob-nailed boots on the glacier.'

Chapter 13

In which Drummond receives an addition to his library

It was four days later. During that four days Drummond's usual bright conversational powers had been limited to one word – 'Stung'. And now as he drew his second pint from the cask in the corner of his room in Brook Street, he elaborated it.

'Stung in the centre and on both flanks,' he remarked morosely. 'And biffed in the jaw into the bargain.'

'Still, old dear,' murmured Algy brightly – Algy's world was bright again, now that there was no further need to postpone his marriage – 'you may meet him again. You'd never really have forgiven yourself if you'd watched him passaging down a glacier. So near and yet so far, and all that sort of thing. I mean, what's the good of a glacier, anyway? You can't use the ice even to make a cocktail with. At least, not if old man Peterson was embalmed in it. It wouldn't be decent.'

'Stung,' reiterated Drummond. 'And not only stung, my dear boy, but very nearly bitten. Are you aware that only by the most uncompromising firmness on my part did I avoid paying his bill at the Palace Hotel? The manager appeared to think that I was responsible for his abrupt departure. A truly hideous affair.'

He relapsed into moody silence, which remained unbroken till the sudden entrance of Professor Goodman. He was holding in his hand an early edition of an evening paper, and his face was agitated.

'What's up, Professor?' asked Drummond.

'Read that,' said the other.

Drummond glanced at the paper.

'DEATH OF WELL-KNOWN ENGLISH FINANCIER IN PARIS'. Thus ran the headline. He read on:

'This morning Sir Raymond Blantyre, who was stopping at the Savoy Hotel, was found dead in his bed. Beside the deceased man an empty bottle of veronal was discovered. No further details are at present to hand.'

The paragraph concluded with a brief description of the dead man's career, but Drummond read no farther. So Blantyre had failed to face the music. As usual, the lesser man paid, while Peterson got off.

'Suicide, I assume,' said the Professor.

'Undoubtedly,' answered Drummond. 'It saves trouble. And I may say I put the fear of God into him. Well, Denny – what is it?'

'This letter and parcel have just come for you, sir,' said his servant.

Drummond turned them both over in his hand, and a faint smile showed on his face. The postmark was Rome; the writing he knew. It was the letter he opened first:

> I have threatened often: I shall not always fail. You have threat-
> ened once: you could hardly hope to succeed. I shall treasure some
> edelweiss. *Au revoir*.

Still smiling, he looked at the parcel. After all, perhaps it was as well. Life without Peterson would indeed be tame. He cut the string; he undid the paper. And then a strange look spread over his face – a look which caused the faithful Denny to step forward in alarm.

'Beer, fool – beer!' cried his master hoarsely.

On the table in front of him lay a book. It was entitled *Our Tiny Tots' Primer of Geography*.

THE END

THE FINAL COUNT

Introduction

In endeavouring to put before the public for the first time the truth concerning the amazing happenings of the summer of 1927, I feel myself to be at a disadvantage. In the first place I am no story-teller: so maybe my presentation of the facts will fail to carry conviction. Nay, further: it is more than likely that what I am about to write down will be regarded as a tissue of preposterous lies. And yet to those who condemn me offhand I would say one thing. Take the facts as you know them, and as they appeared in the newspapers, and try to account for them in any other way. You may say that in order to write a book – gain, perhaps, a little cheap notoriety – I have taken the ravings of a madman around which to build a fantastic and ridiculous story. You are welcome to your opinion. I can do no more than tell you what I know: I cannot make you believe me.

In one respect, however, I feel that I am in a strong position: my own part was a comparatively small one. And it is therefore from no reason of self-aggrandisement that I write. To one man, and one man only, is praise and honour due, and that is the man who led us – Hugh Drummond. But if unbelievers should go to him for confirmation, it is more than probable they will be disappointed. He will burble at them genially, knock them senseless with a blow of greeting on the back, and then resuscitate them with a large tankard of ale. And the doubter may well be pardoned for continuing to doubt: I myself, when I first met Drummond, was frankly incredulous as to his capabilities of being anything but a vast and goodnatured fool. I disbelieved, politely, the stories his friends told me about him: to be candid, his friends were of very much the same type as himself. There were four of them whom I got to know intimately: Algy Longworth, a tall young man with a slight drawl and an eyeglass; Peter Darrell, who usually came home with the milk each morning, but often turned out to play cricket for Middlesex; Ted Jerningham, who fell in love with a different girl daily; and finally Toby Sinclair, who was responsible for introducing me into the circle.

Finally, there was Drummond himself, of whom a few words of description may not be amiss. He stood just six feet in his socks, and turned the scales at over fourteen stone. And of that fourteen stone not one ounce was made up of superfluous fat. He was hard muscle and bone clean through, and the most powerful man I have ever met in my life. He was a magnificent boxer, a lightning and deadly shot with a revolver, and utterly lovable. Other characteristics I discovered later: his complete absence of fear (though that seemed common to all of them); his cool resourcefulness in danger; and his marvellous gift of silent movement, especially in the dark.

But those traits, as I say, I only found out later: just at first he seemed to me to be a jovial, brainless creature who was married to an adorable wife.

It was his face and his boxing abilities that had caused him to be nicknamed Bulldog. His mouth was big, and his nose was small, and he would not have won a prize at a beauty show. In fact, it was only his eyes – clear and steady with a permanent glint of lazy humour in them – that redeemed his face from positive ugliness.

So much, then, for Hugh Drummond, D.S.O., M.C., who was destined to play the leading part in the events of that summer, and to meet again, and for the last time, the devil in human form who was our arch-enemy. And though it is not quite in chronological order, yet I am tempted to say a few words here concerning that monstrous criminal. Often in the earlier stages of our investigations did I hear Drummond mention his name – a name which conveyed nothing to me, but which required no explanation to the others or to his wife. And one day I asked him point blank what he meant.

He smiled slightly, and a dreamy look came into his eyes.

'What do I mean by saying that I seem to trace the hand of Carl Peterson? I'll tell you. There is a man alive in this world today – at least he's alive as far as I know – who might have risen to any height of greatness. He is possessed of a stupendous brain, unshakable nerve, and unlimited ambition. There is a kink, however, in his brain, which has turned him into an utterly unscrupulous criminal. To him murder means no more than the squashing of a wasp means to you.'

He looked at me quietly.

'Understand me: that remark is the literal truth. Three times in the past have he and I met: I'm just wondering if this will prove to be the fourth; if, way back, at the foundation of this ghastly affair, there sits

Carl Peterson, or Edward Blackton, or the Comte de Guy, or whatever he calls himself, directing, controlling, organising everything. I haven't seen him now or heard of him for three years, and as I say – I wonder.'

At the time, of course, it was Greek to me; but now that the thing is over and the terror is finished, it may be of interest to those who read to know before I start what we did not know at the time: to know that fighting against us with every force at his command was that implacable devil whom I will call Carl Peterson.

I say, we did not *know* it, but I feel that I must mitigate that statement somewhat. Looking back now I think – and Drummond himself admits it – that deep down in his mind there was a feeling almost of certainty that he was up against Peterson. He had no proof: he says that it was just a guess without much foundation – but he was convinced that it was so. And it was that conviction that kept him at it during those weary weeks in London, when all traces seemed to be lost. For if he had relaxed then, as we others did, if he had grown bored, thinking that all was over, a thing would have occurred unparalleled in the annals of crime.

But enough of this introduction: I will begin my story. And in telling it I shall omit nothing; even at the risk of boring my readers I shall give in their proper place extracts from the newspapers of the day which dealt with that part of the affair which is already known to the public. If there is to be a record, let it be a complete one.

Chapter 1

In which I hear a cry in the night

It was on a warm evening towards the end of April 1927 that the first act took place, though it is safe to say that there has never been any connection in the public mind up till this day between it and what came after. I was dining at Prince's with Robin Gaunt, a young and extremely brilliant scientist, and a very dear friend of mine. We had been at school together and at Cambridge; and though we had lost sight of one another during the war, the threads of friendship had been picked up again quite easily at the conclusion of that foolish performance. I had joined the Gunners, whilst he, somewhat naturally, had gravitated towards the Royal Engineers. For a year or two, doubtless bearing in mind his really extraordinary gifts, the powers that be ordained that he should make roads, a form of entertainment of which he knew less than nothing. And Robin smiled thoughtfully and made roads. At least he did so officially: in reality he did other things, whilst a sergeant with a penchant for rum superintended the steam-roller. And then one day came a peremptory order from G.H.Q. that Lieutenant Robin Gaunt, R.E., should cease making roads, and should report himself at the seats of the mighty at once. And Robin, still smiling thoughtfully, reported himself. As I have said, he had been doing other things during that eighteen months, and the fruits of his labours, sent direct and not through the usual official channels, lay on the table in front of the man to whom he reported.

From then on Robin became a mysterious and shadowy figure. I met him once on the leave boat going home, but he was singularly uncommunicative. He was always a silent sort of fellow, though on rare occasions when he chose to talk he could be brilliant. But during that crossing he was positively taciturn.

He looked ill and I told him so.

'Eighteen hours a day, old John, for eleven months on end. That's what I've been going, and I'm tired.'

He lit a cigarette and stared over the water.

'Can you take it easy now?' I asked him.

He gave a weary smile.

'If you mean by that, have I finished, then I can – more or less. But if you mean, can I take it easy from a mental point of view, God knows. I'll not have to work eighteen hours a day any more, but there are worse things than physical exhaustion.'

And suddenly he laid his hand on my arm.

'I know they're Huns,' he said tensely: 'I know it's just one's bounden duty to use every gift one has been given to beat 'em. But, damn it, John – they're men too. They go back to their womenkind, just as all these fellows on this boat are going back to theirs.'

He paused, and I thought he was going to say something more. But he didn't: he gave a short laugh and led the way through the crowd to the bar.

'A drink, John, and forget what I've been saying.'

That was in July '18, and I didn't see him again till after the Armistice. We met in London, and at lunch I started pulling his leg over his eighteen hours' work a day. He listened with a faint smile, and for a long while refused to be drawn. And it was only after the waiter went off to get change for the bill that he made a remark which for many months stuck in my mind.

'There are a few things in my life that I'm thankful for, John,' he said quietly. 'And the one that I'm most thankful for is that the Boches broke when they did. For if they hadn't . . . '

'Well – if they hadn't?'

'There wouldn't have been any Boches left to break.'

'And a damned good thing too,' I exclaimed.

He shrugged his shoulders.

'They're men too, as I said before. However, in Parliamentary parlance the situation does not arise. Wherefore, since it's Tuesday today and Wednesday tomorrow, we might have another brandy.'

And with that the conversation closed. Periodically during the next few months that remark of his came back to my mind.

'There wouldn't have been any Boches left to break.'

An exaggeration, of course: a figure of speech, and yet Robin Gaunt was not given to the use of vain phrases. Years of scientific training had made him meticulously accurate in his use of words; and, certainly, if one-tenth of the wild rumours that circulated round the military Hush-Hush department was true, there might be some justification for his remark. But after a time I forgot all about it, and when Robin alluded to the matter at dinner on that evening in April I had to rack my brains to remember what he was talking about.

I'd suggested a play, but he had shaken his head.

'I've an appointment, old man, tonight which I can't break. Remember my eighteen hours' work a day that you were so rude about?'

It took me a second or two to get the allusion.

'Great Scott!' I laughed, 'that was the war to end war, my boy. To make the world safe for heroes to live in, with further slush *ad nauseam*. You don't mean to say that you are still dabbling in horrors?'

'Not exactly, John,' he said gravely. 'When the war was over I put the whole of that part of my life behind me. I hoped, as most of us did, that a new era had dawned: now I realise, as all of us realise, that we've merely gone back a few centuries. You know as well as I do that it is merely a question of time before the hatred of Germany for France boils up and cannot be restrained. Any thinking German will tell you so. Don't let's worry about whose fault it is: we're concerned more with effects than causes. But when it does happen, there will be a war which for unparalleled ferocity has never before been thought of. Don't let's worry as to whether we go in, or on whose side we go in: those are problems that don't concern us. Let us merely realise that primitive passions are boiling and seething in Europe, backed by inventions which are the last word in science. Force is the sole arbiter today: force and blazing hate, covered for diplomacy's sake with a pitifully thin veneer of honeyed phrases. I tell you, John, I've just come back from Germany and I was staggered, simply staggered. The French desire for *revanche* in 1870 compared to German feeling today is as a tallow dip to the light of the sun.'

He lit a cigar thoughtfully.

'However, all that is neither here nor there. Concentrate on that one idea, that force is the only thing that counts today: concentrate also on the idea that frightfulness in war is inevitable. I've come round to that way of thinking, you know. The more the thing drags on, the more suffering and sorrow to the larger number. Wherefore, pursuing the argument to a logical conclusion, it seems to me that it might be possible to arm a nation with a weapon so frightful, that by its very frightfulness war would be impossible because no other country would dare to fight.'

'Frightfulness only breeds frightfulness,' I remarked. 'You'll always get counter-measures.'

'Not always,' he said slowly. 'Not always.'

'But what's your idea, Robin? What nation would you put in possession of such a weapon – granting for the moment that the weapon is there?'

He looked at me surprised. It was a silly remark, but I was thinking of France and Germany.

'My dear old man – our own, of course. Who else? The policemen of the world. Perhaps America too: the English-speaking peoples. Put them in such a position, John, that they can say, should the necessity arise – 'You shall not fight. You shall not again blacken the world with the hideous suffering of 1914. And since we can't prevent you fighting by words, we'll do it by force."

His eyes were gleaming, and I stared at him curiously. That he was in dead earnest was obvious, but the whole thing seemed to me to be preposterous.

'You can't demonstrate the frightfulness of any weapon, my dear fellow,' I objected, 'unless you go to war yourself. So what the devil is the good of it anyway?'

'Then, if necessary, go to war. Go to war for one day – against both of them. And at the end of that day say to them – "Now will you stop? If you don't the same thing will happen to you tomorrow, and the next day, and the next, until you do!" '

'But what will happen to them?' I cried.

'Universal, instantaneous death over as large or as small an area as is desired.'

I think it was at that moment that I first began to entertain doubts as to Robin's sanity. Not that people dining near would have noticed anything amiss with him: his voice was low-pitched and quiet. But the whole idea was so utterly far-fetched and fantastic that I couldn't help wondering if his brilliant brain hadn't crossed that tiny bridge which separates genius from insanity. I knew the hideous loathing he had always felt for war: was it possible that continual brooding on the idea had unhinged him?

'It was ready at Armistice time,' he continued, 'but not in its present form. Today it is perfected.'

'But damn it all, Robin,' I said, a little irritably, 'what is this IT?'

He smiled and shook his head.

'Not even to you, old man, will I tell that. If I could I would keep it entirely to myself, but I realise that that is impossible. At the moment there is only one other being in this world who knows my secret – the great-hearted pacifist who has financed me. He is an

Australian who lost both his sons in Gallipoli, and for the last two years he has given me ceaseless encouragement. Tonight I am meeting him again – I haven't seen him for three months – to tell him that I've succeeded. And tomorrow I've arranged to give a secret demonstration before the Army Council.'

He glanced at his watch and stood up.

'I must be off, John. Coming my way?'

Not wanting to go back so early I declined, and I watched his tall spare figure threading its way between the tables. Little did I dream of the circumstances in which I was next to meet him: a knowledge of the future has mercifully been withheld from mortal man. My thoughts as I sat on idly at the table finishing my cigar were confined to what he had been saying. Could it be possible that he had indeed made some stupendous discovery? And if he had, was it conceivable that it could be used in the way he intended and achieve the result he desired? Reason answered in the negative, and yet reason didn't seem quite conclusive.

'Universal instantaneous death.'

Rot and rubbish: it was like the wild figment of a sensational novelist's brain. And yet – I wasn't satisfied.

'Hullo, Stockton! How goes it? Has she left you all alone?'

I glanced up to see Toby Sinclair grinning at me from the other side of the table.

'Sit down and have a spot, old man,' I said. 'And it wasn't a she, but a he.'

For a while we sat on talking, and it was only when the early supper people began to arrive that we left. We both had rooms in Clarges Street, and for some reason or other – I forget why – Sinclair came into mine for a few minutes before going on to his own. I mention it specially, because on that simple little point there hung tremendous issues. Had he not come in – and I think it was the first time he had ever done so – had he not been with me when the telephone rang on my desk, the whole course of events during the next few months would have been changed. But he did come in, so there is no good speculating on what might have happened if he hadn't.

He came in and he helped himself to a whisky and soda and he sat down to drink it. And it was just as I was following his example that the telephone went. I remember wondering as I took up the receiver who could be ringing me up at that hour, and then came the sudden paralysing shock.

'John! John! Help. My rooms. Oh my God!'

So much I heard, and then silence. Only a stifled scream and a strange choking sound came over the wire, but no further words. And the voice had been the voice of Robin Gaunt.

I shouted down the mouthpiece, and Sinclair stared at me in amazement. I feverishly rang exchange, only to be told that the connection was broken and that they could get no reply.

'What the devil is it, man?' cried Sinclair, getting a grip on my arm. 'You'll wake the whole bally house in a moment.'

A little incoherently I told him what I'd heard, and in an instant the whole look on his face changed. How often in the next few weeks did I see just that same change in the expression of all that amazing gang led by Drummond, when something that necessitated action and suggested danger occurred. But at the moment that was future history: the present concerned that agonised cry for help from the man with whom I had just dined.

'You know his house?' said Sinclair.

'Down in Kensington,' I answered.

'Got a weapon of any sort?'

I rummaged in my desk and produced a Colt revolver – a relic of my Army days.

'Good,' he said. 'Stuff some ammunition in your pocket, and we'll get a move on.'

'But there's no necessity for you to come,' I expostulated.

'Go to hell,' he remarked tersely, and jammed his top hat on his head. 'This is the sort of thing I love. Old Hugh will turn pea-green with jealousy tomorrow when he hears.'

We were hurtling West in a taxi, and my thoughts were too occupied with what we were going to find at the other end to inquire who old Hugh might be. There was but little traffic – the after-supper congestion had not begun – and in less than ten minutes we pulled up outside Robin's house.

'Wait here,' said Toby to the taxi-driver. 'And if you hear or see nothing of us within five minutes, drive like blazes and get a policeman.'

'Want any help now, sir?' asked the driver excitedly.

'Good lad!' cried Sinclair. 'But I think not. Safer to have someone outside. We'll shout if we do.'

The house was in complete darkness, as were those on each side. The latter fact was not surprising as a 'To be Sold' notice appeared in front of each of them.

'You know his rooms, don't you?' said Sinclair. 'Right! Then what

I propose is this. We'll walk straight in as if we're coming to look him up. No good hesitating. And for the love of Allah don't use that gun unless it's necessary.'

The front door was not bolted, and for a moment or two we stood listening in the tiny hall. The silence was absolute, and a light from a lamp outside shining through a window showed us the stairs.

'His rooms are on the first floor,' I whispered.

'Then let's go and have a look at 'em,' answered Toby.

With the revolver in my hand I led the way. One or two stairs creaked loudly, and I heard Sinclair cursing under his breath at the noise. But no-one appeared, and as we stood outside the door of Robin's sitting-room and laboratory combined, the only sound was our own breathing.

'Come on, old man,' said Toby. 'The longer we leave it the less we'll like it. I'll open the door, and you cover anyone inside with your gun.'

With a quick jerk he flung the door wide open, and we both stood there peering into the room. Darkness again and silence just like the rest of the house. But there was one thing different: a faint, rather bitter smell hung about in the air.

I groped for the switch and found it, and we stood blinking in the sudden light. Then we moved cautiously forward and began an examination.

In the centre of the room stood the desk, littered, as usual, with an untidy array of books and papers. The telephone stood on one corner of it, and I couldn't help thinking of that sudden anguished cry for help that had been shouted down it less than a quarter of an hour before. If only it could speak and tell us what had happened!

'Good Lord! Look at that,' muttered Toby. 'It's blood, man: the place is running in blood.'

It was true. Papers were splashed with it, and a little trickle oozed sluggishly off the desk on to the carpet.

The curtains were drawn, and suddenly Toby picked up a book and hurled it at them.

'One of Drummond's little tricks,' he remarked. 'If there's anyone behind you can spot it at once, and with luck you may hit him in the pit of the stomach.'

But there was no-one there: there was no-one in the room at all.

'Where's that door lead to?' he asked.

'Gaunt's bedroom,' I answered, and we repeated the performance. We looked under the bed, and in the cupboard: not a sign of anybody. The bed was turned down ready for the night, with his pyjamas laid in readiness, and in the basin stood a can of hot water covered with a towel. But of Robin or anyone else there was no trace.

'Damned funny,' said Toby, as we went back into the sitting-room. 'What's that scratching noise?'

It came from behind the desk, and suddenly a little short-tailed, tawny-coloured animal appeared.

'Holy smoke!' cried Toby, 'it's a guinea-pig. And there's another of 'em, Stockton: dead.'

Sure enough a little black one was lying rigid and stretched out close to the desk.

'Better not touch it,' I said warningly. 'Leave everything as it is.'

And then a thought struck Toby.

'Look here, Stockton, he can't have been whispering down the 'phone. Isn't there anyone else in the house who would have heard him?'

'There is no other lodger,' I said. 'His landlady is probably down below in the basement, but she's stone deaf. She's so deaf that Gaunt used generally to write things down for her in preference to talking.'

'I think we ought to see the old trout, don't you?' he said, and I went over and rang the bell.

'She may or may not hear it,' I remarked, as we waited. 'Incidentally, what on earth is this strange smell?'

Sinclair shook his head.

'Search me. Though from the look of those bottles and test-tubes and things I assume your pal was a chemist.'

A creaking on the stairs, accompanied by the sounds of heavy breathing, announced that the bell had been heard, and a moment later the landlady appeared. She stared at us suspiciously until she recognised me, which seemed to reassure her somewhat.

'Good evening,' I roared. 'Have you seen Mr Gaunt tonight?'

'I ain't seen him since yesterday morning,' she announced. 'But that ain't nothing peculiar. Sometimes I don't see 'im for a week at a time.'

'Has he been in the house here since dinner?' I went on.

'I dunno, sir,' she said. 'He comes and he goes, does Mr Gaunt, with 'is own key. And since 'e pays regular, I puts up with 'im in spite of all those 'orrors and chemicals and things. I even puts up with 'is dog, though it does go and cover all the chairs with white 'airs.'

'Dog,' said Toby thoughtfully. 'He'd a dog, had he?'

'A wire-haired terrier called Joe,' I said. 'Topping little beast.'

'Then I wonder where the dickens it is?' he remarked 'Good Lord! What's all that?'

From the hall below came the sound of many footsteps, and the voice of our taxi-driver.

'This will give the old dame a fit,' said Toby with a grin. 'I'd forgotten all about our instructions to that stout-hearted Jehu.'

There were two policemen and the driver who came crowding into the room amidst the scandalised protests of the landlady.

'Five minutes was up, sir, so I did as you told me,' said the driver.

'Splendid fellow,' cried Toby. 'It's all right, constable: that revolver belongs to my friend.'

The policeman, who had picked it up suspiciously from the desk, transferred his attention to me.

'What's all the trouble, sir?' he said. 'Don't be alarmed, mother: no-one's going to hurt you.'

'She's deaf,' I told him, and he bellowed in her ear to reassure her.

And then, briefly, I told the two constables exactly what had happened. I told them what I knew of Gaunt's intentions after he had left me, of the cry for help over the telephone, and of our subsequent movements. The only thing I did not feel it incumbent on me to mention was the object of his meeting with the Australian. I felt that their stolid brains would hardly appreciate the matter, so I left it at business.

'Quarter of an hour you say, sir, before you got here. You're sure it was your friend's voice you heard?'

'Positive,' I answered. 'Absolutely positive. He had an unmistakable voice, and I knew him very well.'

And at that moment from the window there came a startled exclamation. The second constable had pulled the curtains, and he was standing there staring at the floor.

'Gaw lumme,' he remarked. 'Look at that.'

We looked. Lying on the floor, stone dead, and twisted into a terrible attitude was Robin's terrier. We crowded round staring at the poor little chap, and it seemed to me that the strange smell had become much stronger.

Suddenly there came a yell of pain, and one of the policemen, who had bent forward to touch the dog, started swearing vigorously and rubbing his fingers. 'The little beggar is burning hot,' he cried. 'Like touching a red-hot coal.'

He looked at his fingers, and then there occurred one of the most terrible things I have ever seen. Literally before our eyes the fingers with which he had touched the dog twisted themselves into knots: then the hand: then the arm. And a moment later he crashed to the ground as if he'd been pole-axed, and lay still.

I don't know if my face was like the others, but they were all as white as a sheet. It was so utterly unexpected, so stunningly sudden. At one moment he had been standing there before us, a great, big, jovial, red-faced man: the next he was lying on the carpet staring at the ceiling with eyes that would never see again.

'Don't touch him,' said a hoarse voice which I dimly recognised as my own. 'For God's sake, don't touch him. The poor devil is dead anyway.'

The other policeman, who had gone down on his knees beside the body, looked up stupidly. Ordinary accidents, even straightforward murder, would not have shaken him, but this was something outside his ken.

'I don't understand, sir,' he muttered. 'What killed him?'

'He was killed because he touched that dead dog,' said Sinclair gravely. 'We can none of us tell any more than that, officer. And this gentleman is afraid that if you touch him the same thing may happen to you.'

'But it's devil's work,' cried the constable, getting dazedly to his feet. 'It ain't human.'

For a while we stood there staring at the dead man, while the landlady rocked hysterically in a chair with her apron over her head. Of the four of us only I had the remotest idea as to what must have happened: to the others it must have seemed not human, as the policeman had said. And even to me with my additional knowledge the thing was almost beyond comprehension.

Robin's wonderful invention; the strange smell which seemed to be growing less, or else I was getting accustomed to it; the dead dog, from which the smell obviously came; and finally the dead police-man, were all jumbled together in my mind in hopeless confusion. That Joe had been killed by this damnable thing his master had perfected was fairly obvious; but why in Heaven's name should Robin have killed a dog whom he adored? The guinea-pig I could understand – but not Joe.

'It looks as you say, constable, like devil's work,' I said at length. 'But since we know that that does not happen we can only conclude that the devil in this case is human. And I think the best thing to do is to ring up Scotland Yard and get someone in authority here at once. This has become a little above our form.'

'I agree,' said Sinclair soberly. 'Distinctly above our form.'

The constable went to the telephone, and the taxi-driver stepped forward.

'If it's all the same to you, gents,' he said, 'I think I'll wait in the cab outside. I kind of feel safer in the fresh air.'

'All right, driver,' said Sinclair. 'But don't go away: they'll probably want your evidence as well as ours.'

'Inspector MacIver coming at once, sir,' said the constable, replacing the receiver with a sigh of relief. 'And until he comes I think we might as well wait downstairs. Come along, mother: there ain't no good your carrying on like that.'

He supported the old landlady from the room, and when we had joined him in the passage he shut and locked the door and slipped the key in his pocket. And then, having sent her down to her basement, we three sat down to wait for the Inspector.

'Cigarette, Bobby?' said Sinclair, holding out his case. 'Helps the nerves.'

'Thank you, sir: I don't mind if I do. It's fair shook me, that has. I've seen men killed most ways in my time – burned, drowned, hung – not to say nothing of three years in the war; but I've never seen the like of that before. For 'im just to go and touch that there dead dog, and be dead 'imself.' He looked at us diffidently. 'Have you got any idea, gentlemen, as to what it is that's done it?'

'It's some ghastly form of poison, constable,' I said. 'Of that I'm pretty certain. But what it is, I know no more than you. Mr Gaunt was a marvellous chemist.'

'A damned sight too marvellous,' said the policeman savagely. 'If it's 'im what's done it I'm thinking he'll find himself in Queer Street when he comes back.'

'I think it's *if* he comes back,' I said. 'There's been foul play here – not only with regard to that dog, but also with regard to Mr Gaunt. He idolised that terrier: nothing will induce me to believe that it was he who killed Joe. Don't forget that cry for help over the telephone. Look at all that blood. It's my firm belief that the clue to the whole mystery lies in the Australian gentleman whom he was going to meet tonight. He left me at Prince's to do so. Find that man, and you'll find the solution.'

'Have you any idea what he looks like?' asked Toby.

'That's the devil of it,' I answered. 'I haven't the slightest. All I can tell you is that he must be a fairly wealthy man who had two sons killed in Gallipoli.'

The policeman nodded his head portentously.

'The Yard has found men with less to go on than that, sir,' he remarked. 'Very likely he'll be putting up at one of the swell hotels.'

'And very likely he won't,' put in Toby. 'If what Mr Stockton thinks it right, and this unknown Australian is at the bottom of it all, stopping at one of the big hotels is just what he wouldn't do. However, there's a taxi, so presumably it's the Inspector.'

The constable hurriedly extinguished his cigarette, and went to the front door to meet MacIver. He was a short, thick-set, powerful man with a pair of shrewd, penetrating eyes. He gave a curt nod to each of us, and listened in silence while I again repeated my story. This time I told it a little more fully, emphasising the fact that Robin Gaunt was at any rate under the impression that he had made a far-reaching discovery which would revolutionise warfare.

'What sort of a discovery?' interrupted MacIver.

'I can't tell you, Inspector,' I said, 'for I don't know. He was employed during the war as a gas expert, and when the Armistice came he had, I believe, invented a particularly deadly form which, of course, was never used. And from what he told me at dinner tonight, this invention was now perfected. He described it to me as causing universal, instantaneous death.'

The Inspector fidgeted impatiently: imagination was not his strong point, and I admit it sounded a bit fanciful.

'He left me to come and interview an Australian who has helped him financially. His idea was that the appalling power of this discovery of his could be used to prevent warfare in future, if it was in the sole hands of one nation. He thought that no other nation would then dare to go to war. And his intention was to demonstrate before the Army Council tomorrow, with the idea that England might be that one nation. That is what he told me this evening. How far his claims were justified I don't know. What his discovery was I don't know. But two things I do know: first, that Robin Gaunt is a genius, and, second, that his claim can be no more fantastic than what we all of us saw take place before our very eyes half-an-hour ago.'

MacIver grunted and rose from his chair.

'Let's go and have a look.'

The constable led the way, and once again we entered the room upstairs. Everything was just as we had left it: the dead man still stared horribly at the ceiling: the terrier still lay a little twisted heap in the window: the blood still dripped sluggishly off the desk. But the strange smell we had noticed was considerably less powerful, though the Inspector noticed it at once and sniffed. Then with the method born of long practice he commenced his examination of the room. And it was an education in itself to see him work. He never spoke; and at the end of ten minutes not a corner had been overlooked. Every drawer had been opened, every paper examined and discarded, and the net result was – nothing.

'A very extraordinary affair,' he said quietly. 'I take it you knew Mr Gaunt fairly intimately?'

He looked at me and I nodded.

'Very intimately,' I answered. 'We were at school together, and at college, and I've frequently seen him since.'

'And you have no idea, beyond what you have already told me, as to what this discovery of his was?'

'None. But I should imagine, Inspector, in view of his appointment with the Army Council tomorrow, that someone at the War Office may be able to tell you something.'

'It is, of course, possible that he will keep that appointment,' said MacIver. 'Though I admit I'm not hopeful.'

His eyes were fixed on the dead dog.

'That's what beats me particularly,' he remarked. 'Why kill the terrier? A possible hypothesis is that he didn't: that the dog was killed accidentally. Let us, for instance, imagine for a moment that your friend was experimenting with this device of his. The dead guinea-pig bears that out. Then some accident occurred. I make no attempt to say what accident, because we have no idea as to the nature of the device. He lost his head, snatched up the telephone, got through to you – and then realising the urgent danger rushed from the room, forgetting all about the dog. And the dog was killed.'

'But surely,' I objected, 'under those circumstances we should find some trace of apparatus. And there's nothing.'

'He might have snatched it up when he left, and thrown it away somewhere.'

'He might,' I agreed. 'But I can't help thinking, Inspector, that it is more sinister than that. Why all that blood? If I may say so, I believe that what happened is this. The Australian whom he was going to meet was not an Australian at all. He was possibly a German or some foreigner, who was deeply interested in this device, and who had deceived Gaunt completely. He came here tonight, and overpowered Gaunt: then he carried out a test on the dog, and found that it acted. After that he, probably with the help of accomplices, removed Gaunt, either with the intention of murdering him at leisure or of keeping him a prisoner.'

'Another hypothesis,' agreed the Inspector, 'but it presents one very big difficulty, Mr Stockton. Your friend must have suspected foul play when he rang you up on the telephone. Now you're on a different exchange, and it must have taken, on a conservative estimate, a quarter of a minute to get through. Are we to assume that during those fifteen seconds this Australian, or whatever he is, and his accomplices stood around and looked at Mr Gaunt doing the one thing they didn't want him to do – getting in touch with the outside world?'

It was perfectly true, and I admit the point had not struck me. And yet in the bottom of my mind I still felt convinced that in the Australian lay the clue to everything, and I said as much.

'Find that man, Inspector,' I repeated, 'and you've solved it. There are difficulties, I know, of which not the least is the telephone. Another is the fact that Gaunt is a powerful man: he'd have struggled like a tiger. And except for the blood there's no sign of a struggle.'

'They may have tidied up after,' put in Toby. 'Hullo! What's the matter, constable?'

The policeman, who, unnoticed by us, had left the room was standing in the door, obviously much shaken.

'This affair gets worse and worse, sir,' he said to MacIver. 'Will you just step over the passage here, and have a look in this room?'

We crowded after him into the room opposite – one which belonged to the corresponding suite to Robin's. Instantly the same faint smell became noticeable, but it was not that which riveted our attention. Lying on the floor was a man, and we could see at a glance that he was dead. He was a great big fellow, and his clothes bore witness to the most desperate struggle. His coat was torn, his waistcoat ripped open, and there was a dark purple bruise on his forehead. But in the strange rigidity of his limbs, and in the fixed staring eyes, he resembled exactly the unfortunate constable in the room opposite.

A foot or so away from his head was a broadish-brimmed hat, and MacIver turned it over with his foot. Then he bent down to examine it.

'I'm thinking, Mr Stockton,' he remarked grimly, 'that we've done what you wanted to do. We've found the Australian. That hat was made in Sydney.'

He whistled softly under his breath.

'And that effectively knocks both our hypotheses out of court.'

He made a sudden dart into the corner.

'Constable, give me those tongs. I guess I'm not touching anything I can avoid in this house tonight.'

He took the tongs and lifted up what appeared to be an india-rubber glove. It was a sort of glazed white in colour, and was obviously new, since the elastic band which fitted round the wrist was quite clean, and there was no sign of scratches or dirt anywhere.

'Put this on the desk in the other room,' said MacIver to the policeman. 'And now we'll go over every single room in this house.'

We did: we explored the attic and the basement, the sitting rooms and the scullery. And it was nearly three before we had finished. But not another thing did we discover: quite obviously everything that had happened had occurred in those two rooms. MacIver grew more and more morose and uncommunicative, and it was obvious that he was completely baffled. Small blame to him: the whole thing seemed like the figment of an incredible nightmare.

And even when Toby Sinclair put forward what seemed on the face of it to be a fairly plausible explanation he merely grunted and expressed no opinion.

'I'll bet you that's what happened,' Toby said as, the search concluded, we stood once again in Robin's room. 'The two of them were in here – Gaunt and the Australian – when they were surprised by someone. The Australian, whom we've suspected unjustly, fought like a tiger, and gained just sufficient time for Gaunt to get through on the telephone. Then they killed the Australian, and got at Gaunt. Don't ask me to explain the dog, for I can't.'

It seemed plausible, as I say, and during the drive home behind our patiently waiting taxi-driver I could think of nothing better. We'd both been warned that our evidence would be required the following day, and the constable, reinforced by another, had been left in possession of the house.

'I believe you've hit it, Sinclair,' I said, as the car turned into Clarges Street. 'But what's worrying me is what has happened to that poor devil Gaunt.'

He shrugged his shoulders.

'If I am right, Stockton,' he answered gravely, 'I'm thinking I wouldn't issue a policy on his life if I was in the insurance business. In fact, what I don't understand is why they didn't kill him then and there.'

The car pulled up at the door of my rooms, and I gave the driver a fiver.

'You've been splendid,' I said, 'and I'm much obliged to you.'

'Don't mention it, sir,' he answered. 'But I guess there's one thing you might like to know.'

He pointed to a taxi which had just driven slowly past and was now turning into Curzon Street.

'It's empty; but that there car was down in Kensington all tonight, just about a 'undred yards along the road. You two gents have been followed.' He handed me a slip of paper. 'And that's the number of the car.'

Chapter 2

In Which I Meet Hugh Drummond

I have purposely alluded at some length to that last conversation between Robin Gaunt and myself at Prince's. Apart altogether from the fact that he was my friend, it's only fair that his true character should be known. At the time, it may be remembered, there were all sorts of wild and malicious rumours going round about him. From being an absolutely unknown man as far as the general public was concerned, he attained the notoriety of a popular film star.

It was inevitable, of course: the whole affair was so bizarre and extraordinary that it captivated the popular fancy. And the most favourite explanation was the most unjust of all to Robin. It was that he was a cold-blooded scientist who had been experimenting on his own dog. A sort of super-vivisectionist: a monster without a heart, who had been interrupted in the middle of his abominable work by the Australian, whom he had murdered in a fit of rage; and then, a little alarmed at having killed a man as well as a dog and a guinea-pig, he had rung me up on the telephone as a blind, and fled.

Apart from ignoring the question of the blood, it was ridiculous to anyone who knew him, but there is no doubt that as an explanation of what had occurred it was the one that had most adherents. Certainly the possibility of Robin having killed the Australian – it transpired that he was one David Ganton, a wealthy man, who had been staying at the Ritz – was entertained for a considerable time. Until, in fact . . . But of that in due course.

I wish now to show how it was that theory started, and why it was that at the inquest I made no mention of the conversation I have recorded. For my lips were sealed by the interview which occurred the following morning. I was rung up on the telephone at eleven o'clock, and an unknown voice spoke from the other end.

'Is that Mr Stockton? It is Major Jackson speaking. I hope it won't be inconvenient for you to come round at once to the War Office in connection with the affair last night. Ask for G branch, Room 38. Instructions will be sent down, so you will have no delay at the door.'

To Room 38, G Branch, I accordingly went, there to find four people already assembled. Seated at a desk was a tanned, keen-faced man who had soldier written all over him; whilst standing against the mantelpiece, smoking a cigarette, was a younger man, whom I recognised, as soon as he spoke, as the man who had rung me up. The other two consisted of Inspector MacIver and a thin-lipped man wearing pince-nez whose face seemed vaguely familiar.

'Mr Stockton?' Major Jackson stepped forward and shook hands. 'This is General Darton' – he indicated the man at the desk – 'and this is Sir John Dallas. Inspector MacIver I think you know.'

That was why Sir John's face had seemed familiar. As soon as I heard the name I remembered having seen his photograph in a recent copy of the *Sphere*, as the author of an exhaustive book on toxicology.

'Sit down, Mr Stockton,' said the General, 'and please smoke if you want to. You can guess, of course, the reason we have asked you to come round . . .'

'I told him, sir,' put in Major Jackson.

'Good! Though I expect it was unnecessary. Now, Mr Stockton, we have heard from Inspector MacIver an account of last night and what you told him. But we think it would be more satisfactory if we could hear it from you first hand.'

So once again I told them everything I knew. I recalled as far as possible, word for word, my conversation with Robin at dinner, and I noticed that the two officers glanced at one another significantly more than once. But they listened in silence save for one interruption when I mentioned his notion of fighting indiscriminately against both sides.

It was the General who smiled at that and remarked that as an idea it had at any rate the merit of novelty.

Then I went on and outlined what had happened up till the arrival of the Inspector, paying, naturally, particular attention to the death of the constable. And it was at that point that Sir John spoke for the first time.

'Did you happen to see what part of the dog the constable touched?' he said.

'Roughly, I did, Sir John. He laid his hand on the dog's ribs just above the left shoulder.'

He nodded as if satisfied.

'I thought as much. Now another thing. You saw this man die in front of your eyes. Did the manner of his death create any particular impression on your brain apart from its amazing suddenness?'

'It produced the impression that he had acute pain spreading from his fingers up his arm. The whole arm seemed to twist and writhe, and then he was dead.'

And once again Sir John nodded as if satisfied.

'There is only one other point which I might mention,' I concluded. 'The Inspector can tell you everything that happened while he was there. As we got out of our taxi in Clarges Street, another car drove slowly by. And our driver told us that it was the same car that had been standing for hours about a hundred yards further down the road. It was empty, and this is the number.' I handed the slip of paper to MacIver, who glanced at it and gave a short laugh. 'It struck us both that we might have been followed.'

'This car was found deserted in South Audley Street this morning,' he said. 'Its rightful owner was arrested for being hopelessly drunk in Peckham last night at about half-past nine. And he swears by all his gods that the only drink he'd had was one whisky-and-soda with a man who was a stranger to him. His car was standing in front of the pub at the time, and he remembers nothing more till he woke up in his cell with his boots off.'

'That would seem to prove outside influence at work, Inspector,' said the General.

'Maybe, sir,' said MacIver cautiously. 'Maybe not. Though it does point that way.'

'But, good Heavens, General,' I cried, 'surely there can be no doubt about that. What other possible solution can there be?'

For a moment or two he drummed with his fingers on the desk.

'That brings us, Mr Stockton,' he said gravely, 'to the main reason which made us ask you to come round here this morning. We have decided to take you into our confidence, and rely upon your absolute discretion. I feel sure we can do that.'

'Certainly, sir,' I said.

'In the first place, then, you must know that the Army Council regard this as a most serious matter. There is no doubt whatever that Gaunt was a most brilliant man: his work during the war proved that. But, as you know yourself, the Armistice prevented any practical test. And there is a vast difference between theory and practice. However, with a man like that one is prepared to take a good deal on trust, and when he asked to be allowed to give us a demonstration today we granted his request at once. I may say that at the time of the Armistice there were still two points where his discovery failed. The first and lesser of the two lay in the stuff itself; the second and greater lay in the method of distributing it. In applying to us for his demonstration he claimed to have overcome both these difficulties.

'At the time when the war ended it was, as you can guess, a very closely guarded secret. Not more than four men knew anything about it. And then, the war over, and the necessity for its use no longer existing, the whole thing was rather pigeon-holed. In fact it was only the day before yesterday, on the receipt of Gaunt's request, that the matter was unearthed again. Naturally we imagined that it was still just as close a secret as ever. The events of last night prove that it cannot have been, unless my alternative theory should prove to be correct. And if that is so, Stockton, we are confronted with the unpleasant fact that someone is in possession of this very dangerous secret. Even in its Armistice stage the matter would be serious enough; but if Gaunt's claims are correct, words are inadequate to express the dangers of the situation. Now, as anyone who is in the slightest degree in touch with the European pulse today knows, we are living on the edge of a volcano. And nothing must be done to start an eruption. Nothing, you understand. All personal feelings must go to the wall. In a moment or two I shall ask Sir John to say a few words, and from him you will realise that the first and lesser of the two points has evidently been rectified by Gaunt. What of the second and greater one? Until we know that, nothing must even be hinted at in the papers as to the nature of the issues at stake. And that brings me to my point. When you give your evidence at the inquest, Stockton, I want you to obliterate from your mind the conversation you had with Gaunt last night. The whole force of Scotland Yard is being employed to try and clear this thing up, and secrecy is essential. And we therefore rely entirely on your discretion and that of your friend, Mr Sinclair.'

'You can certainly rely on him, sir,' I said. 'But what am I to say then? I must give some explanation.'

'Precisely: you must give some explanation,' he agreed. 'But before I suggest to you what that explanation might be, I will ask Sir John to run over once more the conclusions he has arrived at.'

'They are quite obvious,' said the celebrated toxicologist. 'As you may be aware, the vast majority of poisons must either be swallowed or injected to prove fatal. With the first class we are not concerned, but only with the second. In this second class the primary necessity is the introduction of the poison into a vein. You may have the bite of a snake, the use of a hypodermic syringe, or the prick of a poisoned dart – each of which causes a definite puncture in the skin through which the poison passes into a vein. And in each of those cases the puncture is caused mechanically – by the snake's fang, or the dart, as the case may be.

'Now there is another tiny class of poisons – it is really a sub-division of the second class – of which, frankly, we know very little. Some expert toxicologists are even inclined to dismiss them as legendary. I'm not sure that I myself didn't belong to their number until this morning. Evidence is in existence – but it is not reliable – of the use of these poisons by the Borgias and by the Aztecs of Mexico. They were reputed to kill by mere external application, without the necessity of a puncture in the skin. They were supposed to generate some strange shattering force, which killed the victim by shock. Now that is absurd: no poison can kill unless it reacts point-blank on the heart. In other words, a puncture is necessary, and this class supplies its own punctures.

'You remember the policeman's last words – 'The dog is burning hot.' What he felt was a mass of small open blisters breaking out on his hand, through which the poison passed into his veins and up his arm to his heart. Had he touched the dog anywhere else nothing would have happened: as bad luck would have it he put his hand on the very spot where the poison had been applied to the dog.

'So much is clear. In all three cases that eruption of open blisters is there: in the dog above its shoulder, in the policeman on his hand, and in the case of the Australian on his right temple. And excepting in those places it is perfectly safe to touch the bodies.

'Now I was in that house at four o'clock this morning: the Inspector, very rightly, judged that time was an important factor and called me up. I took down with me several guinea-pigs, and I carried out a series of tests. I held a guinea-pig against the danger spot in each body, and the three guinea-pigs all died. I did the same an hour later. The one I put against the dog died: the one I put against the police-man's hand died, but the one I put on the Australian's forehead did not. It is possible that that means that the Australian was killed some time before the dog: on the other hand, it may merely prove that the dog's long coat retained the poison more effectively. Finally, I used three more guinea-pigs at six o'clock, and nothing happened to any of them.

'My conclusions, therefore, are as follows: and, needless to say, they concern only the poison itself and not what actually happened last night. Mr Gaunt has discovered a poison which, judging from the few tests I have carried out already, is unknown to science. It kills almost instantaneously when applied externally to the bare skin. Its effect lingers for some time, but only on the actual place on the body where it was applied. And after a lapse of seven or eight hours no further trace of it remains. As to the method of application I can give no positive opinion. One thing, however, is clear: the person using it would have to exercise the utmost caution. If it is fatal to his victim, it is equally fatal to the operator should it touch him. It is therefore probable that the glove found on the floor was worn by the man using the stuff. And I put forward as a possible opinion the idea of something in the nature of a garden syringe which could be used to throw a jet in any required direction.'

He paused and glanced at the General.

'I think that that is all I've got to say, except that I propose to carry on further with experiments to see if I can isolate this poison. But I confess that I'm not hopeful. If I was able to obtain some of the liquid neat I should be more confident, but I can only try my best.'

'Thank you very much, Sir John,' answered the soldier. 'Now, Stockton, you see the position. It seems pretty clear, as I said before, that Gaunt has solved one difficulty, by perfecting the stuff: has he solved the other as to the means of distribution? A syringe such as Sir John suggests may be deadly against an individual in a room: used by an army in the field anything of the sort would be useless; just as after the first surprise in the war, *flammenwerfer* were useless. Until we know that second point, therefore, the less said about this matter the better. And so we come to what you are going to say. It will be distasteful to you, for Gaunt was your friend, but it is your plain and obvious duty. We are faced with the necessity of inventing a plausible explanation, and the Inspector has suggested the following as filling the bill.'

And then he put forward the theory to which I have already alluded. He admitted that he didn't believe in it himself: he went so far as to say that he wished to Heaven he could.

'It will, of course, be unnecessary and undesirable for you to ad-vance this theory yourself,' he concluded. 'All that is required of you is that you should keep your mouth shut when it is advanced. Because the devil of it is, Stockton, that the signs of struggle on the Australian preclude any idea of accident and subsequent loss of head on the part of Gaunt.'

For a time I sat in silence whilst they all stared at me. To deliberately allow one's pal to be branded as a murderer is not pleasant. But it was clear that there were bigger issues at stake than that, and at length I rose. What had to be, had to be.

'I quite understand, sir,' I said. 'And I will get in touch with Sinclair at once, and see that he says nothing.'

'Good,' said the General, holding out his hand. 'I knew I could rely on you.'

'Inquest tomorrow,' put in MacIver. 'I'll notify you as to time and place.'

And with that I left and went in search of Toby Sinclair. I found him in his rooms consuming breakfast, whilst, seated in an easy-chair with his feet on the mantelpiece, was a vast man whom I had never seen before. It was my first meeting with Drummond.

'Hullo! old man: take a pew,' cried Toby, waving half an impaled sausage at a chair. 'That little fellow sitting opposite you is Drummond. I think I mentioned him to you last night.'

'Morning,' said Drummond, uncoiling himself and standing up. We shook hands, and I wished we hadn't. 'Hear you had some fun and games last night.'

'I've been telling him, Stockton, about our little effort,' said Sinclair, lighting a cigarette.

'Well, don't tell anyone else,' I remarked. 'I've just come from the War Office, and they're somewhat on the buzz. In fact, they regard the matter devilishly seriously. It's bound to come out, of course, that a new and deadly form of poison was in action last night, but it's got to rest at that.'

I ran briefly over what General Darton and Sir John had said, and they both listened without interruption. And though it did not strike me particularly at the time, one small fact made a subconscious impression on my mind which subsequent knowledge of Drummond was to confirm. As I say, they both listened without interruption, but Drummond listened without movement. From the moment I started speaking till I'd finished he sat motionless in his chair, with his eyes fixed on me, and I don't believe he even blinked.

'What do you think of it, Hugh?' said Sinclair, after I'd finished.

'This beer ain't fit to drink, Toby. That's what I think.' He rose and strolled over to the window. 'Absolutely not fit to drink.'

'Very interesting,' I remarked sarcastically. 'The point is doubtless of paramount importance, but may I ask you to be good enough to promise me that what you've heard goes no further. The matter is somewhat serious.'

'The matter of this foul ale is a deuced sight more serious,' he answered genially. 'Toby, old lad, something will have to be done about it. In fact, something is going to be done about it now.'

He strolled out of the room, and I looked at Sinclair in blank amazement.

'What on earth is the man up to?' I said angrily. 'Does he think this thing is a jest?'

Toby Sinclair was looking a bit surprised himself.

'You can never tell what old Hugh thinks,' he began apologetically, only to break off as a loud squealing noise was heard on the stairs. And the next moment Drummond entered holding a small and very frightened man by the ear.

'Foul beer, Toby,' he remarked. 'Almost foul enough for this little lump of intelligence to be made to drink as a punishment. Now, rat face, what excuse have you got to offer for living?'

'You let me go,' whined his prisoner, 'or I'll 'ave the perlice on yer.'

'I think not, little man,' said Drummond quietly. 'Anyway I'll chance it. Now who told you to watch this house?'

'I ain't watching it, governor: strite I ain't.'

His shifty eyes were darting this way and that, looking for a way of escape.

'I'm an honest man, I am, and – oh Gawd, guv'nor, lemme go. You're breaking my arm.'

'I asked you a question, you little swine,' said Drummond. 'And if you don't answer it, I will break your arm. And that thing you call a face as well. Now, who told you to watch this house?'

'A bloke wot I don't know,' answered the man sullenly. ' 'E promised me 'arf a quid if I did wot 'e told me.'

'And what did he tell you to do?'

'Foller that there gent if he went out.' He pointed at Sinclair with a grimy finger. 'Foller 'im and mark down where 'e went to.'

'And how were you to recognise me?' asked Toby.

' 'E showed me a photer, 'e did. A swell photer.'

For a moment or two Sinclair stared at the man in amazement: then he crossed over to a writing-table in the corner.

'Well, I'm damned,' he muttered, as he opened a big cardboard cover with a photographer's name printed on it. 'I'll swear there were six here yesterday and there are only five now. Was that the photograph he showed you?'

He held one up in front of the man.

'That's it, guv'nor: that's the very one.'

'There is a certain atmosphere of rapidity about this,' muttered Drummond, 'that appeals to me.'

He thoughtfully contemplated his captive.

'Where were you to report the result of what you found out?' he went on. 'Where were you going to meet him, to get your half-quid?'

'Down at the Three Cows in Peckham, guv'nor: tonight at nine.'

I gave a little exclamation, and Drummond glanced at me enquiringly.

'Not now,' I said. 'Afterwards,' and he nodded.

'Listen here, little man,' he remarked quietly. 'Do you want to earn a fiver?'

'You bet yer life I do, sir,' answered the other earnestly.

'Well, if you do exactly what I tell you to do, you shall. This gentleman whose photo you have seen is shortly going out. He is going to lunch at Hatchett's in Piccadilly. After lunch he will take a little walk in the Park, and after that he will return here. He will probably dine at the Berkeley. At nine o'clock tonight you will be in the Three Cows at Peckham, and you will report this gentleman's movements to the man who promised you half a quid. If you do that – exactly as I have told you – you can come back here tomorrow morning about this time and you'll get a fiver.'

'You swear there ain't no catch, guv'nor?' said the other.

'I swear there's no catch,' said Drummond quietly.

'Right, sir, I'll do it. Is that all you want with me now?'

'Yes: clear out. And don't make any mistake about what you've got to do.'

'Trust me, sir.'

He touched a finger to his forehead and dodged out of the room.

'A distinct air of rapidity,' repeated Drummond thoughtfully. 'I wonder if he'll do it.'

'How did you know he was watching the house?' I asked curiously.

'It stuck out a yard,' he answered. 'He was on the pavement when I came here an hour ago, and he's not a Clarges Street type. What was it hit your fancy over the Three Cows?'

'The real driver of the taxi that followed us last night was drugged in a Peckham pub by a man he didn't know. Presumably it was the Three Cows.'

'Then possibly we shall meet the man who followed you last night at nine o'clock this evening. Which will be one step up the ladder at any rate.'

He picked up his hat and lit a cigarette.

'By the way, what's the number of your house?'

'3B. It's about ten doors down towards Piccadilly.'

And suddenly he gave a grin of pure joy.

'Is it possible, my jovial bucks,' he cried, 'that once again we are on the warpath? That through the unpleasant object who has lately honoured us with his presence we shall be led to higher and worthier game? Anyway we can but baptise such a wonderful thought in a Martini or even two.'

We followed him down the stairs, and Toby smiled as he saw the look on my face.

'It's all right, old man,' he remarked. 'He's always like this.'

'And why not, forsooth?' boomed Drummond, waving his stick joyfully in the air. 'Eat, drink and be merry . . . Don't you agree with me, sir?'

He stopped suddenly in front of a complete stranger, who stared at him in blank amazement.

'Who the devil are you, sir?' he spluttered. 'And what do you mean by speaking to me?'

'I liked your face,' said Drummond calmly. 'It's the sort of face that inspires confidence in canaries and white mice. Good-morning; sorry I can't ask you to lunch.'

'But the man is mad,' I murmured helplessly to Toby as we turned into Piccadilly.

'There is generally method therein,' he answered, and Drummond smiled.

'He knows not our ways, Toby,' he remarked. 'But judging by appearances you're evidently the important one, Stockton. That one only stuck out a foot.'

'Do you mean to say that that man you spoke to was on the look-out for me?' I stammered.

'What the dickens did you think he was doing? Growing water-cress on the pavement?'

He dismissed the matter with a wave of his hand.

'Yes, Toby,' he went on. 'I have distinct hopes. Matters seem to me to be marching well. And if we adopt reasonable precautions this afternoon it seems to me that they may march even better this evening under the hospitable roof of the Three Cows.'

He turned in to Hatchett's.

'We may as well conform to the first part of the programme at any rate. And over some oysters we'll discuss the first move.'

'Which is?' I asked.

'How to get you two fellows to my house without your being followed. Because I feel that for any hope of success in the salubrious suburb of Peckham we must effect one or two changes in our personal appearance, and I have all the necessary wherewithal in Brook Street. Toby's little pal, I think, we can neglect: it's that other bloke who is after you that will want watching.'

He gave a short laugh.

'Talk of the devil; here he is. Don't look round either of you, but he's taken a table near the door. Well, well: now the fun begins. He is ordering the *plat du jour* and a whisky-and-soda: moreover, he is adopting the somewhat unusual custom of paying in advance. Most thoughtful of him. It goes to my heart to think that his money will be wasted.'

He signalled to the head waiter, who came at once.

'Add this little lot to my account,' said Drummond. 'We've suddenly remembered we're supposed to be lunching in Hampstead. Now, you two – up the stairs: through Burlington Arcade, into a taxi and straight to Brook Street. I'll deal with this bloke.'

Looking back on things now after the lapse of many months, one of the strangest things to me is the habit of unquestioning obedience to Drummond, into which I dropped at once. If someone tells me to do a thing, my nature as a general rule impels me to do the exact reverse. In the Army I never took kindly to discipline. And yet when Drummond gave an order I never questioned, I never hesitated. I mention this fact merely to emphasise the peculiar influence he had on people with whom he came in contact, and the extraordinary personality which he tried to obscure by an air of fatuous nonsense. And though it took me some weeks to realise it, yet the fact remains that that first day I met him I did what he said with the same readiness as I did in days to come after I had grown to know him better.

And I remember another thing which struck me very forcibly that day. I stopped at the top of the stairs for a moment or two to see the fun. Drummond was half-way up when he dropped his stick. And in stooping to pick it up he completely blocked the gangway. Behind him, dancing furiously from side to side in his endeavours to pass, was the other man.

'Why, it's the man with the charming face,' cried Drummond genially. 'But I wish you wouldn't hop, laddie. It's so damned bad for the tum-tum.'

I heard no more: Toby Sinclair, swearing vigorously under his breath, dragged me into Piccadilly.

'Confound you, Stockton, why the devil don't you do what you're told? I was half-way along Burlington Arcade before I realised you weren't there. You'd better take it here and now that if Hugh tells you to do a thing he means it to be done exactly as he said. And he said nothing about standing and watching him.'

'Damn Drummond and everything connected with him,' I said irritably. 'Who is he anyway to give me orders?'

He laughed quietly as we got into the taxi.

'I'm sorry, old man,' he said. 'I was forgetting for the moment that you only met him for the first time today. You'll laugh yourself in a few days when you recall that remark of yours.'

I did; but at the time I was peevish.

'If there's a man living in England today,' he went on, 'who is more capable than Hugh of finding out what happened last night I'd like to meet him.'

And I smiled my incredulity. To tell the truth, the things that had happened since my return from the War Office had rather driven that interview from my mind. But now I had leisure to recall it, and the more I thought of it the less I liked it. It is all very well in theory to say that there are occasions when an individual must suffer for the good of the State, but in practice it is most unpleasant when that individual is your own particular friend. You friend, too, who has called to you for help and whom you have failed. Mercifully Robin had neither kith nor kin, which eased my mind a certain amount: by allowing this false impression to be given at the inquest I was harming no-one, except Robin himself. And if he was dead, sooner or later his body would be found, which would prove beyond doubt that he was not the original culprit: whereas if he was alive the time would come when I should be able to explain. For all that, nothing could alter the fact that I disliked my rôle, and not the less because it was compulsory.

I said as much that afternoon as we sat in Drummond's study. He had come in about two hours after us, and he seemed a bit silent and thoughtful.

'You can't help it, Stockton,' he said. 'And probably Gaunt if he knew would be the first man to realise the necessity. It's not that

that's worrying me.' He rose and went to the window. 'I'm thinking I've made a fool of myself. I don't see a sign of anyone: I haven't for the last hour – and I took Ted's car out of St. James's Square, and have been all round London in it; but I'm afraid I've transferred attention to myself. There was just a second or two on the stairs at Hatchett's when our little lad of the genial face looked at me with the utmost suspicion.'

He resumed his chair and stretched out his legs.

'However, we can but chance it. It may lead to something.'

'It's very good of you,' I said a little doubtfully. 'But I really don't know if – I mean, the police and all that, don't you know. They've got the thing in hand.'

He gazed at me in genuine amazement.

'Good Lord! my dear man,' he remarked, 'if you want to leave the thing to old MacIver and Co., say the word. I mean it's your palaver, and I wouldn't butt in for the world. Or if you want to handle the thing yourself I'm away out from this moment. And you can have the free run of my various wardrobes if you want to go to Peckham tonight.'

I couldn't help it: I burst out laughing.

'Frankly, it would never have dawned on me to go to Peckham tonight,' I said. 'Incidentally if it hadn't been for you I shouldn't have known anything about Peckham, for I should never have had the nerve to pull that little blighter into Toby's rooms even if I'd realised he was watching the house – which I shouldn't have. What I meant was that it seemed very good of you to worry over a thing like this – seeing that you don't even know Gaunt.'

An expression of profound relief had replaced the amazement.

'By Jove! old man,' he remarked, 'you gave me a nasty fright then. What on earth does it matter if I know Gaunt or not? Opportunities of this sort are far too rare to stand on ceremony. What I was afraid of was that you might want to keep it all for yourself. And I can assure you that lots of amusing little shows I've had in the past started much less promisingly than this. You get Toby to tell you about 'em while I go and rout out some togs for tonight.'

'What an amazing bloke he is,' I said as the door closed behind him. And Toby Sinclair smiled thoughtfully.

'In the words of the American philosopher, you have delivered yourself of a perfectly true mouthful. And now, if you take my advice, you'll get some sleep. For with Hugh on the warpath, and if we have any luck, you won't get much tonight.'

He curled himself up in a chair, and in a few minutes he was fast asleep. But try as I would I could not follow his example. There was a sense of unreality about the whole thing: events seemed to be moving with that queer, jumbled incoherence that belongs to a dream. Robin's despairing cry: the policeman crashing to the floor like a bullock in a slaughterhouse: the dead Australian who had fought so fiercely. And against whom? Who was it who had come into that room the night before? What was happening there even as Robin got through to me on the phone?

And suddenly I seemed to see it all. The door was opening slowly, and Robin was staring at it. For a moment or two we watched it, and then I could bear the suspense no longer. I hurled myself forward, to find myself in the grip of a huge black-bearded man with a yellow handkerchief knotted round his throat.

'You swine,' I shouted, and then I looked round stupidly.

For the room had changed, and the noise of a passing taxi came from Brook Street.

'Three hours of the best,' said the big man genially, and a nasty-looking little Jew behind him laughed. 'It's half-past seven, and time you altered your appearance.'

'Good Lord!' I muttered with an attempt at a grin. 'I'm awfully sorry: I must have been dreaming.'

'It was a deuced agile dream,' answered Drummond. 'My right sock suspender is embedded about half-an-inch in my leg. Toby saw you coming and dodged.'

He turned to the little Jew, who was lighting a cigarette.

'Make some cocktails, old man, while I rig up Stockton.'

'Great Scott!' I said. 'I'd never have known either of you.'

'You won't know yourself in twenty minutes,' answered Drummond. 'You're going to be a mechanic with Communistic tendencies, and my third revolver.'

Chapter 3

In which some Excellent Advice is Followed

The Three Cows at Peckham proved an unprepossessing spot. It was a quarter to nine when we entered the public bar, and the place was crowded. The atmosphere reeked of tobacco-smoke and humanity, and in one corner stood one of those diabolical machines in which, for the price of one penny, a large metal disc rotates and delivers itself of an appalling noise.

Involuntarily I hesitated for a moment; then seeing that Drummond had elbowed his way to the bar and that Toby was standing behind him, I reluctantly followed. I really had half a mind to chuck up the whole thing: after all the police were already on the matter. What on earth was the use of this amateur dressing-up business?

'Three of four-'alf, please, Miss,' said Drummond, planking down a shilling on the counter. 'Blest if you ain't got much thinner since I was last 'ere.'

'Come off it,' returned the sixteen-stone maiden tersely. 'You ain't a blinking telegraph pole yourself. Three whiskies and splash, and a Guinness. All right! All right! I've only got two hands, ain't I?'

She turned away and I stared round the place with an increasing feeling of disgust. Racing touts, loafers, riffraff of all descriptions filled the room, and the hoarse hum of conversation, punctuated by the ceaseless popping of corks for the drinkers of Bass, half deafened one. But of either of our friends of the morning there was no sign.

I took a sip of the glass in front of me. Drummond was engaged with a horsy-looking gentleman spotting winners for next day; on my other side Toby Sinclair, in the intervals of dispassionately picking his teeth, was chaffing the sixteen-stoner's elderly companion. And I wondered if I appeared as completely at ease in my surroundings and as little noticeable as they did. A cigarette might help, I reflected, and I lit one. And a moment or two later Drummond turned round.

' 'Ear that,' he remarked in a confidential whisper. 'Strite from the stables. Why the devil don't you smoke a Corona, you fool! Put

out that Turk. And try and look a bit less like a countryman seeing London for the first time. Absolutely strite from the stables.
Stargazer – for the two-thirty. 'E can't lose.'

'Like to back yer fancy, Mister?' The horsy-looking gent leaned
forward with a wink.

'What's that? I mean – er . . . ' I broke off, completely bewildered.
Mechanically I put out my cigarette. For Drummond's words had
confused me. They both laughed.

' 'E ain't been in London long, 'ave yer, mate?' said Drummond. '
'E comes from up North somewhere. What this gentleman means is
that if you'd like to 'ave five bob or 'alf a Bradbury on a 'orse for to-
morrer 'e can arrange it fer yer.'

'And wot's more,' said the horsy man, 'I can give you the winner of
the Derby. As sure as my name is Joe Bloggs I can give you the
winner. You may not believe it, but I 'ad it direct from the stewards
of the Jockey Club themselves. "Bloggs," they says to me, they says,
"it ain't everyone as we'd tell this to. But you're different; we knows
you're a gentleman." '

'Did they now?' said Drummond in an awed voice.

'But wot they said to me was this. "We don't object to your a-
passing of it on, if you can find men wot you trust. But it ain't fair to
give anyone this information for nothing. We don't want the money,
but there are 'orspitals that do. The price to you, Bloggs, is one thick
'un; to be paid to the London 'Orspital." So I said to 'em, I said –
"Done with you, your Graces; a thick 'un it is." And at 'ome, mates,
now – locked up along with my marriage lines and the youngster's
christening certificate is a receipt for one pound from the London
'Orspital. I shall tike it with me to Epsom, and it'll be a proud day for
me if I can tike receipts for two more. It's yer chance, boys. Hand
over a couple of Brads, and the hinformation is yours – hinformation
which the King himself don't know!'

'I'll bet 'e doesn't,' agreed Drummond. 'It's a pleasure to 'ave met
yer, Mr Bloggs. 'Ave another gargle? I guess me and my mate 'ere
will come in on that little deal. Money for nothing I calls it.'

It was at that moment that I saw them enter the bar – the man who
had been in Hatchett's, and another one. Of the squealing little
specimen who had been dragged into Toby's room I saw no sign, but
doubtless he would come later. However, the great point was that
the others had arrived, and I glanced at Drummond to make sure he
had noticed the fact.

To my amazement he was leaning over the bar calling for Mother to replenish his glass and that of his new friend. So I dug him in the ribs covertly, at the same time keeping a careful eye on the two new-comers. It was easy to watch them unperceived, as they were talking most earnestly together. And by the most extraordinary piece of good fortune they found a vacant place at the bar itself just beside the horsy man.

Again I dug Drummond in the ribs, and he looked at me knowingly.

'All right, mate, o' course we'll take it. But wot I was just wonder-ing was whether, seeing as 'ow there are two of us like, this gentle-man wouldn't let us 'ave his hinformation for thirty bob. Yer see, guv'nor, it's this way. You tells me the name of the 'orse, and I pays you a quid. Wot's to prevent me passing it on to him for nothing, once I knows it?'

'The 'Orspital, mate. Them poor wasted 'uman beings wot looks to us for 'elp in their sufferings. As the Duke of Sussex said to me, "Bloggs!" 'e said – "old friend of my youth . . . " '

I could stand it no longer: I leant over and whispered in Drum-mond's ear – 'Do you see who has just come in? Standing next to this awful stiff.'

He nodded portentously. 'I quite agree with you, mate. Excuse me one moment, Mr Bloggs.'

He turned to me, and his expression never varied one iota.

'Laddie,' he murmured wearily, 'I saw them ten minutes ago. I felt London shake when you gave your little start of surprise on seeing them yourself. With pain and gloom I have watched you regarding them as a lion regards the keeper at feeding time at the Zoo. All that remains is for you to go up to them and let them know who we are. Then we'll all sing "Auld Lang Syne" and go home. Well, then, that's agreed. Seeing as 'ow it's for an 'orspital, Mr Bloggs, my mate 'ere says 'e'll spring a thick 'un.'

'Good for both of yer,' cried the tipster. 'And you may take it from me, boys, that it's dirt cheap at the price.'

'Come in 'ere between us, Mr Bloggs,' said Drummond confid-entially. 'It wouldn't do for no-one else to 'ear anything about it. We don't want no shortening of the odds.'

'I sees you knows the game, mate,' said the other appreciatively as they changed places, thereby bringing Drummond next to our quarry. 'You're right: the Duke would never forgive me if we was to do that. "Spread your money amongst all yer bookmakers, Joe, and keep them damned stiffs from bilking honest men like you and me" – them were his very words.'

'Wait a moment, mate,' cried Drummond. 'Mother – give me a pencil and a bit o' paper, will yer? I've got a shocking memory, Mr Bloggs, and I'd like to 'ave this 'ere 'orse's name down in writing, seeing as 'ow I'm springing a quid for it. There it is, and now let's 'ear.'

He produced a one-pound note which he laid on the bar, from which it disappeared, with a speed worthy of Maskelyne and Cook, into Mr Bloggs' pocket. And then the momentous secret was whispered in his ear.

'You don't say,' said Drummond. 'Well, I never did.'

'And if yer gets on now yet gets on at 66 to 1,' said the tipster triumphantly.

'Lumme! It's like stealing the cat's milk.' Drummond seemed suddenly to be struck with an idea. 'Why, blow my dickey, if I ain't been and forgotten young Isaac. 'E's careful with 'is money, Mr Bloggs, is Isaac – but for a cert like this 'e might spring a quid too. Isaac – 'ere.'

'Whath the matter?' said Toby, glancing round.

'Do you want the winner of the Derby 'orse-race, my boy? That's the matter.'

'Go on,' said Toby suspiciously. 'I've heard that stuff before.'

'It's the goods this time, my boy,' said Mr Bloggs impressively. 'Strite from my old pal the Duke of Essex – I mean – er – Sussex – 'imself.'

His back was turned to Drummond, and the movement of Drummond's face was almost imperceptible. But its meaning was clear: Toby was to accept the offer. And for the life of me, as I stood there feeling bored and puzzled, I couldn't make out the object of all this tomfoolery. This palpable fraud had served his purpose; what on earth was the use of losing another pound for no rhyme or reason? The two men behind Drummond were engrossed in conversation, and there was still no sign of the third.

For a moment or two I listened half mechanically to Toby bargaining for better terms, and then something drew my attention to a man seated by himself in a corner. He had a tankard of beer at his side, and his appearance was quite inconspicuous. He was a thick-set burly man, who might have been an engine-driver off duty or something of that sort. And yet he seemed to be studying the occupants of the bar in a curiously intent manner. At any ordinary time I probably shouldn't have noticed him; but then at any ordinary time I shouldn't have been in the Three Cows. And after a while I began to watch him covertly, until I grew convinced that my suspicions were correct. He was watching us. Once or twice I caught his eye fixed on me with an expression which left no doubt whatever in my mind that his presence there was not accidental. And though I immediately looked away, lest he should think I had noticed anything, I began to feel certain that he was another of the gang – possibly the very one we had come to find. Moreover, my certainty was increased by the fact that never once, as far as I could see, did the two men standing next to Drummond glance in his direction.

Drummond noticed nothing: he and Toby were still occupied in haggling with the Duke of Sussex's pal. And I couldn't help smiling slightly to myself as I realised the futility of all this ridiculous masquerade. However, I duly paid my pound, as I didn't want to let them down in their little game, and thought out one or two sarcastic phrases to put across at Drummond later. Though I had said nothing at the time I had not been amused by his remark about 'Auld Lang Syne'.

And then another idea dawned on me – why should I say anything about it? Though I would never have thought it, there was a certain amount of fun in this dressing-up game. And one thing seemed pretty obvious without any suggestion of self-conceit. If Drummond could succeed at it, I certainly could. An excellent fellow doubtless, and one possessed of great strength – but there it ended. And I even began to wonder if he had really spotted the arrival of the two men until I told him. It's easy to be wise after the event, and there is such a thing as jealousy. So I decided that I would have a shot at it myself the following evening. At the moment I was not very busy, and doubtless I'd be able to borrow my present disguise from Drummond. After all he'd offered to lend it to me whenever I wanted it, and even to give me the run of his wardrobe.

'Well, I'm off.' It was Toby speaking, and with a nod that included all of us he slouched out of the bar, to be followed shortly afterwards by Mr Bloggs.

'Don't forget, mate,' said that worthy to me earnestly as he put down his empty glass, 'that it's the goods: 66 to 1 is the price today, so that if yer backs it each way you lands a matter of eighty quid, which is better than being 'it in the eye with a rotten hegg.'

I agreed suitably with this profound philosophical fact, and omitted to tell him that I hadn't even heard the name of this fortune-maker, owing to slight deafness in the ear which I had presented to him.

'One of the lads,' remarked Drummond, as the swing-doors closed behind Mr Bloggs and our three quid. 'Another of the same, Mother, and a drop of port for yourself.'

'Closing time,' bellowed a raucous voice, and a general move towards the door took place. The two men next to Drummond finished their drinks, and then, still engrossed in conversation, went out into the street along with the rest, but he made no movement to follow them, which rather surprised me. In fact, he seemed to have completely lost all interest in them, and he stayed on chaffing the two women behind the bar until a general turning down of lights showed that it was closing time in earnest.

And since my principal interest lay in the thick-set burly man, who was one of the last to leave, it suited me very well. In him I felt convinced lay the first clue to what we wanted, and when I saw a second man, whom I had not previously noticed, and who had been sitting in another corner of the bar, whisper something in his ear as he went out, it seemed proof positive. However, true to my decision, I said nothing about what I had discovered, and, smiling inwardly, I waited to hear what Drummond proposed to do.

'Not bad,' he remarked in his normal voice, as we strolled towards the nearest Tube station. 'Almost too good. In fact – I wonder.'

'Whether the London Hospital will benefit to the extent of three pounds,' I remarked sarcastically, and he laughed.

'He was one of mother's bright boys, wasn't he? It was a bit too blatant, Stockton. That's the trouble.'

'As I'm afraid I didn't even catch the name of the horse I can't argue the point.'

'The name of the horse was 10 Ashworth Gardens,' he answered.

'What on earth do you mean?' I remarked, staring at him blankly.

'10 Ashworth Gardens,' he repeated, 'wherever that may be. Shortly we will get into a taxi and follow Toby there.'

'I say, do you mind explaining?' I demanded. 'Is that what that tout fellow told you?'

He laughed again, and hailed a passing taxi.

'Victoria Station, mate – Brighton Line. And 'op it. Now,' he continued, as the man turned his car, 'I will endeavour to elucidate. Just before Mr Joe Bloggs gave me a whisky shower-bath in the ear, and told me that my uncle's horse, which was scratched late this afternoon, was the winner, our two friends on my right mentioned that address. They mentioned it again when I changed my position and stood next to them. Now my experience is that people don't shout important addresses at one another in public – at least not people of that type. That's why I said that it struck me as being a little too blatant. However, it may have been that they thought they were perfectly safe, so that it's worth trying.'

He put his head through the window.

'I've changed my mind, mate. I want to go to Hashworth Gardens. Know 'em?'

'Know my face,' answered the other. 'Of course I do. Up Euston way.'

'Well, stop afore you get there, and me and my pal will walk.'

'So that was what you wrote on the paper and showed Sinclair,' I exclaimed as he resumed his seat.

'Bright lad,' said Drummond, and relapsed into silence.

For a while I hesitated as to whether I should tell him of my suspicions, but I still felt a bit riled at what I regarded as his offhand manner. So I didn't, and we sat in silence till Piccadilly Circus and Shaftesbury Avenue were left behind us.

'Look here, Stockton,' said Drummond suddenly, 'this is your palaver principally, so you'd better decide. We're being followed.'

He pointed at the little mirror in front of the driver.

'I rather expected we might be, and now I'm sure. So what do you propose to do? It's only fair to warn you that we may be putting our noses into a deliberate and carefully prepared trap.'

'What would you do yourself if I wasn't here?' I remarked.

'Put my nose there, of course,' he answered.

'Then mine goes too,' I said.

'Good man,' he cried. 'You'll be one of the firm in no time.'

'Tell me,' I said, laughing, 'do you do this sort of thing often? I mean in this case, for no rhyme or reason as far as I can see, you are running the risk of certain death.'

'Oh! I dunno,' he answered casually. 'Probably not as bad as that. Might lead to a scrap or something of that sort, which helps to pass away the time. And, really, when you come to think of it, Stockton, this show was positively asking for it. When a man whose lunch you have spoilt literally bawls an address in your ear, it's not decent to disregard it. Incidentally, I wonder if little rat face will have the gall to come and demand his fiver tomorrow.'

The car pulled up and the driver stuck his head round the door.

'Second on the left up that road,' he said, and we watched his red tail lamp disappearing down the almost deserted street. At the far end just before a turn stood another stationary car, and Drummond gave a sudden little chuckle.

'Our followers, unless I'm much mistaken. Let's get a move on, Stockton, and see what there is to be seen before they arrive.'

He swung off down the turning, and at the corner of Ashworth Gardens a figure detached itself from the shadows. It was Toby Sinclair.

'Fourth house down on the left, Hugh,' he said. 'And there's something damned funny going on there. I haven't seen the sign of a soul, but there's the most extraordinary sort of sound coming from a room on the first floor. Just as if a sack was swinging against the blind.'

It was an eerie sort of noise, such as you may hear sometimes in old houses in the country when the wind is blowing. Creak, shuffle, thud – creak, shuffle, thud, and every now and then a sort of drumming noise such as a man's heels might make against wood-work. For a while we stood listening, and once it seemed to me that the blind bulged outwards with the pressure of something behind it.

'My God! you fellows,' said Drummond quietly, 'that's no sack. I'm going in, trap or no trap; there's foul play inside that room.'

Without a second's hesitation he walked up the steps and tried the front door. It was open, and Sinclair whistled under his breath.

'It is a trap, Hugh,' he whispered.

'Stop here, both of you,' he answered. 'I'm going to see.'

We stood there waiting in the hall, and I have no hesitation in confessing that the back of my scalp was beginning to prick uncom-fortably. The silence was absolute: the noise had entirely ceased. Just once a stair creaked above us, and then very faintly we heard the sound of a door opening. Simultaneously the noise began again – thud, shuffle, creak – thud, shuffle, creak, and the next moment we heard Drummond's voice.

'Come up – both of you.'

We dashed up the stairs, and into the room with the open door. At first I could hardly see in the faint light from a street lamp outside, and then things became clearer. I made out Drummond holding something in his arms by the window, and then Toby flashed on his torch.

'Cut the rope,' said Drummond curtly. 'I've freed him from the strain.'

It was Toby who cut it: I just stood there feeling dazed and sick. For the sack was no sack, but our rat-faced man of the morning. He was hanging from a hook in the ceiling, and his face was glazed and purple, while his eyes stared horribly. His hands were lashed behind his back and a handkerchief had been thrust into his mouth.

'Lock the door,' ordered Drummond, as he laid the poor devil down on the floor. 'He's not quite dead, and I'm going to bring him round if every crook in London is in the house. Keep your guns handy and your ears skinned.'

He unknotted the rope and pulled out the gag, and after ten minutes or so the breathing grew less stertorous and the face more normal in colour.

'Take a turn, Stockton,' said Drummond at length. 'Just ordinary artificial respiration. I want to explore a bit.'

I knelt down beside the man on the floor and continued the necessary motions mechanically. It was obvious now that he was going to pull round, and if anything was going to be discovered I wanted to be in the fun. Sinclair had lit a cracked incandescent light which hung from the middle of the ceiling, and by its light it was possible to examine the room. There was very little furniture: a drunken-looking horsehair sofa, two or three chairs and a rickety table comprised the lot. But on one wall, not far from where I knelt, there was hanging a somewhat incongruous piece of stuff. Not that it was valuable, but it seemed to have no reason for its existence. It was the sort of thing one might put up to cover a mark on the wall, or behind a washstand to prevent splashing the paper – but why there? Someone upset the ink, perhaps: someone . . .

My artificial respiration ceased, and my mouth grew dry. For the bit of stuff was moving: it was being pushed aside and something was appearing round the edge. Something that looked like a small-calibre revolver, and it was pointed straight at me. No, not a revolver: it was a small squirt or syringe, and behind it was a big white disc. Into my mind there flashed the words of Sir John Dallas only that morning – 'something in the nature of a garden syringe' – and with a great effort I forced myself to act. I rolled over towards the window, and what happened then is still more or less a blur in my mind. A thin jet of liquid shot through the air, and hit the carpet just behind where I'd been kneeling, and at the same moment there came the crack of a revolver, followed by a scream and a heavy fall. I looked up to see Drummond ejecting a spent cartridge, and then I scrambled to my feet.

'What the devil,' I muttered stupidly.

'Follow it up,' snapped Drummond, 'and shoot on sight.'

He was out in the passage like a flash, with Toby and me at

his heels. The door of the next room was locked, but it lasted only one charge of Drummond's. And then for a moment or two we stood peering into the darkness – at least I did. The others did not, which is how one lives and learns. I never heard them: I never even realised they had left me, and when two torches were flashed on from the other side of the room, I shrank back into the passage.

'Come in, man, come in,' muttered Drummond. 'Never stand in a doorway like that. Ah!'

He drew in his breath sharply as the beam of his torch picked up the thing on the floor. It was the man who had been in Hatchett's that morning, the man who had stood behind him at the Three Cows, and he was dead. The same terrible distortion and rigour was visible: the cause of death was obvious.

'Don't touch him, for Heaven's sake,' I cried, as Drummond bent forward. 'It's the same death as we saw last night!'

'And you were darned nearly the victim, old man,' said Drummond grimly.

'By Jove! Hugh, it was a good shot,' said Toby. 'You hit the syringe itself, and the stuff splashed on his face. You can see the mark.'

It was true: in the middle of his right cheek was an angry red circle, in which it was possible to see an eruption of tiny blisters. And the same strange, sweet smell hung heavily about the air.

On each hand was a white glove of the same type as the one we had found the previous night, and it was evidently that which had seemed to me like a white disc around the syringe.

'So things begin to move,' said Drummond quietly. 'The whole thing was a trap, as I thought. They evidently seem to want you pretty badly, Stockton.'

'But why?' I asked angrily. 'What the devil have I got to do with it?' He shrugged his shoulders.

'They may think you know too much; that Gaunt told you things.'

'But why hang that poor little toad in the next room?' said Toby.

'Ask me another,' answered Drummond. 'Possibly they found out we'd got at him, and they hanged him as a punishment for treachery: possibly to ensure our remaining here some time to bring him round. And incidentally – who hanged him? The occupants of the car that followed us couldn't have got to this house before we did, and he was triced up before Toby arrived here. That means there were people here before and the occupants of that car have yet to arrive.'

Suddenly his torch went out, and I felt his hand on my arm warningly. 'And unless I mistake,' he whispered, 'they've just come. Stick by me, Stockton: you're new to this game. Get by the window, Toby, and keep against the wall.'

A half-breathed 'Right' came from the darkness, and I felt myself led somewhere. Once the guiding hand drew me to the right, and I realised that I had just missed a chair. And then I felt the wall at my back, and a faint light coming round the blind showed the window close by. It was shut, and I could see the outline of Drummond's head as he peered through it.

What had caused his sudden action, I wondered? I hadn't heard a sound, and at that time I had yet to find out his almost uncanny gift of hearing. To me the house was in absolute silence; the only sound was the heavy pounding of my own heart. And then a stair creaked as it had creaked when Drummond left us in the hall.

I glanced at Drummond: his hand was feeling for the window-catch. With a little click it went back, and once more he crouched motionless. Again the stair creaked, and yet again, and I thought I heard men whispering outside the door. Suddenly with a crash that almost startled me out of my senses Drummond flung up the sash and the whispering ceased.

'Stand by to jump, when I give the word,' muttered Drummond, 'and then run like hell. There's about a dozen of 'em.'

He was crouching below the level of the window-sill; dimly on his other side I could see Toby Sinclair. And then the whispering started again; men were coming into the room. There was a stifled curse as someone stumbled against a chair, and at that moment Drummond shouted 'Jump.'

Just for a second I almost obeyed him, for my leg was over the sill. And then I heard him fighting desperately in the room behind. He was covering our retreat, a thing which no man could allow.

There may have been a dozen in all: I know there were three of them on me. Chairs went over as we fought on in the dark, and all the time I was thinking of the liquid on the floor and the dead man's face and what would happen if we touched it. And as if in answer to my thoughts there came Drummond's voice.

'I have one of you here powerless,' he said. 'In this room is a dead man who died you know how. Unless my other two friends are allowed to go at once I will put this man's hand against the dead man's cheek. And that means death.'

'Who is that speaking?' came another voice out of the darkness.

'Great Scott!' Drummond's gasp of surprise was obvious. 'Is that you, MacIver?'

'Switch on the lights,' returned the other voice angrily.

And there stood my burly thick-set man of the Three Cows.

'What is the meaning of this damned foolishness?' he snarled. He glared furiously at Drummond and then at me.

'Why are you masquerading in that rig, Mr Stockton?' he went on suspiciously. And then his eyes fell on the dead man. 'How did this happen?'

But Drummond sprawling in a chair was laughing helplessly.

'Rich,' he remarked, 'extremely rich. Not to say ripe and fruity, old friend of my youth. Sorry, Mac' – the detective was glowering at him furiously – 'but my style of conversation has become infected by a gent with whom I dallied awhile earlier in the evening.'

'I didn't recognise you at the Three Cows, Captain Drummond,' said MacIver ominously.

'Nor I you,' conceded Drummond. 'Otherwise we'd have had a spot together.'

'But I think it's only right to warn you that you're mixing yourself up in a very serious matter. Into Mr Stockton's conduct I propose to inquire later.' Once again he looked at me suspiciously. 'Just at the moment, however, I should like to know how this man died.'

Drummond nodded and grew serious.

'Quite right, MacIver. We were in the next room – all three of us ... Good Lord! I wonder what's happened to rat face. You see, an unfortunate little bloke had been hanged in the next room ... '

'What?' shouted MacIver, darting out into the passage. We followed, crowding after him, only to stand in amazement at the door. The light was still burning: the rope still lay on the carpet, but of the man we had cut down from the ceiling there was no sign. He had absolutely disappeared.

'Well, I'm damned,' muttered Drummond. 'This beats cock-fighting. Wouldn't have missed it for a thousand. Look out! Don't go near that pool on the floor. That's some of the juice.'

He stared round the room, and then he lit a cigarette.

'There's no good you looking at me like that, MacIver,' he went on quietly. 'There's the hook, my dear fellow; there's the rope. I'm not lying. We cut him down, and we laid him on the floor just there. He was nearly dead, but not quite. For ten minutes or so I put him through artificial respiration – then Mr Stockton took it on. And it was while he was doing it – kneeling down beside him – that that bit of curtain stuff moved. I'd be careful how you touch it; there may be some of that liquid on it.'

He drew it back, covering his hand with the tablecloth.

'You see there's a hole in the wall communicating with the next room. Through that hole the man who is now lying dead next door let drive with his diabolical liquid at Mr Stockton. By the mercy of Allah he rolled over in time, and the stuff hit the carpet – you can see it there, that dark stain. So then it was my turn, and I let drive with my revolver.'

'We heard a shot,' said MacIver.

'That's his syringe, or whatever you like to call the implement,' continued Drummond. 'And it obviously wasn't empty, for some of the contents splashed back in his face. The result you see in the next room, and I can't say I regret it.'

'But this man who you say was hanging? What on earth has become of him?'

'Search me,' said Drummond. 'The only conclusion I can come to is that he recovered after we had left the room, and decided to clear out. When all is said and done he can't have had an overpowering affection for the house, and he probably heard the shindy in the next room and did a bolt.'

MacIver grunted: he was obviously in an extremely bad temper. And the presence of his large group of stolid subordinates, who were evidently waiting for orders in a situation that bewildered them, did not tend to soothe him.

'Go and search the house,' he snapped. 'Every room. And if you find anything suspicious, don't touch it, but call me.'

He waited till they had all left the room; then he turned to Drummond.

'Now, sir,' he said. 'I want to get to the bottom of this. In the first place, what brought you to this house?'

'The bird in the next room shouted the address in my ear,' returned Drummond, 'that time we were having one at the Three Cows.'

'Damn it,' exploded MacIver, 'what took you to the Three Cows? In disguise too.'

'Just vulgar curiosity, Mac,' said Drummond airily. 'And we felt that our presence in evening clothes might excite rude comment.'

'Your presence in that rig excites my comment,' snapped the detective.

'Undoubtedly, old lad,' said Drummond soothingly. 'But there's no law against toddling round in fancy dress as far as I know, and you ought to be very grateful to us for bringing you here. We've presented you with a new specimen, in a better state of preservation than the others you've got. Moreover, he's the only one who deserved his fate. The fact of the matter, MacIver, is that we're up against some pretty unscrupulous swine. Their object tonight was to kill Mr Stockton, and they very nearly succeeded. Why they should view him with dislike is beyond me, but the fact remains that they do. They set a deliberate trap for us, and we walked into it with our eyes open. You followed on, and in the darkness everybody mistook everybody else.'

The detective transferred his gaze to Toby Sinclair.

'You're Mr Sinclair, ain't you?'

'I am,' returned Toby affably.

'I thought you were both of you told not to pass this matter on. How is it that Captain Drummond comes to know of it?'

'My fault entirely, Inspector,' said Toby. 'I'd already told him before Mr Stockton returned from the War Office this morning.'

'So I thought I'd help you unofficially,' murmured Drummond, 'the same as I did at the time of the Black Gang.'

MacIver's scowl grew positively ferocious.

'I don't want your help,' he snarled. 'And in future keep out of this matter or you'll find yourself in trouble.'

'Well!' He swung round as some of his men came into the room.

'Nothing, sir. The house is empty.'

'Then, since the hour is late, I think we'll leave you,' remarked Drummond. 'You know where to find me, Mac; and you'd better let me know what I'm to say about that bloke's death. From now on, I may say, we shall drop this, and concentrate exclusively on the breeding of white mice.'

For a moment I thought MacIver was going to stop us; then apparently he thought better of it. He favoured us with a parting scowl, and with that we left him. By luck we found a taxi, and Drummond gave his own address.

'There are one or two things we might discuss,' he said quietly, as we got into the car. 'MacIver's arrival is an undoubted complication. I wonder how he spotted you, Stockton?'

'That's what beats me,' I remarked. 'I spotted him – not as MacIver, of course – down at the Three Cows. He struck me as a suspicious character, so I kept my eye on him casually while you were talking to that racing tout.'

'Oh Lord!' Drummond began to laugh. 'Then that accounts for it.

The effect of your casual eye would make an archbishop feel he'd committed bigamy. It has a sledge-hammer action about it, old man, that would make a nun confess to murder.'

'I'm very sorry,' I said huffily. 'But please remember that this sort of thing is quite new to me. And the practical result seems to be that we've got ourselves into a very nasty hole. Why – that confounded Inspector man suspects me.'

'He doesn't really,' said Drummond reassuringly. 'He was merely as mad as thunder at having made an ass of himself.'

And then he started laughing again.

'Poor old Mac! Do you remember when we laid him out to cool on his own doorstep, Toby?'

'I do,' returned Sinclair. 'And I further noticed that your allusion to the Black Gang was not popular. But, joking apart, Hugh – what's the next move?'

'It rests on a slender hope, old boy,' said Drummond. 'And even then it may lead to nothing. It rests on the reappearance of little rat face. Of course he may be able to tell us nothing: on the other hand, there must have been some reason for tricing him up. And that reason may throw some light on the situation.'

'But are you really going on with it?' I asked.

They both stared at me in amazement.

'Going on with it!' cried Drummond. 'What a question, my dear man. Of course we are. Apart altogether from the fact that they're bound to have another shot at you, and probably at us too, there is all the makings of a really sporting show in this affair. Wash out MacIver's unfortunate entrance for the moment, and concentrate on the other aspects of the case. Evidently what I feared this afternoon was correct, and our friend at Hatchett's – now defunct – got on to us at Brook Street. He may have asked the head waiter who I was – that's a detail. He follows us to the Three Cows; he lays a deliberate trap into which we fall – admittedly with our eyes open. The sole object of that plot is to kill you and possibly us. It fails, and somewhat stickily for the originator. But you don't imagine that we can allow the matter to rest there, do you? It wouldn't be decent.'

'Still,' I persisted, 'it seems to me that we may be getting ourselves into hot water with the police if we go on.'

Drummond laid his hand reassuringly on my knee.

'It's not the first time, old lad,' he remarked. 'Mac and I are really bosom friends. Still, if you feel doubtful, you can back out. Personally I propose to continue the good work.'

'Oh! If you're going on I'm with you,' I said, a little ungraciously. 'Only please don't forget I'm reputed to be a lawyer.'

'Magnificent,' returned Drummond imperturbably. 'We'll come to you for legal advice.'

The car pulled up in front of his house and we got out.

'Come in and change,' he went on, 'and we'll have a nightcap.'

I noticed that his eyes were searching the street. The hour was two, and as far as I could see it was deserted. And yet I couldn't help a distinct feeling of relief as the stout front door shut behind us. It gave one a feeling of safety and security which had been singularly lacking during the preceding part of the evening: no-one could get at us there.

I lit one of my prohibited Turkish cigarettes, and as I did so I saw that Drummond was staring with curious intentness at a letter and a parcel that lay on the hall table. The parcel was about the size of a cigar box, and the label outside proclaimed that it came from Asprey's.

He led the way upstairs, carrying them both with him. And then having drawn himself some beer, and waved his hand at the cask in the corner for us to help ourselves, he slit the envelope open with a paper knife.

'I thought as much,' he said after he had read the contents. 'But how very crude; and how very untruthful. Though it shows they possess a confidence in their ability, which is not so far justified by results.'

We looked over his shoulder at the typewritten slip he held in his hand. It ran as follows:

Mr Stockton is dead because he knew too much: a traitor is dead because he was a traitor. Unless you stop at once, a fool will die because he was a fool.

'How crude,' he repeated. 'How very crude. I'm afraid our opponents are not very clever. They must have been going to the movies or something. It is rare to find three lies in such a short space. Toby, bring me a basin chock-full of water, will you? There's one in the bathroom.'

His eyes were fixed on the parcel, and he was smiling grimly.

'To be certain of success is an admirable trait, Stockton,' he murmured, 'if you succeed. If, on the contrary, you fail, it is ill-advised to put your convictions on paper. Almost as ill-advised, in fact, as to send livestock disguised as a cigarette-case.'

'What on earth do you mean?' I asked.

'Put your ear against that parcel and listen,' he answered shortly.

And suddenly I heard it – a faint rustling, and then a gentle scraping noise.

'You're having an excellent blooding to this sort of game,' he laughed. 'In fact, I've rarely known events come crowding so thick and fast. But crude – oh so crude, as I said before.'

'Here you are, old man. Is there enough water?'

Toby had re-entered the room with the basin.

'Ample,' answered Drummond, picking up the parcel and holding it under the surface. 'Give me that paperweight, Stockton, and then we can resume our beer.'

Fascinated I watched the bubbles rise to the surface. At first they came slowly, then as the water permeated the wrappings they rose in a steady stream. And then clear and distinct there came a dreadful hissing noise, and the surface of the water became blurred with a faint tremor as if the box itself was shaking.

'A pleasant little pet,' murmured Drummond, watching the basin with interest. 'There's no doubt about it, you fellows, that the air of rapidity grows more and more marked.'

At last the bubbles ceased; the whole parcel was waterlogged.

'We'll give it five minutes,' said Drummond, 'before inspecting Asprey's latest.'

We waited, I at any rate with ill-concealed impatience, till the time was up and Drummond took the parcel out of the water. He cut the string and removed the paper. Inside was a wooden box with holes drilled in it, and the water was draining out of it back into the basin.

With the paper-knife he prised open the lid, and even he gave a startled exclamation when he saw what was inside. Personally it filled me with a feeling of nausea, and I saw Toby Sinclair clutch the table.

It was a spider of sorts, but such a spider as I have never dreamed of in my wildest nightmares. Its body was the size of a hen's egg; its six legs the size of a crab's. And it was covered with coarse black hair. Even in death it looked the manifestation of all evil, with its great protruding eyes and short sharp jaws, and with a shudder I turned away.

'A jest I do not like,' said Drummond quietly, tipping the corpse out into the basin. 'Hullo! Another note.'

He was staring at the bottom of the box, and there sure enough was an envelope. It was sodden with water, but the letter inside was legible. And for a while we stared at it uncomprehendingly.

'This is to introduce William. If you decide to keep him, his favourite diet is one of small birds and mice. He is a married man and since I hated to part him from his wife I have sent her along too. She is addressed to the most suitable person in the house to receive a lady.'

As I say, for a moment or two we stared at the note uncomprehendingly, and then Drummond gave a sudden strangled grunt in his throat and dashed from the room.

'Phyllis,' he flung at us hoarsely, from the door.

'Good Lord! His wife,' cried Toby, and with sick fear in our hearts we followed him.

'It's all right, darling,' came his voice from above us, but there was no answer. And when we got to the open door and looked into the room the silence was not surprising.

Cowering in a corner, her eyes dilated with horror, there stood a girl. She was staring at something on the carpet – something that was hidden from us by the bed. Her lips were moving, but no sound came from them, and she never lifted even her eyes to look at her husband.

And I don't wonder. Even now, though eighteen months have passed, my skin still creeps as I recall that moment. If the dead thing below had been horrible, what words can I use for the living? As with many spiders, the female was larger than the male, and the thing which stood on its six great legs about a yard from her feet looked the size of a puppy. It was squat and utterly loathsome, and as Drummond with the poker in his hand dashed towards it, it scuttled under the bed, hissing loudly.

It was I who caught Mrs Drummond as she pitched forward in a dead faint, and I held her whilst her husband went berserk. It was my first acquaintance with his amazing strength. He hurled heavy pieces of furniture about as if they were out of a doll's house. The two beds flew apart with a crash and the foul brute he was after sidled under a wardrobe. And then the wardrobe moved like Kipling's piano, save that there was only one man behind and not several.

But at last he had it, and with a grunt of rage he hit it with the poker between the beady staring eyes. He hit it again and again and then he turned round and stared at us.

'If ever I lay hands on the man who sent these brutes,' he said quietly, 'I will do the same to him.'

He took his wife from me and picked her up in his arms.

'Let's go out of here before she comes to,' he went on. 'Poor kid; poor little kid!'

He carried her downstairs, and a few minutes later she opened her eyes. Stark horror still shone in them, and for a while she sobbed hysterically. But at length she grew calmer, and disjointedly, with many pauses, she told us what had happened.

She'd come in from a dance, and seen the two boxes lying on the hall table. She'd taken hers upstairs, thinking it was a present from her husband. And she'd opened it at her dressing-table. And then she'd seen this awful monster staring at her. Her maid had gone to bed, and suddenly it had scrambled out of the box and flopped off the table on to the floor at her feet.

'I tried to scream, Hugh, and I couldn't. I think I was half mesmerised. I just rushed blindly away, and I went to the wrong corner. Instead of going to the door, I went to the other. And it followed me. And when I stopped it stopped.'

She began to shudder uncontrollably; then she pulled herself together again.

'It just squatted there on the floor and its eyes seemed to grow bigger and bigger. And once I found myself leaning forward towards it, as if I was forced against my will. I think if it had touched me I should have gone mad. Who sent it, Hugh: who was the brute who sent it?'

'If ever I find that out,' said Drummond grimly, 'he will curse the day that he was born. But just now, darling, I want you to take some sleep dope and go to bed.'

'I couldn't,' she cried. 'I couldn't sleep with a double dose.'

'Right ho!' he answered. 'Then stop down here and talk to us. By the way, you don't know Mr Stockton, do you? He's really quite good-looking when you see his real face.'

'I'm afraid, Mrs Drummond,' I said apologetically, 'that I am indirectly responsible for those two brutes being sent to you tonight.'

'Two,' she cried. 'Your parcel had one, too?'

'Yes, my dear, it did,' said Drummond. 'Only I took the precaution of drowning mine before inspecting it.'

'Look here, Hugh,' cried his wife, 'I know you're on the warpath again. Well, I tell you straight I can stand most things – you've already given me three goes of Peterson – but I can't stand spiders. If I get any more of them I shall sue for divorce.'

Her husband grinned and she turned to me pathetically. 'You wouldn't believe what he's like, Mr Stockton, once he gets going.'

'I can hazard a pretty shrewd guess,' I returned. 'We haven't exactly been at a Sunday School treat this evening.'

'Life is real and life is earnest,' chanted her husband. 'And Stockton's becoming one of the boys, my pet. We've had a really first-class show tonight. I've got the winner of the Derby, if it hadn't been scratched a little tactlessly by old Uncle Bob. And MacIver – you remember that shining light of Scotland Yard – has chased us all over London, and is very angry in consequence. And – oh well, lots of other things. What's that you're grasping in your hand, Toby?'

'Another note, old boy. He's a literary gent, is our spider friend.'

'Where did you find it?'

'In the box on Phyllis's dressing-table. And I don't think it will amuse you.'

It did not.

A little nervy? Lost your temper? Well, well! They were quite harmless, both of them, though I admit Mary's claim to beauty must not be judged by ordinary standards. But let that be enough. I don't want meddlers. Next time I shall remove you without mercy. So cease being stupid.

'An amazingly poor judge of human nature,' said Drummond softly. 'Quite amazingly so. I wonder which of the two it was. I trust with all my heart that it was not our friend of Hatchett's and Ashworth Gardens. I should hate to think we would never meet again.'

'But why won't you?' said his wife hopefully.

'Well, we had a little game tonight, darling,' answered Drummond. 'And he has taken his own excellent advice. He has ceased being stupid.'

Chapter 4

In which Hugh Drummond discovers a new aunt

And at this point I feel that I owe my readers an apology. In fact Hugh Drummond, who has just read the last chapter, insists on it.

'What an appalling song and dance about nothing at all,' is the tenor of his criticism. 'My dear fellow, concentrate on the big thing.'

Well, I admit that in comparison with what was to come it was nothing at all. And yet I don't know. After all, the first shell that bursts near one affects the individual more than a bombardment later on. And the events I have described constituted my first shell, so that on that score alone I crave indulgence.

But there is another reason too which, in my opinion, renders it impossible to concentrate only on the big thing. Had these words been penned at the time, much that I am writing now would have been dismissed in a few lines, simply because the position of certain episodes in the chain of events would not have been obvious. But now looking back, and armed with one's present knowledge, it is easy to see how they all fitted in; and how the two chains of events, the big one and the one that Drummond calls little, ran side by side till they finally met. And so I give them both, merely remarking that if certain things appear obscure to the reader, they appeared even more obscure to us at the time.

We were confronted then, on the morning after our visit to the Three Cows, with the following position of affairs. The secret of a singularly deadly poison had been stolen, and in the process of the theft the inventor of the poison had disappeared, his dog had been killed, and the man who, according to his own story, had not only been his friend but had also been financing his experiments, had been murdered. The death of the constable was an extraneous matter, and therefore did not affect the position, save that it afforded proof, if further proof was needed, of the deadliness of the poison.

Sinclair and I, owing to the fact that we had come to Gaunt's rooms, had been followed; and, of the two of us, I was regarded as the more dangerous. So much the more dangerous, in fact, that my death had been deliberately decided on under circumstances which our enemies imagined did not admit of failure.

They had clearly added Drummond to our list, probably, as he surmised, owing to the incident at Hatchett's. And the fact that the head waiter knew him rendered his efforts to throw them off his track abortive. We were undoubtedly followed to the Three Cows, with the idea of inveigling us to Ashworth Gardens. MacIver was there simply and solely because he knew it was the pub in which the taxi-driver had been drugged the night before, and he hoped to pick up a thread to follow.

And there came our first query. Did MacIver recognise the two men, and did they recognise him? To the first of these questions we unhesitatingly answered – No. There was no reason that he should know them at all as far as we could see; and the fact that MacIver's worst suspicions were at once concentrated on me rendered it less probable that he would notice them. To the other question we again answered – No, but with less certainty. It didn't appear a very important one, anyway, but it struck us that it would be taking an unnecessary and dangerous risk on their part to carry on with their programme if they thought they were being watched. And human nature being what it is, they would, with their guilty conscience, if they had recognised MacIver, have assumed he was after them.

As far as we were concerned they didn't care – in fact, they wanted to be recognised. They wanted us to assume that they didn't know us – that our disguises were perfect. And so what more natural than that they should discuss things openly in our hearing? In fact, they had been very sure of themselves, had those two gentlemen.

All that was clear: it was over the subsequent events that there rested the fog of war. Why hang the poor little brute when obviously they had a supply of the poison? If they wished to kill him, that would have been a far surer and more efficacious method. And why the spiders?

We were holding a council of war, I remember, at which I met Peter Darrell and Algy Longworth for the first time, and we discussed those two points from every angle. And it was Drummond who stuck out for the simplest explanation.

'You're being too deep, old lads,' he remarked. 'The whole of this thing has been done with one idea, and one idea only – to frighten us. They think I'm a positive goop – a congenital whatnot. They intended to kill Stockton – who they are afraid knows too much;

and they intended to inspire in me a desire to hire two nurses and a bath-chair and trot up and down the front at Bournemouth. The mere fact that they have brought off a double event in the bloomer line doesn't alter the motive.'

He rose and pressed the bell, and in a moment or two his butler entered.

'Did you take in those two parcels from Asprey's last night, Denny?'

'I did, sir.'

'What time did they come?'

'About midnight, sir.'

'Who brought 'em?'

'A man, sir.'

'You blithering juggins, I didn't suppose it was a tame rhinoceros. What sort of a man?'

'Don't know that I noticed him particularly, sir. He just handed 'em in and said you'd understand.'

Drummond dismissed him with a wave of his hand.

'No help there,' he remarked. 'Except as to time. Obviously they had everything prepared. As soon as they saw we were going to Ashworth Gardens, one of them came here, and the other followed us.'

'Granted all that, old bean,' said Toby. 'But why hang rat face? That's what beats me.'

Drummond lit a cigarette before replying.

'There's a far more interesting point than that,' he remarked. 'And I mentioned it last night. *Who* hanged him? There were people in that house before we got there: men don't hang themselves as a general rule. Those people left that house before we arrived there, just as the man who tried to murder Stockton got there after we arrived there. And on one thing I'll stake my hat: the latter gentleman did not come up the stairs, or I'd have heard him. If he didn't come up the stairs he entered by some unusual method: presumably the same as that by which the others left, or else Toby would have seen them. And houses with unusual entrances always interest me.'

'There's generally a back door,' said Algy Longworth.

'But only one staircase, laddie,' returned Drummond. 'And the man I killed did not come up that staircase. No: the old brain has seethed, and I'm open to a small bet that what they intended to do is clear. They meant to kill Stockton, and then they assumed that Toby and I would dash into the next room to catch the fellow who did it.

Owing to the door being locked he would have time to get away. Then probably we should go for the police. And when we got back I'm wondering if we would have found either body there. On the other hand, we should have had to admit that we were masquerading in disguise, and doubts as to our sanity if nothing worse would be entertained. That, coupled with the spiders, they thought would put me off. Instead of that, however, he didn't kill Stockton and got killed himself. Moreover, the police came without our asking, and found a dead body.'

'But look here, Hugh,' interrupted Peter Darrell, 'you said he'd have time to get away. How? The door is off, and if he'd jumped out of the window you could have followed him.'

Drummond grinned placidly.

'The window was shut and bolted, Peter. That's why I think I shall return to Ashworth Gardens in the very near future.'

'You mean to go back to the house?' I cried.

'No – not to Number 10,' he answered. 'I'm going to Number 12 – next door. And there's very little time to be lost.'

He stood up and his eyes were glistening with anticipation.

'It's clear, boys: it must be. Either I'm a damned fool, or those blokes belong to the genus. If only old MacIver hadn't arrived last night we could have followed it through then. There must be a means of communication between the two houses, and in Number 12 we may find some amusement. Anyway it's worth trying. But, as I say, there's no time to be lost. They've brought the police down on themselves in a way that shows no traces of insanity on our part, and they'll change their quarters. In fact, I wouldn't be surprised if they've done so already.'

'You aren't coming to the inquest?' said Toby.

Drummond shook his head.

'I haven't been warned to attend. And when it comes to the turn of our friend last night, doubtless MacIver will tell me what to say.'

The door opened and Denny entered.

'Inspector MacIver would like to see you, sir.'

'Show him up. Dash it all – that's a nuisance. It means more delay.'

However, his smile was geniality itself as the detective entered.

'Good-morning, Inspector. Just in time for a spot of ale.'

But our visitor was evidently in no mood for spots of ale.

'Look here, Captain Drummond,' he said curtly, 'have you been up to your fool tricks again?'

'Good Lord! What's happened now?' said Drummond, staring at him in surprise.

'The body of the man you killed last night has completely disappeared,' answered MacIver, and Drummond whistled softly.

'The devil it has,' he muttered. And then he began to laugh. 'You don't imagine, do you, my dear fellow, that I've got it lying about in the bathroom here? But how did it happen?'

'If I knew that I shouldn't be here,' snapped the Inspector, and then, with the spot of ale literally forced on him, he proceeded to tell all that he did know.

Three of his men had been left in the house, and owing to the smell from the poison they had none of them been in the room with the dead man. Also the window had been left open and the door locked. MacIver had left to ring up Sir John Dallas, but he was out of London. And when he finally got through to the house of a well-known scientist in Hampshire where Sir John was staying for the night, in order, as it transpired, to discuss the very matter of this poison, it was nearly five o'clock in the morning. And Sir John had decided that so much time had already elapsed that the chances of his being able to discover anything new were remote. So he had adhered to his original plan and come up by an early train, which the Inspector met at Waterloo. Together they went to 10 Ashworth Gardens, and MacIver unlocked the door. And the room was empty: the body had disappeared.

The three men who had been left behind all swore that they hadn't heard a sound. The front door had been locked all the night and the men had patrolled the house at intervals.

' 'Pon my soul,' cried MacIver, 'this case is getting on my nerves. That house is like a cupboard at a conjuring show. Whatever you put inside disappears.'

I glanced at Drummond, and I thought I detected a certain suppressed excitement in his manner. But there was no trace of it in his voice.

'It is possible, of course,' he remarked, 'that the man wasn't dead. He came to: found the door locked and escaped through the window.'

MacIver nodded his head portentously.

'That point of view naturally suggests itself. And, taking everything into account, I am inclined to think that it must be the solution.'

'You didn't think of finding out if the blokes next door heard anything?' said Drummond casually.

'My dear Captain Drummond!' MacIver smiled tolerantly. 'Of course I made inquiries about the occupants of neighbouring houses.'

'You did, did you?' said Drummond softly.

'On one side is a clerk in Lloyd's with his wife and two children; on the other is an elderly maiden lady. She is an invalid, and, at the moment, has a doctor actually in the house.'

'Which is in Number 12?' asked Drummond.

'She is: her name is Miss Simpson. However, the point is this, Captain Drummond. There will now, of course, be no inquest as far as the affair of last night is concerned.'

'Precisely,' murmured Drummond. 'That is the point, as you say.'

'So there will be no necessity . . . '

'For us to concoct the same lie,' said Drummond smiling. 'Just as well, old policeman, don't you think? It's really saved everyone a lot of bother.'

MacIver frowned, and finished his beer.

'At the same time you must clearly understand that Scotland Yard will not tolerate any further activities on your part.'

'From now on I collect butterflies,' said Drummond gravely. 'Have some more beer?'

'I thank you – no,' said MacIver stiffly, and with a curt nod to us all he left the room.

'Poor old MacIver's boots are fuller of feet than usual this morning,' laughed Drummond as the door closed. 'He simply doesn't know which end up he is.'

'A rum development that, Hugh,' said Sinclair.

'Think so, old man? I don't know. Once you've granted what I maintain – namely that there's some means of communication between the two houses – I don't think it's at all rum. Just as MacIver said – the point is that there will be no inquest. Inquests mean notoriety: newspaper reporters, crowds of people standing outside the house staring at it. If I'm right that's the one thing that the occupants of Number 12 want to avoid.'

'But dash it all, Hugh,' cried Darrell, 'you don't suggest that the invalid Miss Simpson –'

'To blazes with the invalid,' said Drummond. 'How do we know it's an invalid? They may have killed the old dear, for all we know, and buried her under the cucumber frame. Of course that man was dead: I've never seen a deader. Well, dead bodies don't walk. Either he went out through the window, or he went into Number 12. The first would be an appalling risk, seeing it was broad daylight; in fact, without making the devil of a shindy it would be an impossibility. So that's where I get the bulge on MacIver. I can go into Number 12, and he can't without a warrant. That's so, isn't it, lawyer man?'

'He certainly can't enter the house without a warrant,' I agreed. 'But I don't see that you can go at all.'

'My dear old lad,' he answered, 'I am Miss Simpson's long-lost nephew from Australia. If she is all that she pretends to be, I shall buy her some muscatel grapes, kiss her heartily on each cheek and fade gracefully away. But if she isn't . . . '

'Well,' I said curiously. 'If she isn't?'

'Then there will be two damned liars in the house, and that's always a sound strategical position if you're the lesser of them. So-long, boys. Tell me all about the inquest, and stand by for a show tonight.'

He lounged out of the room, and I sat looking after him a little helplessly. His complete disregard for any normal methods of procedure, his absolute lack of any conventionality, nonplussed me. And yet I couldn't help admitting to myself that what he said was perfectly correct. If she was the genuine article he merely retired gracefully: if she wasn't, he held the whip hand, since the last thing the occupants of the house could do was to send for the police. And after a time I began to find myself hoping that she would prove to be an impostor, and that there would be another show tonight. It struck me as being more exciting than the legal profession . . .

But at this point, in order to keep to the sequence of events, I must digress for the moment and allude to the inquest. It was an affair of surpassing dullness, chiefly remarkable for the complete suppression of almost all the facts that mattered. I realised, of course, that it was part of the prearranged plan: though even I, knowing as I did that there is a definite understanding between the coroner and the police in all inquests where murder has occurred, was surprised at the result when compared to the facts.

But bald as that result was, the reporters got hold of it. The few central facts which concerned the death of the policeman and the finding of the dead bodies of the dog and the Australian had to come out. Also the disappearance of Robin Gaunt. (In fact, as anyone who cares to look up the account can see for himself, no mention occurred of the War Office or things military throughout the whole of the proceeding. I saw Major Jackson in the body of the court, but, since he was in mufti, he was indistinguishable from any ordinary spectator.)

I told of the cry over the telephone; and, in short, I told with the omissions I have mentioned the story I have already put down in these pages up to the moment when Inspector MacIver arrived. And Toby Sinclair confirmed it.

Then Sir John Dallas gave his evidence, which consisted of a series of statements of fact. The deaths had been due to an unknown poison administered externally: he was unable to say how it had been applied. He could give no opinion as to the nature of the poison, beyond saying that it punctured the skin and passed up an artery to the heart. He was continuing his experiments in the hopes of isolating it.

Then MacIver was called, and I must say that I admired the almost diabolical cunning with which he slurred over the truth, and advanced the theory that had been decided upon. He didn't say much, but the reporters seized it with avidity, and turned it from a weakly infant into a lusty child.

'No trace has been discovered of Mr Gaunt?' said the coroner.

'None,' admitted MacIver.

Though naturally a full description had been circulated all over the country.

The verdict, as may be remembered, was 'Wilful murder by some person or persons unknown' in the case of the Australian – David Ganton: and 'Death by misadventure' in the case of the constable. And in the latter case expressions of sympathy were tendered to his widow.

'Well done, Stockton.' Major Jackson and I went out of the court together.

'I suppose you know they had a shot at me last night,' I said.

'The devil they did,' he remarked, looking thoughtful. 'Where?'

'It's too long a story to tell,' I answered. 'Have you heard anything about the selling of the secret abroad?'

'Couldn't have yet,' he said. 'Of course, strictly between ourselves, we're on to it in every country that counts. But the devil of it all is that unless old Dallas can isolate this poison, the mere fact of finding out that some other Power has got the secret isn't going to help, because we can't make it ourselves. We've given him all the data we possess at the War Office, but he says it isn't enough. He maintains, in fact, that if that formula represents the whole of Gaunt's discovery at the time of the Armistice, then it would have been a failure.'

'Gaunt said he'd perfected it,' I remarked.

'Quite,' answered Jackson. 'But, according to Dallas, it isn't merely a process of growth along existing lines, but the introduction of something completely new. I'm no chemist, so I can't say if the old boy is talking out of the back of his neck or not.'

He hailed a passing taxi.

'It's serious, Stockton; deuced serious. Our only hope lies, as the General said yesterday, in the fact that the distribution question may defeat them. Because we've gone through every single available paper of Gaunt's, and that point doesn't appear anywhere. You see' – his voice dropped to a whisper – 'aeroplanes are impracticable – they travel too fast, and they couldn't take up sufficient bulk. And a dirigible – well, you remember sausage balloons, don't you, falling in flames like manna from the heavens in France? One incendiary bullet – and finish. That's the point, but don't pass it on. Has he solved that? If so . . . '

With a shrug of his shoulders he left his sentence uncompleted, and I stood watching the car as it drove away towards Whitehall.

'Universal, instantaneous death.'

Robin's words came back to me, and they continued to come back to me all through the day, when, for very shame's sake, I was making a pretence of work. They danced between my eyes and the brief in front of me, till in despair I gave up trying to concentrate on it.

'Universal, instantaneous death.'

I lit a pipe and fell to reviewing the events of the past few days. And after a time the humour of the situation struck me. My elderly clerk, I felt, regarded me with displeasure: evidently he thought that a man of law displayed carelessness in getting mixed up in such a matter. As a set-off against that, however, I realised that I had seriously jeopardised Douglas Fairbanks in the office boy's estimation.

But the point I had to consider was my own future action. It was all very well for Hugh Drummond and a crowd of his irresponsible friends to go about committing breaches of the peace if they chose to: it was a very different matter for me. And Inspector MacIver had definitely told him that such activities were to cease. Yet, dash it all . . .

I took a pull at myself and lit another pipe. Undoubtedly it was folly on my part to continue. The police had it in hand: almost certainly I should be getting myself into trouble. Yes, I'd be firm: I'd point out exactly to Drummond and the others how matters stood: my reputation as a lawyer and the impossibility of my countenancing such irregularities. Besides, this brief . . .

And at that stage of my deliberations I heard a loud and well-known voice in the office outside.

'Is Mr Stockton in? I can't help it if he is busy. I've just killed my grandmother and I want his advice.'

I went to the door and opened it. Drummond stood there beaming cheerfully at my outraged clerk, and as soon as he saw me he waved his hand.

'Bolted the badger,' he cried. 'My boy, I must have words with you. Yonder stout-hearted lad says you're busy.'

'A brief,' I said a little doubtfully, 'which I ought to get on with. However, come in.'

'Blow your old brief,' he answered. 'Give the poor girl custody of the children and be done with it.'

He sat down and put his legs on the desk, whilst I, with a glance at my clerk's face of scandalised horror, hurriedly shut the door.

'Look here, Stockton,' said Drummond, lowering his voice. 'I thought I'd rout you out here, because it was a bit too long to say over the telephone. And since you're really the principal in this affair, you ought to know at once. To start at the end of the matter, I haven't the faintest doubt in my own mind now that my suspicions about Number 12 are correct.'

He lit a cigarette and I felt my determination weakening. At any rate I wasn't committed to anything by hearing what he had to say.

'As you know,' he continued, 'I went up to see my long-lost aunt – Miss Simpson. I put on a slouch hat, and made one or two slight alterations in my appearance. The first thing I did was to call at one or two of the local food shops, and at the greengrocer's who supplied the house. I discovered her name was Amelia. Apparently she sometimes paid by cheque – in fact, they'd had one only last week.

'Well, that was a bit of a jolt to start off with: however, I thought I'd have a shot at it since I'd got so far. So off I strolled to Number 12. Two of the most obvious policemen I've ever seen in my life are watching Number 10, but they paid no attention to me as I went past.

'I rang the bell, and for some time nothing happened. And then a curtain in the room next the front door moved slightly. I was being inspected, so I rang again to show there was no ill-feeling. An unpleasant-looking female opened the door about four inches, and regarded me balefully.

' "Good-morning," I remarked, getting my foot wedged in that four inches. "I've come to see Aunt Amelia."

' "Who are you?" she said suspiciously.

' "Aunt Amelia's nephew," I answered. "It's ten years now since my father – that's her brother Harry – died, and his last words to me were, 'Wallie, my boy, if ever you go back to England, you look up my sister Amelia.' "

'You see, Stockton, I'd already decided that if it was a genuine show I'd get out of it by pretending that it must be another Miss Simpson.

' "Miss Amelia's ill," said the woman angrily.

' "Too bad," I said. "I reckon that seeing me will be just the thing to cheer her up."

' "She's not seeing anyone, I tell you," she went on.

' "She'll see little Wallie," I said. "Why, according to my father, she was clean gone on me when I was a child. Used to give me my bath, and doses of dill water. Fair potty about me was Aunt Amelia. Besides I've got a little memento for her that my father gave me to hand over to her."

'As a matter of fact I'd bought a small pearl necklace on the way up.

' "I tell you she can't see you," snapped the woman. "She's ill. You come back next week and she may be better."

'Well, there was nothing for it: I leaned against the door and the door opened. And I tell you, Stockton, I got the shock of my life. Standing at the foot of the stairs was a man with the most staggering face I've ever thought of. Tufts of hair sprouted from it like whin bushes on a seaside links: he was the King Emperor of Beavers. But it wasn't that that stopped me in my tracks, it was the look of diabolical fury in his eyes. He came towards me – and he was a heavyweight all right – with a pair of great black hairy fists clenched at his sides. And what he resembled most was a dressed-up gorilla.

' "What the devil do you want?" he snarled at me from the range of about a foot.

' "Aunt Amelia," I said, staring him in the eyes. "And I reckon you're not the lady in question."

'I saw the veins beginning to swell in his neck, and the part of his face not covered with vegetation turned a rich magenta.

' "You infernal puppy," he shouted. "Didn't you hear that Miss Simpson was ill?"

' "The fact is hardly to be wondered at with you about the house," I retorted, getting ready, I don't mind telling you, Stockton, for the father and mother of scraps.

'But he didn't hit me: he made a desperate effort and controlled himself.

' "I am Miss Simpson's doctor," he said, "and I will tell her of your visit. If you leave your address I will see that you are communicated with as soon as she is fit to receive visitors."

'Now that told one beyond dispute that there was something wrong. If he really had been the old lady's doctor, if she really was ill upstairs, my intentionally insulting remark could only have been received as vulgar and gratuitous impertinence. So I thought I'd try another.

' "If this is a sample of your bedside manner," I said, "she won't be fit to receive visitors for several years."

'And once again I thought he was going to hit me, but he didn't.

' "If you come back tomorrow morning at this hour," he remarked, "I think your aunt may be fit to receive you. At the moment I fear I must forbid it."

'Well, I did some pretty rapid thinking. In the first place I knew the man was lying: he probably wasn't a doctor at all. No man with a face like that could be a doctor: all his patients would have died of shock. In the second place I'd had a fleeting glimpse out of the corner of my eye of a couple of men upstairs who were examining me through a mirror hanging on the wall – a mirror obviously placed for that very purpose with regard to visitors.

'And another thing stuck out a yard: throughout the whole of our conversation he had kept between me and the stairs. Of course it might have been accidental: on the other hand, it might not. The way it struck me, however, was that he was afraid, seeing that I was obviously a breezy customer, that I might make a dash for it. And I damned nearly did, Stockton – damned nearly.

'However, not quite. I'd seen two men upstairs and there might be more: moreover, the bird I was talking to – if he was as strong as he looked – would have been an ugly customer by himself. And even if I'd got to the top and been able to explore the rooms, it wouldn't have done much good. I couldn't have tackled the show single-handed.

'So I pulled myself together, and did my best to appear convinced.

' "Well, I'm real sorry Aunt Amelia's so sick," I said. "And I'll come round tomorrow as you say, Doctor. Just give her my love, will you, and on my way back I'll call in and tell 'em to send along some grapes."

'His mouth cracked in what I presume was a genial smile. "That is very good of you," he answered. "I feel sure Miss Simpson will appreciate your kind attention."

'And with that I hopped it, sent up some grapes, and that's that.'

He lit a cigarette and stared at me with a smile.

'But didn't you tell the police?' I cried excitedly.

'Tell 'em what?' he answered.

'Why, that there's foul play going on there,' I almost shouted.

'Steady, old man,' he said quietly. 'Your lad outside will die of a rush of blood to the head if he hears you.'

'No, but look here, Drummond,' I said, lowering my voice, 'you may have hit on the key of the whole affair.'

'I think it's more than probable that I have,' he answered calmly. 'But that seems to me to be quite an unnecessary reason to go trotting off to the police.'

'But I say, old man,' I began feebly, mindful of my previous resolutions. And then the darned fellow grinned at me in that lazy way of his, and I laughed.

'What do you propose to do?' I said at length.

'Anticipate the visit to Aunt Amelia by some nine or ten hours, and go there tonight. Are you on?'

'Confound you,' I said, 'of course I am.'

'Good fellow,' he cried. 'I knew you'd do it.'

He took his feet off the desk and leaned towards me.

'Stockton,' he said quietly, 'we're hot on the track. I know we are. Whether or not we shall find that unfortunate old lady upstairs I haven't a notion. True she signed a cheque quite recently, but there's such a thing in this world as forgery. And murder. What induced them to select that particular house and her I know not. But one thing I do know. Tonight is going to be a pretty stiff show. Be round in Brook Street at eight o'clock.'

Chapter 5

In which we pay the aunt an informal visit

I was there to the minute. For a while after Drummond had gone, I told myself that I would have nothing more to do with the business, but it was a feeble struggle. The excitement of the thing had got hold of me, and poor old Stevens – my clerk – had never seemed so intolerably prosy and long-winded.

'Splendid,' said Drummond as I walked in. 'That completes us. Stockton, this is Ted Jerningham, a lad of repulsive morals but distinctly quick on the uptake.'

He brought our numbers up to six, and when I look back now and think of the odds against which, in all ignorance, we were pitting ourselves I could almost laugh. And yet I know one thing. Even had Drummond realised what those odds were, it would not have made an iota of difference to him. With him it was always a question of the more the merrier.

'We will now run over the plan of operations,' he went on, when I had removed two dogs from a chair and sat down. 'I've told these birds what I told you this afternoon, Stockton, so it only remains to discuss tonight. In the first place we've had a stroke of luck which is a good omen. The street running parallel to Ashworth Gardens is called Jersey Street. And the back of Number 13 Jersey Street looks on to the back of 12 Ashworth Gardens. Moreover, the female who owns Number 13 Jersey Street lets rooms, and I have taken those rooms. In fact, I've taken the whole bally house for a week – rent paid in advance – for a party of divinity students who have come up to this maelstrom of vice to see the Mint and Madame Tussaud's and generally be inconceivably naughty.

'Separating the backs of the houses are two brown patches of mud with a low wall in the middle which a child of four could climb with ease. And since there is no moon tonight, there oughtn't to be much difficulty in getting over that wall unseen – should the necessity arise.

'And since the spectacle of four of you dashing down the stairs and out of the old girl's back door might rouse unworthy suspicions in her breast, I have stipulated that we must have the use of a ground floor sitting-room at the back of the house. She doesn't usually let it, but I assured her that the wild distractions of Jersey Street would seriously interfere with our meditations.'

'Four?' interrupted Jerningham. 'Why four?'

'I'm coming to that,' said Drummond. 'I want someone with me in Number 12. And since the sport will probably be there, I think it's only fair to let Stockton have it, as this is really his show.'

A chorus of assent greeted his remark, and for the life of me I couldn't help laughing. I had formed a mental picture of Drummond's pal of the afternoon with the whin bushes sprouting from his face, and I could see him being my portion for the evening. But the whole tone of the meeting was one of the most serious gravity: it might have been a discussion before a shoot when the principal guest was being given the best position. So I suppressed the laugh and accepted with becoming gratitude.

'Right,' said Drummond. 'Then that's settled. Now to the next point.'

He picked up from his desk a cowl-shaped black mask, and regarded it reminiscently.

'Lucky I kept a few of these: do you remember 'em, you fellows? Stockton wouldn't, of course.'

He turned to me.

'Years ago we had an amusing little show rounding up Communists and other unwashed people of that type. We called ourselves the Black Gang, and it was a great sport while it lasted.'

'Good Heavens!' I said, staring at him. 'I dimly remember reading something about it in the papers. I thought the whole thing was a hoax.'

They all laughed.

'That's when we chloroformed your pal MacIver and left him to cool on his own doorstep. Happy days, laddie: happy days. However, taking everything into account, the going at the moment might be worse. And it struck me that these things might come in handy tonight. If we wear our old black gauntlets, and these masks well tucked in round the collar, it will afford us some protection if they start any monkey tricks with that filthy juice of theirs. At any rate there is no harm in having them with us in case of accidents: they don't take up much room and we can easily slip them into our pockets. So it all boils down to this. Stockton and I will deposit you four in Jersey Street, where you will take up a firm position in the back sitting-room. Bearing in mind that you are destined for the Church, and the penchant of landladies for keyholes, you will refrain from your usual conversation. Under no circumstances is Toby to tell any of his stories, nor is Ruff's Guide to be placed in a prominent position on the table when she brings you in your warm milk at ten. Rather should there be an attitude of devotion: possibly a notebook or two in which you are entering up your impressions of the Wallace Collection – '

A struggling mass of men at length grew quiescent in a corner, with Drummond underneath.

'It takes five of us to do it,' panted Darrell to me. 'And last time the chandelier in the room below fell on Denny's head.'

'That being quite clear,' pursued Drummond from his place on the floor, 'we will pass on. Should you hear shouts as of men in pain from the house opposite; or should you, on glancing through the crack of the blind, see me signalling you will abandon your attitude of devotion and leg it like hell over the wall. Because we may want you damned quick. Wear your masks: Ted to be "in charge", and I leave it to you as to what to do once you arrive in Number 12.'

'And if we neither hear nor see anything?' asked Jerningham. 'How long are we to give you?'

They had resumed their normal positions, and Drummond thoughtfully lit a cigarette.

'I think, old boy,' he remarked, 'that half-an-hour should be long enough. In fact,' he added, rubbing his hands together in anticipation, 'I'm not at all certain it won't be twenty-nine minutes too long. Let's get on with it.'

We pocketed our masks and gauntlets and went downstairs. There was no turning back for me now: I was definitely committed to go through with it. But I have no hesitation in admitting that our taxi-drive seemed to me the shortest on record. We had two cars and Drummond stopped them several hundred yards short of our objective. Then leading the way with me we walked in pairs to Jersey Street.

Number 13 was typical of all the houses in the neighbourhood – an ordinary drab London lodging-house of the cheaper type. But the landlady, when she finally emerged, was affability itself. The strong odour of gin that emerged with her showed that the rent had not been wasted, and led us to hope that sleep would shortly overcome her. At the moment it had merely made her thoroughly garrulous, and only the timely advent of an acute attack of hiccoughs stemmed the reminiscences of her girlhood's happy days. But at last she went, and instantly Drummond was at the window peering through a chink in the blind.

'Lower the light, someone, and then come and reconnoitre. There's the house facing you: there's the wall. No lights: I wonder if the birds have flown. No, by Jove! I saw a gleam then from that upstairs window. There it is again.'

Sure enough a light was showing in one of the rooms, and I thought I saw a shadow move across the blind. Downstairs all was dark, and after a few moments' inspection Drummond stepped back into the room.

'Come on, Stockton,' he said. 'We'll go round by the front door. Don't forget I'm an Australian, and you're a pal of mine whom I met unexpectedly in London today. And if I pretend to be a little blotto – pugnaciously so – back me up. Ted – half-an-hour; but keep your eye glued on the house in case we want you sooner.'

'Right ho! old man. Good luck.'

We walked through the hall cautiously, but the door leading to our landlady's quarters was shut. And in three minutes we were striding down Ashworth Gardens. A figure detached itself from the shadows outside the scene of last night's adventure, and glanced at us suspiciously. But Drummond was talking loudly as we passed him of his voyage home, and the man made no effort to detain us.

'One of MacIver's men,' he muttered to me as we turned into Number 12. 'Now, old man, we're for it. If I can I'm going to walk straight in.'

But the front door was bolted, and perforce we had to ring. Once more he started talking in the aggressive way of a man who has had something to drink, and I noticed that the detective was listening.

'I tell you my Aunt Amelia will just be charmed to see you, boy. Any pal of mine is a pal of hers. And I haven't come twelve thousand miles to be told that my father's sister isn't well enough to see Wallie. No, sir – I have not.'

The door suddenly opened and a man stood there looking at us angrily.

'What do you want?' he snapped. 'Are you aware, sir, that there is an invalid in this house?'

'I'm perfectly well aware of it,' said Drummond loudly. 'But what I'm not aware of – and what I'm going to be aware of – is how that invalid, who is my aunt, is being treated. I'm not satisfied with the attention she is receiving' – out of the corner of my eyes I saw the detective drawing closer – 'not at all satisfied. And I and my friend here are not going to leave this house until Aunt Amelia tells me that she's being well looked after. There's such a thing as the police, sir, I tell you . . . '

'What on earth are you talking about?' said the man savagely, and I noticed he was looking over our shoulders at the detective, who was now listening openly. 'However, you'd better come inside, and I'll consult the doctor in charge.'

He closed the door behind us, and Drummond gave me an imperceptible wink. Then he went on again aggressively: 'How many doctors are there in this house? I saw a man this afternoon with a face like a hearth-rug – is he here? And do you all live here? I tell you, I'm not satisfied. And until I see my Aunt Amelia . . . '

A door opened and the man whom Drummond had described to me in my office came out into the hall.

'How dare you return here, sir?' he shouted. 'You're the insolent, interfering young swine who was here this afternoon, and if you aren't out of this house in two seconds I'll throw you out.'

'You'd better try,' answered Drummond calmly. 'And why don't you let your face out as a grouse moor? I'm your patient's nephew and I want to know what all you ugly-looking swabs are doing in this house?'

With a quick movement he stepped past the man into the room beyond, and I followed him. Three other men were there sitting round a table, and they rose as we entered. Two packed suitcases lay on the floor waiting to be strapped up, and on the table were five glasses and a half-empty bottle of whisky.

'Five of you,' continued Drummond. 'I suppose you'll be telling me next that my aunt runs a boys' school. Now then, face fungus, what the hell does it mean?'

'It means that if you continue to make such a row your aunt's death will probably be at your door,' answered the other.

'I noticed that you were whispering yourself in the hall,' said Drummond. 'You're a liar, and a damned bad liar at that. You aren't doctors, any of you.'

The men were glancing at one another uneasily, and suddenly the whole beauty of the situation flashed on me. They knew as well as we did that there was a Scotland Yard man outside the house, and the fact was completely tying their hands. Whatever they may have suspected concerning Drummond's alleged relationship, we were, as he had himself remarked, in the sound strategical position of being the lesser liars of the two. Our opponents could do nothing, and the fact that they were utterly nonplussed showed on their faces. And I waited with interest to see what their next move would be. What answer were they going to make to Drummond's definite charge that they were none of them doctors?

They were saved the trouble, and in, to me at any rate, the most unexpected way. In my own mind I was firmly convinced by this time that there was no Miss Simpson, and that even if there was she was no sickly invalid ailing in bed. And yet at that moment there came a weak querulous woman's voice from the landing upstairs.

'Doctor Helias! Doctor Helias, I've been woken up again just as I was going off to sleep. Who is it making that terrible noise downstairs?'

The black-haired man swung round on Drummond.

'Now are you satisfied?' he said savagely. 'And if my patient has a relapse and dies, by Heavens! I'll make it hot for you at the inquest.'

He strode to the door, and we heard him speaking from the foot of the stairs.

'It's the nephew I told you about, Miss Simpson, who called to see you this afternoon. He seems to be afraid you aren't being properly looked after. Now I must insist on your going back to bed at once.'

He went up the stairs, and I glanced at Drummond. His eyes had narrowed as if he too was puzzled, and he told me afterwards that a woman's voice was the last thing he expected to hear. But his voice was perfectly casual as he addressed the room at large.

'Dangerous place London must be. Do you – er – doctors always carry revolvers with you?'

'What the devil are you talking about?' snapped the man who had let us in.

Without a word Drummond pointed to one of the suitcases, where the butt of an automatic Colt was plainly visible.

'I suppose when your surgical skill fails you merely shoot your patients,' went on Drummond affably. 'Very kind and merciful of you, I call it.'

'Look here,' said the other grimly, 'we've had about enough of you, young man. You've forced your way into this house: you've insulted us repeatedly, and I'm thinking it's about time you went.'

'Are you?' said Drummond. 'Then you'd better think all over again.'

'Do you mean to say that now you've heard what your aunt has said to Doctor Helias, you still are not satisfied?'

'Never been less so in my life,' he replied genially. 'This house reeks of crooks like a seaside boarding-house of cabbage at lunch-time. And since we've wakened poor Auntie up between us, I'm going to see her before I go.'

'By all manner of means,' said Doctor Helias quietly. He was standing in the door, and his voice was genial. 'Your aunt would like to see you and your friend. But you must not alarm her or excite her in any way. And incidentally, when your interview is over, I shall await an apology for your grossly insulting remarks.'

He stood aside and I followed Drummond into the passage.

'The first door on the left,' murmured the doctor. 'You will find your aunt in bed.'

'For God's sake, keep your eyes skinned, Stockton,' whispered Drummond as we went up the stairs. 'There is some trap here, or I'll eat my hat.'

But there was no sign of anything out of the ordinary as we entered the room. A shaded lamp was beside the bed, and the invalid was in shadow. But even in the dim light one could see that she was a frail old lady, with the ravages of pain and disease on her face.

'My nephew,' she said in a gentle voice. 'My brother Harry's boy! Well, well – how time does pass. Come here, nephew, and let me see what you've grown into.'

With an emaciated hand she held up the electric lamp so that its rays fell on Drummond. And the next instant the lamp had crashed to the floor. I bent quickly and picked it up, and as I did so the light for a moment shone on her face. And I could have sworn that the look in her eyes during that brief instant was one of sheer, stark terror . . . So vivid was the impression that I stared at her in amazement. True, the look was gone at once, but I *knew* I had not been mistaken. The sight of Drummond's face had terrified the woman in the bed. Why? Crooked or not crooked, it seemed unaccountable.

'I'm so weak,' she said apologetically. 'Thank you, sir – thank you.' She was speaking to me, as if she realised that I was staring at her curiously. 'It was quite a shock to me to see my nephew grown into such a big man. I should never have known him, but that's only natural. You must come again when I'm better, nephew, and tell me all about your poor dear father.'

'I certainly will, Aunt Amelia,' said Drummond thoughtfully.

'Harry was always a little wild, but such a dear lovable boy,' went on the old lady. 'You're not very like him, nephew.'

'So I've been told,' murmured Drummond, and I saw his mouth beginning to twitch. 'I'm much more like my mother. She'd just about have been the same age as you, Auntie, if she'd been alive. You remember her, don't you – Jenny Douglas that was, from Cirencester?'

'It's a long time ago, nephew.'

'But my father always said that you two were such friends?'

For a moment the woman hesitated, and from downstairs came the sound of an electric bell rung twice.

'Why, of course,' she said, 'I remember her well.'

'Then you must have a darned good memory, Auntie,' said Drummond grimly. 'It was conceivable that you might have had a brother called Harry who went to Australia, though I did happen to invent him. But by no possible stretch of imagination could you have had a sister-in-law called Jenny Douglas from Cirencester, for I've just invented her too.'

'Look out, Drummond,' I shouted, and he swung round. Stealing across the floor towards us was the black-haired Doctor Helias with a piece of gas-piping in his hand, and behind him were three of the others.

And then like a flash it happened. It was the men we were watching; we'd forgotten the invalid in bed. I had a momentary glimpse of bed-clothes being hurled off, and a woman fully dressed springing at Drummond from behind. In her hand was something that gleamed and suddenly the overpowering smell of ammonia filled the room. But it was Drummond who got it straight in the face. In an instant he was helpless from the fumes, lurching and staggering about blindly, and even as I sprang forward to help him I heard the woman's voice –

'Put him out, you fool, and do it quick.'

And the black-haired man put him out easily and scientifically. He was obviously an expert, for he didn't appear to use much force. He just applied his piece of piping to the base of Drummond's skull, and it was over. He went down as if he was pole-axed and lay still.

'My God!' I muttered, 'you've killed him.'

And that was my last remark for some hours. The three men who applied themselves to me were also experts in their line, and I estimated it at half-a-minute before I was gagged and trussed up, and thrown into a corner. But I was still able to hear and see.

'You damned fool,' said the woman to the man called Doctor Helias. 'Why didn't you tell me it was him?'

She was pointing at Drummond, and he stared at her in surprise.

'What do you mean?' he answered. 'I don't know who he is any more than you do. Isn't he the nephew?'

She gave a short laugh.

'No more than I am. And you can take it from me I know him only too well. He suspected, of course: that's why I rang.'

She flung the water pistol which had contained the ammonia on to a table, and going to the cupboard took out a hat.

'Put 'em both below, and for Heaven's sake get a move on. Is he dead?' Once again she pointed at Drummond, and the big man shook his head. 'If I'd known he was coming I'd have been out of this house four hours ago. Mon Dieu! Helias – you have bungled this show.'

'But I don't understand,' stammered the other.

'Throw 'em below,' she stormed at him. 'With your brain you wouldn't understand anything.'

'Take 'em downstairs,' snarled Helias to the others. He was glaring sullenly at the woman, but he was evidently too afraid of her to resent her insults. 'Hurry, curse you.'

And at that moment the fifth man dashed into the room.

'Men coming across the wall at the back,' he said breathlessly. 'Listen: they're getting in now.'

From below came the sound of a window opening, and muttered voices.

'Police?' whispered the woman tensely.

'Don't know: couldn't see.'

'How many?'

'Three or four.'

'Out with the light. Whoever they are – do 'em down one by one as they come into the room. But no noise.'

And then ensued the most agonising minute I have ever spent in my life. Helpless, unable to do anything to warn them, I lay in the corner. It was Ted Jerningham, of course, and the others – I knew that, and they were walking straight into a trap. The room was dark: the door was open, and outlined against the light from the passage I could see the huge form of Doctor Helias crouching in readiness. Dimly I saw the others waiting behind him, and then the woman moved forward and joined them. But before she did so I had seen her stand on a chair and remove the bulb from the central electric light.

The steps on the stairs came nearer, and now the shadow of the two leaders fell on the wall. There was a click as the switch was turned on – and then, when nothing happened, they both sprang into the room. For a moment they were clearly visible against the light, and even I gave a momentary start at their appearance. In the excitement of the past few minutes I had forgotten about the black masks, and they looked like two monstrous spectres from another world. The woman gave a little scream, and then the other two came through the door.

Thud! Thud! Swiftly Helias' arm rose and fell with that deadly piece of piping in his hand, and the two last arrivals pitched forward on the floor without a sound.

'At him, Peter.' It was Jerningham's voice muffled by the covering over his face, and I saw the two of them spring at the doctor.

But it was hopeless from the start. Two to five: the odds were impossible, especially when one of the five was a man with the strength of three. It may have been half-a-minute, but it certainly wasn't more before the bunch of struggling men straightened up, and two more unconscious and black-cowled figures lay motionless.

With a feeling of sick despair I watched the woman put back the bulb and flood the room with light. What an ignominious conclusion to the night's work. And what was going to happen now? We were utterly powerless, and our captors were not overburdened with scruples.

Already Helias had taken off the masks, and was staring at the unconscious men on the floor with a savage scowl.

'What's all this damned tomfoolery?' he muttered. 'Who are these young fools, and why are they rigged up like that?'

And then something made me look at the woman. She was leaning against the table, and in her eyes was something of that same look of terror that I had seen before.

'Kill them. Kill them all: now – at once.'

Her voice was harsh and metallic, and the others stared at her in amazement.

'Impossible, Madame,' said Helias sharply. 'It would be an act of inconceivable folly.'

She turned on him furiously.

'It would be an act of inconceivable folly not to. I tell you they are more dangerous far, these men, than all the police of England.'

'Well, they are not particularly dangerous at the moment,' said the other soothingly. 'Think, Madame: reflect for a moment. We have difficulties already, severe enough in all conscience. And are we to add to those difficulties by murdering six young fools in cold blood?'

'I tell you, I know these men,' she stormed, 'And that one' – she pointed to Drummond – 'is the devil himself.'

'I can't help it, Madame,' returned the doctor firmly. 'I have no scruples as you know, but I am not a fool. And to kill these men or any of them would be the act of a fool. We have to get away at once: there is no possible method of disposing of the bodies. Sooner or later they are bound to be discovered in this house, and a hue and cry will start, which is the last thing we want. Pitch them into the cellar below and leave them there, by all means. But no unnecessary killing.'

For a moment I thought she was going to continue the argument: then with a little shrug of her shoulders she turned away.

'Perhaps you're right,' she remarked. 'But, mon Dieu! I would sooner have seen all Scotland Yard here than that man.'

'Who is he?' said Helias curiously.

'His name is Drummond,' answered the woman. 'Get on with it, and put them below.'

And from the darkness of the cellar where they pitched us I listened to the sounds of their departure. How long it was before the last footstep ceased above I don't know, but at length the house was silent. The stertorous breathing of the unconscious men around me was the only sound, and after a while I fell into an uneasy doze.

I woke with a start. Outside a wagon was rumbling past, but it was not that which had disturbed me: it was something nearer at hand.

'Peter! Algy!'

It was Ted Jerningham's voice, and I gave two strangled grunts by way of reply.

'Who's there?'

Once more I grunted, and after a pause I heard him say, 'I'm going to strike a match.'

The feeble light flickered up and he gave a gasp of astonishment. Sprawling over the floor just where they had been thrown lay the others, and as the match spluttered and went out Algy Longworth groaned and turned over.

'Holy smoke!' came his voice plaintively. 'Have I been passed over by a motor bus or have I not?'

It was Drummond himself who had taken it worst. The cowls had broken the force of the blows in the case of the others, whilst I had come off almost scot free. But Drummond, poor devil, was in a really bad way. His face was burnt and scalded by the ammonia, and the slightest movement of his head hurt him intolerably. In fact it was a distinctly pessimistic party that assembled upstairs at half-past six in the morning. We none of us asked anything better than to go home to bed – none of us, that is, save the most damaged one. Drummond wouldn't hear of it.

'We're here now,' he said doggedly, 'and even if my neck is broken, which is more than likely by the feel of it, we're going to see if we can find any clue to put us on the track of that bunch. For if it takes me five years, I'll get even with that damned gorse bush.'

'I think the lady disliked us more than he did,' I remarked. 'Especially you. She went so far as to suggest killing the lot of us.'

'The devil she did,' grunted Drummond.

'She knew you. She knew your name. I think she knew all of you fellows by sight, but she certainly knew Drummond.'

'The devil she did,' he grunted again, and stared at me thoughtfully out of the one eye that still functioned. 'You're certain of that?'

'Absolutely. You remember she dropped the lamp in her agitation when she first saw your face. I saw the look in her eyes as I picked it up: it was terror.'

And now they were all staring at me.

'Why,' I went on, 'she alluded to you as the devil himself.'

'Good Lord!' said Drummond softly, 'it can't be . . . Surely, it can't be . . . '

'There's no reason why it shouldn't,' said Jerningham. 'It's big enough for them to handle.'

'We're talking of things unknown to you, Stockton,' explained Drummond. 'But in view of what you saw and heard, it may be that a very extraordinary thing has taken place . . . Confound my neck! . . . '

He rubbed it gently, and then went on again.

'As far as I know there is only one woman in the world who is likely to regard me as the devil himself, and be kind enough to suggest killing me. And if it is her . . . Great Scott! boys – what stupendous luck.'

'Marvellous!' I ejaculated. 'She must love you to distraction.'

But he was beyond my mild sarcasm.

'If it's her – then Helias . . . oh my sainted aunt! Don't tell me that old gorse bush was Carl Peterson.'

'I don't know anything about Carl Peterson,' I said. 'But it was old gorse bush, as you call him, who flatly refused to kill you and us as well. Moreover, he didn't know you.'

'Then gorse bush wasn't Carl. But the woman . . . Ye Gods! I wonder. Just think of the humour of it, if it really was Irma. Not knowing it was me, she thought I possibly was the genuine article – the real Australian nephew. She made herself up into a passable imitation of Aunt Amelia, kept the light away from her face, and trusted to luck. Then she recognised me, and saw at once that I was as big a fraud as she was, and that the game was up.'

'I don't know your pals, as I said before,' I put in, 'but that's exactly what did happen.'

'If I'm right, Stockton, you'll know 'em soon enough. And further-more, if I'm right my debt of gratitude to you for putting me in the way of this little show will be increased a thousandfold.'

His voice was almost solemn, and I began to laugh.

'Mrs Drummond's debt of gratitude will wilt a bit when she sees your face,' I said. 'Don't you think you'd better get home and have it attended to?'

'Not on your life,' he remarked. 'My face can wait: examining this house can't. So let us, with due care as befits five blinking cripples, see what we can find. Then a bottle of Elliman's embrocation and bed.'

'Damnation!' roared a furious voice from the door. 'What the devil are you doing here again?'

'MacIver's little twitter,' said Drummond. 'I would know that fairy voice anywhere.'

He rose cautiously and turned round.

'Mac, we have all taken it in the neck, not only metaphorically but literally. Any sudden movement produces on the spot an immediate desire for death. So be gentle with us, and kind and forbearing. Otherwise you will see the heartrending spectacle of six men burst-ing into tears.'

'What on earth has happened to your face?' demanded the de-tective.

'Aunt Amelia sprayed it with ammonia from point-blank range,' said Drummond. 'A darned unfriendly act I think you'll agree. And then a nasty man covered with black hair took advantage of my helpless condition to sandbag me. Mac, my lad, in the course of a long and blameless career I've never been so badly stung as I was last night.'

'What do you mean by Aunt Amelia?' growled the other.

'The official occupant of this house, Mac.'

'Miss Simpson. Where is she?'

'I know not. But somehow I feel that the sweet woman I interviewed in bed last night was not Miss Amelia.' Then with a sudden change of tone – 'Have you found the communication between the two houses?'

'How do you know there is one?'

'Because I'm not a damned fool,' said Drummond. 'It was principally to find it that I came here.'

He glanced at the detective's suspicious face and began to laugh.

'Lord! man: it's obvious. That fellow the other night was dead, so how did the body disappear? It couldn't have gone out by the window in broad daylight, and unless your men are liars or asleep it couldn't have gone out by the door. So there must have been some way of communication.'

'I found it by accident a few minutes ago from the next house,' said MacIver. 'It opens into the bedroom above.'

'I thought it must,' said Drummond. 'And I wouldn't be surprised if dear Aunt Amelia's bed was up against the opening.'

'There was a woman here, was there?'

'There was.' For a moment or two Drummond hesitated. 'Look here, MacIver,' he said slowly, 'we've had one or two amusing little episodes together in the past, and I'm going to tell you something. After they knocked me out last night, Mr Stockton, who was only bound and gagged, heard one or two very strange things. This woman who was here masquerading as Miss Simpson evidently knew me. She further evinced a strong wish to have me killed then and there. Now who can she have been? MacIver, I believe – and mark you, there is nothing inherently improbable in it – I believe that once more we are up against Peterson. He wasn't here; but the girl – his mistress – was. I may be wrong, but here and now I'd take an even pony on it.'

'Perhaps you're right,' acknowledged the other. 'We've heard nothing of the gentleman for two or three years.'

'And if we are, MacIver,' continued Drummond gravely, 'this whole show, serious as it is at the moment, becomes ten times more so.'

'If only I could begin to understand it,' said the detective angrily. 'The whole thing seems so utterly disconnected and pointless.'

'And it will probably remain so until we reach the end, if we ever do reach the end,' said Drummond. 'One thing is pretty clear: this house was evidently the headquarters of that part of the gang which lived in London.'

'I'm getting into touch with Miss Simpson at once,' said MacIver. Drummond nodded.

'She may or may not be perfectly innocent.'

'And two of my fellows are searching this house now,' went on the detective. 'But damn it, Captain Drummond, I'm defeated – absolutely defeated. If whoever is running this show wanted to get away with Gaunt's secret – why all this? Why didn't they go at once? Why waste time?'

He swung round as one of his men came into the room. He was carrying in his arms a metal tank of about four gallons capacity, which was evidently intended to be strapped to a man's back. To the bottom was attached a length of rubber tubing, at the end of which was fixed a long brass nozzle with a little tap attached. On one side of the tank a small pump was placed, and we crowded round to examine it as he placed it on the table.

'Two or three more of them in the cellar below, sir,' said the man.

'Pretty clear what they are intended for,' said Drummond gravely. 'It's nothing more nor less than a glorified fruit sprayer. And with that liquid of theirs inside . . . '

'There is this too that I found,' went on the man. 'I'd like you to come yourself, sir, and see. There was blood on the walls and on the floor – and this – '

From his pocket he took a handkerchief, and it was stained an ominous red. It was quite dry, and MacIver opened it out and laid it beside the tank.

'Hullo!' he muttered, 'what's this mean?'

Scrawled over part of the material were some red letters. The ink used had been blood: the pen might have been the writer's finger.

$$3 P 7 A N T$$

A smear completed it: evidently he'd collapsed or been interrupted.

'I found it in a crack in the wall, sir,' said the man. 'It had been pushed in hard.'

MacIver's eyes had narrowed, and without a word he pointed to the corner of the handkerchief. Clearly visible through the blood were two small black letters. And the letters were R.G.

Chapter 6

In Which We get a Message from Robin Gaunt

Robin Gaunt! It was his blood-soaked handkerchief that lay in front of us. He too had been thrown into the same cellar where we had spent the night. And where was he now?

I picked up the handkerchief, and a sudden wave of bitterness swept over me. I pictured him, wounded – perhaps dying – scrawling his message down there in the darkness, whilst outside men said vile things about him and papers fanned the flame.

'Your super-vivisector, Inspector,' I remarked. 'It's damned well not fair.'

'But just at present it's necessary, Mr Stockton,' he answered. 'By Jove! If only that handkerchief could speak! 3 P 7 A N T . . . What on earth was he trying to write?'

He turned and went briskly out of the room.

'Show me exactly where you found it,' he said to his subordinate.

We all trooped after him, and by the light of an electric torch we explored the cellar. The officer pointed to the crack in the wall where he had found the handkerchief, and to the dark stains below and on the floor.

'I'm thinking,' said Drummond gravely, 'that the poor devil was in a pretty bad way.'

Torch in hand, MacIver was carrying out his examination systematically. An opening in one wall led to a smaller cellar, and it was there that three other spraying cisterns, similar to the one upstairs, were standing. They differed in small details, but their method of action was the same. In each design there was a pump for producing the necessary pressure, and a small stopcock at the end of the spraying pipe which allowed the jet of liquid to be turned on or off at will.

The main points of difference lay in the arrangement of the straps for securing the reservoirs to the shoulders, and the shape and size of the reservoirs themselves. Also the rubber piping varied considerably in length in the different models.

'Take these upstairs,' said MacIver to the officer, 'and put them alongside the other one.'

Once more he resumed his examination, only to stop abruptly at the startled exclamation that came from his man. He was standing at the top of the cellar steps tugging at the door.

'It's locked, sir,' he cried. 'I can't make it budge.'

'Locked!' shouted MacIver. 'Who the devil locked it?'

'It's been locked from the other side, and the key is not in the keyhole.'

MacIver darted up the steps, and switched his torch on to the door.

'Who came in last?' he demanded.

'I did,' said Toby Sinclair. 'And I left the door wide open. I can swear to it.'

In a frenzy of rage the Inspector hurled himself against it, but the result was nil.

'Not in a hundred years, Mac,' said Drummond quietly. 'No man can open a door as stout as that at the top of a flight of stairs. You can't get any weight at the top of a flight of stairs. You can't get any weight behind your shoulder.'

'But, damn it, man,' cried the other, 'we haven't been down here ten minutes. Whoever locked it must be in the house now.'

'Bexton is there too, sir,' said the officer. 'He was exploring upstairs.'

'Bexton!' bellowed the Inspector, through the keyhole. 'Bexton! Lord! is the man deaf? Bexton – you fool: come here.'

But there was no answer.

'Steady, MacIver,' said Drummond, 'you'll have a rush of blood to the head in a minute. He's possibly up at the top of the house, and we'll get him as soon as he comes down. No good getting needlessly excited.'

'But who has locked this door?' demanded the other. 'That's what I want to know.'

'Precisely, old lad,' agreed Drummond soothingly. 'That's what we all want to know. But before we have any chance of knowing, we've got to get to the other side. And since we can't blow the blamed thing down there's no good going on shouting. Let's have a look at it: I'm a bit of an authority on doors.'

He went up the stairs, and after a brief examination he gave a short laugh.

'My dear Mac – short of a crowbar and a pick-axe we're stung. And since we've none of us got either in our waistcoat pockets there's no good worrying. The bolt goes actually into the brickwork: you can see it here. And the lock on the door has been put on from the other side, so a screwdriver is no good.'

He came down again laughing.

'I can't help it – I like these people. They are birds after my own heart. They've bitten us properly, and got away with their expensive set of uppers and lowers complete intact. I shall sit down and ruminate on life, and if anyone feels strong enough to massage my neck, I shall raise no objections. Lord! What a game we'll have when I meet gorse bush again.'

He lit a cigarette, and deposited himself on the floor with his back against the wall.

'Mac, if that's our only means of illumination you'd better switch it off. We may want it later – you never know.'

'Bexton must be down in a moment or two,' said the Inspector angrily.

'True,' answered Drummond. 'Unless he's down already.'

'What do you mean?'

'I mean that there are some people knocking about in this district who are no slouches in the sandbag game. And I should think it was quite on the cards that the worthy Bexton has already discovered the fact.'

'If that's the case we're here for hours.'

'Just so,' agreed Drummond. 'Which is all the more reason for preserving that air of masterly tranquillity which is the hallmark of the Anglo-Saxon in times of stress. Men have won prizes ranging from bulls-eyes to grand pianos for sentiments less profound than that. We are stung, Mac: we are locked in, and we shall remain locked in until some kindly soul comes along to let us out. And since the betting is that the key has been dropped down the nearest drain-pipe, and that our Mr Bexton has taken it good and hard where I took it last night, I think we can resign ourselves to a fairly lengthy period of rest and meditation . . . Damn my neck!'

'Supposing we all shouted together,' I suggested, after we had sat in silence for several minutes. 'Someone must hear surely.'

We let out a series of deafening bellows, and at length our efforts were rewarded. A heavy blow was struck on the other side of the door, and an infuriated voice shouted through the keyhole.

'Stop that filthy row. You'll have plenty of time to sing glees when you're breaking stones on Dartmoor. If you do it any more now I'll turn a hose on you.'

We heard the sound of retreating footsteps, and MacIver gave a gasp of amazement.

'Am I mad?' he spluttered. 'Am I completely insane? That was Fosdick's voice – the man on duty next door.'

And then every semblance of self-control left him, and he raved like a lunatic.

'I'll sack the fellow! I'll have him out of the force in disgrace. He's been drinking: the fool's drunk. Fosdick – come here, damn you, Fosdick!'

He went on shouting and beating on the door with one of the tin reservoirs, till once again came a blow from the other side followed by Fosdick's voice.

'Look 'ere, you bally twitterer: I'm getting fair fed up with you. There's a crowd outside the door now asking when the performing hyenas are going to be let out. Now listen to me. Every time I 'ears a sound from any of you, you stops down there another 'alf-hour without your breakfasts. The van when she comes can easily wait, and I ain't in no hurry.'

'Listen, you fool,' roared MacIver. 'You're drunk; you've gone mad. I order you to open the door. It's me – Inspector MacIver.'

'Inspector my aunt,' came the impassive reply. 'Now don't you forget what I said. The van oughtn't to be long now.'

'The van,' said MacIver weakly, as the footsteps outside departed. 'What van? In the name of Heaven, what is the man talking about?'

'Oh Lord, Mac,' cried Drummond helplessly, 'don't make me laugh any more. As it is I've got the most infernal stitch.'

'I fail to see the slightest humour in the situation,' said MacIver acidly. 'The only possible conclusion I can come to is that Fosdick has suddenly lost his reason. And in the meantime I, sir, am locked in here at a time when every moment is of value. In the whole of my career such a thing has never happened.'

'There's no doubt about it, old man,' agreed Drummond in a shaking voice, 'that up-to-date our investigations have not yet met with that measure of success which they justly deserve. We can muster between us five stiff necks, one parboiled face, and an excessively uncomfortable floor to sit on.'

'The whole thing is entirely owing to your unwarrantable inter-ference,' snapped the detective.

'My dear Mac,' said Drummond, 'if, as you think, your Fosdick has gone off the deep end you really can't blame me. Personally I don't think he has.'

'Then perhaps you'd be good enough to explain what he's doing this for,' said MacIver sarcastically. 'A little game, I suppose.'

'Nothing of the sort,' answered Drummond. 'My dear man, cease going off like a steam-engine and think for a moment. The whole thing is perfectly obvious. The van is to take us to prison.'

'What on earth . . .' stuttered MacIver.

'No more and no less,' went on Drummond calmly. 'Yonder stout-hearted warrior is under the firm impression that he has a band of bloodthirsty criminals safe under lock and key. He sees promotion in store for him: dazzling heights – '

'Inspector MacIver! Inspector MacIver. Are you there?'

It was Fosdick's agitated voice from the other side of the door.

'I should rather think I am,' said MacIver grimly. 'Open this door, you perishing fool . . .'

'I will, sir, at once. It's all a mistake.'

'Damn your mistakes! Open the door.'

'But I haven't got the key. Wait a bit, sir, I'll get a screwdriver.'

'Hurry,' roared MacIver. 'May Heaven help that man when I get at him.'

'I wouldn't be too hasty if I was you, Mac,' said Drummond quietly. 'Better men than he have been caught napping.'

It was a quarter of an hour before the door was opened and we trooped upstairs, followed by the trembling Fosdick.

'Now, you fool,' said MacIver, 'will you kindly explain this little jest of yours?'

'Well, sir,' answered the man. 'I'm very sorry I'm sure – but I acted for the best.'

'Get on with it,' stormed the Inspector.

'I was on duty outside Number 10, when I saw you come out of the house . . .'

'You saw me come out of this house? Why, you blithering idiot, I've been locked up in the cellar all the morning.'

'I know that now, sir, but at the time I thought it was you. You passed me, sir – at least the man did – and you said to me, "We've got the whole bunch". It was your voice, sir; your voice exactly. "They're in the cellar in Number 12 – locked in, and I've got the key. I'm going round to the Yard now, and I'll send a van up for 'em. They can't get out, but they may make a row." And then you went on – or rather the other man did – "By Jove! this is a big thing. I've got one of 'em in there that the police of Europe and America are looking for. I had him once before – and do you know how he got away? Why, by imitating my voice over the telephone so well that my man thought it was me!" '

'How perfectly gorgeous,' said Drummond ecstatically.

'And then you see, sir, when I heard your voice in that there cellar I thought it was this other bloke imitating you.'

'I see.' Despite himself MacIver's lips were beginning to twitch. 'And what finally made you decide that I wasn't imitating my own voice?'

'Well, sir, I waited and waited and the van never came – and then I went upstairs. They've knocked out Bexton, sir; I found him unconscious on the floor in the room above. So then I rang up the Yard: nothing had been heard of you. And then I knew I'd been hoaxed. But I swear, sir, that bloke would have deceived Mrs MacIver herself.'

'He certainly put it across you all right,' said MacIver grimly. 'I'd give quite a lot to meet the gentleman.'

'I wonder what the inducement was,' said Drummond. 'No man was going to run such an infernal risk for fun.'

'By Jove!' cried MacIver, 'that cistern is gone. It's lucky I had the handkerchief in my pocket.'

'He was carrying a tin with straps on it when he spoke to me,' said Fosdick, and MacIver groaned.

'Literally through our fingers,' he said. 'However, we've got the other three cisterns. Though I'd much sooner have had the man.'

'Anyway that's a point cleared up,' remarked Drummond cheerfully. 'We know why he came here – '

'We don't,' snapped MacIver. 'The fact that he took the blamed thing is no proof that he came for that purpose.'

'True, my dear old policeman,' said Drummond. 'But it is, as they say, a possible hypothesis. And, as I remarked before, he didn't come here for fun, so in default of further information we may as well assume that he came for the cistern. In the hurry of their departure last night they forgot these little fellows down in the cellar, so someone came back to get them. He found one nicely put out for him on the table, and a personally conducted Cook's party in the cellar inspecting the others. So in addition to taking his property he locked the cellar door. Easy, laddie: easy.'

'Yes; isn't it?' said MacIver sarcastically. 'And perhaps you'll explain what he'd have done if we hadn't been in the cellar.'

'My dear Mac, what's the good of making it harder? I haven't the faintest idea what he'd have done. Stood on his head and given an imitation of a flower-pot. He *did* find us in the cellar, and that's all we're concerned with. He took a chance – and a darned sporting chance – and it came off. You're up against something pretty warm, old lad. I don't pretend to be a blinking genius, but if my reconstruction of what has happened up to date is right, I take off my hat to 'em for their nerve.'

'What is your reconstruction?' said MacIver quietly, and I noticed his look of keen attention. Whatever may have been his official opinion of our interference, it was pretty clear that unofficially he was under no delusions with regard to Drummond. In fact, as he told me many months later, there was no-one he knew who had such an uncanny faculty for hitting the nail on the head.

'Well, this is how I see it,' said Drummond. 'Their first jolt was the fact that Gaunt managed to get through on the telephone to Stockton. Had that not happened they'd have been in clover. It might have been a couple of days before the Australian was found dead in that house. The old woman is deaf, and probably the first thing she'd have known about it was when she showed a prospective lodger a dead man in her best bedroom and a dead dog across the passage. But Gaunt getting through on the 'phone started it all, and everything that has happened since is due, I'm certain, to their endeavour to fit in their previous arrangements with this unexpected development. They brought Gaunt here: that's obvious. Why did they bring Gaunt here particularly? Well – why not? They had to take him somewhere. They couldn't leave him lying about in Piccadilly Circus.

'They brought him here, and then for reasons best known to themselves they decided to murder Stockton. Well, we all know what happened then, and it was another unexpected development for them. The last thing they wanted was your arrival on the scene. And you wouldn't have arrived, Mac – unless you'd followed Stockton. That's what huffed 'em: old Stockton giving his celebrated rendering of a mechanic at the Three Cows. Naturally you suspected him at once: it was without exception the most appalling exhibition of futility I've ever seen.'

'Thanks so much,' I murmured.

'That's all right, old bean,' he said affably. 'I expect you're the hell of a lawyer. However, to continue. You arrived, Mac, with most of the police force of London next door – and you can bet your life the people in here began to sweat some. Why didn't they go away at once, you say? I don't know. Instead of their quiet little backwater the whole glare of Scotland Yard was beating on the next-door house. And what was even worse for them was, that not only had they failed to murder Stockton before you came, but one of their own men was dead. Inquests: newspaper publicity. All the more reason for them to go at once. Why didn't they? What was their reason for stopping on when they must have realised their danger? I don't know; but it must have been a pretty strong one. Anyway they chanced it – and, by Jove! they've pulled it off. That's why I take off my hat to 'em. They were ready to go last night, and they went last night, and the last twenty-four hours they spent in this house must have been pretty nerve-racking.'

'May I ask what you are doing in my house?' came in an infuriated female voice from the door.

A tall, thin, acidulated woman was standing there regarding us balefully, and MacIver swung round.

'May I ask your name, madam?'

'Simpson is my name, sir. And who may you be?'

'I'm Inspector MacIver from Scotland Yard, and I must ask you to answer a few questions.'

'Scotland Yard!' cried Miss Simpson shrilly. 'Then you're the very man I want to see. I have been the victim of a monstrous outrage.'

'Indeed,' remarked MacIver. 'I'm sorry about that. What has happened?'

'Three weeks ago a female person called to see me in this house. She wished to know if I would let it furnished for a month. I refused, and told her that I considered her request very surprising, as I had not told any house-agent that I wanted to let. I further asked her why she had picked on my house particularly. She told me that she had just returned from Australia, and was spending a month in London. She further said that before going to Australia she had lived with her father in this house, and that since he was now dead she wished to spend the month under the old roof for remembrance' sake. However, I told her it was impossible, and she went away. Two days afterwards occurred the outrage. Outrage, sir – abominable outrage, and if there is any justice in England the miscreants should be brought to justice. I was kidnapped, sir – abducted by a man.'

'Is that so?' said MacIver gravely. 'How did it happen, Miss Simpson?'

'In a way, sir, that reflects the gravest discredit on the police. I was returning from the Tube station late in the evening – I had been to a theatre – and as I reached the end of the road a taxi drew up beside me. At the time the road was deserted: as usual no adequate protection by the police was available against gangs of footpads and robbers. From the taxi stepped a man, and before I had time to scream, or even guess their fell intention, I was bundled inside by him and the driver – a handkerchief was bound round my mouth and another round my eyes and we were off.'

'You have no idea, of course, who the men were?' said MacIver.

'Absolutely none,' she remarked indignantly. 'Do you imagine, sir, that I should number among my acquaintances men capable of such a dastardly act?'

'No-one who knew you would ever be likely to abduct you,' agreed Drummond soothingly. 'Er – that is, in such a violent manner, don't you know. What I was going to say' – he went on hurriedly – 'is what about the servants? Didn't they start running round in circles when you failed to roll up?'

'That is one of the very points I wish to clear up,' she said. 'Jane – I keep only one maid – had received a telegram only that morning stating that her mother in Derbyshire was ill. So she had gone off, and there was therefore no-one in the house. But that was three weeks ago. Surely she must have returned in that time, and if so, when she failed to find me here, why did she say nothing to the police?'

'An interesting point, Miss Simpson,' said MacIver, 'and one that we will endeavour to clear up. However, let's get on now with what happened to you. I hope these men used no unnecessary violence.'

'Beyond forcibly placing me in the car,' she conceded, 'they did not. And I may say that during the whole period of my imprisonment I was treated very well.'

'Where did they take you?' demanded MacIver eagerly.

'I don't know: I can't tell you. It was a house in the country: that's all I can say. It stood by itself among some trees – but I was blindfolded the whole way there. And when they brought me back this morning I was again blindfolded. They brought me as far as the Euston Road: whipped off the handkerchief from my eyes, pushed me out on the pavement, and then drove off at a furious rate. Now, sir, what is the meaning of this inconceivable treatment?'

'If you'll come upstairs, Miss Simpson, you'll understand,' answered MacIver. 'The meaning of the whole thing is that you happened to be living in this house. And it wasn't you they wanted: it was the house. Had you agreed to let it to that woman who called to see you, none of this would have happened.'

'But why did they want the house?'

'That's why.'

MacIver stepped into the room where Drummond and I had interviewed the bogus invalid, and pointed to an opening in the wall.

'You knew nothing of that, of course?'

'Good Heavens, no.' She was staring at it in amazement. 'What's through on the other side?'

'The next house: Number 10.'

'And that's been there all these years. Why! I might have been murdered in my bed.'

'It's a carefully done job, MacIver,' said Drummond, and the detective nodded.

The wall of each room consisted of imitation oak boarding, and the opening was made by means of two sliding panels. The brickwork between them had been removed to form the passage, and the opening thus made crowned with a small iron girder. The two panels moved in grooves which had been recently oiled, and when closed it was impossible to notice anything unusual.

'A bolt-hole, Miss Simpson,' explained MacIver. 'A bolt-hole, the existence of which was known to the gang that abducted you. And a bolt-hole is very useful at times. That's why they wanted your house.'

'Do you mean to say that a gang of criminals has been living in my house?'

'That is just what I do mean,' said MacIver. 'But I don't think they are likely to return. If they intended to do so they wouldn't have let you go. They lived here and they used the empty house next door. The thing I'm going to find out now is the name of your predecessor. Can you tell me the agent through whom you got this house?'

'Paul and Paul in the Euston Road.'

'Good. That saves time.'

'And now I shall be glad, sir, if you would kindly go,' she said. 'I presume I may expect to hear in time that the police have a clue to account for my treatment. It would be too much to expect any more. But at the moment my house resembles a bear garden, and I would like to start putting it into some semblance of order – '

And then occurred a most embarrassing incident. It was so sudden and unexpected that it took us all by surprise, and it was over before anyone could intervene.

Drummond became light-headed. We heard a dreadful noise from an adjoining room: he had burst into song. And the next moment – to our horror – he came dancing through the door, and made a beeline for Miss Simpson.

'My Tootles,' he cried jovially. 'My little flower of the east.'

Miss Simpson screamed: Ted Jerningham gave an uncontrollable guffaw.

'Dance with me, my poppet,' chanted Drummond, seizing her firmly round the waist.

Protesting shrilly, the unfortunate woman was dragged round the room, until between us we managed to get hold of Drummond. The poor chap was completely delirious, but fortunately for all concerned not violent. We explained to the almost hysterical woman that he had had a very bad blow on the head the preceding night, from one of the same gang of scoundrels who had abducted her – and that, of course, he was suffering from concussion. And then we got him downstairs and into a taxi. He was still humming gently to himself, and playing with a piece of string, but he offered no resistance.

'Extraordinary thing his going like that so suddenly,' I said to Darrell, who was sitting opposite.

'Frightfully so,' agreed Drummond. 'Just hold that end of the string.'

'Good Lord!' I stammered. 'Do you mean to say . . . '

'Hold the end,' he said tersely. 'I want to see something.'

With his fingers outstretched he measured the distance between my end and the point he was holding, whilst I still stared at him in amazement.

'I thought as much,' he said quietly. 'Tell the taxi to stop at the first small hotel we come to. You go back, Peter, and bring MacIver along there at once. Tell him it's urgent, but don't let that woman hear you.'

'Who – Miss Simpson?'

'She's no more Miss Simpson than I am.'

The car pulled up, and we all got out.

'Go back in it, Peter: make any old excuse. Say I left my hat – but get MacIver quickly. Now Stockton – let's have a drink, and think things over.'

'I say, Drummond,' I said weakly, 'do you mind explaining?'

'All in good time, old man – all in good time. I refuse to utter until I've got outside a pint.'

'What on earth is the meaning of this?' said MacIver a few minutes later as he came into the room where we were sitting.

'Only that you apologised for my attack of insanity so convincingly that I think the lady believed it. I sincerely hope so at any rate. While you were holding forth, Mac, about the secret opening I went on a little voyage of exploration. And I found a cupboard full of female clothes. They were all marked A. Simpson, and right in front three or four skirts were hanging. I don't know why exactly, but it suddenly occurred to me that the skirts seemed singularly short for the lady. So I took one down and measured it round the waistband. And allowing the span of my hand to be about ten inches I found that Miss Simpson's waist was approximately forty inches. Now that woman is thinner than my wife – but I thought I'd make sure. I took her measurement with this bit of string when I was dancing with her, and if that is Amelia Simpson she's shrunk thirteen inches round the tum-tum. Laddie – it can't be done. But, by Jove, it was a fine piece of acting. She's got every man jack of us out of the house as easily as peeling a banana.'

MacIver rose and walked towards the door.

'What are you going to do?' said Drummond.

'Have that woman identified by somebody,' answered the detective. 'Ask her some more questions, and if the answers aren't satisfactory, clap her under lock and key at once.'

'Far be it from me to call you an ass, dear boy, but that doesn't alter the fact that you are one. At least you will be if you arrest that woman.

'Well, what do you suggest? We'll have got one of them anyway.'

'And if you give her sufficient rope, we may get a lot more. Think, man, just think. What did that fellow who impersonated you run his head into a noose for this morning? Not for the pleasure of locking us into a cellar. What has that woman turned up for so quickly, pretending she is the rightful owner? If those garments belong to Miss Simpson – as they surely must do – the two women must be utterly unlike. True, they would assume – and rightly so as it happened – that none of us had ever seen Miss Simpson. All the same, if they hadn't been in a tearing hurry they would surely have sent someone a little less dissimilar. They *are* in a tearing hurry – but what for? There's something in that house that they want – and want quickly: something they forgot last night when they all flitted. And when that woman finds it – or if she finds it – she'll go with it – to them. And we shall follow her. Do you get me, Steve? We can watch the house in front from Number 10. We can watch it from behind from Number 13 Jersey Street, in which six respectable divinity students have taken rooms for the week. We are the noble half-dozen. Let's get rid of the young army that we've had tracking around up to date, and be nice and matey. But we insist, Mac, on seeing the fun. Out of the kindness of my heart I've put you wise as to what I discovered, and you've got to play the game. You and I and Stockton will go to Number 10; Ted, Peter and Algy to Jersey Street. Toby, you trot back and tell Phyllis what is happening – and tell her to put up some sandwiches and half a dozen Mumm '13. Then come back to Jersey Street, and tell the old geyser there that it's a new form of Apenta Water. And send all the rest of your birds home to bed, Mac.'

'It's strictly irregular,' he said, grinning, 'but, dash it all, Captain Drummond, I'll do it.'

'Good fellow!' cried Drummond. 'Let's get on with it.'

'I'll keep a couple of my men below in 10 to follow her if she goes out,' went on MacIver.

'Excellent,' said Drummond. 'And Toby can tell my chauffeur to bring the Hispano up to Jersey Street. For I'll guarantee to keep in sight of anything in England in her.'

And so, once more, we returned to Number 10. No-one had entered the house next door during our absence – and no-one had come out, at any rate at the front. Of that Fosdick, who was still on duty, was sure. And then there commenced a weary vigil. Personally, I make no bones about it, I dozed through most of the afternoon. We were in the room which communicated with Number 12, but though we pulled back the panel on our side, no sound came from the next house. If she was carrying out her intention of restoring some semblance of order she was being very quiet about it.

Just once we heard the noise of drawers being pulled out, and what sounded like their contents being scattered on the floor; and later on footsteps in the next room caused MacIver noiselessly to slide back the panel into its closed position. But that was all we heard, while the sleepy afternoon drowsed on and the shadows outside grew longer and longer.

I think MacIver was nodding himself when there suddenly came the sound that banished all sleep. It was a scream – a woman's scream – curiously muffled, and it came from Number 12. It was not repeated, and as we dashed open the other panel the house was as silent as before. We rushed through into the passage and thence into the bedrooms: everywhere the same scene of disorder. Clothes thrown here and there: bedclothes ripped off and scattered on the floor.

'She's restored a semblance of order all right,' said MacIver grimly, as we went downstairs.

And then he paused: a light was filtering out from the half-opened cellar door.

'The end of the search, Mac,' said Drummond. 'Go easy.'

At first as we stood on the top of the stairs we could see nothing. A solitary candle guttered on the floor, throwing monstrous shadows in all directions: and then we smelt it once again – that strange bitter sweet smell – the smell of death.

MacIver's torch flashed out – to circle round and finally concentrate on something that lay just beyond the buttress wall still stained with Robin Gaunt's blood. And there was no need to ask what that something was: the poison had claimed another victim.

She lay there – the woman who had taken Miss Simpson's place – and the scream we had heard had been with her last breath. The same dreadful distortion: the same staring look of horror in the eyes – everything was just the same as in the other cases. But somehow with a woman it seemed more horrible.

'My God! but it's diabolical stuff,' cried MacIver fiercely as he bent over the woman. 'How did it happen, I wonder?'

'It's on her hand,' said Drummond. 'She's cut it on something. Look, man – there's a bit of a broken bottle beside her with liquid in it. For Heaven's sake be careful: the whole place is saturated with the stuff.'

'We'll leave the body exactly as it is,' said the Inspector, 'until Sir John Dallas comes. I'll go and telephone him now. Captain Drummond, will you and Mr Stockton mount guard until I return?'

'Certainly,' answered Drummond, and we followed the Inspector up the stairs.

'So that's what they came to look for,' I remarked as the front door closed behind MacIver.

'Seems like it,' agreed Drummond, lighting a cigarette thoughtfully. 'And yet it's all a little difficult. A fellow may quite easily forget his handkerchief when he goes out, but he ain't likely to forget his trousers. What I mean, Stockton, is this. The whole thing has been done from the very beginning with the sole idea of getting the secret of that poison. Are we really to believe that after committing half-a-dozen murders and a few trifles of that description they went off and left it behind? Is that the only sample in existence? And if it isn't, what is the good of worrying about it? Why send back for it at all? It looked as if it was quite a small bottle.

'There's another point,' he went on after a moment. 'Where was that bottle this morning? I'll stake my dying oath that it wasn't lying about in the cellar. It was either hidden there somewhere, or that woman took it down there with her. Great Scott! but it's a baffling show!'

We sat on in silence, each busy with his own thoughts. For me it was Robin who filled them: what had happened to him – where was he now? Or had they killed him? Or had he died as the result of his injuries? It was a possible solution to many things.

'If Gaunt is dead, Drummond,' I said after a while, 'it may account for a lot. It's not likely that he had very large supplies of the stuff in his rooms. And we know anyway that a lot of it was wasted when you shot our friend the night before last. So it seems to me to be perfectly feasible that that bottle down below contained the only existing sample – which in the event of Gaunt's death would become invaluable to them. They may not know his secret: in which case their only hope would be to get a sample.'

'But why leave it behind?' he objected. 'Why go to the worry and trouble of hiding it in the cellar? For I think it must have been hidden there: the idea that that unfortunate woman should have carried it down there seems pointless. It's just my trouser example, Stockton.'

'Each one may have thought the other had it,' I said, but he shook his head.

'You may be right,' he remarked, 'but I don't believe it was that that she was looking for. And my opinion is that the clue to the whole thing is contained in that blood-stained handkerchief, if only one could interpret it. 3 P 7 A N T. It's directions for something: it can't be meaningless.'

Once again we relapsed into silence, until the sound of a taxi outside announced the arrival of someone. It was MacIver, and with him was Sir John carrying some guinea-pigs in cases.

'Sorry to have been so long,' said the Inspector, 'but I couldn't get Sir John on the telephone, so I had to go and find him. Anything happened?'

'Not a thing,' said Drummond.

MacIver had brought another torch and several candles, and by their light Sir John proceeded to make his examination. He had donned a pair of stout india-rubber gloves, but even with their protection he handled things very gingerly.

First he poured what was left of the poison into another bottle, and corked it with a rubber cork. Then he took a sample of the dead woman's blood, which he placed in a test-tube and carefully stoppered. And finally, after a minute examination of the cut in her hand and the terrible staring eyes, he rose to his feet.

'We can now carry her upstairs,' he remarked. 'There is nothing more to be seen here. But on your life don't touch her hand.'

We lifted her up, and MacIver gave a sudden exclamation. Underneath where the body had been lying, and so unseen by us until then, was a hole in the floor. It had been made by removing a brick, and the brick itself, which had been concealed by the body, lay beside the hole. At the bottom of the hole was some broken glass and the neck of the bottle from the base of which Sir John had removed the poison. So it was obviously the place where the poison had been hidden. But who had hidden it – and why?

'Obviously not a member of the gang,' said MacIver, 'or she would have known where it was and not wasted time ransacking the house.'

'Therefore obviously Gaunt himself,' said Drummond. 'Great Scott! man,' he added, 'It's the third brick from the wall. Give me your stick, Sir John. The handkerchief, MacIver – 3 and 7.'

He tapped on the seventh brick, and sure enough it sounded hollow. With growing excitement we crowded round as he endeavoured to prise it up.

'Careful – careful,' cried Sir John anxiously. 'If there's another bottle we don't want any risk of another casualty. Let me: I've got gloves on.'

And sure enough when the seventh brick was removed, a similar hole was disclosed, at the bottom of which lay a small cardboard pillbox. With the utmost care he lifted it out, and removed the lid. It was filled with a white paste, which looked like boracic ointment.

'Hullo!' he said after he'd sniffed it. 'What fresh development have we here?'

And suddenly Drummond gave a shout of comprehension.

'I've got it. It's the message on the handkerchief. 3 P. The third brick – poison: 7 A N T – the seventh brick, antidote. That's the antidote, Sir John, you've got in your hand; and that's what they've been after. That woman came down to look for it – and she only found the poison. Gaunt must have hidden them both while he was a prisoner down here, and then left that last despairing message of his . . .'

'We'll try at once,' said Sir John quietly.

He handed me the pill-box, and took the poison himself.

'Take a little of the ointment on the end of the match,' he said, 'and I'll take a little of the poison. You hold one of the guinea-pigs, MacIver. Now the instant I have applied the poison, you follow it up with your stuff in the same place, Stockton.'

But the experiment was valueless. With a sudden convulsive shudder the little animal died, and when we tried with another the result was the same.

'Not a very effective antidote,' said Sir John sarcastically.

'Nevertheless,' said Drummond doggedly, 'I'll bet you it is the antidote. Couldn't you analyse it, Sir John?'

'Of course I can analyse it,' snapped the other. 'And I shall analyse it.'

He slipped the box into his bag, followed by the bottle of poison.

'I wonder if I might make a suggestion,' said Drummond. 'I don't want to seem unduly alarmist, but I think we've seen enough to realise that we are up against a pretty tough proposition. Now do you think it's wise to have all one's eggs in one basket, or rather all that stuff in one box. It might get lost: it might be stolen. Wouldn't it be safer, Sir John, to give, say, half of it to MacIver – until at any rate your analysis is concluded? I see you have a spare box in your bag.'

We were going up the steps as he spoke and he was in front. And suddenly he paused for a moment or two and stared at the door. Then he went on into the hall, and I noticed that he glanced round him in all directions.

'A most sensible suggestion,' said Sir John, 'with which I fully agree.'

'Then come in here, Sir John,' said Drummond. He led the way into one of the downstairs rooms, and shut the door. And it seemed to me that he was looking unduly grave. He watched the transfer of half the paste to another box, and he waited till MacIver had it in his pocket. Then –

'Please send for Fosdick, MacIver.'

A little surprised, the Inspector stepped to the window and beckoned to the man outside.

'Anyone been in this house, Fosdick, during the last half-hour?' said Drummond.

'Only Sir John's assistant, sir.'

'I haven't got an assistant,' snapped Sir John.

'My sainted aunt, Mac,' said Drummond grimly, 'we're up against the real thing this time. He's gone I suppose?'

'Yes, sir,' said Fosdick. 'About ten minutes ago.'

'Then I tell you, Sir John, your life is not safe. It's the stuff in the pill-box that they are after. Perhaps we've put it on wrong: perhaps you've got to eat it. Anyway that man who posed as your assistant knows you've got it. I beg of you to put yourself under police protection day and night. If possible, at any rate, until you have analysed the stuff don't go near your house. Remain inside Scotland Yard itself.'

But what Sir John lacked in inches he made up for in pugnacity.

'If you imagine, sir,' he snapped, 'that I am going to be kept out of my own laboratory by a gang of dirty poisoners you're wrong. If the Inspector here considers it necessary he can send one of his men to stand outside the house. But not one jot will I deviate from my ordinary method of life for twenty would-be murderers. Incidentally' – he added curiously – 'how did you know a man had been here?'

'The position of the cellar door,' answered Drummond. 'It's a heavy door, and I know how I left it when we went in. It was a foot farther open when we came out – and there is no draught.'

Sir John nodded approvingly.

'Quick: I like quickness. What in the name of fortune have you done to your face?'

'Don't you worry about my face, Sir John,' said Drummond quietly: 'you concentrate on your own life.'

'And you mind your own business, young man,' snapped the other angrily. 'My life is my own affair.'

'It isn't,' answered Drummond. 'It's the nation's – until you've analysed that stuff. After that, I agree with you: no-one is likely to care two hoots.'

Sir John turned purple.

'You insolent young puppy,' he stuttered.

'Cut it out, you silly little man,' said Drummond wearily. 'But don't forget – I've warned you. Come on, Stockton: we'll rope in the others and push off. Mount Street finds me, Mac; but I must have some sleep. Let me know how things go, like a good fellow.'

'Sorry I lost my temper with the little bloke,' he said to me, as he spun the Hispano into the Euston Road. 'But really, old man, this stunt of yours is enough to try anybody's nerves.'

The other four were behind, all more or less asleep, and I was nodding myself. In fact I hardly noticed where he was taking us until we pulled up in front of his house.

'My warrior can take you round and drop you,' he said, yawning prodigiously. 'And tomorrow we might resume the good work.'

Personally I didn't even get as far as bed. I just fell asleep in an easy-chair in my room, until I woke with a start to find the lights lit and someone shaking me by the shoulder.

It was Drummond, and the look on his face made me sit up quickly.

'They got him,' he said, 'as I knew they would. Sir John was stabbed through the heart in his laboratory an hour ago.'

'My God!' I muttered. 'How do you know?'

'MacIver has just rung up. Stockton – as I've said before – we're up against the real thing this time.'

Chapter 7

In which I appear to become irrelevant

I think it was the method of the murder of Sir John that brought home to me most forcibly the nerve of the gang that confronted us. And though there will be many people who remember the affair, yet, for the benefit of those people who do not, I will set forth what happened as detailed in the papers of the following day. The cutting is before me as I write.

Another astounding and cold-blooded murder occurred between the hours of nine and ten last night. Sir John Dallas, the well-known scientist and authority on toxicology, was stabbed through the heart in his own laboratory.

The following are the facts of the case. Sir John, as our readers will remember, gave evidence as recently as the day before yesterday in the sensational Robin Gaunt affair. He described in court the action of the new and deadly poison by means of which the dog, the policeman and the Australian – David Ganton – had been killed. He also stated that he was endeavouring to analyse the drug, and there can be little doubt that he was engaged on that very work when he met his end.

It appears that yesterday afternoon a further and, at present, secret development occurred which caused Sir John to feel hopeful of success. He returned to his house in Eaton Square in time for dinner, which he had served in his study – the usual course of procedure when he was busy. At eight-thirty he rang the bell and Elizabeth Perkins, the parlour-maid, came and removed the tray. He was apparently completely absorbed in his research at that time, since he failed to answer her twice-repeated questions as to what time he would like his milk. On the desk in front of him was a bottle containing a colourless liquid which looked like water, and a small cardboard box.

These facts are interesting in view of what is to follow, and may prove to have an important bearing on the case. At between nine o'clock and a quarter-past the front-door bell rang, and it was answered by Perkins. There was a man outside who stated that he had come to see Sir John on a very important matter. She told him that Sir John was busy, but when he told her that it was in connection with Sir John's work that he was there, she showed him along the passage to the laboratory. And then she heard the stranger say distinctly, "I've come from Scotland Yard, Sir John."

Now there can be but little doubt that this man was the murderer himself, since no-one from Scotland Yard visited Sir John at that hour. And as walking openly into a man's house, killing him, and walking out again requires a nerve possessed by few, the added touch of introducing himself as a member of the police is quite in keeping with the whole amazing case.

To return, however, to what happened. Perkins, having shown this man into the laboratory, returned to the servants' hall, where she remained till ten o'clock. At ten o'clock she had a standing order to take Sir John a glass of warm milk, if he had not rung for it sooner. She got the milk and took it along to the laboratory. She knocked and, receiving no answer, she entered the room. At first she thought he must have gone out, as the laboratory appeared to be empty, and then, suddenly, she saw a leg sticking out from behind the desk. She went quickly to the place to find, to her horror, that Sir John was lying on the floor with a dagger driven up to the hilt in his heart.

She saw at a glance that he was dead, and rushing out of the house she called in a policeman, who at once rang up Scotland Yard. Inspector MacIver, who, it will be recalled, is in charge of the Robin Gaunt mystery, at once hurried to the scene. And it was he who elucidated the fact that the bottle containing the colourless liquid, and the little cardboard box, had completely disappeared. It seems, therefore, impossible to doubt that at any rate one motive for the murder of this distinguished savant was the theft of these two things with their unknown contents. And further, since we know that Sir John was experimenting with this mysterious new poison, the connection between this dastardly crime and the Gaunt affair seems conclusive.

The matter is in the capable hands of Inspector MacIver, and it is to be hoped that before long the cold-blooded criminals concerned will be brought to justice. It is an intolerable and disquieting state of affairs that two such appalling crimes can be committed in London within three days of one another.

Which was a fair sample of what they all said. The *Daily Referee* offered a reward of a thousand pounds to the first person who discovered a clue which should lead to the arrest of the murderer or murderers. 'Retired Colonel' and 'Frankly disgusted' inflicted their opinions on a long-suffering public; and as day after day went past and nothing happened, Scotland Yard began to get it hot and strong in the Press.

Somehow or other MacIver managed to hush up the death of the woman at Number 12 Ashworth Gardens, but there was no getting away from the fact that the authorities were seriously perturbed. Their principal cause of anxiety lay, as I have shown, in a fact unknown to the public; and whereas the latter were chiefly concerned with bringing the murderers to book, Scotland Yard and the Secret Service's chief worry was as to what had happened to the secret. Had it been disposed of to a foreign Power? If so, to which?

The only ray of comfort during the weeks that followed lay in Drummond's happy idea of dividing the antidote – if it was an antidote – into two portions. For MacIver's specimen had been analysed, and its exact composition was known. The trouble lay in the fact that it was impossible to carry out further experiments, since we possessed none of the poison. For an antidote to be efficacious it is advisable to know how to use it, and since the most obvious way was not the correct one, we were not much further advanced. Still, the general opinion was that Drummond's theory was correct, and all the necessary steps were taken to allow of its immediate manufacture on a large scale, should occasion arise.

Gradually, as was only natural, public interest died down. Nothing further happened, and it seemed to all of us that the events of those few days were destined to have no sequel. Only Drummond, in fact, continued to do anything: the rest of us slipped back into the normal tenor of our ways. He still periodically disappeared for hours at a time – generally in a disguise of some sort. He was not communicative as to what he did during these absences, and after a time he, too, seemed to be losing interest. But the whole thing rankled in his mind: he made no secret of that.

'Put it how you like,' he said to me on one occasion, 'we got very much the worst of it, Stockton. They got away with everything they wanted, right under our noses. And positively the only thing we have to show for our trouble is the antidote.'

'A pretty considerable item,' I reminded him.

He grunted.

'Oh, for ten minutes with gorse bush alone,' he sighed. 'Or even five.'

'You may get it yet,' I said.

Off and on we saw a good deal of MacIver, in whose mind the affair rankled also. The comments in the Press concerning Scotland Yard had not pleased him, and I rather gathered that the comments of his immediate superiors had not pleased him either. It was particularly the murder of Sir John Dallas that infuriated him, and over which criticism was most bitter. The other affair contained an element of mystery; a suspicion, almost of the uncanny. There seemed to be some excuse for his failure in connection with Robin Gaunt. But there was no element of mystery over stabbing a man to death. It was just a plain straightforward murder. And yet it remained wrapped in as dense a fog as the other. It was perfectly true that Elizabeth Perkins stated that she would recognise the man again. But, as MacIver said, what was the use of that unless he could first be found? And as she was quite unable to describe him, beyond saying that he was of medium height, clean-shaven and dark, the prospect of finding him was remote. At a conservative estimate her description would have fitted some ten million men.

The case of the man called Doctor Helias held out a little more prospect of success. Drummond and I separately described that human monstrosity to MacIver, and within two days a description of him was circulated all over the world. But, as Major Jackson pointed out a little moodily, it wasn't likely to prove of much use. If our fears were justified: if the secret of the poison had been handed over to a foreign Power, it was clear that Doctor Helias was an agent of that Power. And if so they wouldn't give him away.

It certainly proved of no use: no word or trace of him was discovered. He seemed to have disappeared as completely as everyone else connected with the business.

Another thing MacIver did was to turn his attention to the genuine owner of Number 12. First he tracked the maid, and we found out that part, at any rate, of the story told us by the woman who had died was true. Someone had come round and asked Miss Simpson to let the house: she had talked it over later with the maid. And on a certain morning a wire had come stating that her mother was ill, and summoning the maid to her home in Devonshire. To her surprise she found her mother perfectly fit. The wire had been sent from the village by a woman; that was all they could tell her at the Post Office. And then next morning, when she was still puzzling over the affair, had come a letter in Miss Simpson's handwriting. It was brief and to the point, stating that she had decided after all to let her house, and was proposing to travel. And it enclosed a month's wages in lieu of notice. The maid had felt hurt at such a brusque dismissal, and was shortly going to another place.

'That's really all I got out of her,' said MacIver, 'except for a description of Miss Simpson. She is short and fat, as Captain Drummond surmised. Also, according to the maid, she has no near relatives and very few friends. She hardly went out at all, and no-one ever came to the house. Moreover, the description the maid gave me of the woman who came to ask to rent the house would fit the woman who impersonated Miss Simpson and was killed, which may be poetic justice, but it doesn't help us much.'

Inquiries as to Miss Simpson's predecessors helped as little. Messrs. Paul & Paul were the agents right enough; but all they could say, having consulted their books, was that the house had belonged to a Mr Startin, who, they believed, had gone abroad. And they knew absolutely nothing about him.

'A dead end everywhere,' said MacIver despondently. 'Never in the whole course of my career have I seen every trace so completely covered. They set the whole Press blazing from end to end in the country, and then they disappear as if they were wiped out.'

And then on the 20th of June occurred the next link in the chain. It was an isolated one, and it is safe to say that the few people who may have read the paragraph in the papers never connected it with the other issues.

A fisherman named Daniel Coblen made a gruesome discovery late yesterday afternoon. He was walking over the rocks near the Goodrington Sands at Paignton when he saw something floating in the sea. It proved to be the body of a woman in an advanced stage of decomposition. He at once informed the police. From marks on the unfortunate lady's garments it appears that her name was A. Simpson. Doctor Epping, who made an examination, stated that she must have been dead for considerably over a month.

As I say, the few people who may have read the paragraph would assuredly have traced no connection between it and Sir John Dallas being stabbed to death, but MacIver went down post haste to Paignton. It transpired at the inquest that death was due to drowning: no marks of violence could be found on the body. But the point of interest lay in how it had happened. How had she been drowned?

No local boatman knew anything about it: no ship had reported that any passenger of that name was missing. How then had Miss Simpson been drowned?

That it was a question of foul play seemed obvious – but beyond that one bald fact everything seemed blank. The gang had decided to get rid of her, and they had chosen drowning as the method. Why they had done so was a totally different matter.

It was well-nigh inconceivable that they would have taken the trouble to put her on board a boat merely to take her out to sea and drown her, when their record in London showed that they had no hesitation in using far more direct methods. It seemed to add but one more baffling feature to a case that contained no lack of them already.

And the sole result was that Drummond's interest which had seemed to be waning, revived once more. Sometimes I wonder if Drummond, with that strangely direct brain of his, didn't have a glimmering of the truth. Not the final actual truth – that would have been impossible at that stage of the proceedings; but a glimpse of the open ground through the trees. He said nothing then, and when I asked him the other day he only shrugged his shoulders. But I wonder . . . Day after day he disappeared by himself until his wife grew quite annoyed about it. As a matter of fact I, too, thought he was wasting his time. What he was doing, or where he went, he would never say. He just departed in the morning or after lunch, and often did not return till two or three in the morning. And since there seemed to be nothing particular to look for, and no particular place to look for it in, the whole thing struck me as somewhat pointless.

It was about that time that I began to see a good deal of Major Jackson. His club had been closed down for structural repairs, and the members had come to mine. So I saw Jackson two or three times a week at lunch. General Darton, too, was frequently there, and sometimes we shared the same table. On the whole I thought they were fairly optimistic: nothing had as yet been heard from any of our agents abroad which led them to suspect any particular Power of having acquired the secret.

'Somebody must have it presumably,' said the General. 'Crimes of that sort aren't perpetrated for fun. But the great point, Stockton, is this – we've got the antidote. It might be quite useful if we could discover how it worked,' he added sarcastically.

'Anyway those squirting machines must have a very small range, and there still are rifles left in the world amidst this mass of filthy chemicals.'

The worthy infantryman snorted, and Jackson kicked me gently under the table. He was off on his favourite topic, and he required no assistance from us. Only now as I look back on that conversation, which was only one of many similar ones, that big fundamental mistake of ours looms large. It was a natural mistake, particularly since the War Office had been concerned in the affair from the very beginning. Automatically their gaze was fixed on the foreign target; and it was tacitly assumed by us all that the direction was right. Until, that is, Drummond proved it wrong.

At the time, however, all of us who knew the inner history of the affair had our attention fixed abroad; and for the rest – the great general public – the Robin Gaunt mystery had become a back number. The Press had buried him in a final tirade of obloquy and turned its attention to other things – principally, as will be remembered, the Wilmot dirigible airship.

It was in July, I see after reference to my files, that the Wilmot airship publicity stunt was first started. Up to that date airships were regarded as essentially connected with the fighting services. And it was then that the big endeavour was made to popularise them commercially.

The first difficulty which the promoters of the scheme had to overcome was a distinct feeling of nervousness on the part of the public. Aeroplanes they were accustomed to: the magnificent Croydon to Paris service was by this time regarded as being as safe as the boat train. But airships were a different matter. Airships caught fire and burned: airships broke their backs and crashed: airships had all sorts of horrible accidents.

The second difficulty was financial nervousness in the City, doubtless induced largely by the physical nervousness of the public. Would a fleet of airships – six was the number suggested – pay? They were costly things to construct: a mooring mast worked out at about £25,000 – a shed at more than £100,000. Would it prove a commercial success?

And the promoters of the scheme, rightly realising that the first difficulty was the greater, took every step they could to reassure the public. Who can fail to remember that beautiful, graceful ship circling over London day after day: going long trips over the Midlands and down to the West Country: anchored to the revolving top of the lattice-work mooring mast?

And then came the celebrated trip on July 25th, when representatives from every important London paper were taken for a trial voyage, and entertained to a luncheon during the journey which the Ritz itself could not have beaten.

I have before me a copy of the *Morning Herald* of the 26th in which an account of the trip is given. And I cannot refrain from quoting a brief extract. Having described the journey, and paid a glowing tribute to the beauty and the comfort of the airship, the writer proceeds as follows:

Then came the culminating moment of this wonderful experience. Lunch was over, a meal which no restaurant *de luxe* could have bettered. The drone of the engines ceased, and, as we drifted gently down wind, the whole gorgeous panorama of English woodland scenery unfolded itself before our eyes. It was the psychological moment of the day: it was the fitting moment for Mr Wilmot to say a few words. He rose, and we tore our eyes away from the view to look at the man who had made that view possible. Tall, thick-set, and with greying hair and eyes gleaming with enthusiasm he stood at the end of the table.

"I am not going to say much," he remarked, in his deep steady voice – a voice which holds the faintest suspicion of American accent – "but I feel that this occasion may mark the beginning of a new epoch in British aviation. Today you have seen for yourselves something of the possibilities of the airship as opposed to the aeroplane: I want the public to see those possibilities too. The lunch which you have eaten has been prepared entirely on board: not one dish was brought into the kitchen ready-made. I mention that to show that the domestic arrangements are, as I think you will agree, passably efficient. But that, after all, is a detail. Think of the other possibilities. A range of 3000 miles carrying fifty passengers in the essence of comfort. Australia in a fortnight; America in three days. And it is safe, gentlemen – safe. That is the message I want you to give the British public."

And at this point I can imagine the reader laying the book down in blank amazement. What, he will say, is the fellow talking about? What on earth has the Wilmot dirigible got to do with the matter? We all know that any hope of success for the scheme was killed when the airship crashed in flames. There were ridiculous rumours of Wilmot going mad, though for some reason or other the thing was hushed up in the papers. Anyway, what has it got to do with Gaunt and his poison?

Don't get irritable, my friend. I warned you that I am no story-teller: maybe if I was I could have averted your anger by some trick of the trade. And I admit it looks as if I had suddenly taken leave of my senses, and that a dissertation on the habits of ferrets would have been equally relevant. I will merely say that at the time I would have agreed with you. The Wilmot dirigible had as little to do with Robin Gaunt in my mind as the fact that my clerk's name was Stevens. If I ever thought of Mr Wilmot, which I presume I must have done, I pictured him as an ordinary businessman who saw a great commercial future in the rigid airship. I take it that such was the picture in everybody's mind. I know that I heard of him lunching in the City: I know that I heard rumours of a company being actually floated. (The Duke of Wessex was to be one of the directors.)

The principal thing I did not know at the time was the truth. So bear with me, my irritated friend: in due course you shall know the truth yourself. Whether you believe it or not is a totally different matter.

Furthermore, I'm now going to make you angry again. More apparent red herrings are going to be drawn across the trail: herrings which, I once again repeat, seemed as red to me then as they will to you now.

On the 31st of July the celebrated American multimillionaire, Cosmo A. Miller, steamed into Southampton Water in his equally celebrated yacht, the *Hermione*. He had with him on board the type of a party that a multi-millionaire might have been expected to entertain. To take the ladies first, there was his wife, for whom he had recently bought the notorious Shan diamonds. The diamonds of death, they had been christened: strange, wasn't it, how they lived up to their evil reputation! Then there was Angela Greymount, a well-known film star: Mrs Percy Franklin, a New York society woman and immensely wealthy; and finally Mrs James Delmer, the wife of a Chicago millionaire. The feminine side of the party was to be completed by the Duchess of Sussex – also an American, and Lady Agatha Dawkins, an extremely amusing woman whom I knew slightly. These last two were to join the yacht at Southampton, and it was to pick them up that the *Hermione* called there.

The men consisted of the owner, three American business friends, the Duke of Sussex and Tony Beddington, who was, incidentally, a pal of Drummond's. He and the Duke also joined the yacht in England.

Cowes week was in progress at the time, of course – so the eyes of social England and the pens of those who chronicle the doings of the great were already occupied in that quarter. But the arrival of the *Hermione* was something which dwarfed everything else. Never had so much wealth been gathered together in a private yacht before. Mrs Tattle, in that bright and breezy column which she contributed daily to the *Morning Express*, stated that the jewellery alone was worth over two million pounds sterling. And it is, I gather, a fact that a dear friend of Mrs Cosmo Miller's once stated that she'd lunched with Minnie's diamonds and she believed Minnie was inside.

The yacht itself was a miniature floating palace. It had a swimming pool and a gymnasium: it had listening-in sets and an electric piano encrusted in precious stones – or almost. There was gold plate for use at dinner, and the plebeian silver for lunch. In fact it was the supreme essence of blatant vulgarity.

In addition to the guests there were the Wallaby Coon Quartette, the Captain, the wireless operator, four maids, the chef and the writer of 'The Three Hundred Best Cocktails' as barman. The crew numbered sixteen.

So that when the *Hermione* steamed slowly down Southampton Water there were in all forty souls on board. The sea was like a mill-pond; the date was August 2nd. On August 4th a marconigram was received in London by the firm of Bremmer and Bremmer. It was from Mr Miller, and is of interest merely because it is the last recorded message received from the *Hermione*. From that moment she completely disappeared with every soul on board.

At first no-one worried. When the *Hermione* failed to arrive at the Azores, which was originally intended, it was assumed that Mr Miller and his guests had changed their route. But when, on August 10th, Bremmer and Bremmer having obtained the information required by Mr Miller proceeded to wireless to the *Hermione*, no response whatever was received from her. The sea was still beautifully calm: no report of any storms had been received from the Atlantic. And somewhere in the Atlantic the *Hermione* must be, since it was definitely certain she had not passed Gibraltar and entered the Mediterranean.

By August 12th the whole Press – English and American – was seething with it.

'Mysterious Disappearance of Multi-Millionaire's Yacht'

'Cosmo A. Miller beats it with Wallaby Quartette'

'S.Y. *Hermione* refuses wireless calls'

etc., etc.

Still no-one took it seriously. The yacht was fitted with a Marconi installation: the sea was still like glass. The general opinion was that there had been a breakdown in the engines, and that for some obscure reason the wireless was out of action.

But by August 20th, when the silence was still unbroken, the tone of the Press began to change. Once again I will refer to my file of cuttings, and quote from the *Morning Herald* of that date.

The mysterious silence of the S.Y. *Hermione* has now become inexplicable. The last communication from her was received more than a fortnight ago. Since then nothing further has been heard, though Mr Cosmo Miller, her owner, has been repeatedly called up on important business matters. It is impossible to avoid a feeling of grave anxiety that all is not well.

But what could have happened? The wireless operator was known to be a first-class man, and it seemed impossible that such damage could have happened to his instruments, in a perfectly calm sea, that he would be unable to effect a temporary cure.

Then some bright specimen had an idea which held the field for quite a while. It was just an advertisement – an elaborate publicity stunt. They were receiving all these messages, and taking no notice of them merely in order to keep the eyes of the world focussed on them. Such a thing, it was argued, was quite in keeping with, at any rate, Mrs Miller's outlook on life. And it wasn't until August 25th came and went that one of the officials at Southampton Docks shattered that theory. The *Hermione's* bunkers only held sufficient coal for a fortnight, and that only when steaming at her economic speed. And it was now twenty-four days since she had sailed.

By this time the public on both sides of the Atlantic were very gravely perturbed. The wildest rumours were flying round: from pirates to sea serpents all sorts of suggestions were put forward.

Both the British and American navies despatched light cruisers to discover what they could; and it may be remembered that when Mr Wilmot's patriotic offer to place his airship at the disposal of the authorities was refused, he himself, at his own expense, went far out into the Atlantic to see if he could find out anything.

Nothing was ever discovered; no trace was found of the yacht. And no trace ever will be; for she sank with every soul on board.

Now for the first time I will put down what happened, and show the connection between the two chains of events – the big and the so-called little: between the disappearance of the *Hermione* and

Robin Gaunt's cry over the telephone. I will tell of the death of
Mr Wilmot, and of what happened to the man called Helias in
that lonely spot in Cornwall. And, perhaps, most important of all,
certainly most interesting, I will set down word for word the last
statement of Robin Gaunt.

Chapter 8

In Which We Come to Black Mine

But before I go on to pick up the thread of my story, I wish again to reiterate one thing. On September 5th, when Drummond rang me up at my office asking me to go round to his house at once, there was no inkling in my mind that there was any connection. Nor was there in his. The events I have just recorded were as irrelevant to us as they appear to be on these pages. In fact the last thing known to us which was connected in any way with Robin Gaunt in our minds was the discovery of Miss Simpson's body at Paignton.

So it was with a considerable feeling of surprise that I listened to what Drummond had to say over the telephone.

'Found out something that may be of value: can you come round at once?'

I went, to find, to my amazement, a man with him whom I had never expected to see again. It was little rat face, who had been put to watch Toby Sinclair and whom we had saved from hanging in Number 10. He was sitting on the edge of his chair, plucking nervously at a greasy hat in the intervals of getting outside a quart of Drummond's beer.

'You remember Mr Perton, don't you, old boy?' said Drummond, winking at me. 'I happened to meet him this morning, and reminded him that there was a little matter of a fiver due to him.'

'Well, gentlemen,' said Mr Perton nervously, 'I don't know as 'ow I can call it due, for I didn't do wot you told me to. But I couldn't, sir: I 'ad a dreadful time. You won't believe wot them devils did to me. They 'ung me.'

'Did they indeed?' said Drummond quietly. 'They don't seem to have done it very well.'

'Gawd knows 'ow I escaped, guv'nor. They 'ung me, the swine – and left me swinging. I lost consciousness, I did – and then when I come to again, I was laying on the floor in the room alone. You bet yer life I didn't 'alf do a bolt.'

'A very sound move, Mr Perton. Have some more beer? Now do you know why they hanged you?'

'Strite I don't, guv'nor. They said to me, they said – 'You're bait, my man: just bait.' They'd got me gagged, the swine: and they was a-peering out of the window. "Here they come," says one of 'em: "trice 'im up!" So they triced me up, and then they give me a push to start me swinging. Then they does a bunk into the next 'ouse.'

'How do you know they bunked into the next house?' said Drummond.

'Well, guv'nor, there was a secret door, there was – and they'd brought me from the next house.'

He looked at us nervously, as if afraid of the reception of his story.

'How long had you been in the next house, Mr Perton,' asked Drummond reassuringly, 'before they brought you through the secret door to hang you?'

'Three or four hours, sir: bound and gagged. Thrown in the corner like a ruddy sack of pertaters. Just as I told you, sir.'

'I know, Mr Perton; but I want my friend to hear what you have to say also. During those three or four hours whilst you were thrown in the corner, you heard them talking, didn't you?'

'Well, I didn't pay much attention, sir,' said Mr Perton apologetically. 'I was a-wondering wot was going to 'appen to me too 'ard. But there was a great black-bearded swine, who was swearing something awful. And two others wot was sitting at a table drinking whisky. They seemed to be fair wild about something. Then the other bloke come in – the bloke wot had been in Clarges Street that morning, and the one wot had brought me from the Three Cows to the 'ouse. They shut up swearing, though you could see they was still wild.

'"You know wot to do," says the new man, "with regard to that thing." He points to me, and I listened 'ard.

'"We knows wot to do," says the black-bearded swab, "but it's damned tomfoolery."

'"That's for me to decide," snaps the new bloke. "I'll get the others next door, and I'll do the necessary once they're there." They didn't say nothing then abaht making me swing, you see, so . . . '

'Quite, Mr Perton,' interrupted Drummond. 'But they did say something else, didn't they?'

'Wot, that there bit about Land's Hend? Wot was it 'e said, now – old black beard? Yus – I know. "We'll all be in 'ell's end," he said, "not Land's Hend if we goes on like this." And then someone cursed 'im for a ruddy fool.'

'You're sure of that, Mr Perton, aren't you?' I could hear the excitement in Drummond's voice. 'I mean the bit about Land's End?'

'Sure as I'm sitting 'ere, sir.'

He took a large gulp of beer, and Drummond rose to his feet.

'Well, I'm much obliged to you, Mr Perton. I have your address in case I want it, and since you had such a rotten time, I must make that fiver a tenner.' He thrust two notes into the little man's hand, rushed him through the door, and bawled for Denny to let him out. Then he came back, and his face was triumphant.

'Worth it, Stockton: worth day after day, night after night searching London for that man. Heavens! The amount of liquor I've consumed in the Three Cows.'

'Great Scott!' I cried, 'is that what you've been doing?'

'That – and nothing else. And then I ran into him this morning by accident outside your rooms in Clarges Street. Still, it's been worth it: we've got a clue at last.'

'You mean?' I said, a little bewildered.

'Land's End, man: Land's End,' he cried. 'I nearly kicked the desk over when he said it first. Then I sent for you: I wanted him to repeat his story for confirmation. He did – word for word. The fog is lifting a little, old boy: one loose end is accounted for at any rate. I always thought they hanged the poor little swine in order to get a sitting shot at us. As they told him – bait. But, anyway, that is all past, and a trifle. He's got a tenner in his pocket and two quarts of beer in his stomach – and we can let him pass out of the picture. We, on the contrary, I hope and trust, are just going to pass into it again.'

'You really think,' I said a little doubtfully, 'that we're likely to find out anything at Land's End?'

'I'm going to have a damned good try, Stockton,' he said quietly. 'On his own showing the little man was listening with all his ears at that time, and it seems incredible to me that he would invent a thing like that. We know that the rest of the story was true – the part that he would think us least likely to believe. Very well, then assuming that black beard did make that remark it must have had some meaning. And what meaning can it have had except the obvious one? – namely, that the gang was going to Land's End. Why they went to Land's End, Heaven alone knows. But what this child knows is that we're going there too. I've warned the boys: Toby, Peter and Ted are coming with us. Algy is stopping behind here to guard the fort.'

'What about MacIver?' I asked.

Drummond grinned.

'Mac hates leaving London,' he remarked. 'And if by any chance we do run into gorse bush, I feel MacIver would rather cramp my style. When can you start?'

'Well,' I said doubtfully.

'After lunch?'

'I've got a rather important brief.'

'Damn your brief.'

I did, and after lunch we started. We went in the Hispano, and spent the night in Exeter.

'Tourists, old lads,' remarked Drummond. 'That's what we are. Visiting Penzance. Let's make that our headquarters.'

And so at four o'clock on the 6th September five tourists arrived at Penzance and took rooms at an hotel. But should any doubting reader who dwells in that charming West Country town search the various hotel registers I can tell him in advance that he will find no record of our names. Further, I may say that mine host at Exeter would have been hard put to it to recognise the five men who got out of the Hispano in Penzance. There was no point in handicapping ourselves unnecessarily, and Drummond and I at any rate would certainly be recognised by the gang, even if the others weren't.

The next day we split up. The plan of action we had decided on was to search the whole of the ground west of a line drawn from St. Ives to Mount's Bay. We split it into five approximately equal parts with the help of a large-scale ordnance map, and each part worked out at about ten square miles.

'To do it properly should take three or perhaps four days,' said Drummond. 'It's hilly going, and the north coast is full of caves. If anybody discovers anything, report to the hotel at once. Further, in order to be on the safe side we'd better all return here every night.'

We drew lots for our beats, and I got the centre strip terminating to the north in the stretch of coast on each side of Gurnard's Head. Having a very mild sketching ability I decided that I would pose as an artist. So I purchased the necessary gear, slung a pair of Zeiss field-glasses over my shoulder and started off. I had determined to work my strip from north to south, since I felt sure that if the gang was there at all they would have chosen the desolate country in the north or centre rather than the comparatively populous part near Penzance itself.

The weather was glorious, and since I happen to love walking I foresaw a very pleasant holiday in store. I admit frankly that I did not share the optimism of the others. It struck me that, considering over four months had elapsed, we were building altogether too much on a chance remark.

This is not a guide-book, so I won't bore my readers with rhapsodies over the scenery. The granite cliffs carved and indented into fantastic shapes by countless centuries of erosion: the wild rugged tors rising from the high moorland – it is all too well known to need any further description from my pen. And the desolation of it! Here and there a deserted mine-shaft – tin, I supposed, or copper. No longer a paying proposition: not even worth the labour of dismantling the rusty machinery.

I stopped for a few moments to light my pipe, and a passing shepherd touched his cap.

'Going sketching, sir,' he said in his delightful West Country burr. 'There certainly do be some fine views round these parts.'

I walked with him for a while, listening absentmindedly to his views on men and matters. And, in common with a large number of people in many walks of life, he was of the opinion that things were not what they were. The good old days! Those were the times.

'I remember, sir, when each one of them was a working concern.' He paused and pointed to a derelict mine below us. 'That was Damar Mine, that was, and two hundred men used to work there.'

'Bad luck on them,' I said, 'but I think as far as the scenery is concerned it's better as it is. Didn't pay, I suppose?'

'That's it, sir: didn't pay. Though they do say as how the men that are working Black Mine are going to make it pay. A rare lot of money they're putting into it, so Peter Tregerthen told me. He be one of the foremen.'

'Where is Black Mine?' I asked perfunctorily.

'Just over this hill, sir, and you'll see it. Only started in May, they did. Queer people too.'

I stared at him: it was impossible, of course – just a coincidence . . .

'How do you mean – queer people?' I asked.

'Peter Tregerthen he tells me as how they've got queer ideas,' he answered. 'Scientific mining they're a-going for: carrying out lots of experiments secretly – things which the boss says will revolutionise the industry. But so far nothing seems to have come of them: they just goes on mining in the old way. There it is, sir: that's Black Mine.'

We had reached the top of the tor, and below us, a quarter of a mile away, lay the road from Land's End to St. Ives. On the other side, half-way between the road and the edge of the cliffs, stood the works, and for a moment or two a sudden uncontrollable excitement took hold of me. Was it possible that our search was ended almost before it had begun? And then I took a pull at myself: I was jumping ahead with a vengeance. To base such an idea on a mere coincidence in dates and a Cornish miner's statement that the owners were queer people was ridiculous. And anything less nefarious than the peaceful appearance of Black Mine would have been hard to imagine. Smoke drifted lazily up from the tall chimney, and lines of trucks drawn by horses passed and repassed.

'How many men are employed there?' I asked my companion.

'Not many, sir, yet,' he answered. 'It's up in that wooden building yonder on the edge of the cliffs that they be experimenting as I told you. No-one aren't allowed near at all. In fact Peter Tregerthen he did tell me that one day he went up and there was a terrible scene. He wanted for to ask the boss something or t'other, and the boss very nigh sacked him. Well, sir, I reckons I must be a-going on. Be you waiting here?'

'Yes,' I said. 'I think I'll stop here a bit. Good-morning to you.'

I watched him go down the hill and strike the road: then, moved by a sudden impulse, I retraced my steps to the reverse slope of the tor, and lying down behind a rock I focussed my field-glasses on the wooden building which was so very private in its owners' estimation. It seemed a perfectly ordinary erection, though considerably larger than I had thought when I saw it with the naked eye. I could see now that it stretched back some distance from the edge of the cliff, though, being foreshortened, it was hard to guess any dimensions.

Of signs of life in it I could see none. No-one entered or left, and on the land-side – the only one I could observe properly – there were no windows as far as I could make out. And then a sudden glint, such as the sun makes when its light strikes something shining, came from up near the roof. It was not repeated, though I kept my glasses glued on the spot for ten minutes.

It was as I was coming to the conclusion that I was wasting time, and that an inspection from closer range was indicated (after all they couldn't sack me), that a man came out of the building and walked towards the mine. I saw, on consulting the ordnance map, that the mine itself was just over half a mile from where I lay, and the cliff's edge was distant a farther half-mile. And it was just about ten minutes before the man reappeared on my side of the mine building. I watched him idly: he was still too far off for me to be able to distinguish his features. After a while he struck the road, but instead of turning along it one way or the other he came straight on, and commenced to climb the hill. In fact it suddenly dawned on me that he was coming directly for me. I slipped backwards out of sight, and hurriedly set up my easel and camp stool, only to see another man approaching from my right rear. And the second man must have seen my hurried preparations. However, I argued to myself that there is no law that prevents a man admiring a view through field-glasses preparatory to sketching it. And though as an argument it was perfectly sound, the presence of Drummond would have been far more comforting.

'Good-morning.'

The man who had come from the mine breasted the rise in front of me, and I glanced up. He was a complete stranger, with a dark rather swarthy face, and I returned the compliment politely.

'Sketching, I see,' he remarked affably.

'Just beginning,' I answered. And then I took the bull by the horns. 'I've been admiring the country through my glasses most of the morning.'

'So I perceived,' said another voice behind my shoulder. It was the second man, whom again I failed to recognise. 'You seemed to decide to start work very suddenly.'

'I presume,' I remarked coldly, 'that I can decide to start work when I like, where I like, and how I like. The matter is my business, and my business only.'

A quick look passed between the two men, and then the first arrival spoke.

'Of course,' he remarked still more affably. 'But the fact of the matter is this. By way of experiment a small syndicate of us have taken over Black Mine. We believe, I trust rightly, that we have stumbled on a method which will enable us to make a large fortune out of tin-mining. The information has leaked out, and we have had several people attempting to spy on us. Please wait' – he held up his hand as I began an indignant protest. 'Now that I have seen you, I am perfectly sure that you are not one of them. But you will understand that we must take precautions.'

'I would be obliged,' I remarked sarcastically, 'if you would tell me how you think I can discover your secret – even granted I knew anything about tin-mining, which I don't – from the range of a mile.'

'A very natural remark,' he replied. 'But, to adopt military terms for a moment, there is such a thing as reconnoitring a position, I believe, before attempting to assault it.'

'Which it seems to me, sir, you have been doing pretty thoroughly this morning,' put in the other.

I rose to my feet angrily.

'Look here,' I said, 'I've had about enough of this. I'm an Englishman, and this is England. If you will inform me of any law which prohibits me from looking through field-glasses at anything I like for as long as I like, I shall be pleased to listen to you. If, however, you can't, I should be greatly obliged if you'd both of you go to blazes. I may say that the question of tin-mining leaves me even colder than your presence.'

Once again I saw a quick glance pass between them.

'There is no good losing your temper, sir,' said the first man. 'We are speaking in the most friendly way. And since you have no connection with the tin-mining industry there is no need for us to say any more.'

'I certainly have no connection with the tin-mining industry,' I agreed. 'But for the sake of argument supposing I had. Is that a crime?'

'In this locality, and from our point of view,' he smiled, 'it is. In fact it is worse than a crime: it is a folly. Several people have proved that to their cost. Good-morning.'

I watched them go, and my first thought was to pack up and walk straight back to the hotel. And then saner counsels prevailed. That second man – where had he come from? I felt certain now that that flash had been a signal. Or an answer. He must have been lying up in that high ground behind me on the right. And glancing round I could see hundreds of places where men could lie hidden and watch my every movement.

Was it genuine? That was the whole point. Was all this talk about revolutionising tin-mining the truth, or merely an elaborate bluff? There below me was an actual tin mine going full blast, which substantiated their claim. Anyway the main thing was to give them no further cause for suspicion. And in view of the fact that for all I knew unseen eyes might still be watching me, I decided to stop on for a couple of hours, eat my lunch, and then saunter back to Penzance. Moreover, I determined that I wouldn't use the field-glasses again. I had seen all I could from that distance, so there was no object in rousing further suspicion in the event of my being watched.

Was it genuine? The question went on reiterating itself in my mind. And it was still unanswered when I returned to the hotel about tea-time. I had seen no trace of any other watcher; the high ground on each side of me had seemed silent and deserted while I ate my lunch and sketched perfunctorily for an hour or so. Was it genuine? Or did the so-called secret process cloak something far more sinister?

We weighed up the points for and against the second alternative over a round of short ones before dinner.

Points for – Coincidence of dates and the very special precautions taken to prevent outsiders approaching. Point against – Why come to a derelict tin mine in the back of beyond, and incur all the expense of paying miners when on the face of it a far more accessible and cheaper location could be found?

'In fact,' remarked Drummond,' the matter can only be solved in one way. We will consume one more round of this rather peculiar tipple which that sweet girl fondly imagines is a Martini: we will then have dinner: and after that we will go and see for ourselves.'

'Supposing it is genuine?' I said doubtfully.

'Then, as in the case of Aunt Amelia, we will apologise and withdraw. And if they refuse to accept our apologies and show signs of wishing to rough-house, Heaven forbid that we should disappoint them.'

We started at nine in the car. There was no moon and we decided to approach from the west, that is, the Land's End direction.

'We'll leave the car a mile or so away – hide it if possible,' said Drummond. 'And then, Stockton, call up your war lore, for we're going to have a peerless night creep.'

'Do we scatter, Hugh, or go in a bunch?' asked Jerningham.

'Ordinary patrol, Ted. I'll lead: you fellows follow in pairs.'

His eyes were gleaming with excitement; and if my own feelings were any criterion we were all of us in the same condition. My doubts of the morning had been replaced by a quite unjustifiable optimism: I felt that we were on the track again at last. Undoubtedly the wish was father to the thought, but as we got into the car after dinner I was convinced that these were no genuine experimenters in tin.

'Carry a revolver, but don't use it except as a last resort.'

Such were Drummond's orders, followed by a reminder of the stringent necessity for silence.

'On their part as well as our own,' he said quietly. 'If you stumble on anyone, don't let him give the alarm.'

In our pockets we each of us had a gag, a large handkerchief, a length of fine rope, and a villainous-looking weapon which Drummond alluded to as Mary. It was a short, heavily loaded stick, and as he calmly produced these nefarious objects from his suitcase, followed by five decent-sized bottles of chloroform, I couldn't help roaring with laughter.

'Always travel hoping for the best,' he grinned. 'Don't forget, boys –

no shooting. To put it mildly, it would be distinctly awkward if we killed a genuine tin merchant.'

It was ten o'clock when we reached a spot at which Drummond considered it sound to park the car. For the last two miles we had been travelling without lights, and with the aid of a torch we confirmed our position on the map.

'I make out that there is another ridge beyond the one in front of us before we get to Black Mine,' said Drummond. 'If that's so and they've got the place picketed, the sentry will be on the farther one. Manhandle her in, boys: she'll make a noise on reverse.'

We backed the car off the road into a small deserted quarry and then, with a final inspection to see that all our kit was complete, we started off. Toby and I came five yards behind Drummond, with the other two behind us again, and I soon began to realise that the yarns I had heard from time to time – told casually by his pals about our leader – were not exaggerated. I have mentioned before his marvellous gift of silent movement in the dark; and I had myself seen an exhibition of it in the house in Ashworth Gardens. But that was indoors: that night I was to see it in the open. You could hear nothing: you could see nothing, until suddenly he would loom up under your nose with whispered instructions.

Toby had had previous experience of him, but the first time it happened I very nearly made a fool of myself. It was so utterly unexpected that, never dreaming it was he, I lunged at him viciously with my loaded stick. The blow fell on empty air, and I heard him chuckle faintly.

'Steady, old man,' he whispered from somewhere behind me. 'Don't lay me out at this stage of the proceedings. We're just short of the top of the first ridge: spread out sideways until we're over. Then same formation. Pass it back.'

We waited till the other two bumped into us, I feeling the most infernal ass. And then, even as we were passing on the orders, there came a faint snarling noise away to our left. We stared in the direction it came from, but it was not repeated. All was silent save for the lazy beat of the breakers far below.

'By Gad! you fellows, we've bumped the first sentry.' Drummond materialised out of the night. 'Fell right on top of him. Had to dot him one. What's that?'

A stone moved a few yards away from us, and a low voice called out – 'Martin! Martin – are you there? What was that noise? God! This gives me the jumps. Martin – where are you? Ah – '

The beginnings of a scream were stifled in the speaker's throat, and we moved cautiously forward to find Drummond holding someone by the throat.

'Put him to sleep, Ted,' he whispered, and the sickly smell of chloroform tainted the air.

'Lash him up and gag him,' said Drummond, and then, with infinite precaution, he switched his torch for a second on to the man's face. He was one of the two who had spoken to me that morning.

'Good,' said Drummond cheerfully. 'We won't bother about the other: he will sleep for several hours. And now, having mopped up the first ridge, let us proceed to do even likewise with the second. Hullo! What the devil is that light doing? Out to sea there.'

Three flashes and a long pause – then two flashes. That was all: after that, though we waited several times, we saw nothing more.

'Obviously a signal of some sort,' remarked Drummond. 'And presumably it is to our friends in front. By Jove! you fellows, is it possible that we've run into a bunch of present-day smugglers? What a perfectly gorgeous thought. Let's get on with it. There's not likely to be anyone in the hollow in front, but go canny in case of accidents. Same formation as before, and spread out when we come to the next ridge.'

Once more we started off. Periodically I glanced out to sea, but there was no repetition of the signal. Whatever boat had made it was lying off there now without lights – waiting. And for what? Smugglers? Possible, of course. But what a coast to choose! And yet was it a bad one? Well out of the beaten track: full of caves: sparsely populated. One thing anyway seemed certain. If the signal had been intended for the present owners of Black Mine, it rather disposed of the genuineness of their claim. The connection between tin-mining secrets and mysterious signals out at sea seemed rather too obscure to be credible.

'Hit him, Stockton.'

Toby Sinclair's urgent voice startled me out of my theorising just in time. I had literally walked on a man, and it was a question of the fraction of a second as to whether he got away and gave the alarm.

'Good biff,' came in Drummond's whisper as the man crashed. 'I've got the other beauty. We're through the last line.'

The other two had joined us, and for a while we stood there listening. Ahead of us some three hundred yards away was the Black Mine: to the left, on the edge of the cliff, the wooden house stood outlined against the sky. And even as we stared at it a door opened for a second, letting out a shaft of light as someone came out.

'So our friends are not in bed,' said Drummond softly. 'There is activity in the home circle. Let's go and join the party. We'll make for the edge of the cliff a bit this side of the house.'

It was farther than it looked, but we met no more sentries. No further trace of life showed in the wooden house as we worked our way cautiously forward.

'Careful.' Drummond's whisper came from just in front of us. 'We're close to the edge.' He was peering in front, and suddenly he turned round and gripped my arm. 'Look up there towards the house. See anything? Underneath a little – just below the top of the cliff.'

I stared at the place he indicated, and sure enough there was a patch which seemed less dark than its surroundings.

'There's a heavily screened light inside there,' he muttered. 'It's an opening in the cliff.'

And then, quite clearly audible over the lazy beat of the sea below, we heard the round of rowlocks.

'This is where we go closer,' said Drummond. 'It strikes me things are going to happen.'

We crept towards the house, and I know that I at any rate was quivering with excitement. I could just see Drummond in front well enough to conform to his every movement. He paused every now and then, but not for long, and I pictured him peering into the darkness with that uncanny sight of his. Once, I remember, he stopped for nearly five minutes, and while I lay there trying to stop the pounding of my heart I thought I heard voices below. Then he went on again, until the house seemed almost on top of us.

At last he stopped for good, and I saw him beckoning to us to come and join him. He was actually on the edge of the cliff, and when I reached his side and passed over, I very nearly gave the show away in my surprise. Not twenty feet below us a man's head was sticking out of the face of the cliff. We could see it outlined against a dim light that came from inside, and he was paying out something hand over hand. At first I couldn't see what it was. It looked like a rope, and yet it seemed singularly stiff and inflexible.

'Form a circle,' breathed Drummond to the other three. 'Not too near. For Heaven's sake don't let us be surprised from behind.'

'What on earth is it that he's paying out?' I whispered in his ear as he once more lay down beside me.

'Tubing of sorts,' he answered. 'Don't talk – watch.'

From below came a whistle, and the man immediately stopped. Then a few seconds later came another whistle and the man disappeared. Something must have swung into position behind him, for the light no longer shone out; only a faint lessening of the darkness marked the spot where he had been. And then, though it may have been my imagination, I thought I heard a slight gurgling noise such as a garden hose makes when you first turn the water on.

For some time nothing further happened; then again from below came the whistle. He must have been waiting for it from behind the screen, for he reappeared instantly. As before the light shone on him, and suddenly I felt Drummond's hand close on my arm like a vice. *For the man was wearing india-rubber gauntlets.*

Coil by coil he pulled the tubing up until it was all in: then again he disappeared and the screen swung down, shutting out the light.

'Stockton,' whispered Drummond, 'we've found 'em.'

'What are you going to do?' I asked.

'Explore,' he said quietly. 'If we'd got through without bumping their sentries, I'd have given it a chance till daylight tomorrow. As it is, it's now or never.'

'Then I'm coming with you,' I remarked.

'All right,' he whispered. 'But I'm going down to reconnoitre first.'

He collected the other three and gave his orders. He, Jerningham and I would go down and force an entrance through the front of the cliff: the other two would guard our retreat and hold the rope for us to ascend again. But Toby was adamant. There was a large post rammed into the ground for some purpose or other to which the rope could be attached, and he and Peter insisted on coming too. And even in the darkness I could see Drummond's quick grin as he agreed.

'As soon as I signal all right, the next man comes down. And if they find the bally rope and cut it we'll fight our way out through the back door. One other thing: instructions *re* revolvers cancelled. It's shoot quick, and shoot often. Great Heavens! What's that?'

From somewhere near by there came a dreadful chattering laugh followed by a babble of words which died away as abruptly as it had started. To the others it was merely a sudden noise, staggering because of the unexpectedness of it, but to me it was a paralysing shock which for the moment completely unnerved me. For the voice which had babbled at us out of the night was the voice of Robin Gaunt.

Chapter 9

In Which We are Entertained Strangely In Black Mine

'You're certain of that?' muttered Drummond tensely, for even his iron nerves had been shaken for the moment.

'Absolutely,' I answered. 'That cry came from Robin Gaunt.'

'Then that finally proves that we're on to 'em. Let's get busy: there's no time to lose.'

We made fast the rope and then lay peering over the edge of the cliff as he went down hand over hand. For a moment the light gleamed out as he drew aside the screen, and then we heard his whispered 'Come on'. One after another we followed him till all five of us were standing in the cave. Behind us a curtain of stout sacking, completely covering the entrance, was all that separated us from a hundred-feet fall into the Atlantic: in front – what lay in front? What lay round the corner ten yards away? Even now, though many months have elapsed since that terrible night, I can still feel the pricking at the back of my scalp during the few seconds we stood there waiting.

Suddenly Drummond stooped down and sniffed at something that lay on the floor. Then he beckoned significantly to me. It was the end of the tubing which we had seen the man paying out, and from it came the unmistakable scent of the poison. More confirmation of the presence of the gang: and another piece in this strange and inexplicable jigsaw.

I straightened up to see that Drummond had reached the corner and was peering cautiously round it. He was flattened against the rough wall, and his revolver was in his hand. Inch by inch he moved forward with Jerningham just behind him, and the rest of us following in single file.

The passage went on bending to the left and sloping downwards. The floor was smooth and made of cement, but the walls and roof were left in their natural condition just as they had been blasted out. It was not new except for the floor, and as we crept forward I wondered for what purpose, and by whom, it had been originally made. The illumination came from somewhere in front, and it was obvious through the light getting brighter that that somewhere was very close.

Suddenly Drummond became motionless: just ahead of us a man had laughed.

'Damned if I see what there is to laugh at,' snarled a harsh voice. 'I'm sick to death of this performance.'

'You won't be when you get your share of the stuff,' came the answer.

'It's an infernal risk, Dubosc.'

'You don't handle an amount like that without running risks,' answered the other. 'What's come over you tonight? We've been here four months and now, when we're clearing out, you're as jumpy as a cat with kittens.'

'It's this damned place, I suppose. No report in from the sentries? No-one about?'

'Of course there's no-one about. Who would be about in this God-forsaken stretch of country if he hadn't got to be?'

'There was that sketching fellow this morning. And Vernier swears that he was lying there on the hill examining the place for an hour through glasses.'

'What if he was? He couldn't see anything.'

'I know that. But it means he suspected something.'

'It's about time you took a tonic,' sneered the other. 'We've gone through four months in this place without being discovered; and now, when we've got about four more hours to go at the most, you go and lose your nerve because some stray artist looks at the place through field-glasses. You make me tired. Devil take it man, it's a tin mine, with several perfectly genuine miners tinning in it.'

He laughed once again, and we heard the tinkle of a glass.

'There was every excuse if you like for being windy when we were in London. And it served that cursed fool Turgovin right. What did we want anyway with that man – what was his name – Stockton, wasn't it? What was the good of killing him, even if the fool had done it, and not got killed himself? I tell you that when I saw the Chief a week later, he was still apoplectic with rage. And if Turgovin hadn't been dead, the Chief would have killed him, himself. We ought to have done what Helias said, and cleared out as soon as we got Gaunt.'

'What are we going to do with that madman when we go?'

'Kill him,' said the other callously. 'If he hadn't gone mad, and suffered from his present delusion, he'd have been killed weeks ago. Hullo, here he is. Why ain't you tucked up in the sheets, looney?'

And then I heard old Robin's voice.

'Surely it's over by now, isn't it?'

'Surely what's over? Oh! the war. No: that's not over. The Welsh have gained a great victory over the English and driven 'em off the top of Snowdon. Your juice doesn't seem to be functioning quite as well as it ought to.'

'It must succeed in time,' said Robin, and his voice was the vacant voice of madness. 'How many have been killed by it?'

'A few hundred thousand,' answered the other. 'But they're devilish pugnacious fighters, these Englishmen. And the General won't give up until he's got those legs of Welsh mutton for his dinner. By the way, looney, you'll be getting slogged in the neck and hurt if I hear you making that infernal noise again. Your face is bad enough without adding that filthy shindy to it.'

'That's so,' came in a new deep voice. I saw Drummond's hand clench and he glanced round at me. Doctor Helias had come on the scene. 'If it occurs again, Gaunt, I shall hang you up head downwards as I did before.'

A little whimpering cry came from Robin, and suddenly the veins stood out on Drummond's neck. For a moment I thought he was going to make a dash for them then and there, which would have been a pity. Sooner or later it would have to come: in the meantime, incomprehensible though much of it was, we wanted to hear everything we could.

'Get out, you fool,' snarled Helias.

There was the sound of a heavy blow, and a cry of pain from Robin.

'Let him be, Helias,' said one of the others. 'He's been useful.'

'His period of utility is now over,' answered Helias. 'I'm sick of the sight of him.'

'But there isn't enough,' wailed Gaunt. 'Too much has gone into the sea, and it is the air that counts.'

'It's all right, looney; there's plenty for tonight. Go and put your pretty suit on so as to be ready when he comes.'

A door closed and for a time there was silence save for the rustling of some papers. And then Helias spoke again.

'You've neither of you left anything about, have you?'

'No. All cleared up.'

'We clear the instant the job is finished. Dubosc – you're detailed to fill the tank with water as soon as it's empty. I'll deal with the madman.'

'Throw him over the cliff, I suppose.'

'Yes; it's easiest. You might search his room, Gratton: I want no trace left. Look at the fool there peering at his gauge to see if there's enough to stop the war.'

'By Jove! This is going to be a big job, Helias.'

'A big job with a big result. The Chief is absolutely confident. Lester and Degrange are in charge of the group on board the *Megalithic*, and Lester can be trusted not to bungle.'

'Boss! Boss! Vernier is lying bound and gagged on the hill outside there.'

Someone new had come dashing in and Drummond gave us a quick look of warning. Discovery now was imminent.

'What's that?' We heard a chair fall over as Helias got up. 'Vernier gagged. Where are the others?'

'Don't know, boss. Couldn't see them. But I was going out to relieve Vernier, and I stumbled right on him. He's unconscious. So I rushed back to give the warning.'

'Rouse everyone,' said Helias curtly. 'Post the danger signal in the roof. And if you see any stranger, get him dead or alive.'

'Terse and to the point,' remarked Drummond. 'Just for the moment, however, stand perfectly still where you are.'

He had stepped forward into the room, and the rest of us ranged up alongside him.

'Well, gorse bush – we meet again. I see you've removed your face fungus. Very wise: the police were so anxious to find you.'

'By God! It's the Australian,' muttered Helias. He was standing by the table in the centre of the room, and his eyes were fixed on Drummond.

'Have it that way if you like,' answered Drummond. 'The point is immaterial. What my friends and I are principally interested in is you, Doctor Helias. And when we're all quite comfortable we propose to ask you a few questions. First of all, you three go and stand against that wall, keeping your hands above your heads.'

Dazedly they did as they were told: our sudden appearance seemed to have cowed them completely.

'Feel like sitting down, do you, Doctor? All right. Only put both your hands on the table.'

He pulled up a chair and sat down facing Helias.

'Now then: to begin at the end. Saves time, doesn't it? What exactly is the game? What are you doing here?'

'I refuse to say,' answered the other.

'That's a pity,' said Drummond. 'It would have saved so much breath. Let's try another. Why have you got Gaunt here, and why has he gone mad?'

'Ask him yourself.'

'Look here,' said Drummond quietly, 'let us be perfectly clear on one point, Doctor Helias. I know you, if not for a cold-blooded murderer yourself, at any rate for a man who is closely connected with several of the worst. I've got you and you're going to the police. What chance you will have then you know best. But if you get my goat you may never get as far as the police. For only a keen sense of public duty restrains me from plugging you where you sit, you ineffable swine.'

'In which case you would undoubtedly hang for it,' snarled the other. His great hairy hands kept clenching and unclenching on the table: his eyes, venomous with hatred, never left Drummond's face.

'I think not,' said Drummond. 'However, at present the point does not arise. Now another question, Helias. Who was the woman who impersonated the wretched Miss Simpson the first time?'

'I refuse to say.'

'She knew me, didn't she? I see you start. You forget that Stockton was not unconscious like the rest of us. Helias – do you know a man called Carl Peterson?'

He fired the question out suddenly, and this time there was no mistaking the other's agitation.

'So,' said Drummond quietly. 'You do. Where is he, Helias? Is he at the bottom of all this? Though it's hardly necessary to ask that. Where is he?'

'You seem to know a lot,' said Helias slowly.

'I want to know just that one thing more,' answered Drummond. 'Everything else can wait. Where is Carl Peterson?'

'Supposing I told you, would you let me go free?'

Drummond stared at him thoughtfully.

'If I had proof positive – and I would not accept your word only – as to where Peterson is, I might consider the matter.'

'I will give you proof positive. To do so, however, I must go to that cupboard.'

'You may go,' said Drummond. 'But I shall keep you covered, and shoot without warning on the slightest suspicion of trickery.'

'I am not a fool,' answered the other curtly. 'I know when I'm cornered.'

He rose and walked to the cupboard, and I noticed he was wearing a pair of high white rubber boots.

'Been paddling in your filthy poison, I suppose,' said Drummond. 'You deserve to be drowned in a bath of it.'

The other took no notice. He was sorting out some papers, and apparently oblivious of Drummond's revolver pointing unwaveringly at the base of his skull.

'Strange how one never can find a thing when one wants to,' he remarked conversationally. 'Ah! I think this is it.'

He came back to the table with two or three documents in his hand.

'I have your word,' he said, 'that if I give you proof positive you will let me go.'

'You have my word that I will at any rate think about it,' answered Drummond. 'Much depends on the nature of the proof.'

Helias had reseated himself at the table opposite Drummond, who was looking at the papers that had been handed to him.

'But this has got nothing to do with it,' cried Drummond after a while. 'Are you trying some fool trick, Helias?'

'Is it likely?' said the other. 'Read on.'

'Keep him covered, Ted.'

And then suddenly Drummond sniffed the air.

'There's a strong smell of that poison of yours, Helias.'

I caught one glimpse on Helias's face of unholy triumph, and the next moment I saw it.

'Lift your legs, Drummond,' I yelled. 'Lift them off the floor.'

The advancing wave had actually reached his chair; another second would have been too late. I have said that the passage sloped down abruptly from the opening in the cliff to the room, and pouring down it was a stream of liquid. It came surging over the smooth floor and in an instant there ensued a scene of wild confusion. Drummond had got on the table: Toby Sinclair and I scrambled on to chairs, and Jerningham and Darrell just managed to reach a wooden bench.

'You devil,' shouted the man Dubosc, 'turn off the stopcock. We're cut off.'

Helias laughed gratingly from the passage into which he had escaped in the general scramble. And then for the first time we noticed the three other members of the gang. They were standing against the wall – completely cut off, as they said. Owing to some irregularity in the floor they were surrounded by the liquid, which still came surging into the room.

And then there occurred the most dreadful scene I have ever witnessed. They screamed and fought like wild beasts for the central position – the place which the poison would reach last. It was three inches deep now under our chairs, and it was within a yard of the place where the three men struggled.

Suddenly the first of them went. He slipped and fell right into the foul stuff, and as he fell he died. Without heeding him the other two fought on. What good they could do by it was beside the point: the frenzied instinct of self-preservation killed all reason. And forgetful of our own danger we watched them, fascinated.

It was Dubosc who managed to wrap his legs round the other's waist, at the same time clutching him round the neck with his arms.

'Carry me to the cupboard, you fool,' he screamed. 'It's the only chance.'

But the other man had completely lost his head. In a last frenzied attempt to get rid of his burden he stumbled and fell. And with an ominous splash they both landed in the oncoming liquid. It was over; and we stared at the three motionless bodies in stupefied silence.

'I don't like people who interfere with my plans,' came the voice of Helias from the passage. 'Unfortunately I shan't have the pleasure of seeing you die because the thought of your revolver impels me to keep out of sight. But I will just explain the situation. In the cupboard is a stopcock. In the building beyond you is a very large tank containing some tons of this poison. We use the stopcock to allow the liquid to pass through the pipe down to the sea – on occasions. Now, however, the end of the pipe is in the passage, which, as you doubtless observed, slopes downwards into the room where you are. And so the liquid is running back into the room, and will continue to do so until the stopcock is turned off or the tank is empty. It ought to rise several feet, I should think. I trust I make myself clear.'

We looked round desperately: we were caught like rats in a trap. Already the liquid was so deep that the three dead men were drifting about in it sluggishly, and the smell of it was almost overpowering.

'There's only one thing for it,' said Drummond at length. His voice was quite steady, and he was tucking his trousers into his socks as he spoke.

'You're not going to do it, Hugh,' shouted Jerningham. 'We'll toss.'

'No, we won't, old lad. I'm nearest.'

He stood up and measured the distance to the cupboard with his eye.

'Cheer oh! old lads – and all that sort of rot,' he remarked. 'Usual messages, don't you know. It's my blithering fault for having brought you here.'

And Peter Darrell was crying like a child.

'Don't!' we shouted. 'For God's sake, man – there's another way. There must be.'

And our shout was drowned by the crack of a revolver. It was Drummond who had fired, and the shot was followed by the sound of a fall.

'I thought he might get curious,' he said grimly. 'He did. Poked his foul face round the corner.'

'Is he dead?' cried Ted.

'Very,' said Drummond. 'I plugged him through the brain.'

'Good Lord! old man,' said Peter shakily. 'I thought you meant that other stuff.'

'Dear old Peter,' Drummond smiled: 'I did. And I do. But I'm glad to have paid the debt first. You might – er – just tell – er – you know, Phyllis and all that.'

For a moment his voice faltered: then with that wonderful cheery grin of his he turned to face certain death. And it wasn't only Peter who was sobbing under his breath.

His knees were bent: he was actually crouching for the jump when the apparition appeared in the door.

'Hugh,' shouted Ted. 'Wait.'

It was the figure of a man clothed from head to foot in a rubber garment. His legs were encased in what looked like high fishing waders: his body and hands were completely covered with the same material. But it was his head that added the finishing touch. He wore a thing that resembled a diver's helmet, save that it was much less heavy and clumsy. Two pieces of glass were fitted for his eyes, and just underneath there was a device to allow him to breathe.

He stood there for a moment with the liquid swirling round his legs, and then he gave a shout of rage.

'The traitor: the traitor. There will not be enough for the air.'

It was Robin Gaunt, and with sudden wild hope we watched him stride to the cupboard. Of us he took no notice: he did not even pause when one of the bodies bumped against him. He just turned off the stopcock, and then stood there muttering angrily whilst we

wiped the sweat from our foreheads and breathed again. At any rate
for the moment we were reprieved.

'The traitor. But I'll do him yet. I'll cheat him.'

He burst into a shout of mad laughter.

'I'll do him. There shall be enough.'

Still taking no notice of us, he waded back to the door and disappeared up the passage. What wild delusion was in the poor chap's
brain we knew not: sufficient for us at the moment that the liquid had
ceased to rise.

Half-an-hour passed – an hour with no further sign of Gaunt. And
the same thought was in all our minds. Had we merely postponed the
inevitable? The fumes from the poison were producing a terrible
nausea, and once Darrell swayed perilously on his bench. Sooner or
later we should all be overcome, and then would come the end. One
thing – it would be quick. Just a splash – a dive . . .

'Stockton,' roared Drummond. 'Wake up.'

With a start I pulled myself together and stared round stupidly.

'We must keep awake, boys,' said Drummond urgently. 'In an
hour or two it will be daylight, and there may be someone about who
will hear us shout. But if you sleep – you die.'

And as he spoke we heard Gaunt's voice outside raised in a shout of
triumph.

'He is coming: he is coming. And there will be enough.'

We pulled ourselves together: hope sprang up again in our minds;
though Heaven knows what we hoped for. Whoever this mysterious
he proved to be, it was hardly likely that he would provide us with
planks or ladders by which we could walk over the liquid.

'What's that noise?' cried Toby.

It sounded like a motor bicycle being ridden over undulating
ground, or a distant aeroplane on a gusty day. It was the drone of
an engine – now loud, now almost dying away, but all the time
increasing in volume. Shout after shout of mad laughter came from
Gaunt, and once he rushed dancing into the room with arms outstretched above his head.

'He comes,' he cried. 'And the war will cease.'

And now the noise of the engine was loud and continuous and
seemed to come from close at hand. Gaunt in a frenzy of joy was
shouting meaningless phrases whilst we stood there marooned in his
foul poison, utterly bewildered. For the moment intense curiosity
had overcome all other thoughts.

Suddenly Gaunt reappeared again, staggering and lurching with something in his arms. It was a pipe similar to the one which had so nearly caused our death, and he dropped the nozzle in the liquid.

'I'll cheat him,' chuckled Gaunt. 'The traitor.'

It was Drummond who noticed it first, and his voice almost broke in his excitement.

'It's sinking, you fellows: it's sinking.'

It was true: the level of the liquid was sinking fast. Hardly daring to believe our eyes we watched it disappearing: saw first one and then another of the dead men come to rest on the floor and lie there sodden and dripping. And all the time Robin Gaunt stood there chuckling and muttering.

'Go on, pump: go on. I will give you the last drop.'

'But where's it being pumped to?' said Jerningham dazedly. 'I suppose we aren't mad, are we? This is really happening. Great Scott! Look at him now.'

Holding the pipe in his hands, Gaunt went to pool after pool of the poison as they lay scattered on the uneven floor. His one obsession was to get enough, but at last he seemed satisfied.

'You shall have more,' he cried. 'The tank is still half full.'

He lurched up the passage with the piping, and a few seconds later we heard a splash.

'Go on,' came his shout. 'Pump on: there is more.'

'Devil take it,' cried Drummond. 'What *is* happening? I wonder if it's safe to cross this floor.'

'Be careful, old man,' said Jerningham. 'Hadn't we better let it dry out a bit more? Everything is still wringing wet.'

'I know that. But what's happening? We're missing it all. Who has pumped up this stuff?'

He gave a sudden exclamation.

'I've got it. Chuck me a handkerchief, someone. These two books will do.'

He sat down on the table, and tied a book to the sole of each of his shoes. Then he cautiously lowered himself to the ground.

'On my back – each of you in turn,' he cried.

And thus did we escape from that ghastly room, to be met with a sight that drove every other thought out of our mind. Floating above the wooden hut so low down that it shut out the whole sky was a huge black shape. It was Wilmot's dirigible.

Standing by the tank of which Helias had spoken was Robin Gaunt, and the piping which had drained the liquid from the room was now emptying the main reservoir.

'Enough: there will be enough,' he kept on saying. 'And this time he will succeed. The war will stop. Instantaneous, universal death. And I shall have done it.'

'But there isn't any war, Robin,' I cried.

He stared at me vacantly through his goggles.

'Instantaneous, universal death,' he repeated. 'It is better so – more merciful.'

We could see the details of the airship now: pick out the two central gondolas and the keel which formed the main corridor of the vessel. And once I thought I saw a man peering down at us – a man covered with just such a garment as Robin was wearing.

'Pumping it into a ballast tank,' said Toby, going to the door. 'You see that: they're letting water out as this stuff goes in.'

He pointed to the stern of the vessel, and in the dim light it was just possible to see a stream of liquid coming out of the airship.

'To think,' he went on dazedly, 'that ten days ago I went for one of Wilmot's Celebrated Six-hour Trips and had Lobster à l'Américain for lunch.'

Suddenly the noise of the engine increased, and the airship began to move. I glanced at Robin and he was nodding his head triumphantly.

'I knew there would be enough,' he cried. 'Go: go, and stop the senseless slaughter.'

The poor devil stood there, his arms thrown out dramatically while the great vessel gathered speed and swung round in a circle. The she flew eastwards, and five minutes later was lost to sight.

'Well, I'm damned,' said Jerningham, sitting down on the grass and scratching his head.

'You're certain it was Wilmot's?' said Drummond.

'Absolutely,' said Toby. 'There's no mistaking her.'

'Can't we get any sense out of Gaunt?' cried Jerningham. 'Where is he anyway?'

And just then he appeared. He had taken off his suit of india-rubber, and I gave an exclamation of horror as I saw his face. From chin to forehead ran a huge red scar; the blow that gave it to him must have well-nigh split his head open. He came towards us as we sat on the ground, and stopped a few yards away, peering at us curiously.

'Who are you?' he said. 'I don't know you.'

'Don't you know me, Robin?' I said gently. 'John Stockton.'

For a while he stared at me: then he shook his head.

'It doesn't matter,' I went on. 'Tell us why your poison is pumped up into the airship.'

'To stop the war,' he said instantly. 'It flies over the place where they are fighting and sprays the poison down. And everyone touched by the poison dies.'

'It sounds fearfully jolly,' remarked Drummond. 'And what happens if a shell bursts in the airship; or an incendiary bullet?'

A sudden look of cunning came on Robin's face.

'That would not matter,' he answered. 'Not one: nor even two. And an incendiary bullet is useless. Just death. Instantaneous, universal death.'

He stared out over the sea, and Drummond shrugged his shoulders hopelessly.

'Or better still, as I have told them all,' went on Robin dreamily, 'is a big city. The rain of death. Think of it! Think of it in London . . . '

'Good God!' With a sudden gasp Drummond got to his feet. 'What are you saying, man? What do you mean?'

'The rain of death coming down from the sky. That would stop the war.'

'But there isn't a war,' shouted Drummond, and Robin cringed back in terror.

'Steady, Drummond,' I said. 'Don't frighten him. What do you mean, Robin? Is that airship going to spray your poison on London?'

'I don't know,' he said. 'Perhaps if the war doesn't stop he will do it. I have asked him to.'

He wandered away a few paces, and Jerningham shook his head.

'Part of the delusion,' he said. 'Why, damn it, Wilmot is trying to float a company.'

'I know that,' said Drummond. 'But why has he got that poison on board?'

'It's possible,' I remarked, 'that he is taking the stuff over to some foreign Power to sell it.'

'Then why not make it over there and save bother?'

To which perfectly sound criticism there was no answer.

'Anyway,' said Drummond, 'there is obviously only one thing to do. Get out of this, and notify the police. I should think they would like a little chat with Mr Wilmot.' And then suddenly he stared at us thoughtfully. 'Wilmot! Can it be possible that Wilmot himself is Peterson?'

He shook both his fists in the air suddenly.

'Oh! for a ray of light in this impenetrable fog. Who was down there last night? Whom did we see signalling from the sea? Why did they want the poison? Why does the airship want it? In fact, what the devil does it all mean? Hullo! What's Ted got hold of?'

Jerningham was coming towards us waving some papers in his hand.

'Just been into another room,' he cried, 'and found these. Haven't examined them yet, but they might help.'

With a scream of rage Robin, who had been standing vacantly beside us, sprang at Jerningham and tried to snatch the papers away.

'They're mine,' he shouted. 'Give them to me.'

'Steady, old man,' said Drummond, though it taxed all his strength to hold the poor chap in his mad frenzy. 'No-one is going to hurt them.'

'It's gibberish,' I said, peering over Jerningham's shoulder. He was turning over the sheets, on which disconnected words and phrases were scrawled. They had been torn out of a cheap note-book and there seemed to be no semblance of order or meaning. Stray chemical formulae were mixed up with sentences such as 'Too much to the sea. I have told him.'

'Just mad gibberish,' I repeated. 'What else can one expect?'

I turned away, and as I did so Jerningham gave a cry of triumph.

'Is it?' he said. 'That's where you're wrong. It may not help us much, but this isn't gibberish.'

In his hand he held a number of sheets of paper covered with Robin's fine handwriting. He glanced rapidly over one or two, and gave an excited exclamation.

'Written before he lost his reason,' he cried. 'It's sense, you fellows – sense.'

And the man who had written sense before he lost his reason was crying weak tears of rage as he still struggled impotently in Drummond's grip.

Chapter 10

In Which We Read the Narrative of Robin Gaunt

Many times since then have I read that strange document, the original of which now lies in Scotland Yard. And whenever I do my mind goes back to that September morning, when, sitting in a circle on the short clipped turf two hundred feet above the Atlantic, we first learned the truth. For after a while Robin grew quiet, though I kept an eye on him lest he should try and snatch his precious papers away. But he didn't: he just sat a little apart from us staring out to sea, and occasionally babbling out some foolish nonsense.

Before me as I write is an exact copy. Not a line will be altered: not a comma. But I would ask those who may read to visualise the circumstances under which we first read that poor madman's closely guarded secret with the writer himself beside us, and the gulls screaming discordantly over our heads.

I am going mad.
[thus it started without preamble]

I, Robin Caxton Gaunt, believe that I shall shortly lose my reason. The wound inflicted on me in my rooms in London, the daily torture I am subjected to, and above all the final unbelievable atrocity which I saw committed with my own eyes, and for which, so help me God, I feel a terrible personal responsibility, are undermining my brain. I have some rudimentary medical knowledge: I know how tiny is the dividing line between sanity and madness. And I have been seeing things lately that are not there: and hearing things that do not exist.

It may be that I shall never complete this document. Perhaps my brain will go first: perhaps one of these devils will discover me writing. But I am making the attempt, and maybe in the future the result will fall into the hands of someone who will search out the arch-monster responsible and kill him as one kills a mad dog. Also – for they showed me the newspapers at the time – it may help to clear my character from the foul blot which now rests on it. Though why John Stockton, who I thought was my friend, didn't say what he knew at the inquest I can't imagine.

[that hurt, as you may guess.]

I will begin at the beginning. During the European war I was employed at Headquarters on the chemical branch. And just before the Armistice was signed I had evolved a poison which, if applied subcutaneously, caused practically instant death. It was a new poison unknown before to toxicologists, and if it were possible I would like the secret to die with me. God knows, I wish now I had never discovered it. Anyway I will not put down its nature here. Sufficient to say that it is the most rapid and deadly drug known at present in the civilised world.

As a death-dealing weapon, however, it suffered from one grave disadvantage: it had to be applied under the skin. To impinge on a cut or a small open place was enough, but it was not possible to rely on finding such a thing. Moreover, the method of distribution was faulty. I had evolved a portable cistern capable of carrying five gallons, which could be ejected through a fine-pointed nozzle for a distance of over fifty yards when pressure was applied by means of a pump, on the principle of a pressure-fed feed in a motor-car. But a rifle bullet carries considerably more than fifty yards, and therefore rifle fire afforded a perfectly effective counter except in isolated cases of surprise.

The possibilities of shells filled with the liquid, of distribution by aeroplane or airship, were all discussed and rejected for one reason or another. And the scheme which was finally approved consisted of the use of the poison on a large scale from fleets of tanks.

All that, however, is ancient history. The Armistice was signed: the war was over: an era of peace and plenty was to take place. So we thought – poor deluded fools. Six years later found Europe an armed camp with every nation snarling at every other nation. Scientific soldiers gave lectures in which they stated their ideas of the next war: civilised human beings talked glibly of raining down myriads of disease germs on huge cities. It was horrible – incredible: man had called in science to aid him in destroying his fellow-men, and science had obeyed him – at a price. It was a price that had not been contemplated: it was a case of another Frankenstein's monster. Man had now to obey science, not science man: he had created a thing which he could not control.

It was in the summer of 1924 that the idea first came to me of inventing a weapon so frightful that its mere existence would control the situation. The bare fact that it was there would act as the presence of the headmaster in a room full of small boys. One very forgetful lad might have to be caned once, after that the lesson would be learned. At first it seemed a wildly fanciful notion, but the more I thought of it the more the idea gripped me. And quite by chance in the July of that year when I was stopping in Scotland playing golf I met a man called David Ganton – an Australian – whose two sons had been killed in Gallipoli. He was immensely wealthy – a multi-millionaire, and rather to my surprise when I mentioned my idea to him casually one evening he waxed enthusiastic over it. To him war was as abhorrent as it was to me: and he, like me, was doubtful as to the efficacy of the League of Nations. He immediately placed at my disposal a large sum of money for research work, and told me that I could call on him for any further amount I required.

My starting-point, somewhat naturally, was the poison I had discovered during the war. And the first difficulty to be overcome was the problem of the subcutaneous injection. A wound, or an opening of some sort, must be caused on the skin before the poison could act. For months I wrestled with the problem till I was almost in despair. And then one evening I got the solution – obvious, as things like that so often are. Why not mix with the poison an irritant blister which would make the little openings necessary?

Again months of work, but this time with renewed hope. The main idea was, I knew, the right one: the difficulty now was to find some liquid capable of blistering the skin, which when mixed with the poison would not react with it chemically and so impair its deadliness. The blister and the poison had, in short, though mixed together as liquids, each to retain its own individuality.

In December 1925 I solved the problem: I had in my laboratory a liquid so perfectly blended that two or three drops touching the skin meant instantaneous death.

Then came the second great difficulty – distribution. The tank scheme, however effective it might have been when a war was actually raging, was clearly an impossibility in such circumstances as I contemplated. Something far more sudden, far more mobile was essential.

Aeroplanes had great disadvantages. Their lifting power was limited: they were unable to hover: they were noisy.

And then there came to my mind the so-called silent raid on London during the war when a fleet of Zeppelins drifted down-wind over the capital with their engines shut off. Was that the solution?

There were disadvantages there too. First and foremost – vulner-ability. Silent raids by night were not my idea of the function of a world policeman. But by day an airship is a comparatively easy thing to hit; and once hit she comes down in flames.

The solution to that was obvious: helium. Instead of hydrogen she would be filled with the non-inflammable gas helium.

Which brought me to the second difficulty – expense. Hydrogen can be produced by a comparatively cheap process – the electro-lysis of water: helium is rare and costly.

I met Ganton in London early in 1926 and told him my ideas. His enthusiasm was unbounded: the question of expense he waved aside as a trifle.

'That's my side of the business, Gaunt: leave that to me. You've done your part: I'll do the rest.'

And then, as if it was the most normal thing in the world, he calmly announced his intention of having a rigid dirigible con-structed of the Zeppelin type.

For many months after that I did not see him, though I was in constant communication with him by letter. Difficulties had arisen, as I had rather anticipated they might, but with a man like Ganton difficulties only increased his determination. And then there came on the scene the man – if such a being can be called a man – who goes by the name of Wilmot. What that devil's real name is I know not; but if these words are ever read, then to the reader I say, seek out Wilmot and kill him, for a man such as he has no right to live.

From the very first poor Ganton was utterly deceived. Letter after letter to me contained glowing eulogies of Wilmot. He too was heart and soul with me in his abhorrence of war; and, what was far more to the point, he was in a position to help very considerably with regard to the airship. It appeared that a firm in Germany had very nearly completed a dirigible of the Zeppelin type, to be used for commercial purposes. It was to be the first of a fleet, and the firm was prepared to hand it over when finished provided they secured a very handsome profit on the deal. They made no bones about it: they were constructing her for their own use and they were not going to sell unless it was really made worth their while.

Ganton agreed. The exact figure he paid I don't know – but it was enormous. And his idea, suggested again by Wilmot, was to employ the airship for a dual purpose. Ostensibly she was to be a commercial vessel, and, in fact, she was literally to be employed as one. But, in addition, she was to have certain additions made to her water ballast tanks which would enable those tanks to be filled with my poison if the necessity arose. The English Government was to be informed and the vessel was to be subjected to any tests which the War Office might desire. After that the airship would remain a commercial one until occasion should arise for using her in the other capacity. Such was the proposition that I was going to put before the Army Council on the morning of April 28th of this year. The appointment was made, and mentioned by me to John Stockton when I dined with him at Prince's the preceding evening. Why did he say nothing about it in his evidence at the inquest?

As the reader may remember, on the night of April 27th, a ghastly tragedy occurred in my rooms in Kensington – a tragedy for which I have been universally blamed. That I know: I have seen it in the Press. They say I am a madman, a cold-blooded murderer, a super-vivisectionist. They lie, damn them, they lie.

[in the original document it was easy to see the savage intensity with which that last sentence was written.]

Here and now I will put down the truth of what happened in my rooms that night. It must be remembered that I had never seen Wilmot, but I knew that he was coming round with Ganton to see the demonstration. Ganton had written me to that effect, and so I was expecting them both. He proved to be a big, thick-set man, clean-shaven, and with hair greying a little over the temples. His eyes were steady and compelling: in fact the instant you looked at him you realised that his was a dominating personality.

I let them both in myself – Mrs Rogers, my landlady, being stone deaf – and took them at once up to my room. I was the only lodger in the house at the time, and looking back now I wonder what that devil would have done had there been others. He'd have succeeded all right: he isn't a man who fails. But it would have complicated things for him.

He professed to be keenly interested, and stated that he regarded it as an honour to be allowed to be present at such an epoch-making event. And then briefly I told them how matters stood. Since I had perfected the poison, I had spent my time in searching for an antidote: a month previously I had discovered one. It was not an antidote in the accepted sense of the word, in that it was of no use if applied *after* the poison. It consisted of an ointment containing a drug which neutralised not the poison but the blister. So that if it was rubbed into the skin *before* the application of the poison the blister failed to act, and the poison – not being applied subcutaneously – was harmless. I pointed out that it was for addit- ional security, though the special india-rubber gloves and overalls I had made were ample protection.

He was interested in the matter of the antidote, was that devil Wilmot.

Then I showed them the special syringes and cisterns I had designed more out of curiosity than anything else, for our plan did not include any close-range work.

And he was interested – very interested in those – was that devil Wilmot.

Then I experimented on two guinea-pigs. The first I killed with the poison: the second I saved with the antidote. And I saw one fool in the papers who remarked that I must obviously be mad since I had left something alive in the room!

'Most interesting,' remarked Wilmot. He went to the window and threw it up. 'The smell is rather powerful,' he continued, leaning out for a moment. Then he closed the window again and came back: he had signalled to his brother devils outside from before our very eyes and we didn't guess it. Why should we have? We had no suspicions of him.

'And tomorrow you demonstrate to the War Office,' he said.

'I have an appointment at ten-thirty,' I told him.

'And no-one save us three at present knows anything about it.'

'No-one,' I said. 'And even you two don't know the composition of the poison or of the antidote.'

'But presumably, given samples, it would be easy to analyse them both.'

'The antidote – yes: the poison – no,' I remarked. 'The poison is a secret known only to me, though, of course, I propose to tell you. I take it that there will be no secrets between us three?'

'None, I hope,' he answered. 'We are all engaged on the same great work.'

And just then a stair creaked outside. Now I knew Mrs Rogers slept downstairs, and rarely if ever came up at that hour. And so almost unconsciously – certainly suspecting nothing – I went to the door and opened it. What happened then is still a confused blur in my mind, but as far as I can sort it out I will try and record it.

Standing just outside the door were two men. One was the man whom I afterwards got to know as Doctor Helias: the other I never saw again till he was carried in dead to the cellar where they confined me.

But it was the appearance of Helias that dumbfounded me for a moment or two. Never have I seen such an appalling-looking man: never have I dreamed that such a being could exist. Now that a description of him has been circulated by the police he has shaved off the mass of black hair that covered his face; but nothing can ever remove the mass of vile devilry that covers his black soul.

But to go back to that moment. I heard a sudden cry behind me, and there was Ganton struggling desperately with Wilmot. In Wilmot's hand was a syringe filled with the poison, and he was snarling like a brute beast. For a second I stood there stupefied; then it seemed to me we all sprang forward together – I to Ganton's assistance, the other two to Wilmot's. And after that I'm not clear. I know that I found myself fighting desperately with the second man, whilst out of the corner of my eye I saw Wilmot, Helias and Ganton go crashing through the open door.

'Telephone Stockton.'

It was Ganton's voice, and I fought my way to the machine. I was stronger than my opponent, and I hurled him to the floor, half stunning him. It was Stockton's number that came first to my head, and I just got through to him. I found out from the papers that he heard me, for he came down at once; but as for me I know no more. I can still see Helias springing at me from the door with something in his hand that gleamed in the light: then I received a fearful blow in the face. And after that all is blank. It wasn't till later that I found out that little Joe – my terrier – had sprung barking at Wilmot as he came back into the room and had been killed with what was left of the poison after Ganton had been murdered in the next room.

How long afterwards it was before I recovered consciousness I cannot say. I found myself in a dimly-lit stone-floored room which I took to be a cellar. Where it was I know not to this day. At first I could not remember anything. My head was splitting, and I barely had the strength to lift a hand. Now I realise that the cause of my weakness was loss of blood from the wound inflicted on me by

Helias: at the time I could only lie in a kind of stupor in which minutes were as hours and hours as days.

And then gradually recollection began to come back – and with it a blind hatred of the treacherous devil who called himself Wilmot. What had he done it for? The answer seemed clear. He wished to get the secret of the poison in order to sell it to a foreign Power. Ganton had confided in him believing him to be straight, and all the time he had been waiting and planning for this. And if once the secret was handed over to a nation which could not be trusted to use it in the way I intended – God help the world. I imagined Russia possessing it – Russia ruled by its clique of homicidal alien Jews. And it would be my fault – my responsibility.

In my agony of mind I tried to get up. It was useless: I was too weak to move. And suddenly I happened to look at my hands in the dim light and I saw they were covered with blood. I was lying in a pool of it, and it was my own. Once again time ceased, but I did not actually lose consciousness. Automatically my brain went on working, though my thoughts were the jumbled chaos of a fever dream. And then out of the hopeless confusion there came an idea – vague at first but growing in clearness as time went on. I was still in evening clothes, and in the pockets of my dinner jacket I had placed the two samples – the bottle containing the poison, and the box full of the antidote. Were they still there? I felt, and they were. Would it be possible to hide them somewhere in the hopes of them being found by the police? And if they were found, then at any rate my own country would be in the possession of the secret too.

But where to hide them? Remember, I was too weak to even stand, much less walk, so the hiding-place would have to be one which I could reach from where I sat. And just then I noticed, because my hand was resting on the ground, that some of the bricks in the floor were loose.

Now I know from what Wilmot has told me since that the hiding-place was discovered by the authorities. Was it my handkerchief. I wonder, on which I scrawled the clue in blood with my finger? But oh, dear Heavens, why did they lose the antidote? Why didn't they guard John Dallas? He was murdered, of course: you know that. He was murdered by Wilmot himself. He was murdered by that devil – that devil – that . . . I must take a pull at myself. I must be calm. But the noises are roaring in my head: they always do when I think that it was all in vain. Besides, I'm going on too fast.

I buried the two things under two bricks, and I pushed the handkerchief into a crack in the wall behind me. And then I think I must have slept – for the next thing I remember was the door of the cellar opening and men coming in carrying another in their arms. They pitched him down in a corner, and I saw he was dead. Then I looked closer, and I saw it was the man I had fought with at the telephone.

But how had he died? Why did his eyes stare so horribly? Why was he so rigid?

It was Helias who told me – he had followed the other two in.

'Well, Mr Pacifist,' he remarked, 'do you like the effects of your poison? That man died of it.'

Until my reason snaps, which can't be long now, I shall never forget the horror of that moment. It was the first time I had seen the result of my handiwork on a human begin. Since then, God help me, I have seen it often – but that first time, in the dim light of the cellar, is the one that haunts me.

For a while I could think of nothing else: those eyes seemed to curse me. I think I screamed at them to turn his head away. I know that Helias came over and kicked me in the ribs.

'Shut that noise, damn you,' he snarled. 'We've got quite enough to worry us as it is without your help. I'll gag you if you make another sound.'

Then he turned to the other two.

'That fool has brought the police into the next house,' he raved, and wild hope sprang up in my mind. 'That means we must get these two out of it tonight. Get his clothes.'

One of the men went out, to come back almost at once with a suit of mine.

'Look here, Helias,' he said, 'if we're to keep him alive we'd better handle him gently. He's lost about two buckets of blood.'

'Handle him how you like,' returned Helias, 'but he's got to be out of this in an hour.'

And so they took off my evening clothes and put on the others. Then one of them put a rough bandage on my head and face, and here and now I would say – if ever that vile gang be caught – that I hope mercy will be shown him. I don't know his name, and I have never seen him since, but he is the only one who has treated me with even a trace of kindness since I fell into their clutches.

I think I must have become unconscious again: certainly I have no coherent recollection of anything for the next few hours. Dimly

I remember being put into a big motor-car, seeing fields and houses flash past. But where I was taken to I have no idea. Beyond the fact that it was somewhere in the country and that there were big trees around the house I can give no description of the place in which I was kept a prisoner for the next few weeks.

Little by little I recovered my strength, and the ghastly wound on my face healed up. But I was never allowed out of doors, and when I asked any question, no answer was given. The window was barred on the outside: escape was impossible even had I possessed the necessary strength.

But one night, when I was feeling desperate, I determined to chance things. I flashed my electric light on and off, hoping possibly to attract the attention of some passer-by. And two minutes later Helias came into the room. I had not seen him since the night in the cellar, and at first I did not recognise him, for he had shaved his face clean.

'You would, would you?' he said softly. 'Signalling! How foolish. Because anyway no-one could see. But you obviously need a lesson.'

He called to another man, and between them they slung me up to a hook in the wall by my feet, so that I hung head downwards. And after a while the pressure of blood on the partially healed wound on my face became so terrible that I thought my head would burst.

'Don't be so stupid another time,' he remarked as they cut me down. 'If you do I'll have your window boarded up.'

They left me, and in my weakness I sobbed like a child. Had I had any, I would have killed myself then and there with my own poison. But I hadn't, and they took care to see that I had no weapon which could take its place. I wasn't allowed to shave: I wasn't even allowed a steel knife with my meals.

The days dragged on into weeks, and weeks into months, and still nothing happened. And I grew more and more mystified as to what it was all about. Remember that then I had seen no papers, and knew nothing. I wasn't even sure that David Ganton was dead. Why did they bother to keep me alive? was the question I asked myself again and again. They had the secret: at least I assumed they must have, for the paper on which I had written the formula of the poison was no longer in my possession. So what use could I be to them?

And then one day – I'd almost lost count of time, but I should say it was about the 10th of June – the door of my room opened and Helias came in, followed by Wilmot.

'You certainly hit him pretty hard, Doctor,' said Wilmot, after he'd looked at me for some time. 'Well, Mr Gaunt – been happy and comfortable?'

'You devil,' I burst out, and then, maddened by his mocking smile, I cursed and raved at him till I was out of breath.

'Quite finished?' he remarked when I stopped. 'I'm in no particular hurry, and as I can easily understand a slight feeling of annoyance on your part, please don't mind me. Say it all over again if it comforts you in any way.'

'What do you want?' I said, almost choking with sullen rage.

'Ah! that's better. Will you have a cigar? No. Then you won't mind if I do. The time has come, Mr Gaunt,' he went on, when it was drawing to his satisfaction, 'when you must make a little return for the kindness we have shown you in keeping you alive. For a while I was undecided as to whether I would dispose of you like your lamented confrère Mr Ganton, but finally I determined to keep you with us.'

'So Ganton is dead,' I said. 'You murdered him that night.'

'Yes,' he agreed. 'As you say, I killed him that night. I have a few little fads, Mr Gaunt, and one of them is a dislike to the word murder. It's so coarse and crude. Well – to return, Mr Ganton's sphere of usefulness as far as I was concerned was over the moment he had afforded me the pleasure of meeting you. But for the necessity of his doing that, he would have – er – disappeared far sooner. He had very kindly paid a considerable sum of money to acquire an airship, and as I wanted the airship and not Mr Ganton, the inference is obvious. You've no idea, Mr Gaunt, how enormously it simplifies matters when you can get other people to pay for what you want yourself.'

I found myself staring at him speechlessly: in comparison with this cold, deadly suavity Helias seemed merely a coarse, despicable bully.

'In addition to that,' he went on quietly, 'the late Mr Ganton presented me with an idea. And ideas are my stock-in-trade. For twenty years now I have lived by turning ideas into deeds, and though I have accumulated a modest pittance I have not yet got enough to retire on. I trust that with the help of Mr Ganton's idea – elaborated somewhat naturally by me – I shall be able to spend my declining years in the comfort to which I consider myself entitled.'

'I don't understand what you're talking about,' I muttered stupidly.

'It is hardly likely that you would at this stage of the proceedings,' he continued. 'It is also quite unnecessary that you should. But I like everyone with whom I work to take an intelligent interest in the proceedings. And the thought that your labours during the next few weeks will help to provide me with my pension should prove a great incentive to you. In addition you must remember that it will also repay a little of the debt you owe to Doctor Helias for his un-remitting care of you during your period of convalescence.'

'For God's sake, don't go on mocking,' I cried. 'What is it you want me to do?'

'First, you will move from here to other quarters which have been got ready for you. Not quite so comfortable, perhaps, but I trust they will do. Then you will take in hand the manufacture of your poison on a large scale, a task for which you are peculiarly fitted. A plant has been installed which may perhaps need a little alteration under your expert eye: anything of that sort will be attended to at once. You have only to ask.'

'But what do you want the poison for?' I asked.

'That, as Mr Gilbert once said – or was it Mr Sullivan – is just like the flowers that bloom in the spring, tra-la-la. It has nothing to do with the case. In time you will know, Mr Gaunt: until then, you won't.'

'Is it for a foreign country?' I demanded.

He smiled. 'It is for me, Mr Gaunt, and I am cosmopolitan. But you need have no fears on that score. I am aware of the charming ideal that actuated you and Mr Ganton, but, believe me, my dear young friend, there's no money in it.'

'It was never a question of money,' I cried.

'I know.' His voice was almost pained. 'That is what struck me as being so incredible about it all. And that is where my elaboration comes in. Now there is money in it: very big money if things work out as I have every reason to hope they will.'

'And what if I refuse?' I said.

He studied the ash on the end of his cigar.

'In the course of the twenty years I have already mentioned, Mr Gaunt,' he said, 'I wouldn't like to say how many people have made that remark to me. And the answer has become monotonous with repetition. Latterly one of your celebrated politicians has given me an alternative reply, which I will now give to you. Wait and see. We've been very kind to you, Gaunt, up to date. You gave me a lot of trouble over that box of antidote which you hid in the cellar' –

how my heart sank at that – 'though I realise that it was partially my fault – in not remembering sooner that you had it in your pocket. In fact, I had to dispose of an eminent savant, Sir John Dallas, in order to get hold of it.'

'Then the authorities got it?' I almost shouted.

'Only to lose it again, I regret to say. By the way,' he leaned forward suddenly in his chair – 'do you know a man called Drummond – Captain Hugh Drummond?'

From beside me as I read, Drummond heaved a deep sigh of joy.

'It is Peterson,' he said. 'That proves it. Go on, Stockton.'

'Hugh Drummond! No, I've never heard of the man. But do you mean to say you murdered Sir John?'

'Dear me! That word again. I keep on forgetting that you have been out of touch with current affairs. Yes, Sir John failed to see reason – so it was necessary to dispose of him. Your omission of the formula for the antidote on the paper containing that of the poison has deprived the world, I regret to state, of an eminent scientist. However, during the sea-voyage which you are shortly going to take I will see that you have an opportunity of perusing the daily papers of that date. They should interest you, because really, you know, your discovery of this poison has had the most far-reaching results. Still, if you will give me these ideas . . . '

He rose shrugging his shoulders.

'Am I to be taken abroad?' I cried.

'You are not,' he answered curtly. 'You will remain in England. And if I may give you one word of warning, Mr Gaunt, it is this. I require your services on one or two matters, and I intend to have your services. And my earnest advice to you is that you should give that service willingly. It will save me trouble, and you – discomfort.'

With that they left me, if possible more completely bewildered than before. I turned it over from every point of view in my mind, and I could see no ray of light in the darkness. The only point of comfort was that at any rate I was goin to change my quarters, and it was possible that I might escape from the new ones. Vain hope! It is dead now, but it buoyed me up for a time.

It was two days later that Helias entered the room and told me to get ready.

'You are going in a car,' he said. 'And I am going with you. If you make the slightest endeavour to communicate or signal to anyone I shall gag you and truss you up on the floor.'

And that brings me to the point . . . Eyes, those ghastly staring eyes. And the woman screaming . . . Oh! God, my head . . .

At this point the narrative as a narrative breaks off. It is continued in the form of a diary. But it has given rise to much conjecture. Personally I think the matter is clear. I believe, in fact from a perusal of the original it is obvious, that 'head' was the last coherent word written by Robin Gaunt. The rest of the sheet is covered with meaningless scrawls and blots. In fact I think that at that point the poor chap's reason gave way. How comes it, then, that the diary records events which occurred *after* he had been taken away in the motor-car? To me the solution is clear. The diary, though its chronological position comes after the narrative given above, was actually written first.

Surely it must be so. Up to the time when he was removed in the car he was in such a dazed physical and mental condition that the mere effort of keeping a diary would have been beyond him. Besides, what was there to record? His mind, as he says, was hopelessly fogged. He knew nothing when he left the house in which he had been confined as to what had happened in his rooms in London – or rather shall I say he knew nothing as to what had been reported in the papers? And yet the narrative already given was obviously written with a full knowledge of those reports.

Besides – take his first paragraph, 'Daily torture.' There had been no question of daily torture. 'Final unbelievable atrocity.' There had been none. No: it is clear. When things began to happen Gaunt kept a diary. And when, at the end he felt his reason going, he wrote the narrative to fill in the gap not covered by the subsequent notes. Had he not gone mad we might have had the whole story in the form in which he presented the first half.

I know that certain people hold a different view. They agree with me that he went mad at this point, but they maintain that the diary was written by him when he was insane. They say, in fact, that he scrawled down the disordered fancies of his brain, and for confirmation of their argument they point to the bad writing – sometimes well-nigh illegible: to the scraps of paper the notes were made on: to the general untidiness and dirt of the record.

I can only say that I am utterly convinced they are wrong. The bad writing, the scraps of paper were due, I feel certain, to the inherent difficulties under which they were written. Always he was trying to escape detection: he just scribbled when he could and where he could. Then for some reason which we shall never know he found himself in the position of being able to write coherently and at length. And the fortunate thing is that he brought his narrative so very close to the point where his diary starts.

Chapter 11

In which we read the diary of Robin Gaunt

I am on board a ship. She is filling with oil now from a tanker alongside. No lights. No idea where we are. Thought the country we motored through resembled Devonshire.

They're Russians – the crew – unless I'm much mistaken. The most frightful gang of murderous-looking cut-throats I've ever seen. Two of them fighting now: officers seem to have no control. Difficult to tell which are the officers. Believe my worst fears confirmed: the Bolsheviks have my secret. May God help the world!

Under weigh. Just read the papers Wilmot spoke about. Is Stockton mad? Why did he say nothing at the inquest? And Joe – poor little chap. How dare they say such things about me? The War Office knew; why have they kept silent?

The murderers! The foul murderers! There was a wretched woman on board, and these devils have killed her. They pushed her in suddenly to the cabin where I was sitting. She was terrified with fear, poor soul. The most harmless little short fat woman. English. They hustled her through – three of them, and she screamed to me to help her. But what could I do? Two more of the crew appeared, and one of them clapped his hand over her mouth. They took her on deck – and with my own eyes I saw them throw her overboard. It was dark, and she disappeared at once. She just gave one pitiful cry – then silence. Are they going to do the same to me?

Four men playing cards outside the door. Certain now that they are Russians. What does it all mean?

It is incomprehensible. There must be at least fifty rubber suits on board with cisterns and everything complete for short-range work with my poison. An officer took me to see them, and one of the men put one on.

'Good?' said the officer, looking at me.

I wouldn't answer, and a man behind me stuck a bayonet into my back.

'Good now?' snarled the officer.

I nodded. Oh! for a chance to be on equal terms . . .

But they are good: far too good. They have taken my rough idea, and improved upon it enormously. A man in one of those suits could bathe in the poison safely. But what do they want them for, on board a ship?

Thank Heavens! I am on shore again. They dragged me up on deck and I thought it was the end. A boat was alongside, and they put me in it. Then some sailors rowed me away. It was dark, and the boom of breakers on rocks grew louder and louder. At last we reached a little cove, and high above me I could see the cliffs. The boat was heaving, and then the man in charge switched on an electric torch. It flashed on the end of a rope-ladder dangling in front of us, and swaying perilously as the swell lapped and then receded. He signed to me to climb up it, and when I hesitated for a moment, he struck me in the face with his boat-hook. So I jumped and caught the ladder, and immediately the boat was rowed away, leaving me hanging precariously. Then a wave dashed me against the cliff, half stunning me, and I started to climb. An ordeal even for a fit man . . . Exhausted when I reached the top. I found myself in a cave hewn out of granite. And Helias was waiting for me.

'Your quarters,' he said. 'And no monkey tricks.'

But I was too done in to do anything but sleep.

The mystery deepens. This place is too amazing. Today I have been shown the plant in which my poison is to be made. It is a huge tank capable of holding I know not how many tons concealed from view by a wooden building built around it. The building is situated on the top of the cliff and the cliff itself is honeycombed with caves and passages. One in particular leads down from the tank to a kind of living-room, and thence up again to another opening in the cliff similar to the one by which I entered. And from the bottom of the tank there runs a pipe – yards and yards of it coiled in the room. Enough to allow the end to reach the sea. There is a valve in the room by which the flow can be stopped. It must be to supply the vessel below. But why so much? I will not make it: I swear I will not make it, even if they torture me.

Dear God! I didn't know such things were known to man. Four days – four centuries. Don't judge me . . . I tried, but the entrance was guarded.

[In the original this fragment was almost illegible. Poor devil – who would judge him? Certainly not I. Who can even dimly guess the refinements of exquisite torture they brought to bear on him in that lonely Cornish cave? And I like to think that behind that last sentence lies his final desperate attempt to outwit them by hurling himself on to the rocks below. 'But the entrance was guarded.']

It is made. And now that it is made what are they going to do with it? They've let me alone since I yielded, but my conscience never leaves me alone. Night and day: night and day it calls me 'Coward'. I am a coward. I should have died rather than yield. And yet they *could* have made it themselves: they said so. They knew the formula. But they thought I'd do it better. If any accident took place I was to be the sufferer.

Should I have ended it all? It would have been so easy. It would be so easy now. One touch: one finger in the tank and everything finished. But surely sooner or later this place must be discovered. I lie and look out over the grey sea, and sometimes on the far horizon there comes the smoke of a passing vessel.

Always far out – too far out. Anyway I have no means of signalling. I'm just a prisoner in a cave. They don't even give me a light at night. Nothing to do but think and go on thinking, and wonder whether I'm going mad. Is it a dream? Shall I wake up suddenly?

Yesterday I had a strange thought. I must be dead. It was another world, and I was being shown the result of my discovery on earth. Cruelty, death, torture – that was all that the use of such a poison as mine could lead to. It was my punishment. It's come back to me since – that thought. What was that strange and wonderful play I saw on earth? *Outward Bound*. Rather the same idea: no break – you just go on. Am I dead?

[undoubtedly to my mind the first time that Robin Gaunt's reason began to totter. Poor devil – day after day – brooding alone.]

Things are going to happen. There's a light at sea – signalling. Is it the ship, I wonder? They're letting down the pipe from the cave above me. It's flat calm: there is hardly a murmur from the sea below.

At last I know the truth. At last I know the reason for the tank on the top of the cliff, and all that has happened in the last three months. With my own eyes I have seen an atrocity, cold-blooded and monstrous beyond the limits of human imagination.

Six thousand feet below me gleams the Atlantic: I am on board the dirigible that Wilmot murdered Ganton to obtain. I have locked my cabin door: I hope for a few hours to be undisturbed. And so whilst the unbelievable thing that has happened is fresh in my mind I will put it down on paper.

[I may say that this final portion of Robin Gaunt's diary was written in pencil in much the same ordered and connected way as the first part of his narrative. It shows no trace of undue excitement in the handwriting: nor, I venture to think, does it show any mental aberration as far as the phraseology is concerned.]

I will start from the moment when I saw the signal from the sea. The pipe was hanging down the cliff, and after a while there came a whistle from below. Almost at once I heard the gurgle of liquid in the pipe: evidently poison from the tank was being lowered to someone underneath. Another whistle and the gurgling ceased. Then came the noise of oars; the pipe was drawn up, and for some time nothing more happened.

It was about half-an-hour later that Helias appeared and told me to come with him. I went to the main living-room, where I found Wilmot, and a man whom I recognised as having seen on board. They were talking earnestly together and poring over a chart that lay between them on the table.

'The 2nd or 3rd,' I heard Wilmot say, 'and the first port of call is the Azores.'

The other man nodded, and pricked a point on the chart.

'That's the spot,' he said. 'A bit west of the Union Castle route.'

And just then I became aware of the faint drone of an engine. It sounded like an aeroplane, and Wilmot rose.

'Then that settles everything. Now I want to see how this part works.' He glanced at me as I stood there listening to the noise, which by this time seemed almost overhead. 'One frequently has little hitches the first time one does a thing, Mr Gaunt. You will doubtless be able to benefit from any that may occur when you proceed yourself to stop the next war.'

They all laughed, and I made no answer.

'Let's go and watch,' said Wilmot, glancing at his watch. 'I'll just time it, I think.'

He led the way up the passage towards the tank, and I followed. That there was some devilish scheme on foot I knew, but I was intensely eager to see what was going to happen. Anything was better than the blank ignorance of the past few weeks.

We approached the tank, and then to my amazement I saw that there was a large open space in the roof through which I could see the stars. And even as I stared upwards they were blotted out by a huge shape that drifted slowly across the opening so low down that it seemed on top of us.

'The dirigible that Mr Ganton so kindly bought for me,' said Wilmot genially. 'As I say, it is the first time we have done this and I feel a little pardonable excitement.'

And now the huge vessel above us was stationary, with her engines going just sufficiently to keep her motionless in the light breeze. One could make out the two midship gondolas, and the great central keel that forms the backbone of every airship of her type. And as I stared at her fascinated, something hit the side of the wooden house with a thud. A man clad in one of the rubber suits who was standing on the roof slipped forward and caught the end of a pipe similar to the one in the cave. This he dropped carefully into the tank.

'Ingenious, don't you think, Mr Gaunt?' said Wilmot. 'We now pump up your liquid into the ballast tanks, at the same time discharging water to compensate for weight. You will see that by keeping one tank permanently empty there is always room for your poison to be taken on board. When the first empty tank is filled, another has been emptied of water and is ready.'

I hardly listened to him: I was too occupied in watching the level of the liquid fall in the gauge of the tank: too occupied in wondering what was the object of it all.

'Twelve minutes,' he remarked, as the pump above began to suck air in the tank. 'Not so bad. We will now go on board. Another little device, Gaunt, on which we flatter ourselves. It looks alarming, but there is no danger.'

Swinging above us was a thing that looked like a cage, which had evidently been let down from the airship. In a moment or two it came to rest on the roof, and Wilmot beckoned to me to go up the steps.

'Room for us both,' he remarked.

I made no demur: it was useless to argue. Why he wanted me on board was beyond me, though doubtless I should know in time. So I followed him into the cage, and he shut the door. And the next moment we were being drawn up to the dirigible.

It was the first time I had been outside and I stared round eagerly, but in the faint grey light that precedes dawn it was difficult to see much. Far below us lay the sea, whilst inland the ground was hilly. I saw what I took to be a road in the distance: also a tall chimney which stuck up from the midst of low-lying buildings. And then the cage came to rest: it had been drawn right into the keel of the airship. A metal plate closed underneath us with a clang, and we both stepped out into the central corridor.

'Something to eat and drink, Mr Gaunt,' said Wilmot, and I followed him in a sort of dull stupor.

He led the way to a luxurious cabin which was fitted up as a dining-room. On the table were champagne and a variety of sandwiches.

'We will regard this as a holiday for you,' he remarked. 'And if you behave yourself there is no reason why it shouldn't prove a very pleasant one. After it is over you will have to refill the tank for us, but for the next three or four days let us merely enjoy ourselves.'

We were flying eastwards – I could tell that by the light; and I peered out of the window trying to see if I could spot where we were.

'A beautiful sight, isn't it?' said Wilmot. 'And when the sun rises it is even more beautiful. Lord Grayling and the Earl of Dorset both agreed that to see the dawn from such a vantage-point was to see a very wonderful sight.'

'In God's name,' I burst out, 'what does it all mean?'

He smiled as he selected a sandwich.

'Just your scheme, my dear fellow,' he answered. 'Your scheme in practice.'

'But there's no war on,' I cried.

'No. There's no war on,' he agreed.

'Then why have you filled the ballast tanks with poison?'

'You may remember that I once pointed out to you the weak point in your scheme,' he answered. 'There was no money in it. In the course of the next few days you are going to see that defect remedied, I trust.

'Of course,' he went on after a while, 'this is only going to be quite a small affair. It's in the nature of a trial run: just to accustom everyone to what they have to do when the big thing comes along. And that's why I've brought you along. You have had, I gather, a little lesson over not doing what you're told, and I feel sure that you will give me no further trouble. But one never knows that some little hitch may not occur, and should it do so in your particular department, it will be up to you to rectify it.'

But I haven't the time to give that devil's conversation in full. I can see him now, suave and calm, seated at the table smoking a cigar whilst he played with me as a cat plays with a mouse. Utterly ignorant then as to what was going to happen, much of it was lost on me. Now I can see it all.

It conveyed nothing to me then that the British public was keenly interested in the airship: that tours at popular prices were given twice a week: that there was talk of floating a company in the City.

'Not that that is ever likely to come off, my dear Gaunt,' he remarked, 'though if it did, of course, I should have no objections to taking the money. But it instils confidence in the public mind: makes them regard me as an institution. And an institution can do no wrong. You might as well suspect the Cornish Riviera express of robbing the Bank of England.'

There lies the diabolical ingenuity of it all. Did I not hear from the cabin where they kept me bound and gagged – guarded by two men – did I not hear him showing two members of the Royal Family over the vessel? That was while we were tied up to the mooring mast before we started.

Did we not go for a four-hour trip with thirty people on board, amongst them some of the highest in the land? He told me their names that night, with a vile mocking smile on his face.

'But why,' I shouted at him, 'why?'

'All in good time,' he answered. 'I am just showing you what an institution I am.'

That's it: and will anyone believe what I am going to write down? I see it all now: the tin mine ostensibly being worked as a tin mine; in reality merely a cloak to disguise the making of the poison. As he said, it had to be in a deserted place by the sea, because the ship had to take supplies on board.

He's told me everything: he knows I'm in his power. He seems to take a delight in tormenting me: in exposing for my benefit the workings of his vile brain. But he's clever: diabolically clever.

It was two days ago that they let me out of my cabin. The airship was in flight, and looking out I saw that we were over the sea. They took me into the dining-room, and there I saw Wilmot and a woman. She was smoking a cigarette, and I saw she was very beautiful. She stared at me with a sort of languid interest: then she made some remark to Wilmot at which he laughed.

'Our friend Helias has a strong right arm,' he remarked. 'Well, Gaunt – very soon now your curiosity is going to be satisfied. We have ceased to be commercial: we're going to go and stop your war. But we still remain an institution. Have you ever heard of Mr Cosmo Miller?'

'I have not,' I said.

'He is an American multi-millionaire, and at the moment he is some forty miles ahead of us in his yacht. If you look through that telescope you will be able to see her.'

I glanced through the instrument, and saw away on the horizon the graceful outlines of a steam yacht.

'A charming boat – the *Hermione*,' he went on. 'It goes against the grain to sink her.'

'To do what?' I gasped.

'Sink her, my dear Gaunt. She is, one might say, your war. She is also the trial run to give us practice for other and bigger game.'

I stared at him speechlessly: surely he must be jesting.

'Considerate of Mr Miller to select this moment for his trip, wasn't it? Otherwise we might have had to try our 'prentice hand on less paying game. At any rate he has sufficient jewellery on board to pay for our running expenses if nothing more.'

'But, good God!' I burst out, 'you can't mean it. What is going to happen to the people on board?'

'They are going to sink with her,' he replied, getting up and looking through the telescope.

A man came into the cabin and Wilmot swung round.

'No message been sent yet, Chief.'

Wilmot nodded and dismissed him.

'A wonderful invention – wireless, isn't it? But I confess that it renders modern piracy a little difficult. In this case the matter is not one of vital importance, but when we come to the bigger game the question will have to be very carefully handled. Now on this occasion it may be that the two excellent and reliable men who took the place of two members of the *Hermione's* crew at Southampton have broken up the instrument already; or it may be that the wireless operator hardly considers it worth while to broadcast the information that he has seen us. However, we shall soon know. My dear!' he added to the girl, 'we're getting very close. I think it might interest you now.'

She got up and stood beside him, whilst I stood there in a sort of stupor. I watched Wilmot go to a speaking-tube: heard him give directions to fly lower. And then, drawn by some unholy fascination, I too went and looked out.

Half-a-mile ahead. The passengers were lining the rail staring up at us, and in a few seconds we had come so close that I could see the flutter of their pocket handkerchiefs.

'Come with me, Gaunt,' snapped Wilmot. 'Now comes the business. My dear, you stay here.'

He rushed me along the main corridor till we came to one of the central ballast tanks. The engines were hardly running, and I realised that we must be directly over the yacht and just keeping pace with her. Two men clad in rubber suits stood by the tank: two others were by the corresponding tank on the opposite side of the gangway.

Wilmot himself was peering into an instrument set close by the first tank, and I saw a duplicate by the second. I went to it and found it was an arrangement of mirrors based on the periscope idea: by looking into it I saw directly below the airship.

And of the next ten minutes how can I tell? Straight underneath us – not a hundred feet below – lay the yacht. Everyone – guests, crew, servants – were peering up at the great airship, which must have seemed to fill the entire sky. And then Wilmot gave an order. Two levers were pulled back, and the rain of death began to fall. The rain that I had invented – Oh, God! – it was unbelievable . . .

I saw a woman who had been waving at us fall backwards suddenly on the deck and lie there rigid, her face turned up towards us. A man rushed forward to her help: he never reached her. The poison got him first. And all over the deck it was the same. Men and women ran screaming to and fro, only to crash forward suddenly and lie still as the death rain went on falling. I saw three niggers, their black faces incongruous against their white ducks. They had rushed out at the sound of the pandemonium on deck, and with one accord, as if they had been pole-axed simultaneously, they died. I saw a man in uniform shaking his fist at us. He only shook it once, poor devil . . .

And then as if from a great distance I heard Wilmot's voice – 'Enough'.

The rain of death ceased: it was indeed enough. No soul moved on the yacht; only a white-clad figure at the wheel kept her on her course.

Stumbling blindly, I went back to the central cabin. The girl was still there, staring out of the window, and I think I screamed foolish curses at her. She took no notice: she was watching something through a pair of glasses.

'Quite well timed,' she remarked as Wilmot entered. 'She's only about a mile off.'

I looked and saw a vessel tearing through the water towards us: coming to the rendezvous of death.

'I would never have believed,' said Wilmot, 'that with her lines she would have been capable of such speed.'

Then he turned to me.

'Put on that suit,' he said curtly. 'We're going down on deck.'

He was getting into one himself, and half unconsciously I followed his example. I was dazed: stunned by the incredible atrocity I had just witnessed.

And if it had been terrible from above, what words can paint the scene on deck as we stepped out of the cage? In every corner lay dead bodies; and one and all they stared at me out of their sightless eyes. They cursed me for having killed them: everywhere I turned they cursed me.

The deck was ringing wet: the smell of the poison lay heavy in the air. And again and again I asked myself – What was the meaning of this senseless outrage? I didn't know then of the incredible wealth of the wretched people who had been killed: of the marvellous jewels that were on board.

The other vessel lay alongside: a dozen of the crew clothed in rubber suits had come on board the yacht. It was the ruthless efficiency of it all that staggered me: they worked like drilled soldiers. One by one they carried the bodies below and piled them into cabins. And when a cabin was full they shut the door. They damped down the stoke-room fires: they blew off what head of steam remained. They stove in the four ship's boats and sank them: they moved every single thing that would float and put it below in such a place that when the ship sank everything would go down with her. And all the while the dirigible circled overhead.

Once, and only once, did anything happen to interrupt them. Heaven knows where he had been hidden or how he had escaped, but suddenly, with a wild shout, one of the crew darted on deck. In his hands he held a pick: he was a stoker evidently. Gallant fellow: he got one of them before he died. In the head – with his pick, and then another of the pirates just laid his glove wet with the poison against the stoker's face. And the work went on.

At last Wilmot appeared again. He was carrying a suitcase, and I saw him signal to the airship. She manoeuvred back into position and the cage was lowered on to the deck of the yacht. And a minute later we were in the dirigible once more.

'A most satisfactory little experiment,' said Wilmot. 'We will now examine the spoils more closely.'

Sick with the horror of it all, I stood at the cabin window, whilst he and the woman went over the jewels on the table behind me. We had circled a little away from the yacht, and the other vessel no longer lay alongside, but a hundred yards or so away. And suddenly there came a dull boom, and the yacht rocked a little on the calm sea.

'A sight, my dear, which I don't think you've ever seen,' said Wilmot, and he and the woman came to the window. 'A ship sinking.'

Slowly the yacht settled down in the water: they had blown a great hole in her bottom. And then at last with a sluggish lurch her bows went under and she turned over and sank. For a time the water swirled angrily to mark her grave: then everything grew quiet. No trace remained of their devilish handiwork: the sea had swallowed it up.

'Most satisfactory,' repeated Wilmot. 'Don't you agree, Gaunt?' He laughed evilly at the look on my face.

'And you have committed that atrocious crime for those,' I said, pointing at the jewels.

'Not altogether,' he answered. 'As I told you before, this is merely in the nature of a trial trip. Of course it's pleasant to have one's expenses paid, but the principal value of this has been practice for bigger game . . . That is what we are out for, my dear Gaunt: bigger game.'

I watched him with a sort of dazed fascination as he lit a cigar. Then he began to examine through a lens the great heap of precious stones in front of him. And after a while the thought began to obsess me that he was not human. His complete air of detachment: his amused comments when he discovered that a beautiful tiara was only paste: above all the languorous indifference of the girl who only an hour before had witnessed an act of wholesale murder made my head spin.

They are devils – both of them: devils in human form; and I told them so.

They laughed, and Wilmot poured me out a glass of champagne.

'You flatter us, Gaunt,' he remarked. 'Surely you have not been listening to the foolish remarks of the crew. They, poor simple-minded fellows, do, I understand, credit me with supernatural powers, but I am surprised at you. Merely your antidote, my friend: that's all.'

'I don't understand what you're talking about,' I muttered.

'There now,' he said genially, 'I am always forgetting that your knowledge of past events is limited. An amusing little story, Gaunt, and one which flatters your powers as a chemist. I may say that it also flatters my powers as a prophet. My men, as you may know, are largely Russians of the lower classes. Docile, good fellows as a general rule, with a strong streak of superstition in them. And realising that in a concern of this sort one has to control with an iron hand, I anticipated that possibly an occasion might arise when some foolish man would question that control. It was because of that, my dear Gaunt, that I took so much trouble to procure that admirable oint-ment of yours, the existence of which is not known to the members of my crew. In that point lay the little element of – if I may say so –

genius, which separates a few of us from the common herd. Though I admit that it was with some trepidation – pardonable I think you will allow – that I put the matter to the test. Of the efficacy of your poison I had no doubt, but with regard to the antidote I had only seen it in action once, and then on a guinea-pig. If I remember aright, my darling,' he said to the girl, 'we drank to Mr Gaunt's skill as a chemist in one of our few remaining bottles of Imperial Tokay, at the conclusion of the episode. A wonderful wine, Gaunt; but I fear extinct. These absurd revolutions that take place for obscure reasons do a lot of harm.'

That's how he talked: the man is *not* human. Then he went on.

'But the episode in question will, I am sure, interest you. As I had foreseen, some stupid men began to question my authority. In fact, though you will hardly believe it, it came to my ears that there was a conspiracy to take my life. It is true I had had a man flogged to death, but what is a Russian peasant more or less? Apparently this particular fellow sang folk-songs well, or tortured some dreadful musical instrument better than his friends. At any rate he was popular, and his death was a source of annoyance to the others. So, of course, it became necessary to take the matter in hand at once in a way which should restore discipline, and at the same time prevent a recurrence in the future. My dearest, this caviare is not so good as the last consignment. Another devastating example of the harm done by revolutions, I fear. Even the sturgeons have gone on strike.

'However, to return to my little story. I bethought me of your antidote. "Here," said I to myself, "is an opportunity to test that dear chap Gaunt's excellent ointment in a manner both useful and spectacular." So I rubbed it well into my face and hands – even into my hair, Gaunt – and strode like a hero of old into the midst of the malcontents. You perceive the beauty of the idea. A man not gifted with our brains might reasonably remark, "Why not don a rubber suit, which you know is quite safe?"

'True, but besides being hot and uncomfortable – I think we shall have to try and improve those suits, Gaunt – it is very clumsy in the event of the wearer being attacked with a knife. And though I anticipated from what I had heard that they proposed to use your poison, one has to allow for all eventualities. Also there was that mystic vein in them which I wanted to impress.

'Behold me then, my dear fellow, apparently as I am now, striding alone and unarmed to their quarters. For a moment they stared at me dumbfounded – my sudden appearance had cowed them. And then one of them pulled himself together and discharged a syringe full of the liquid at me. It hit me in the cheek – a most nervous moment, I assure you. I apologise deeply to you now for my qualms; I should have trusted your skill better.

'Nothing happened, and the men cowered back. I said no word; but step by step I advanced on the miscreant who had dared to try and rob the world of one of its chief adornments. And step by step he retreated till he could retreat no further. Then I took his hand and laid it on my cheek. And that evening we tied him in a weighted sack, and buried him at sea.'

He smiled thoughtfully and studied the ash on his cigar.

'It was most successful. Rumours about me vary amongst these excellent fellows. The one I like best is that I am a reincarnation of Rasputin. But there has been no further trouble.'

He rose from the table and swept the jewels carelessly into the suitcase.

'Not a bad haul, my little one. We shall have to be very careful over the disposal of the Shan diamonds: they're notorious stones.'

They both walked over to one of the windows together, and . . .

[at this point the narrative breaks off abruptly. Evidently Gaunt was interrupted and crammed the papers hurriedly into his pocket. And the only other document – the most vital of all – was scrawled almost illegibly on a torn scrap of paper. Whether it was written on the airship or at Black Mine will never be known. Of how he got back to the mine there is no record. Who were the men alluded to as 'them' is also a mystery, though I have no doubt that one of them was Wilmot. Possibly the other was Helias.]

I heard them today. They didn't know I was listening. The *Megalithic* with thirty of the gang on board. Attack by night. The bigger game. He will succeed: he is not human . . . Hydrogen not helium . . . Not changed . . . Sacrifice ship . . . Fire . . .

That is all. Those are the papers that we read, sitting on the edge of the cliff with the writer beside us staring with vacant eyes over the grey sea below. Those were the papers, stumbled on by the merest accident, on which we had to base our plans. Was it true or were we the victims of some gigantic delusion on the part of Gaunt? That was the problem that faced us as the first rays of the early sun lit up Black Mine on the morning of September 8th.

Chapter 12

In which the final count takes place

How much of it was true? We had confirmation of a certain amount
with our own eyes. We had seen the pipe, lowered over the cliff:
we had seen the mysterious signal from the sea. Above all we had
seen Wilmot's dirigible actually filling up with the poison. So much,
therefore, we knew. But what of the rest?

What of the astounding story of the *Hermione*? Had we discovered
the solution of the yacht's disappearance, or had we been wasting our
time reading the hallucination of a madman's brain? Had Gaunt –
having read in the papers of the loss of the *Hermione* – imagined the
scene he had described?

Against that theory was the fact – as I have mentioned before – that
neither in the writing nor the phraseology could we detect any sign
of insanity. And surely if the whole thing was a delusion, traces of
incoherence and wildness would have been bound to appear.

So we reasoned, and still could come to no conclusion. It seemed so
wildly fantastic: so well-nigh incredible. And if those epithets could be
used in connection with the *Hermione*, what was to be said concerning
the amazing fragment about the *Megalithic*? Even granted for the
moment that the description of the loss of the *Hermione* was correct,
were we seriously to imagine that the same thing could be done to a
great Atlantic liner?

From the very first moment Drummond made up his mind and
never changed it. I admit that I was sceptical until the last damning
proof came to us, but he never hesitated.

'It's the truth,' he said quietly. 'I am convinced of it. The mystery
of the *Hermione* is solved. And with regard to the *Megalithic* it is the
truth also.'

I suppose he saw my look of incredulity, for he then addressed
himself exclusively to me.

'Stockton, ever since the time in Ashworth Gardens when that
woman recognised me, I've known that we were up against Peterson.

I've felt it in every fibre of my being. Now it's proved beyond a shadow of doubt. Whatever may or may not be true in that diary of Gaunt's, that fact is obvious. Wilmot is Peterson: nothing else could account for his asking Gaunt if he knew me.'

He lit a cigarette, and I was struck by the gravity of his face.

'You've asked once or twice about Peterson,' he went on after a while. 'But though we've told you a certain amount, to you he is merely a name. To us, and to me particularly, he's rather more than that. That is why I am certain in my own mind that that scrawled message about the *Megalithic* is true. And the principal reason for making me think it is true lies in the last few words. That is Peterson all over.'

I glanced at the scrap of paper.

'Hydrogen not helium . . . Not changed . . . Sacrifice ship . . . Fire . . . '

'My God! you fellows' – Drummond was almost shouting in his excitement – 'it's stupendous. Don't you see the tear in the paper there between sacrifice and ship? Ship doesn't refer to the *Megalithic*: the word "air" has been torn out. It's the airship he is going to sacrifice. It is still full of hydrogen: Peterson wasn't going to the expense of refilling with helium.'

He was pacing up and down, his hands in his pockets.

'That's it: I'll swear that's it. It's the Peterson creed. It's the loophole of escape that he always leaves himself. He has decided to attack the *Megalithic*; why, we don't know. Possibly a boat-load of American multi-millionaires on board. He's got thirty of his own men in the ship, and that strange craft of his alongside. Let's suppose the attack is successful. The liner disappears: sinks with all hands. Right: there's nothing further to worry about. But supposing it isn't successful. With the best of luck and arrangement it's a pretty big job to tackle – even for Peterson. What's going to happen then? In a few seconds the astounding news will be wirelessed all over the world that Wilmot's dirigible is carrying out an act of piracy on the high seas of such unbelievable devilry that it would make our old pal Captain Hook rotate in his coffin if he heard of it. Suppose another thing too. Suppose it is successful, but that the wireless people in the *Megalithic* manage to get a message through before their gear is put out of action. Peterson gets that message on his own installation. What's he going to do? He may be an institution all right at the moment, but he won't have the mayor and a brass band out to welcome him on his return once the truth is known. So he descends from his airship either into this mysterious vessel of his, or else on to dry land. We know he can do that. What he does with the crew is immaterial. Probably leaves them with a few ripe and fruity instructions, and a bomb timed to explode a little later. And so Wilmot's dirigible pays the just retribution for an astounding and diabolical crime, while Wilmot himself retires to Monte Carlo on the proceeds thereof. It's what he has always said: there's nothing like dying to put people off the scent. No police in the world are going to bother to look for the blighter if they think he is a perfectly good corpse in his own burnt-out airship. It's a pity in a way,' he concluded regretfully, 'a great pity. I should have liked to deal with him personally.'

'Well, why not?' said Jerningham.

'It's too big altogether, Ted,' answered Drummond. 'I never mind chancing things a certain amount with MacIver, but I don't think we'd be justified this time. The consequences of failure would be too appalling. Let's dump the sentries inside the hut, and then push off and have some breakfast. After that we'll make for London and MacIver. Whatever is believed or is not believed, there's one thing that Peterson is going to find it hard to explain. Why are his ballast tanks full of Gaunt's poison?'

So we carried the men, who still lay bound and gagged, into the wooden hut. And there, having locked the door, we left them, with the scent of death still heavy in the air and their four gruesome companions.

'It breaks my heart,' said Drummond disconsolately as we strolled towards the car, 'to think that we've got to pull in Scotland Yard. Still, we've had a bit of fun . . . '

'We have,' I agreed grimly. 'Incidentally what on earth are we going to do with Gaunt?'

'Well, since the poor bloke is bug house, I suppose we'll have to stuff him in a home or something. Anyway that comes later: the first thing is to lead him to an egg or possibly a kipper. We can pretend he's eccentric if the staff go up the pole when they see him.'

And so we returned to the hotel, which I certainly had never expected to see again. Now that it was all over the reaction had set in, and I even found myself wondering whether it hadn't all been some terrible nightmare. Only there sat Robin Gaunt to prove the reality, and in my pocket I could feel the sheets of his diary.

Sleep! I wanted it almost more than food: sleep and something to rid me of the racking headache which the fumes of that foul liquid had produced. And even as I waited for breakfast I found my head nodding on to the table. It was over: the strain and tension was past. One could relax . . .

'Good Lord!' Drummond's startled exclamation roused us all. He was staring at a newspaper, whilst his neglected cigarette burnt the table-cloth beside him.

'What's the day of the week?'

'Thursday,' said someone sleepily.

'Look here, you fellows,' he said gravely, 'pull yourselves together and wake up. The *Megalithic* sails today from Liverpool for New York.'

We woke up all right at that and his next remark completed the arousing process.

'Today, mark you – carrying thirty million in bullion on board.'

'Instantaneous, universal death,' babbled Gaunt, but we paid no attention. We just sat there – all ideas of sleep banished – staring at Drummond.

'They must be warned,' he said decisively. 'Even at the risk of making ourselves look complete and utter fools. The *Megalithic* must be wirelessed.'

He put his hand into his pocket and pulled out some letters.

'Give me a pencil: I'll scribble down a message.'

And then suddenly he broke off, and sat looking blankly at something he held.

'Well, I'm damned,' he muttered. 'I'd forgotten all about that. Tonight is the night of Wilmot's Celebrated Farewell Gala Night Trip. Somebody sent me two complimentary tickets for it. Couldn't think who'd done it or why. Phyllis was keen on going.'

Once more he fell silent as he stared at the two tickets.

'I've got it now,' he said at length, and his voice was ominously quiet. 'Yes – I've got it all now. Peterson sent me those two tickets, and there's no need to ask why.'

He turned to the girl, who was putting the breakfast on the table.

'How long will it take to get through to London on the telephone? Anyway I must do it. Get me Mayfair 3XI. Now then, you fellows – food. And after that we'll drive to London as even the old Hispano has never moved before.'

'What are you ringing up Algy for?' said Darrell.

'I want four more tickets, Peter, for tonight's trip. And above all I want some of that antidote. Peterson is not the only man who can play that particular game.'

'What about wirelessing the *Megalithic*?' I asked.

He looked at me with a queer smile.

'No necessity now, Stockton. If there is one thing in this world that is certain beyond all others it is that Wilmot's dirigible will be at the aerodrome when we get back to London. For I venture to think – without undue conceit – that there is one desire in Mr Wilmot's heart that runs even the possession of thirty million fairly close. And that desire is my death.'

I stared at him incredulously, but he was perfectly serious.

'Had I not known that he was going to be there, it would have been imperative to warn the *Megalithic*. Now the situation is different. If we wireless, don't forget that he will get the message. We warn him equally with the ship.'

'Yes, but even so,' I objected, 'dare we run the risk?'

'There is no risk,' said Drummond calmly. 'Now that I know who Wilmot is – there is no risk. And tonight I'm going to have my final settlement with the gentleman.'

He would say no more: all the way back to London, when he drove like a man possessed with ten devils, he hardly opened his lips. And sitting beside him, busy with my own thoughts, the spell of his extraordinary personality began to obsess me. Never had he seemed so completely sure of himself – so absolutely confident.

And yet the whole thing was bizarre and strange enough to cause all sorts of doubts. I, too, had forgotten the much-advertised final trip of the airship, until Drummond had pulled the tickets out of his pocket. The dinner was to be even more wonderful than usual, and every guest was to receive a memento of the occasion from Mr Wilmot himself. The thing that defeated me was why Wilmot should waste the time. Granted that Drummond's theory was correct, and that after having attacked the *Megalithic* the airship was to come down in flames, why fool around with a two or three hours cruise beforehand? There was no longer any necessity to pose as an 'institution.'

Drummond smiled at my remarks.

'Why of necessity should you assume that it's going to be three hours wasted? You don't imagine, do you, that a man like Peterson would consider it necessary to return to the aerodrome and deposit his passengers?'

'But, great Scott, man,' I exploded, 'he can't carry out an attack on the *Megalithic* with fifty complete strangers on board his airship.'

'Can't he? Why not? Once granted that he's going to carry out the attack at all, I don't see that fifty or a hundred and fifty strangers would matter. You seem to forget that an integral part of his plan is that none of them should return alive to tell the tale.'

'It's inconceivable that such a man can exist,' I said.

'He's mother's bright boy all right is Carl Peterson,' agreed Drummond. 'I confess that I'm distinctly intrigued to see what is going to happen tonight.'

'But surely, Drummond,' I said, 'we're not justified in going through with this. An inspection of his ballast tanks will prove the presence of the poison. And then the matter passes into the hands of Scotland Yard.'

'I'm perfectly aware that that is what we ought to do,' he said gravely. 'Moreover, it is what we would do if it was possible.'

'But why isn't it possible?' I cried.

'Think, man,' he answered. 'At a liberal estimate we shall have an hour in which to change and get to the aerodrome. If we puncture we shan't have as much. Let us suppose that during that hour we can persuade MacIver and Co. that we are not mad – a supposition which I think is very doubtful. But for the sake of argument we will suppose it. What is going to happen then? MacIver appears at the aerodrome with a bunch of his pals, and attempts to board the airship. Peterson, who can spot MacIver a mile off, either sheers off at once in his dirigible, leaving MacIver dancing a hornpipe on the ground; or, what is just as likely, lets him come on board and then murders him. Don't you see, Stockton, the one fundamental factor of the whole thing is that that airship is never going to return. It doesn't matter one continental hoot to Peterson whether he is suspected or whether he isn't suspected – once he has started. He may be branded as the world's arch-devil: what does he care? A just retribution has over-taken him: he has perished miserably in the flames of his machine. No – I've thought it over, and I'm convinced that our best chance is to let his plans go on as he has arranged them. Don't let him suspect that we suspect. It won't seem strange to him that I turn up: he'll merely assume that I've utilised the ticket he sent me in utter ignor-ance of who he is. And then . . . '

'Yes,' I said curiously as he paused. 'And then – what?'

'Why – just one thing. The one vital thing, Stockton, which knocks the bottom out of his entire scheme. If we're right, and I *know* we're right, his whole plan depends on his ability to leave the airship. And he's not going to leave the airship . . . '

'For all that,' I argued, 'he may cause the most ghastly damage to the *Megalithic*.'

'I think not,' said Drummond quietly. 'I've made out a rough time-table, and this is how I see it. He plans to attack her somewhere off the south coast of Ireland, probably in the early hours of tomorrow morning. Long before that the guests will have realised that something is wrong. The instant that occurs he will show his hand, and matters will come to a head. One way or another it will be all over by eleven o'clock.'

'My God! It's an awful risk we're running,' I muttered.

'And an unavoidable one,' he answered. 'There's not a human being in England who would not believe us to be absolutely crazy if we told them what we know. So that any possibility of preventing people going on board that airship tonight may be ruled out of court at once.'

It was half-past five when we arrived, and we found Algy Longworth waiting for us at Drummond's house.

'Done everything you told me, old lad,' he cried cheerfully. 'They thought I was mad at the War House. Great Scott!' he broke off suddenly as he saw Gaunt, 'Who's your pal?'

'Doesn't matter about him, Algy. You've got the antidote?'

'A bucket of it, old boy. Saw Stockton's pal – one Major Jackson.'

'And you've got four tickets for Wilmot's dirigible this evening?'

'Got 'em at Keith and Prowse. What is the fun and laughter?'

'Peterson, Algy. Our one and only Carl. He's Wilmot.'

Algy Longworth stared at him incredulously.

'My dear old bird,' he said at length, 'you're pulling my leg.'

'Wilmot is Carl Peterson, Algy. Of that there is no shadow of doubt. And that's why you've got four tickets. We renew our acquaintance tonight.'

'Good Lord! Well, the tickets are a tenner each, including dinner, and I got the last. So we must get our money's worth.'

'You'll get that all right,' said Drummond grimly. 'Have you brought everybody's clothes round? Good. Get changed, you fellows: we start at six.'

And now I come to the final act in the whole amazing drama. Though months have elapsed, every detail of that last flight is as clear in my mind as if it had happened yesterday.

We started at six, leaving Denny in charge of Robin. Each of us had in our pockets a pot of the antidote and a revolver; and no-one talked very much. Drummond, his face set like granite, stared at the road in front of him. Algy Longworth polished and repolished his eyeglass ceaselessly. In fact, in sporting parlance – I don't know about Drummond, but as far as the rest of us were concerned – we had got the needle.

The evening was calm and still as we motored into the aerodrome. Great flaring arc lights lit up everything with the brightness of day, whilst above our heads, attached to the mooring mast, floated the graceful vessel, no longer dark and sinister as we had seen her the night before, but a blaze of light from bows to stern.

She was due to start at seven o'clock, and at ten minutes to the hour we stepped out of the lift at the top of the mast into the main corridor of the dirigible. Everywhere the vessel was gaily decorated with festoons of brightly coloured paper and fairy-lights. And in the first of the big cabins ahead we caught a glimpse of a crowd of fashionably dressed women gathered round a thick-set good-looking man in evening clothes. Mr Wilmot was welcoming his guests.

'Is that Peterson?' I whispered to Drummond.

He laughed shortly.

'Do you mean – do I recognise him? No, I don't. I never have yet, by looking at his face. But it's Peterson all right.'

Drummond was handing his coat and hat to a diminutive black boy in a bright red uniform, and I glanced at his face. A faint smile was hovering round his lips, but his eyes were expressionless. And even the smile vanished as he strolled towards the group in the ante-room: he was just the ordinary society man attending some function.

And what a function it proved. It was the first time that I had ever been inside an airship, and the thing that impressed me most was the spaciousness of everything – and the luxury. Even granting that it was a special occasion, one had to admit that the whole thing was marvellously well done. The lighting effect was superb; and in every corner great masses of hothouse flowers gave out a heavy scent.

'It's Eastern,' I said to Drummond. 'Oriental.'

'Peterson has always been spectacular,' he answered. 'But I agree that he has spared no pains with the coffin.'

'I simply can't believe it,' I said. 'Now that we're actually here, surrounded by all this, it seems incredible that he proposes to sacrifice it all.'

'There are a good many things about Peterson that strike one as incredible,' said Drummond quietly. 'But I wish I had even an inkling of what he's going to do.'

Suddenly the eyes of the two men met over the heads of the women. It was the moment I had been waiting for and I watched Wilmot intently. For perhaps the fraction of a second he paused in his conversation and it seemed to me that a gleam of triumph showed on his face: then once again he turned to the woman beside him with just the correct shade of deference which is expected of those who converse with a Duchess.

Drummond also had turned away and was chatting with someone he knew, but I noticed that he continually edged nearer and nearer to the place where Wilmot was standing a little apart from the others. At last he stopped in front of them and bowed.

'Good-evening, Duchess,' he remarked. 'Why aren't you slaughtering birds up North?'

'How are you, Hugh? Same thing applies to you. By the way – do you know Mr Wilmot? – Captain Drummond?'

The two men bowed, and Jerningham and I, talking ostensibly, drew closer. I know my hands were clammy with excitement, and I don't think the others were in much better condition.

'Your last trip, Mr Wilmot, I believe,' said Drummond.

'That is so,' answered the other. 'In England, I regret to say, the weather is so treacherous that after the early part of September flying ceases to be a pleasure.'

'He has got some wonderful surprises for us, Hugh,' said the Duchess.

'Merely a trifling souvenir, my dear Duchess,' answered Wilmot suavely.

'Of what has become quite an institution, Mr Wilmot,' put in Drummond.

Wilmot bowed.

'I had hoped perhaps to have made it even more of an institution,' he answered. 'But the public takes to new things slowly. Ah! We're off.'

'And what,' asked Drummond, 'is our course tonight?'

'I thought we would do the Thames Valley. Duchess – a cocktail?'

A waiter with a row of exquisite glasses containing an amber liquid was handing her a tray.

'Captain Drummond? You, I'm sure, will have one.'

'Why, certainly, Mr Wilmot. I feel confident that what the Duchess drinks is safe for me.'

And once again the eyes of the two men met.

Personally I think it was at that moment that the certainty came to Wilmot that Drummond knew. But just as certainly no sign of it showed on his face. All through the sumptuous dinner that followed, when he and Drummond sat one on each side of the Duchess, he played the part of the courteous host to perfection. I was two or three places away myself, so much of their conversation I missed. But some of it I did hear, and I marvelled at Wilmot's nerve.

Deliberately Drummond brought up the subject of the Robin Gaunt mystery, and of the fate of the *Hermione*. And just as deliberately Wilmot discussed them both. But all the time he knew and we knew that things were moving inexorably towards their appointed end. And what was that end going to be?

That was the question I asked myself over and over again. It seemed impossible, incredible, that the suave, self-possessed man at the head of the table could possess a mind so infamously black that, without a qualm, he would sacrifice all these women. And yet he had not scrupled to murder the women in the *Hermione*.

It seemed so needless – so unnecessary. Why have brought them at all? Why not have flown with his crew alone? Why have drawn attention to himself with his much-advertised gala night?

'Have you noticed the rate at which we are going? She's positively quivering.'

Jerningham's sudden question broke in on my thoughts, and I realised that the whole great vessel was vibrating like a thing possessed. But no-one seemed to pay any attention: the band still played serenely on, scarcely audible over the loud buzz of conversation.

At last dinner was over, and a sudden silence fell as Wilmot rose to his feet. A burst of applause greeted him, and he bowed with a faint smile.

'Your Grace,' he began, 'Ladies and Gentlemen. It is, believe me, not only a pleasure but an honour to have had such a distinguished company tonight to celebrate this last trip in my airship. I am no believer in long speeches, certainly not on occasions of this sort. But, before distributing the small souvenirs which I have obtained as a memento of this – I trust I may say – pleasant evening, there is one thing which as loyal subjects of our gracious Sovereign it is our duty to perform. Before, however, requesting the distinguished officer on my right' – he bowed to Drummond, and suddenly with a queer thrill I noticed that Drummond's face was shining like an actor's with greasepaint – 'to propose His Majesty's health, I would like to mention one fact. The liqueur in which I would ask you to drink the King is one unknown in this country. It is an old Chinese wine the secret of which is known only to a certain sect of monks. Its taste is not unpleasant, but its novelty will lie in the fact that you are drinking what only two Europeans have ever drunk before. One of those is dead – not, I hasten to assure you, as a result of drinking it: the other is myself. I will now ask Captain Drummond to propose the King.'

In front of each of us had been placed a tiny glass containing a few drops of the liqueur, and Drummond rose to his feet, as did all of us.

'Ladies and Gentlemen,' he said mechanically, and I could tell he was puzzled – 'the King'.

The band struck up the National Anthem, and we stood there waiting for the end. Suddenly on Drummond's face there flashed a look of horror, and he swung round staring at Wilmot. And then came his mighty shout – drowning the band with its savage intensity.

'Don't drink. For God's sake – don't drink. It's death.'

Unconsciously I sniffed the contents of my glass: smelt that strange sickly scent: realised that the liquid was Gaunt's poison.

The band stopped abruptly, and a woman started to laugh hysterically. And still Drummond and Wilmot stared at one another in silence, whilst the great vessel drove on throbbing through the night.

'What's all this damned foolery?' came in angry tones from a red-faced man half-way down the table. 'You're frightening the women, sir. What do you mean – death?'

He raised the glass to his lips, and before any of us could stop him, he drained it. And drinking it he crashed forward across the table – dead.

It was then that real pandemonium broke loose. Women screamed and huddled together in little groups, staring at the man who had spoken – now lying rigid and motionless with broken glass and upset flower vases all round him.

And still Drummond and Wilmot stared at one another in silence.

'The doors, you fellows,' Drummond's voice reached us above the din. 'And line up the servants and keep them covered.'

With a snarl that was scarcely human Wilmot sprang forward. He snatched up the Duchess's liqueur glass and flung the contents in Drummond's face. And Drummond laughed.

'Your mistake, Peterson,' he said. 'You only got half the antidote when you murdered Sir John Dallas. Ah! no – your hands above your head.'

The barrel of his revolver gleamed in the light, and once again silence fell as, fascinated, we watched the pair of them. They stood alone, at the head of the table, and Drummond's eyes were hard and merciless, while Peterson plucked at his collar with hands that shook.

'Where are we driving to at this rate, Carl Peterson?' said Drummond.

'There's some mistake,' muttered the other.

'No, Peterson, there is no mistake. Tonight you were going to do to the *Megalithic* what you did to the *Hermione* – sink her with every soul on board. There's no good denying it: I spent last night in Black Mine.'

The other started uncontrollably, and the blazing hatred in his eyes grew more maniacal.

'What are you going to do, Drummond?' he snarled.

'A thing that has been long overdue, Peterson,' answered Drummond quietly. 'You unspeakable devil: you damnable wholesale murderer.'

He slipped the revolver back in his pocket, and picked up his own liqueur glass.

'The good host drinks first, Peterson.' His great hand shot out and clutched the other's throat. 'Drink, you foul brute: drink.'

Never to my dying day shall I forget the hoarse yell of terror that Peterson uttered as he struggled in that iron grip. His eyes stared fearfully at the glass, and with a sudden stupendous effort he knocked it out of Drummond's hand.

And once again Drummond laughed: the contents had spilled on the other's wrist.

'If you won't drink – have it the other way, Carl Peterson. But the score is paid.'

His grip relaxed on Peterson's throat: he stood back, arms folded, watching the criminal. And whether it was the justice of fate, or whether it was that previous applications of the antidote had given Peterson a certain measure of immunity, I know not. But for full five seconds did he stand there before the end came. And in that five seconds the mask slipped from his face, and he stood revealed for what he was. And of that revelation no man can write . . .

Thus did Carl Peterson die on the eve of his biggest coup. As he had killed, so was he killed, whilst, all unconscious of what had happened, the navigator still drove the airship full speed towards the west.

And now but little remains to be told. It was Drummond who walked along the corridor and found the control cabin. It was Drummond who put a revolver in the navigator's neck, and forced him to swing the airship round and head back to London. It was Drummond who commanded the dirigible till finally we tied up once more to the mooring mast.

And then it was Drummond who, revolver in hand to stop any rush of the crew, superintended the disembarkation of the guests. Lift-load after lift-load of white-faced women and men went down to the ground till only we six remained. One final look did we take at the staring glassy eyes of the man who sprawled across the chair in which he had sat to entertain Royalty, and then we too dropped swiftly downwards.

News had already passed round the aerodrome, and excited officials thronged round us as we stepped out of the lift. But Drummond would say nothing.

'Ring up Inspector MacIver at Scotland Yard,' he remarked curtly. 'Leave all the rest of them on board till he comes. I will stop here.'

But, as all the world knows, it was decreed otherwise. Barely had we sat down in one of the waiting-rooms when an agitated man rushed in.

'She's off,' he cried. 'Wilmot's dirigible is under weigh.'

We darted outside to see the great airship slowly circling round. She still blazed with light, and from the windows leaned men, waving their arms mockingly. Then she headed north-east. And she was barely clear of the aerodrome when it happened. What looked to me like a yellow flash came from amidships, followed by a terrible rending noise. And before our eyes the dirigible became a roaring furnace of flame. Then, splitting in two, she dropped like a stone.

What caused the accident no-one will ever know. Personally I am inclined to agree with Drummond that one of the crew, realising that Wilmot was dead, decided to ransack his cabin to see what he could steal. And in the cabin he found some infernal device for causing fire, which in his unskilful hands exploded suddenly. It is a possible solution: that is all I can say for it. Anyway the point is immaterial. For twelve hours no man could approach the wreckage, so intense was the heat. And when at length it was possible, the bodies were so terribly burned as to be unrecognisable. Two only could be traced: the two in evening clothes. Though which was the red-faced man who had drunk and which was Wilmot no-one could say. And again the point is immaterial. For when a man is dead he's dead, and there's not much use in worrying further. What did matter was that one of those two charred corpses was all that remained of the super-criminal known to the world as Wilmot – and known to Drummond as Carl Peterson.

Chapter 13

In which I lay down my pen

I have finished. To the best of my ability I have set down the events of that summer. At the outset I warned my readers that I was no literary man: had there been anyone else willing to tackle the job I would willingly have resigned in his favour.

There will be many even now who will in all probability shrug their shoulders incredulously. Well, as I have said more than once, I cannot *make* any man believe me. If people choose to think that Gaunt's description of the sinking of the *Hermione* is a madman's delusion based on what he had read in the papers, they are welcome to their opinion. But the *Hermione* has never been heard of again, and it is now more than a year since she sailed from Southampton. And I have, at any rate, put forward a theory to account for her loss.

What is of far more interest to me is what would have happened had the attack been carried out on the *Megalithic*. What would have happened if Drummond had not chanced to pick out the scent of death in his glass, from the heavy languorous smell of the hothouse flowers that filled the cabin in which we dined? Can't you picture that one terrible moment, as with one accord every man and woman round that table pitched forward dead, under the mocking cynical eyes of Wilmot, and the great airship with its ghastly load tore on through the night?

And then – what would have happened? Would the attack have been successful? I know not, but sometimes I try to visualise the scene. The dirigible – no longer blazing with light – but dark and ghostly, keeping pace with the liner low down on top of her. Those thirty desperate men; the shattered wireless: and over everything the rain of death. And then the strange craft capable of such speed in spite of her lines, alongside. Everywhere, panic-stricken women and men dashing to and fro, and finding no escape. Perhaps the siren blaring madly into the night, until that too ceased because no man was left to sound it.

Then in the grey dawn the transfer of the bullion to the other vessel: the descent of Wilmot from the airship: perhaps a torpedo. A torpedo was all that was necessary for the *Lusitania*.

And then, last of all, I can see Wilmot – his hands in his pockets, a cigar drawing evenly between his lips – standing on the bridge of his ship. The swirling water has calmed down: only some floating wreckage marks the grave of the *Megalithic*. Suddenly from overhead there comes a blinding sheet of flame, and the doomed airship falls blazing into the sea.

Guesswork, I admit – but that is what I believe would have happened. But it didn't, and so guesswork it must remain to the end. There are other things too we shall never know. What happened to the vessel with the strange lines? There is no-one known to us who can describe her save Robin Gaunt, and he is incurably insane. Where is she? What is she doing now? Is she some harmless ocean-going tramp, or is she rotting in some deserted harbour?

What happened to the men we had left bound in Black Mine?. For when the police got there next day there was no sign of them. How did they get away? Where are they now? Pawns – I admit; but they might have told us something.

And finally, the thing that intrigues Drummond most. How much did Peterson think we knew?

Personally I do not think that Peterson believed we knew anything at all until the end. Obviously he had no idea that we had been to Black Mine the night before, until Drummond told him so. Obviously he believed himself perfectly safe, and but for the discovery of Gaunt's diary he would have been. Should we, or rather Drummond, ever have suspected that liqueur except for the knowledge we had? I doubt it, and so does Drummond. Even though we knew that smell so well – the smell of death – I doubt if we should have picked it out from the heavy exotic scent of the flowers.

They are questions which for ever will remain unanswered, though it is possible that some day a little light may be thrown on them.

And now there is but one thing more. Drummond and his wife are in Deauville, so I must rely on my memory.

It was four days after the airship had crashed in flames. The scent of the poison no longer hung about the wreckage: the charred bodies had all been recovered. And as Drummond stood looking at the debris a woman in deep black approached him.

'You have killed the man I loved, Hugh Drummond,' she said. 'But do not think it is the end.'

He took off his hat.

'It would be idle to pretend, Mademoiselle,' he said, 'that I do not know you. But may I ask why you state that I killed Carl Peterson? Is not that how he died?'

With his hand he indicated the wreckage.

She shook her head.

'The airship came down in flames at half-past one,' she said. 'It was ten o'clock that Carl died.'

'That is so,' he said gravely. 'I said the other to spare your feelings. You have seen, I presume, someone who was on board?'

'I have seen no-one,' she answered.

'But those details have been kept out of the papers,' he exclaimed.

'I have read no paper,' she replied.

'Then how did you know?'

'He spoke to me as he died,' she said quietly. 'And as I said before, it is not the end.'

Without another word she left him. Was she speaking the truth, or was there indeed some strange *rapport* between her and Peterson? Did the personality of that arch-criminal project itself through space to the woman he had lived with for so many years? And if so, what terrible message of hatred against Drummond did it give to her?

He has not seen her since: the memory of that brief interview is getting a little blurred. Perhaps she too has forgotten: perhaps not. Who knows?

THE END